DRAGON KNIGHT

THE SKYSTONE CHRONICLES BOOK 4

BLAKE & RAVEN PENN

GOOD LUX CREATIVE

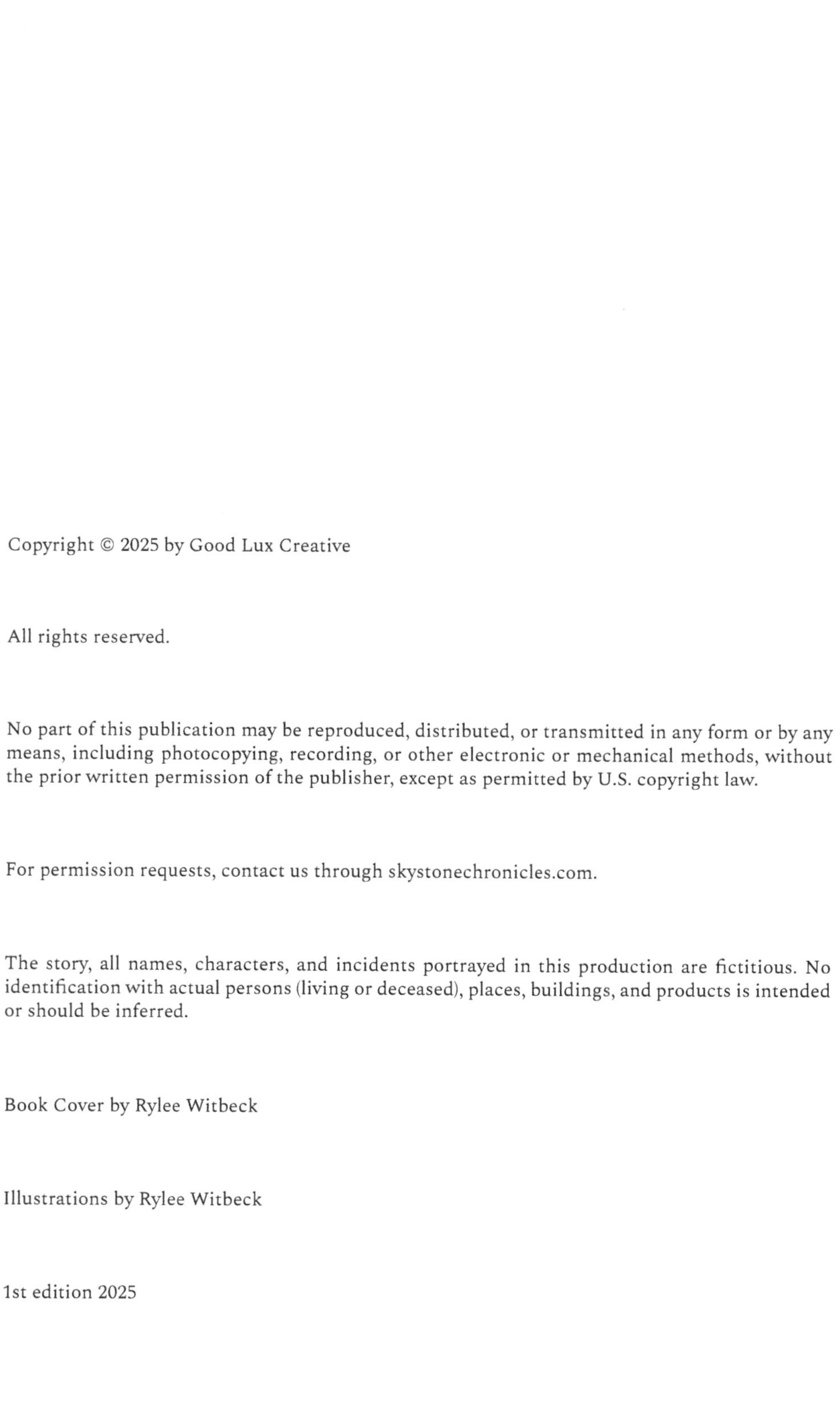

Book Cover by Rylee Witbeck

Illustrations by Rylee Witbeck

1st edition 2025

Dedication

For you, Team Skystone

We couldn't have gotten this far without you. For Evgard, unite!

Contents

Dear reader,

In our travels across worlds, we've gathered many stories of heroes. Those heroes always face an unseen enemy.
May this book help you face yours.

Sincerely,

Blake Penn

Raven Penn

THE SKYSTONE CHRONICLES

The Land of EVGARD

THE SKYSTONE CHRONICLES

Ley Lines

Considered the lifeblood of the spirit plane, Etheria, "ley lines" are floating rivers of pure ether. As the flow freely throughout the spirit world, ley lines are the source from which magi draw their ether, even if those on the physical do not recognize it.

A place where many ley lines intersect is called a "nexus." The first Evgardians tended to build capital Keeps on or near these.

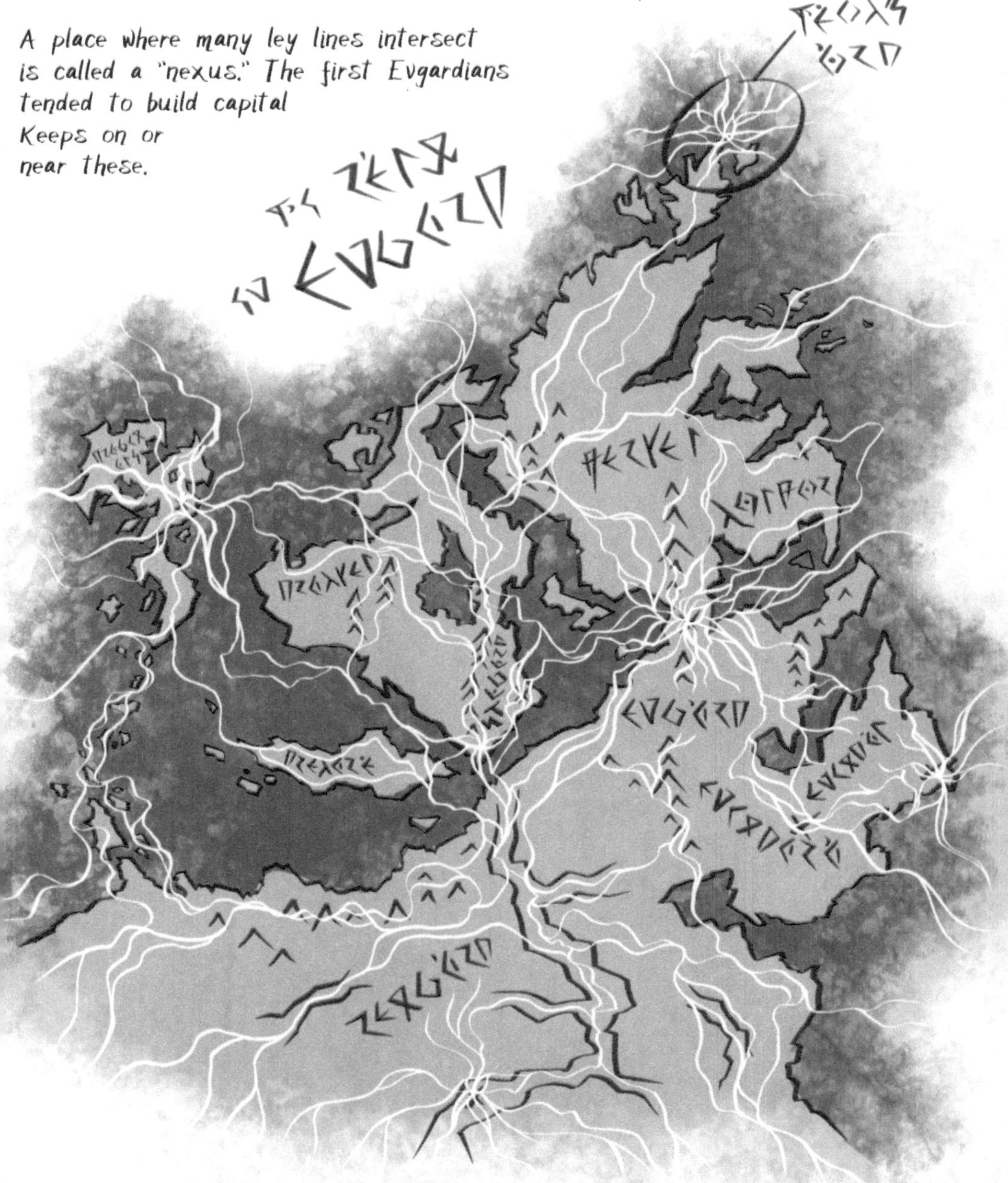

The Ethereal Triad

The chart below shows the nine types of etherarchy common among worlds. Your world tends to call these effects "magic" or "supernatural." We use the term etherarchy because it is the command of ether that accomplishes these mythic effects.

Any person who can command etherarchy is a magi. They fall into one of three groups:

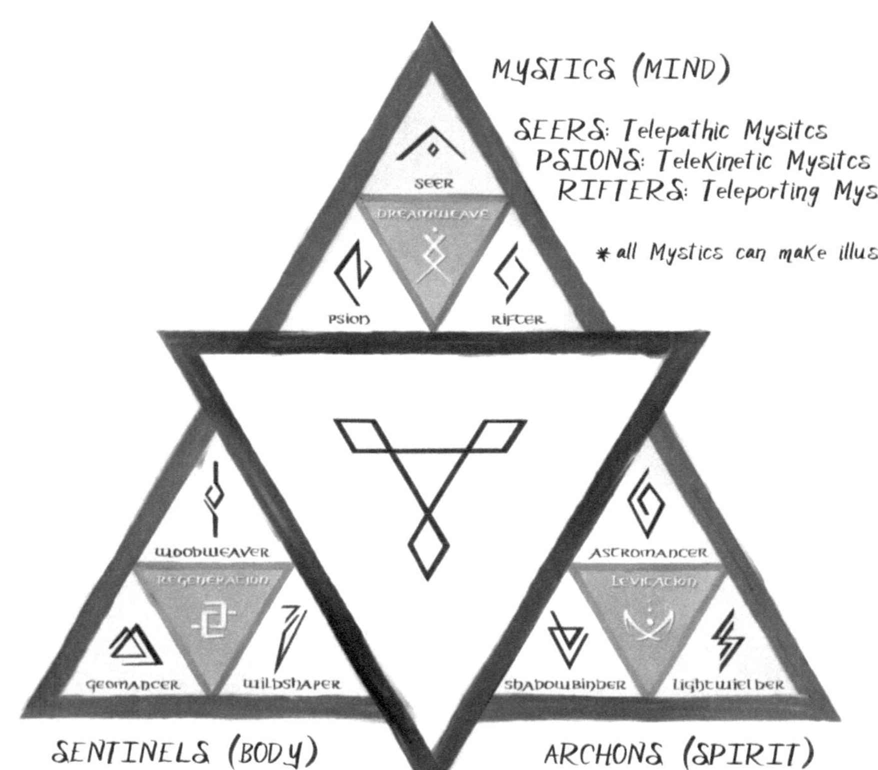

GEOMANCERS: Earth-based Sentinels
WILDSHAPERS: Fauna-based Sentinels
WOODWEAVERS: Flora-based Sentinels

*all Sentinels can regenerate

LIGHTWIELDERS: Light Archons
SHADOWBINDERS: Dark Archons
ASTROMANCERS: Ether Archons

*all Archons can levitate

* A note on silver: It is common Knowledge that all etherarchy is nullified on contact with silver. This is why Mage Hunters wield silver weapons, and why Evgardian Keeps have silver lined cells designed to hold magi.

Preface

A Brief Guide to Evgard is included in the back of the book, or you can check out skystonechronicles.com for more information on the world.

Sign up for our newsletter to get updates on our writing journey and the world of the Skystone Chronicles.

Now, without further ado, we hope you enjoy *Dragon Knight!*

Earlier in the Skystone Chronicles...

In the shadows of the Mirror Forest, the forces of the Rebel Knights of the Torch are growing.

Princess Eliana and her rare true dragon act as a beacon, drawing more soldiers and loyal followers alike. Meanwhile, Asher prepares to duel the general of the Drekai army, hoping to turn their fight to the death into an opportunity for the Knights to learn more about the strange Gray beings that threaten the land. The only problem is, if Asher loses... the Drekai will take Eliana and her dragon.

Outside the forest, the Mage Hunters are increasing their numbers as well. Meleya, Jax, and others serve as members of the Black Valkyrie's entourage, but Meleya has a secret. A dark, powerful weapon lies inside her rift hold: the Soul Reaper's voidshard.

After months of resisting, Meleya gives in to the darkness. But revealing the voidshard makes her a target. The Black Valkyrie and those loyal to her have no choice but to flee the Mage Hunter Academy to escape the wrath of High Prince Mason. Unable to reconcile with his mother, Jax remains behind.

In a fiery clash of enemies, the Rebel Hunters seek refuge with the Rebel Knights. Though their alliance is tenuous at best, both sides must pull together in hopes of reclaiming a pair of valuable prisoners. Asher, Meleya, and their friends embark on a journey across Evgard.

Tensions high, Asher and Meleya infiltrate the Orothion stronghold. But what began as a simple rescue mission explodes into a battle that ultimately reunites the fractured Knights of the Torch. As for Asher and Meleya, an accident leaves them stranded—not in the physical plane, but in Etheria, the realm of spirits.

With High King Magnus on their side, the wraiths have pierced the very heart of the realm. Evgard and the Dragon Isles alike now stand on the brink of ruin. Will the Gray Ones reclaim the Soul Reaper's voidshard before the fated convergence of mythic stars? And how can the Knights of the Torch hope to stop them when the Gray threatens to tear them apart from within?

Echo I

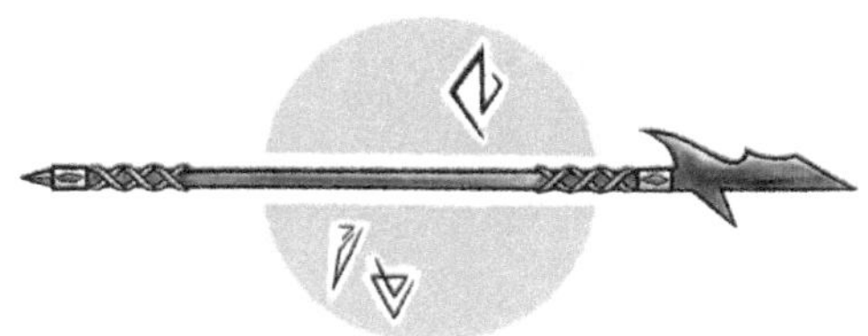

Vidya

Red coals.

What was once a tasteful tavern had been leveled to the ground. The smoking pile of splintered wood and glass was practically unrecognizable. A charred plank bearing the former establishment's name, The Cattledrake Cantina, lay smoldering at Vidya's feet.

"So much for a hot meal and a bed for the night." Beside Vidya, Solrac stood looking over the remains of the Knights of the Torch safehouse. Though he wore a hood to hide his face, Vidya could see that even Solrac's perpetual optimism was faltering.

"What happened here?" Vidya asked.

"Something very bad," Solrac replied. Vidya rolled her eyes.

"You're a Seer," she said. "Why don't you touch the wood and read its memories or something?"

"Ah," Solrac said. "I could do that, yes. But the memory of a chunk of wood would be quite inferior to that of a person, wouldn't you agree?"

"A person?" Vidya followed Solrac's gaze to find that a man was indeed making his way toward them from a fairly long way off, his silhouette just visible through the smoke rising from the still-hot embers of what had just been the Cattledrake Cantina.

Instinctively, Vidya tensed, gripping her dragonhook spear. Their journey from the Mirror Forest had thus far proven dangerous, and no wonder—Solrac's face was plastered on wanted posters in every town square, citadel wall, and back alley all across Evgard. The bandits drawn by the thousand-mark reward for the Farseer's capture was enough to ensure the two of them hadn't gotten a good night's sleep in weeks.

Perhaps you should have remained at the safehouse, the feminine voice taunted in Vidya's head. *Or better yet, at our true master's side, preparing for our eternal reign.*

I no longer serve the Soul Reaper. Vidya's mental reply was quick and harsh.

For now, Exusha conceded. *But it is only a matter of time before I regain control.*

Vidya swallowed, and the wraith laughed. *I sense that you fear this. It is why you cowered so long within the walls of that safehouse, where I could not touch your mind. But now, you are mine for the taking.*

If I were so malleable, Vidya shot back, *you'd have taken control already. I know your tricks, Exusha. My mind is no longer your playground.*

Exusha hissed and Vidya winced. Still, her willpower held out, and she felt the Gray One's presence retreat—for now.

Vidya's shoulders slumped from the effort. From the very beginning of their journey westward toward Orothion, Vidya felt she'd been fighting a battle. Not a physical one, but a mental war for control over her own actions.

Exusha was right about one thing—Perhaps she should have remained at the safehouse. Rhana's cabin was protected from wraiths, and while there, Vidya had enjoyed the longest stretch of mental peace she'd had in years. But when Solrac declared that the omens told him they needed to get to Orothion, Vidya's wraith had returned stronger than ever, having fed on lesser wraiths while waiting for Vidya to leave the cabin's safety.

But she hadn't been about to let Solrac go alone. While her marriage to Solrac had been rash—a rebellious decision made by two youthful runaways nearly twenty years ago—they had made the choice to give it another chance.

For Vidya, that meant putting twenty years' worth of bitterness and revenge-seeking aside. Part of her still resisted, but the greater part of her now realized that the consequences of her anger hadn't only hurt Solrac, but their son Jax as well.

Drak, but Vidya worried about Jax. Vidya still remembered how sick she'd felt when she'd seen Jax's eyes flash with sapphire light right before she'd left him at the Mage Hunter Academy. The dark path he walked... It was all her fault.

Now, she'd give anything to fix things for her son—starting with forgiving his father. Despite Vidya's best efforts, she still very much loved Solrac.

And for whatever reason, he still loved her back.

Repairing their marriage had been anything but easy so far, and Vidya could only hope it was worth it.

That *she* was worth it.

But she felt tainted now... her additional ether wells had brought her power, it was true... but they had also poisoned her very soul.

That's right, Exusha whispered, already restarting her mental advances. *You are corrupted beyond repair—*

"My friend!" Solrac's chipper voice cut through the wraith's darkness like a ray of light. He was waving to the man, who'd finally reached them. Solrac extended an arm, which the stranger grasped at the elbow.

"Who do I meet on this eve of darkness?" Solrac asked.

Without hesitation, the man replied, "One who carries the light."

Proper passphrases exchanged, Solrac beamed and pulled back his hood. The man's mouth fell open at the sight of him, and Vidya readied her etherarchy in case he made a move against her husband.

But Solrac's charm and that scorchingly endearing accent of his quickly put the man at ease. Apparently, he'd been a barkeep at the cantina. When Solrac asked him what had become of this place, a shadow crossed his face.

"They moved like a storm," the man said. "A psionic force the likes of which I've never seen before. Windows shattered, the very beams holding the building together crumbling in his wake."

"His?" Vidya prompted.

"The masked ones that followed him... they called him the Gray Knight."

"Show me," Solrac said. With the man's permission, Solrac activated a mind-reading rune, then extended his hand to touch the man's shoulder. Solrac took Vidya's hand with his other so that she too could see into the man's memories.

It was just like he'd said—a psionic storm of incredible proportions, led by an imposing figure clad in ornate plate armor from head to toe. Detailed, angular designs covered his chestplate, tassets, and gauntlets, and a gray robe swept out behind him. His helmet had a jagged ridge running along its breadth, his eyes darkened within the slits as an intricate blue rune shone over his forehead.

"He's using voidarchy for sure," Vidya said. "And his cohorts are definitely acolytes of the Coven of the Gray Ones." Vidya recognized their blank masks and gray robes.

"How many of our Knights were lost?" Solrac asked soberly.

"None, thankfully," the man replied. "The Gray Knight seemed to only be interested in eliminating the safehouse, thank Streya."

"Well, that is a bright side if I ever saw one," Solrac said, stroking his beard. He did that a lot ever since he started growing it out at the start of their journey.

"There's more," the man said as Solrac let him go, allowing the mental images to dissolve. "The Cattledrake Cantina's not the only Knights of the Torch safehouse the Gray Knight and his followers have left in shambles. We got word of at least three others in Evyndara, plus a few more in Rengard and the Capital Keepdom's southwestern shores. The Gray Knight's been at the head of all of them—Must be working with rift anchors of some kind to get to so many so fast. But more importantly, it goes to show that our safehouses are no longer safe. Someone's been telling him exactly where we are. Someone's betrayed the Knights."

"Stars," Solrac muttered, his countenance falling. "I believe you are right."

Solrac gave the unfortunate barkeep some marks, then took Vidya's hand and moved along. While Solrac had been joking about missing out on a meal and a bed for the night, Vidya felt that loss more keenly than she wanted to admit. Night would soon fall, and they needed to find a place to camp.

They found sanctuary in a clearing where the dense cindercone pines made room for an ether vent. This vent was not particularly large, but it chronically spouted a short geyser of pure ether, which made the earth surrounding the hot spring shimmer with various colors: White, gold, and blood red.

Vidya hadn't been sure about the spot, but Solrac insisted. They needed to camp somewhere where ether was abundant, so that it could aid him in his omen reading.

"We must consult the omenfires," Solrac said, setting the coals on the ground before the ether geyser's spring. In order to augment his visions, he'd slipped into the red robes of the Farseer, as well as the red-scaled gauntlets. He even clutched his iconic antler-handled staff while the mysterious black mythraven perched atop his shoulder.

But before he put up the hood, Solrac pulled out a small, diamond-shaped hand mirror—the very one he'd gifted to Vidya soon after they were married. Vidya had carried the mirror around for years, her sole keepsake of a bygone era. Now, Solrac was holding it up while he messed with his hair. With the unwieldy gauntlets, he looked objectively ridiculous.

"Why in the stars would you care what your hair looks like," Vidya started, "when you'll be hiding it under a hood?"

"It gives me great confidence to know that even beneath the hood, my hair looks fantastic."

Solrac continued fussing, and eventually Vidya took pity on him and strode up to his side. Her thin fingers worked far better than Solrac's gauntleted ones, and he seemed quite pleased—both with his hair's results and with Vidya's proximity.

"I know you know this," Solrac said, "but I must warn you: Omens can be confusing even at the best of times. What we see within these fires—especially concerning the future—might seem quite dark."

"I can handle it," Vidya assured him, feeling mildly insulted that he found such a warning necessary. She'd seen more darkness than Solrac ever would. She felt her wraith creeping closer.

But rather than turn this into an argument, Vidya took a mental step back. Solrac was only speaking this way out of an earnest desire to protect her. She could hardly fault him for that. Opportunity lost, Exusha retreated into the shadows.

Together, Solrac and Vidya sat on the sandy earth. Solrac traced a complicated rune, prompting a heatless, golden flame to burst to life over the coals.

Solrac put up his red hood and his face melted into the darkness within as two glowing white eyes shone, a brilliant skystone shining from his forehead between the two. When Solrac next spoke, his voice had deepened into that of the Farseer.

"First, a vision of the past."

Images flickered within the flame so quickly Vidya couldn't decipher any of them. Finally, they slowed, revealing a man sitting alone at the bar of the seediest tavern that Vidya had ever seen. The man belched, pushing aside one bottle and gesturing for the bartender to bring him another.

Vidya and Solrac exchanged glances. Both had no trouble recognizing Torsten, the man whom Vidya had pretended was Jax's father in her efforts to get back at Solrac. Torsten's bad habit of getting blackout drunk had made him easy to trick but, to be fair, twenty years ago he'd been far less sloppy and overweight. As Vidya and Solrac watched him get to work on his next bottle, he barely fit in his chair. This vision of the past must've been fairly recent, sometime soon after Keep Rengard's Winter Solstice Ball.

The omens projected a dark, gray aura around Torsten, within which hovered several sets of haunting blue eyes. Voices rose from the golden flames, and Vidya knew the grating speech was what Torsten was hearing within his mind:

We knew you'd end up back here—you always do.
You are weak. Foolish. A failure.
They will never accept you.
Freedom is not within your grasp.

Torsten's expression grew more and more tense until it was clear he couldn't stand it any longer. Desperate to drown out the voices, he downed another gulp of his drink.

Vidya winced, hating how much she could relate to unfortunate Torsten's plight. She hadn't turned to the drink, but she'd lost herself in her roles, from the Black Valkyrie persona to the many others she'd taken on over the years. She hated recalling what she'd done while absorbed in the escapism that such roles offered, particularly while playing Shaya. She'd hurt so many people, especially Asher.

Such dreary reminiscences were ample cause for Exusha to make another play for Vidya's mind. Her icy presence seemed to send a layer of frost across Vidya's soul as she kept watching the scene unfolding within the omenfire.

A man and a woman wearing gray robes approached, standing directly behind Torsten in the bar. Though they weren't wearing masks, Vidya was certain they were members of the Coven of the Gray Ones, with whom Torsten had collaborated in southern Rengard.

Torsten didn't turn around, his northern drawl dark as he asked, "How'd y'all find me?"

"A drunk is never hard to find," the robed man sneered.

"I ain't with the Coven no more," Torsten said, knuckles whitening as he gripped his bottle. "Not now that Lorelai's gone."

"Oh, Torsten..." The female Coven member shook her head. "It's not that simple. We still need you."

At that, Torsten let out a sudden, too-loud whoop that got both Coven members to jump. The few patrons of the dilapidated tavern cast them annoyed, sidelong looks.

"Y'all hear that?" Torsten hollered, speech slurring. "Says she needs me!" He took another swig, then exhaled as his watery eyes met those of the Coven. "Soot if it ain't nice to be needed, right?"

Both Coven acolytes turned up their noses at Torsten's display. "Believe me," the man said, "if we had a choice, we'd let you pickle yourself with draquila here. But magi like you are scarce, and you're our only option."

Vidya knew exactly what the acolyte meant. Ever since the late High Queen's Rifter purge, magi with the ability to teleport were all but extinct. Those few remaining were in high demand, and the Coven wasn't the first group to try to force a Rifter to serve their ends.

"We don't need your precious Liberator—er, Lorelai—anymore," the female acolyte went on. "Our new benefactors are far less volatile, and promise to pay handsomely."

"And just who are these 'new benefactors'?" Torsten asked.

"We can't speak openly here, but suffice it to say that these are... particularly high-ranking officials from the Mining Keepdom." The acolyte's prideful reply only confirmed Vidya's suspicion that the Kolbohrian nobles were in league with the Soul Reaper.

The hypocrisy of it all disgusted Vidya. Just last winter, the Liberator had riled up the southern Coven, convincing them to turn their ire on the noble class. Now, it seemed they were turning to royalty like greedy dragonmutts looking for a bone.

"Come with us, Torsten," the male acolyte said. "It's not like you've got somewhere better to be. Besides, things are changing, truly this time. Magi like us will at last be properly worshiped for our gifts, not scorned and made into outcasts. Come next spring, *we* will be on the winning side. All our Seers say so."

Torsten cleared his throat, then spat toward the acolyte's feet, making him jump back once again. "I don't give a flyin' scale what y'all's drakkin' Seers say. I ain't comin'."

No sooner had the words left Torsten's mouth than the Coven woman lurched forward and snapped a pair of silver cuffs around Torsten's wrists.

The big man wailed in protest, but the dingy bar's small handful of other patrons just moved to tables further away, utterly indifferent.

"You know," the male acolyte said condescendingly, "if you'd only let a Gray One choose you, silver's sting would mean nothing to you, too."

Torsten grunted. "That may be true. But unlucky for you, silver don't change my size."

At that, Torsten crossed his arms and stubbornly settled deeper into his chair. The Coven acolytes exchanged annoyed glances. Neither stood a chance of physically transporting him against his will.

The woman turned to her companion, then whispered, "Knock him out with your lightwielding. Then levitate him and we'll drag him out of here."

"Why you—"

That was as far as Torsten got before blue lightning crackled and the images within the omenfire vanished.

"Poor Torsten," Solrac said, his regular voice coming from within the Farseer's hood. "Truly, the lot of a Rifter in Evgard is a heavy one."

"What does the Coven need Torsten to do for them?" Vidya asked.

Solrac gulped. "I was hoping you could tell me."

Vidya shook her head. The golden flames flared once more, indicating that they had more to share.

Solrac put on the Farseer's deep, resonant tone once more. "Now, a vision of the present."

The fires depicted one of the most beautiful women Vidya had ever seen. From her dewy, innocent eyes to her shining curls and perfect, heart-shaped lips, Vidya recognized Queen Ilona, the widowed ruler of the Keepdom of Rengard. At present, she was bustling about her white adobe citadel, giving one of her servants a stack of letters bearing Rengard's orange seal.

"Invitations to the annual council meeting on the Rise," Queen Ilona explained. "Please ensure they arrive in a timely manner—I want each of the highest ranking noble houses present. For the meeting of course, as well as the splendid gala afterward. Everyone *must* be there."

The queen beamed and fluttered her thick, dark eyelashes as the servant hurried to obey.

"What's so important about this meeting?" Vidya mused as the scene dissolved.

"Rengard is a key player in Evgard," Solrac said. "The Canyonlands boast one of the strongest militaries the realm over—An alliance with them could change the tides for the Knights of the Torch and the coming war with the Gray. Prior to his untimely death, I was in talks with Queen Ilona's husband, King Axel."

Here Solrac's tone grew somber, and Vidya's already chilly mood darkened further as she recalled the night of the king's death.

"Perhaps the omens are trying to tell us that this is a second chance to sway the Canyonlands to our side," Solrac said. "We must have a seat at that meeting."

"You mean, we're not going to Orothion after all?" Vidya asked.

"Orothion first," Solrac nodded eagerly, which appeared strange while he was wearing the epic Farseer getup. "Akayto is there, and can provide us with rift anchors to ensure that the two of us make it to the Rise in time for the meeting."

Vidya's heart sank. It felt as if the sanctuary from her wraith she'd been looking forward to in Orothion was a rug, and Solrac had just ripped it out from under her.

He's as oblivious to your pain now as he was at the start. The thought flickered in the back of Vidya's mind. Vidya bit her cheek as she realized she wasn't sure if that thought had come from her wraith or herself.

Before she could reply, however, the omenfire flared once more.

"And now," Solrac said, gazing into the golden flames, "a vision of the future—Brace yourself, these tend to get complicated."

Light flashed within the flames, emerald green like dragonfire. Vidya quickly realized she was looking at a skyfall, one of the great meteors that frequently fell in Evgard, bringing both valuable skystone as well as the eggs of wild dragonkind.

As this skyfall streaked across the darkened heavens, the vision was overlaid with the starry outline of a powerful woman. She sat astride a mighty true dragon, an ornate crown atop her head. The great, ancient longsword she wielded bore a unique celestial pattern on its hilt.

"The Veilblade." Vidya recognized the legendary sword. "Is that supposed to be the mind goddess, Streya?"

"Yes," Solrac confirmed. "The skyfall... This is Streya's Comet. It is supposed to pass over Evgard in the coming months—Something significant must be occurring on that day."

Vidya wasn't much of an astronomer, but she knew that Streya's Comet had long circled the heavens, passing Evgard once every century or so.

But besides the great comet, apparently the vision had other things to say about the future as well.

Within the fire, the comet gave way to Asher of Steel Rim lying on a table, chained by mist and bathed in the eerie blue light of a thousand stars. Meleya of Misthaven was there too, that same blue reflected in her eyes as her expression twisted in rage.

"I've seen this scene many times before," Solrac said, eyes fixed on the vision. "At first, Asher appeared in the clothing of a Mage Hunter, but now, that is not the case. More drakking symbolism, I suppose... Meleya and Asher's conflict did begin at the Mage Hunter Academy, after all. But now, the scope has grown. Note the skies—" Solrac traced them with his finger. "Those are the three constellations of the convergence of mythic stars. Once they fully align, the Soul Reaper will make his play for Evgard."

Vidya saw no shapes in the jumble of stars. Solrac might've seen all this before, but Vidya watched with trepidation as Meleya advanced on Asher, who screamed when the snowheaded young woman trained a glimmering seaxe on his chest. Vidya's heart thudded. She'd seen Meleya while under the influence of her own powerful wraith before, and the horrible things she'd done.

Things that pale compared to what you *have done,* Exusha reminded her. Vidya clenched her hands, the nails of her fingers digging into her palms.

Now the vision swirled, and Asher disappeared in a flash of light while Meleya was overcome by mists. Light and mist coalesced to form a massive, ash gray dragon. Vidya startled when the dragon's expression turned savage before leaping from the omenfire and enclosing its wide, shadowy jaws around Solrac's head.

At once, the fire went out.

When the gray smoke had dissipated, Solrac was perfectly alright. Still, Vidya's eyes were narrowed when they met her husband's.

"I know what you're going to say," Vidya said in the darkness. "You think the dragon signifies your death, don't you?"

Solrac sighed. They'd had this conversation several times before, ever since he'd confided in her regarding this particular recurring vision.

"It is not uncommon for Farseers to receive omens of their own demise," Solrac said. "Mine will come, that much is clear."

Before Vidya could respond, the omenfire suddenly blazed back to life, casting the cindercones in a brilliant, golden glow. Solrac and Vidya's attention snapped back to the flames.

Now the omenfire showed them a glorious, shining city wrought from pure, white crystal. Within the crystals, Vidya thought she could see more stars—no doubt symbolic of the convergence again. Then the city began to tremble, pieces shattering. Vidya, too, struggled not to shake as Exusha pressed harder against her consciousness.

Next, a great curtain appeared to cut the city in half. The fabric was of thin gauze, and through its glowing fibers Vidya could see thousands of pairs of eyes. Then the Veilblade appeared again, this time to slice directly into the thin curtain. The once-white city began to turn sapphire, as if blue blood were saturating it from the inside out.

At the heart of it all, Vidya saw a swan, its white wings dripping with black blood that fell like rain over the city. The vision carried on with more symbolic soot and nonsense, but the sight of the swan blurred Vidya's vision with tears so she could no longer see it.

You will never be free, Exusha's voice echoed within. *Your name is etched on my voidshard. You are already mine, Vidya.*

The visions, the wraith, the blood... the *guilt.* It was all too much. Vidya inhaled sharply, her heart all but stopping as she felt Exusha's cold presence fill her limbs.

Vidya rose. Solrac was still focused on the omenfire, his red Farseer's robes taunting her. At once, all her old pain and hatred for the Knights resurfaced. Everything she'd done as the Black Valkyrie... it was because of them. Because of *him.* She had to believe that her past deeds weren't completely her fault, or she'd lose her mind.

The omenfire flickered before going out for good this time. The only light now came from the dim red coals. That, and Vidya's glowing sapphire eyes.

"Vidya?" Solrac said, suddenly becoming aware of her looming over him. At Exusha's command, Vidya's hand rose, shadow encompassing it as she summoned a ragged dragonhook spear. The spear was a wraith-blade, forged from gray mist, with black shadowfire rippling along its edge.

No, Vidya thought, wrestling to regain control. *My past actions were* mine. *No one else's. Drak you, wraith!*

With an exhausting surge of sanity, Vidya expelled Exusha from her mind and body, the exertion leaving her eyes dull and her limbs wobbly and spasmodic. Solrac hurried to his feet to steady her.

"Scorch," Vidya swore through clenched teeth. "You see? I can barely control her. What if... what if I'm not strong enough to go to Rengard with you? What if I give in and do something unforgivable, as I have so many times before?"

"Hush your fears, my dear," Solrac soothed, his hand in hers helping to keep her grounded. "I believe you can do this. Truly."

Vidya leaned into his embrace as her heartbeat steadied. She had deep, gnawing doubts regarding her ability to control the wraith, but for now, Solrac's belief in her would have to be enough.

As she stared into the dying red coals of the omenfire, Vidya couldn't help but wonder what exactly the visions had meant. But amidst all the flashing images and frankly frustrating symbolism, one thing was certain: Evgard was about to change forever.

Chapter I: The Spirit Plane

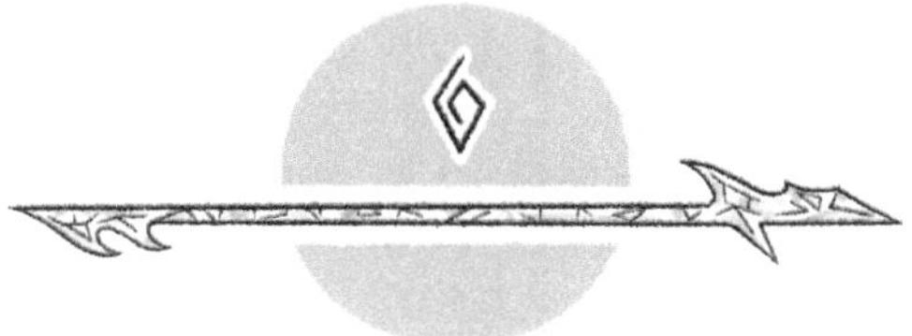

Asher

I didn't *feel* dead. Then again, I'd never been dead before, so for all I knew, this was just what death was.

None of it made any sense. One moment, Meleya and I had been looking down into the depths of the Skyforge from the overhanging terrace, and the next, Zel was pointing a dreamweave-infused crossbow in our faces. The bolt blasted us in the head, then...

This happened.

White etherdust from the portal-powered super-bomb I'd named 'the eclips-plosion' dusted the ground of the Skyforge terrace, its glow even more powerful than it had been upon first exploding. At least, that's how it looked to me now, as a sort of extra layer of white-gold mist swirled all around it.

Muddled voices assaulted my ears like the roaring of a hundred wild dragons. Soldiers and nobles raced back and forth in the chaotic aftermath of the battle we'd just waged against Zel and his followers, but there was something very off about the sight of them. Blindingly bright colors trailed each person, and no one so much as looked my way. I yelped as someone darted directly *through* me, as if I were a ghost.

Which, I guess I kind of was.

But at least I wasn't alone. Meleya of Misthaven stood—or floated—beside me, her spirit form as translucent as mine. Her long white braid streamed behind her, looking almost as if it was suspended in water rather than air. I'd heard of ethereal auras before, but I'd never imagined anything half as vibrant and beautiful as the spiraling, indigo-colored mists that surrounded her.

But in the internal battle between awe and sheer panic, the latter unequivocally won out.

"What in the stars is going on?" I cried. "Why can't anyone see us? And why do you look like a bottle of purplish-blue ink sneezed all over a cloud?"

"I already told you," Spirit-Meleya snapped back, clearly dissatisfied with my comparison. "We're in Etheria, the spirit plane. At least, this is what it looks like when I use the Sight."

Her large, round eyes darted all around, trying to drink in everything. Meanwhile, I squeezed mine shut. There were colors and patterns everywhere, all moving a million miles a minute, and my already distractible brain was finding it impossible to focus. I pressed my spirit-hands to my spirit-temples.

"*This* is what it's like for Rifters?" I asked. "How can you stand it?"

"Well, it's a lot easier to swallow in bite-sized flashes of color rather than whatever is happening to us now."

"That's it!" I half-marched half-hovered over to the edge of the newly shattered Skyforge dome. It was strange—moving here was like a more natural version of levitating, and I could direct where I wanted to go just by willing it.

I peered over the mostly demolished ledge. Far below, I could see the smoky interior of the ancient forge, its floor littered with debris from the battle.

There was still a lot going on down there. I saw Aradan, the brother of the King of Drakfell, and his trio of bonded dragons fighting alongside my father to take down our enemy, Zel, and his great red wyvern once and for all.

I winced as more of those glaring auras shrouded the action. It was like trying to squint through paint-spattered glasses, only the paint was alive.

Dad fought fiercely, his crossbow bolt taking Zel in the shoulder. The sinister old Shadowbinder fell into King Rodan's waiting grip, where he dropped his weapons and held up his hands.

Enraged, Zel's wyvern thrashed, his ruddy aura going ballistic here on the ethereal side of things. My heart skipped when his thick tail whipped around, knocking my father into the stony wall. Fortunately, that gave

Aradan's dragons the opening they needed to entrap Zel's wyvern for good.

"Dad!" I said, nearly jumping in to get to him right then and there, but more misty, aura-shrouded people had already clustered around him and the other wounded fighters. A couple of medics checked on my father, one signaling the other that he was breathing. Nodding, the medic's assistants carefully lifted Dad onto a cot, then carried him and several others from the Skyforge.

Relief filled my spirit-body. The battle was over, and Dad was going to be okay.

Just as quickly, dread replaced that relief. *I* was *not* okay.

"There we are!" I shouted, pointing into the Skyforge below, where my and Meleya's bodies remained caught up in that insane salad of colors and mist, lying dangerously still. Only the faintest, dullest wisps of aura mist still clung to us. More medics surrounded us, along with Thorn and Sniff, my black-and-copper dragon bond and Meleya's golden-yellow one. They must've helped to break our falls. Was that Elle beside us, too? It was hard to tell through the shiny purple cloud.

"What in the void are you doing?" Meleya's spirit called to me from behind.

"I'm going to get back into my body, thank you very much!"

My spirit feet had just left the floor in what was sure to have been a wild leap when I felt Meleya tackle me from behind.

"Drak, Asher!" she cried, yanking me back onto solid ground. "You can't just go jumping off of things whenever it suits you!"

"I do it all the time!" I countered. "Besides, I'm not just going to *float* here. We have to get out of this place, starting with... uh..."

"Starting with *what?*" Meleya asked, and I could tell she was panicking too—a lot more than she'd initially let on. "What's your plan exactly?"

"I don't know—Try to realign my spirit with my body or something? What's *your* plan then, Etheria-expert?"

"I haven't had time to make one, as I've been too busy keeping you from getting yourself killed."

"For all we know, I'm already dead!"

Whatever Meleya said next faded into the background as a voice pierced the chaos:

"Asher! Asher!"

It was a feminine voice, with the distinct accent of someone from the Dragon Isles. Each second, it came closer.

"Asher!"

Even after all these years, I recognized the voice instantly. My spirit literally began to tremble as I turned around.

It was her. Bright, dragonfire green eyes the same shade as mine. Where the tips of my pointed ears had dark teal scales, hers did too, though she had a short pair of horns sprouting from within her hair. She was a full half-born, whereas I was technically only one-quarter Drekai.

She was radiant, aglow with a vibrant dark turquoise light, and her face... Stars, her face looked the same as it had the last time I'd seen her over four years ago.

I closed the distance between us faster than a shooting star. Her laughter sounded like the melody from an old favorite song.

"*Vaaro,* careful, my *laaksi rakaai,*" she said as she embraced me back. "You've gotten so much stronger since the last time I saw you! That is, since the last time I *really* saw you, face to face."

"Mom!" I cried, the word tasting sweeter than cinderberries on my tongue. "It's really you! Stars, if I'd known this awaited me, I wouldn't have been so afraid of death!"

"Oh, my *laaksi...*" Mom pulled back, wiping the spirit-tears from her eyes. "I don't know why the Allfather's favor has given me the chance to see you now, but I can assure you, you're not dead."

"I'm not?" Confusion flooded me, along with a wave of relief.

Mom shook her head, then gestured to follow her. In the tumultuous aftermath of the battle, the action here on the Skyforge terrace was still making my head spin. Still, I was glad that it seemed everyone would be alright.

Once we'd moved to a quieter corner, Mom offered further explanation. "The fact that you haven't moved on to Deep Etheria already is evidence that you are very much alive."

My heart leaped. "You're here, too. Does that mean—"

"*Nii,* no, Asher. I truly passed on all those years ago. The only reason I'm here is... well..."

"What is it?"

"We can speak of that later. For now, aren't you forgetting something?"

I raised a spirit-eyebrow, and Mom laughed again. Dark turquoise mists trailed as she raised an arm to point over my shoulder.

At once, I realized that Meleya was still standing there, hanging back with her mouth open as she watched the scene unfold. When I turned to look at her, she shrank away as if embarrassed to have been intruding on the reunion.

I, on the opposite scale, broke into a wide, crooked grin. Darting over to Meleya, I grabbed her by the hand and pulled her back to where Mom stood. Then, I got to do something I never thought I would:

I introduced a girl to my mother.

Not that Meleya and I were... Well, I wasn't entirely sure *what* Mel and I were to each other. Friends, for sure. After all, I *had* just died saving her. Then again, I guess I hadn't actually saved her. Or died, for that matter. Stars. I was all sorts of confused.

Either way, I could hardly keep the tremor from my voice. "Mom, I'd like you to meet Mel—That is, Meleya."

"Hi," Meleya said with a shy wave.

Mom, on the other hand, pulled Meleya right in for an embrace, speaking a hundred miles a minute in her native tongue:

"*Taaket, uuta kuii kauuni ehta siina! Ehta siilma kaau ehlka, ja zehki kaau vaava. Min Asher jan kun oniia janehl-zi joiita.*"

Meleya blinked a few times as the Drekai words went right over her head. She glanced at me expectantly, but I just gave a nervous chuckle. Mom had essentially just raved about how beautiful Meleya was, then remarked on how lucky I was to have found someone like her.

Not sure I wanted to translate that one for Meleya, I smoothly changed the subject. "This doesn't feel real. Are you two sure you're not part of some insane dream I'm having?"

I reached out with each hand and gave both Mom and Meleya a good pinch. Meleya wrenched her arm away and shot me a glare, but Mom laughed heartily and pinched me right back. I darted away to avoid several more playful pinches while my heart filled with joy. Mom hadn't changed a bit.

Meanwhile, Meleya had float-walked back over to the shattered edge of the Skyforge dome. Some of the chaos had died down, and she now peered in the same way I'd done before.

"Zerana," Meleya called to my mother. "Can spirits like us still access our powers?"

Mom raised a lively eyebrow. "Why don't you find out?"

Meleya's translucent finger trailed gold light as she runetraced. I'd seen her trace similar runes a hundred times before, but from the spirit world side of things, the etherarchy looked even brighter. Each line of light was filled with infinite coiling tendrils, a little like an intricate snowflake or a nebula in the night sky. When Meleya's portal appeared, its gold rim of light was the same, full of unfathomable detail.

That wasn't all, however—While on the physical side of things, only the entrance and exit portals themselves were visible. Here in Etheria, I could actually *see* the connection between rifts, like a thin, twisting golden slide spanning the space between Meleya's entrance portal up here and the exit portal near our bodies.

"Where do you think you're going?" I asked.

Meleya gave me a quick, sheepish glance. "I was going to try aligning my spirit with my body to see if... you know."

I broke into a wide, crooked grin. "You mean my plan that you so harshly rejected a few minutes ago?"

Meleya rolled her eyes. "Are you coming or not?"

I turned to Mom, questioning.

She smiled. "You're eighteen now, Asher. You don't need your mother's permission anymore."

Next, I held out a hand to Mom. I wasn't about to move an inch unless I knew she was coming with me.

Meleya's portal took us right to where a misty throng surrounded our bodies. My vision must've been getting used to Etheria, because the longer I spent here, the harder it was becoming to make out people's physical forms. I could make out tiny flickers of multicolored light, busily floating about from place to place, but it was only when I intentionally focused on each small flame that they expanded, taking shape as the unique aura around the form of a living person in the physical plane.

Still, it wasn't hard to focus on my own physical body lying still on the ground. My best friend, Kai, was down here now, carefully cradling my head. At least, I was pretty sure the neat, goldish aura was his. Stars, the way it clung to him in even rows like writing, mostly concentrated around his head, practically screamed 'Kai.'

I stood by, watching as Spirit-Meleya carefully floated into place over her body. It was a strange sight, watching her spirit settle into her physical form. I bit the inside of my spirit-cheek as the two aligned.

For a second, I couldn't see Mel's spirit anymore. Had it worked?

Then her spirit-form suddenly sat up, a deep frown on her face. She tried a couple more times, essentially doing spirit-sit-ups over her own body. I laughed so hard I snorted.

No. It most definitely hadn't worked.

After sufficiently teasing Meleya for looking so 'cool', I gave it a try myself. After seeing Mel's attempts fail, I wasn't surprised when I didn't have any more success than she had.

Looking over at Mom, I was absolutely okay with that.

There was clearly a lot of commotion going on in the physical plane as medics carted our bodies out of the Skyforge. Soldiers were still everywhere, and I mean everywhere. I certainly didn't enjoy the feeling of being incorporeal as people swept through me as if I didn't exist.

"Yeesh," I shuddered, step-floating to the side to avoid someone running through me once more. "Do you ever get used to that?"

"Not really." Mom wrinkled her nose and, stars, even that felt so wonderfully familiar. "Though it does get easier once you learn how to focus. Right now, your full attention is split between both planes, but once you learn to hone in on just Etheria, the elements of the physical plane fade to something more like... suggestions."

"Fascinating," Meleya said.

"Isn't it?" Mom beamed. Then she turned to me. "They took your father to the medical wing. He'll be alright, though we ought to give him some time to recover before we overwhelm him."

"That's right," I said, eyes widening. "Dad... he'll be able to see us!"

"One of very few who can." Mom nodded. "For now, I know a place we can go. Down on the cliffs below the castle, near the dragon stables."

"Sounds good to me," I said.

"How do we get there?" Meleya asked.

The words had no sooner left her lips than a *whoosh* of wind blew through me. As in, right *through* me, sending a chill straight to my core. The long-ish black hair on the top of my head blew into my eyes the same way it usually did, but the sensation felt different without my physical body. Less touch-based, and more temperature-based, somehow.

At first, I tensed at the sudden sight of a big, silvery aura. In my experience, silver was a color to be avoided at all costs. Not only did silver metal burn like ice when it touched magi like me, but it usually came with Mage Hunters.

But Meleya didn't seem fearful at all as she squealed with excitement and rushed toward the large, silvery aura. An aura that belonged to a four-winged dragon now perching beside us on the Skyforge floor.

"Stars," I muttered. The dragon was translucent, but I could see it perfectly. That had to mean it wasn't a physical evren, but a spirit one.

Meleya flung herself at the creature, wrapping her arms around its neck. In turn, the dragon rubbed its head against her a few times in quick succession, and I heard a distinct, draconic purr.

Beside me, Mom was beaming. I suddenly got the feeling this wasn't the first time she was seeing this silver spirit dragon.

"Who's this?" I asked.

"Blink," came Meleya's animated reply. "Sniff's twin sister."

Pieces started coming together. I saw Meleya eagerly clutching a silver heartscale—at least, the spirit version of one—where it hung from a cord around her neck. It was clear that the golden-yellow-scaled Sniff wasn't the only dragon Meleya had bonded.

Meleya was already mounting her dragon, Blink, and beckoning for Mom and I to join her. For a moment I was worried the evren, clearly only on her first ascension, wouldn't be able to carry all three of us. But it turned out spirits weighed next to nothing, and Blink had no trouble spreading her four wide wings and taking to the skies.

Soot, the sky in Etheria was *incredible*.

Where the sky appeared blue in the physical plane, I now realized I'd never even understood what true blue was before now. The shade was so vibrant and pure I felt like I could stare infinitely into its depths. Cutting across the blue canvas was the sun, which left a blazing golden arc in its wake. The arc spanned from the east horizon to the west, creating a great celestial ring around us like a comet chasing its own tail. Shimmering orange, pink, and green fringed the ring in nebulous clouds. The sun was setting, but the sky remained bright. I could've stared at it for hours.

At least, I could have if there wasn't so much other stuff to look at.

Creatures native to the spirit plane soared all around us. Some were semi-familiar, like the translucent flying foxes, complete with ethereal feathered wings, which trailed red-and-yellow auras behind them. Others were completely foreign, like these rabbit-sized draconic insects in every imaginable shade of violet. They looked like small, carapaced dragons, with translucent, butterfly-esque wings and glittering, kite-like tails.

"Avias," Mom called them.

It was like Mom had said: The more I focused on the ethereal side, the more the physical plane faded into the background. When I tried to, the physical side was easy to see, but for now, the spirit world filled my vision.

Meleya was absolutely loving our flight. Her long, white braid floated out behind her as she drank it all in, asking Mom about everything.

"What's that?" Meleya pointed to a mass of tiny, snake-like lime green auras flying in a spiral pattern as they corkscrewed across the painted sky.

"A flurry of skywinders," Mom explained.

"What about that?" Meleya directed our gazes downward and to the west, where a brilliant white column of what looked like pure ether twisted along with the landscape, floating just above the array of earthy auras below.

"Is that... a river of ether?" I asked.

"*Jhi*, yes," Mom said eagerly. "*Ku zuuta liija ji taaika, ja ziinan kun alkuuja ji etehr. Zama kal zuuo ji zidaan*—"

"Mom," I said, using my head to gesture toward a very confused Meleya. "*Ehta ziina kuuvat Drekai*—You're speaking in Drekai."

"*Antiik*—I'm so sorry," Mom said.

"She does that sometimes when she gets excited," I said as I leaned closer to Meleya. I felt a little rush as I got to speak this way about my mother. I'd thought I'd forgotten all of her endearing little habits, and I was thrilled by how familiar they felt now.

"That river of ether is called a 'ley line'," Mom repeated in accented Evgardian. "Rivers of pure ether that provide for all of Etheria. They are the source from which magi refill their ether wells, even in the physical plane. Once, I believe I even saw a great ship sailing along the ley lines, though it was too far away to reach. Many things in Etheria are still a mystery even to me."

"Amazing," I said, already feeling tempted to dive straight into the floating white river just to see what would happen.

"Drak," Meleya suddenly cursed. "What's *that?*"

I craned my neck to get a look at what she was pointing to, and what I saw made my stomach churn. While everything we'd seen in Etheria thus far had been full of life and light, what lay in the far distance to the northeast was exactly the opposite.

It was a vast swath of earth, completely blanketed in dull, lifeless gray. Spiraling storm clouds brewed within it, as if we were looking at a massive, turbulent, gray hurricane. Even from here, I could see bright blue lightning crackling.

"That's a Haze," Mom said. "One of many. All of Etheria is broken up into Hazes and Havens, which are locked into an endless war with one another. Here, we are in a Haven, where everything is vibrant. Even now, night falls, but we remain in the light."

"I noticed that," I said, glancing once more at the gorgeous sun on its ring, now sinking beneath the horizon.

"But if we were to set foot within a Haze," Mom continued, "everything would go dark and cold. There, it is eternally night. Our entire perception of the world would change."

"What's in the Haze?" I asked.

"Storms," Mom replied. "And umbral spirit creatures, poisoned by the Gray. I've never ventured far into a Haze—it's too dangerous. Spirits who stay in one for too long go gray and numb."

Meleya's tone was worried. "Spirits can get the shadow wasting, too?"

"*Jhi,* they certainly can. Ah—" Mom pointed downward. "Land here, Blink!"

Meleya's spirit dragon gave a roar, then angled her wings so that we began to coast. Before long, we alighted on a grassy knoll atop the ledges of Skygard's rugged southern coastline and I hurried to slide off of Blink's back to get a better view.

The Orothion stronghold stood proudly on the cliffside above us, and I could see the castle's dragon stables on a ledge of its own a little further up as well.

Below us, the ocean waves of the Scarlet Straight crashed against the rock. As I focused on seeing both the physical and the spiritual waves, I realized that while the churning water was mostly synchronized, there were slight discrepancies between the cool, gray-blue physical water and the playful aquamarine aura misting all around it. It was fascinating—everything here seemed more alive than I'd ever realized. Even the winds seemed to shimmer, and I could've sworn I heard laughter from them as they whipped up the waves and made the auras of the pale green grasses dance.

Meleya smiled as she stroked the spirit scales along Blink's neck. Mom joined me at the edge of the cliff to put an arm around me. That wasn't enough for me, so I gave her yet another tight embrace.

"Mom," I started. "Earlier you mentioned that there was a reason you hadn't yet moved on. Into... what did you call it?"

"Deep Etheria," Mom supplied.

"That's it. What did you mean?"

Meleya took a few steps closer to listen in, and her dragon crept along with her.

Mom took a deep breath before responding. "Did I ever tell you about my people's legends regarding the *khaviila jhi Zolehi?*"

"Solei's protectors," I translated. It was incredible how quickly the language was coming back. The words sparked a mental image of a spitfire, a draconic, winged snake with a frill, native to the Dragon Isles. "Yeah, I think so. There was a story about an ethereal spitfire who battled monsters. Jet was the spitfire's name, right?"

Mom grinned and ruffled my hair. "You *would* remember that part. Do you remember why Jet the spitfire battled monsters?" I shook my head. "It was to protect Jihn, the man who tried to save his life as a hatchling. Though Jihn's attempts to save the young spitfire failed, even in death, the creature pledged to protect Jihn. With a fang as an anchor for Jet's spirit, the pair ventured across the Dragon Isles, fighting darkness and umbrals on both the spiritual and physical sides of the earth."

"Jet and Jihn," I nodded, remembering late nights of eagerly taking in every word of Mom's stories. "That was one of my favorites. But what does it have to do with why you're still here?"

"Even in death, Jet chose not to move on, but to become a *khaviila.* A protector, tethered to a living soul through an object."

Meleya made a sudden noise; something between a gasp and a shriek.

"Of course!" she said, beaming. "*That's* what Blink is! And her heartscale... that's what tethers her to me!"

She clutched the heartscale as Blink began to purr once more, nuzzling Meleya with her silvery nose. Her foxlike draconic ears twitched with contentment.

"That's right." Mom nodded. "As for me, my situation is... unique. When I passed into Etheria, I found I could not move on as most spirits do."

"Why?" Meleya asked.

My heart sank as I understood. "It was because of the Black Valkyrie, wasn't it?" I said. "Vidya... she still had your ether well, which meant..."

"I was trapped," Mom finished. "Even if I'd wanted to, I can't leave the first level of Etheria for what lies beyond. But I soon learned that this left me with an opportunity that few human spirits ever get."

Meleya's eyes widened. "You became a *khaviila*."

Mom put a hand on my back. "Even in death, I swore to remain by my son's side. Stars, I'm glad I did, too. You wouldn't believe how many *khaamu*, how many wraiths, hunger to control you, Asher."

"What?" I asked with a frown.

Mom squeezed my shoulder affectionately. "Why do you think you've never heard a whisper from a Gray One while so many of your fellow Knights of the Torch suffer? It seems being a human *khaviila* makes me even more of a threat to those shade-cursed wraiths."

At that, Mom's hand went to her hip. For the first time, I realized a sword hung there—a curved, Drekai-style scimitar made entirely of crystals and starglass. Soot, it looked cool, with streaks of spirit-quartz, topaz, and emerald running through the crisp starglass blade. But Mom was no Astromancer, so where had she gotten ahold of a weapon like that?

For a moment, I wondered how the starglass didn't dissolve into ether-dust after a certain amount of time, but then I realized that a few of the crystals embedded in its hilt were actually skystone. With a perpetual power source like that, her weapon would last indefinitely.

"Where did you get that sword?" I asked. "It's made of starglass, right?"

"*Jhi*, yes. Starglass and *krystaali*—that is, the Ethereal equivalent of gemstone."

"Only Astromancers can make starglass, so how...?" I cocked my head.

Zerana gave a smile as she patted the hilt of her blade. "I may be trapped on this level of Etheria, the one most closely linked to the physical plane, but I'm not completely isolated here. Traders from Deep Etheria pass through every now and then, and I was able to get this off of one who deals in Ethereal weaponry. It's been incredibly useful for fighting off wraithkind. Some Gray Ones got very close to you last year when you were seeking revenge on Vidya for what she did to me. I hate to think what might've happened if they'd succeeded and were there to egg you on."

"Soot," I muttered, putting a hand to my head. "This is a lot to take in."

"I know," Mom said apologetically. "I was overwhelmed at first as well."

"So if you're my spirit protector," I began, latching onto the first question that came to mind, "what object anchors you to me?"

Mom arched a dark eyebrow, her lips quirking into a smile. "What do you think?"

It took me another second, but then it hit me like a ton of scales. Of course, I thought as my fingers closed around the familiar fabric of Mom's old turquoise dust scarf. My heart swelled, and I thought I noticed the sparkle of spirit-tears in Mom's dragonfire green eyes.

While the night here didn't leave the spirit plane any darker than twilight, I got to watch the crescent moon rise. Like the sun, it spun on a ring of its own light, though it was dimmer than that of the sun. When I focused on it, I thought I could almost see the spindly, wire-like connection between the moon and the tides, like the strings of a puppet. The moon glowed with a color I couldn't quite place... Something like violet mixed with the color of ashes.

And stars, the *stars.*

They glowed as brightly as the sun, just smaller. Each had its own glorious, nebulous aura in a different color, a lot like the human auras I'd seen running around the Skyforge terrace when we'd first gotten blasted into Etheria. Maybe it was just my imagination, but when I focused, they seemed to emit sound as well. A faint, celestial chorus like a choir singing in harmony.

My mouth fell open when a sudden burst of emerald fire streaked across the sky. "Whoa," I said aloud, and Meleya got up from where she'd been sitting with Blink.

"It's a skyfall," she said, just as awestruck as I was. We'd both seen skyfalls before, but watching the comet race toward Evgard from this side was both breathtaking and terrifying all at once. As it fell, it sent out pulses of pure ether, which raced across the air in cascading waves. And while the stars' song had been harmonious and otherworldly, the skyfall thrummed like a lute playing a note far lower and more resonant than it had any right to play.

The skyfall landed somewhere in the distant Izmara Ocean to the west, sending out one last pulse of ether that rippled across the sea. Even all the way at Skygard's southern tip, I could feel the faintest wave of its power. All that valuable skystone—and all those draconic eggs—that the meteor carried were now at the bottom of the sea.

"*Ehta ehlka*—Incredible, isn't it?" Mom said, joining Meleya and me at the ledge.

"It's *all* incredible," I replied. "The skyfall, the sea, the moon...are just—"

"*Zaavu!* The moon!" Mom smacked her forehead. "That reminds me. Shades, but he'll be so worried!"

"What?" Meleya asked at the same time I said, "Who?"

Only I understood as Mom muttered to herself in Drekai, as if she hadn't heard us, "*The moon is only a waxing quarter, so that will make things fairly tricky. Still, we ought to try.*"

Meleya looked at me with confusion, but in this case, translating wouldn't exactly fix that.

"Come on!" Mom tugged at both my arm and Mel's. "We have to get back to the stronghold!"

It took us a little while to figure out exactly where they'd taken our physical bodies. But once Meleya began to look for clues, she quickly noticed the super-fine aura threads in indigo and turquoise that connected our spirits to our bodies. Those led us straight to the outside window of Orothion's medical wing. Blink dropped us off and the three of us climbed inside.

We spotted our bodies right away, spread out on adjacent cots near the window. Both Meleya and I were lying as still as we had been in the Skyforge earlier, our breathing shallow and even. When our spirits came close, they seemed to regain a tiny bit of color. We looked so peaceful.

After finally getting the hang of tuning the physical plane out, it took considerable concentration to get it to come back into focus now. What had just recently been barely-visible flickers of color took shape, and I watched, intrigued, as the tiny lights grew into full auras that trailed behind medics as they rushed around the wing, attending those who'd been wounded during the battle of the Skyforge. Many beds were filled, and I hoped they'd be able to help everyone in need.

"Look!" The sight of a red, waterfall-like aura got Meleya jumping up and down. She rushed over to it and I blinked a few times to help me hone in more effectively on the physical plane.

"It's Brigan," I said upon recognizing the aura's source. From his broad shoulders to his tidy ridgeknot hairstyle, there was no mistaking the Heir Duke of Solhelm. He was one of a very short list of nobles I found almost tolerable. Okay, okay—I had to admit I really respected, and even liked, Brigan. Who wouldn't like the realm's most genuine, intelligent, debate-obsessed guy?

Continuing to hone my senses, I heard Brigan calling out orders.

"We need some more scaleroot tincture over here, and can someone track down the extra bandages? You, keep watch over this soldier until you're sure he's stable, then report to me for a second check. As for you, bring out another bottle of liquid light. We're gonna need it."

He spoke with such authority and confidence that everyone obeyed without question. I had to admit, I was impressed.

Meleya reached out toward him but, of course, her hand slipped right through his body. Brigan and Meleya had been best friends for years, and between watching him, the various auras, and all of the action inside the medical wing, Meleya was sufficiently occupied.

Meanwhile, I took a few steps back toward our bodies. A cloud of steady, unassuming cobalt-colored mists hovered over me. The blue didn't look at all like the vivid lightning-blue of voidarchy, nor did it appear dusky like the cloaks Mage Hunters wore.

I inhaled deeply as ever so gradually the physical form of a man sitting beside my cot began to take shape. A man whose posture was somehow both proud and strong, yet weighed down by years of heavy burdens.

Dad.

And he was staring right at me.

Not just looking my way, but actually making eye contact, in a way his blind eyes could no longer manage in the physical plane. It was jarring. Not once since arriving in Etheria had a single living soul—that is, a living *physical* soul—so much as flinched at my spirit's presence. But Dad... he was different.

Years ago, when the Black Valkyrie took Mom, Dad had fought back, which resulted in him losing his sight completely. He'd lost his job at the mines, and for too long, I'd thought he was losing his mind as well. As a Rifter like Meleya, Dad was able to use his powers to access 'the Sight', which allowed him glimpses into the spirit plane. All these years, I'd thought his claims of being able to detect Mom's presence were nothing more than the delusions of a poor, grief-stricken widower, desperate to believe his wife wasn't really gone.

Stars, did I ever stand corrected.

He must've recovered from whatever minor wound had left him injured right after the battle, because he got to his feet as soon as he saw me and Mom. A glowing golden rune shone over his forehead, its light penetrating both the physical and spiritual planes.

"Akayto, my dearest *rakaai!*" Mom beamed as she floated beside me. "Look who I've found! I'm so sorry for not finding you sooner—things have been so chaotic and I knew you needed to be seen by the medics, so I thought I'd let Asher and Meleya take a moment to get used to Etheria, then I just got distracted. I know, I know, that's no surprise—"

"Oh, Zerana, Asher's with you?" Dad's whisper cut in before Mom finished, his unseeing eyes bright with worry. "Soot... does that mean..."

Dad trailed off and I did a double take. Had he not heard a word Mom just said?

Beside me, Mom shook her head, then replied slowly and articulately. "Not. Dead."

She pointed my way, but Dad still looked very confused.

My brow furrowed. "He can't hear us, can he?"

Mom sighed. "It's called 'the Sight' not the 'sound'." She chuckled weakly at the joke before continuing. "But I digress—Your father *can* hear me, but only at certain times. The veil between worlds is a tricky thing. It ebbs and flows with the tides. When the moon is new, he can't even see me very well. But when the moon is full, that's when the barrier between the spiritual plane and the physical world is the thinnest. Then, we can practically communicate in full sentences."

Mom glanced longingly out the window where the crescent moon hung in the bright ethereal sky. "But that won't be for another week or so," she said.

Dad was looking at me with such pain it made my heart ache. He thought I was dead. I smiled at him, hoping to reassure him.

I saw him turn back toward my physical body. He fumbled to find my chest, then placed a gentle hand atop it, feeling it rise and fall, however slowly. His aura churned, and I realized he didn't know *what* to think.

After a moment, Dad got up from his chair and went to stand by the window. He tilted his chin upward toward the night sky.

In the physical world, the sky was dark. But for us—Dad included—the endlessly deep amethyst sky was a canvas for about a zillion stars speckling it with infinite shades of splattered paint.

Dad had always been interested in the heavens, I realized, as I recalled all the times Dad had invited me to join him stargazing. Before I was born, Dad had been part of a crew of skyseekers—men and women who tracked skyfalls, fought off any dreklings or other wild dragonkind at the site, then pillaged the skystone and sold it to the highest bidder. Dad had always referred to skyseeking as 'privateering', but I liked to drive him crazy by calling him an 'ex-pirate'.

Dad had been the navigator of his skyseeker crew. He knew everything and then some about the stars, and though he couldn't use it anymore, I knew he still kept his old astrolabe—the runemark-enhanced device he'd once used for navigation—back at our family home in Steel Rim.

Each time Dad had asked me to join him under the stars, however, I'd said no. I just wasn't interested in constellations and all that the way he was. But now... I was starting to wish I hadn't turned him down. In fact, as I focused on the stars now, I thought I could even see a gossamer, shimmering light, as if outlining the constellations. The drawings of dragons and birds and archers I'd seen in Kai's astrology books had always looked like artistic nonsense to me—there was no way anyone really saw such images in all those dots... right? But my whole view on the stars was rapidly shifting.

Mom joined Dad at the window. I watched them standing side by side, one corporeal and the other spirit, looking up at the moon together. Mom leaned her head onto Dad's shoulder, and though I knew he couldn't truly feel her, I saw him tilt his head ever so slightly her way, too.

My heart felt both pained and full at the same time. There was so little separating them, yet what was there seemed as vast and endless as the ethereal night sky.

Chapter 2: Astral Sleep

Meleya

As it turned out, there were actually a surprising number of perks to being a ghost.

Okay, we weren't ghosts, just spirits. Bodiless souls, trapped in Etheria with no idea when or if we would ever get back to the physical plane. Honestly, if it weren't for Blink, I would probably still be panicking inside. For one thing, I was partially see-through. For another, it was really taking me a minute to get used to this whole 'floating' thing, directing my motion more with willpower than actual walking. Luckily, we didn't float away with the winds, since our spirits seemed to generally adhere to most of the basic principles of gravity.

But with my spirit dragon by my side, I was keeping it together. Almost enjoying myself, even.

First off, the views were spectacular. Each new aura was like a neverending pool of color, texture, and depth, and I wanted to learn everything about each one. My old mentor, Torsten, had given me a book filled with runes designed to help Rifters like me access our powers, but I couldn't help but wish I'd asked him more about the Sight. The book didn't have much information regarding aura interpretation, but I recalled that Torsten used to weave blankets based on various auras he'd seen in the spirit plane. I wondered if I'd ever see him again.

Another fascinating aspect of being a spirit was how we didn't need to sleep for nearly as long as physical beings did. After only three or so hours a day, I felt completely refreshed.

Time passed quickly for Asher, Zerana, Blink, and me in Etheria. We set up a makeshift camp in the spot Zerana had shown us on the cliffside just below the Orothion stronghold, near the dragon stables. I was happy about that, since it meant I could visit Sniff often.

My bond with Sniff felt strange, and Asher felt the same regarding his bond with Thorn. I could still feel my golden-yellow evren and sense his general state of being through the spirit version of the golden heartscale I wore around my neck beside Blink's silver one. That said, our communication had degraded significantly, similar to when Asher and Zerana had tried to get through to Akayto. Whenever my spirit got close, Sniff would perk up and let his tongue hang out, then fold up his four wings and use the talons on the hinges to scurry around the stables in search of me. I could almost hear the faint sound of flute-like notes through our bond, but it was never quite solid enough. He couldn't see, feel, or hear me, but I talked to him every day anyway. It was odd, because my connection with Blink seemed to work even when I was in the physical plane, but I figured it was because of how new this development was. Even communicating with Blink had taken some time to solidify at first.

Each day our communication seemed to improve, and once I even got Sniff to sit down while I gave him a scratch on the neck the way he liked. He sensed it so strongly that he immediately launched himself a few feet in the air with excitement and began chasing his tail. It was like Zerana had said—the veil between worlds thinned and thickened with the phases of the moon.

As Sniff got so riled up that he began to sneeze his trademark ether blasts through his nose, I couldn't help but wonder if I'd ever get to ride him again. I loved being here with Blink, but stars, I missed my Sniff.

Would we ever get back into our bodies? Our physical forms were in some kind of stasis—We didn't need to eat or drink, and all other functions had come to a stop as well. None of the medics knew quite what to make of it. I'd tried to align my spirit with my body several times since that first day, but of course, nothing ever changed.

I noticed that Asher hadn't tried again even once. In those first moments after the blast had hit us, he'd been so eager to make things right. But now that he had his mother back, he clearly wasn't ready to risk losing her again so soon. Frankly, I couldn't blame him.

Zerana, for her part, was the ideal guide to the spirit plane. Each passing hour was filled with wonder. Everything had its own unique aura, from the wildflowers to the waters to the wind.

One day, Zerana took us walking-slash-floating along the ledge near the Orothion stronghold. There was a little grove of trees, and I was just admiring their mixed red-and-forest green auras when suddenly one of the tree auras pulsed, almost as if it were shuddering.

"What was that?" I asked.

"Focus on the physical plane," came Zerana's answer.

When I did, I saw a man—He must've been one of the groundskeepers at Orothion. He'd just chopped the tree down, and was now dragging it away.

"Stars," Asher said. "But the tree's aura is still upright in the spirit plane."

"While the physical and spiritual form of the earth are eternally entwined," Mom began, "they are not always in perfect synchronization. It may take months or even years for the tree's spiritual form to fall. And by fall, I do not mean die, I mean its essence will simply take a new form. But without its physical form to anchor it, the tree's aura is far more volatile, more likely to follow in its physical footsteps at the slightest disturbance."

"Fascinating," I said as I reached out to touch the aura of the fallen tree. To me, it still felt solid, at least for now.

I tapped my chin. "I've seen Blink fly straight through solid ground before, as if it were nothing but air."

"In the spirit plane, it likely was." Zerana smiled. "It's why spirits like us can so often float through walls, if they're thin enough. It's especially easy in newer buildings, where the structure's spiritual form hasn't yet taken shape."

There was so much about Etheria that was difficult to grasp, but I was loving learning as much as I could.

A few days later, after visiting the dragon stables, I spotted something peculiar a little lower down the cliff. A soft white glow seemed to be coming from a gap in the stone, and curiosity drove me to rift down to it.

Stars, was I glad I did! Through a crack in the cliffside, I found a secluded cove filled to bursting with what appeared to be pure ether.

In the center of the cove was a crystal spring, only instead of water, it flowed with glowing white ether. Ethereal plants surrounded it, from purple emberferns to earthy green moss, to a whole row of delicate bushes laden with plump berries. Each berry was round, and glowed with a whitish inner light like tiny stars.

Dozens of spirit creatures gathered around the spring. A misty, translucent doe fed on the plants while little draconic foxes curled up near the water. Dainty dragonflies flitted to and fro while scaled hummingbirds' wings vibrated faster than my eyes could track.

I didn't waste a second scurrying back out of the cove to find Asher and Zerana. Blink flew us down, and with some handy portalling, I managed to get her large form into the cove along with us. Blink's fiery green eyes shone in the mystical etherlight, as did Asher's and Zerana's.

True to form, Asher couldn't help but hurry over to the spring and touch it. His whole aura pulsed with light, and I watched with wonder as his ether well—the translucent crystal tethered to his spirit near his heart—went from about half-empty to completely full.

"Wow," Asher said. "It's like the ether vents back home in Steel Rim!"

"That's exactly right." Zerana nodded eagerly. "Well spotted! This is an ether oasis. They pop up in Havens wherever enough ley lines intersect. Sometimes the ether is plentiful enough to penetrate the physical plane, too. I wonder if that's the case here..."

Zerana trailed off as she squinted. I'd come to recognize that look. She was focusing on the physical plane.

I did the same, and soon, things began to take shape. Drak, I wasn't sure what I'd expected to see in the physical world, but it certainly wasn't a comfortable armchair set before a hearth.

Asher chuckled. "What's a cozy living room doing in a random seaside cove?"

"I'm not sure," Zerana admitted. "They say the ancients built sacred or important structures at the places where ley lines intersect. According to some contacts of mine, the Guardians built the great High Citadel over the most powerful ether oasis in the realm, at the heart of Evgard. I've never seen it myself—Been too busy keeping an eye on you."

She gave Asher a teasing tickle, and he laughed.

As he did, I noticed a great red bloodhusky curled up near the armchair on the physical side. He was watching us with intelligent eyes, and I recognized him right away.

"His Majesty?" I said, hurrying up to him. What was Solrac's dog doing here? His Majesty the bloodhusky woofed as my spirit knelt beside him.

"You can see me," I marvelled. "Zerana, can all animals in the physical plane see spirits?"

"Some can," Zerana answered. "Though in my experience, their interactions tend to be fairly limited. His Majesty's a smart one."

As if on cue, His Majesty's ruddy tail began to wag, and I laughed as I stroked his fur. At least, I went through the motions. I didn't really feel anything, though I thought I felt the slightest resistance, and His Majesty gave a contented sigh, curling up to resume his nap.

Now, as interesting as the cozy cove's physical elements were, I had more questions. I stopped concentrating on the physical plane and hurried over to one of the spirit bushes—the kind with the glowing berries.

"What're these, Zerana?" I asked.

"Etherberries," Zerana said as she plucked one and popped it into her mouth. "Mmm. *Kuliinen!* Easily one of the best parts about Etheria."

As I watched her eat, my mind instantly began to race. Asher noticed and gave an amused snort.

"Already thinking up recipes for an etherberry pie, Mel?"

"Shut up," I quipped. But Asher wasn't wrong. That was one of the things I'd been missing most since getting blasted into the spirit plane: cooking for my friends and family.

I knew spirits didn't need to eat the same way a physical being did. According to Zerana, we could thrive indefinitely on light, be it sunlight, starlight, or—apparently—etherlight. Still, after sampling an etherberry myself, I couldn't help but pick a little handful of them.

Next, I traced a medium-complexity rune. As I did, a tiny, floating particle that had been following me just over my shoulder ever since our arrival floated into place before me and began to sparkle with golden light.

Soon, it elongated into a crack that split apart to reveal a spacious, white interior. I saw the familiar shelves of ingredients, from sacks of potatoes to jars of preserves, to the little canisters of spices all clustered together near the front. There were strips of dried drakalope jerky and a whole row of peppers that Asher and I had bought together at the festival in Topaz Sierra during our journey to Skygard. I'd neatly arranged those in order of spiciness, from the cool poblanos all the way to the dangerously hot ghost pepper I had warned Asher not to even touch. While we'd been camped with the refugees on the lava fields, I'd gotten some help drying out some of the peppers and then grinding them into powders. I couldn't help but look at the canisters with pride and longing. They were practically begging to be used.

"Meleya of Misthaven," Asher said, laughing as he peered over my shoulder, "I'd bet good marks that no other Rifter in the history of Evgard has ever used their rift hold as a pantry."

My lips quirked into a grin—Asher was probably right about that. Rift holds were like one-way personal portal pockets, used for storing valuable things that only the Rifter who made it could access.

Then a sudden coldness pricked my heart. While almost everything inside my rift hold pantry brought me joy, there was one item in the far back corner that filled me only with dread.

From the Etheria side of things, the little sack of rice pulsed with a sinister blue light. That was where I'd stashed it—one of the darkest, most powerful objects the realm over:

The Soul Reaper's voidshard.

Even just thinking about the thin blue crystal sent a shudder running through my spirit. I knew that, more than anything, the Soul Reaper wanted his shard back. It was vital to his success in tearing down Evgard as we knew it. Numerous Mage Hunters had pursued us across the realm trying to get it back.

While keeping the shard in my hold was a heavy burden, I felt it was my duty. Besides Akayto, I was the only Rifter among the Knights of the Torch. The Farseer—that is, Solrac—said that the safest place for it was in the spirit plane where the Soul Reaper couldn't detect it, which meant I had to hang onto it. I had no idea for how long, but I was determined not to let the shard's dark influence drag me down as it had before.

I hadn't realized I'd been staring at the sack until I felt something brush against my hand. When I saw that it was Asher, the back of his fingers coming to rest against mine, my heart nearly jumped into my throat.

"You okay?" he asked, real concern evident in his voice. He'd caught on to my sudden mood shift. My aura must've given me away.

"Uh..." I started. Drak, why was I finding it so difficult to put together a sentence? This was *Asher*, the obnoxious, messy, erratic scarf-wearer who enjoyed spending his free time driving me up a wall. Yeah, I *might* have kissed him after a spar out on the lava fields right before our group of formerly 'Rebel' Knights infiltrated the Orothion stronghold. But that kiss had practically been an accident—the result of my getting caught up in the moment. Those fiery emerald eyes of his certainly didn't help.

As it turned out, I wasn't the only one with doubts about the two of us being together. Just then, Blink's head slowly rose up just behind Asher and me, her large eyes narrowed as they shifted back and forth between us.

Boom-boom... dum, Blink's thoughts came like determined drumbeats through our bond, channeled so that only I could sense them. Though she was only a first ascension dragon and couldn't communicate with words, her meaning was clear: Blink was *not* a fan of Asher and me.

Brrum, ba-dum, Blink clarified, reminding me that she very much liked Asher and me—Seperately. As if validating this conclusion, Blink not-so-subtly nosed her way between us, effectively separating our hands. Asher raised an eyebrow.

Blink! I thought through the bond, cheeks burning. My dragons had always had strong opinions about where I placed my feelings.

My silvery evren gave me a pointed look, prompting me to look down at my belt. Even in the spirit plane, a white quartz crystal hung there, and I instinctively clutched it. The crystal had been a gift from someone who, despite everything, I doubted I'd ever fully forget. Still...

That ship has sailed, Blink, I thought stubbornly. *It's time to move on.* Blink's glare didn't exactly fade, but the emotion behind her eyes did soften just a bit.

"I think I'll go check on Akayto," Zerana suddenly said, thankfully ending the standoff between my dragon and me.

"I can join you if you'd like," Asher said, taking a step toward his mom.

"No need. I'll catch up with you two later."

Then she was gone, leaving Asher and me with my uncompromising evren, who was still watching Asher with suspicion. Asher was looking at me again, his expression unreadable.

Aware that the fringes of my aura were turning a shade of soft red, no doubt reflective of my quickly warming spirit-cheeks, I gave a somewhat pitiful fake cough.

"Uh," I started, "I think I'll take Blink for a ride."

For a second, Asher seemed to wilt. His turquoise aura, normally in constant, energetic motion, slowed its churning as he replied, "Oh. Okay." Had he wanted me to stay?

Without thinking, I asked, "Wanna come?"

At that, Asher's whole soul brightened. "Yeah!"

Blink straightened right up, narrowing her eyes again as she sent a whole string of skeptical drumbeats through our bond.

Please don't be weird, I begged through the bond as the three of us headed back outside.

Soon, Asher and I were soaring over the Scarlet Strait. It was the first time we'd flown through Etheria together without Zerana and, for whatever reason, that changed the tone of the flight entirely.

Blink wasn't nearly as wild in her flight patterns as Sniff was. Where Sniff would ride the winds up and down, occasionally throwing in a spiral or a loop, Blink's track was smooth and graceful, her wings cutting through the air as if it were melting butter. Actually, the sky was currently a gorgeous shade of pale gold, a lot like butter. Drak, I needed to stop thinking about food.

As usual, Asher couldn't just sit back and enjoy the ride. So far, our flight had been simple, but he suddenly had an idea for how to spice things up.

"Check this out," he said, scooting backward along Blink's spine. I twisted my body to get a better look.

Asher's eyes flashed with gold etherlight as he accessed his powers. As an Astromancer, he was one of the Archonic magi types, which meant he didn't have to runetrace like I did. I watched as he willed his powers into manifesting through his hands.

He pulled ether from his well—literally, I realized, as streams of white flowed from his heart to his hands as he formed it into tangible links of pure, crystalline starglass. His precision was impressive as he formed a fine, chain-link rope, then fashioned a starglass harness around his chest and shoulders, fusing the end of the chain to its center.

"What in the void are you doing?" I asked.

Asher shot me a wide, crooked grin. "Ever seen a human kite?"

"Oh no."

Despite my misgivings, Asher hurriedly began fusing the other end of the chain to a clump of starglass he was attempting to secure on one of Blink's spines.

"What if it slips off?" I asked.

"It won't sl—"

I barely flicked the crystalline apparatus and it fell right off of Blink's spine. Blink gave a satisfied, purr-like dragon chuckle.

Asher put a finger to his lips and narrowed his eyes to melodramatic slits. "That... was not how I pictured it working."

"Here," I said, "use me."

"What?"

"I'll be your anchor."

Asher's eyes lit up as he understood what I was saying. More ether coalesced in his hands, and he carefully formed another starglass harness on me.

I stared straight ahead, not daring to look Asher in the eye as his etherarchy sent my spirit-heart speeding. He didn't even so much as touch me, but it was enough that even the temperature of my aura seemed to rise.

"What're those?" Asher asked.

I turned slightly to see that he was pointing to a series of tiny indigo bursts that were jumping off of my aura and onto his own. Oh stars—those weren't literal sparks flying, were they?

Blink huffed in annoyance.

"Just fuse the chain to my harness," I said, pretending not to have heard him.

Asher did so, then crouched with his feet on Blink's back. Then, with a mighty whoop, he launched himself into the sky.

Even in his usual form, Asher was never especially gravity-bound, but as a spirit he was practically lighter than air. He didn't waste a second as he activated his levitation powers, the air warping behind him as he propelled himself through a series of somersaults, spirals, swoops, and dives that made me laugh out loud. Even Blink found his antics amusing. The harness worked perfectly, allowing me to be his anchor while he soared.

"Mel, you've got to try this!" Asher called out.

"Not on your life!" I shouted back.

"But how about on my starglass?"

Even as it was happening, I wasn't sure how Asher convinced me to do it. He made some adjustments to the starglass chain's connection points, then strung the chain around Blink's body, the chain securing itself between her dual sets of wings.

Then Asher offered me his hand, and with *great* hesitation, I took it.

A scream ripped from my throat as Asher channeled his levitation power into me. The rush was something I'd never experienced before—Was this how it felt to be an Archon?

The winds lifted me up while carrying straight through my spirit, tossing my hair and clothing, but not affecting me the same way they would have in the physical plane. A mild, not unpleasant coolness filled my soul.

I clung to Asher's hand so tightly I'd have cut off circulation if spirit-veins flowed with blood. He was laughing his head off, and I could feel Blink sending me comforting drumbeats through our bond, assuring me that she'd keep our flight smooth and safe, even if she thought Asher was crazy.

"You have to open your eyes, Mel," Asher said.

"Technically, that's not true," I countered, keeping them squeezed tight.

"Fair. But I don't think you'll want to miss this."

I allowed myself another few seconds of precious caution before cracking one eyelid. When I did, I found Asher's crooked smile waiting for me.

I inhaled and it gave me the courage to let go. Not of Asher's hand, but of my anxiety.

I threw out my arms and let out a 'whoop' mixed with just a hint of terrified screaming. Asher whooped back with confidence, and I called out again, this time with genuine thrill. This *was* pretty fun!

Hand in hand Asher and I soared, rising and falling with the winds, with Blink leading the way. The picture we painted transcended anything I'd ever seen before, as our respective auras in silver, indigo, and turquoise splashed across the golden ethereal sky.

That was when I caught sight of a green-tailed meteor streaking across the distant heavens, pulses of pure power rippling off of it as it sailed. It wasn't quite like the skyfall we'd seen that first day in Etheria, mostly because this one wasn't actually falling, rather, it stuck to the atmosphere as if watching over Evgard. Through my ethereal eyes, I noted a gold tinge surrounding the celestial wonder, as if the power it carried was too strong to be contained.

"I think that's Streya's Comet," Asher said, catching sight of the meteor as well. "It passes Evgard once every hundred years or something. My dad once told me that you can see it in the skies for several weeks."

"Incredible," I marvelled.

I wasn't sure how long we stayed up there, spinning spirals, flying loops, and turning somersaults. Eventually, I even built up enough courage to let go of Asher's hand and soar on my own ethereal wings.

"Look!" Asher said, pointing to the east.

I found the moon had risen, looking positively enormous through my ethereal eyes. Its mysterious, multicolored aura shrouded its corporeal face, like something straight out of a dream.

"Whoa," I said as I nearly collided with one of those ethereal butter-fly-dragons Zerana had called 'avias', its feather-like antennae tickling my face and sending me into a slight panic. I swatted madly and nearly went spiraling out of control.

Luckily, a certain scarf-wearing Astromancer was there to catch me.

"Now Mel," he said, arm wrapped around my waist. "I know you miss cooking, but I don't think bug dragon paste would make a very good ingredient."

Asher laughed at his own joke while I struggled to choose between doing the same and rolling my eyes. But then something distracted me enough that I forgot about doing either. Asher got distracted too, based on the way his laughter trailed off.

As he held me, Asher's aura sent a volley of bright turquoise sparks toward mine. His gaze was fixed on my spiraling indigo aura and, so softly I could barely hear it, he breathed, "Wow."

My heart began to pound. But then, Asher seemed to notice the turquoise sparks. He immediately blinked himself out of whatever trance he'd been in.

"So..." he started, his tone jarringly insincere, "not many people know this, but dragon dung is extremely flammable. Some citadels even use it to fuel furnaces that provide heat to the entire castle."

I stared blankly. Both of our auras immediately dimmed, though Blink's perked up a bit in satisfaction.

"How... interesting," I replied. Stars, had I just been imagining the captivated light in his eyes? I suddenly felt embarrassed for... for... I wasn't sure exactly.

Asher gave a deeply awkward smile. "The more you know, right?"

"Right."

Just then, a loud, long whistle pierced the air. Asher and I looked down at Orothion's southernmost tower, where we spotted Zerana waving us down.

Asher and I floated back onto Blink's back, and she flew us to the tower. Zerana was practically jumping up and down with excitement.

"What's going on, Mom?" Asher asked as he dismounted.

"It's Solrac," Mom replied. "He's just arrived at the stronghold from the Mirror Forest."

"Solrac's *here*?" I asked, my interest piquing. Though it made sense—We'd seen His Majesty in the cozy cove, after all.

Zerana nodded vigorously. "He's in the medical wing now, talking with Akayto."

Solrac looked like he'd been through a lot on his journey to Orothion. His medium-length dark hair, normally so immaculately styled, was a bit tangled, and I saw a bruise on his sharp jaw.

That made sense, I thought. Given the bounty of one-thousand gold marks on his head, I was willing to bet that every farmer, dragonslayer, and even nobleman the realm over wanted to be the one to deliver the great Farseer to High King Magnus.

But despite Solrac's state, his rich scarlet aura burned with a commanding fire. He gave orders to his fellow Knights with the confidence and authority of a natural-born leader:

"We'll also need to send a team to Bitter Valley, due northeast. There's a backwater apothecary there that sells moonwillow bark—Drak, I hope it's still around. Arcocado oil should be easier to come by, but we'll need to start it steeping beneath tonight's full moon as *quickly* as possible. I'm talking within the hour. You got all that?"

A chorus of agreement rose from the cluster of aura flickers surrounding Solrac's. I focused on the physical plane and saw a team of medics with Brigan at their head, taking careful note of each new ingredient Solrac asked for.

"Be careful," Solrac warned. "If you must stay the night while out procuring the ingredients, be extra vigilant. Our safehouses may not be as safe as we once thought—On our journey here, Vidya and I encountered the aftermath of one they're calling the Gray Knight."

A few medics nodded as if they'd heard the news as well. They promised to be careful, then Brigan hurriedly led the group of medics from the wing.

"What's going on?" I asked Zerana.

"They're working on a remedy," she explained. "Something that will return you to your bodies. Solrac called your state 'astral sleep'."

"Astral sleep..." I repeated, and suddenly, pieces began to fall into place.

I filled Asher and Zerana in on what had happened to the King of Rengard last year. A blast of dream energy to the head had put him into a strange coma for months, and the only way to wake him was by administering a special remedy provided by the Farseer. Er, Solrac.

"This must've been what happened to King Axel!" I exclaimed. Relief filled my heart. He'd awoken, and with Solrac and Brigan on the job, so would we—eventually.

"But when will this remedy be ready?" Asher asked, a note of worry in his tone.

"I'm not sure, my *laaksi-rakaai*," Zerana replied. She put a gentle hand on his arm.

"Solrac?" said a newcomer, sounding a little out of breath. "Stars, it *is* you!"

It was Kai of Steel Rim, skidding into the medical wing with his ever-present black notebook tucked under his arm. His other hand was occupied, holding the hand of my best friend and Kai's new girlfriend, Solvai. I noticed the way their auras interacted, with Solvai's feathery cerulean spirit doing wonders to release the clear tension in Kai's rigid goldenrod one. Meanwhile, where Kai's aura touched Solvai's, her sky blue mists brightened with confidence.

Kai and Solvai hurried over to where Asher and I lay on our cots.

"They said you asked to see us in the medical wing." Solvai gulped. "Asher and Meleya—Are they alright?"

"Quite alright," Solrac said. "The remedy for astral sleep is being brewed as we speak."

"Thank the goddesses," Solvai said.

"Astral sleep," Kai repeated. "What does that mean?"

"It means that while their bodies sleep, their spirits wander Etheria, very much alert," Solrac said somberly. "There's really no way to know where their spirits are now."

"Actually..." From his place beside Asher's bed, Akayto coughed. "I can tell you exactly where they are now."

The entire gathered assembly responded with shock, glee, and a bit of trepidation as Akayto explained that he could see our auras and even hear our voices. And not only ours, but Zerana's as well. Eager to confirm this, Kai sent one of his many copies of Glint, his ethereal gecko familiar, scurrying across the floor and into Akayto's hand. I was familiar with Kai's gecko-powered mindlink, and knew he already had Glint copies with Solrac and Solvai.

Before long, Kai had connected himself and the others to Akayto's mind. Their surprise and excitement multiplied as they took in our misty, indigo and turquoise forms.

Asher gave an over-the-top salute. "Hello there, Kai, Solrac, and Solvai! If you can hear me, say, 'Asher is the best!'"

Solvai just snorted at that, while Kai was too busy taking notes with wide eyes. Only Solrac replied with a vehement, "Asher is the best!"

"Why didn't you mention anything earlier, Akayto?" Kai asked, still scribbling furiously in his notebook.

"Until Solrac showed up with his astral sleep theory, I really thought they might be dead," Akayto said. "Besides, I haven't been able to see or hear them clearly until tonight—The veil between worlds is at its thinnest during a full moon. Not to mention, they only showed back up quite recently!" He gestured toward the window. "They must've found out somehow that Solrac has come."

Kai's pen was flying as he muttered his rapidly-forming hypotheses about the celestial cycles' influence on the Sight. "I wonder," he murmured, "how much Akayto's personal connection with Zerana enhances his perception... likely accounts for at least fifty-two to eighty-nine percent of the communicative clarity in this particular instance..."

"Meleya?" Solvai said, taking a cautious step closer. She clearly felt a little silly since she was only seeing me thirdhand through Akayto and Glint.

"I'm right here," I responded. When my spirit-hand touched her cerulean aura, it pulsed. Solvai smiled, and I got the feeling that even without the mindlink, she could sense me, much like His Majesty had. For as long as I'd known Solvai, she'd had some of the strongest instincts I'd ever witnessed. As a Wildshaper, it was part of her. The leaders of the Knights of the Torch had seen such potential in my friend too, which is why she'd been appointed to the Triarchy council that led the Knights in spite of both her youth and her prior status as a Mage Hunter.

"By the way," Asher was saying, "I'm loving the beard, Solrac. Very tasteful."

"Why, *thank you,* Asher!" Solrac beamed. "Would you believe that no one has mentioned the beard yet?"

"A crime," Asher said, shaking his head with mock disbelief. Solrac laughed. As I looked at their respective auras, I realized that Solrac's and Asher's had a similar pattern. Both spun with a concentrated, authoritative sort of energy that demanded people pay attention.

"And Zerana," Solrac said, bowing his head toward where she floated. "How long it has been. Truly, I did not think I would get to speak with you again while I still walked this plane."

"Nor I." Asher's mother smiled warmly.

"I am certain you have been taking excellent care of these two—" Solrac gestured toward Asher and me. "And I hope you continue to do so for as long as it takes to brew the remedy that will awaken them. For now, Asher and Meleya, I suppose the two of you can sit back, relax, and enjoy Etheria! After what you did to reclaim Orothion for the true Knights, you've certainly earned a respite."

"Actually..." Solvai started, and everyone turned toward her.

At the sudden onslaught of attention, Solvai's freckled cheeks turned slightly pinker and her sky blue aura visibly trembled. Still, she swallowed and said what she had to say.

"Actually, with Meleya and Asher in the spirit plane, we might have a unique opportunity on our hands. Solrac, how long did you say it would take to brew the remedy?"

"At least a couple of weeks," Solrac said. "To be precise, nine days from the day Brigan and the medics begin to steep the ashroot in the arcocado oil and star blossom extract, which I predict will be..." He paused, stole Kai's notebook and skipped a few pages back, then casually flung it back onto the young Seer's lap, "approximately three days from now, when our lovely, medically inclined sharpshooter, Trickshot, arrives to take charge."

"That's twelve days total," Kai summed up. "Why, Solvai? What are you thinking?"

"Well," Solvai continued, "I've been keeping in contact with a group of falcondrakes living on the cliffs within the lava fields just north of here. They only moved to that spot when something forced them from their old nesting grounds."

"What forced them out?" I asked.

Solvai's expression was thoughtful. "Do you remember the refugees in the lava fields talking about a Haze?"

A few of us nodded—Before we'd infiltrated Orothion, Brigan had mentioned that some of the refugees had seen parts of the land itself going Gray, losing all life and color. I'd seen the way the shadow wasting disease infected humans, even tasted of the numbness once for myself. The idea that the land might be similarly suffering put a pit into my stomach.

All at once, the pieces began to click into place. I remembered that great, gray expanse that Zerana had pointed out when we first got trapped in Etheria. *All of Etheria is broken up into Hazes and Havens,* she'd said, *which are locked into an endless war with one another.*

"Zerana," I spoke quickly. "The Ethereal Hazes you told us about... what if they're starting to show up in the physical plane too?"

Zerana's eyes widened, and she nodded. She explained the concept of Ethereal Hazes and Havens to the 'corporeals', as I was beginning to think of our non-spirit friends, and soon they were all as convinced as I was that the Gray that had once been trapped here was beginning to leak into the physical plane.

"But how?" Kai asked. "And why now? What could be causing these Hazes in the first place?"

"That," Solvai said, "is what I'm hoping Meleya and Asher might be able to find out."

"Us?" Asher asked.

Solvai nodded. "The falcondrakes are sensitive to Etheria—I think that the answers we're looking for about the Hazes might be something the two of you can find while you're still spirits."

"You want them to go into the Haze," Solrac said, stroking his short beard. "If they can find out what's causing them..."

"It'll be the first step in stopping them once and for all." Solvai nodded eagerly, and Solrac's eyes lit up.

Solvai was absolutely right. With the Hazes growing, our whole land was in danger. According to the refugees, the Hazes housed many umbral creatures, whose bites infected people with the shadow wasting. If it had displaced the falcondrakes, there was no doubt it had done the same to hundreds of others, human and animalkind alike. And if it continued to spread, there might not be anywhere else to go.

"It's possible," Zerana said, dragonfire eyes bright. "On this side, the nearest Haze is only a few days' flight northeast from here in the

Stormshadow Desert."

Solrac raised an eyebrow. "The Stormshadow Desert? That sky-forsaken place *would* be a spiritual wasteland." He spoke quickly, clearly enthused about Solvai's idea. "Finding out what lies at the center of the Hazes would benefit our cause *greatly.*"

The pit in my stomach was growing. Zerana had said that the Hazes were dangerous, and that being in one for too long could leave our very spirits stricken with the shadow wasting. I was about to voice my concerns when Kai spoke back up.

"Twelve days..." He tapped his pen against his chin. "Is that enough time for Asher and Meleya to travel to the center of the Haze and back?"

"They won't need to travel back," Solrac said. "Once the remedy is administered, their spirits will return to their bodies, no matter where they are. That is, unless their spirits are killed while they're in the Haze, of course. In that case, Asher and Meleya will never wake up, and we'll all get bombarded with random ingredients as little by little, the contents of Meleya's strange-but-delightful rift hold reverts to the physical plane!"

"Soot and scales." I grimaced.

"More like 'flour and summer squash'," Asher corrected with exaggerated horror, and I rolled my eyes.

"That... doesn't make me feel any better about this plan," Akayto grumbled to Solrac. It seemed I wasn't the only one with doubts.

"Is that really how rift holds work?" Kai asked, pen poised to take notes.

"Indeed," Akayto said. "When a Rifter's spirit... *expires*... anything within their hold drops to the ground, first within the Ethereal plane, then, over the next hour or so, each item fades back into the physical plane to surround the body of the hold's creator. Sometimes the items instead revert to a location that is meaningful to the Rifter, but now we're getting into the sootweeds."

"Fascinating." Kai scribbled in his notebook.

"But Akayto is right to be cautious about the plan," Solrac went on. "We cannot move forward unless Asher, Meleya, and Zerana are on board." He turned our way, light glinting in his eyes. "What say you three? Take a moment to consider if you wish."

There was a moment of silence. Asher and his mother locked gazes, then they floated over to Akayto, whose cobalt aura was swirling with discontent.

"It's not safe," Akayto grumbled. "Asher should just stay put and wait until the remedy is ready."

"That is the easier option," Zerana agreed. Asher looked deep in thought, his expression uncharacteristically serious.

As for me, a bundle of nerves pounded inside my chest. Without thinking, I went to the window where Blink was still perched. Her snout against my cheek brought some comfort.

What do you think, girl? I channeled the thought to my spirit dragon through our bond. While I couldn't see the great gray Haze that lay to the northeast from here, even just picturing it made me shudder.

Ba-doom doom, came Blink's thrumming reply, letting me know that if I did this, I wouldn't be doing it alone. Blink had a lot of experience fighting darkness by now, and if I chose to go, she would do everything she could to keep me safe.

I meandered over to where my body lay. Drak, it was strange seeing myself like this. My long, white hair was splayed out over a pillow, my arms laid neatly at my sides.

Examining my own face, I couldn't help but focus on the Rifter's silvermark on my cheek. When they'd discovered I was a magi, the Mage Hunters' special, silver-infused knife-pen had carved the mark, branding me forever.

Absently, I touched my spirit-cheek, and startled when I felt no mark there. I hadn't had the chance to see my spirit's reflection, and I guess I had assumed the mark would have cut to my soul, too.

For a moment, I wondered why Asher hadn't told me. As I glanced his way, we made eye contact, and I realized, of course he wouldn't have mentioned it. Asher didn't care about things like brands or scars. He wouldn't see my spirit self as healed, because he'd never seen my physical self as broken.

"I know it's risky," Solvai said apologetically, breaking the relative silence.

"Most things worth doing are," Asher answered. He floated over to where our bodies lay too.

"Yes, it would be easier to just wait here, enjoying Etheria's sights and sounds while we wait for the remedy," Asher went on, his voice growing in confidence. "But if I have the chance to help the realm, I've got to take it. Isn't that what it means to be a Knight of the Torch? To Choose Light."

"Burn Bright," I added, giving the second pillar of the Knight's Code.

"And this would 'Drive Out Darkness' for sure," Asher continued. By now, his aura shone like a beacon, and I felt it inspiring mine to do the same. It was as if his light was amplifying mine and, looking around the room, I realized I wasn't the only one. Asher was sharing light with everyone, though I didn't think he noticed.

"I'm in too," I said.

"Me too," Zerana echoed. Blink roared in agreement as well, and Solvai, Kai, and Solrac beamed, their auras fiery. Only Akayto still frowned.

"I'll keep him safe, my *rakaai,*" Zerana whispered to her husband. "As I always have."

Solrac clapped his hands together so loudly that sparks spiraled from his aura on impact. "Excellent! It seems that many of us must now prepare for journeys—Vidya and I must soon depart for Keep Rengard—Speaking of which, Akayto, I hoped to ask for your help in making some rift anchors to speed our journey along. Perhaps another to get us back quickly in a pinch as well. With all the skystone here that Zel hoarded, we should have plenty of ether to power the anchors."

"Of course." Akayto nodded.

"Excellent. Now, for the final piece of business..." Solrac trailed off dramatically, clearly waiting for someone to prompt him to continue.

I bit. "What's that?"

Solrac grinned. "I have already come up with the perfect name for your quest."

Solvai and I both snorted. Asher and Zerana leaned forward with anticipation. Kai seemed ready to write it down, while Akayto rolled his eyes.

"Ladies and gentlemen," Solrac announced with perfect ceremony, "it is time for the opening night of *Braving the Haze: A Tale of Triumph, Turbulence, and Tenacity.*"

Fragment: Gloomhaven

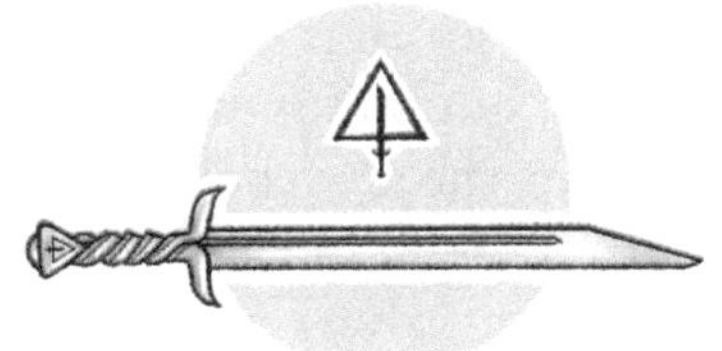

Zoren

Zoren wasn't sure which was bleaker: the streets of Kolbohr or the expressions worn by its inhabitants.

He'd been in the thick of it for days now—the dismal, gray wastes some were calling the Haze. Here, everything from the vegetation to the earth to the skies appeared colorless and misty. While traveling through less populous areas, Zoren had needed to fight off more than a few umbral dreklings; He suspected that, after hatching, many of the bipedal, draconic monsters were gathering around the entrances to Kolbohr's mines, hungry for the skystone veins hidden deep within the earth. But before long, the bites of umbral creatures within the Haze had left them gray and even more savage. After a particularly nasty encounter had nearly cost Zoren his leg, he'd stuck to more well-traveled roads on his trek northeast. Thank the Allfather for Rekoa, or he might've lost his life.

The large, dark purple evren hummed as she used the foreclaws on the hinges of her four wings to walk beside her rider. Zoren and Rekoa had been together since his touch had hatched her egg many moons ago in the dragon hatcheries of Zolehiinu. Her presence was like an anchor to him—For so long, he'd counted his dragon bond as his only true friend.

"*Alright, Rekoa,*" Zoren spoke in his native Drekai. "*I'll meet you here at sundown. But for now, I must go on alone.*"

The third ascension evren's humming grew louder as she replied to Zoren through their bond. *Can I not accompany you?*

"*No,*" Zoren said with finality. "*Gloomhaven is no place for a dragon—Even one belonging to a respected Mage Hunter. The north is filled with dragonslayers looking to turn a quick profit on scales, whether they come from wild dragons or bonded ones like you. Stay hidden."*

She sent a thrumming like a deep didgeridoo through their bond so that even as he left Rekoa behind, Zoren could still sense her comforting humming.

The town of Gloomhaven had given into the Haze completely. Not only was its plantlife dull and gray, but so too were its buildings, streets, and canals. Mist enshrouded even the bedrock, and Zoren could taste the thick, salty air coming in from the eastern sea. This was nothing like the warm, abundant beaches that ran along the Scarlet Strait or the coastal Dragon Isles. This place was cold and overcast, and it was not altogether uncommon to see a set of sapphire eyes from an umbral rat lurking in the gutter.

But as unsettling as Gloomhaven's general ambiance was, it wasn't the part Zoren found most unsettling. For though the Haze left all who lived here perpetually miserable, the people of Kolbohr still managed to summon the requisite energy to shun Zoren. One look at his Drekai horns and tail got them casting dirty looks as they crossed to the other side of the foggy street. Some muttered 'scale-skin' while others whispered 'demon.'

If only they knew.

Suddenly, displacing Rekoa's comforting internal hum came an icy, invisible hand that clenched Zoren's heart. The feeling was, unfortunately, not unfamiliar. Zoren had long known the Gray Ones were drawn to him, feeding off of his loneliness and stoking his bitterness and jealousy. He'd been glad to leave Rengard behind, for being so near to Freya and that scoundrel husband of hers, Ivar, had only provided the *khaamu* with an even more tempting array of human misery than usual.

Things hadn't been nearly this bad when Zoren had been a young man back in the Dragon Isles. Back then, his cares and worries—though they'd felt weighty at the time—had been so simple. He recalled how nervous he'd been about trying to join the Emerald Eye, the secret group of Drekai agents bound to serve the Drekai royal family. But at one particular friend's encouragement, he'd finally plucked up the courage.

Of course, Zoren recalled, everything had gone sideways during his first assignment in Evgard's Mirror Forest. Out of his whole unit, Zoren had been the lone survivor, though even he hadn't made it through the wraith's attack unscathed. Even now, as Zoren splashed through the muddy streets of Kolbohr, his old shadow wasting wound was acting up, its inky gray tendrils leeching up his arm and spreading their pervasive, numbing venom. Each day it crept nearer to his heart until one day it would encapsulate it and leave Zoren completely devoid of will and emotion. One of the Hollow.

For the umpteenth time, Zoren wished his old Mage Hunter partner, Trickshot, was with him. While Rekoa was his oldest friend, she wasn't the only one who'd stood by him here in Evgard. As the best healer to come out of the Mage Hunter Academy in a decade, Trickshot had always been diligent about treating Zoren's wound with liquid light, and had even given him a large supply before he'd left the Rise in Keep Rengard. She'd offered to come with him, wherever he was going, but Zoren had refused. Not even Trickshot knew of Zoren's true allegiance to the Drekai—that his true goal was still the same one that had brought him to Evgard nearly twenty years ago.

It seemed like a blessing from the Allfather and the three goddesses that Freya's daughter, Meleya of Misthaven, had been able to at least glimpse, if not obtain, the Soul Reaper's voidshard for long enough to read the names scratched onto its surface. Her temporary banishment to the deadly Dragon Mists—which, at the time, Zoren had attributed to more of his inescapable bad luck—had granted her the knowledge Zoren's unit had been searching for so long ago in the Mirror Forest of Evyndara.

Kjell and Agnai, she'd said. The names were now burned into Zoren's steel trap of a mind. And now, after months of searching, they'd led him here, to the abandoned Sanctuary of Streya at the edge of the town of Gloomhaven.

The building had fallen into disrepair, the moist seaside air having badly damaged the wood over the years. Part of the star-adorned spire atop the building now lay in the dirt, with moss and fungi clawing at it from below. At first, it was clear that everyone in town was right about no one having come to the sanctuary since it ran out of marks and had to send away the orphans it once housed.

But then Zoren began to look more closely. While the foot of most of the doors to the sanctuary were overgrown with more gray moss and mushrooms, one skid mark in the mud stood out. This door had been opened as recently as a day or two ago.

Zoren entered, soon discovering a certain staircase whose railing was the only one not coated in a layer of dust. Up the stairs of the cluttered, abandoned sanctuary he went, until at last he found a door that had been left ajar. Within, the warm orange flame contrasted with the endless gray, and silently, Zoren slipped inside.

Set before the hearth in a large, creaky chair sat a small and comparably creaky old woman. She was frail, hunched, and possessed skin so wrinkled Zoren could only just make out her milk-white, cataract-riddled eyes. But from the way she watched the fire, Zoren was certain right away that she wasn't completely blind.

She wore the black robes of a Sister of Streya, and the black, crystal-adorned circlet on her brow denoted that she'd achieved high rank. A pail of partially frozen water sat at the edge of the fireplace, and a meager slice of brown bread sat partially eaten on a tin plate on her lap.

Zoren's movement snapped her gaze to the doorway. Her plate fell to the floor with a metallic *clang.*

"Who goes there?" the Sister asked, her northern accent thick. She squinted his way, age keeping her from being able to see him properly.

"I mean you no harm," Zoren assured her, adopting a traditional Evgardian accent in place of his native Dragon Isles accent. He bent down, gathering up her fallen meal and handing it back to her. For good measure, he retrieved an ashpear from his pack and handed it to her.

"Thank you kindly, stranger," she said as she sank her teeth into the soft fruit. "And may Streya bless you. It's been many a moon since Old Olga done tasted somethin' sweet. Tell me, what brings you to Gloomhaven?"

"I seek information," Zoren replied, pulling up a chair beside Old Olga, "about a boy who once lived here."

Her mouth full, the woman replied, "Old Olga's been here at this sanctuary a right long time. Tell me, kind stranger, what was this boy's name?"

"Did you ever know a child called Kjell?"

At that, Olga inhaled sharply, nearly dropping her food again. She hissed, her wrinkled face twisting into a skeletal scowl.

Zoren let out a breath. "You know him," he said, trying not to sound too eager.

"Of course..." Old Olga trembled, her clouded eyes growing wide and unfocused. "Can't nobody forget the boy who spoke with shadows."

Chapter 3: Oasis

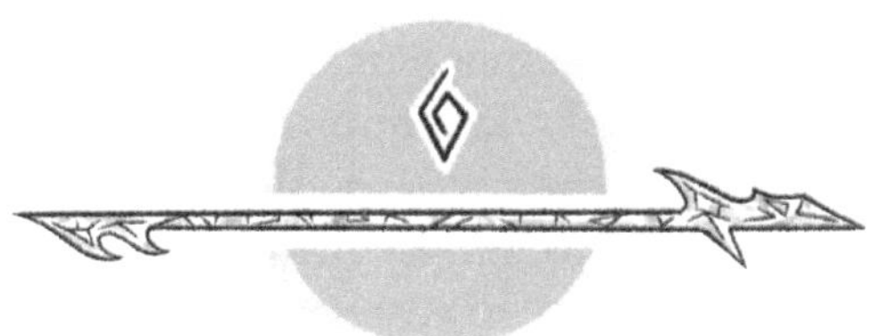

Asher

For a spirit with literally no physical possessions, Meleya had put together quite the packing list.

She was so deep in thought as she crouched between the ether spring and the etherberry bushes that she had no idea I was watching her from the other side of the oasis. It was the perfect opportunity for me to ambush her. I knew I shouldn't—We were about to embark on a dangerous mission, plus I was eighteen now, technically 'of age', and probably should've been above such pranks.

And yet, here we were.

Meleya was muttering to herself, largely gibberish numbers: "With four of us, times three etherberries per day... let's round up to five just to be safe... times twelve days equals... Oy."

Meleya began harvesting etherberries with such speed that her spirit-hands were practically blurs. There was a sort of halo around her head, a focused crown of mist that indicated she was deeply focused.

Time for a show.

My spirit-eyes burned with golden etherlight as I prepared to channel my powers. I held out my hands at the ready.

Then, all at once, I thrust my hands forward.

Ether flowed through me, and while in my semi-translucent spirit form, I could actually see the powerful white substance racing from my ether well and out through my fingertips like veins. White light coalesced above the spring, taking shape as crystalline starglass.

Meleya yelped as the curving pipes of starglass solidified all around her. I willed the ether from the spring to sweep up the pipes at high speed, its glowing power illuminating them section by section.

The pipes ended in an ether-cascade set a few feet above Meleya's head. As expected, she looked up just as the waterfall started in full force.

Meleya's yelp turned full scream when she got a face-full of pure, shimmering liquid ether. She thrashed, dropping her arm full of etherberries as her white braid twisted in the air. Her ether well, which manifested as a translucent crystal tethered to her forehead, refilled to bursting.

It wasn't like a regular bucket of water to the face. My exploring thus far in the spirit plane had taught me that the ether from the spring was pleasantly warm, like the sun emerging from behind a cloud to gently kiss your skin. But from the way Meleya ripped into me, I might as well have dropped a chunk of ice down the back of her tunic.

"Asher of Steel Rim, you maniacal son of a dragonmutt, what is wrong with you?!"

Her aura had gone from indigo spirals to indigo flames. Her glare wasn't exactly shooting literal daggers, but when I looked closely, I thought I could make out little shards of her essence bolting toward mine.

I, on the opposite scale, was laughing so hard my aura was spinning.

"I *will* destroy you," Meleya threatened.

"If you can catch me!" I winked, then hover-launched into the air. As a spirit, it was quite the launch. Practically flying, I zipped across the ceiling as Meleya...

...pointedly *didn't* chase me.

Instead, she sat back down and resumed gathering and re-counting her scattered etherberries, keeping her eyes narrowed in my direction all the while.

That only made me laugh harder. I hover-dashed to a stop before her and dismissed my starglass pipe contraption.

Meleya pursed her lips. "We've got a schedule to keep, you know. Can't you just be normal for a second?"

"Not even one, I'm afraid." I shrugged, then plopped down beside her at the edge of the ether spring. I scooped up a handful of fallen etherberries and offered them to her, a look of apologetic innocence on my face.

For a second, I thought she'd refuse my help just to prove a point. But my crooked smile seemed to do the trick. In the end, she sighed and took the berries, and I even thought I saw a ghost of a smile desperately fighting for a place on her face.

"Thanks," Meleya said, with only the faintest hint of a remaining grudge.

"*Jehl zitaan*—You're welcome," I replied, and together, we continued re-gathering etherberries.

"Being around your Mom is bringing the Drekai language back, I see," Meleya said.

"Absolutely," I agreed. "I'd gotten rusty. It used to be so natural." Once we'd recouped all the fallen berries, we started plucking more of the tiny, glowing spheres from the bushes.

"You know, despite your obvious obnoxiousness..." Meleya started. I was about to teasingly protest her opening claim, but she rushed to cut me off. "...Despite that, I wanted to tell you how much I appreciated what you said last night in the medical wing—About doing the right thing instead of the easy thing." In the movement of her aura, I sensed that she'd felt that sentiment deeply, and I felt a tug on my heartstrings.

"You know something about that, don't you?" I said seriously. "You joined the guard at thirteen to save your parents from execution, right?"

Meleya's spirit cheeks reddened. "Uh, yeah. Although at the time, I didn't really feel as though I were making the 'right' choice. Rather, I saw it as my *only* choice."

She looked at me as if deciding whether or not to go on. Something in my eyes or aura must've given her the confidence to continue.

"Honestly, I've never felt like I'm truly in control of my own choices. First I was a nomad because my family was in hiding. Then I became a guard to save my parents, and after that a Mage Hunter to try to get my mother back, only to learn she was no longer herself. And... I don't know. My whole life has been a series of cloaks, none of them a color I chose for myself."

I was about to tell Meleya that at least she was a free Knight of the Torch now. But the words died on my lips as I recalled the dark, powerful voidshard she kept inside her rift hold on the Knights' behalf. No doubt she still felt trapped, obligated to keep the shard to protect those she cared about.

A wave of sympathy mixed with admiration washed over me as I watched Meleya furiously pick etherberries, counting to herself as she went. Her brow was knit, and I could all but see the weight of her burdens on her ethereal shoulders.

Before her busy hand could take another berry, I reached out to hold it.

Meleya's gaze snapped to me. "What are you doing? We have to pack enough for—"

"Wait," I said.

"But if I don't—"

"*Wait.*"

Once I was mostly sure Meleya wouldn't go right back to her furious berry harvest, I let go of her hand. My eyes flashed gold as I formed a little spade out of starglass, which I then used to dig around the base of the nearest etherberry bush. Thanks to Mom and her cactus garden, I knew to be careful not to cut any major roots.

Before long, I was able to pull up the berry-laden bush, along with a sizable clump of ethereal dirt. Glowing white roots curled and spiraled as they hung from it.

With a flourish of my hand, I formed a starglass pot and transplanted the etherberry bush. I figured the ether from the berries would sustain the starglass as well as skystone would. By now, Mel had caught onto my plan. The two of us gently packed more dirt into the pot.

Next, I pointed to the small ball of light that hovered over Meleya's shoulder. In response, Meleya runetraced to open her rift hold, and together we lifted the etherberry bush into a bright corner of the pantry. While everything else in there was physical and therefore untouchable, the etherberry bush was made of pure spirit. The plant seemed to be thriving, its leaves as robust as ever and its hundreds of etherberries ripe and shining.

I smiled, giving Meleya a light shove. "How's that, scale-in-the-mud?"

Meleya jabbed me with her elbow, unable to keep the smile from her face. "Not bad, scarf-wearer."

Just then, a rustle from the neighboring etherberry bush—the one still planted in the ground—made us both whirl. Meleya dismissed her rune and her rift hold winked back into its sparkle form.

Suddenly, Blink's enormous, draconic head emerged from between the bushes. Both Meleya and I startled, falling backward and away from each other. Blink's glare evaporated at once, as if startling us had been her plan all along.

"Blink!" Meleya berated her dragon. "Are you trying to give us heart attacks?"

Blink gave a low growl, and I could tell by the way they looked at each other that they were communicating through their bond. At once, Meleya's spirit-cheeks flushed.

"What is it?" I asked.

"Nothing," Meleya replied, giving Blink a meaningful look as she stood and dusted off her clothes. "Just that your mom is waiting for us. It's time."

The thunder of drums thrummed from Blink as she launched from the Skyforge terrace carrying me, Mom, and Meleya on her back. Since Blink was only on her first ascension, the ride was just a *little* snug.

The sun had barely risen, the golden orb just visible along its fiery gold ring that encircled the earth. I took note—According to Solrac, we had exactly twelve days to figure out what was causing the Hazes. This sunrise marked the start of day one.

Blink's four wide wings took us higher until I felt it. The air shimmered and there was a strange shift, as if someone had pulled a lever that instantly dropped the temperature by a few degrees. It wasn't enough to make me cold, but it definitely caught my attention.

When I glanced behind us, I realized what had just happened. We'd crossed the boundary of Orothion's protective wards. I knew a bit about the etherlocks, the ancient, triangular, metal devices forged by the Guardians of old. These etherlocks had been set at intervals all around the stronghold to ward off darkness, including wraithkind, while in the spirit plane, their power manifested as a translucent golden bubble encompassing the area surrounding the castle.

I felt Meleya's spirit tense as she sat astride Blink just in front of me, and knew she must've just realized the same thing. I knew wraiths had given Meleya trouble in the past, so I leaned closer to remind her she wasn't alone.

"Ow," I said as Blink suddenly jostled us.

Higher and higher Blink flew, and once again, the glory of Etheria sprawled before us as far as the eye could see. Dozens of spirit creatures roamed both the land and the skies. There were more flying foxes and avias, the butterfly-dragons Mom had shown us that first day. Far below, I saw a spirit-dragon moose and a family of spirit-drakalope, their auras trailing behind them as they bounded over the land with impossible agility.

"Stars," Meleya said. "I can see so much more actually *being* here than I can with the Sight."

As I looked at the glorious landscape set before us, awe overcame me as well. The ruddy, proud auras of the giant redwood trees coated the forest canopy like a thin gauze, covering the earth like a spydra-silk blanket. Not far off, I could see the onyx-colored aura of the lava beds, a huge swath of long-dead lava flows. Likewise, the aura coming from that area flowed, twisting and turning on itself as if the spirit of the lava beds hadn't quite realized that the magma had long since cooled.

Then there were the ley lines. From here, I could see dozens of the white rivers of pure ether as they floated just over the land, bending and twisting with the landscape. Where the ethereal rivers crossed, I could often see an extra-bright spot, indicating more ether oases, similar to the one in the cozy cove beneath Orothion's cliffs. At those spots, there were ethereal waterfalls, geysers, springs... all sorts of beautiful features. Mom animatedly pointed out each one.

There was so much to look at, I hardly noticed how much time was passing. By the time Meleya suggested that we camp out for a few hours to give Blink's wings a rest and get a little sleep, the sun was already low on its golden arc in the western sky.

We continued our journey like that throughout day two and most of day three. Meleya checked on her etherberry bush religiously, and I was pleased to see the pot was holding up well. In the perpetually sunny Haven, we didn't need the etherberries' power; not like we surely would once we reached the Haze. Each day, we drew closer to the vast gray storm, its heavy, turbulent clouds crackling with the occasional flash of ominous blue lightning.

While we saw an abundance of spirit wildlife in Etheria, we didn't see any other humans. It was like Mom said: Besides her, they'd all moved on to Deep Etheria.

We *did* pass several towns, though. Not Ethereal towns, but cities in the physical plane that manifested here in a massive flurry of flickering aura lights. Focusing made it clear that each light belonged to a different living soul, rushing from place to place as they went about their business.

It was utterly fascinating, as some towns were old enough that certain buildings—usually the citadels and sanctuaries—manifested in the spirit plane, too. We stopped briefly once to explore the ethereal version of a Sanctuary of Solei, the spirit goddess. A golden, sun-like aura filled the building, and the flowers there flourished on both the spirit and physical sides.

As we flew over a particularly large town, filled with flickering aura lights darting this way and that, I heard Meleya speak.

"The auras... they look just like they did in the giant crystals in Scryer's Grotto," she muttered.

"What's Scryer's Grotto?" I asked.

"Nothing," Meleya said quickly, as if she regretted even mentioning it. "Just... I'd rather not talk about it if that's okay."

Meleya's aura was shrinking closer to her spirit form. I could tell whatever she was talking about held painful memories, so I didn't press her.

By the end of day three, we'd nearly made it to the outskirts of the Haze. The next town we passed seemed... different. While the flickers of multicolored auras still bustled about as usual, there was a dingy gray cloud hovering over one building near the far northeast corner of the city. Curiosities aroused, we went to check it out.

It turned out to be some kind of small hospital. There were a few brightly-colored aura lights there, but many were surprisingly dim, shrouded in gray clouds of their own.

"That's not..." I started, pointing to one.

"Shadow wasting," Mom said grimly. "This is what it looks like on the spirit side."

Sure enough, when I focused on one of the gray-shrouded flickers, a physical being came into focus. A man sat with his head in his hands as inky gray patches leeched along the skin of his forearms, neck, and jaw. The pale green of his aura was muted by the miasma of sickly gray clouds that clung to it like a leech.

"The shadow wasting cuts deep," Meleya observed.

"But watch this," Mom said, pointing.

On the physical side, a medic approached the stricken man. Carefully, she administered a few drops of a glowing golden substance I knew well: liquid light.

From the Etheria side, the empowered healing medication, made by Lightwielder magi, seemed to be imbued with a life of its own. Vivid gold threads shimmered and danced all around the vial and wherever the liquid light touched the man's skin, the inky gray patches swiftly shrank back. They didn't completely disappear, but at the golden touch, the man's whole soul seemed to lift. The shadowy cloud around his aura dispersed, and a smile graced his face.

"Stars," Meleya and I said in unison.

"Really gives you hope, eh?" Mom agreed. "Unfortunately, too many of the victims of the shadow wasting suffer from cases that liquid light cannot permanently cure. It alleviates the symptoms, but it's not a lasting solution."

More shadow wasting victims huddled together in the building, their auras similarly grayed out. Near the back, I saw a handful of people whose auras appeared to have been completely consumed, every drop of color smothered by drab gray clouds.

Focusing hard on the physical plane, I saw that the people's physical forms were entirely gray as well. Their expressions were blank, their eyes vacant.

"What's wrong with them?" I asked.

"They've gone hollow," Mom replied, deep sorrow coloring her tone. "The shadow wasting has pricked their hearts, leaving them devoid of emotion, personality, and even will. Not even liquid light can do anything for the hollow."

Sure enough, as we watched, the hollow only moved when healers prompted them to. They only ate at their suggestion too. It was like Mom had said—they were completely devoid of will.

The sight struck both Meleya and me with a deep sense of sorrow. I couldn't imagine anything worse than losing what made me *me*.

We pressed on, the looming Haze soon growing so close that my spiritual fingertips began tingling with anticipation. But before we could reach the stark edge of the churning, gray storm, I noticed something on the Haven side.

It was one last ether oasis, and this one was *huge.* At least four ley lines intersected here, each one tumbling over, around, and under the others to form wild rapids in the ether rivers. When I focused, I saw that the whitewater rapids corresponded on the physical side, too, though not quite as gravity-defying as the floating network of ley lines.

Just then, a series of gleeful chirps fell on my ears. My eyes went wide with excitement when I saw them—ethereal, draconic otters with auras in every conceivable shade of blue, splashing and chuckling as they rode the rapids.

"Etherotters," Mom said, pointing.

"Can we stop?" I asked. The otters were practically *begging* to be played with.

"Of course not," Meleya said. "We're on an important mission, and we've already stopped so many times. We should do our best to stay ahead of schedule, right, Zerana?"

But Mom didn't hear Meleya—she was too busy launching off of Blink's back. She whooped, then landed with a satisfying splash in the warm, ethereal river. The etherotters chittered with delight.

"Aww yeah!" I cried, then swung my leg over Blink and slid off her back, whooping as I hover-dove to join her. The ley line's pure ether felt like a refreshing breeze on my spirit skin, and my ether well was positively bursting.

Mom cupped her hands around her mouth, calling for Meleya to join us. After an obligatory eye roll, Meleya shrieked as she, too, slipped from her dragon's back to land with a blue-violet splash in the ethereal river.

I had no idea how much time passed as we laughed and played with the etherotters at the oasis. Some of the draconic spirit-otters were only as long as my forearm, but others were big enough to ride. They chuckled as we raced them down the zigzagging rapids.

I'd just playfully pushed Meleya into the ether when Blink suddenly decided to get in on the action too. She dove into the river directly between us, then soared back out again with a draconic chuckle. The white ether mingled with the silver of her aura as it sprinkled off her wings and onto our faces.

We quickly learned that the etherotters had some minor Archonic abilities—that is, they could levitate like me. Eyes flashing with gold light, they launched from the ley lines, then coiled around them as they left glorious spiral patterns in the air with their trailing auras.

They were having so much fun, I activated my levitation powers to give it a try myself. Meleya used portals to keep up, swimming in and out of the gold-rimmed tears connected by twisting golden warps while Blink flew alongside us in an almost chaperone-like fashion. Mom laughed and cheered us on from the sidelines.

Tired out and practically glowing with ether, we left the river network when Meleya suggested we get a look at the etherberry bushes growing here. Thanks to the bush inside her rift hold, we had plenty of berries in our supplies, so collecting more wasn't her aim. But she'd noticed a few fallen berries drying out in the sun here had become shriveled, a little like raisins. That had gotten her cooking-mind going, and she started drying out some mashed berries to essentially make ethereal fruit leather.

I had no choice but to tease her. "Who's the one going off-schedule now?"

"Shut up." Meleya hurried off with Blink to try out her recipe.

Meanwhile, Mom and I sat together on the bank of one of the ley lines. This particular one almost perfectly matched a river in the physical plane. After only a short rest, some of the otters were already back at it, using their draconic tails to splash at each other.

I laughed at the sight. "They never get tired, do they?"

"Like someone else I know." Mom winked.

I tapped my chin with mock curiosity. "Wonder where I got that from..."

Mom nudged me affectionately, and as I looked into her bright green eyes, I felt the tiniest twinge of sadness. Of course, Mom noticed.

"What's wrong?"

"Doesn't matter."

"Asher..." Stars, could all mothers do that, or did some have to practice saying their children's names like that?

I caved. "It's just... I remember hiking with you all the time by the cliffs near Steel Rim. You were a *legend* with levitation powers. I learned everything I know from you, and I wish you still had that. It's not fair."

Mom's tone was soft. "Don't go down that road again, Asher."

"I won't, I swear," I said. "Even after what she did to you, I don't wish Vidya dead anymore. I had my chance to end her, and..."

I trailed off, and Mom put a hand on my shoulder. "And you chose light."

I gave her a sidelong glance. "In the geyser fields outside of Keep Drakfell, when everyone was practically screaming at me to kill the Black Valkyrie, but I didn't... In that moment, were you there?"

"Yes," Mom replied. "Doing all I could to lend you strength. But *khaviila* like me cannot push you to action, the same way the wraiths cannot force their host's action unless that host grants them control. Your choices have always been—and will always be—your own. You made that decision yourself, and in doing so, made me so very proud of you."

"After losing you, all I wanted for years was to end the Black Valkyrie," I said, absently forming and reforming a piece of starglass in my hands into a miniature dragonhook spear. "At first, I struggled when that desire went away. If I wasn't after her to avenge you, what was I good for? Who was I? But... I really think I've finally figured it out. Who I am, I mean."

Mom smiled, her grip tightening on my shoulder. "And who is that, my *laaksi-rakaai*?"

"Well, for one, I'm the realm's most impressive etherotter rider," I said. Mom's ensuing laugh was like sweet bells ringing out across the oasis.

"But for real," I said, "I'm Asher of Steel Rim. I'm a thief turned Knight of the Torch. I'm a halfway-decent Astromancer, and a dragon rider to a powerful, mildly-sarcastic wyvern who I miss like crazy right now. I'm also a friend to some of the strongest magi and most brilliant minds in the realm, and, of course..." I looked Mom in the eye, a crooked smile a lot like my father's on my face. "I'm the son of the two most kind, wise, and scorching fun outlanders Drakfell's ever seen."

Mom smiled back, but there was something deeper behind it. Sadness? Regret? Her aura was churning.

I cocked my head. "Mom?"

"Asher," she started. "There's something I have to tell you."

"What's that?"

Mom inhaled deeply. "Once you wake from astral sleep, you'll be going to the Dragon Isles. The capital city, Zolehiinu, to be specific."

A jumble of dragonflies appeared in my spirit stomach at the thought. "For my duel with the Drekai General—I almost forgot."

Mom nodded. "I've been watching you train for months. You've gotten *very* good—Better than I ever was."

"Yeah, right." I chuckled, then tapped Mom's forearm. At that, she pulled up her spirit sleeve to show off the series of tattoos that adorned the underside of her wrist: over a dozen interlocking diamonds called 'honor marks', one for each duel she'd ever won.

"Do all Drekai have so many?" I asked.

Mom tilted her head. "I *may* have more than most. Though not all are from honor duels—Most are from duels of wills."

"What's the difference?" I asked, intrigued at this rare glimpse into my mother's past. She'd always avoided talking too much about the Dragon Isles, and used to always find a way to change the subject.

She sighed. "A duel of honor is a duel to the death over a matter of utmost significance. Battles over the fates of lives, tribes, or even the nation. The extreme consequence corresponds to the extremity of what's at stake."

Those dragonflies in my stomach rapidly turned into full-on wyverns. I knew there was *a lot* riding on my *zhaku*, or honor duel, with General Kheradok. A possible alliance between the Dragon Isles and the Knights of the Torch, for one. An alliance everyone thought I was crazy for even bringing up in the first place, since—as so many people liked to remind me—Drekai and Evgardian didn't mix.

But I was living proof against that, right?

Besides that, the outcome of my duel would also determine whether Princess Eliana, true dragon rider of Evgard, and her rare, powerful mount, Aurora, would remain free, or become captive to the Drekai nation.

The thought of Elle made my heart twist. For a second, I wondered how she was doing, and whether or not she cared that I was trapped in astral sleep.

She had to care at least a little, I decided, since I'd seen her come by to visit me in the medical wing every day without fail. A few days before we'd left for the Haze, she'd even brought a stout little flowering cactus in a pot to set at my bedside.

She'd had no idea I was there in spirit form, watching as she took my hand, then sang to me her old song about dragons dancing in Etheria. Elle's voice had been captivating, visually manifesting in the spirit plane as dancing, shimmering strings that filled the room.

Stars, thinking of Elle made my heart ache, and I banished the memories as quickly as they'd surfaced. Elle, or rather, Princess Eliana, had made her intentions very clear: There couldn't be anything between the two of us—Our worlds were just too different. I had to accept that our carefree days mucking out stables and hover-dancing at festivals were behind us. She had far more important duties to attend to than spending time with someone like me.

I looked up, hoping to find a distraction, and spotted Meleya in the distance. She was squatting on the ground at the foot of an etherberry bush, her right arm working double time as she madly mashed a pile of etherberries in the shallow cavity of a stone. She was focused, and clearly didn't give a flying scale about appearing sophisticated.

Just seeing her like that was like a breath of fresh air. Meleya was just so... normal. Perfectly, blessedly, and beautifully normal.

"Asher?"

I jolted back to the moment when Mom started waving a hand in front of my face. I blinked a few times, then offered a salute.

"Reporting for duty," I said melodramatically. "What were we talking about?"

Mom smiled at my distractability as she continued. "The distinction between a duel of honor—like the one you'll be fighting come autumn—and a duel of wills," Mom gently reminded me. "A *zhavoi,* or duel of wills, does not end in death, but at first blood. These are meant to settle matters of lesser consequence: Disputes over things like land, dragons, or personal disagreements. Every true Drekai knows they must honor the results of the duel."

"I understand." I nodded. The starglass in my hands continued to change shape and, as I listened, I carefully crafted a tiny model of my wyvern, Thorn.

"So, what was it you were going to tell me in the first place?" I asked as I worked.

"Oh," Mom said. "Right. Where to begin..." Her aura tensed up, and once again began storming almost as much as the distant Haze.

She spoke carefully. "I never got the chance to speak to you about... your Drekai Life Path."

"Life Path?" I repeated.

Mom nodded, her aura storm calming as she launched into another explanation about her people's customs.

"At sixteen, Drekai—and half-borns like us, too—must choose an *Elaaka Kuu,* or Life Path. It's a pillar or principle to which we dedicate our lives. Those who wish to become warriors often choose a Life Path like Strength, Skill, or Loyalty. Others may choose Truth, Creativity, Generosity, or Family. There are many paths to choose from, but whatever the choice, we Drekai must serve our Life Path with every gift we've been given. To fail one's path is to fail one's self. Not just in mortality, but into eternity."

The dark teal clouds of Mom's aura seemed to become heavier with every word. I was no aura-reader, but I could tell she was feeling deep sadness. I almost didn't dare ask, but I couldn't help it.

"What was your Life Path?"

When she replied, Mom's mind seemed a million miles away. "Courage. Courage was my path in life, and it remains so even now, despite my... Despite..."

Mom trailed off, and though I waited patiently, she didn't continue. I could tell from her face and aura just how intensely difficult this was for her to talk about. Though I couldn't for the life of me imagine why—After all, Courage was the perfect path for Mom. I'd seen her face down wild ridgerunners, hostile warriors, and a host of other threats without a second thought. She was the bravest person I knew.

I hated seeing Mom suffer like this, and passed her my little starglass wyvern.

"We can talk about this later," I assured her.

Absently holding the starglass dragon, she rushed to reply, "*Nii*, no. I've long prayed for another chance to speak with you. What I have to say, I couldn't pass through your father, either. I've needed to say this to you directly, so that you can be sure of the truth. I feel... I feel I've let you down as a mother."

"Let me down?" My jaw actually dropped. "Are you kidding? You were—you *are*—the greatest mother in the realm! You gave me everything, and look how I turned out."

I tapped my chin, tilting my head back and forth as I went on. "I mean, I guess I *did* turn out to be a thief, but that wasn't your fault. I never stole anything until after you were gone and Dad stopped being able to work. And even then I only ever stole from good-for-nothing, selfish nobles. Stars, Mom, it's not you, it's *them* letting me down. Baron Eidan and the rest of the sooty noble class let all people like us down, and then stomp on us to make sure we stay down. All nobles are that way."

But even as I said it, the words rang false. Not *all* nobles were like that. My friends Brigan and Elle were good and kind, as was King Rodan, who'd saved my life in Orothion.

Still, I turned to Mom, hoping that my statement had at least made her feel better. But instead of a smile on her face, she looked like she was going to be sick.

My brows knit with concern. "Mom, are you okay—"

"*Taaket*—Stars, it's later than I thought!" Mom suddenly got to her feet. "Where did Meleya and Blink get off to? If we're going to reach the Haze before sundown, we'd better get going."

“Mom,” I started. But she was already floating down the riverbank toward Meleya.

All was eerily quiet at the edge of the Haze.

The four of us stood together on the Haven side, where all was still bright and sunny. But only about a foot in front of the tips of our boots, everything was different.

Skygard’s forsaken Stormshadow Desert stretched out before us. Its dry earth, littered with hundreds of small fissures, had a dusty yellow aura clinging to it on the Haven side, yet appeared fully gray on the Haze side.

Wherever the Haze met the Haven, the ground churned as inky grayness tried to eat its way into the light. But the light fought back, the two sides ebbing and flowing like a tumultuous ocean tide. Even the air seemed to be doing battle: the warm golden side versus the cool gray.

This was it. Our little crew exchanged glances, and Blink let out a disconcerted growl.

I took Mom’s hand on one side and Meleya’s on the other. Then, together, we stepped into the Haze.

Chapter 4: Stormshadow

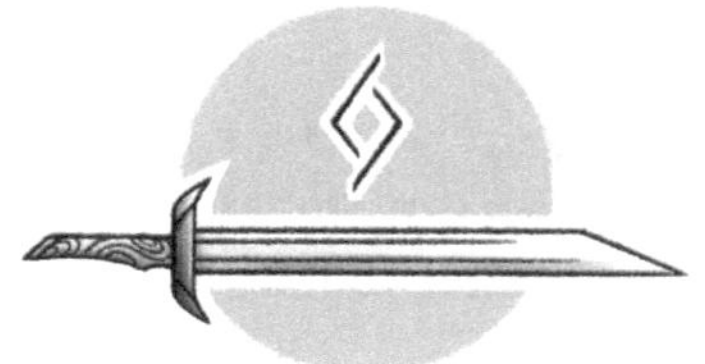

Meleya

Whoosh!

A gust of wind buffeted my long, white hair as we stepped over the line between Haven and Haze. My spirit-ears popped, and the temperature dropped. Zerana had been right—One step into the Haze had changed my perspective on the whole world around me.

Where the whole sky had once appeared bright and sunny, it now took on the dark blue-gray tinge of perpetual twilight. The sun and the ring it rode was no longer fiery yellow-gold, but that horrible shade of void-blue I'd come to both loathe and fear.

The nearest ley line, which had looked so pure and white from the other side, now shone with blue-tinged energy. Not fully tainted, but as I followed the ether river with my gaze, it seemed to become bluer with corrupted voidarchy the nearer it flowed toward the center of the Haze.

The sound of distant thunder peppered my ears as plumes of thick, toxic-looking smoke wafted up from behind craggy rocks along the horizon. I felt like I'd just entered a war zone, or worse: One of the old nightmares I used to get when I was a cadet at the Mage Hunter Academy.

The air was thin and misty, too, with crackles of blue lightning occasionally illuminating the fog. Everything felt too familiar. Too much like the Dragon Mists.

My surroundings instantly set my teeth on edge and got my spirit-blood pulsing. Old fears bubbled up inside my chest, and my hand that held

Asher's began to squeeze his fingers so tightly I heard him protest, though I couldn't make out words through my mental haze.

My other hand went automatically to the quartz crystal clipped to my belt. As memories of running for my life in the Dragon Mists surfaced, I couldn't help but think of him:

Jax.

Jax had been my lifeline when our commander had banished the pair of us to the deadly, monster-filled mists that ran along the southern edge of the Canyonlands. We'd stood by each other's sides, protecting one another and being there when we'd needed it most.

So, yes, my memories of the Dragon Mists were charged with shadows, exhaustion, and terror. But they also held a spark of warmth. The Mists were where Jax and I had really fallen for each other. He'd been my sanctuary, but now, he was gone.

I squeezed my eyes shut, trying to expel all thoughts of Jax from my mind. As a spirit, I didn't need to breathe per say, but my lungs felt constricted anyway, which was somehow worse. I forced myself to take slow, even breaths to try and counter the feeling, but drak, it wasn't easy. The Haze threatened to close in on me.

"Mel?" Asher's voice finally pierced the fog. "Are you okay?"

My first reaction was to tell him I was fine, but I realized that wasn't really true. I'd learned the hard way that lying about how I was doing never ended well.

I met Asher's sincere, dragonfire eyes. "It's just... this place is a lot like the Dragon Mists. It's... I'm..." My next breaths came in stilted gulps.

Asher's expression softened. Then, he broke into a sudden grin, of all things.

"Desert, mountains, or beach?" he asked.

I instantly knew what he was doing, and I clung desperately to the distraction. "I already told you that I'm not much a fan of the beach. At least, it's alright for visiting, but I couldn't live there."

"Me neither," Asher agreed. Zerana watched our exchange with curiosity as Blink nuzzled against my side.

"What about you?" I asked. "Which would you choose?"

"Easy—Mountains. There are peaks to climb and endless places to explore. I could breathe better there. Besides, look around—" Asher gestured to the dry, dismal landscape surrounding us. "This isn't exactly a point in favor of deserts."

I chewed my lip. "Well, if it's *this* desert against some idyllic mountainside, we know which wins. But I grew up travelling with the nomads throughout the redrock of the Canyonlands. The desert has a wild, beautiful side too."

Asher got a teasing glint in his eye. "Meleya of Misthaven, part-time experimental etherberry chef, part-time desert fangirl."

I rolled my eyes and gave Asher a jab with my elbow, but to my utter relief, his ploy had worked. My spirit lungs relaxed once more, and the Haze no longer seemed quite so oppressive.

"We should move quickly," Zerana said quietly. "Cover as much ground as we can before the sun sets. That's when things will get really—"

A growl from Blink cut Zerana short. I whirled to where my spirit evren stood and saw several gray, shadowy... *things* had begun to seep from the fissures within the dry, sunken earth.

At first, I thought they were wraiths. The way their smoky forms leeched and curled was very wraithlike, but these were too small, and far less put together. Besides, wraiths were human-shaped from the waist up, whereas these were amorphous masses, featureless other than the pair of glowing sapphire eyes hidden within their misty bodies.

It was as if a whole slew of these things had been guarding the border, just waiting for the chance to attack anything that dared cross into the Haze.

I gasped—At least six of them were climbing onto Blink's flank. Their foggy forms flared as the wretched things appeared to be sucking the light out of my dragon.

"Shades!" Zerana hissed the word as if it were both an explanation and a curse. She unsheathed the deadly starglass-and-gemstone scimitar she kept on her hip and dashed toward the creatures.

But with his hover-speed, Asher was faster. He was at Blink's side in an instant, having summoned his go-to weapon: his starglass dragonhook spear.

He windmilled the spear, taking out at least three of the shadowy wraithlings. Each one disintegrated in a satisfying poof of smoke, leaving nothing but a tiny, crystalline core that dropped to the earth, then faded from blue to white. Stars, it was just like killing an umbral creature.

Next, Asher trained his blade upon the largest wraithling in the bunch and sent a pulse of pure white ether shooting straight into it. The shapeless monster burst, its essence curling into nothingness as it dropped its core.

Asher continued his steady barrage, the wraithlings vanishing in the wake of his channeled Archonic power. Zerana quickly arrived to assist, her starglass scimitar slashing. I hated feeling so useless, but between the two of them, only a few more moments left us mini-gray-shadow-beast-free once again.

"Blink!" I rushed to my evren's side to check her over. Reassuring drumbeats thrummed through our bond, but her left hind wing appeared duller than the rest of her silvery spirit form. Blink stretched her wings out to give them a test flap, but hurriedly folded them up again, her emerald eyes betraying her pain. Without wasting another second, I opened my rift hold and fed her an etherberry.

Brrrum, Blink drummed to me, and I nodded with understanding. She'd heal, but it might be best to avoid flying for at least a few hours.

"Stars," Asher said, sweeping his hair out of his eyes. "What were those creepy things?"

"Shades," Zerana repeated what she'd said earlier. "They're minor wraith-kind that seek to slowly garner enough power to take a full wraith form, and eventually be able to whisper to a human. The larger, more humanoid ones are called echoes, and some of them can even talk."

"Yikes." Asher cringed, and a shiver made the spirit-hairs on my spirit-arms stand on end.

"Yikes is right." Zerana gave one last look around before sheathing her scimitar.

Then, Asher stepped up to me. His eyes glowed gold as he began to reshape his starglass spear into something much shorter and more stout.

"Here, Mel," Asher said as he handed me a pure starglass long seaxe, much like the one I usually fought with. "I get the feeling you might want this."

"Thank you." I took the weapon eagerly. But I knew the starglass wouldn't hold forever, not without some kind of perpetual power source like skystone.

But wait...

I bent down to pick up one of the tiny fragments of crystal left by one of the shades. When it had fallen from its core, the shard had been blue, but now it had reverted to a soft, glowing white.

"Shades have the beginnings of a voidshard forming in them, but when they're killed, it reverts to a small skystone the same way full voidshards do," Zerana explained.

I passed it to Asher, and he quickly embedded it plus the rest of the scattered skystone pieces into the hilt of my new blade. Now it would last indefinitely.

Asher's precision with starglass was impressive. Each groove in the starglass seaxe was in exactly the same place as it would've been on a standard-issue guard's long seaxe. But Asher had added a little extra flair to the hilt, giving it a three-dimensional design that reminded me of snowflakes. My lips quirked into a smile when I noticed it.

"We ought to get a move on," Zerana said, glancing upward toward the strange, blue sun on its ring. "Staying in one place too long will only draw more shades and echoes. Can you walk, Blink?"

Blink gave a proud little roar, then used the hinges on the joints of her four wings as claws to take the first few steps. The rest of us fell in line, following the ley line as it flowed deeper toward the center of the storm.

With Blink's wing recovering, we covered less ground than we'd hoped to by nightfall. Once the cold blue sun set, the ring that trailed it thinned to a thread, and the already dim sky became almost as black as pitch. Only the faintly glowing ley line and the odd flashes of blue lightning lent any meaningful light to the bleak landscape.

As we traveled, Asher and Zerana took point on fighting off any shades that tried to come for us. I sent a few back to the void with my new starglass seaxe, but I mostly watched over Blink. She was improving, but clearly needed rest in order to get that hind wing back in fighting shape.

Eventually, we stopped in a secluded area where the floating ether river wound in and out of a network of tall, ragged hoodoos. There was some debate on whether or not this was a good place to set up camp, since there were so many places for things to hide. But it was for that very reason that we chose to hide out here ourselves. It felt safer here than out in the open, anyway.

I volunteered to take the first watch, promising the others that I'd wake them the second I saw something even vaguely threatening. Before they lay down, I passed both Asher and Zerana a piece of my experimental etherberry fruit leather to replenish their stamina. At the first bite, their auras visibly brightened.

"Soot, Mel," Asher said as he chewed. "I'll admit, I thought you were wasting your time mashing up those berries—they were already so good. But this isn't half bad."

"It's a nice texture, huh," I said, taking a bite from a strip.

"It's more than that," Zerana said. "I think you've made their power more potent by concentrating the berries. I'd wager we could last an entire day on one piece of this."

Despite being in the oppressive darkness of the Haze, their comments left me in a good mood as I settled in for watch duty. Asher and his mother lay down at the base of a wide hoodoo rock spire, and Blink hung upside-down from a ledge near the hoodoo's top, her wings enclosing her body like a bat as she slept. The ether river cast a soft, white-blue glow onto their faces.

I chose a perch a short distance in front of them where I could watch over my team while still getting a decent view of our surroundings. I'd see if anything was coming our way and I was far enough away that, with any luck, I'd be able to dispatch any shades without waking my companions.

The series of eroded rock hoodoos were actually quite majestic, especially with the ley line weaving through the valley. It reminded me of a place where my parents and I had spent a lot of time while travelling with the Copperhead Caravan, on the outskirts of a keep called Red Glen, named for the veritable forest of redrock spires that surrounded it.

Thinking of my parents sent a pang of longing through my being. I hadn't seen them in so long, and we hadn't exactly parted on good terms. My last real conversation with my mother had ended with her weeping while I practically yelled at her for teaching me to hate my etherarchy.

I felt awful for the way I'd treated her, but I'd been too stubborn to smooth things over. Then I'd left on the quest to Orothion, and now... well, I couldn't help but wonder if I'd missed my chance for good.

Umbral spirit-lizards crept along the rocks, but kept their distance. I saw a spirit-scorpio, too, but it was small—Nothing compared to the huge monsters we'd faced on our journey west. I tensed at the sight of it anyway, but it passed me by.

Meanwhile, the faint howling of dragon coyotes punctuated the quiet of the night, along with more of that low, rumbling thunder that followed each flash of lightning. While the misty air out here near the far side of the Haze was in constant, swirling motion, the hurricane-like storm seemed to become more and more fierce the closer it got to its center. There, the clouds were so thick I couldn't see beyond them. What could they be hiding? What was the source of this great, encroaching grayness? If all went according to plan, we'd find out in a matter of days.

"Mind if I join you?" Zerana's voice was soft as she materialized beside me.

"Sure," I replied. "Shouldn't you be resting?"

"I'll get to it," Zerana said, "but first I wanted to tell you something. How grateful I am."

"For what?"

At that moment, Spirit-Asher stirred in his sleep. Through the fringe of his dark eyelashes, soft, gold light flashed. For just a split second, Asher floated an inch or two in the air before he settled back down, his etherarchy no longer subconsciously activated.

Zerana and I shared a quiet laugh. "He hasn't changed a bit. That's actually what I wanted to thank you for, Meleya. Asher's always been a free spirit with a penchant for adventure. I'm glad he has you to keep him grounded."

I caught Zerana's implication, and a blush bloomed on my cheeks so strong it tinged my aura red. "Oh. Well, I mean, to be clear, Asher and I aren't... well, I don't *think* we're exactly... you know. But that's not to say I wouldn't want to be, unless... Oy. Asher and I... it's complicated."

Zerana laughed so hard she snorted, her aura dancing with shimmering teal lights. "*Rentuuki,* relax. I know things can get tricky around your age. Decisions of that nature are finally starting to really matter, right?"

I exhaled with relief as I nodded. "I really care about your son. There's something in me that's drawn to him—As if when he's around, the stars give me permission to smile as much as I want."

"He does have that effect," Zerana agreed. She was smiling now as she watched bright turquoise clouds drift slowly around Asher's sleeping form.

As I watched her watching him, I felt tears spring to my eyes. I wondered how many times my own mother had watched me sleeping like that, all those years we'd traveled with the caravans. The desire to make things right with her nearly overwhelmed me.

"You're an amazing mom," I told Zerana.

"Trust me, I've made my fair share of mistakes." I suddenly realized Zerana's eyes were moist as well. "I only hope Asher can forgive me."

I nearly asked what she meant, but the way her aura tossed like the stormy sea stopped me short. I didn't want to pry.

Instead, I put a hand on her shoulder. "Asher loves you more than anything in the whole world, and he always will," I said. "Trust him. He's made of strong stuff."

Zerana swallowed, then covered my hand with her own and squeezed it for support. We stayed that way for a while, her thinking of her son, and me thinking of my mom.

"*Zaavu,* I think I will get some rest after all," Zerana finally said. "I'll take the next watch in an hour or so."

I agreed. Zerana lay down near Asher, and I settled back into my post.

There was no real need to build a fire, but just for the sake of it, I put a little trio of etherberries from the bush in my rift hold into a little circle of stones. Their soft, pure white light buoyed my spirits as I sat up alone, keeping watch in the darkness.

As I scanned our surroundings, I kept myself alert by thinking about cooking up a big pot of spiced scorchapple cider. That'd warm our crew right up. I nearly started salivating as I imagined adding cinnamon, sugar, and a tiny sprinkle of smoked paprika to the big, hearty pot. I had all of the ingredients inside my rift-pantry now, and I couldn't stop my finger from runetracing to open the hold.

The golden crack split open just wide enough for me to get a look at all my favorite spices. I spotted a basket of scorchapples, and frowned when I noticed a few bruises on them. They'd probably go bad while we were in the Haze, and I hated the thought of wasting perfectly good ingredients. I should've bought fewer of them.

I was just about to put out my rune when I felt it. The already chilly air got even colder as an aura that looked like icy gray frost crept around my feet, then started up my calves and along my fingertips, reaching for my core.

Then I heard her raspy voice. "Don't close the rift hold just yet, Meleya."

I didn't even jump at the sound. I'd been expecting her.

"Get away from me, Xan," I said. At my words, the icy gray aura momentarily retreated. Though when I turned around, I could see her standing before me.

Xan was no minor shade or echo, but a full-fledged wraith. From the waist up, her turbulent, smoky essence formed a woman with curling, misty hair. Glittering sapphire eyes stared out from an otherwise featureless face, and I could make out a faintly glowing, blue crystal core shrouded within her chest. Where her legs should have been were only wispy tendrils of shadow.

"What took you so long?" I asked as I reflexively assumed a defensive stance.

Xan laughed, and now that we were both ethereal beings, the sound wasn't just bouncing off of the walls of my head. She was really here, truly facing me for the first time.

"Did you miss me?" Xan taunted.

"No," I replied firmly, standing and moving even further from my sleeping companions so that Xan wouldn't disturb them. The golden crack that led to my rift hold followed. "But now that I'm on the Etheria side of things, I just figured you'd be around to harass me the second I left the safety of Orothion's etherlock shield."

"I have been... busy." Xan inched closer. "I had certain matters to attend to among my kind. Would you like to know more?"

"No."

"Pity," Xan replied. "Here I was thinking you were finally taking an interest. There is so much I could teach you. Together, we would be unstoppable."

Xan suddenly hissed and lunged toward me. Or rather, toward my rift hold.

But I was used to her tricks, and readily dissolved my rune as well as the corresponding entrance to my rift hold. Xan wouldn't be getting a hold of the Soul Reaper's voidshard today.

Xan gave another guttural hiss as she dove through empty space. She spun on me, mists sparking as she stretched a smoky hand upward.

Only her hand was no longer hand-shaped. Before my eyes, it roiled, twisting and elongating into a long, jagged sword. My eyes widened at the sight of it.

Xan laughed once more. "A wraithblade. Like it? I have only just begun to be able to form one of this magnitude. It's powerful enough to match even the Elders, and certainly enough to cross you."

Xan struck at me with the speed of an ashviper. But as a trained soldier in the dragon guard, my reactions were quick. My starglass seaxe blocked

Xan's wraithblade with a sound like breaking crystal, but Asher's creation held strong. We were far enough by now that Asher and the others couldn't hear us.

Dark fog swirled around my feet as I engaged my demon in a literal fight, spirit to spirit. Xan slashed and I parried several times before she darted around a hoodoo and out of sight. When I followed, she lashed out from her hiding place.

I inhaled sharply as her wraithblade cut into my arm, leaving a grey slash that leaked ethereal light instead of blood.

"What do you plan to do once you kill me?" I asked. "That won't get you the Soul Reaper's shard."

This time, I landed a cut along Xan's arm with my starglass blade. While the wound to my spirit bled light, Xan's spewed shadow.

"It might, if I'm quick enough," Xan hissed. "Were your spirit to pass into the deeper beyond, that which lies within your rift hold will linger here before returning to your body in the physical realm. But do not fear, Meleya of Misthaven, for I do not wish to kill you. I merely want you to be a more willing host."

Wraithblade met starglass seaxe in a flurry of blows. I portalled on top of a stony hoodoo, but Xan swept upward to float at my level, and we continued our battle. Moving like the snowstorm Vidya named me for, I rifted from hoodoo to hoodoo while Xan struggled to keep up.

"I can take you where you wish to go," Xan said as she caught my blade with her own. "I've been to this netherstone. Tasted its ancient power."

"What are you talking about?" I grunted, shoving Xan back and stabbing toward her core. Xan's shadowy form swirled to the side, avoiding my blade. She then backed up, gesturing deeper into the Haze with her wraithblade.

"The source of the Haze," she said. "Is that not your quest? To discover what great power lies at the center of the gray storm and claim it for the Knights of the Torch?"

"The Knights aren't interested in claiming any drakking voidarchy," I retorted, opening a portal to her side and stabbing for her center once again. This time, my strike grazed her back, and Xan shrieked as more of her essence burned away.

Despite that, Xan laughed. "You have seen for yourself what these so-called Knights are capable of. They are all susceptible to the Gray. You cannot trust them, Meleya."

"It's *you* I can't trust!"

From my perch atop the somewhat distant hoodoo, I ripped open a trio of portals at once, three corresponding exits appearing all around Xan to trap her. Two were false portals, but Xan froze, unable to tell which one I'd strike through.

Crying out, I slashed through the true portal. My white starglass blade caught her sword arm, and I felt like I was hacking into a blanket. But to Xan, the blow was enough to fiercely burn away at her essence. Within a moment, her jagged wraithblade sword had become more of a wraith-dagger.

Xan thrashed in rage. "I need that voidshard. *We* need it!"

As I leaped to a perch closer to Xan, sword at the ready, my aura blazed with indigo fire. I spoke with power. "Give it up, Xan! You can't tempt me anymore!"

Xan growled, her misty form tensing when she realized I had her backed against a wall. Literally—I'd trapped her against a particularly tall and wide hoodoo with nowhere to go. "But we want the same thing!" she rasped.

"And what's that?"

"To take down the Wraith King, of course. The all-powerful top wraith who has bound himself to the Soul Reaper. His voidshard is the key. *Only we* have the power to end him, and our window is closing quickly. The Wraith King will not stop until he retrieves that shard."

"He can't do that," I countered. "Not as long as the voidshard is locked away inside my rift hold."

I gripped my sword, ready to plunge it once and for all through Xan's shadowy chest. She knew it, too, yet still, she forced a single peal of laughter.

"For now."

A tiny stab of doubt pricked my heart. Did Xan know the Wraith King's plans? Or was she just stalling to keep me from burning away more of her essence?

I hesitated. "What do you mean?"

Xan's eyes glittered with pleasure, and some of the fear seemed to leave her trembling form. "King Agnai is relentless and his servants are loyal. One of his most powerful ancients is coming for you, Meleya."

My heart began to thunder in my chest.

Xan pressed on. "He plans to ensure you do not leave Etheria alive. But I can protect you. With our powers combined—"

I gave a roar of protest. This was nothing more than Xan's usual sinister drivel. Sharp starglass sword glittering in the light of the ley line that twisted through the hoodoos around us, I lunged toward her glowing blue heart.

But while I moved fast, Xan had been ready. She spun away from me, throwing herself into the rushing river of blue-tinged ether, which swept her away like a dark shooting star.

"Drak!" I cried, plunging my sword into the dry, cracked earth at my feet.

I was breathing heavily, my aura spinning all around me. I'd been so close—at least, I'd felt like I'd been so close—to destroying Xan. Hopefully now she'd think twice before taking me on again, at least while I was in Etheria.

I fell to my knees in exhaustion. That fight, while brief, had taken a lot out of me.

I floated-slash-dragged myself back to my makeshift fire pit and popped one of the glowing etherberries I'd left there into my mouth. The wound on my arm from Xan's wraithblade seemed to improve after that; at least it wasn't leaking light anymore, though there was still a thin line of gray on my translucent arm as well as my aura.

The etherberry lifted my mood somewhat, but I still felt chilled to the... Well, I didn't currently have any bones, but if I did, I would have been chilled to them.

As I sat down and resumed my watch, my mind latched onto the sack of rice sitting inside my rift hold, hiding the most dangerous weapon in the realm. According to Xan, the voidshard was the key to the Soul Reaper's—and the Wraith King's—undoing. What if I *was* meant to use it in order to bring him down?

"No," I whispered aloud. There had to be another way. There was *always* another way.

For now, all I had to do was keep the shard out of enemy hands until the convergence of mythic stars this spring. According to Solrac, that was when we needed to be ready to fight the Soul Reaper and his accumulated forces. But the convergence was many months from now, and it felt like a lifetime away.

I'd no sooner had the thought than a wispy, silvery cloud played at the edges of my vision. In a second, I felt Blink's snout nuzzling its way under my arm. I was glad she'd slept through the fight. Her wing was almost better, but I knew Xan wouldn't hold back against her.

Thrum, Blink sent a low, comforting beat through our bond as she curled up beside me. I leaned against her flank and began to stroke the spirit-scales along her spine. Blink purred. I'd learned she liked that better than a scratch behind the ears like Sniff did. It was intriguing—Sniff and Blink were twins, but their personalities were as different as the sun and moon.

As I thought about Sniff, holding the spirit version of his golden-yellow heartscale, I could practically hear the ghost of a flute-like melody through our bond. I missed our connection, and couldn't wait to get back to my body.

With the increasingly blue ley line as our guide, we pressed on through the Stormshadow Desert. The ether river was too corrupted for us to refill our ether wells, so we had to rely mostly on our etherberry supply. The winds got stronger with every passing hour as we approached the heart of the storm, and our encounters with shades and echoes became more frequent. Still, they usually only attacked in small groups, and between the four of us, we were able to fight them off fairly easily.

When Blink's wing had fully healed, we traded off between flying on her back and walking to give her some rest. I wanted to use rifting to get us closer to the center faster, but it was hard to see far through the turbulent fog.

Once, the mists cleared just enough that I gave our old skyskipping technique a go. Blink flew through my portal with the three of us on her back to then reappear miles ahead. But I hadn't seen the circling swarm of umbral spirit-buzzards, and I portalled us directly into them. We escaped with only a few minor scratches, but we decided it would be best to keep skyskipping into the unknown to a minimum from then on.

Asher diligently kept track of the passing days by way of the sun, and every morning, he somehow found the energy to announce each new day in a new, dorky way:

"Day four hath come, mine fair companions!"

"Wait guys, do you hear that? It sounds like... day five."

"Day six, day six, your feet smell like dragon-bricks."

I was impressed by his diligence, but far less impressed by his untrue foot commentary and rhyming skills. Also, what were 'dragon-bricks' anyway? I didn't dare ask.

First thing each morning, I'd distribute our daily etherberries. Then we'd fly for several hours before giving Blink's wings a break while we walked.

Before long, we nearly stumbled right into a massive trench. Asher got really excited and hover-dashed, following the gouge in the landscape, which ended in a skyfall crater about the size of a lake. In the dead center was a meteor, the odd plume of dragonfire green smoke still rising from it, though it was clear the thing had landed a day ago or more.

When I focused on the physical plane, I could see evidence of a fierce battle between wild dragonkind. Asher and Zerana tiptoed among the fragments of drekling and wild dragon eggshells that littered the ground near the crater's center. Surrounding them were claw marks and about a half-dozen scaled bodies. The dead dragonkind, from wild dragons, to ashvipers, to the hunched, long-armed dreklings, were only visible on the physical side. Here in Etheria, no auras hung around them anymore.

Except...

Far below, tucked away near the bottom of the crater, was a tiny clutch of unhatched dragon eggs, with little bits of meteor still clinging to the shells. I counted two scale-covered drake eggs, two leathery wyvern eggs, and one perfectly spherical evren egg, adorned with a thousand crystalline planes.

From the Etheria side of things, I could see auras glowing through the eggshells. They were so sweet and frail, in bright colors that would match the scales of the dragons that would one day hatch from them. Beside me, Blink gave a low purr of motherly adoration. While some dragon eggs came from skyfalls like this, I couldn't help but feel a pang of sorrow that Blink would never get to have a clutch of her own.

Unable to stop myself, I reached for a little periwinkle-colored wyvern egg. As a spirit, my hand went straight through the shell to gently caress the spirit of the unhatched dragon inside.

At my touch, he—I could somehow tell that the aura was masculine—gave a little wiggle of contentment. Blink reached out too, nudging the baby dragon with her snout, which made his aura pulse with light.

Drak, it was beautiful. I knew this young dragon would more than likely end up wild, ferocious, and of lesser sentience. But I found myself secretly hoping he would find a good rider to bond so that he could experience life to its fullest.

The fight's victors had fled hours before, though not before taking as much skystone as they could pry from the fallen star. Still, I saw quite a few pockets of harder-to-reach skystone still embedded in the rock. Each chunk of crystal shimmered, emitting an aura of pure white power. I joined Asher as he stood staring at a shard of it.

"Skyseekers will probably show up at this site soon," Asher mused. "Use their daggers to pick over the stuff the wild dragons and dreklings left behind."

At that, Asher pulled out the spirit version of the dagger he always kept sheathed at his belt. It was a skyseeker's blade, I realized, noting the unique, curved chisel on its handle.

Since the dagger was merely spirit, a shadow of the real thing that'd stayed with Asher's physical form at Orothion, I naturally expected it to go right through the skystone. But when Asher moved to pry it from the fallen star, it stuck.

"What in the void?" I asked, eyes going wide as I watched an equally surprised Asher chisel the skystone from the rock. Pretty soon, he was holding—yes, actually holding—a large chunk of shimmering skystone in his now-trembling spirit-hands.

"How...?" he asked.

Zerana was beaming. "*Naat, kiiviziiva javaali kun—*"

"Evgardian, Mom," Asher reminded her.

"Ah, *antiik,* I'm sorry. You see, skystone spans the veil between worlds. Its power comes from this plane, Etheria, after all, so both spirits and corporeals can interact with them. That is part of why they are so powerful."

"No kidding," Asher murmured, following which his aura seemed to pulse with light near his head.

"Hey Blink!" He turned to my dragon. "You hungry?"

Blink's eyes lit up. Asher tossed her the skystone, which she snapped up in her jaws. I beamed, knowing what was coming.

I'd seen Sniff ascend, so this time, I knew what to expect. Mystic runes, Sentinel markings, and the telltale burn of golden irises that came from using Archonic power coalesced as Blink rose several feet into the air. White light and a golden cloud surrounded her, and the *plinking* sound of her spirit-scales shedding onto the ground was like literal music.

Then Blink spread her four wings and the golden cloud dissipated. She was now larger, her scales and ridges tougher, and her horns longer. From the Etheria side, the transformation was all the more enchanting.

She may not have had a physical form, but when the light had fully subsided, Blink's spirit had grown every bit as strong as Sniff's now that they both were on their second ascension. But the best part came when Blink spoke to me through our bond, for the first time, with words:

Would like to see that wraith try to get my Meleya now! Her usual drumbeats punctuated her challenge, and I rushed to embrace my dragon bond's neck.

"Thank you, Asher," I said. He responded with his very best crooked smile.

That was when I noticed Zerana was on the ground, meticulously gathering Blink's shed scales, each one like a glowing silver coin.

I cocked my head. "What are you doing?"

"We've got to keep these, of course," Zerana replied as she scooped the scales into a sack. "When a rider's bond ascends, is it not tradition to use the shed scales to forge armor for the rider?"

Asher's mouth fell open. "You can make *spirit* ascension armor?"

Zerana raised an eyebrow. "Not myself, but I know where I can get the job done. That is, if you don't mind me holding onto these, Meleya? Even if your spirit ascension armor isn't ready before you return to your physical body, I'll make sure to get it to you."

My pulse was racing with excitement, and all I could manage was a grateful nod.

Fragment: The Rise's Fall

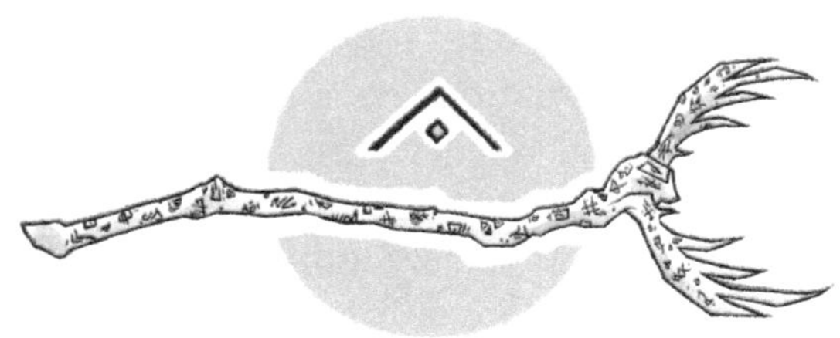

Solrac

Solrac wasn't sure what was higher—the desert temperatures, or the tension between the Canyonlands' noble houses.

He and Vidya sat at the far end of the incredibly long table set on the spacious balcony atop Keep Rengard's famed Rise. Once again, they were in disguise, this time as the Lord and Lady of Rengard's twelfth house. The pair was notoriously reclusive, so while no one had expected their presence, neither did they bat an eye when they waltzed in.

A dragonhide canopy stretched overhead to protect them from the sun, but even the light breeze wasn't enough to keep everyone present from sweating.

"I will not hear another word on the subject!" The Duchess of Keep Scarlet Shore pounded the table. "Ally with the Knights of the Torch? The very idea is ludicrous!"

"What's ludicrous is being so closed-minded as to not consider such a proposal," the Duke of Gray Fen snapped back. "I don't like the Knights much myself, but it cannot be denied that we are in dire need of allies. If Skygard's forces might aid us in the war with the Drekai—"

"But that's the very crux of the issue!" interrupted a young noble representative from Keep Mesa. The Lord must've only just turned eighteen, his parents sitting to his left and right. At Queen Ilona's request, many of the noble families had brought their heirs in an effort to give them more experience.

The young man continued. "Why are we fighting this war with the Dragon Isles? Was it not the Coven of the Gray Ones who attacked the Rise's dragon stables last summer? Our quarrel is not with the Isles, but magi!"

"Another reason to avoid allying with the Knights of the Torch!"

The arguing continued, and the frown Solrac had worn since the meeting's onset deepened. As a nobleman himself, Solrac had attended his fair share of councils, but never before had things become so heated so quickly.

"Something is wrong," Solrac muttered to Vidya sitting beside him.

She didn't respond, her hand sweating as it gripped his beneath the table. Her expression was troubled, but Solrac got the feeling it wasn't related to what was happening here at the table.

Solrac worried for her, but knew that if anyone had a shot at uniting this discordant group, it was Vidya. Or rather, the Black Valkyrie. It was why the omens had shown them this meeting in the first place, he was sure of it.

"It is time," Solrac whispered.

"I don't think I can," Vidya murmured.

Solrac bit his tongue. As much as he wanted Vidya to carry out their plan, he wouldn't force her.

At the head of the table, Queen Ilona sat alone, the picture of beauty. Until today, Solrac had only ever seen the queen in vision, but drak, the visions hadn't done her justice. The woman's face was soft, her eyes large and innocent. Each curl shone, as did her heart-shaped lips. While the conflict around the table disturbed Solrac, Queen Ilona simply sat there, contentedly watching with her dainty hands clasped before her atop the table.

Vidya caught Solrac staring and gave him a subtle kick. Solrac turned his gaze onto his wife, whose knowing glare momentarily put an amused grin right back onto his face.

"Forgive me," said a somewhat timid noblewoman seated at the far end of the table, near Solrac and Vidya, "but I agree that the Coven of the Gray Ones ought to retain our true focus. Not just the Coven, but every Gray force that threatens the Canyonlands. Have we not all heard of the Gray Knight whose masked army terrorizes Rengard's northern cities?"

Mutters broke out, and Solrac and Vidya exchanged glances. It seemed that while the Rengardians hadn't yet realized that the mysterious Gray Knight was targeting Knights of the Torch safehouses specifically, his notoriety was growing.

"Besides that," the noblewoman continued, "back home in Keep Saguaro, a strange gray sickness leeches the life out of our outlying towns. The Haze, they call it."

"I've heard of this Haze as well," said another noble, stroking his chin thoughtfully. A few others murmured their agreement. Perhaps Solrac could change things without Vidya needing to appear as the Black Valkyrie today...

Solrac cleared his throat, then spoke with a traditional Evgardian accent to aid in his disguise. "I've heard that the Knights of the Torch are well aware of this Haze, and are working on solutions that might combat it. Discovering its source, for one."

For a moment, the tension in the room seemed to soften. Solrac seized his opportunity.

"Don't you see?" he went on. "War with the Drekai, the crusade against magi... it's all only serving to distract us from what truly matters: defeating the Gray. But if we were to follow the example of King Rodan of Drakfell, as well as the Queen of Behrfell, who recently pledged her allegiance to the Knights as well—"

A soft cough yanked control over the discussion straight to the head of the table. Queen Ilona's charm was magnetic, and everyone turned their heads away from Solrac with surprising uniformity.

"In these troubling times, we cannot allow ourselves to act in haste." Queen Ilona glanced down, lashes fluttering over her large, sympathetic eyes. "The Knights of the Torch have long been regarded as reckless, dealing in secrets and conducting their activity behind closed doors. How can we trust rebels such as these?"

That was when Solrac felt it—a pinprick at the back of his consciousness. Few knew how to recognize the subtle tap of a Seer trying to infiltrate their mind, but Solrac had endured extensive training in preparation to become the Farseer. His mental wards were strong, his mind impossible to penetrate without his notice.

Pretending to be focused on what Ilona was saying, Solrac subtly runetraced below the table. Two runes took shape: one to locate the source of the mental assault, and another to cloak both runes so that no one would realize Solrac was channeling etherarchy.

The mental picture of a starmoth resting in his hair just behind his ear appeared in Solrac's mind. It must have been the ethereal familiar of some other Seer. Solrac traced another rune that would allow him to work his way into the starmoth's mind to tap into the mindlink it was forming.

Solrac had to fake a cough to cover his shock. Whatever Seer this ethereal familiar belonged to had planted starmoth copies on every person present today. Soot, could that be the reason for discord? Was a powerful Seer working to sow discontent amongst the Canyonlands' nobility?

Solrac narrowed his eyes as he scanned the faces of the gathered nobles, trying to locate the Seer via the physical realm as well as through the mindlink. He had to know whether they were simply reading minds, or affecting people's minds more deeply. It was difficult to be certain, but he thought he could see a pale blue sheen flashing occasionally across some people's eyes. That could easily be the result of cleverly concealed mind control.

Queen Ilona demurely continued. "But our High King has always dealt fairly with the Canyonlands. Think of his kindness in facilitating the evacuation of our shadow wasted to Kolbohr, where they will have shelter and work. The Great Uniter, he is called, for what he did to restore the realm to vitality after the Dragon Wars. A mighty true dragon rider, whose forces are the stuff of legends. Tell me, what do we fear more? A vague, gray threat that we have already defeated? Or the wrath of a High King who has only ever done his best to see the Canyonlands thrive?"

"The queen makes excellent points," said the plump Duke of Scarlet Shore seated near the table's head. "Her reason matches her beauty." He made eyes at the queen, who gave a prim bat of her lashes.

Some were agreeing while others loudly voiced their disapproval. Solrac narrowed his eyes at Ilona, who seemed equally pleased with both responses. His runetracing finger secretly flew once more.

"But the Knights of the Torch have a true dragon rider as well," another lord piped up, eliciting a glare from the plump Duke at his side. "Princess Eliana of Drakfell."

That caused another uproar. Everyone and their drake had an opinion about the Princess, who had been doing her best to recruit small, sympathetic towns to the Knights' cause. Little by little, those small towns were adding up. Her presence had caused no small stir, and the bounty on her head set by the jealous Magnus was a hefty one.

"Excuse me," one noblewoman practically shouted to be heard. "But Duke Brodrik—Isn't your son betrothed to this Drakfellian princess?"

All eyes turned to a man with russet skin and smooth, thick black hair. He and his wife exchanged glances before Duke Brodrik cleared his throat.

"That was once true, yes. But an alliance with the traitorous King Rodan is no longer in our stars. I'd like nothing more than to see justice for the High King and see the rebel true dragon rider apprehended."

"Social climber," someone muttered.

"Do not mock my loyalty to the High Crown," Duke Brodrik snapped. "I will not see the great Canyonlands fall to the bottom of the ranks alongside the traitorous Badlands. I stand with Queen Ilona—I will not cast my lot with the Knights of the Torch."

"Hear hear!" someone agreed, and another din broke out.

Meanwhile, the queen's smile was the epitome of delighted innocence. Solrac was almost certain of her guilt even before the cleverly masked black mythraven's feather floated into *Ilona's* hair.

The mental connection bloomed, and though Ilona did have some simple mental wards in place, Solrac was the Farseer. While the ever-growing uproar around the table was all discord, the sinister, otherworldly voice within Ilona's mind was completely in harmony with Ilona's own thoughts.

Yes, yes! They'll be at each other's throats by the end of the meeting! Then tonight...

The Canyonlands will fall, Ilona's voice relished the thought. *My brother foresees great power coming to the Gray in the wake of Streya's Comet. As for me, I will put these arrogant nobles in their places. Magi like us will at last sit in our rightful place above the rabble.*

The Soul Reaper will be pleased, the voice answered back.

Solrac cursed under his breath. He'd heard all he needed to.

First, he quickly traced a semi-complex rune that would nullify the power of the starmoth Ilona had planted on him, then another to stop the one he sensed was on Vidya. Soot, this was a lot of etherarchy. Then, using his and Vidya's interlaced fingers and yet another rune to connect their minds, Solrac filled his wife in.

What I cannot understand, Solrac thought to Vidya, *is why she would use her abilities to sow discord rather than simply push everyone to take her side. When it comes to mind control, it's far more difficult to force someone to do something they normally wouldn't. But these nobles seem uncertain enough that swaying them should be easy.*

It's because her true goal is *discord,* Vidya thought back grimly. *Chaos. It's the aim of all wraiths. A realm in chaos is a realm left vulnerable.*

Beside Solrac, Vidya took a deep breath. *I have to stop this,* she thought, then let go of Solrac's hand.

As she stood, blue wildshaper marks appeared on her skin as a sapphire mist melted away her disguise. When it dissipated, Vidya stood in her usual black armor, from her swan-emblazoned pauldron to her black feathered cloak. In her hand, she gripped her fierce, pitch-colored dragonhook spear as she commanded the people's attention even more powerfully than Ilona had. The Black Valkyrie's posture was straight, her expression haughty, and murmurs broke out as people recognized her.

The Black Valkyrie proudly addressed the gathered nobles. "Nobility of the Canyonlands, I know I was not invited to your council, but I hope you can accept me at your table. Perhaps some of you recognize me from last year's Winter Solstice Ball, when I and my loyal Mage Hunters defeated the wildshaping Liberator who would have seen you all dead."

That did it. Solrac watched with pride as the murmurs swelled. The nobles indeed remembered that night well, and how without the Black Valkyrie, many would not be sitting here today. Only Ilona appeared dismayed, and through the mental connection via the mythraven feather, Solrac caught her scattered thoughts:

The Black Valkyrie... Not supposed to be here... Must listen to what she has to say... She's one of us... Servant of the Wraith King.

Vidya cooly pressed on. "Now then—High King Magnus and his son, Mason Drakeslayer, are leading this realm down the path of ruin. Those of you who attended last winter's ball know just how ruthless the Coven of the Gray Ones can be. Well, mark my words: the High King has put himself in league with the very same powers, and desires the Canyonlands to do the same. I can assure you that what we saw that night will be nothing compared to what's in store. Therefore, as the only party taking this threat seriously and resolved to fight back, the Knights of the Torch have my full support, and they should have yours too!"

This provoked more lively conversation, and—to Solrac's pleasure—much of it was in the Knights' favor. Many still could not fathom the idea of turning their backs on the Capital as Drakfell and Behrfell had done, but while the hero of Rengard stood before them, their dissenting comments had become far more subdued.

Traitorous Black Valkyrie! Solrac heard Ilona's wraith screech in her mind. *It appears Exusha has lost control. We will destroy her along with these pampered fools.*

Tonight? came Ilona's reply.

No need to wait—Let us annihilate them now and blame the Knights of the Torch.

Solrac hadn't even had time to wonder what she meant before the sickening sound of blade cutting flesh garnered gasps and screams. The whole table turned to see that the Duke of Scarlet Shore had the tip of a sword sprouting from his chest.

The perpetrator was none other than the lord sitting beside him. The lord's eyes appeared glassed over for only a moment longer before he blinked, then looked down in horror at his own hands.

"Scorch," the lord cursed. "I... How..."

Before he could finish, another jeweled sword silenced the lord, as another glassy-eyed noble exacted revenge on behalf of the fallen Duke of Scarlet Shore. Before long, more weapons were drawn, and utter chaos ensued as the nobles scrambled, shouting and screaming as they clambered to escape.

"Stop!" Vidya shouted, drawing her black dragonhook blade. "Stop this madness!"

But the nobility weren't in control of their actions—Ilona was. And while the wickedly beautiful queen's mental laughter echoed within, on the outside, she had a hand over her heart, eyes round with well-practiced shock and horror.

Vidya started drawing a psionic rune, planning to disarm as many mind-controlled nobles as she could. But the one next to her swung at her with his seaxe, interrupting her runetracing.

"This is *your* doing!" Vidya leaped onto the table and trained her spear on Queen Ilona. "End this!"

Queen Ilona gasped as fat—likely illusory—tears slid down her cheeks. "Me? Impossible!"

Solrac didn't waste another second. He too shed his disguise so that he wouldn't have to split his focus more than necessary, then stood, flinging a dreamweave spell across the long table toward Ilona. Violet light pulsed as the powerful illusion-breaking enchantment hit her square in the chest.

At once, the facade melted away to reveal the truth about the queen. While still beautiful, the seamless perfection of Ilona's face and hair dulled to reflect reality. Gray seemed to emanate from her wraith-bound form, and her irises glowed vivid sapphire blue. But still, the starkest difference was in the queen's expression. What had once been tender innocence gave way to a heartless sneer.

Livid that her secret had been revealed, Queen Ilona's void blue eyes pulsed with light. She rose to her feet, then slammed her hands down upon the table.

"Let them all die," Ilona hissed, her voice doubled with her wraith's.

The nobility turned on one another in a horrific massacre. Solrac runetraced frantically, pinpointing starmoths and dreamblasting them to restore the nobles to their own control.

Suddenly, the Farseer's great black mythraven swooped in, runes aglow on its feathers. The creature did what it could to dreamblast the starmoths, but the nobles were cutting each other down faster than he could stop them. Meanwhile, Vidya summoned her six ethereal starswans, who attacked the most aggressive nobles, trying to keep them away from each other.

Guards now flooded the courtyard, both ones who'd been standing by and others from within the citadel. Some tried to intervene, but inevitably fell as the vicious blades of the mind-controlled nobility turned on them too. Scorch, Ilona's skill was incredible, no doubt the result of years of training.

Vidya meanwhile swept toward Ilona, determined to end the source of the bloodbath. Shadowfire lit up the edge of her spear, though Solrac noticed that it wasn't as vivid as he'd seen from her before. It seemed that Vidya was trying to limit her use of voidarchy, to keep her wraith from taking control.

Rather than take on the Black Valkyrie herself, Ilona forced more nobles to impede Vidya's way. Vidya had to stay her hand, trying to break through the barrier without doing the hypnotized nobles significant bodily harm. Ilona's eyes glittered. She had no such restriction, and stars if her skill in mind control wasn't beyond any Solrac had ever seen. Of course, most Seers found such a use of their powers immoral, and for good reason.

Unable to effectively destroy all of Ilona's starmoths, Solrac shifted his focus into targeted dream blasts. He fired bolts of pure violet energy at every nobleman or woman he could, knocking them out cold. That effectively broke Ilona's hold over them, and she snarled as more and more of her puppets dropped.

"Alright then, Exusha," Ilona snarled in her doubled timbre, all guises of innocence long gone. "Let us see which of us best serves the Wraith King now."

Ilona rose to join Vidya on the tabletop, clearly using telekinesis to propel her own clothing. It seemed Vidya wasn't the only one operating with multiple ether wells.

Ilona's irises blazed with sapphire light as a gray shroud of mist appeared to surround her. Her right arm became shadow, sprouting a long, jagged blade. Solrac could hardly believe he'd once thought this woman demure and fragile.

Solrac's heart skipped a beat when, likewise, Vidya's eyes flashed void blue. The very light around her seemed to disappear as Vidya took on the telltale reverse glow of someone being steered by a powerful wraith.

While Solrac worked with the mythraven and starswans to save as many nobles and their guards as they could, his wife did battle with the Queen of the Canyonlands.

The two wraith-bound women's clash of power was blinding. Blue runes glowed from both their foreheads as their blades met, shadow grinding against shadow. At last, the Black Valkyrie sprouted a pair of mighty gray swan wings and took to the air.

Sweeping down with mounting momentum, she stabbed toward Ilona. But Ilona was prepared, no doubt using her seership to foresee Vidya's next moves. Moving with otherworldly grace, the queen sidestepped the Black Valkyrie, then parried her attack with a swift slash from her jagged arm blade, cleaving Vidya's spear in two and slashing against Vidya's armor.

Hissing seemed to emit from both women, as if the wraiths themselves were locked in battle. Vidya and Ilona were lost within the Gray's contest of might.

Despite Ilona's skill with foresight, the Black Valkyrie's wraith-enhanced power gave her certain advantages that Solrac knew firsthand were virtually impossible to defeat. Though Vidya fought with her own black dragonhook spear, gray mist coiled around it, infusing it with the same power as Ilona's wraithblade. Though Ilona tried to dodge, Vidya's psionically charged stab pierced the queen's torso, and raw shadowfire overcame her.

As Ilona took her last, shuddering breath, the sapphire light flickering within her irises, she spoke.

"At least... our master will know... we accomplished what we set out to do. The Canyonlands... in ruin."

Then, her soul left her body lifeless as it lay upon the table.

Solrac felt a wave of momentary relief. Though chaos still ruled the courtyard around him, he rushed toward his wife, who remained standing over the fallen queen, breathing heavily as she gripped her shadowspear.

"Vidya!" Solrac called as he reached out to touch her. "Vid—"

Solrac shouldn't have moved so quickly. The Black Valkyrie suddenly whirled on him, gray wings beating as she grabbed Solrac by the collar. Using telekinesis to enhance her might, she slammed Solrac down against the table and trained her shadowy spear upon his throat.

Eyes still aglow with dark power, the Black Valkyrie spoke with a doubled tone. "It is time to take you to the Surgeon, great Farseer. Oh, how we have longed for this moment—Seeing you helpless. It's only fair that you taste the poison you once fed us."

The Black Valkyrie's hold was so tight Solrac couldn't speak. All he could do was look into those cold sapphire eyes, searching for the woman he knew was underneath.

That, and runetrace.

Rather than employ an aggressive defense, Solrac connected his mind with Vidya's. Memories began to flow between them in rapid succession. Some came from long ago: their early days performing with *Marelda's Mythica* circus, their runaway marriage. Days spent in the waterfall inn.

Then followed memories that were far more recent: helping each other survive the journey from the Mirror Forest to Orothion. Solrac re-gifting her the diamond-shaped hand mirror he'd recently 'borrowed'. Finally, a memory from just a few nights ago at the ether geyser outside the ruins of the Cattledrake Cantina, when she'd leaned into Solrac's arms while he'd soothed her.

I believe you can do this, Solrac had said. *Truly.*

He'd meant every word, and he still believed them now.

Little by little, Vidya's heavy breathing slowed, until soon the glow of sapphire covering her midnight blue irises faded away entirely. Then, blessedly, the wraith-like mists surrounding her dragonhook spear dissipated into wisps, and she cast the weapon aside.

Tears welled as Vidya released her hold over Solrac. He sat up just in time to catch her as she fell into his arms.

Too quickly, the sound of shouts and anguished cries wrenched both Solrac and Vidya back to reality.

The scene beneath the now-shredded canopy was one of nightmares. Those who Solrac had knocked out with dreamweave energy were slowly rising, but far too many lay still, especially those nearest the head of the table.

More and more soldiers were rushing onto the courtyard, trying to piece together what had happened. Frantic, terrified nobles trembled beneath the table and in the corners of the room. Vidya refused to let go of Solrac's hand.

"Ilona's wraith got what she wanted," Vidya said soberly. "Chaos."

"The fate of Rengard is forever altered," Solrac agreed, his heart aching. "Just as the omens said."

Before long, one of the soldiers approached Solrac and Vidya. He stood out from the others, the insignia on his shoulder pauldron setting him apart as the Captain of the Guard.

"Black Valkyrie," he said, nodding respectfully. "And Solrac, Duke of Glacia... Great Farseer. I'm Captain Gunnar, leader over the guard here on the Rise."

Solrac and Vidya told Gunnar everything they'd discovered about Ilona and how the meeting had gone so horribly wrong. Gunnar seemed to be a reasonable man, nodding as he took in the information.

"Captain Gunnar," Solrac said thoughtfully, "I know there is much to attend to, but it cannot have escaped your notice that the Canyonlands finds itself without a ruler."

"I was thinking the same thing," Captain Gunnar responded gravely. "I've checked myself to see who's been lost, and scorch, it's not looking good. King Axel had no other kin, and the whole second house and their heir are gone. The third house is in the same state."

"And the fourth house?" Vidya asked.

"The Duke and Duchess of Solhelm were lost as well." Gunnar glanced sorrowfully toward the ground near the table, where the fallen couple still lay. "But their children were not present."

Solrac started. Solhelm rang a bell...

"Well, that's a blessing," Vidya said. "Is their heir of age?"

"Only as of a few months ago," Gunnar responded.

"Who is it?" Vidya asked.

Gunnar swallowed. "Brigan of Solhelm is now King of Rengard."

Fragment: Tides

Brigan

As usual, Brigan couldn't sleep.

Typically on such nights, Brigan would gravitate toward the library. If he couldn't get rest, he might as well get some knowledge. But they'd been a little understaffed in Orothion's medical wing lately, so Brigan figured he ought to roll up his sleeves and put his healing skills to good use.

"Brigan! Glad to see you," said Trickshot, the talented medic and best sharpshooter in the eight keepdoms. She hurried to meet Brigan at the door.

"I've got to mix up some tonics that need to be delivered first thing in the morning, and I'm all out of star anise," Trickshot went on, tucking her thick auburn hair behind one ear. A white streak stood out among the strands, the result of taking an ether blast to the head during battle. "I sent the other medics to bed, but since you're up..."

"I can keep an eye on things here," Brigan assured her.

"You're a lifesaver." She hurried to gather her supply-filled satchel. "Things are pretty quiet tonight," she said on her way out. "All you'll really need to do is keep an eye on the usuals."

There was the expected tightening of Brigan's chest as he slowly strode toward 'the usuals.' Two figures, lying perfectly still on adjacent cots at the back of the medical wing. The first, a half-born with messy, jet black hair and dark teal scales on the tips of his pointed ears. Asher's chest moved rhythmically up and down, unchanging, the same way it had for weeks.

Then, there was Meleya.

Her long hair cascaded over the side of the bed like a white waterfall. Her large, round eyes were closed as if in slumber, but Brigan didn't have any trouble picturing the deep brown shade he'd seen almost every day for years. He wished he could see it now.

Immediately, he reminded himself not to wish *too* hard.

Brigan and Meleya had been close friends ever since they'd met in basic training at age thirteen. Now, five years later, Brigan was more sure than ever that 'friends' was all they'd ever be. He'd come to grips with the fact that Meleya didn't reciprocate his feelings, and had assured her that their friendship didn't hinge on any potential romance. Despite that, the hole in his heart remained sore. Brigan wondered how long it would take to heal, and whether he really wanted it to.

Carefully, he went through the routine checklist to ensure that Meleya and Asher were still stable. Their breathing, movement, and temperatures were all normal. They weren't like normal coma patients—they were in what Trickshot and the others called 'astral sleep.' Brigan had read up on it thoroughly, and had practically memorized the definition in *Noric and Simetra's Manual for Mystical Medicine*:

Astral sleep is a rare condition during which the patient's spirit separates from his or her body, typically as a result of a dream energy-charged blow to the head. During astral sleep, the body exists in a static state, so no atrophy is expected to occur. All regular functions neutralize during the sleep period, which can last anywhere from a fraction of a second (if regenerative etherarchy is applied immediately and the case is mild) to months or even years (for more severe cases).

It is said that the spirit may remain active during this state, though trapped in the spirit plane, Etheria. There is debate among experts regarding the accuracy of this claim, as few victims of astral sleep reawaken. Some speculate that this is because, while in Etheria, the afflicted spirits encounter horrors they are ill-equipped to face, and therefore expire, causing death to the corresponding physical body as well.

To wake a patient suffering from astral sleep, a specific remedy is required. The ingredients and method are as follows: Add three parts moonwillow bark to two parts arcocado oil (or crystalized lightberry extract). Steep beneath a full moon for three to five hours, or until the color shifts to a clouded pale violet...

The instructions went on. Solrac had given Brigan this information along with detailed instructions for how to ensure the remedy was prepared properly and in a timely manner. Brigan wished Solrac himself was here to oversee it all, but he and Vidya had been needed in Rengard on some top-secret assignment. Brigan hoped that their mission was going well.

Trickshot's arrival had helped immensely. Brigan's skill as a healer was growing, but she knew far more than he did, and he enjoyed learning from her.

Momentarily, Asher twitched. His eyes partially opened for a moment before closing again, and his breathing sped up ever so slightly. A gray mark suddenly appeared on the back of his hand.

Brigan frowned. That almost looked like a slash mark from a blade, just... gray. There was no blood either.

Worried, Brigan strode to the store cupboard. As he spotted the small handful of vials of liquid light, he couldn't stop the small pit from forming in his stomach. Their liquid light supply was dwindling fast. He wondered if the Lightwielders would be able to keep up with demand, especially as cases of the shadow wasting proliferated throughout the realm.

Rather than draw from Orothion's stores, Brigan pulled out his personal vial of liquid light. The tiny crystal bottle had been specially forged using the shed scales from Brigan's drake, Bolt. Bolt was a Lightwielder, and her scales empowered the vial to continuously refill with light. Back at the refugee camp in the lava fields, Brigan had essentially demolished his own ascension armor to create as many new perpetually-refilling vials as he could. He'd given most of them away, keeping only three for when he inevitably came across others in need. For what he'd done, they called him 'Brigan the Lightbringer.' The moniker had stuck, carrying over to the staff here at Orothion as well.

Brigan was as sparing as he could be when applying the precious healing substance to Asher's hand. The moment it touched his skin, the gray slash mark vanished, and Brigan rested easier. As he carefully replaced the vial in his medical bag, he made note of the occurrence so that he could tell Trickshot about it later.

Brigan was just adjusting the pillow beneath Meleya's head to ensure she was comfortable when the sound of someone rushing into the medical wing made him jump. Scorch, who would be running in at this hour?

"Is it still here... yes! Stars, this'll be perfect!"

For such a late hour, Kari of Steel Rim sure had a lot of energy as she spilled into the medical wing, arms full of random things: tools, bits of scrap metal, some blocks of wood, and a whole bag full of crystals. Even more things stuck out from the massive, grease-smeared pockets of her blacksmith's apron.

Kari didn't even seem to notice Brigan's presence as she barreled toward Asher's bedside. Still muttering to herself, she plopped down on the nearest empty cot and began sorting through her items.

Brigan winced. Her tools would undoubtedly stain the bedsheets, and he was fairly certain it would be down to him to change them out once she finished... whatever it was she was doing. Still, the way Kari's eyes blazed with energy was enough to coax an amused smile onto his face.

Brigan watched her work for a few more seconds before clearing his throat.

"Gauntlet down—"

"Holy mother of the sky goddesses!" Kari practically fell off the bed at the sound of Brigan's voice. A few miscellaneous cogs and screws clattered to the ground, and Kari threw a hand to her mouth as if covering it would somehow help mute the noise.

Brigan snorted, then bent down to help her retrieve the fallen items. "Sorry. Didn't mean to break your concentration."

"I can't believe I didn't see you there," Kari shook her head, making black curls bounce all around her shoulders.

"Don't worry about it." Brigan set her things back on the definitely-stained blankets as Kari got right back to work, pulling out a measuring stick. "What *are* you doing anyway?"

"Putting together a longevity promotion device for this!" Kari eagerly began to measure a small, squat, potted cactus sitting on a tray-sized table beside Asher. "Elle left it here the other day, but I noticed it wasn't getting enough sunlight. But I just had the most brilliant idea for how to fix the problem!"

"One that couldn't wait until morning?" Brigan asked good-naturedly.

Kari shrugged. "I don't control when inspiration strikes. Do you mind?"

Brigan smiled. "Be my guest."

Kari set to work, applying her careful measurements to thin metal rods which she connected using adjustable hinges. She spent a long time attaching small mirrors to certain points along the contraption, along with little shimmering panels of crystal.

“Is that starglass?” Brigan asked as she worked.

“Mmhm.” Kari nodded. “I had an Astromancer make me some to keep on hand a while back. They’re infused with fractional amounts of skystone so that they don’t fade over time.”

“Ah,” Brigan said, leaning closer to examine the panels. “Similar to the way the starglass panels worked at Rhana’s safehouse cabin.”

“Exactly! I never got to see the cabin, but I’ve heard amazing things. In fact, it was learning about the rooftop starglass panels that power the lightwielder’s torches there that spurred the idea for this!”

“Brilliant.”

Kari looked up from her tools just long enough to beam at Brigan. As she did, she cocked her head.

“Sorry I didn’t see you at first,” Kari said. “I tend to get a little... obsessive. I got it from my parents, Solei rest their souls.”

“I didn’t realize your parents had passed,” Brigan said. “Kaidan and Kalari, were their names, right? I thought Kai mentioned them disappearing on some sort of quest.”

“Kai’s never given up hope that they’re still out there somewhere.” Kari shrugged. “I guess I’m more of a realist.”

“I can’t imagine what you and Kai have gone through,” Brigan shook his head. “Without my parents, I’d be lost.”

Brigan and Kari exchanged smiles. “It’s Brigan, right?” Kari asked. “You were one of the ones helping Asher and my little brother, Kai, to free Orothion.”

“Yeah.”

“Aren’t you a duke or something?”

“Heir Duke to Keep Solhelm,” Brigan said with a casual wave of his hand. He wasn’t all that interested in talking about titles and ranks at the moment.

Kari kept working as she asked, “So, how did someone like you end up becoming a Knight of the Torch?”

Ah, now *that* was something Brigan enjoyed discussing.

“Someone gave me this,” Brigan said, digging into his deep tunic pocket to pull out a thin red book. The well-worn cover read, *The Knight’s Code.*

“It’s all about the creed every Knight swears to live by,” Brigan went on passionately. “Choose light, Burn bright...”

“Drive out darkness, and Light the way,” Kari finished. “I know the Code well.”

"Really?"

"I joined the Knights years before Kai and Asher did. All because I fell in love with the Code."

Brigan's eyes were bright. "So did I! All my life, I've felt aimless. Bound by the obligations of the title to which I was born. Taught that playing political games to advance my own station was the proper way to live a fulfilling life. But once I found the Knights..."

"Everything fell into place." Kari nodded. "I feel like the Knight's Code, while simple, is the one thing I could keep learning about forever without ever completely having it all figured out."

"I love that."

Brigan and Kari continued to discuss the finer points of the Knights of the Torch's code, from its controversial history to the intellectual applications of living by its pillars. Kari's opinions were strong and well-researched, which Brigan found deeply refreshing.

Finally, Kari was ready to set up her cactus-preserving contraption. The device was complicated, and she had to mount it upon the mottled red-and-gray stone of the walls to get it all the way around Asher's cot.

"All that's left now is to wait for the sun to rise," Kari said.

While she waited, she took Asher's measurements. Asher's dragon bond, Thorn, had recently risen to third ascension, which meant he'd shed his old scales, which Kari planned to forge into new ascension armor for him as soon as she got a spare moment.

Eventually, just as the first rays of morning light began to stream through the wide window of the medical wing, it became clear that Kari's 'longevity promotion device' worked. Light bounced from one mirror to the next, filling the starglass panels and ultimately shining bright, soft golden light onto the cactus. The squat plant seemed to stand taller beneath its glow.

"Well, what do you think of that?" Kari said, smacking her palms together.

"It's genius, of course," Brigan replied. Then he tapped his chin. "Although..."

Brigan strode toward the small side table that held the plant. He plucked up the pot, then moved it to the side table on the other side of Asher's bed. There, it was in full sunlight, just as bright as that of Kari's complex reflector.

Kari's mouth fell open. She and Brigan locked eyes for a moment before she burst into laughter.

"I guess that works too," she snickered.

Brigan chuckled as he moved the cactus back under her contraption. "But your way is more exciting. Gauntlet down: Sometimes it's best to bring the light to you, and other times—"

"—all you've got to do is step into the light," Kari finished.

Brigan smiled, about to say more when thundering footsteps sounded from the doorway of the medical wing. Moments later, Trickshot appeared, with several others close behind her. What were Solrac and Vidya doing here? Weren't they supposed to be in Rengard? Brigan knew that Asher's father, Akayto, had given them a skystone-powered rift anchor that could get them back to Orothion at a moment's notice, but why had they returned in such a rush?

Besides Solrac and Vidya, another familiar face made Brigan balk.

"Commander Gunnar?" Brigan said. His old instructor had a few cuts on his face and his cloak was torn as if he'd recently been in a fight. Gunnar was part of the guard at Keep Rengard. What in the stars was he doing at the Knights of the Torch's headquarters?

"It's Captain Gunnar now," Gunnar replied. "But that doesn't matter." Then, for some reason, Gunnar bent down on one knee before Brigan.

Brigan frowned as his pulse immediately began to race. Throughout basic training and his time in the guard, Gunnar had never once bowed to him.

"What's going on?" Brigan asked.

Vidya's expression was grim as she approached. "We returned as quickly as we could. Brigan... we come with news."

Solrac's eyes were watery. When he put his hand on Brigan's shoulder, Brigan's heart sank.

Brigan stood alone on the gray, cloudy beach. Behind him, the high cliffs loomed, the Orothion stronghold at their peak.

The salty sea air filled Brigan's lungs as the spray of crashing waves speckled his face. He'd always breathed better when he was near the ocean.

Captain Gunnar and the others hadn't liked the idea of Brigan going off on his own. Word traveled fast, and there could already be assassins wanting to take out the barely eighteen-year-old King of Rengard.

King of Rengard.

Scorch, the very idea seemed impossible. Especially since it meant that everyone else was... that his parents were...

Brigan dropped to his knees in the dense sand. The ocean surf racing along the shore was jarringly cold as it rushed in to drench his pants and legs.

But even that wasn't enough to distract from the pounding in his head. To try and ease the pressure, Brigan pulled the loop from his tidy ridgeknot, letting the wind whip his tight curls. Brigan felt strange—He almost never let his thick, natural coils free.

Then, Brigan yelled as loudly as he could.

The sounds of the wind and sea were loud enough to drown him out entirely, and the deserted early-morning beach meant no one was there to witness his tears. Brigan felt like his heart had been ripped from his chest and replaced with a weight so heavy he wondered if he'd ever be able to get back up.

Brigan threw off his tailored jacket, then lay down on his back, letting the shallow, foaming water surround him. He shut his eyes, allowing the rhythmic sounds to comfort him.

His heartscale felt cool over his collarbone as he heard it—a mighty roar from further up the beach.

Brigan cracked an eyelid to see orange scales in the distance. It was Bolt, Brigan's bonded drake. She roared again, and Brigan felt a surge of empathy from her through their bond. Why didn't she come closer?

As water rushed in his ears, Brigan realized he'd been drifting out to sea. It was something he used to do for fun as a kid in Keep Solhelm. Ah, that was why Bolt hadn't come closer—As a wingless drake, even she couldn't reach him here. Rather than return to his dragon, Brigan clung to the vulnerable rawness of being one with the waves.

As he floated, a cold darkness seemed to encircle and clamp around his heart. He'd never felt so lost. Helpless to turn back time. Powerless to face what was to come. Wouldn't it be easier to let the waves just drag him under?

No, it wouldn't, came the soft, electrifying voice of Bolt through her bond with Brigan. As Brigan drifted, he felt an invisible force lifting him from below, keeping him afloat. Through her heartscale, she was using her Archonic power to levitate him.

It wasn't long before the exhaustion from staying up all night caught up with Brigan. Not just last night, but nearly every night since he'd left home those many years ago. Not caring what happened to him, he let the waves and his dragon's low humming through their bond lull him into sleep.

Brigan awoke in a sandy alcove just off shore. He had no idea how much time had passed. A day, maybe? Though Brigan's heart still ached, the sharpness of the pain had eased somewhat. At least now he could think clearly as he processed what had happened—both to his family, and to himself.

Bolt was curled up beside him, her dragonfire green eyes soft as she watched over her rider. Brigan sent gratitude flowing through their bond.

Squinting, Brigan rubbed his eyes. The clouds must have cleared while he slept, because he could now just see a dark green silhouette across the Scarlet Strait to the south.

Keep Solhelm, he thought. Home.

Brigan! a bright note suddenly pierced the din of wyverngull cries, straight to Brigan's mind. Scorch, that sounded like...

"Sniff?" Brigan asked aloud, voice husky from sleep. Sure enough, the vivid yellow dragon was perched on a craggy rock to Brigan's other side. Sniff was Meleya's dragon, but he and Brigan had always shared a special connection. After all, Brigan had bonded Bolt the same day Meleya had bonded Sniff.

Practically blinding sunlight glinted off of Sniff's scales, and more flute-like musical notes filled Brigan's mind as Sniff flapped his four wings to hover just off the ground.

"What are you doing here?" Brigan asked Sniff.

He's here to take you back to the stronghold, Bolt thought to Brigan through their bond. Sniff turned a spastic circle in the air to confirm Bolt's words.

Brigan glanced up the sheer cliff face where Orothion's castle stood overlooking the sea. It was a long way up, and the mere sight of such a height made Brigan's stomach turn. While he was perfectly at ease in the water, he'd never liked heights.

Choose light, my rider, she said.

With Bolt's encouragement ringing through their bond like a powerful wave, Brigan got to his feet, then brushed off the sand from his clothes and pushed his hair out of his face, gathering it once again into a tight knot—all but that stray little curl over the side of his forehead.

Sniff landed in the sand, turning so that Brigan could mount him. Without another moment's hesitation, Brigan did.

Then, they took to the skies.

Once he arrived at the castle, there was hardly time to breathe. Protective guards surrounded Brigan, with Captain Gunnar at their head. Solrac and several others were there, too, and everyone wanted to speak with him. Some offered condolences. Most simply bombarded him with orders thinly disguised as advice.

Another claimed he had fresh news from the Canyonlands—Apparently, what had happened at Queen Ilona's ill-fated meeting, which folks were already calling 'The Rise's Fall', had triggered an uprising in the southwest. Threats had trickled in from several prominent keeps stating that unless young Brigan abdicated the throne in favor of their candidate, the old, grizzled Duke of Skullheim, they would secede. That set Brigan's teeth on edge, but he didn't show it.

Others insisted that Brigan needed more time to himself to process what had just transpired, and that he ought to be left alone again. Whether or not that was true, Brigan knew he wasn't the only one hurting. The Canyonlands needed to regain stability, and it was up to him to provide it the best way he knew how.

Captain Gunnar's voice rose above the others. "Your majesty, we must not delay in getting you safely to Keep Rengard. As the new King of the Canyonlands, you will be expected to move into the capital on the Rise post-haste."

"He can't do that," Vidya put in with a scowl. "If it's expected, there will undoubtedly be assassins there."

"We will bring guards enough to quell anyone who dares to harm our king."

"But—"

"I will not be returning to Keep Rengard," Brigan cut in firmly. "As of today, the new capital city of the Canyonlands is Keep Solhelm."

There was a general uproar, and someone asked, "Is that wise? The Rise has been the prime seat of Rengard for decades."

“The Rise is vulnerable now after the Coven’s attack. And long term, it is too near the Dragon Mists. Meanwhile, Solhelm lies just across the Scarlet Strait from this very stronghold, and is the perfect place from which to orchestrate the Canyonlands’ new alliance with the Knights of the Torch.”

This was enough to bring those surrounding Brigan to silence. Then, Solrac clapped his hands together.

“I know this situation is difficult,” he said genuinely, “but *you*, Brigan of Rengard, just might be the greatest thing that could have possibly happened to the Canyonlands.”

“I hope so,” Brigan replied with solemnity. “I am certain the leaders here will be well-equipped to help me end Rengard’s war with the Dragon Isles. Surely that will bode well for the upcoming duel between Asher of Steel Rim and General Kheradok of the Dragon Isles, and the potential agreement between the Knights and the Drekai.”

Brigan’s remarks were met with considerable applause, but he shrugged off the Knights’ praise and sent for someone to prepare a longship to take them across the strait as quickly as possible. After the Rise’s Fall, there were a lot of keeps in crisis, and Brigan wanted to ensure that his subjects could look to their king for hope.

Chapter 5: Umbruffalo

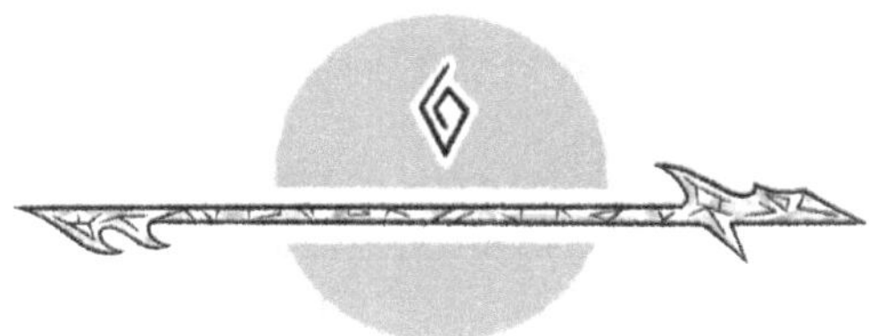

Asher

We'd been getting close to the massive hurricane at the center of the Haze when a sudden thunderous sound had sent us running. It seemed the stampede of savage, sapphire-eyed ghost buffalo really didn't want us to reach our destination.

"Over here!" Mom called, and Meleya and I dove for shelter inside the rocky alcove in which she'd ducked.

We huddled together, watching the herd of wild, draconic spirit bison continue their rampage, the ground quaking beneath their hooves. Curious, I blinked a few times to focus my vision on the physical side of things.

"Whoa!" I exclaimed. "The ground—It's still here in Etheria, but on the other side, it's collapsed. A total chasm."

"Soot," Meleya cursed, pushing her back more tightly against the rock, as if that would somehow help if the Ethereal ground were to collapse as well.

"No doubt caused by physical dragon buffalo stampeding through the same way these ones are here," Mom said over the thunder of hooves. "No wonder the spirit version is so unstable."

"They almost seem to be driving us away on purpose," Meleya said. "What's got the stormchargers all riled up, you think?"

"Stormchargers?" Mom repeated.

Meleya shrugged. "That's what my dad calls them."

I chimed in, "Since these ones are umbral, I think we should call them 'umbruffalo'."

I gave an open-mouthed grin and pointed Mom and Meleya's way with both index fingers, hoping to get a reaction, but then the ground shook again and we clung to the rock to stabilize ourselves.

"We shouldn't stay here long," Mom said. "Is Blink ready to fly?"

"That okay, girl?" Meleya asked her dragon, who—now that she was on her second ascension—had to perch atop our alcove rather than attempt to squeeze inside.

Instead of a response, Blink let out a warning roar. Instantly, all three of us were on our feet, peering around the rock as the last of the umbral bison passed us by.

I followed Blink's gaze to find a solitary figure standing atop the rim of a cliff. A man, shrouded in gray mists—Wraith mists. Soot. So far, we'd only come up against minor shades and echoes. This would be our first actual wraith, and scorch if he didn't appear menacing.

He exuded power like one of Meleya's signature soups exuded deliciousness, and wore full plate armor decorated in some kind of jagged, twisting design I couldn't make out from here. A helmet covered his face, but his glowing void-blue eyes stared right at us from across the volcanic plains. All at once, I found myself wondering if Meleya was right and the umbruffalo stampede had been no mere accident.

Then suddenly, the wraith-man was no longer alone. A veritable army of shades and echoes appeared over the ledge, writhing and roiling like a tumultuous, bubbling mud pot as they flanked him. Hundreds of scratchy voices whispered in an otherworldly muttering:

We serve the Gray Knight.

"The Gray Knight," I repeated. "Didn't Solrac mention something about a Gray Knight?"

Meleya nodded. "He's who Solrac warned the medics about—the man targeting Knights of the Torch safehouses."

"It seems his reach isn't limited to the physical plane." Zerana swallowed.

"Could this be his wraith form or something?" Meleya asked, but nobody had an answer.

Then, as if the slew of subservient shades weren't enough, the Gray Knight lifted a shadowy finger. Void blue light trailed behind it, the rune he traced burning over his forehead like a jewel in his helm.

Then in one abrupt motion, he flung both arms out to either side as a storm of blades seemed to rip from his misty, gray form to telekinetically float in mid-air all around him. More jagged axes than I could count, all forged from pure shadow.

"Wraithblades," Meleya breathed. Mom nodded her agreement, eyes wide. It looked like she was about to say something more when suddenly the Gray Knight thrust both hands forward.

At once, the several dozen weapons raced our way like a flock of vicious, hungry ashfalcons. At the same moment, the shades and echoes burst forward like a raging, sinister waterfall pouring over the cliffside.

There were *way* too many of them for our puny starglass weapons to take head-on. Neither could we outpace them, especially in a terrain they knew better than we did. That left us only one option.

I spread my feet wide to ground myself, my eyes flashing with golden etherlight as I stretched my hands outward and channeled starglass with everything I had.

Roaring with the effort, I formed a pure starglass dome from the ground upward, fully encapsulating Mom, Meleya, Blink, and myself. The moment the all-encompassing starglass shield sealed together at the top, the first of those—what had Mel called them? Right—wraithblades hacked into the starglass. None broke through, but haphazard cracks crept like bolts of lightning across the improvised hemisphere as more and more of the jagged, misty axes struck its pliable Archonic surface.

"Soot, that wraith-man packs a punch!" I said, draining more ether from my well as I worked to seal the cracks. Was it just me, or did my ether well drain faster than normal here in the Haze?

"What do we do?" Meleya asked. Her fingers twitched as if she were just itching to runetrace, but wasn't sure how teleportation would help in this situation.

"You wouldn't happen to have left a rift anchor anywhere particularly safe, would you?" I asked.

"Not on this plane," Meleya responded, cursing. "We'll never be able to take down all those shades. Not to mention the wraith who leads them."

"*Nii ju khaamu*—That's no wraith," Mom said grimly. "At least, he's not *just* a wraith. *Kaatzo*—Look."

I split my focus, keeping an eye on the starglass shield repairs while trying to get a look through the crystalline panels to where the Gray Knight was slowly, methodically making his way toward us.

At first, I saw only what I'd already noticed from a distance: A powerful, misty Gray One, inky shadows rising from his heavy plate armor. But on second look, there was something... *more* to him. His legs didn't taper off into an amorphous cloud, his whole body appearing hauntingly solid, given the ethereal context. His form appeared somewhat translucent, almost like Mom, Meleya, and me, as if he were straddling the line between wraith and human.

"A wraith indeed, but one bound to a human host," Mom said ominously. "More powerful than even the greatest *khaamu.*"

"But how can someone who's bonded a wraith be here in Etheria? Shouldn't that be impossible?" Meleya asked.

Mom shrugged. "Until a few weeks ago, I'd have said the same thing about the two of you."

Then Meleya went white as dragon bone. "This must be what Xan warned me about... My wraith," she elaborated in response to my confused head tilt. "She said the Wraith King wants his voidshard back, and that one of his most powerful servants would come for me."

Right on cue, a wicked wraithblade axe pierced the starglass dome right beside her shoulder, nearly puncturing the floating gold sparkle that was her rift hold. Instantly, a shade managed to squeeze through the cracks, its formless arm reaching for Meleya...

Zap! I sent a blast of pure ether straight toward it. It dissolved with a hiss, and I hastily sealed the crack in the starglass.

"Well that's not going to happen on my watch," I growled.

Mine either! Blink's voice resounded inside our heads as the evren took a protective step closer to Meleya.

Mom gripped the handle of her crystalline scimitar. "If that really is one of the Soul Reaper's most powerful servants, Meleya, then I doubt even the four of us together can scatter such an ancient spirit's essence."

Another round of the gray axes embedded themselves into my starglass shield, and I grunted as I drew from my ever-dwindling ether supply to blast them into nothing and patch the cracks. I turned to the others.

"No offence, but these lovely wraith-musings aren't exactly helping to solve our current problem. Anyone got a plan? Stars, where's Kai when you need him?"

Silence met me.

I set my jaw. "Fine then—I'll try something."

Warning given, my eyes blazed with golden etherlight once more. Only this time, I channeled nearly everything I had into the starglass shield dome until it positively glowed with power.

Then, I executed a move I'd aptly named the 'astro-nova'.

White ether burst from the dome in a crackling shockwave. The ripple threw every shade and echo in the vicinity backward, and I watched dozens of them instantly dissolve, their crystal cores plinking against the starglass shrapnel before softly thudding to the ground. I'd even put the Gray Knight flat on his back.

I tried to give a celebratory 'whoop', but the move had almost completely drained me of my ether. I wobbled, and would've fallen hard on my knees if Meleya and Mom hadn't appeared to hold me up on either side. My spirit-chest felt so tight I thought it might burst, and I almost thought I saw my practically-empty ether well pulsing with a reddish light of warning.

Thankfully, Meleya was already runetracing, ripping open her rift hold and pulling a fresh ether berry from its bush. She closed the hold, then shoved the berry into my mouth.

With more ado than I'd have liked, I managed to swallow the berry, which gave me a slight lift. It wasn't enough to refill my ether well more than a fraction, but it eased the tension in my chest and I could at least stand on my own again. I could tell Meleya wanted to shove more and more berries into me, but according to Mom, consuming more than one etherberry at a time didn't make too much of a difference, and we were all out of Meleya's special fruit leather; I'd have to wait until my spirit was once again able to absorb more ether.

"Drak you," Meleya cursed, but I could hear notes of relief in her tone. "What was *that* supposed to be?"

I exhaled through my nose. "That was me stopping the wraiths. You should probably be impressed..."

I trailed off as a series of hail-like thuds pelted against the starglass dome. Soot—It seemed that while my astro-nova had depleted more wraithlings than I could count, there were nevertheless fresh waves of them incoming. Likewise, the Gray Knight was back on his translucent, armored feet, approaching us with angry purpose. It seemed the Soul Reaper was *really* bent on getting that shard back this time.

With my ether well this low, attempting another astro-nova was out of the question. When the next wraithblade axe hacked into the starglass bubble, I didn't even have it in me to repair the fissures. I tried, of course, but Mel restrained my hand while Mom and Blink took on the shades squeezing in through the crack.

"Soot," Meleya muttered beside me, so quiet only I could hear. "What happens if we die here again?"

"You heard Solrac," I muttered back, my pulse picking up. "We never wake up."

I looked at Mom, panic rising in my stomach. If the Gray Knight and his shades took out Mel, Blink, and me, we'd just move on to Deep Etheria. But Mom... she couldn't move on. What would happen to her? I didn't want to find out.

"Hand over the Wraith King's voidshard, and I will let you live!" the disembodied voice spoke with a strange, inhuman deepness, as if voidarchy was distorting it.

The voice belonged to the Gray Knight, who was now standing mere feet away from us, shades, echoes, and ragged wraithblade axes spinning all around him. Only an increasingly fragile wall of starglass separated us.

Meleya stood her ground directly in front of him on the other side of the starglass shield. "I'll die first!" she cried.

"That's just what he wants, Meleya!" Mom called from where she and Blink continued dispatching the shades who'd managed to slip through the cracks. "Remember? If a Rifter dies while in Etheria, the contents of their hold empties—for a brief window—into this plane. That must be this ancient wraith's plan: Kill you, then take the shard before it reappears in the physical plane."

Thwack!

The Gray Knight moved with a trance-like quality as he used his newly-formed wraithblade to hack at the walls of the dome. The cleft he left was massive, more than I'd be able to repair even if I ran my poor ether well dry.

"What do we do?" Meleya asked again, the shake in her tone betraying her panic.

Thwack! The Gray Knight sent chunks of starglass dropping from the breach in the dome, which dissolved upward into tiny flecks of etherdust as they hit the ground. A few more good hits and we'd be done for.

That's when I spotted the source of my next very bad idea. There were so many enemies to deal with that I'd almost completely forgotten about the stampeding umbruffalo. Through the starglass, I could just see the smoke rising from the still-stampeding herd.

"Mel!" I shouted over the din. "If I leave, can you do anything to hold them off, even for a minute?"

Meleya yelped as the Gray Knight swung once more. "Well, I know a rune that can help me make a sort of portal-bubble. I've done it before, but not this big, and not in the drakking Haze—"

"Perfect!" I cut her off before she could make any more excuses. "On my word, light it up. Three..."

Meleya's finger sprang into action.

Ready to bolt, I went on, "Two... Oh, and can I borrow Blink?"

"What?"

"*One!*"

Everything happened all at once. The Gray Knight gave one final, mighty swing, promptly shattering my whole starglass dome. Meanwhile, I leaped onto Blink's back, urging her to take to the skies and then using *just* enough hover-flying propulsion to launch us through the wall of shades, but not so much that I'd pass out due to ether overuse.

At the same time, Meleya's bubble-shaped portal shield went up to cover her and Mom. The Gray Knight, as well as several shades, float-walked right into it, only to be ejected through the exit portal, which Meleya had placed as far away as she could see. The thick, permanent fog here made it so that wasn't all that far away, but still, I had to trust that she could keep them at bay long enough for me to fulfill my part of the shoddy plan that was still forming inside my head.

Blink and I shot across through the Haze like a skyfall. A handful of rogue wraithlings tried to follow us, but Blink's raking claws sent them spiraling into oblivion. One wraithblade axe sliced the back of my hand, leaving a faint gray mark on my spirit.

It didn't take us long to catch up with the umbruffalo herd. At my instruction, Blink gave an enthusiastic roar, then exhaled a stream of vivid green spirit-dragonfire.

Blink's fire made the bison at the head of the herd grunt in surprise, and gradually, she was able to redirect them. Pretty soon, we'd gotten them all turned around, so that they were stampeding straight toward the Gray Knight and his swarm of shades and echoes. I was willing to bet the Gray Knight and his wraithlings had used a similar tactic to get the umbruffalo to chase us into the valley in the first place and, to my relief, these creatures weren't intelligent enough to distinguish between friend and foe.

"Yes!" I cried, watching from above as the umbral stormchargers utterly scattered the shades. Oh, the chaotic mass of wraiths was still there, more concentrated than ever. But rather than being focused on getting to Meleya, the sea of Gray was now being thrown into the skies or trampled beneath the umbruffalos' hooves. Even the Gray Knight got swept away by the stampede, struggling to telekinetically push on his armor to get himself to safety atop the bluff we'd initially used for shelter.

Meanwhile, a few bison had the misfortune of running into Meleya's portal bubble, only to find themselves stumbling, then getting tossed as they charged at their own herd from the side. I let out a breath. As I'd hoped, Meleya's portal had kept her and Mom safe.

At least, it did until the ground fell out beneath them.

My heart dropped along with the earth. Meleya's portal vanished in an instant, and both she and Mom screamed as they plummeted downward. Soot, I'd forgotten how unstable the ground was here on the ethereal side, and this final, mad stampede had apparently been the straw that broke the aldraka's back.

The umbruffalo caught in the rockslide screamed as well, and a horrific sound—something like a dying dragon-horse mixed with a grunting javelina—tore out of them.

I could hardly blame them, especially seeing as the rapidly forming chasm had opened to reveal *a lake of magma* below. This stuff wasn't like the cold lava fields further south—It was very much active.

My heart stilled when Mom was able to grab hold of the side of the rock, but Meleya kept falling. She was clearly trying to runetrace, but rocks and debris kept jostling her, interrupting her runes.

I cried out, willing Blink to go faster, though I knew the etherberry hadn't given me enough power to funnel any more etherarchy into the pair of us.

But maybe I had enough to hover-boost just me.

I used every ounce of strength my legs could give—which was a lot, given that I was a super-light spirit—to launch off of Blink's back. Ether warped the air behind me as I shot toward Meleya, hoping to catch her as I had once before in that grove of firemaple trees during our journey to Orothion. Only this time, there was no chance I'd be able to land us gently on the forest floor.

I vanished into the chasm, doing my best to dodge the larger falling rocks and the odd wailing umbruffalo. When I felt Meleya securely in my arms, a rush of relief hit me.

That relief was short-lived. Meleya and I careened into the chasm, with me doing my absolute best to arrest our momentum so that we wouldn't splash into that red-hot lake of lava at the bottom. Would spirits burn to death like a physical person would? I didn't want to find out.

But there were also enormous falling boulders and bovines to consider. Then again, now that Meleya wasn't getting pelted on all sides, she was doing her best to use a portal shield she'd placed at our backs to keep stray debris from hitting us. She had my back as much as I had hers.

At the moment, I could only see one place that would keep us from being either scorched or squashed: a smallish alcove in the side of the chasm near the shore of the lake of lava.

Using the last bit of levitation etherarchy I could muster, I slung us toward it, and we skidded into the alcove. And not a moment too soon, I realized as a veritable avalanche of spirit stone collapsed over the entrance to our little nook, at long last matching its physical counterpart.

Meleya kept a portal going between us and the rocks to ensure none crushed us. Trembling, we held onto each other while we waited for the tumbling stone to finally settle.

When it did, there was silence. Silence, and darkness, but for the faint glowing of our auras, which cast a moonlike glow onto the walls of the alcove. The avalanche had fallen hard and fast, entirely blocking the way we'd come in.

Finally, I dared to speak. "Are you okay?" I asked.

"Yeah," Meleya replied. "You?"

"Other than the fact that I'm currently lower on ether than Jaira of Whitestone Hall is on general jolliness, I'm great!"

My dumb joke broke whatever spell we'd been under, and both Meleya and I released our hold on each other. A quick shot of disappointment hit me, and I wished I'd held my tongue just to make the moment last a little longer.

At once, I remembered the cut on my hand from the wraithblade axe. But when I looked at my hand, it was completely gone. Huh.

"I can't stop thinking about the Gray Knight," Meleya said, the glowing mists of her aura highlighting her furrowed brow.

"Trust me," I replied, "if he manages to get to us down here, he deserves to take us out."

"That's not what I'm worried about." Meleya shook her head. "Your mom mentioned that he was like us."

"I remember."

"There's just something about him that feels wrong," she said.

"I can name three: One, the glowing blue eyes. Two, the villainous, garbled, illusory voice thing. And three, the flag he was waving around that said, 'Warning: I'm evil!'"

"He wasn't waving any flag."

"He might as well have been."

By now, both Meleya and I were instinctively examining the stack of boulders blocking our exit. We shifted a few of the smaller ones, only to find several gigantic ones—way larger than we could ever hope to move without telekinesis— completely sealing us inside. We tried to focus and somehow float our spirits through the stones, but the stones were too thick, rendering any ghost-like moves impossible, especially when we were this drained. Maybe once we had time to recover, we'd be able to get through then? But what if we couldn't? If there was one thing I knew about Etheria, it was that its rules and its ether were wildly unpredictable.

Anyhow, I could barely stand in here without banging my head on the lumpy stone ceiling.

"Uh oh," I said, going for exaggerated drama but letting too much real concern eke into my tone. "This isn't good."

I pulled on a few more stones, but of course, it was useless. "No..." I muttered as real panic began to set in. "Mom! Mom, where are you? She was okay, right? Blink? Blink, tell me you got to her in time!"

"She did," Meleya assured me. She was holding Blink's silver heartscale. "Zerana and Blink are finding cover and waiting for the lingering shades to disappear. There's no sign of the Gray Knight so, with any luck, he fell into the lava. I'm letting Blink and Zerana know we're fine too—"

"We're *what* now?" I cut Meleya off as my hands began to twitch. "We're not fine. We're not fine at all! In fact, I can't remember ever being *less* fine, and I've nearly been executed multiple times! Don't you see how *trapped* we are?"

The tight walls seemed to be closing in around me. Maybe I could blast our way out of here with ether... but that would probably just make the stones collapse on us. If spirits could sweat, I was sweating scales as I began to shove against the rocks, willing them to budge.

Obviously, it was useless. And soot, I was so drained from overdoing my etherarchy that I felt like I could hardly breathe—As if the boulders around me were pressing down on my ribcage and suffocating me.

"Soot!" I said, way louder than I'd meant to. "Where's the sky? I can't breathe. Do I even need to breathe? Stars, this won't be my tomb!"

I was full-on flailing at this point, patting down every wall in hopes of finding something—anything besides solid rock.

"Asher," Meleya spoke forcefully, as if she'd had to repeat herself several times already. "Calm down. This *won't* be your tomb."

"You don't know that!"

She took matters into her own hands—literally. Meleya grabbed me by the shoulders and held me in place.

She spoke with surety. "Yes I do, because—worst case scenario—in five days from now they'll finish brewing the remedy for astral sleep and we'll get pulled right back to our bodies."

I latched onto her eyes like they were the last longship out of the void. Even in the darkness of the alcove, the swirling indigo light of her aura accentuated the deep, earthy color of her large, round eyes.

"Four," I said.

"What?" Meleya raised an eyebrow.

"This morning was our eighth sunrise. They'll finish up with the remedy in four days, not five."

"Well, there you go then. Four."

Our spirits didn't need to breathe the same way our bodies did, but I'd found not breathing left me feeling stale and somehow hollow. Maybe spirits *did* still need breath—at least, in their own way. Now, Meleya was breathing slowly and deliberately, and I caught on, focusing on matching my breath with hers. The walls still felt far too near, but, thanks to her, the panic had passed.

My next thought tumbled from my lips before I could stop it. "Your soul is insanely beautiful, you know."

At my words, Mel's breath caught. But I hardly noticed that—I was too busy watching her spirit. The intricate, dancing strands of blue-violet light began to glow even brighter, reaching toward the turquoise mists of my aura. Wherever the two met, tiny, dual-colored sparks erupted like luminous, breaching dragonwhales.

We both leaned in closer. Suddenly, I had a deep and urgent desire to find out what it felt like to kiss a spirit.

But just before I could touch my lips to hers, Meleya suddenly backed away.

"Ouch," Meleya said, rubbing the back of her head as she bonked it against the wall of rocks. Then she nervously swallowed before speaking very quickly, not daring to make eye contact.

"Um, so maybe if we work together we can shift some of these smaller stones first..."

"Nah," I said. "We aren't doing this again."

"Moving rocks? Obviously, odds are we won't make a dent, what with these huge boulders in the way, but it sure beats sitting around doing nothing down here for the next four—"

I cut her off by pressing my lips against hers.

Maybe it was too soon, too reckless, but at the moment, I didn't give a flying scale. I was tired of the constant back and forth between us, all the while pretending not to care.

Yep. There were a thousand reasons I shouldn't have been kissing her, and I sent them all scattering to the stars.

Chapter 6: Lava Turtles

Meleya

Asher was kissing me. Asher was kissing me? *Asher* was kissing *me*!

When I'd kissed him on the lava fields during our journey to Orothion, it had been impulsive and, frankly, one-sided. But this time, *he'd* been the one to make the first move. This time, there was no hesitation, and no holding back.

Obviously, I had no idea what our future held—Neither of us did. There were infinite factors to consider, but for now, I put them all out of my mind as I eagerly pulled Asher close by the lapels of his jacket. This release... we both needed it. The chilliness of the Haze thawed until I hardly remembered it at all.

I couldn't help it—I cracked my eyes open to get a look at our auras. Turquoise and indigo twisted together to create something like a glowing, ethereal cocoon, each strand laced with a line of sparkling, translucent fire.

Then Asher and I pulled away and rested our foreheads together. Our spirit-hearts were pounding so loudly I worried they'd cause another rockslide.

"We have to get out of here," I whispered. "Zerana and Blink—They'll need etherberries soon."

"Not to mention Solvai and the others need us to finish this mission, and fast," Asher agreed. He was right. Whether or not we succeeded in reaching the center of the Haze, we'd return to our bodies once they administered the cure back at Orothion.

But besides that, I wasn't about to let Asher leave Etheria without a nice, long-winded goodbye to the mother he'd once thought he'd lost forever. It's what I would've wanted for myself, after all.

I narrowed my eyes and scanned the alcove. There had to be something, some way to...

"There!" I pointed.

Asher squinted in the general direction I'd indicated. "Hm, nice bit of rock, Mel. Very igneous. But I don't see how that's going to help us."

I rolled my eyes, then moved directly behind Asher and used my hands to steer his face. "*Look.*"

They were hard to see at first, but sure as scales, they were there: Auras *through* the spirit-stone. They were faint, but about a dozen or so reddish-orange lights distinctly stood out, the spirits of whatever they were stronger than that of the rock.

"Alright," Asher started, "so there's something else in here. We still can't..."

I started to runetrace.

"Oh, nice," Asher said sarcastically. "Yes, let's rift ourselves two inches, from one side of the alcove to the other. Why not, right?"

But my exit portal didn't appear inside the alcove. I could just see its golden light faintly through the stone where those red-orange auras were. Here on the spirit side, we could see that the two rifts were connected by a twisting, golden translucent path cutting straight through the stone.

Asher saw it too. "Stars! You can do that?"

"I can rift to anywhere I can see, even without an anchor," I replied enthusiastically. "I've rifted through stone to an aura before. Of course, then it took me and my friends to a deadly cave network filled with umbral dreklings and the secret hideout of the Coven of the Gray Ones."

"Let's hope it's not a pattern," Asher replied.

He and I grasped hands, and while we'd technically held hands before, this time it felt different. Maybe, it even *meant* something different.

I wasn't sure what to expect, but when Asher and I emerged through the exit end of my rift, I certainly hadn't foreseen stepping right onto the back of an enormous turtle.

And I most definitely hadn't pictured said turtle floating in the middle of a lake of smoking hot lava.

There were dozens of them—gargantuan spirit lava turtles, leisurely swimming in a red-hot lake of churning magma. The cavern here was tall and wide, stretching off into the distance, flowing right alongside...

"The ley line!" I cried, jumping up and down and squeezing Asher's hand tight. "It must connect to the one above! If we follow it—"

"It'll eventually lead us back to Mom and Blink!" Asher finished, jumping even higher.

"Exactly," I laughed.

Asher got that adventurous look in his eye. He let go of my hand then, true to form, he took a wild flying leap onto the back of the adjacent lava turtle's shell. It was a long jump, impossible to make even as a super-light spirit without a little extra boost of levitation. As he landed, smoke rose from the spirit-turtle's shell, though the creature itself gave little more than a mildly amused twist of its head.

"Woohoo!" Asher exclaimed, thrusting both hands into the air. "Well, what are you waiting for? Ready for the realm's most intense game of *laava laati?*"

"Lava what?"

"Lava floor! Mom and I used to play with Kai and Kari all the time."

I shrugged.

"Stars, I forgot you missed out on being a kid!" Asher gave his forehead a melodramatic smack.

He was teasing, but it was true. All those years travelling with the nomadic caravans, we'd never stayed in one place long enough for me to build any lasting friendships. I'd played cards with my parents, but never anything like the kind of games Asher remembered from his childhood.

He briefly explained the rules, which were simple: Don't touch the lava. Apparently the floor usually served as imaginary 'lava' in the game, but in this case, there was no need for imagination. I was pretty sure as spirits the lava wouldn't affect us the same way it would a physical person, but still, Asher insisted that to touch the lava would incur a fate worse than death.

I chuckled. This game was weird, but it sounded like fun.

Knowing Asher wouldn't be able to resist using his levitation, I checked his ether well. He'd drained it pretty severely earlier, and I'd been worried. But it was already refilled nearly halfway. Stars, this guy was a magnet for light!

Before getting started, I insisted on testing the lava to see how our spirits would handle it if we did so happen to fall in during this medium-reckless game. When I dipped the tip of my starglass seaxe into the flowing red-orange spirit lava, it sizzled. Asher went so far as to put a pinkie finger within a centimeter of it. He quickly pulled his finger back and put it in his spirit-mouth to cool it.

"Yeah, let's not touch that," he said.

Despite the somewhat-elevated stakes, I was confident our etherarchy would keep us from singeing our spirits while we played. With the ley line to guide us, Asher and I made our way through the underground tunnel, leaping like wild drakalopes from shell to shell. Asher used his levitation to span the wide gaps, while I employed rifts, connected via golden warps in the ethereal plane, to drop me exactly where I wanted to go.

Our tunnel seemed to wind endlessly through the earth, and there were always more scaled, spirit lava turtles casually swimming through the thick magma. Not one of them seemed to mind that we were using their shells for our game.

"That all you got, Mel?" Asher teased as he hover-launched himself onto a faraway turtle's back.

I rifted myself beside him, then narrowed my eyes. "Not even close!"

With that, I became the Snowstorm, rifting in and out of portals so quickly I left a trail of indigo mists in my wake. Asher whooped and took off after me.

I laughed as the rush of letting go of every woe and worry completely fled my soul. It may have taken Asher awhile to get me out of my shell, but now, as we zoomed from shell to shell, mine felt long gone.

Pretty soon, we entered a long, narrow passage. The lava turtles became more sparse, but there were also no more curves or bends in our way for a very long stretch. This was my opportunity.

I chose a spot as far as I could see and placed my exit portal. I'd have to be careful to ensure I landed somewhere safe, but Asher had triggered a deeply competitive nerve.

When Asher saw me about to dive through the rift, his competitive side came out swinging as well. Just before I vanished into the warp, his eyes burned with a gold brighter than any I'd ever seen, as if they were on fire.

I emerged on the far side of the natural corridor, and turned around to get a look at Asher. Expecting him to be all the way on the other side where I'd left him, I wasn't prepared when he came flying into me—*Actually* flying.

Asher was soaring, airborne as if he were a dragon, propelled by his own levitation prowess. His aura left a trail streaking all the way down the tunnel. What was the term Archons used when they unlocked new abilities within their powers? That's right—Asher just had a breakthrough.

When his spirit collided with mine, it left a cascading shower of blue-violet and turquoise particles. Fear bloomed in my stomach as I felt like we were spiraling out of control.

But Asher had things well in hand. He straightened me out, gripping my hand and channeling etherarchy into me so that we were flying in spirals together through the air. It was like when we'd flown with Blink like kites, only this time without the harnesses. The rush of energy made me laugh out loud.

We only flew like that for another moment before Asher started slowing down. At my urging, we landed on a wide, flat patch of earth at the shore of the magma. Sure enough, Asher's ether well was once again nearly empty.

"You need to rest," I declared as I pulled a fresh etherberry from my rift hold and handed it to him. I ate one myself, all the while worrying about Blink and Zerana. No doubt they could use an etherberry boost right about now too.

Clutching my silver heartscale, I reached out to Blink through our bond. Her response came through almost immediately, loud, clear, and thoroughly annoyed.

Boom-boom, dum. Meleya sneaky.

I was taken aback. *Excuse me?*

Blink's drumbeats increased, and I suddenly understood even before she explained herself. *The moment I'm gone, you and Asher... brrrum!*

Before I could defend myself, I heard another musical note trill in my heart. It was faint, but my soul lit up when I recognized Sniff.

Trrring! Meleya happy! This is good!

Sniff! I cried through the bond. It seemed that time was working to restore our communication, though I could tell our connection was still a bit hazy. I vaguely sensed that he was in the dragon stables at Orothion.

How are you doing, buddy?

A series of musical notes played through our bond, but I could tell they weren't all cheerful. Sniff couldn't quite articulate the details, but I could tell that something had happened. Something to do with...

Is Brigan alright? I asked, my heart leaping into my throat.

He will be, Sniff thought. *Brigan brings light.*

Try as I might, I couldn't discern quite what Sniff meant. Still, I was just glad that our connection had been at least somewhat restored.

For now, Sniff emoted, his voice growing fainter with every word as our connection faded. *Meleya focus on mission...*

Yes, focus on mission, Blink pointedly agreed. *Not—*

"Are Blink and Mom okay?" Asher asked, gesturing to Blink's silver heartscale in my hand.

"They're alright," I said, dropping the scale and shaking my head to clear it. "We can take a little while to rest, but then we should keep going."

"Sounds good." Asher's reply was understandably drowsy, his typically fast-moving aura slowing down as well. We'd been going nonstop since long before our encounter with the Gray Knight and the umbral storm-chargers, and even I was really starting to feel it.

We set up a makeshift camp right there between the lava lake and the side of the tunnel. Asher fell asleep pretty quickly, but not me. For one, we were still in the Haze. Not that these lava turtles seemed at all aggressive, but still, someone needed to stay up to keep watch.

For another... I was still reeling from the release of jumping from turtle to turtle over the literal lava floor. And, despite Blink's beratement, I couldn't help but think about the unforgettable way Asher's turquoise aura had collided with my indigo one.

"That's it! That's our way out!"

Asher pointed up the great, towering waterfall. An ether waterfall, where the ley line flowed upward in a churning reverse-cascade. Just above the falls, I could make out the slightest change in light. Ever since we'd left the magma lake behind, we'd been relying on the light of the corrupted ley line to guide us through the dark underground. But up there, the blue-gray light of the Haze's perpetual twilight lit the walls. That must be where all these tunnels would finally breach the surface.

"One rift, coming right up," I said, my fingers already runetracing as Asher and I rode the golden warp right to the top of the waterfall. Sure enough, we could see straight through to the end of the cavern where our subterranean branch of the ley line connected with the one above.

Not only that, but we also saw a pair of wonderfully familiar faces.

"Mom!" Asher said, hover-dashing to clear the distance.

Meanwhile, I started running for Blink. Her eyes shone with joy as she swept deeper into the mouth of the cave to meet me halfway.

I was used to Sniff's style of greeting: an out-of-control, puppy-like collision that often put me flat on my back. While Blink was more reserved, she was every bit as affectionate. Despite her earlier reprimands regarding my love life, she nuzzled me with her snout, urging me to sit down. She then plopped her great second ascension head into my lap so that I could stroke the scales along her spine. The firm drumbeats sounding through our bond tipped me off that she didn't plan to move—or allow me to move—until she was good and ready.

Smiling, I used the hand that wasn't occupied with soothing my dragon to open my rift hold and pull out a handful of etherberries. I fed one to Blink and tossed another to Zerana, then watched as the latter's entire aura perked up.

"*Taaket,* stars, I needed that," she said. I handed her several more, and gave some to Asher as well. Backups, in case we got separated again.

"How long were you and Blink waiting here, Mom?" Asher asked.

"We only arrived about an hour ago," Zerana said. "We ran into a few shades along the way, but not nearly as many as I'd have expected, honestly, and no sign of the Gray Knight. The cave mouth here was a welcome sight, though. A sort of last refuge before things take a turn for the worse."

Zerana gestured toward the opening in the rock, and I immediately saw what she meant—The storm out there was *bad.* Harsh winds whistled, whipping up the Haze's smoky mists. Thunder rumbled while blue lightning crackled, and I even thought I saw the odd shade rush by, riding the winds on its way to suck the light out of some poor, unsuspecting creature.

"We should camp here," Zerana went on. "Regain all our strength before heading into the storm. Once we go in, that's it. *Nii laata,* no turning back."

"In that case," I started, already scouring the ground for a suitable spirit stone, "I'm going to make a rift anchor and leave it here. That way, if things go wrong, we'll be able to get right back."

"Good thinking," Zerana said.

Meanwhile, Asher boldly strode to the very edge of the cave mouth, just a scale's breadth away from those awful winds. He squinted skyward.

"Day nine," he declared. "We should have just enough time to complete our mission. Three days left before they administer the remedy."

I caught the slight waver in his aura and knew what he was really thinking: that only three days remained before he'd have to say goodbye to his mom again. My heart grew tight, and I cuddled closer to Blink.

As we settled in, I couldn't help but stare at those turbulent, stormy skies, wondering what might be lurking in there that was strong enough to cause all this grayness and gloom?

It seemed we were about to find out.

Fragment: The Book Dragon

Valla

The blizzard raged around the white polar wolf as she bounded over the fresh snowpack. Valla was uncertain whether she was more intent on what she was running toward, or what she was running from.

Either way, she kept going, afraid that if she lost her momentum even for just a moment, she might turn back. Valla's sharp wolf eyes let her see through the cutting snowstorm, and her enhanced senses ensured that she continued pressing due north.

Valla wasn't entirely sure how long she'd been going like this. She hadn't shifted back to her human form since her arrival at the northernmost safehouse of the Knights of the Torch, a ramshackle saloon called the Untamed Ursadon, set on the edge of a glacial river. That had been sometime in the last few... weeks? Months? Maybe longer.

Valla kept pushing forward.

Of course, Kaidan and Kalari's trail had long since gone cold—they'd disappeared over two years ago—but Valla had found a map that the pair had left in the secret Knights-only basement of the saloon. The map had been unlike any Valla had ever seen before, depicting Evgard crisscrossed with white, squiggly pathways labeled 'ley lines.'

Valla didn't know what on Selene's green earth a 'ley line' was, but several of them seemed to align with rivers, while others converged at the various capital cities throughout Evgard's eight keepdoms. An enormous convergence of white lines appeared directly over Evgard's Capital city where the High Citadel's famed Waterfall Keep lay.

But Valla was more intent on a different set of converging ley lines. As far north as could be, Kai and Kari's parents had circled a spot they'd labeled 'Theok's Hoard.'

Valla knew as much about Theok as the next Evgardian. He was said to have been a legendary Guardian, the one who'd saved their forefathers from their old, dying land and brought them here. It was hard to be sure, what with so many legends regarding mysterious northern treasures, but Valla was certain she'd heard tell of the great Theok's mythical wealth, preserved somewhere in Behrfell's white wastes. Over the centuries, countless skyseekers and dragonslayers had been lost in search of Theok's ancient riches. But Valla wasn't seeking personal gain. All she hoped was that Kaidan and Kalari were right about this hoard including the treasure Evgard needed most:

The Everflame.

The mythical flame of the first true dragon, the Everflame was said to have the power to restore light and purge voidarchy. In reality, Valla thought all the tales of treasure and mystical restorative flames were nothing more than bardic fantasy.

And yet, here she was, chasing them like her very sanity depended on it.

Though Valla's limbs ached, she kept running. Logic told her that she should stop for the night, get some rest, perhaps even pull out her copy of Glint the mirror gecko—No doubt the Knights would be craving an update on her progress—but Valla still couldn't bring herself to speak with any of them, Solrac most of all. She wasn't literally going to the ends of the earth to avoid him for nothing. Solrac had insisted that Valla take a dreamweb with her, enchanted to allow her to contact the great Farseer across any distance, but Valla had no intention to use that either.

Keep running, Valla told herself whenever the exertion threatened to overcome her. *Just keep running.*

Suddenly, a flash of something wispy and red streaked past Valla. Next, a flicker of gold. Then, a whole flurry of multicolored flickers appeared, just as Valla felt not snow beneath her padded paws, but soft, green grass. Drak, the whole snowstorm had ceased, giving way to warmth. She could now see straight up to the heavens, where the emerald green tail of Streya's Comet cut across the distant horizon.

Valla skidded to a stop. Glancing backward, she confirmed that the blizzard hadn't actually ceased, but had seemingly been stopped by some stark, invisible barrier.

What *was* this strange oasis?

Ahead of her, Valla saw a spring, with glorious, natural fountains of both water and pure ether bubbling up from its center. When she touched the edge of the spring, her ether well instantly refilled.

Valla now realized that the glowing flickers she'd seen on the way in belonged to various creatures that surrounded the oasis. Colorful mist clung to many of them. It was as if some beasts were corporeal, while others were only translucent spirits.

A baby drakalope wiggled her nose and trembled at Valla's intrusion, and she saw a handful of other animals cowering as well. At once, she realized that most of these creatures were small, prey animals, while she'd remained an intimidating polar wolf. Desiring to put these creatures at ease, Valla shifted back to her human form for the first time in far too long.

As she drew closer, she saw a grand pavilion beyond the spring. With its towering pillars and oversized, open doors, it looked to be Guardian-made. An odd contraption ran from the pavilion down to the spring, consisting of some kind of hydraulic pulley system for gathering the water and ether in small buckets before bringing it back to the pavilion.

But as Valla got closer, she saw that it wasn't water at all. The spring was full of liquid ether. She'd come across a few ether geysers during her travels, and seen the ether vents in Steel Rim as well as the waterfall in Veil Falls, but this spring was on a whole new level.

Just then, a shadow loomed over Valla, and she heard a low, rich voice enter her mind.

Greetings, weary traveler. Would you like some hot chocolate?

The voice startled Valla right back into polar wolf form. She whirled around and found herself face to face with an enormous, third ascension true dragon.

Well, not exactly face to face... more like 'snout to draconic knee.' This thing was *huge.*

Huge, and beautiful. His brilliant ruby red scales caught the etherlight, as did his long, spiraling horns. His wide wings were tucked behind him, and his deep, ancient-looking eyes appeared magnified, thanks to the starglass lenses balanced on his scaled, draconic nose.

There is no need for alarm, my wildshaping friend. The dragon's voice was surprisingly gentle. *Welcome to my hoard.*

"*Your* hoard?" Valla reverted to her human form. "For a moment I thought I'd finally found Theok's Hoard."

Ha! The true dragon's laughter echoed through the spring. *In that case, allow me to dispel your disappointment. You see, I am the very Theok whom you seek!*

"Theok?" Valla's mind raced. "But... Theok was an ancient philosopher. The last of the Guardians, who helped build Orothion."

The red true dragon laughed again, a strange, growly sound coming from a third ascension dragon. *I'm not sure how I feel about 'ancient'—I'd prefer 'finely aged', or perhaps 'well stricken with wisdom'—but yes. History can get a little muddled at times, but since you've traveled this far, by the skies, you deserve to know the truth! Thanks to a series of minor misadventures, my rider ended up receiving the credit for both my literary works and my name. I don't mind this—Few would've allowed a dragon to publish philosophical texts at the time anyway.*

Theok the dragon laughed again, and his strange spectacles nearly fell off his nose. He righted them with a bit of psionics before going on.

Although, to be clear, the feats my rider accomplished as both a Guardian and the first Farseer are entirely his own. A greater man this realm never saw, despite his aversion to the written word and the occasional misstep during courtship.

Valla just blinked up at the dragon for a moment, slow to take in the dragon's history-shattering musings.

"Wait..." She shook her head. "Are you saying that you are *the* dragon bond of a Guardian? The founder of Evgard, no less?"

Correct! the dragon cheerfully replied.

"And Theok is *your* name, not his?"

Correct again!

"And furthermore... Did you say your rider was the first *Farseer?*"

The red robes were my idea, the dragon said, proudly puffing out his ruby-scaled chest.

"Soot," Valla muttered, taking it all in. "How are you... you know..."

Ahh, Theok chuckled. *Everyone's always curious about the immortality thing.* He paused, and Valla waited with bated breath to hear what he would say next. Instead, Theok gave a warm, draconic grin. *Would you like some hot chocolate?*

It was clear the previous topic of conversation was closed. Thoroughly taken aback, Valla allowed the welcoming true dragon to lead her through the grand double doors and into the pavilion.

Please forgive the state of things, Theok said, slight embarrassment radiating through his words. *It's been a few years since a human has visited my library.*

Despite his caveat, Valla's mouth fell open at the sight of the vast, towering half-circle of shelves utterly filled with books. Translucent spheres in a variety of colors floated all throughout the library, much like those Valla had seen before in Ghost Lake's arcanum. Still, that library paled in comparison to this.

A veritable mountain of fur blankets and cushions lay before one shelf. That must've been where the great dragon slept, surrounded by that which he valued most. Not gold and jewels, but knowledge—That was the treasure hidden away in Theok's legendary hoard. Valla was certain most treasure seekers would've been unimpressed, but Valla appreciated the care Theok clearly took of his library.

More small animals, some corporeal and others spirit, scurried about, and Valla could've sworn some were reading. One evren hung near a cleft in the domed sealing, reading a psionically-enchanted book while hanging upside-down.

Please, Theok said, using a foreclaw to gesture to a smaller stack of cushions and furs. *Make yourself comfortable.*

Valla still felt the urgency of her quest, and though the luxurious blankets were tempting, she remained standing. "Actually, I'm here because I need something."

A mug of creamy, delicious hot chocolate, I know. Drak, did this dragon just wink?

"No," Valla said. "I'm here looking for information."

Well, Theok beamed, spreading his wings to gesture to his vast collection of books, *you came to the right place! What is it you wish to know, my friend?*

"I seek the Everflame," Valla replied.

Ahh, you're not the first.

Valla's fingers twitched in anticipation. "My friends, Kaidan and Kalari, were here, weren't they?"

Kaidan and Kalari, yes! Theok's magnified, draconic eyes lit up. *Has it been years already? It feels like only yesterday they were browsing my hoard in search of the very information you now seek. I lent them my very best copy of* 'Grammaton Arkaeon.' *It's long past overdue, now that I think about it...*

"Do you remember where they went?" Valla said, already preparing to shift forms and continue her trek.

Of course! Theok replied.

Valla waited, but the dragon simply kept looking at her. She narrowed her eyes to slits, but the dragon only blinked back, daring her to break the silence.

At last, Valla relented. "Well?"

Do you prefer your hot chocolate traditional, or would you like a sprinkle of cinnamon in it?

"Cinnamon, I guess..." Valla sighed, her resolve utterly crumbling beneath the dragon's relentless hospitality. "But just one mug!"

Before Valla knew it, she was three mugs deep and halfway through a pile of warm, buttery rolls—surprisingly tender for having been baked by a dragon using telekinesis—bawling her eyes out as her life's story fell from her lips like rain from a too-dense cloud. Even Valla's copy of the mirror gecko, Glint, had popped out to listen, her large, reflective eyes as shiny as Valla's own.

Valla wasn't sure how Theok had coaxed it out of her. Then again, maybe the accumulation of years' worth of pent-up feelings was finally coming to a head now that she was comfortably wrapped up in a drakalope fur blanket with a full belly and someone genuinely interested in her tale. No one had ever asked about her life and innermost thoughts before. In fact, Valla had ensured that no one had dared.

She'd told the kind, bookish dragon everything. About running away from her family when she'd learned about her powers in order to protect them from Mage Hunters. About hiding out in the forests of White Cliff, nearly starving to death before being discovered by a beautiful white polar wolf. The wolf had been hunting, but when Valla connected with her mind via her wildshaping, the creature had taken pity on her and led her to its well-concealed hideout. Within, Valla had found more polar wolves, many of whom weren't just animals, but were actually fellow Wildshapers. Valla had found her pack.

They had taught Valla to use her powers until eventually she found the Knights of the Torch. Almost right away, she'd met Solrac and ultimately become his bodyguard. The pair had become inseparable, and Valla had... She'd...

You fell for him, didn't you? Theok prompted, not at all mocking, judgmental, or pitying. From her perch on Valla's knee, Glint Seven watched for Valla's response.

Theok was right, of course, and Valla swallowed the long-suppressed lump in her throat as she nodded. For years, she'd hoped Solrac would return her affection, but deep down, she'd always known she was doomed to be alone.

Theok didn't tell her everything was fine or try to solve all her problems—For that, Valla was grateful. Rather, he offered her and Glint Seven more snacks and stoked the hearth.

As the plate of rolls emptied and the sky darkened outside the pavilion, Valla felt a massive sense of relief. Her eyelids were heavy.

Rest, Theok said, a low hum reverberating from his throat like a comforting strum from a harp. *I'll take care of everything. For now, you need sleep.*

"But—" Valla weakly protested.

But then Theok began to hum more earnestly. His voice was low and rich, the melody ancient. Valla almost thought she could *see* the song riding the warm, sweet air of Theok's library, appearing as dancing strands of golden light. Glint Seven was already asleep, and before she knew it, Valla too was snuggling down into the furs and letting her eyes drift shut.

Valla awoke feeling more refreshed than ever, like she'd inexplicably gotten lighter as she slept. Stretching, she found Theok reading a little book that he had set levitating in front of him. His spectacle-magnified eyes blinked down at the small print, but when he saw that Valla was awake he telekinetically guided his book through the air where it settled open on one of his spiraling horns to save his place.

Excellent. Theok gave a satisfied smile. *That heaviness that you carried will not weigh you down where you go now. I trust you are ready to continue on your path toward the Everflame?*

At once, Valla was fully alert. She stood as the great red true dragon continued.

I must warn you; the path to the Everflame can be unpredictable and fraught with danger. But I know you are ready. And before you embark, I have a gift for you.

At once, Theok sent a small, bright red object psionically floating toward Valla. She opened her hands, ready to receive the gift, and watched as a single scale dropped into her outspread palms, clearly one of Theok's own. Not a heartscale, of course, though Valla did notice that his heartscale was missing—Evidence that he'd once been bound to a rider. At the very least, that part of his story had been true.

Now, Theok said, *few wildshapers can master a full shift into a true dragon, nor do I believe you'll be able to access any other forms of etherarchy through this. But once you attune to it, my wildshaping friend, I believe my scale will make an excellent totem that can enhance the gifts you already have. Use it well.*

"I will," Valla replied, clutching the scale with reverence.

Splendid! Theok's tone shifted instantly from serious to jovial. *Now, I'm sure you're anxious to get on with your journey.* A new golden rune appeared over Theok's forehead as a rift hold tore open beside him. He reached inside with one of his deft foreclaws and pulled out a white crystalline statue, small enough to hold in one's hand and beautifully adorned with the sun, moon, and stars. Mystic runes were etched along its surface.

Valla squinted, recognizing some of the runes. "Is that a rift anchor?" Besides the runes, the stone had what looked like Sentinel patterns carved along it, and the whole thing shone with a telltale Archonic glow.

Of sorts, Theok replied. *The etherarchy held within this relic is very old, even older than myself. It will take you to your friends.*

With that, Theok carefully carried the relic over to a large stone basin filled with ether-laced water, carried over from the spring outside using the bucket pulley contraption. Gently, he placed the statue in the basin.

The pooling ether rippled, then swirled as a point of golden light expanded from the place where he'd set the relic, leaving an almost mirrored, white-tinged surface in its wake, surrounded by what looked like the golden flames of an omenfire. It was a portal, Valla realized, the likes of which she'd never before seen.

At once, Valla remembered something. She checked her boot, but already knew intuitively that Glint was not inside it. Valla scanned Theok's Hoard, Sentinel patterns tracing out around her eyes as they took on the enhanced vision of a polar wolf.

Aha! She spotted the tiny violet gecko perched atop one of the translucent bubbles that floated throughout the library. A telekinetically-enchanted book about ten times Glint's size hovered open in front of her, and Valla spotted a whole stack of books hovering in wait nearby—Evidently, Glint Seven was nowhere near ready to leave the ancient library. In any case, she was out of range, and Valla was certain she wouldn't 'work' wherever Theok was sending her anyhow.

Theok followed Valla's gaze, then gave a draconic chuckle. *I'll look after our bookish little friend for as long as she wishes to stay.*

Valla nodded.

As for you, Valla of White Cliff. Theok brought his enormous face close to hers and offered a leisurely, sagely wink. *Take care.*

Valla gave Theok one last look. Though she'd only just met the dragon, she felt she'd truly found a friend in him.

"Thank you," she said, then decisively stepped into the pool.

Although Valla fell through the entrance portal going down, she came through the exit sideways. The experience was jarring, and got her landing flat on her back.

Below Valla were planks of wood, while above her the midday sun glowed with a blinding golden light that left a fiery trail arcing across the sky. The sky appeared strange too, swirling with a thousand shades of blue. Odd, translucent butterfly dragons flew in a V-formation overhead, a myriad of colorful mists streaming out behind them.

Where in the stars *was* she?

Valla sat bolt upright. More wooden planks, full, white sails, a dragon figurehead... She was on the deck of a ship.

Grabbing hold of the ship's rail to steady herself, Valla peered over the side. Drak—the ship was floating in mid-air! Well, not mid-air exactly. Rather than cutting through water, this ship was sluicing through a wide, flowing river of pure ether that hovered a good distance above the land below.

Valla was still processing it all when voices and footsteps began to swell around her. She whirled, so caught off guard that she didn't even shift into polar wolf form as she faced down what must've been the ship's crew.

They marvelled at the sight of her, and fragments of their conversation reached Valla's ears.

"Where did she come from?"

"She's corporeal, like us!"

"Someone get the captains!"

"We're here," one woman's voice rose above the rest, and the crew parted to reveal their leaders. One was a woman with thick, dark curls. The other was a man, clutching a notebook in his hand. Both of them gaped at the sight of Valla.

Valla gaped right back.

"Kaidan and Kalari," she murmured. "You're alive!"

CHAPTER 7: THE NETHERSTONE

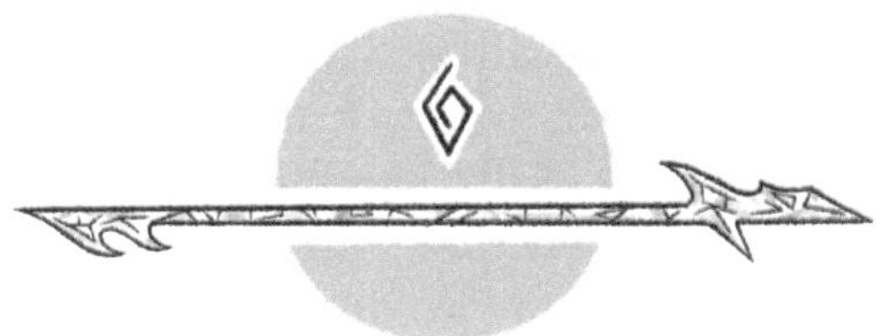

ASHER

"Bet you thought you were going to get some nice alone time over here, didn't you? Well, think again," I said as I joined Mom on the ledge overlooking the ley line's backwards-waterfall, our feet dangling over the side.

Mom laughed—quietly, so as not to wake Meleya and Blink. "*Ehta mehna!* I thought no such thing. My father used to say, 'Our breed withers when lonely, but thrives with quality companionship'. That's not a perfect translation, but alas."

Mom's statement gave me pause. Well, not the statement itself, but its source. In all my life, Mom had never so much as mentioned her father. She'd always said that her past was behind her, and that that included her old family. I felt silly now that I thought about it, but I'd never even really pictured what Mom's parents—my grandparents—were like. I guess I'd subconsciously assumed Mom just appeared as a fully realized adult or something.

"What was your father like?" I asked, half-certain she wasn't going to answer.

To my surprise, Mom smiled. "He was proud and strong, but a more loving parent never drew breath. Every free moment he had he spent with me and my sisters."

"You had sisters?"

"Two." Mom nodded. "Though I was the only half-born. Not that such things mattered—to us, at least. We had our differences, but we loved each other very much. Family is the strongest bond of them all."

Sighing, Mom fearlessly peered over the edge and into the faraway expanse below. Down there, faint glows from thorny spirit-wildflowers, tainted blue by the corrupted ley line, winked back at us. Despite the vastly different circumstances, I still found myself thinking of the stony ledge that overlooked a secret, lush valley back home. Only Mom, Dad, Thorn and I knew about that valley, where the dragon buffalo grazed and drank from the lake, and wildflowers in every color grew abundantly. Mom had named the overlook 'Kiivi Zariika', Drekai for 'Cozy Rock.'

"Are you thinking of the valley too?" Mom asked.

I nodded. "It feels like a faraway dream or something. Part of me worries I'll never see it again."

For a long while, Mom and I just talked about the old days: Hiking the cliffs around Steel Rim in search of new cactus varieties for Mom's home garden. Waiting for Dad to come home from working in the iron mines, then surprising him with a picnic on Kiivi Zariika.

"You should see Thorn fish in the lake," I said fondly. "He's a natural—Brings in enough dragonbass for Dad, Kai, Kari, and me without even breaking a sweat. Not that dragons sweat. Or do they? Stars, I'll have to ask Thorn sometime."

Mom smiled and gave me a nudge. "I'm glad you and Thorn found each other."

"Me too."

A faint scraping sounded behind us, and I turned back toward the raging storm that lay just beyond the mouth of the cave, but it was only a loose tumbleweed rolling by. I instinctively checked on Meleya, but she was sound asleep, curled up against snoozing Blink's flank.

Mom smiled. "She's a very smart girl."

"Yeah," I agreed.

"And beautiful."

"Yeah."

"And *very* curious about my old Drekai recipes. She even got me to give up the secret ingredients in *anuukas.*" Mom got a twinkle in her eye.

I quirked a smile. "Really? My old favorite birthday breakfast?"

"The very same," Mom chuckled. I did too.

Mom continued. "You know, she really does believe in you."

"Yeah..." I repeated, my heart thudding just thinking about Meleya. I didn't regret kissing her in the alcove, not a bit. But that didn't mean I felt sure about the two of us. Not yet.

Mom gave my hair a teasing ruffle, then immediately began to smooth the wild locks back into place.

"What makes you say she believes in me?" I asked, my tone growing more serious.

"Just something she brought up the other night," Mom replied. "That you're made of strong stuff. She's right."

Mom finished fixing my hair, then spent some time examining my face, looking over every detail. In her gaze I saw more of that fear I'd seen just before we'd entered the Haze, but also notes of pride. My aura glowed brighter.

Then Mom began to sing. As ever, her voice was sweet and clear, and I just sat back and listened, drinking in every note. I knew the song well; it was the old Drekai one written in tiny, ancient script hidden amidst the detailed design of my scarf. That was the one other time I remembered Mom mentioning her father—when she'd given me that scarf.

Mom first sang the song in Drekai. Then she sang it again in Evgardian, and I joined her, threads from our auras floating out and riding the waterfall, as if the song itself were dancing in time with the music:

You are a link in a legacy of light
A chain that spans the ages
Sent to tend with wisdom and might
Through bright or darkened stages

We will guide you
Ever beside you
We who've come before
Do not fear
Your time draws near
Share light forevermore

When we finished, Mom pulled me into an embrace. She was trembling.

"I get it now, Mom," I said, trying to reassure her. "For years I doubted, but now I know. You're still with me in ways I never understood, and I swear never to doubt again. I love you."

"I love you too, my *laaksi rakaai*," Mom tearfully replied. "You are capable of anything. Anything, you hear? And I know you'll be stronger than I was."

I wasn't entirely sure what she meant by that, especially because I knew Mom had been plenty strong right up until the end. What had happened with her ether well hadn't been her fault, after all, and I hated to think that she bore any guilt over that.

I squeezed Mom tighter. Three days—That was how long I had before we'd have to say goodbye all over again. It was coming to an end far too quickly.

Still, compared to what I'd thought before this experience, three days felt like a precious gift.

Inside the hurricane, I felt like all my senses had gone into a permanent state of chilly, blue-gray overwhelm.

Flying was out of the question, as Blink's four wings would've no doubt caught the crazy winds and sent us all spinning. Instead, the four of us trekked through the shade-infested, lightning-laden gales, hand in hand. Well, three of us held hands. With the hand that wasn't holding mine, Meleya gripped one of the spines on Blink's tail.

Thank the goddesses for that ley line. Once again, the river of ether became our guide, leading us ever closer to the center of the Haze. The ether river was completely void-blue here, and gave off a sinister energy that very much made me want to give it a wide berth. But we stuck by it as it flowed just above the earth—We had to be close.

The harder we pressed, the fiercer the storm became until all at once... it wasn't fierce at all.

Our party stumbled into a stretch of desert that was starkly still. A wide circle of eerie calmness that stretched about a mile across. I could see the wall of inky, tumultuous mists on all sides, but here, there was nothing. Nothing except a bone-chilling cold. In fact, it was so icy here, our auras seemed to take on an oddly frosty quality.

There was only one explanation: We'd reached the eye of the storm.

And there in the center of the circle of deadened plants and dry, cracked earth, was what could only be the Haze's source.

I wasn't sure what I'd expected to find there. Maybe a monster, like a massive, venomous, spydra-wraith or draconic snake? Perhaps a heinous plant, poisoning the ley lines and sowing gray darkness for miles and miles around?

Instead, we stood in awe before a great crystalline monolith. It was a head or two taller than I was and floated several feet off the ground, emitting a harsh blue light across the clearing. It was made from blue starglass, and was clearly an ancient monument of some kind. The design consisted of tall, upright shapes with jagged, curving ridges engraved along the pillar. It reminded me of the Guardian-era buildings and statues I'd seen before in Keep Drakfell and Skygard.

The light came from something at the thing's center—a corrupted skystone, no doubt, lodged within the starglass at its core. Runemarks decorated the monolith's planes, pulsing with more of that otherworldly blue light.

Honestly, it would have been beautiful if it weren't so dangerous.

"Whoa," I said, eloquently voicing all of our thoughts.

Cautiously, we crept closer. As we did, I noticed a faint, hair-raising hum emanating from the monolith. The storm no longer pushed against us, but we still clung to each others' hands.

"What is it?" I asked, my voice practically echoing in this strange space.

"I don't know," Mom muttered. Blue light illuminated her face as she stared upward.

"I do," Meleya said. "My wraith... She said it was called a 'netherstone'."

The word sent chills up my spirit-arms. "Yep, that feels right. Did she give you any other helpful tips regarding its nature?"

Meleya shot me a glare. "Sorry, I was too busy fighting for my soul to ask." I chuckled. It was good to know that our moment in the underground hadn't ruined her sarcastic streak toward me.

Next, I broke free from our hand hold to walk all around the netherstone, examining it from every angle. I bent low to look beneath its floating underside, and even used a little levitation to get a better view of the top. That way, Kai could read my mind later and jot down details to his data-driven heart's content.

"So if this is what's causing the Haze, both here and in the physical plane," Meleya wondered, "do you think, I don't know, that some of its essence is somehow leaking through the veil between worlds? I mean, maybe there are more netherstones, scattered throughout Etheria, all slowly tainting the land." I shuddered at the thought.

"That could very well be." Mom grimaced. "Maybe the Haze seeps through when the veil is thinnest, on the full moon? But these things are clearly remnants from hundreds of years ago. So why are things changing in the physical plane only now?"

Neither Meleya, Blink, or I had an answer.

We stared at the netherstone for another minute or two before I suggested, "Maybe we should try breaking off a piece of it for the others to look over? If we put it in Mel's rift hold, I bet we could—"

"No," Meleya blurted so abruptly I jumped. "Sorry, it's just... my rift hold already has enough darkness in it. Besides, I don't think we should bring something like this back to Orothion."

Based on the way even being in this thing's presence had started turning my aura frosty, I had to agree with that. Even now, I could practically feel the ice creeping along the back of my neck.

Wait—That wasn't just *any* icy feeling. The hairs on my neck were standing on end, as if we were being watched.

Slowly I turned, and my spirit-blood ran cold.

There on the opposite end of the eye of the storm, like a mighty, demonic shadow, stood our old pal, the Gray Knight.

Soot. It seemed he'd recovered from being trampled by a herd of stampeding umbruffalo, and had definitely not fallen to his doom in a lake of boiling magma.

And, of course, he'd brought his friends. A newly replenished army of shades, echoes, and everything in between flanked the Gray Knight.

No, more than that—They lined the entire circle so that we were completely surrounded, with several more wraithlings slowly filling the gaps above our heads so that we couldn't escape by air. Stars, this must've been why so few shades had bothered us over the last day as we'd journeyed through the storm. They'd been busy answering this extra-powerful wraith-guy's call. My heart began to race.

The Gray Knight looked even stronger than before, his whole wraith-empowered form shining with a bone-chilling reverse-glow, as if he were sucking what little light existed here directly out of the air around him. When he spoke, it was with that same deep, inhuman tone he'd used before.

"You will not get away so easily this time, Snowstorm," he warned, then began to mutter in a language I didn't recognize. A smooth, chanting dialect, filled with hair-raising soft 's' and 'sh' sounds. Some kind of awful, ancient wraith-speak. Sure enough, the shades answered back, once again chanting, "We serve the Gray Knight!"

Luckily, this time we'd come prepared. Mom and I looked to Meleya, who didn't hesitate to activate the rift anchor she'd left back at the cave mouth. The gold-rimmed entrance portal opened.

But before we stepped through, Meleya gasped, throwing out her hands to stop us.

"What is it?" I asked, and Meleya pointed straight ahead.

When I realized what was happening, I gasped too. Another gold-rimmed rift—this one with the telltale black-tinged interior of an exit portal—had split open directly beside the Gray Knight. He extended his hand in triumph so that we could see it—the small, runemarked stone Meleya had left in the cave.

He, or at least his servants, had taken it.

So much for our backup plan. Unnerved, Meleya rapidly shut off the portals.

"Soot... Remind me again," I whispered to Mom and Mel from the corner of my mouth. "What exactly happens to us if our spirits die in here?"

Mom replied, "Your bodies die too, and your spirits will move straight into Deep Etheria."

"Cool, that's what I thought." I sucked in my cheeks, once again worried about Mom. She *couldn't* move on to Deep Etheria, not while the Black Valkyrie still had her ether well. What would happen to her if we were overwhelmed here? I took her hand and gave it a long, hard squeeze.

Meleya bravely brandished her starglass seaxe and assumed a perfect battle stance.

"Blink," she said, "whatever happens to me, don't let them get the voidshard. Once I'm... If I... you know. Take it and fly as far away as you can. Promise?" Even I could feel the thundering of drums as Blink roared in pained agreement.

"Asher..." Meleya said, locking eyes with me.

"Meleya," I responded. We didn't say anything else—We didn't need to.

Nor was the Gray Knight and his crew about to give us the chance. With a motion of his armored hand, he let the shades and echoes loose.

At once, the world became a tempest of gray and gold. Shades attacked each one of us with reckless abandon, but we sent them swiftly back to the void in a flurry of starglass, ether blasts, rifts, and dragonfire. My senses went on high alert. Despite the multitude of gray, light-leaking slashes the wraiths left on our spirit forms, we were keeping the horde at bay—It just took every ounce of energy and concentration to do so.

Still, even as I reduced a trio of echoes to nothing but smoke and crystal cores, I kept the corner of my eye trained on the Gray Knight himself. The fully armored warrior was making his way toward us, his movements almost trancelike. He had one goal and one goal only: Get that voidshard. He had to focus, too. He knew as well as we did that he wouldn't have long to snag the shard before it returned to the physical plane near Meleya's body. But that was only if Mel... if she...

No. I wasn't about to let that happen.

Meleya was currently using a series of about nine mini-portals to suck shades in as if she were fishing for them. Each of the nine rapidly racing rifts deposited the shades through a single exit rift right in front of her. There, her starglass seaxe moved like lightning to dispatch whole groups at a time. Stars, rifting was cool!

But as much as I'd have liked to marvel at her ingenious use of etherarchy, the Gray Knight was approaching fast from behind. A sinister, inky wraithblade took shape, replacing his hand with a jagged, shadowed greataxe.

"Mel!" I cried, swiftly disengaging from the battle I'd been waging on a particularly nasty echo and gritting my teeth against the numb, gray mark the creature left on my spirit-leg. I was too busy hover-dashing, coming to a stop directly between Meleya's back and the Gray Knight.

"Sorry, Sir Gray Knight!" I called as I summoned my starglass dragonhook spear and outfitted myself with starglass armor to match. "I'm no Seer, but my forecast predicts a zero-percent chance of snow falling today!"

Feeling pretty proud of my wordplay there, I gave a wide, crooked grin. Meanwhile, the Gray Knight stopped in his tracks as veritable spirit-steam seemed to be rising from his wraith-shrouded aura. Through the slats in his helmet, I could sense deep-seated ire in those void-blue eyes.

My taunting skills must've been better than I thought, because the sight of me completely changed the Gray Knight's course. Like a torradon bull seeing red, he turned away from Mel completely, instead focusing all of his rage on me.

He charged, his finger flying to runetrace. That jagged greataxe wraithblade, along with a whole arsenal of newly formed wraithblades, rose into the air, then surged toward me like a flock of diving demonic dragonbats.

I yelped, hover-dashing to avoid the worst of the first wave of weapons. Only one rogue axe grazed my cheek, leaving a gray mark that leaked light. Huh, that was strange—Some of my initial gray cuts were already healing. Still, more quickly replaced them as the Gray Knight's seemingly endless tide of shades and wraithblades swept through.

By the time the second round of blades were poised to strike, I managed to pull off a small-scale astro-nova. A burst of ether pulsed off of me, dissolving the wraithblades into nothing and even pushing the Gray Knight back a little.

But the third attack wasn't a barrage of wraithblades—It was the Gray Knight himself.

Psionically pushing on his own armor to enhance his force, he slammed straight into me with his heavy shoulder pauldron. I gave a strangled 'oof' as he literally drove my spirit straight into the dirt so hard we made something of a crater.

Stars... I was seeing stars. Also, I was seeing orange for some reason. The Gray Knight... had his gray aura just flashed orange for a second? I had to be seeing things. He reeled back his gauntleted fist, ready to punch me hard in the face.

My starglass spear was somewhere in the dirt, so I raised a hand to block the Gray Knight's blow. My spirit-wrist alone would've snapped against his might, but fortunately I was actively armoring my entire hand and forearm with a starglass gauntlet of my own.

That surprised him just enough for me to get my feet into position against his chest. With a surge of levitation, I kicked him—hard.

The Gray Knight tumbled backward. Before he could get ahold of me again, I scrambled to my feet, resummoning my spear to my hands.

The Gray Knight got to his feet as well, albeit a bit more slowly than me. As he turned back my way, there it was again: Orange. This time, I was certain I wasn't imagining the deep orange mists that glowed through the cracks in his armor.

I was about to make my move when a feminine gasp snapped my attention to the side.

Meleya stood staring at where the Gray Knight and I faced off, her mouth open, her eyes wide. What was going on?

Without a second thought, Meleya disengaged from her fight with the shades and started hurrying our way. In doing so, she sustained a few more gray slashes, which leaked light all along her skin. Stars, why was she—

"Meleya!" I called. "Watch your—"

A slam from the flat of a telekinetically-charged wraithblade—or rather, wraith-*axe* sent me right back to the ground, shattering my starglass chestplate. Where the shadowy weapon had bludgeoned me in the side, a gray bruise formed that extended to my spirit-clothing and aura as well.

I groaned. Stars, it stung, but not in the same way it would have in the physical plane. Had that axe hit my physical form like that, it would have broken ribs for sure. As it was, I felt only an icy numbness.

Then the Gray Knight was above me once more, prepared to hit me while I was down. But I was ready too, and a lot quicker than he was. I hover-rolled out of the way, popping up behind him to thrust my spear directly into his back...

...Until another starglass blade stopped mine.

"Mel!" I said. "What in the stars are you *doing*?"

Before she could answer, the Gray Knight's gray aura flared. He jerked toward her, his wraithblade axe forming once again as an extension of his shadowy arm.

"Meleya, run!" I cried.

She didn't.

Instead, she reached toward the Gray Knight's face, then took hold of his helmet, ripped it off, and tossed it to the side, revealing...

I gasped. That wild, steely hair. The hard, bitter expression.

There was no mistaking him:

Jax.

Fragment: Marked

Trickshot

Trickshot felt the Orothion medical wing was beginning to feel more like a crowded harbor than a peaceful place to convalesce.

"What in the void is going on?" a worried Kai asked.

"That's what I'd like to know, drak-gonit," Meleya's equally worried father, Ivar, agreed. "Where'n the stars are all these gray marks comin' from?"

"Nowhere good, that's for sure!" Kari's dark eyes were wide. Meanwhile, Solvai was practically rubbing the falcondrake charm she wore around her neck raw as she watched over her best friend's body. From the window, Asher's wyvern bond's nose twitched with concern. Behind him, Trickshot thought she could spot Meleya's excitable evren flying nervous circles in the sky.

Even Trickshot couldn't help but feel a sense of growing dread. Earlier this week, the day before he'd left for the Canyonlands, Brigan had noted an instance of a minor gray mark appearing on Asher's hand. According to Brigan, it had healed right up with a drop of liquid light.

Since then, Trickshot had done a good deal of reading up on all that was known regarding the mysterious spirit plane, Etheria. She'd only found one mention of such gray markings in her medical texts, which hypothesized that they were the result of battles being fought among spirits. Battles fierce enough that the damage done to the spirit's aura was enough to affect the body as well.

When the markings had begun to appear in rapid succession all over Asher and Meleya's bodies, Trickshot had administered liquid light to try and stop them. But when they'd just kept coming, she'd sent for Solrac, who'd alerted Kai, who'd told Solvai and Kari, until soon the entire medical wing had grown crowded with worried people seeking answers that even Trickshot herself could only guess at.

"Little is known about markings like these," Trickshot explained. "But I believe that Asher and Meleya's spirits may be in trouble."

"You mean they could die?" Solvai squeaked, hazel eyes swimming with guilt.

"It's possible," Trickshot reluctantly replied.

"Out of the question!" Solrac shook his head.

"Agreed." Asher's father folded his arms from his perch at his son's bedside.

"What can we do?" Ivar tried to refocus their conversation.

Trickshot swallowed, cracking her knuckles as a nasty gray slash appeared along Asher's cheek. There were so many factors at play, but wrong or right, Trickshot knew she had to be decisive.

She pointed to Ivar. "Run up to the skyforge terrace and bring back the moonwillow bark solution that's been absorbing sunlight."

Ivar didn't hesitate. "On it!"

"And you," Trickshot spoke to one of her fellow medics. "Bring me some wyrmwood from the storehouse. It'll help take the edge off, I think."

As soon as the medic had gone, Trickshot took the momentary reprieve to unlock a glass-paneled cabinet near the window. Carefully, she extracted a little glass jar filled with a pale violet liquid. It was going to take a bit more time to make it all come together. Trickshot only hoped they *had* a bit more time.

"But Trickshot," another medic butted in, "the moonwillow bark solution isn't supposed to be added to the remedy until it's ready for administration."

"And that's not for another two days!" Kai added, his finger jabbing a page of his notebook.

"I know." Trickshot grimaced. "We're going to wake them up early."

Chapter 8: Divided

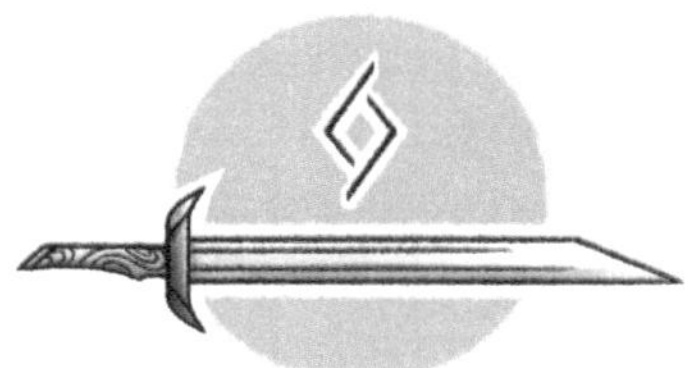

Meleya

"Jax!" I yelled to the so-called Gray Knight. Drak—I'd known it was him the second I'd seen that tangerine aura of his trapped beneath the gray.

My head was spinning, my pulse racing. There was no doubt about it: Jax was wraith-bound. He must've accepted that powerful wraith's voidshard. My hopes for his well-being were dashed to pieces like a jar of preserves that just got knocked down from a high shelf.

At the sound of his name, Jax blinked, and that horrid wraithblade on his arm began to shrink. With his helmet gone, it was clearer than ever that he was translucent too, just like Asher and me. That meant he, too, was in spirit form, caught in some kind of astral sleep state just like we were. His expression was hard to read, but I thought he looked confused. Almost as if he was waking up to find he wasn't where he'd been when he'd fallen asleep.

But that expression quickly gave way to one of anger and determination. His eyes glowed lightning blue—completely sapphire, down to the whites. They unnerved me, especially when he grabbed me by the collar, his jagged wraithblade axe reforming fast.

That was when Asher swept in, starglass spear swinging. He undercut Jax's axe, redirecting the Psion's momentum so harshly that he lost hold of me. Once again, Asher and the Gray Knight crossed blades, dragonhook spear against wraithblade greataxe.

"Asher, stop!" I yelled to no avail. "Asher!"

"No!" Asher shot back.

"But it's—"

"*I don't care!* Mel, he's trying to *kill you!*"

Both Asher's and Jax's expressions were set in rage, and both were out for blood. Each swing was charged with equal parts pent-up animosity and—respectively—ether blasts and telekinetic force. With turquoise trailing hyper-fast Asher and a gray shell riddled with deep tangerine cracks surrounding powerful Jax, it was a sight that would remain with me for the rest of my life—however long or short that may be.

Both fought like dragons, but Jax was fighting two wars at once: His wraith, too, was fighting for control, and while Jax clearly wanted to destroy Asher, the wraith wanted nothing more than to kill *me*.

In a flash of blue light, the wraith overcame Jax's will, and Jax ducked my way before Asher could land his next blow. Jax, eyes fully sapphire, raised his wraithblade, and I had no choice but to block with my seaxe.

Thwack! The Gray Knight's strength dropped me like a sack of scales, and I barely managed to redirect his blade to the side so it didn't end me then and there. Before he could strike again, I rolled out of the way, straight through a portal.

I emerged beside Asher who, thanks to seeing the golden warp connecting my rifts, had anticipated my exit.

"Meleya, get out of here!" he said, an uncharacteristically serious light in his eyes. "He's not going to stop until you're dead!"

"It's not his fault," I replied, desperate to make him understand. I knew firsthand what it felt like to lose yourself to a wraith. The powerlessness. The self-loathing. The regret. I knew Jax, and this wasn't him.

Asher snapped back. "But it is *our* problem. We have to take him down!"

Jax was running toward us again, divided on which of us he wanted to attack. At the last second, Asher and I dove in opposite directions, leaving Jax to stumble forward.

As the fight continued, Jax remained torn between killing me and ripping Asher's head off. Meanwhile, Asher was becoming increasingly furious each time he had to waste precious battle strength on me as I continually stepped in to thwart his deadly blows. Besides that, I had to defend myself from Jax's dark side each time his wraith made a move.

Drak! All of this was awful, complicated, and exhausting.

While we were locked in an impossible three-way battle, Blink and Zerana did their best to hold off the shades and echoes. Blink's dragonfire lit up the clearing, its emerald light clashing with the harsh blue of the netherstone. The wraithlings crumbled to dust in the fire's wake, and was no doubt the reason more shades weren't attacking Asher and me now.

But Zerana didn't have the advantage of dragonfire *or* etherarchy. Gray slash marks and bruises covered her spirit-skin. I could tell she was drained, and dangerously close to being overwhelmed.

I tried to break free and run to her. My finger was already runetracing, preparing a portal for Zerana, though I wasn't sure where I could send her. Everything was so hazy, I couldn't see anywhere safe.

But I didn't get far before my feet suddenly stopped moving. I fell forward, barely catching myself with my hands, all hopes of making a portal dissolving along with my rune.

It took me a moment to realize what was going on, but then I saw that Jax—or rather, the Gray Knight—was telekinetically grounding my spirit-boots to the floor. I tried to wrench free, but I was stuck fast.

"You're not going anywhere, Snowstorm!" the Gray Knight called. Without his helmet, his voice was no longer distorted by some sort of illusion rune. Rather, it was Jax's voice, doubled as his wraith stole it.

Meanwhile, the wraithlings continued to bombard Zerana, and her sword arm was so numb with gray that it fell from her grip.

Blink! I called to my dragon through our bond.

Blink answered the call. She alighted at Zerana's feet, and Asher's mom hurried to pick up her fallen weapon before climbing onto Blink's back. An ounce of relief flooded my spirit. Blink would keep Zerana safe.

But I could tell my dragon was tired too. Her fire continued to ravage the seemingly endless barrage of wraithlings, but several of the stronger echoes had managed to slip through the cracks.

No doubt at the request of the Gray Knight, the incoming storm of echoes rained down on Asher, dragging him away from Jax and forcing him to focus his waning energy and ether on themselves.

With Asher no longer in Jax's sights, it was apparently easier for his wraith to retake control once again. Jax—the Gray Knight—straightened up, his expression going from livid to eerily neutral as he turned toward me once again.

"Jax," I said, pleading with the goddesses that I'd be able to get through to him. Still, though reason was my first choice, I knew the likelihood I'd need a backup weapon was high. Boots still grounded by his telekinesis, I gripped my starglass seaxe in one hand and brandished a portal shield with the other.

There was still some distance between the Gray Knight and me as he telekinetically launched a flurry of wraithblades my way. I blocked a few with my sword, but caught most in the portal shield, which I had to expand to nearly my height in order to keep it effective. Meanwhile, I worked to step out of my boots in hopes that leaving them behind would grant me the chance to escape. Soot, why were the spirit-laces on these things so tight?

"We tire of this, Snowstorm," the Gray Knight said, his voice doubled with his wraith's. "We are the Wraith King's right hand. You are nothing against our power!"

A series of complex runes I'd never seen before burst to life over Jax's forehead as he runetraced faster than lightning. Suddenly, his heavy, intricate plate armor began to telekinetically separate from his form, leaving Jax's spirit in just his long-sleeved tunic, pants, and boots. Each piece of heavy armor hung in the air for just a moment before it swept toward me.

I was halfway through tracing a new portalling rune when the armor hit me. It was far too big for me, but between the thick spirit-metal chestplate, pauldrons, gauntlets, and greaves, I was completely trapped. I panicked as the gauntlets tightened around my wrists, keeping my fingers from being able to trace.

I struggled to wrench myself free, but it was impossible. The Gray Knight's psionic hold was too powerful.

"Hold still," the Gray Knight commanded as he appeared before me. No... not the Gray Knight, I reminded myself.

Jax.

This was Jax, who'd fought by my side at Outcast Outpost. Who'd nearly died protecting me on multiple occasions in the Dragon Mists. The man who cared for me enough to come with me to the Mage Hunter Academy even though the idea left him terrified. And then, when I was at my lowest, it was he who'd brought me above the gray Academy clouds and into that sublime mountain glade.

Yes, things had changed since then, in so many ways. But underneath this gray shell, I knew the real Jax would never be able to live with himself if he went through with this. I had to stop him—not only to save my own skin, but to save Jax's soul.

"Please, Jax," I said, spirit-tears forming at the corners of my eyes as he reformed his greataxe wraithblade, his eyes now fully burning with void-blue fire.

"Please," I repeated, "you need to fight this. I know it seems impossible, but you have to try. You're stronger than he is."

There they were—cracks in the dark gray shell. The wraith aura was powerful, like an earthen mountain, but through dozens of fissures, the tangerine light fought to shatter it. For just a moment, the voidish sapphire light fled Jax's eyes, leaving his irises their natural midnight blue.

One word—technically one letter—fell from Jax's lips: "M."

But just as quickly, his wraith's might filled in the cracks and the void retook his eyes. Tears burned in mine, but at least Jax's resistance had bought enough time for someone to tackle the Gray Knight to the ground.

I gasped when I realized my rescuer was neither Asher, Blink, nor Zerana.

Instead, it was Xan.

"Get away from my host, Calyx!" Xan hissed.

The Gray Knight growled. "She is not your host yet, usurper! Your bond is incomplete!"

Xan narrowed her sinister sapphire eyes at me. "Let me in, Meleya of Misthaven! We can use the shard to defeat him!"

"Never!" I cried back, ready to die fighting before I succumbed to the wraith whom I'd struggled so hard to overcome.

"We'll see about that..." Xan returned her attention to the Gray Knight, her long, jagged wraithblade forming in place of her hand. "In the meantime, let me show you what I can do."

With a savage, netherworldly hiss, Xan lunged toward the Gray Knight. Her foe raised a wraithblade of his own, but his movements were more sluggish than before. Cracks were once again forming in the gray shell, too. Jax was fighting him.

The gray aura began to burn with ire as Xan's blows chipped away at its defenses, scattering pieces of his essence to the winds. Jax's resistance was making it impossible for his wraith to win this fight.

Before long, the Gray Knight dropped to his knees and gave a mighty, voidish cry as the gray aura suddenly shot upward, like an erupting geyser, and took on a shape of its own. I shuddered as I recognized the hulking, massive Gray One, his sapphire eyes narrowed to slits. His face was featureless, but was covered in dozens of bone-chilling ivory markings written in a language I'd never seen before. When he spoke, his voice was as deep as the void itself.

"I will scatter your essence once and for all, foolish, arrogant shade!"

"When I consume your power," Xan rasped back, "even the Wraith King himself will fall before me!"

Where Xan's jagged blade met the greataxe of the ancient Gray One, a shower of fiery gray ashes burst out, releasing a grating, scratching sound that made me want to cover my ears.

To my relief, I could. With the ancient wraith—Calyx, had Xan called him?—occupied, the telekinetic charge within the armor vanished. Each piece fell from my body like autumn leaves from a tree.

I didn't waste a second. First, I checked on my team—Blink wasn't flying as high as she had been before, but her silvery claws still raked against the shades pursuing her and Zerana. Zerana herself clung to Blink's scales with one hand, while with the other she brandished her scimitar, pushing beyond her considerable fatigue. Asher had it the worst, with dozens of echoes drakepiling on top of him. Employing one of his signature astro-nova ether pulses, he managed to blast them backward, but his ether well was so depleted that the blast failed to destroy them all.

I wanted to help each of my friends, but deep down I knew I had to focus on our one chance of stopping all of this. I ran for Jax, who Calyx had left in a heap on the cold, gray ground.

Without the wraith, his tangerine aura flowed around him freely, though its clouds were still wreathed in tumult. I saw his ether well, too, manifesting as a translucent blue crystal near his forehead. It had been corrupted, poisoned by voidarchy. Just the sight of it made me sick.

Jax struggled to prop himself up on his elbows. He seemed disoriented, as if he were wondering how he'd gotten here.

I took his hand and pulled him to a sitting position. When he saw me, his midnight eyes went wide and he clutched my hand like it was the last solid thing on earth.

"M," he said. "I... I..."

Drak. There was so much to say, but no time to say it. I knew my aura was in chaos, too, indigo spirals spinning out of control as my mind raced.

Jax's jaw flexed as clarity filled his vision. "M, the safehouses... Calyx made me—And Streya's comet... skystone... They're going to—"

A hideous shriek yanked my focus back to Xan and Calyx's duel. Calyx had just landed a blow to Xan's side, where her essence burned, rapidly draining into the wind. In this moment, she looked small and pitiful next to a wraith as monstrous as Calyx.

I could tell Xan was furious, but she knew when she was overmatched. As I'd learned, she wasn't above a coward's retreat. Now, she dismissed her wraithblade, concentrating all her might into escaping Calyx's swooping greataxe.

Like a slithering, misty serpent, Xan raced away, once again heading toward the corrupted ley line. Before diving in, she called out to Calyx, or maybe all of us:

"This is not over! Soon, all will bow before me, the Wraith Queen!"

Then she dove into the ether river, retreating to nurse her wounds.

For a wraith of such mass, Calyx was fast. I cried out as suddenly he rushed back toward Jax, whose expression betrayed his panic and dread.

"M—" he managed, but that was all before Calyx's gray swallowed up Jax's tangerine aura like flowing lava overtaking a grassy field. Once again, Jax's expression hardened and his eyes glowed sapphire as the Gray Knight stood to loom over me.

Maybe it was because I was low on ether, or the fact that my emotions were all over the place. The Gray Knight's telekinetic hold over my boots certainly didn't help either. Whatever the case, when the wraithblade greataxe swung my way, I found myself paralyzed and squeezed my eyes shut in anticipation of the blow that never came.

When I dared open them again, I gasped.

"No!" my voice broke along with my heart when I saw Blink stooped over between me and the Gray Knight, the latter's jagged, voidish blade embedded in her flank. Her shining, silvery aura began leaking away, vanishing into the winds. Zerana was nowhere in sight.

Run, Meleya! Blink channeled through our bond. Her whole spirit flickered in and out as she used her rapidly waning strength to spread her wings like a shield between me and the Gray Knight.

For the briefest second, the void blue in the Gray Knight's eyes faltered, and Jax's soulless expression twisted into one of horror over what he was doing, especially when he saw what it was doing to me. Then, as he tried to wrest back control, Blink roared and shoved him backward.

Jax stumbled, but Blink's shove hadn't been enough. Light leaked from her flank, and she was becoming less tangible by the second. Then, Jax's eyes returned to voidish sapphire as the wraith regained control. The

Gray Knight hacked at Blink again, and now her entire form began to fade. It was clear my spirit evren only had a few seconds left.

Through our bond, Blink urged me to get out of here while I still could. Spirit-tears ran down my cheeks.

"I can't leave you!"

Her final drumbeats sounded like thunder in my ears. *GO!*

Refusing to let Blink's sacrifice be in vain, I opened a portal and darted through, emerging where I'd spotted Asher and Zerana banding together. Almost all of the shades were gone now, having been either dispatched or un-summoned while the Gray Knight was distracted, it was impossible to tell.

But *drak*, both Asher and Zerana were in bad shape, gray markings covering both their spirits; in fact, Asher's entire form seemed to be erring more toward trans*parent* than translucent.

"What's happening?" I asked, worry overtaking my already shaky tone. But Asher looked just as confused as me as he studied his arms with knit brows.

I reached for his hand, but mine went straight through it. Panic set in as I cried, "Don't let deeper Etheria take him!"

"It's not deeper Etheria that's taking him," Zerana managed.

Suddenly, Asher's aura appeared to be getting sucked upward. A trail of turquoise appeared, drifting to the south, and I suddenly put the pieces together.

"The remedy," I gasped. "But it's two days early!"

"Mom!" Asher cried as he reached for her.

"Asher!" Zerana cried, desperate to hold onto him a little longer. She clearly had more to say, and her dragonfire green eyes shone with regret. "Asher, forgive me!"

Asher mouthed the word 'mom' once more, but it was too late. His spirit was already being pulled along the turquoise thread like a meteor hurtling earthward in reverse. There was nothing he could do to stop it, just as there was nothing I could do when my own spirit began to turn immaterial.

An indigo thread appeared next, and I felt myself being pulled into the southbound skies. Muddled voices filled my ears, and there were faces. I could almost see faces. Was that Solvai? And Dad?

Blink... I thought. *Jax...*

I couldn't see them anymore. Even Zerana's face was becoming so faint as she softly bade me farewell. But no… I couldn't leave her here, not in the midst of so much danger.

Even as I felt my spirit lifting, I runetraced. A portal appeared in front of her, and as my spirit swept upward along my aura thread, I placed my exit at the edge of the Haven, back at the ether oasis where we'd swam with the etherotters.

I could sense Zerana using my portal, my one last gift to her before we left Etheria.

And then all at once, I was landing hard on my back. At least, that's what it felt like. Though I hadn't closed them, my eyes fluttered open, the lids heavy. My whole body felt stiff, clumsy, and leaden, and I could hear Asher breathing heavily on his cot near mine.

There was no mistaking it:

We were awake.

Fragment: Escape

Jax

Jax gasped for breath, sitting up so quickly he set his head spinning. Where was Meleya? Or that son of a dragonmutt, Asher? For that matter, where was Jax himself?

He felt stifled in his heavy plate armor, so he ripped off the helmet and tossed it aside where it clanged onto the hard floor. Then, wiping sweat from his brow, Jax finally got a disoriented look at his surroundings.

Voidish blue light cast eerie shadows on the walls. Shelves bearing dozens of jars, each filled with a floating crystal Jax had learned were ether wells, forcibly ripped from the souls of magi and pulled into the physical plane where the Soul Reaper kept them on display like trophies. Many of the ether wells were cracked, and a few were even split in two or three pieces—evidence of the difficult, unnatural process that was soul surgery.

Of course. Jax was in the Soul Reaper's—that is, the *Surgeon's* lair. It was all coming back to him... The Mage Hunter, Ilyan, administering some kind of high-powered dream blast to Jax's head... Jaira's cold laughter as he'd slipped from consciousness and into the spirit plane, Etheria.

Footsteps sounded as someone scurried away—A masked, gray-robed servant who must've been ordered to administer the remedy for Astral sleep, but hadn't wanted to hang around the notoriously volatile Gray Knight afterward.

The Gray Knight, who'd become a hero of the Gray for all he'd done to weaken the Knights of the Torch. As he'd ceded more control to Calyx, the merciless wraith had finally used his inside information to pinpoint dozens of Knight safehouses—then utterly annihilate them. At least, thank the stars, Jax had been able to keep Calyx from hurting any Knights directly. The Soul Reaper's rifting abilities had allowed him to travel quickly, his entourage of Coven in tow, to destroy the safehouses one by one before anyone realized what was happening, earning the Gray Knight's reputation as a savage, destructive servant of the Surgeon.

Jax barely remembered most of it. His memory was peppered with long periods of fogginess whenever Calyx had taken over. Still, he remembered pushing back against Calyx's various attempts at violence against the Knights they'd discovered in the safehouses at the times of their attacks. Such resistance had infuriated Calyx, pushing him to use his dark power to keep Jax's will buried even more deeply beneath the surface. That was how he'd ended up on this operating table, being subjected to the induced astral sleep coma so that at last he could retrieve the Soul Reaper's all-important voidshard.

Now, Jax remembered everything that had happened in Etheria with painful clarity. Before, it was as if he'd been watching the events from the outside rather than being an active participant in their unfurling. Until the end, at least, when Jax had ruined everything. Again.

You foolish, worthless excuse of a man! Calyx screamed inside Jax's head, so loud that Jax nearly fell off of the operating table where he'd been lying for the past several days. As ever, Calyx's deep voice was oppressive, leaving Jax feeling as though he'd been punched in the gut.

But Jax had some words for Calyx as well.

"You're a drakking liar!" Though Calyx spoke only within the walls of Jax's mind, Jax shouted aloud, his voice echoing off the sterile laboratory walls.

"I've let you control me ever since I accepted your sooty voidshard," Jax spat. "But you're insane if you think I'd ever let you hurt Meleya!"

The Snowstorm has the Wraith King's shard, Calyx bit back harsher than a blizzard wind. *The shard must be returned to its proper owner.*

"Go back to the void!" Jax cried, sliding from the table with a hand to his forehead. The astral sleep state had made him wobbly on his feet and he had to brace himself for stability. "Scorch you, Calyx—I'm no murderer."

You are not the murderer, Calyx growled. *You are simply a bystander, absolved of any guilt for actions taken while I am in control. You said you wanted to choose nothing, so* choose nothing. *Stop resisting!*

Now that he was no longer in Etheria, Jax couldn't visually see Calyx. But soot, he could *feel* him, looming over him, as if his brawny, shadowy form was glaring back from the other side of the operating table.

What is the girl to you, anyway? Calyx hissed. *You are certainly nothing to her—Not while Asher of Steel Rim draws breath.*

At that, Jax felt a wave of dizziness, nausea, and hate wash over him. He slammed his fist down hard on the operating table as he cried out in anger.

"Why?" Jax said. "Why didn't you just let me take him down in Etheria?"

It is not our *destiny to destroy the half-born,* Calyx replied. *At least, not yet. Your time to hurt him will soon come, but know this: If I had let you fight Asher of Steel Rim in Etheria, he would have bested you and all would have been for naught. He is stronger than you—Meleya certainly thinks so.*

Jax roared, his hands pressing against his temples. But that did nothing to quell the voice coming from within.

If you cannot have her, no one should, Calyx pressed. *Least of all* him.

"Shut up!" Jax shouted, ready to start pounding his own forehead. "Shut up and get the void out of my head!"

Jax's outburst seemed to make a difference as Calyx's icy presence palpably withdrew. Maybe the wraith had been weakened during his fight with Meleya's wraith in Etheria. Working hard to control his breathing, Jax reached for the pile of his belongings that they'd stowed beneath the table.

Part of him wanted to take off the heavy metal chestplate, pauldrons, tassets, and greaves, but something in him didn't dare. The more of himself he covered up, the better hidden he'd be from anyone who might recognize him and expect better than he was capable of giving.

Jax slipped the straps of his old holster across his chest so that his twin fanged axes were securely on his back. Beneath the axes was an extra sheath, one that held a *kalaata,* or Drekai boomerang. This particular one could activate an edge of pure light that made it sharp beyond any ordinary blade.

Just thinking about the boomerang that had once belonged to Zyri made Jax wince. Zyri had been a skilled Drekai woman who'd saved Jax and Meleya's lives multiple times before sacrificing herself in the service of her country, the Dragon Isles. Together, Jax and Meleya had buried the *kalaata* in Zyri's honor, in a glade where they'd spent the last perfect day Jax could remember.

Days after he'd broken up with Meleya, Jax had gone back to that glade and dug up the boomerang. He wasn't entirely sure why he'd done it—probably out of spite for the way she'd lied to him. Maybe that was why he carried it now.

Or maybe, it was something more. Zyri had faced the darkness with courage until her dying breath. Perhaps, deep down, Jax had hoped that some of her steadfast, unbreakable will would transfer to him.

Then again, it was too late for Jax. Far too late. Already, Jax could feel Calyx working his way back into his mind, ready to smother the light of his will under the dark weight of Calyx's own.

Slowly, Jax strode toward his metal helmet, which had rolled across the sterile laboratory portion of the Soul Reaper's lair to the edge of the loft's balcony.

Jax picked up the helmet with its vacant, empty eyes, then looked over the loft's ledge. Below the laboratory was a vast room with high ceilings covered in curving windows. An enormous telescope was pointed toward the windows, the central feature of the observatory portion of the lair. The Surgeon had been using it to track Streya's Comet, which would be passing soon, and with it the most massive payload of skystone the realm had ever seen. One the Surgeon planned to take for himself.

Jax had no clue what sinister plot could possibly require so much skystone. Already, every corner of the lair was filled to bursting with the stuff. Since becoming one of the Soul Reaper's elites, Jax had learned that the skystone tribute the keeps paid the High King went straight to the Soul Reaper—an impressive payment for the Surgeon's having saved the High King's son from the shadow wasting. The Surgeon had become so drakking powerful.

Jax suppressed a shudder. This place... it was all too much. He wanted to leave, but... but...

You have nowhere to go, Calyx whispered. *The Knights left you behind, as did Solrac, your mother, and even Meleya. No one will accept you now after what you've done. I am your only refuge.*

Jax gripped the helmet tightly as the wraith's words took root deep in his chest. When Calyx next spoke, he played right into Jax's greatest fears:

I will ensure you are never left behind again, Jax. Together, we will build the greatest monument this realm has ever seen. History will never forget your name.

Jax hated to admit it, but the wraith's words brought him comfort. Too exhausted to fight back, he exhaled. As he breathed back in, he felt Calyx's icy presence envelop him once more, and his irises began to glow with a dim sapphire light...

ECHO 2

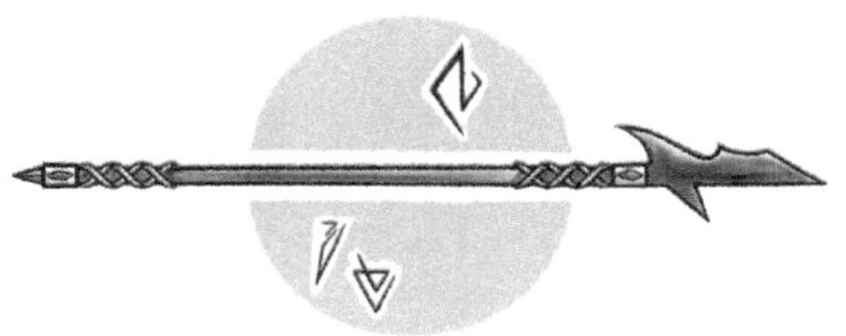

VIDYA

As she listened to Meleya and Asher tell their tale, Vidya's heart grew heavier with each passing second. Meleya's tears cut like blades. Jax... no. He couldn't be the Gray Knight. Goddesses, please, let it not be true.

The other Knights listened with grim acceptance as Vidya's greatest nightmare came true before their eyes: Jax was fighting for the Gray, and it was entirely her fault. She'd pushed him. She'd essentially conned him into attending the Mage Hunter Academy, where everything had gone wrong. So terribly, terribly wrong.

My dear JJ... Vidya thought later as she walked the corridors of Orothion in a sort of trance. She'd stayed until the medics had forced everyone out so that Asher and Meleya could recover in peace. From there, Vidya had been aimlessly wandering Orothion's halls as the guilt and regret piled higher and higher atop her shoulders.

Vidya didn't realize she'd wandered back to the chambers she shared with Solrac until she was instinctively opening the door. Maybe she'd go to bed early—Sleeping often helped chase away the pain.

But a surprise met Vidya inside the room. There on the desk she found a softly flickering candle, two glasses and a bottle of deep red liquid, and a little package neatly wrapped in brown paper.

Vidya picked up the parcel. No doubt Solrac had big plans and wanted her to wait to open it until he returned, but Vidya's curiosity got the better of her.

Vidya's heart began to pound when inside the package she found a delicately woven band. A small wooden panel was woven into the threads, and when Vidya looked closely, she saw that a couplet had been inscribed on it.

"From this moment on, my greatest role," Vidya read aloud.

"Is to be yours, body, mind, and soul," Solrac finished from the doorway. It seemed he hadn't been far behind Vidya.

Solrac closed the door behind him and hurried over to his wife's side. "I was planning all this before we rushed to the medical wing. Still... do you like it?"

Vidya examined the intricate marriage bracelet. "It's not fair. I haven't gotten you a marriage bracelet in return yet."

"That's alright." Solrac blushed. "I took the liberty. Check the drawer."

Inside the desk drawer, Vidya found another package. She opened it too, and found another woven band, only instead of a poem, this one featured an etching of a swan feather.

"You were always rather particular regarding your appearance," Vidya said.

"You too," he replied. With a twinkle in his eye, Solrac plucked the feminine bracelet from Vidya's hand and ceremoniously slipped it onto her wrist. Then he held out his own for Vidya to do the same with the masculine bracelet. The band felt strange and foreign against Vidya's skin.

Glancing back toward the desk, Vidya nodded to the bottle. "Dragonberry tequila?"

"Just like the old days with *Marelda's Mythica* circus," Solrac replied. "I thought we could celebrate one of our last nights together."

"You mean one of our last nights before your trip to the Dragon Isles," Vidya corrected.

"Yes," Solrac said, a shadow crossing his face. "But perhaps beyond that."

Vidya grimaced. "There it is. Your ever-present fixation on your imminent doom. Drakking omens. You're always saying they're never certain, yet when it comes to this you seem to believe your fate is set in scorching stone!" She hadn't meant to get angry, but the bitterness was piling up.

"I cannot stand by and pretend I never saw the omen," Solrac replied, tension creeping into his tone as well. "My only desire is to make the most of the time we have left."

“How in the scorching stars do you expect me to sit here sipping draquila while our son is out there losing his soul?”

“Do not act as if I’m not upset about Jax too,” Solrac said, brows furrowing.

“Then why won’t you *do* something?” Vidya beseeched him. “I can’t leave this drakking stronghold without encountering my wraith, but you? You’re the Farseer! The legendary hero of magi. If you can’t accomplish something as simple as saving your own son, what’s the point of any of it?”

“What am I supposed to do?” Solrac threw up his hands. “Mind control the boy and drag him back to Orothion by force? That would make me no better than his Gray One. Jax must come back to us of his own free will. But he will come back in time, I’m sure of it.”

“How sure? Are there omens you’ve been keeping from me, or is this just more of your insufferable optimism?”

“Don’t take my hope from me, Vidya!” Solrac shot back. “Not when it’s all that’s keeping me together. If these really are my last days—”

“There it drakking is again!” Vidya cut him off. “Why is it that you can muster up hope for everyone but yourself?”

“Scorch!” Solrac ran his fingers through his hair. “What do you want from me?”

“Nothing at all!” Vidya bit. “Just go on then—Go, and leave me behind once again. Maybe losing you will hurt less the second time!”

Vidya could no longer stand it. Without waiting for Solrac’s response, she stormed from the room, trading the warm glow of candlelight for the dim, moonlit halls of Orothion once more.

Instant regret thrummed through Vidya’s chest. Solrac had planned a tender evening together and she’d spoiled it. And without Exusha’s presence, she couldn’t even use her wraith as an excuse for her sullen behavior. Her heart longed to return to that room to try and make things right. Besides, part of her knew Solrac was right—If these *were* their last moments, she certainly didn’t want to spend them arguing. But her pride demanded she keep walking.

And walking. Up staircase after staircase Vidya went, until soon she found herself in the open-air terrace atop the stronghold’s legendary Skyforge. Though reconstruction was underway, the dome was still somewhat in shambles after what Meleya and the others had done winning back Orothion for the true Knights of the Torch. Above, Vidya spotted

Streya's Comet in the distance and, remembering Solrac's vision, her frustration spiked once more.

Vidya climbed onto the rampart where the lighthouse overlooked the Scarlet Strait. Desperate to continue her momentum away from her fight with Solrac—away from her own shame—Vidya dug deep to activate her stolen Wildshaper's ether well.

Wide, gray swan wings unfolded along her back while the rest of her remained in human form. The sound of the wind rushing in her ears was deafening as she flew high above the dark water. Wyverns and evren from Orothion's dragonhold skimmed the sea below her, frolicking and fishing in the Scarlet Strait, blissfully unaware of Vidya's flying form overhead.

Prior to attuning the swan feather she kept as a Wildshaping totem, Vidya hadn't had much experience with flying. She'd never been a dragon rider, after all. Looking down from this high up, the problems she'd left behind on the ground seemed somehow smaller.

As she flew, Vidya's thoughts meandered to her childhood in Evgard's Capital Keepdom. She hadn't grown up in the city proper, but a smaller town north of the famed waterfall city. As the daughter of a baron and baroness, Vidya had been given many opportunities—at least before anyone had learned she was a magi. One of those opportunities had been to travel to the High Citadel to become one of the magnanimous Capital Riders.

Vidya had turned the offer down. Though virtually everyone else in the Capital did it, the idea of forcing a bond with a dragon just didn't sit well with her. If a dragon found her worthy and offered her its heartscale, she'd have gladly accepted it. Yet for all the unspeakable things she'd done as the Black Valkyrie, taking a dragon against its will had been a step too far.

No dragon would take you because they sense your blackened heart.

The voice came with a sudden icy feeling that jarred Vidya from her musings. Her whole body tensed, and she dropped several feet before her wings caught air again.

Exusha, Vidya thought, heart sinking. Had she really flown so far as to leave the protective boundary the etherlocks provided?

Let us fly to the mainland tonight, the wraith whispered. *I can help you save Jax. We will go to the great Surgeon, restore ourselves to his good graces. Under his order, your son will see you as an ally. Was this not once your greatest desire?*

Exusha's will was suffocating. Vidya could feel her control slipping, and when she glanced at her hands, she could've sworn she could see them fading to gray. Though doing so felt like pushing against the flow of a raging river, Vidya turned around and began flying back toward Orothion. Back toward safety, for everyone and herself.

Exusha protested all the while, pressing against Vidya's mind with netherworldly force. When Vidya finally crossed back into the etherlock's sphere of protection, she gasped with relief.

This can't go on, she decided. *Whatever it takes, I need to find a way to rid myself of this Gray poison once and for all. Only then will I be able to save my son.*

Fragment: Home

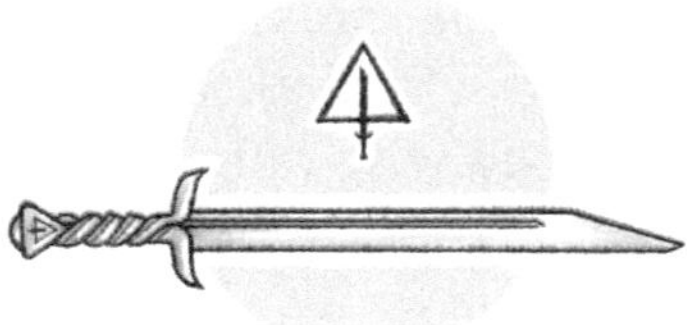

Zoren

For the first time in twenty years, Zoren was going home.

He soared across the sea on the back of his dark amethyst evren, Rekoa. Through their bond, he could feel her elation at seeing the lush silhouette of Zolehiinu on the horizon.

Zoren shared her excitement. Zoren had long been accused of being overly analytical, but even he could not help but admire the abject wonder that was the Drekai capital city. Nowhere else in all his travels had Zoren found such a seamless blending of nature and architecture woven together in perfect harmony.

During his years among the Evgardians, Zoren had grown used to their disdain for magi. That disdain heavily impacted their infrastructure. Here in the Dragon Isles, on the other scale, a preponderance of Psions had led to incredible feats of engineering.

Hovering totem pillars infused with etherarchy dotted the landscape. Elegant buildings with layered roofs, designed to mimic the spines on a dragon's back, sat suspended in the treetops of ancient scale cedars. Still others telekinetically hovered over the many rivers and streams that wound throughout the temperate rainforest of the Drekai islands.

Part of that custom owed to the superstition that flowing water kept the *khaamu*, or wraiths, away. But the Drekai were also a proud people, and liked to flaunt their triumph over nature through architecture.

Loosely connected bridges linked each network of buildings, the slats of which floated individually in the air and could be rearranged through psionics. The multi-tiered roofs, some doubled or even tripled, signified each building's level of importance.

At Zolehiinu's center was the jewel of them all: the palace. The nine-tiered roof of the fortress's core showed it was more important than any of the other buildings in the Dragon Isles. There were about a dozen smaller edifices surrounding the main building, some in treetops, others on the ground, and still others hovering telekinetically over the rushing Lokaai River.

Rekoa gave a gleeful roar when she caught sight of the palace's dragonhold. It was just as she and Zoren remembered, built directly over the river so that the dragons could hunt the bloodsalmon. They alighted on the landing platform and, through their bond, Zoren could tell she wanted to go inside to see if any of her old friends were still here.

"Go on ahead," Zoren murmured to his mount, stroking the scales along her neck as he dismounted. "I'll find you later."

Will you be alright? Rekoa asked through their bond. *Odds are the guards will not remember you from before, and if they do recognize you, it might not be a point in your favor.*

Rekoa hummed, her large, foxlike eyes shining with concern as she looked her rider up and down. She had a point—While he no longer sported the dusky cloak and silver pauldron of the Mage Hunters, his nomadic tunic and light armor were distinctly Evgardian. Not only that, but there was a strong possibility that his fame on the mainland had extended to the Isles. Somehow, he doubted the Ursadon, famous Drekai Mage Hunter, would be welcomed back with open arms.

That was why he needed to speak with Empress Khaisa as quickly as possible. He could use some food and rest himself, not to mention a dose of liquid light...

As if on cue, Zoren cringed as a shock of numbness shot through his veins from shoulder to fingertips. He felt his shadow wasting leeching ever closer to his chest, and the sudden desire to leave this place filled him. His people would no longer accept him. It would be easier to return to Evgard and find some obscure place where he could fade into the background for the rest of his days. Certainly that would be easier.

Zoren could feel the bitter, hateful darkness growing within him. Darkness born of the void—the influence of a lesser wraith, hoping to push him into complacency. The fact that his old wound was worsening certainly didn't help.

Zoren rolled up his sleeve to get a better look, and the sight of the large, inky gray patch was enough to make his stomach drop. Without Trickshot's care, the wound was metastasizing, the darkness clawing ever closer to his heart, trying to overtake him and leave him hollow. He'd completely run out of the supply she'd given somewhere over the Izmara Ocean on his way here.

But even that would have to wait. First, the Empress needed to hear what Zoren had discovered.

Zoren assured Rekoa that he'd manage, then hurried across the floating slats of the bridge that led to the front gates of Zolehiinu's palace. He saw a trio of warriors in battleworn bronze plate armor standing guard there, and prayed to the sky goddesses that they wouldn't give him a hard time.

As usual, Zoren's prayers went unanswered.

"What if instead of granting you entry," one guard said, speaking Drekai, "we lock you up? What say you, *Ursadon?*"

"I thought I recognized him!" another warrior butted in. "Traitor!" Both guards drew their scimitars, and the third copied their action only a second later.

Zoren narrowed his eyes, subconsciously taking in every detail of the warriors' appearances, demeanors, and mannerisms. One was quite young, his armor crisp and new. This was likely his first assignment. The armor of the other two, the ones with the accusing light in their dragonfire eyes, was more battered. Zoren noted tiny flecks of red dirt that hadn't been entirely cleaned from some of the laces that held together the segments. Redrock. These warriors must've recently been deployed in the Canyonlands, which in part explained their recognition of Zoren.

Zoren's shadow wasting wound throbbed while his ever-turbulent mind raced. How could he convince these guards to let him pass?

That was when he noticed the wrapping on the handle of the youngest guard's scimitar. The flaxen yellow color perfectly matched the scales on the tips of the soldier's ears.

"If you won't take me to the Empress," Zoren said, looking directly at the youngest soldier, "then send for your blademaster, Zedek."

The yellow-scaled warrior seemed taken aback. "How do you know—"

"Send for him," Zoren said with the authority of a former captain of the guard. "As for you two, hold me here in the meantime. I will not leave until I've spoken with Zedek."

The moment the elderly blademaster saw Zoren, his face lit up. Zoren, too, felt lighter, the chronic darkness that had lingered in him relenting. Blademaster Zedek thanked the guards, then led Zoren past them and into the palace to a more private alcove.

"*Valo voitakun,*" Zoren said, a lump catching in his throat.

The blademaster repeated the phrase. "*Valo voitakun.*" Let light prevail—the passphrase of the Drekai '*Zaraaki Ziia*', or 'Emerald Eye,' the ancient order of spies working directly for the royal family.

Zedek pulled Zoren into an embrace. "It's so good to see you. Some said you had left the Order—turned your back on us for the Evgardian's Mage Hunters. But not old Blademaster Zedek. I knew you'd never abandon us, even after all these years."

"You know me," Zoren said. "I couldn't come home until I'd accomplished my mission."

It took Zedek a second, but then his eyes widened. "You mean..."

Zoren nodded. "Bring me to the Empress. We must not delay—"

"Shades!" Zedek suddenly cursed, seizing Zoren's arm and pushing up the sleeve. Zoren recoiled, but though Blademaster Zedek was old, his iron grip made it easy to believe he was a former Chief Captain in the Drekai army.

Zedek's gaze scanned the vast patch of inky gray leeching along Zoren's entire arm. Stars, it was numb.

"You're not going anywhere until you've seen a healer," Zedek said, already guiding Zoren toward the palace door.

"But my information—"

Blademaster Zedek cut him off. "—has waited this long. Even the burning sun must rest from his labors come nightfall."

Zoren sighed. He knew better than to argue once Zedek had employed one of his platitudes. Relief softened the darkness's edge as Zoren let himself be dragged along.

Blademaster Zedek took Zoren to one of the many floating totems situated in the Zolehiinu palace. Each of the hovering, ornately carved monuments had been marked, infused with a distinct power that affected anyone standing within its range.

At the blademaster's insistence, Zoren spent a good long while basking in the soft glow of a totem that emitted the healing power of lightwielding. The inky grayness of his wound slowly began its retreat—Not completely, of course. No amount of liquid light could erase Zoren's particularly nasty case of the shadow wasting, and he'd need ongoing treatment his whole life long if he wanted to keep from going hollow.

The numbness having subsided, Zoren and Zedek were at last striding through the rain-dampened scalecedars of the forest behind Zolehiinu's palace. Stars, he'd missed this place.

The path he walked was nearly imperceptible, but Zoren knew it well. It led to what Drekai diplomats referred to as *kun Zuo*—the Bog.

Such a moniker could not have been further from the truth. But thanks to illusion etherarchy, only those who knew about the Emerald Eye Headquarters could see it.

And what a sight it was. Set on the eastern beach was an elegant series of buildings, each telekinetically floating above the sand and surf. The highest was the observatory, its glass dome catching the diffused sunlight. This was where Drekai astronomers tracked everything from constellations to skyfalls. Zoren spotted movement up there now—No doubt they were busy, since historically, skyfalls always increased around the passage of Streya's Comet. Although, in Zoren's estimation, there seemed to be even more skyfalls than usual during this particular cycle. In the back of his mind, Zoren wondered if the Gray would try to take advantage of that, perhaps by wrangling more dreklings and turning them umbral like they had in Rengard.

Zoren had watched Streya's Comet from Rekoa's back on the way here, a distant, green-tailed wonder crossing the sky. It would be visible for another few weeks before vanishing back into the blackness of the heavens.

Mist rose from the water, adding to the mysterious air which was only punctuated by the towering, dark sea stacks—solitary ridges of rock rising out of the sea—that dotted the area.

Like much of the Dragon Isles, psionic bridges connected each of the smaller buildings to the largest one in the center. Seeing the dojo where the Emerald Eye trained their agents sent memories racing through Zoren's mind. Zoren was hardly the same shy young man who'd left the Emerald Eye Headquarters all those years ago.

Zoren and Blademaster Zedek used a large, flat, runemarked stone as a psionic lift from the beach to the balcony of the dojo. Intricate wooden panels served as doors that rotated open on a central axis along all four walls, and windows let in both diffused daylight and the salty scent of the sea.

Empress Khaisa stood at the edge of the central combat training area, calmly looking on as a warrior sparred against several psionically-powered practice dummies, runemarked wooden posts with spinning arms that mimicked an enemy's movement. From her fair skin, elegant draconic horns, and the emerald-green scales lining her hairline and cheekbones, she looked just like the princess Zoren remembered, though older and more careworn. At Khaisa's side, her great, third ascension true dragon sat with his tail curled protectively near her feet. Though it had been decades, Zoren's meticulous mind had no trouble recalling that she'd named the dragon 'Mehtzi' for her forest-like coloring.

Together, Khaisa and Mehtzi watched the action unfolding on the practice floor. They hadn't noticed Zoren and Zekek's entrance yet.

Meanwhile, Zoren took in every detail in the blink of an eye. The swordsman had red-and-black accent scales and a pair of wide wings. He was astonishingly skilled with the blade for one so young, and his ornate armor denoted a position of leadership. A high one at that—Ah, there it was: the insignia of a General. His balance between his blade and his fiery gauntlet was unorthodox, his fighting style unique. He was quite impressive.

The fact that Empress Khaisa herself watched him train signified her personal investment in him, and their features were fairly similar as well. Zoren knew Khaisa had no children herself, so this must've been a cousin or nephew.

The only other person in the dojo was another young man, sitting in a corner with one of the wooden practice dummies in pieces before him. Judging by the numerous grease smears on his fingers, the chipped end of one of his horns, and the tool in his hand, he must've been an inventor of sorts.

"Well done, General Kheradok," Empress Khaisa called to the swordsman as he finished a set of moves. "But next time, I want to see more speed. Your foe is an Astromancer, said to be expert in hover-dashing and the manipulation of starglass. You must decide how you wish to counter this."

"Counter starglass..." the warrior muttered, brows lowered in thought.

The Empress went on, "Don't let Raaku coddle you, either."

"Coddle? Me?" The grease-smeared inventor gave an indignant look. "These practice dummies are set to expert levels! The Chief of Peace here is just that good."

Raaku winked, but Kheradok remained solemn. "I will bring honor to the Isles by defeating the half-born," Kheradok said.

"*I will bring honor to the Isles by defeating the half-born,*" Raaku repeated in a mocking tone. He laughed. "Lighten up, *Raiia*—unless you plan on boring the half-born to death with overly serious chatter in the arena this fall." That got a slight snort out of the sober warrior and, despite how different they were, Zoren sensed a long-time friendship between the two.

"Whether you like it or not, Raaku, this duel is a serious matter," Empress Khaisa said. "It would not bode well for our nation to see my nephew lose. If he's killed, the entire royal family would be vulnerable to further threats, both from within and without. Kheradok is my only heir, and without him, the succession would fall to another family after my death. Above all, I do not wish to see this happen."

"Of course, my Empress," Raaku said.

That was when Zedek cleared his throat to get the Empress's attention. When she turned to face Zedek and Zoren, both men briefly took a knee.

Khaisa's dragonfire eyes were bright as Blademaster Zedek made the introduction. "Zoren, son of Loyalty and agent of the Emerald Eye, has finally returned after twenty long years."

"Rise, Zoren," Empress Khaisa said, looking at him with curiosity. She remembered him, Zoren was certain of it.

"I bring urgent news, esteemed Empress Khaisa," Zoren said.

"Better be *good* news," Raaku said. "If it took you twenty years to get it."

Zoren bit the inside of his cheek before grumbling, "I became somewhat... distracted."

Raaku grinned. "A woman?"

Zoren was surprised to feel his cheeks warming.

"I knew it!" Raaku slapped his knee.

"Please, Raaku." Empress Khaisa put up a hand to end the inventor's antics. Then she turned back to Zoren. "We are eager to hear of your findings."

"But first..." Blademaster Zedek interrupted, and everyone turned to him expectantly. "She'll be here any moment, arriving by rift anchor."

"Who's coming?" Raaku asked.

"Our leading expert on wraiths, of course," Zedek replied. "She's spent the past several years on Isle Haarma, documenting our knowledge of the Gray for our history. When Zoren mentioned that his news dealt with the Gray, I sent for her."

"Very good." Empress Khaisa nodded to the blademaster.

Meanwhile, Kheradok frowned. "What's this woman's name?"

Blademaster Zedek turned to the young general. "Certainly you remember—"

The door of the dojo swinging open cut him off. There stood a woman much younger than Zoren would have expected for a historian. She had sky blue scales, a similar shade to the pet spitfire—the small, snake-like, lesser dragon—coiled over her shoulder. Between the large portfolio of sketching paper under her arm and the trio of pencils sticking out of her blonde draketail hairstyle, Zoren deduced that she was something of an artist.

"Zaria!" Raaku broke into a grin at the sight of her, rushing over to wrap her in a friendly hug.

"You two know each other?" Empress Khaisa asked.

"We *three*," Raaku corrected. "Zaria served in the southern warband with Kheradok and me, what, four, five years ago?"

"Six," Kheradok and Zaria spoke in unison. Both of them seemed entranced, as if recalling a nearly forgotten dream. There was certainly a history between them.

After a too-long moment, Zaria blinked a few times as if to reset her mind. Then, straightening up, she cleared her throat.

"It's good to see both of you again. But if what Zedek and the Empress have said is true, we have much to discuss." Zaria turned to Zoren. "You come bearing information concerning the Gray?"

"I do." All of the Drekai in the dojo gathered nearer in anticipation.

Zoren began, "Many years ago, the former Empress and Emperor—your mother and father, Empress Khaisa—sent me to Evgard in hopes that I might retrieve a dark object. Something that would aid us in our quest to end the Gray ethereal force that threatens these lands."

"The Soul Reaper's voidshard." Empress Khaisa nodded. "You have discovered it at last?"

"Alas, no." Zoren bowed his head. "But I am certain the Soul Reaper does not have it either. I was able to ascertain the names etched on the shard."

Eyes wide, Zaria pulled out a sketchbook in anticipation. Everyone else leaned closer, and Empress Khaisa subtly held her breath.

"I used these names to track and uncover the origins of the Soul Reaper," Zoren continued. He pulled out a dreamweb, silky threads criss-crossing within the wooden hoop etched with runemarks. "Memories of him I've collected within this."

He held out the hoop to the Empress, who took it with both eagerness and trepidation.

Zoren gulped. "It is as we feared, my Empress. Agnai, the Wraith King, has risen again."

Chapter 9: Awake

Asher

The two days it took for the medics at Orothion to deem me 'stable' enough to let out of their sight felt like weeks. Our bodies had been in pretty bad shape after all the craziness our spirits had endured in Etheria, each cut from the shades and echoes leaving gray marks along our skin—even with Brigan and the others actively healing us throughout the ordeal. Trickshot had saved our lives by waking us up when she did, and under her care, my skin was looking nearly as warm and coppery as before. Just a few more treatments and she promised the occasional shivers I'd been feeling would subside, too. She asked us to let her know if we experienced any other strange side effects of being woken up early as well.

When they finally agreed to release me, the first thing I had to do upon leaving the medical wing was submit to a mental evaluation via Seer mind reading. That part I'd been expecting, at least—The Knights needed to learn everything they could about the netherstone we'd found at the center of the Haze.

Lucky for me, the Seer who'd been assigned to sift through my mind was none other than my best friend and resident bookwyrm, Kai.

"Slow down, Asher," Kai huffed as he tried to match my pace. "You don't know where we're going."

"You make a good point," I said, slowing down so that Kai could lead the way through the ever-twisting halls of the Orothion castle. "Even if you walk slower than a sea-kirin."

"Sea-kirin are aquatic—They don't walk at all."

I gave Kai a look that said 'exactly', and he rolled his eyes so hard he nearly dropped the stack of books he carried.

"Good to have you back, Asher," Kai said, and I got the sense that buried deep under all that sarcasm, Kai meant it.

It was strange getting used to having a body again. Kai may have thought I was moving too quickly, but stars, compared to what it had been like in Etheria, I felt like I was walking through sap, and I had to stop myself from simply levitating everywhere I went. Everything felt so drakking *heavy*. Then again, maybe that was because Mom was gone again.

You knew this was coming, I chided myself.

Despite that, the end of our time together in Etheria had felt far too rushed. Meleya assured me that she'd rifted Mom to safety outside the Haze, but I still worried.

Uh oh. A lump threatened to form in my throat, and I knew I needed to stop thinking about Mom before I became a wreck.

Luckily, Kai and I had just arrived at the library.

And what a library it was.

We must've been in one of Orothion's many spires, because the book-laden walls seemed to spiral upward forever. Guardian-era pillars rose at each of the points of a multi-tiered, nine-pointed star etched into the floor. In the center of the star stood three incredibly detailed, life-sized marble statues depicting three unique creatures: A dragon, a phoenix, and a dire wolf.

"Wow," I said.

Kai beamed. "Isn't it *incredible?* It's the second-largest Guardian-era library still in operation in Evgard, behind the one at the Capital citadel, of course."

"Obviously," I replied, but Kai was already leading me away to a quiet alcove where we found a desk laden with neat stacks of books along with several extra quill pens. Diffused sunlight shone through the window behind it, and a terrarium sat in one corner of the desk, a silvery mirror gecko basking in the light from a stony perch inside. It seemed they'd given Kai his own little nerd office, and based on the way Kai proudly drummed his fingers along the desk as he sat down, he was quite pleased with it.

At Kai's request, I drew the curtain to give us some privacy, then took a seat across the table from him. From there, he ordered his original, silvery mirror gecko, Glint, to climb out of her terrarium and onto the back of my hand. That way, she could assist Kai in reading my memories. From there, my interrogation—I mean, *report*—began.

"Now—" Kai opened his notebook, "show me everything you saw from the moment you stepped into the Haze."

I mentally replayed our journey as Kai took furious notes. I knew he'd said to show him 'everything' we'd seen, but growing up with a Seer for a best friend had helped me figure out how to manipulate mind reading, so I was able to hold back a few select details. Most notably, private conversations with Mom, as well as a certain moment in a darkened alcove with Meleya.

Stars, deliberately *not* thinking about the kiss in the alcove really got me thinking about the kiss in the alcove. The way Meleya's and my auras danced as indigo and turquoise sparks flew...

I didn't realize Kai had stopped taking notes to stare at me until way too late. His eyes were wide, one eyebrow raised. Oh soot. So much for keeping that memory to myself.

"You and—" Kai started.

I cut him off. "Shh."

"But you and Meleya... Really? Does that mean..."

"*Shh!*" I looked around to make sure no one was eavesdropping. "I don't know what it means, okay? It's not—It's...complicated. For both of us. Ugh—Just keep watching."

Kai narrowed his eyes and I knew this conversation was far from over, but he kept sifting through my memories of Etheria.

When we got to the netherstone, Kai kept slowing my memories down so he could take more detailed notes. He did his best to sketch it out, labeling each part and jotting down anything that might prove helpful later on. He had about a million questions, from 'How does it work?' to 'Why the ancient design?' to 'How did it get there?' but there was one particular observation that I couldn't believe I'd missed while looking at the netherstone in person:

"It's not native to the spirit plane, that's for sure," Kai observed as he scribbled.

"How do you know that?" I asked.

"It's physical, not spirit," Kai responded, manipulating the memory so that we could focus on the netherstone up close. "See how it's completely opaque? Most things you encountered in the spirit plane were translucent to some degree. Spirit form only—at least, that was the level at which you interacted with them. But this netherstone... While it currently resides exclusively in Etheria, it's almost certainly native to this plane."

"Stars," I said.

"There are likely more of these netherstones at other points within the Ethereal plane, and for some reason, something is triggering them to affect not just the spirit plane—as I suspect they have been for some time—but the physical plane too. The question is: Why?"

"Also 'how'," I added.

"And 'who'," Kai agreed.

"How about 'what'?" I offered.

Kai frowned, his eyes not leaving his notebook as he wrote. "Well, now we know 'what'."

I pressed on with an air of melodrama. "And, of course... 'when?'"

"We know 'when' too, Asher," Kai mumbled, unamused. "Also 'where,' so don't even bother with that one."

I closed my ready mouth. Despite my lame jokes, I couldn't help but feel the heavy weight of what we still didn't know hanging over us like a stormcloud. Yeah, I'd been to the center of the Haze and seen this netherstone thing in Etheria with my own eyes. But rather than provide answers, it seemed the journey had only left us with more questions.

Meanwhile, Kai continued combing through my memories of the battle with the shades and the Gray Knight. He watched Meleya unmask our foe, unsurprised by the face beneath the helm—When Meleya had awakened from her astral sleep trembling and in tears, Jax's treachery had been impossible to hide. The revelation had affected everyone, especially Solrac. He'd been his usual optimistic self when we'd been revived, but the moment he'd learned about Jax, his whole demeanor had shifted. Come to think of it, I'd barely seen him at all over the past couple days.

Solrac, Meleya... everyone seemed so shocked that Jax had betrayed the Knights of the Torch. As for me, I couldn't shake the image of the Gray Knight coming at me, murder in his eyes. I'd seen that very ire directed at me before, and I was willing to bet that it would've been there whether Jax was wraith-bound or not. The wraith he'd bonded may have been after Meleya, but as for Jax himself... his loathing for me felt entirely genuine.

Frustration filled my chest as I thought of the multiple altercations between Jax and myself. I wasn't sure what the others had ever seen in him, but soot if I wouldn't mind never seeing Jax again as long as I lived. And if I ever did...

Soot. All of a sudden... Kai was watching my last moments in Etheria.

Mom! I'd cried as my spirit began to fade.

Mom's eyes were bright with tears as she reached for me. I'd reached back, though I hadn't been able to feel her anymore.

Asher! Asher, forgive me! Stars, what had she meant?

The next thing I knew, I'd found myself in a room full of medics and spectators. The memory was still fresh enough that some pesky tears appeared behind my eyes. I'd been acting extra goofy since waking up, all in an attempt to suppress the pain of losing Mom all over again. But seeing Mom's face in those final moments was too much.

I opened my mouth again, fully planning on making another dumb, lighthearted joke. But when I tried, I got choked up.

I shoved Glint from my hand to sever the mindlink between Kai and me, then turned away. Pressing my palms against my eyes, I could only hope that Kai wouldn't... I wasn't sure exactly. Judge me? Think less of me? Feel uncomfortable?

But my best friend clearly didn't take issue with my reaction. When I finally dared to remove my hands from my red-tinged eyes, I was surprised to see that Kai's dark eyes were almost as wet as mine.

When he spoke, his voice was gentle. "I know it's not the same, but I miss her too."

I sniffled. "You'd think the past four years would've been enough time to get over it."

"Stop thinking you have to 'get over' it. She's your Mom, Asher, not a bridge. Besides... I'd never expect you to forget her when I can't forget mine."

Now it was Kai's turn to look away. His gaze locked onto the black leather notebook clutched in his hands. An elaborate tree design was pressed into its cover, which I knew gave him hope. His parents had joined the Knights of the Torch long before any of us, but they'd disappeared while on a mysterious quest. Their last gift to Kai had been this journal, emblazoned with a tree design that Kai once told me might've been an ancient symbol for the long-lost 'Everflame.'

According to Kai and some of the other Knights, legend said that the Everflame was an ancient torch bearing the mystical, powerful fire of the first true dragon. At the time, I hadn't thought much of the spirit-y, superstitious story. Even when Valla had left on her dangerous quest to find this legendary flame, several of us had thought it was a futile endeavor.

But after my impossible journey into the spirit plane, I wasn't sure of anything anymore. I'd gotten to see my mom again, and I could only pray that Kai would one day be blessed with that same gift.

Kai's and my eyes met, and an understanding passed between us. As I looked at my friend, I noticed for the first time what he was wearing.

"Nice robes," I said, admiring the red fabric that fell to his wrists and his knees over his pale beige pants. Gold threads wove into designs that looked runic along the cuffs, hem, and collar, and finely carved wooden buttons bore the same tree design as his notebook.

I recalled that it wasn't all that long ago that Kai wouldn't go outside without his too-big, heavy plate armor. He'd certainly come a long way. Despite being armor-free, he seemed far less vulnerable and far more confident.

"Thanks," Kai said. "They're the same ones Solrac gave to me before we left the Mirror Forest, but with some additions. Solvai carved the buttons."

"Ooh, *Solvai* carved them for you." With a knowing double eyebrow raise, I gave Kai a shove across the desk. He couldn't hide his smile as he shoved me back. I was about to tackle him when Kai stopped me, reminding me that an ancient, sacred library probably wasn't the best place for a wrestling match.

"We should get you out of here anyway," Kai said, gathering up his notebook and pen.

"Look, Kai, I know I've got a reputation for being a dragon-bull in a crystal shop, but my mere presence won't destroy the library, I promise."

"That's not what I mean." Kai snorted. "I mean, you should probably start packing."

"Packing?"

"Didn't anyone tell you?" Kai frowned, then flipped open his notebook. "I swear Solrac said he was going to remind you..."

"Remind me about what?" Solrac hadn't told me anything, but then again, he must have been distracted by the news about Jax. I got a sudden feeling I knew what was coming and my heart started beating faster.

"Your duel with General Kheradok," Kai said. "You and your party are leaving for the Dragon Isles in two days."

Despite Kai's suggestion, I didn't head off to pack. I still had two whole days, after all—That gave me at least forty-seven-and-a-half hours before I even needed to start thinking about which extra pair of socks to bring with me on the trip to my possible doom.

In the meantime, I found myself wandering up to the terrace above the Skyforge. Overhead, I spotted the green fire of Streya's Comet streaking across the sky, though it looked far duller now compared to the wonder we'd witnessed in Etheria.

While the Skyforge terrace was currently abandoned, it was clear that this was an active construction area. The dome's framework was nearly back in place, though I could tell that the new metal the smiths had added to replace the parts Meleya, Kari, and Enya had blown up was somehow different than before. The original pieces of the intricately-patterned dome were a richer shade of gold, while the new stuff was some kind of shiny brass. Still, they'd made excellent progress. They hadn't started working on replacing the starglass interior that filled the space between the gold frame, though.

I needed something to do, so I took the opportunity.

My eyes flashed as I accessed my etherarchy. Hands outstretched toward the massive structure, I began forming mass quantities of starglass. Without a constant supply of ether, the starglass would dissolve after three days, but it seemed the workers here at Orothion had accounted for that by placing a chest in the far corner of the terrace. When I focused on it, I could've sworn I saw the telltale shimmering white aura of skystone, even through the chest.

I blinked a few times, shaking my head until my vision returned to normal. This had happened a few times since I'd woken up—flashes of the Sight, so brief I thought I was seeing things. It was beginning to worry me.

But this time, it worked to my advantage. I pulled a few skystones from the chest, setting them at intervals along the framework so that my starglass would remain intact indefinitely. It was a clever method, one I was certain the original builders of Orothion had used when they'd first constructed the stronghold.

I lost myself in the construction, letting the task clear my head. My eyes were ablaze with etherlight as I levitated from place to place, lighter than air. I wasn't quite flying the same way as I was able to while in Etheria, but my feet only touched the ground for moments at a time.

The challenge of it all left me so focused that it caught me off guard when Meleya suddenly appeared on the terrace. Startled, I momentarily lost concentration and nearly plummeted through a gap in the framework. I managed to catch myself just in time, hover-jumping to land beside her then clearing my throat as if nothing had happened.

"Morning." I saluted.

"Kai told me I could find you up here," Meleya said.

"Ah," I replied, cracking my knuckles before getting back to work on the portion of the dome near where we stood. "Kai read your memories too?"

Meleya nodded, and I could tell that reliving Etheria had been hard on her as well. Hoping to lighten her mental load, I began channeling starglass into a life-sized, crystalline statue of a dragon buffalo, perching majestically atop the dome.

Meleya cocked her head. "What in the stars are you doing?"

"Commemorating the umbruffalo we encountered in Etheria," I replied matter-of-factly as I put the finishing touches on its vestigial wings. "Looks pretty good, right?"

"Something tells me the Knights wouldn't particularly like a giant dragon-cow overseeing their stronghold."

"You're right." I tapped my chin. "An etherotter would be much better."

From there, I reformed my starglass statue into a giant version of one of the playful draconic otters we'd met on our spirit journey. That coaxed a smile out of Meleya, so I kept going.

"Or better yet, how about this?" I said, ether flaring as I reformed the starglass once again. This time, the otter's scaled back gave way to a curved shell, and before long we were looking at a lava turtle.

I turned to Meleya, a crooked grin on my face as I anticipated her response. To my surprise, Meleya's smile slowly faded as she took in the sight of my latest starglass creation. Meleya and I locked eyes, and I knew she was remembering our ethereal game of lava floor as well—Back when everything between us had seemed so simple. Before...

"Asher," Meleya began, "about what happened at the netherstone..." She trailed off.

I swallowed. "You mean when you stopped me from taking out the guy who was trying to kill you?"

Meleya's cheeks reddened. "He's not just some guy."

"Clearly. He's a wraith-possessed monster now too," I responded, my face growing warm as well. Needing to do something with my hands, I dissolved the starglass lava turtle and replaced it with a figure more suited to the Knights as a whole: Aurora, her magnificent wings outstretched as she gazed upward toward the skies.

There, that was much less personal.

Right?

Meanwhile, I got back to work on filling in the rest of the gaps in the dome. I took hold of another fragment of skystone, embedding it into the framework as I readied another crystalline panel.

I knew I should keep my mouth shut, but I couldn't. Not looking Meleya's way, I continued. "You still have feelings for Jax, don't you? Despite everything."

After sputtering incoherently for a moment, Meleya managed, "You and Jax worked together, right? You know as well as I do that the Gray Knight isn't who Jax really is."

"Do I, though?" I replied tersely. "I seem to recall various punches to the face, rude nicknames, and a whole arsenal of other slights that speak to the opposite."

"You don't know what it's like to have a wraith in your head!"

"That's no excuse. He's still responsible for his own actions. Either that, or he's succumbed to his wraith, and the real Jax isn't even in there anymore, in which case it would be a mercy to stop him."

"And by stop him, you mean *kill* him?"

I accidentally made my next wave of starglass appear directly next to where she stood, which made her jump.

"Drak!" she cursed.

"Sorry," I said halfheartedly as I slammed the lid of the skystone chest so hard it tipped over, scattering several crystals onto the terrace floor.

Within a second, Meleya was already on her knees gathering the fallen skystone. "Soot, Asher. You really haven't changed since that first day in Swan Spire have you?"

"As opposed to Jax, who's gone from a regular jerk to a murderous one," I retorted, grabbing a skystone from the ground and returning to my starglass roofing project with extra vigor. "And for the record, no one's asking you to clean up after me. Just because my real mom isn't around anymore doesn't mean I'm looking for a replacement."

"Ugh!" Meleya glared. "Are you *trying* to be obnoxious, or is that just a natural consequence of you existing?"

"Oh, so now I'm obnoxious for being the realistic one for once? It's not my fault your scale-in-the-mud attitude is rubbing off on me."

"How are *you* being realistic right now?"

"You're so caught up in your emotions that you can't see the truth about that workout-obsessed traitor! Don't think I didn't see what Jax did to Blink—Are you really just going to ignore that?"

"Jax was fighting for control, and Blink knew that!"

"That doesn't change what he did."

"He would never—"

"But he *did*, Meleya."

Meleya sputtered, unable to come up with a good response to that before managing, "Blink cares—she cared—about Jax."

"That makes two of you then!"

I instantly realized I'd taken things too far. Tears sprang to Meleya's large brown eyes, and the etherarchy I'd been about to channel fizzled out in a shimmer of white dust. I'd been levitating too, but now my feet touched back down.

Refusing to look me in the eye, Meleya busily finished gathering the last fragments of skystone and replaced them in the chest. I joined her and, at the same time, we reached for the final piece.

Our hands brushed and Meleya instantly recoiled. Guilt over what I'd said and hurt over what she'd said clashed within my chest.

I put the skystone back into the box and closed it back up once more. The cries of distant wyverngulls and Meleya's sniffling were the only sounds on the terrace as we stood, our gazes naturally drawn to the dome.

I'd finished the job, gleaming starglass set along the brassy framework and catching the sunlight. The fragments of skystone peppered the dome, glistening as they powered the starglass. I had to admit, it looked just as pristine as it had before we'd blown it up. Still, there were a handful of differences between the original and mine—For one thing, the Guardians had somehow enchanted the starglass so that it darkened during the day, while mine was just plain starglass, but that was a secret we didn't know how to replicate.

From there, my eyes wandered to a spot just off to the side of the dome, here on the terrace. That was where, as a spirit, I'd gotten to see Mom again for the first time in years.

As I stared at the spot, it happened again—A flash of something more crossed my vision. For the briefest moment, I could've sworn I saw an avia—one of those spirit butterfly-dragons Mom had shown us—flitting by, its vibrant, misty aura trailing behind it.

I blinked as the flickering creature swept toward me. I flinched when one of its wings seemed to graze me, but of course, it went right through me like wind. I was corporeal again.

Having noticed my strange reaction, Meleya spoke. "I've been seeing things too. Flashes of the spirit plane, like the Sight activating even when I haven't runetraced."

"Stars," I said, relieved that I wasn't going crazy. Or at least, if I *was* going crazy, I wasn't alone. "What do you think's causing it?"

"I talked to Trickshot about it," Meleya said soberly. "She thinks it's the result of us being woken up from our stasis too early. The remedy hadn't fully completed its steeping cycle or some medical soot like that. She says the effects could last months or even longer."

I nodded, not upset to hear this. With any luck, I might get to see Mom again. That thought brought me hope and calmed my inner tumult.

"I'm sorry, Mel," I started. "Coming back from Etheria hasn't been easy, but I sure as stars didn't mean to hurt you."

At that, Meleya wrapped her arms around me in a tight embrace. I hugged her back, her comforting, bread-like smell filling my nostrils as I leaned into her hair. Relief filled me—I hated arguing with her.

"I'm sorry too," Meleya said. "It's like you said: this transition has been tough. Especially knowing that you'll be leaving for the Dragon Isles so soon. Kai told me—two days, right?"

"That's right," I said.

We held each other for a long moment, and I caught sight of the indigo of Meleya's aura over her shoulder. It was as striking as I remembered, though I could tell it was swirling with conflict.

As much as I wished they were, things really weren't as simple as we'd imagined they were while in Etheria. She knew that as well as I did, and only time would tell what our futures held.

At last, we released each other. Mel's tears had dried, and she even managed a soft smile.

Chapter 10: The Surprise

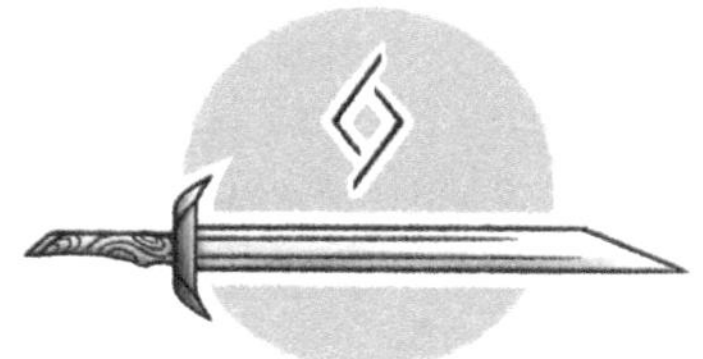

Meleya

Standing there on the Skyforge terrace, I watched Asher disappear back into the castle, his turquoise aura churning. Though I hadn't runetraced, a brief flash of residual Sight let me see just how stressed he was. I hated the fact that I'd added to it.

Looking over what Asher had done to the Skyforge dome, I couldn't help but be impressed. In my estimation, it looked even better than it had before. Asher really was gifted with starglass.

As I examined the intricate way he'd fused the starglass to the framework, my mind replayed our conversation. We'd both spoken out of frustration, sure, but I wondered if there was more truth in Asher's claims than I'd been willing to admit.

Was he right about Jax being gone? I didn't think so. I'd *seen* Jax's hesitation in Etheria—He was still in there somewhere. But while I knew how difficult it was to overcome a wraith's influence once it had taken over, I knew Asher was right: That didn't make Jax guiltless. After all, he was the one who'd handed the wraith control in the first place, just as I had back at the Mage Hunter Academy. And now, his path was his to choose alone.

As for Asher, his path was light. No matter what, I trusted him to never default on that. He was a true Knight of the Torch and a beacon to everyone around him, whether he realized it or not. Still, I had no idea what that meant for *us*. After all, this afternoon had made it abundantly clear that things between us weren't all sunshine, sky-daisies, and ethereal fun and games. I had no idea what I wanted, and clearly, neither did he.

I breathed a long sigh. Drak, it had been a hectic few days. Ever since Asher and I had woken from astral sleep, it had been nothing but medics, treatments and answering questions about the Haze. After talking with Kai I'd wanted to check in on Asher, but now, I knew what I needed to do next:

See my parents.

Sure, Dad had been there when Trickshot had woken us from astral sleep, and he'd stopped by the medical wing several times since then between his training sessions with the Knights of the Torch's steadily-growing, ragtag army. But I hadn't actually seen my mom since leaving Rhana's safehouse in the Mirror Forest. And after seeing the strong bond between Asher and Zerana, it was my turn to make the long overdue choice to make things right in my own family.

As one of the commanding officers of the Knights' army, my father had been offered his pick of some of the choicest rooms in the vast Orothion castle. But my parents had turned the offer down, instead choosing a modest cottage in the town just outside the walls and down the hill. I was glad.

The humble stone cottage was set near the city wall, a tangle of bramblevines climbing along its surface. A neatly swept cobblestone path led to the front door, which looked to have received a fresh coat of dusky red paint.

I'd only just raised my hand to knock when I was ambushed by a borderline-frenzied ball of gray fur and spines. Tiny, claw-like hands clung to my sleeve as a hailstorm of chitters rained down on me.

I laughed. "Come on, Dusty—I swear I came as soon as I was able!"

Dusty the draccoon, my father's ethereal familiar, narrowed his beady eyes and chittered his further disapproval.

"Well, I'm here now." I shrugged and Dusty scampered down my arm to hop onto the windowsill. He crawled through the gap and into the cottage. At the same time, the door swung open and there she was.

Mom's long hair was tied back into a braided bun with a pinkish-red prairie paintbrush flower tucked into it. She wore a comfortable dress with a lacy black shawl draped over her shoulders—a shawl I recognized as one she'd been given by my old Mage Hunter cadet friend, Shaya. Mom's large brown eyes shone brightly as she took in the sight of me.

"Meli," she said. "Meli, my darling. Welcome home."

With those two words, I breathed a contented sigh. I wasn't sure what I'd expected from Mom upon seeing me—the last few years had brought everything from worry and fear to pain and shame. But to see her simply smile and welcome me home... Stars, it filled my whole soul with relief.

Without further ado, Mom took my hand and pulled me right inside. The place wasn't large, only a couple of rooms and a combined kitchen-slash-living area, but Mom had done everything she could to make it special. And to my nomad sensibilities, it was all but an estate. There were pale green curtains in the windows, and even a potted flowering prickly pear on the sill beside where Dusty perched. Judging by the half-finished aldraka wool blanket laid over the back of a chair, Mom had taken up knitting. I wondered if Shaya was teaching her.

The sight of the little cottage warmed my heart. During our time traveling with the nomads, Mom had rarely fully unpacked her bags. This must've been the first time in ages where she really felt safe, stable, and at home.

Dad appeared and promptly wrapped me in a bear hug. "Good to have you here, Mels! Place just ain't a home without all of us together." As if in agreement, Dusty took a flying leap from the window sill and onto Dad's shoulder.

I smiled as I glanced beyond the pair of them toward the kitchen. It was small, but perfectly functional and well-supplied. And with the sun about to reach its zenith, I had no doubt my parents were as hungry as I was. I began to rummage through the cupboards to look for ingredients I could transform into something tasty.

I'd no sooner grabbed a jar of preserved peaches than Mom put a hand on my arm.

"Go on and sit down, Meli," she said fondly. "You don't need to cook for us."

"But I'm happy to—"

"Mels," Dad said, folding his arms. From Dad's shoulder, Dusty mimicked the gesture. "It's time for us to take care of *you* for once."

I thought about protesting again, but I could tell this was important to them. Obediently, I curled up on a wide, comfortable chair, then watched, smiling, as my parents bustled around the kitchen together.

As they worked, we talked. At first, our conversation was a little uneasy as, out of habit, I avoided topics that might upset Mom. It was what I'd had to do for years while in the Canyonlands guard so as not to set her off. But slowly, I began to realize that things had changed. She asked questions about our quest across Evgard from the safehouse to Orothion, and I shared about what we'd done to infiltrate the castle and reunite the fractured Knights. Before I knew it, I was telling Mom all about the beautiful, unforgettable things I'd seen in the spirit plane.

"The colors, Mom," I spoke animatedly. "They're beyond anything I could've ever imagined. The sky is a thousand shades of blue and purple. And the ley lines! Picture floating rivers of pure white ether racing over the landscape."

Mom beamed. "Incredible. Stars, I almost wish..."

She trailed off, but she didn't have to finish her sentence for me to know exactly what she was thinking. Mom had given up her ether well, handing herself over to the Mage Hunters to receive the 'magi cure.' Once, she'd been a Rifter like me, able to use the Sight to see the marvels of the spirit plane all around us. At first, she claimed to feel only relief about having lost her etherarchy. But now that the dust had settled, I wondered if she'd begun to feel the loss more keenly.

Dad put a hand on Mom's back and passed her a stack of bowls. Then she shook herself out of her reverie and served us up.

The breakfast-for-lunch meal was simple, fresh, and smelled divine. Warm, hearty porridge topped with pools of melting, golden butter, sweet honey, and a handful of plump, juicy dragonberries. Heat from the bowl warmed my face as I joined my parents at the table.

Only once we were all seated did I notice a fourth bowl had been set. It wasn't for Dusty either, since he'd returned to the window sill with a pile of stolen dragonberries. The draccoon tucked in while I cocked my head.

"Who's that bowl for?" I asked.

Both Mom and Dad turned toward the window, squinting. Dad frowned.

"Huh," he said. "That old rascal ain't normally this late. Wonder what's keeping him—"

"Ain't' gotta wonder no more!" an unseen voice made me jump, and I whirled around to see Boone letting himself in, half-heartedly tapping the door in an obligatory knock before he shut it behind him.

From there, the wiry old man marched himself over to the fourth chair, plopped down, and took a big bite of breakfast as if it were the most natural thing in the world.

"Mm-mm!" Boone said, swallowing. "If that don't just hit the spot, I ain't a scorchbeetle's uncle!"

I somehow doubted Boone bore any relation to scorchbeetles, but I couldn't help but chuckle. I'd met Boone for the first time during a chaotic battle for our lives atop Keep Rengard's Rise, but I remembered well his... *unique* way of expressing himself.

I looked to my parents, raising one eyebrow. Dad rushed to explain.

"You know that Boone'n I got close while transportin' them magi ex-prisoners from the Canyonlands to safety in the Mirror Forest. Well, since then, we've come to an agreement, us 'n' him."

Mom hurried to elaborate, an amused smile on her lips. "Your father's essentially adopted Boone as his honorary father."

"Woowee!" Boone hollered in agreement between bites. "I tell you what, there ain't been nothin' better for this ol' drakpat than havin' himself a family again. I thank you kindly for that, Ivar my boy."

"Hopefully you don't mind, Mels," Dad said, a slightly nervous look coloring his face.

I broke into a wide grin, then gave Boone the Evgardian soldier's salute, bringing my right fist to my opposite shoulder. "I've always wanted a grandpa."

"Drak-tootin'!" Boone whooped, then responded with a slightly less controlled version of the salute. "Us snowheads gotta stick together!"

We all laughed as we continued eating our porridge. Boone's presence felt more natural than I would have expected, and he and Dad chatted easily regarding plans for upcoming training for the soldiers.

"What about me?" I interrupted them. Both men looked at me with equal parts fatherly pride and fatherly concern, so I went on. "I'm a capable soldier. Where should I report to?"

"Oh, Mels." My father seemed to be at a loss for words. "You've already done more than enough. Not to mention you're already doing your part by keeping that voidshard tucked away in your rift hold."

"I know," I replied, trying to keep my mounting frustration under wraps. I thought about what Asher had said to Solrac the night before we'd left for the Haze, or how I'd felt upon walking through the initiation flames back at the safehouse cabin. Hadn't that been a promise to serve this cause? If I could help banish the Gray from this realm—to keep others from falling prey to wraithkind—I wanted to do it.

Fortunately, Dad seemed to grasp my feelings without my needing to actually say them aloud. "Have it your way. Report to the barracks first thing tomorrow, my darin' li'l darlin'."

"That's some granddaughter I done inherited!" Boone agreed. "Speakin' of, what'd she say when you told her the news?"

"News?" I asked.

Dad gave Boone a look. "We haven't told her yet."

I raised a dark eyebrow. "Told me what?"

All three of them looked at me with eager anticipation. Dad nodded to Mom.

Mom's gaze was filled with light as she set down her spoon. "Meli—you're going to be an older sister!"

It took me a few seconds to process what I'd just heard. But once I had, I leaped out of my chair and practically flew toward my mother to wrap her in a pointedly careful embrace.

"Mom, you're... This means... I'm going to have a..." I could hardly form a sentence, and Mom laughed with glee. Dad and Boone watched on, beaming.

For as long as I could remember, I'd wanted a brother or sister. I'd dreamed of it on those lonely days between nomadic caravans, and now... well, things wouldn't exactly be the same, what with an almost nineteen-year age gap between the two of us, but still. I could hardly believe it. What was more, this confirmed my suspicion that, for the first time probably ever, Mom felt safe. Confident enough to want to bring another child into the world, magi or not. That thought alone filled my heart so much it might've burst.

"I've been so eager to tell you, Meli," Mom started as I knelt beside her to put a hand on her belly. Sure enough, there was the tiniest bit of hard roundness there, visually imperceptible.

"When is the baby due?" I asked, and I couldn't help but notice as traces of worry crept into their otherwise gleeful faces.

"Sometime this spring," my father said meaningfully, and it took me a moment to realize what he meant.

"The convergence of the mythic stars," I breathed more than spoke. "That's when Solrac said the Soul Reaper will—"

"Solrac says a lotta things," Boone put in, then winked at me from across the table. I nodded back, appreciating the interruption. Some things were better left unsaid.

"Oh, Meli?" My mom summoned my attention. "There's been something I've been wanting to ask you. See, when I was expecting you, I used to runetrace, using the Sight so I could watch you. Your sweet little indigo aura was so bright, even then, and seeing the life within me, well, it put me at ease, knowing you were well. I wonder..."

She didn't have to finish—I was already runetracing. Etheria burst to life before my eyes, though not nearly as clearly as it had been only a few short days ago. Still, the auras of everyone in the room were clear enough: Dad's stalwart sage, Boone's the color of a duststorm at midday. Mom's was a beautiful muted mulberry, swirling around her like blooming spring flowers.

Something I saw around Mom's shoulders momentarily drew my attention. A white-gold halo shone there, looking almost like a protective shield, and something about its look felt familiar. At once, I realized it was very similar to the way Asher's scarf had appeared in Etheria. Fascinating... Whatever it was, it seemed to be emanating from Mom's black shawl.

But I couldn't dwell on that, for right near Mom's core was the tiniest, most delicate, perfect aura I'd ever seen.

"Green," I breathed. "Light, springy green, like a meadow of fresh grass."

Mom put a hand to her mouth, and Dad knelt beside her to pull her close while she remained in her chair. Even Dusty joined in, clinging to my upper arm and giving a cheery little chitter. Nearby, Boone beamed. There we stayed for a while, the colors of our auras spinning and weaving together in tight, familial bonds.

Stars, how I'd longed for this—My family, happy, whole, and together. Everything we'd been through had been worth it, if only for this moment.

Chapter 11: The Stars

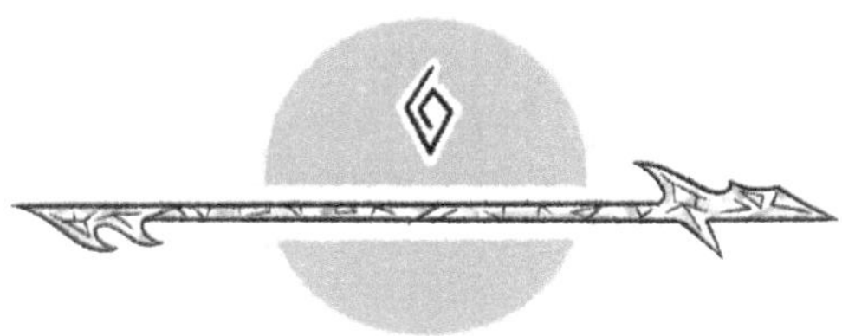

Asher

My nerves were out of control and I couldn't sit still for longer than half a second at a time. After all, we were going to the Dragon Isles in the morning.

Lucky for me, I had a mighty third ascension dragon bond to keep me company. And there was no better place to hide out than in Thorn's stall at the Orothion dragon stables.

Since his ascension, Thorn was *huge*. His proud stag antlers had nine points each now, and the once-coppery patterns along his neck, flank, and eyes now appeared in a dark, shining gold.

But despite all the changes we'd each been through, our bond remained as strong as ever. Laughing, I gripped Thorn's antlers as my dragon playfully wrenched me from side to side. While I'd been in Etheria, our connection had been down to embers, but now it was alive and well like a roaring bonfire.

"You missed me, huh Thorn?" I asked.

I sure did, Thorn replied through our bond. I sensed sincerity, but there was a hint of something more.

I narrowed my eyes. "*I sure did,*" I mimicked in my best Thorn voice. "What were you up to while I was in Etheria?"

Thorn's dragonfire eyes shifted left and right, then all of a sudden, he tossed his head to the side. I lost my grip on his antlers and went flying.

"Whoa!" I called out, activating my levitation and landing myself softly in a pile of hay.

Thorn gave a low wyvern chuckle. *Funny you should ask...*

He glanced sideways toward the entrance to the dragon stables. There, silhouetted in the fading daylight, was another wyvern standing shyly, watching Thorn expectantly. From her sleek pair of wings to her pale, reddish-gold scales, I recognized Rose instantly. Rose was the dragon bond of a fellow Knight of the Torch named Shaya, who must've arrived at Orothion while I'd been in astral sleep.

"Ahh," I said, returning to Thorn's side. "Let me guess—You want to have one last goodbye hunting trip with *her* before we head out to the Dragon Isles in the morning."

Thorn looked at me hopefully.

I laughed. "Well go on then, you big scalehead!"

Thorn gave a giddy roar, then swept toward Rose. Together, the pair of them left the stables and flew off together over the Scarlet Strait for what I hoped would turn out to be a very romantic fishing trip. At least, as romantic as sharing a naga or drakefish could be.

I was watching their silhouettes against the newly risen crescent moon when I heard footsteps approaching. Turning around, I saw my father heading my way, using a cane to feel for obstacles. The rune for the Sight was aglow over his forehead, so I knew he recognized my aura.

"I thought I'd find you here," Dad said.

"Dad!" I hurried over to him, ready to help guide him if needed. I knew he had no trouble getting around our house in Steel Rim, but Orothion wasn't home. Besides that, I'd harbored an extra layer of worry for him ever since Zel had held him captive, using him for his rifting abilities and pushing him beyond his limits. Gold veins no longer stood out along his tan skin, but streaks of gold still mingled with the gray of age along his hairline and temples, evidence of the ethereal trauma he'd been subjected to.

"Thought you were going to head overseas without saying goodbye, did you?" Dad raised a brow.

"Me? Never," I promised. "I just figured you were sick of me after listening to me complain about being stuck in the medical wing for the past two days."

Dad shrugged. "Trust me, I'll be wishing for your voice—complaints and all—in the coming weeks."

Dad's expression was teasing, but I could tell something serious was lurking just beneath the surface. Looking past him through the dragon stables doorway, I could see that the sun had now fully set, and there wasn't a cloud in the sky.

"Hey Dad," I started. "Do you want to... I mean, would you mind going stargazing with me?"

"What?" Dad's brow furrowed.

"I know the stars look different through ethereal eyes, but still. I thought you could show me some of the constellations and all that. You never know when some navigation skills might come in handy."

At that, Dad broke into the widest, crookedest grin I'd seen from him in years.

Soon, Dad and I were lying on our backs in the soft grass atop Orothion's cliffs, not far from where Mom, Meleya, Blink, and I had set up camp on the Etheria side. Sight rune burning over his forehead, Dad was animatedly gesturing to the starry sky overhead.

"Now, that constellation there is the Dragon. That's the first one you're going to want to be able to track. See its wings and serpentine tail?"

"I think so," I replied, imagining a fierce true dragon in flight overlaying the pinpoints of light. "It's the one with the big, bright star right on its chest, right?"

"Right on the heartscale, that's it!" Dad replied. "Now, keep one eye on the heartscale star while you see if you can spot Solei's Blade."

"A sword? What does it look like?"

"Four stars there make up the crossguard, with that row of seven branching out from it."

"I see it!"

"Perfect—Now, trace an imaginary line between the point of Solei's blade and the Dragon's heartscale. See the star right in between the two?"

"The extra bright one?"

"Aye! That's called 'the Anchor' on account of it's the only star in the sky that doesn't appear to move, no matter the time of year. If you can find the Anchor, you'll always know where you are and where you're headed."

I laughed. "Aye? Your old skyfall pirate days are coming back."

Dad gave me a little nudge with his elbow. "Hey, I told you, I'm no pirate. My crew and I were always working for highly reputable private funders."

"As were Kai and I." I winked, and Dad elbowed me harder. I hadn't seen him this relaxed since before we'd lost Mom.

"Stars," he sighed. "Would you just look at Streya's Comet? It's even more glorious than I imagined. One old skyseeker used to say seeing the comet as a child blessed him with long life and great posterity. I always hoped I'd get the chance to see it for myself."

There was a note of sorrow in Dad's voice, and I rushed to assure him, "You're getting the best view from the Ethereal side. Trust me."

That coaxed another smile out of him. "I wish I had my old sextant with me so I could teach you some real navigation skills. Haven't been able to use it for years, for obvious reasons. It's probably locked up in an old trunk somewhere back in Steel Rim."

"We'll have to go back for it one of these days," I assured him. "At least for now I've got this."

I unclipped the dagger from my belt and carefully passed it to Dad so that he could feel the familiar hilt. He sighed as memories washed over him.

"Ah, my old skyseeker's dagger. This thing and I saw many a skyfall site back in our day."

"Do you ever miss it?" I asked, "Skyseeking, I mean."

"Sometimes," Dad replied, still holding the knife built with an extra hook on the hilt to pry skystone from fallen meteors. "But that doesn't mean I have any regrets. When your Mom and I found out you were coming along, we wanted to settle down—Give you one place to grow up in and call home. For me, that meant saying goodbye to the crew and joining Steel Rim's miners. At first I didn't much like the work, I'll admit."

"What changed?" I asked. When Dad didn't answer right away, I turned in the grass to better see his strong profile. His neck was tense with emotion.

"I got a look at you, Asher, that's what," Dad finally said. "You were enough to get me singing on my way to the mine every day for the next fourteen years."

"Singing? You?" I teased.

Dad laughed. "Don't worry, I wouldn't have put my fellow workers through my singing—What I mean is, I suddenly had a reason to try. We didn't have much back home at our little hut in Steel Rim, but between you, me, and your mom... We had everything that mattered."

We lay there in silence for a long while. A light breeze blew through the grasses and tugged at my hair, and I knew both Dad and I were thinking about her. One glance at Dad and I could feel how much he missed her.

"Dad?" I finally asked.

"Yeah?" he replied.

"In Etheria, Mom told me a little bit about growing up in the Dragon Isles. Did she ever talk about that with you?"

"Not much," Dad admitted. "Zerana came to Evgard looking for a fresh start. Speaking of her past pained her, and I hated seeing her hurt so I never pressed. We started over when we got married, and never looked back. Why?"

"She mentioned her Life Path. Her *Elaaka Kuu*."

"Life Paths, aye, she spoke of that a time or two. They're the ideals Drekai pledge themselves to. She always intended to have you choose yours when you turned sixteen, but... Well."

"Mom said her path was Courage, but that she felt she'd failed it," I said, chewing my lip thoughtfully. "While we were in the spirit plane, she wanted to tell me something, and I think it had to do with that. I think that maybe she wanted me to fulfill her life path for her by showing courage during my duel in the Dragon Isles."

Dad turned to me, taking in the sight of my turquoise aura. "I know you will, my *zaaki*." Dad's heavy Evgardian accent as he used the Drekai word for 'son' brought a smile to my face.

Sighing, Dad said, "Hard to believe you'll be shipping out at dawn."

"Let me guess," I said, looking back up at the stars. "You don't want me to go. It's too dangerous and all that."

"No." Dad's reply came fast and vehement, and it took me aback. Dad was *always* worried about me, ever since Kai and I went on our first raid. Things had only gotten worse when I joined up with the Knights of the Torch, and with me about to sail off to a duel to the death with a seasoned Drekai general, and a powerful magi no less, I could hardly believe my scale-tipped ears.

"No?" I repeated.

"I can't hold onto you forever, Asher," Dad said. "Come to think of it, you've always been prone to soaring so high, I doubt I ever truly had ahold of you in the first place." Dad gave a light chuckle. "This duel started out as a hasty challenge made by a well-meaning boy. But when you go to the Dragon Isles, you'll be going as a man, and a worthy representative of the Knights of the Torch. You inspire people more than you realize, and it does my heart good to see you becoming a beacon of light—like your mother was. I only wish I could be there to see you kick that Drekai general's scales."

My heart swelled in my chest, as if I'd unknowingly been longing to hear those words for years. To know that my dad was proud of me.

"Why don't you come, Dad?" I asked. "Come to the Isles with me and see Mom's homeland. Well, 'see' in a manner of speaking."

He chuckled, but hesitated before responding. "I wish I could. But you'll need to travel fast and light to make up for lost time, and an old blind man like me would only slow you down."

"We'll be on a boat for most of the journey. It wouldn't be so—"

"Besides," Dad cut me off, "after this past year, I'm not sure these bones have another sea voyage left in them."

When I next looked at my father, I realized just how tired he was. Zel had put him through so much, using him to rift entire armies across hundreds of miles at a time, all for a corrupt cause. He wasn't all that old, but he'd borne enough burdens to fill multiple lifetimes.

"The Knights need me here anyway—Solrac wouldn't last a week without my rift anchors." He smirked, then palmed my head and ruffled my hair. "And as for you... I know that your path, whatever you choose to make of it, is one that would make any father proud."

Dad couldn't see the tears welling up in my eyes, but I saw the ones in his. I wasn't above embracing my father as we sat together in a peaceful silence, watching the skies.

"Have courage, my son," Dad said. "Courage to choose light, even if it means risking everything."

Overhead, the stars winked down at us. I wasn't having one of my strange Sight flashes and with my physical eyes, they were simple, bright spots of white light. But now I'd seen the night sky with my ethereal eyes, and I knew Dad was seeing so much more. A vast tapestry painted with thousands of multicolored lights, burning with a fire that would last through the ages.

Looking up, it was hard not to feel small. But it was also impossible to feel alone.

A whole slew of well-wishers met our party at Orothion's front gates at dawn. The sun had only just started peeking over the mountains to the east, but already I'd endured lengthy goodbyes from Kai and Kari, Ivar, and so many other Knights I'd lost count. Old, wrinkled Boone saw me off with a bone-crushing hug followed by a thump on the back so hard it nearly knocked the wind out of me.

"Just remember your trainin', m'boy," Boone said in his heavy drawl. "You do that, and you'll be sittin' prettier'n a scaly pronghorn just got his antlers shined, you hear?"

"I hear," I confirmed, placing my hands on either side of my head and using my thumbs and first two fingers to mimic a scaly pronghorn's antlers.

Boone approved, then left to bid the rest of our group farewell. Some diplomatic representatives from the Knights of the Torch, including Rasec, Trickshot, and others, along with a few guard-types stood in a cluster with Solrac nearby. Solrac was giving Vidya a long embrace. He would be traveling in disguise, since the bounty out on the Farseer's head was one even the most loyal of ship captains would be hard-pressed to ignore.

But as the Farseer, Solrac's presence in the Dragon Isles would be vital to securing a potential alliance, while Vidya's would only cause trouble. I knew firsthand that the Drekai were *not* fans of the Black Valkyrie, and besides that, with her wraith still bound to her soul, it was best she stayed at Orothion where she wasn't susceptible to any more advances from the Gray Ones. Word of what had happened on the Rise had reached Meleya and me in the medical wing, and I shuddered at the thought of Vidya facing off against the crazy, wraith-bound Queen of the Canyonlands. Honestly, it felt only fitting that a noble had undermined her own people like that.

Then again, the news about Brigan had me thinking exactly the opposite: Maybe nobles weren't so bad. If anyone was born to lead, it was him. Stars, I could hardly imagine what he must've been going through.

Over Solrac's shoulder, Vidya's gaze met mine and she gave me a single nod. The sight of her still brought mixed feelings, but I nodded back.

Thorn stood nearby, nose to nose with the lovely lady-wyvern, Rose, and a crooked smile appeared on my face as I watched them say goodbye. Near them was Aurora, the majestic, white true dragon who'd caused such a stir both in the Dragon Isles and here in Evgard. Aurora blinked with interest at all the hubbub, and most Knights that passed her inclined their heads with reverence.

Then Aurora shifted, revealing a pair of young women chatting behind her. The sight of them made my heart lurch first into my stomach, then down to my feet.

One was Meleya, who was—for whatever reason—holding an enormous, lumpy burlap sack. The other was Elle.

Where Meleya's long white hair was tied back in its usual scaletail braid, Elle wore her dark hair long and flowing. Meleya's head was bare while a gleaming golden tiara brought out the amber of Elle's eyes. Meleya's slim, athletic form donned light dragonleather armor in the nomadic style over her tunic and pants, while Elle wore a long, white, armored dress accented with Aurora's shed scales. A deep purple flower poked out of her hair, and a matching sash encircled her waist.

Both young women were so different, yet both were like brilliant, shining stars. I had to admit, each of them looked undeniably beautiful.

And scorch if the sight of them laughing together didn't put me on edge. Through my bond with Thorn, I felt a spark of amusement.

How do you always manage to get yourself into these situations? he emoted to me.

I don't get myself *into them,* I protested. *Things just... happen.*

Right.

What should I do, Thorn?

Oh, this wyvern's staying out of this one. All on you, Asher.

On that unhelpful note, my bond emotionally abandoned me, leaving my pulse racing as Elle and Meleya spotted me watching and started pointing my way. My foot started tapping madly, and I gave them the goofiest salute I could muster. Meleya rolled her eyes and Elle laughed harder.

Then they exchanged a few more words I couldn't hear before Elle went to bid farewell to a group of eager Knights. Meanwhile, Meleya started making her way toward me, hefting that ridiculous burlap sack in both arms.

"Meleya of Misthaven." I gave a melodramatic bow to hide my nerves. The pair of us hadn't spoken since our argument on the Skyforge terrace.

"Asher of Steel Rim," she replied.

"First off," I said, "what in the stars is *that?*"

I pointed at the sack, and she grunted as she carefully set it down and opened the top to reveal several smaller sacks, then rifled through them until at last she produced one that had been labeled 'Asher'.

"Lunch and dinner for each of you heading out," Meleya said. "Just a few sandwiches, as well as flatbread filled with sauteed dragonbeef and peppers."

"Ghost pepper?" I asked with a wink.

Meleya smiled. "No. I know you wouldn't be able to handle it. In fact, I put some ghost pepper powder on one of my test flatbreads, and even *I* couldn't handle it. I'll have to think of something to do with the rest."

Mel's face screwed up as she recalled trying the extremely spicy pepper powder, and I laughed.

"Stars." I shook my head. "I don't know what we did to deserve you, but I'm glad. Thanks for the food, Mel."

"You're welcome."

A moment of silence passed between us. It started off relaxed, but quickly grew tense. Dread began to creep up inside me as I realized it was time to continue the conversation we'd started on the Skyforge terrace. Part of me wanted to hover-dash away, but I knew Meleya deserved better than that.

"Asher..." Meleya swallowed. "What happened in Etheria was..."

"Ethereal?" I supplied.

She nodded and wrung her hands. "Something I'll never forget for as long as I—"

"—live?" I finished.

She glared at me. "Is that mouth of yours capable of shutting up for *one* second?"

"Oh, I can shut up," I assured her. "I can shut up so well you won't even know what hit you. You'll say, 'Wow, I had no idea Asher was so good at shutting that mouth of his. We should give him some kind of reward to commemorate—'"

At that point, Meleya threw up her hands and started to walk away. I reached out to stop her, taking hold of her wrist, and she stopped in her tracks.

I let go, then silently mouthed 'sorry.'

Warily, Meleya continued. "I'm still mulling over everything that happened in Etheria. Between us, and otherwise..."

I nodded. I was still figuring out what I felt too. The fact that Meleya had actually met my mother, gotten to spend time with her, and even win her approval might've pushed our relationship forward more quickly than either of us had anticipated. That said, I knew we shared something deep and undeniable. Only time would tell how that might manifest.

"That said," Meleya went on, "there are a few things we should probably talk about before you go."

I grimaced. "You mean... him?"

Meleya grimaced too, and I knew she understood exactly which steely-haired, wraith-bound traitor I was talking about. She looked almost sick, and I couldn't blame her. Even thinking of the way she'd defended Jax in Etheria made my blood begin to boil all over again. I was still angry, both at Jax and—if I was being honest—a little at Mel too.

"Actually," Meleya murmured. "This time, I meant *her*."

At the same time, both Meleya and I looked over to find Elle standing before a crowd of starstruck well wishers, smiling and curtsying at all the right moments as they bade her and our entire entourage farewell. She was the picture of leadership. A perfect princess.

"You know as well as I do that Elle and I are history," I said. "She's said so to my face. Multiple times!"

Meleya was shifting from foot to foot. She had something to say on that score, that much was clear. But for whatever reason, the words refused to tumble out.

"It's not over," Meleya finally spoke. "Not for her, at least."

I was completely taken aback. "What?"

"She still has feelings for you," Meleya rushed, as if afraid that if she didn't speak quickly enough, she might not get the words out. "In fact, it's *because* Elle cares for you that she pushed you away. She doesn't want to trap you in the kind of life she's bound to live as a true dragon rider and a royal."

"But—"

"Asher, look—" She cut me off. "I know you can do anything you set your mind to, and right now that means winning this duel against General Kheradok. I think you're stronger than some people give you credit for—including yourself. I've seen how you've grown through your training with Rhana, Boone, my dad, even me, and there's no one else I'd rather have fighting for our future in your place. Whatever you decide to do with your life after that, I'll always be rooting for you, even if it's something as simple as trying not to make a complete fool of yourself at court. Or... a life that's a little more humble."

Her eyes darted to mine and she smiled briefly before turning away. "I guess I'm just saying that I don't think either of us should feel beholden to what happened between us in Etheria. I don't know what the future holds for any of us, and I sure as the void don't think anything's over. But... well, fate is a pen we all wield for ourselves. So, by the stars, take fate by the reins and fly."

For a long moment, she stared at me, as if waiting for me to say something. Something that might push either of us to make a decision, one way or the other.

But I had nothing, not even a joke or quippy reply.

"Huh." Meleya cracked a smile. "I guess that mouth of yours *is* capable of shutting up for a second."

Then, she took a few steps closer to me, stood on her tiptoes, and kissed me on the cheek.

"Goodbye, Asher. And good luck," Meleya said.

That was enough to whisk me back to my senses. I shook myself out of my stupor and pulled her into a tight embrace.

"Thank you, scale-in the mud," I whispered.

"You too, scarf-wearer." She gave me one final squeeze. "Come back in one piece, okay?"

"Would two or three be acceptable?"

"No."

"Got it. Just checking."

Just then, there was a whistle. It was Solrac, signaling us all that it was time to go. Meleya hurried off to stow our sandwiches while I joined Solrac and the others near the dragons and kirin that would ferry us to the longship.

Solrac gave me a nod. "Ready, my half-born companion?"

I gave a salute. After all, I was merely on my way to a realm-shattering duel across the sea. What was the worst that could happen?

I die, I thought grimly.

Then again, after my time in Etheria, death no longer seemed all that final. Once, I'd seen it as a terrifying end. But now...

Now, I thought, squaring my shoulders as I mounted my dragon, *I'd much rather die fighting for something I believe in than live standing for nothing at all.*

And with that, I patted Thorn's flank and, together, we took to the skies.

Fragment: Streya's Comet

Jax

The Gray Knight stood with the rest of the Soul Reaper's core followers, overlooking the vast, stony plain. In the distance, he could see the silhouette of the High Citadel atop the cliffside where an elaborate network of waterfalls cascaded into the Ridgeback River. The black and white castle was grand, as was the great city sprawling around it.

But out here in the foothills overlooking the stony plain, the earth was already becoming foggy and gray thanks to the ever-encroaching Haze. Jax remembered being in a Haze on the Etheria side, where the darkness was obvious. Here in the Capital Keepdom, however, the netherstones—recently restored to the physical plane—performed their work more subtly. The gray radiated from each dark monument, causing the plants, animals, and even the earth underfoot to pale, little by little. It wouldn't be long before it reached the Capital Keep, suppressing every last ounce of light still fighting to shine out beyond its walls.

It all made Jax sick. But as for the Gray Knight, Calyx ensured he observed it all with utter indifference.

In the higher foothills across the way stood about thirty masked members of the Coven of the Gray Ones. Jax knew that each one of them was a Psion, some born with the power while others only wielded it thanks to a transplanted ether well from a true magi.

At the highest peak overlooking the stony plane stood the Soul Reaper himself, silhouetted against the darkening sky. His features were shrouded by night, but Jax could make out his robes, tattered to threads at the bottom to mimic the look of the misty lower half of the Gray Ones.

Bound to the most powerful wraith of all, the Soul Reaper's sinister energy seemed to emit from him as his eyes glowed with fractured sapphire light. In his hands, he wielded a mighty longsword with a starry hilt. The Veilblade.

The army of Coven Psions looked to the Soul Reaper, awaiting his signal. As a Psion himself, Jax did the same, as did a handful of others with telekinetic powers among the elites, though this latter group sat on dragonback in the more secluded foothills, far removed from where the danger would be.

Not far from where Jax sat on the back of his green evren, Jade, Ilyan eagerly anticipated the Soul Reaper's signal. The former lieutenant of Jax's mother, the Black Valkyrie, preferred to be called by his more sophisticated moniker, 'the Overseer', but Jax and many of the others called him Snake Eyes, thanks to the thick, silvery snake familiar draped in its usual place over his shoulders. He was on dragonback as well, though Jax could tell by the way the drake's short ears flattened back against its head that the creature wasn't especially happy with this arrangement. Beneath Jax, his evren shifted and snorted as she watched the dragon, forced into a bond with a rider she hadn't chosen.

Snake Eyes had always been a skilled Seer, but his psionic ether well was a recent addition. Thanks to High King Magnus's recent mandate that all unregistered magi were to report to Evyndara to receive the magi cure, there were plenty of ether wells to go around. The cure, of course, was no cure at all, but rather a veiled excuse for the Soul Surgeon to consolidate more power for his followers. With rewards posted for each new magi brought in, the Surgeon had kept busy, performing more soul surgeries whenever the moon was at its fullest.

While the very thought of the Surgeon's treachery made Jax sick, it made Calyx hungry. He'd even tried to push Jax to ask the Surgeon for another ether well, against which contingency Jax had fought the hardest. Still, Jax wasn't sure how much longer he could resist. Accepting Calyx's bond was supposed to ease his pain, but instead Jax found his very soul growing more and more exhausted with every passing day.

Ilyan, on the opposite scale, had had no trouble accepting his second ether well. He openly aspired to become the supreme Mystic, eventually hoping to acquire all three Mystic ether wells: Seer, Psion, and Rifter. He'd need to be patient about getting his hands on a Rifter's well, since there weren't exactly a lot of Rifters running around free anymore—and the ones who were were naturally quite difficult to catch. But the Coven swore they had just the Rifter's well in mind for Ilyan the Overseer—they were just waiting for its current owner to finish some dark task for them.

While Snake Eyes was a skilled Seer, Jax had thus far been unimpressed with his ability to channel his new psionic voidarchy. But tonight they needed every ounce of telekinesis they could get.

Down on the stony plain marched a platoon of Capital soldiers in black and white cloaks, their weapons drawn and ready. For now, they were alone there, but soon...

Jax narrowed his eyes skyward. In the west, he could already see Streya's Comet, a faraway ball of fiery green streaking across the darkness. The massive, legendary skyfall passed Evgard once every century, but tonight, that would change.

From his superior vantage point, the Soul Reaper watched the comet as well. Any minute now.

"Glad to see you're back in time for this, Gray Knight."

Jax grimaced as he turned to the Mage Hunter beside him. Bjorn of Skullheim looked as manic as ever, from his mohawk to his wild eyes. Having proven himself loyal to the Gray, Bjorn had recently undergone his first soul surgery, and now sported a Geomancer's silvermark on his left cheek.

Jax found Bjorn's acceptance of the mark both disturbing and hypocritical. Bjorn loathed magi, yet now, he'd become one. The one time Jax asked him about it, he'd said that, the way he saw it, voidarchy wasn't the same as etherarchy.

One drew dragons. The other drew wraiths.

Just then, a feral snort emitted from Bjorn's forcibly bonded dragon. The beast was monstrous, from its fully sapphire eyes to the blue cracks covering its scales like bolts of jagged lightning.

The sight of it chilled Jax to the bone. This wasn't the first empowered, umbral dragon Jax had encountered. While wild dragons typically behaved like any other wild animal when poisoned by umbral venom, *bonded* dragons usually behaved the same way a human suffering from the shadow wasting would. Rather than becoming savage, bonded dragons went first numb, then hollow once the sickness penetrated their hearts.

Back when Jax had been on assignment with Boone in Ghost Lake, they'd glimpsed the dark experiments transpiring within the lake town's Mirror Sanctum. They'd found Mage Hunters inside, working to umbralize dragons while they were still in their shells, then forcing them into bonds once they'd hatched. The result was savage, soulless dragons, wholly subservient to their riders. Jax found the practice despicable, which was why he, Solrac, and the others had destroyed the Sanctum as part of their heist in Ghost Lake. It seemed that while the building had collapsed, the secrets it held regarding the creation of umbral dragons remained.

When Jax didn't reply, Bjorn continued. "Although, we heard even you failed to get the Soul Reaper's voidshard back from that drakking snowheaded ethercursed."

Jax wanted to snap at Bjorn for talking about Meleya that way, but Calyx held his tongue.

From Jax's other side, riding an umbral dragon bond of her own, Jaira chimed in. "The Surgeon was *very* displeased. Here we were thinking you were special for having bonded one of the Elder Wraiths."

Jaira's tone was darkly gleeful on the surface, but that only thinly veiled her deep-seated jealousy. While Jaira had once been wraith-bound, she'd lost her Gray One. Jax knew she hoped to bond another soon, but she was waiting for one of sufficiently high caliber.

"Perhaps forces greater than the Gray are conspiring against the Surgeon, keeping him from acquiring the voidshard. It is, after all, the last artifact he needs, is it not?"

Mason Drakeslayer's words surprised Jax. The High Prince sat on the back of his navy drake, Cosmos, as he tossed his blond curls out of his eyes. The prince's drake eyed Bjorn's umbral mount with distaste, as did Mason himself. Bjorn's unfortunate dragon had been muzzled, and tightly at that, the straps digging into his face in a way that had to've been painful, even for a mount of lesser sentience. Mason looked up and, for the briefest second, he and Jax made eye contact, as if they were both thinking the same thing but remained powerless to stop it.

No, you cannot, Calyx affirmed in Jax's mind, making Jax feel mentally smothered. *Just as that dumb dragon now belongs to Bjorn, you belong to me.*

As they waited for the comet to reach the proper position, Ilyan began making small talk with Jaira, Mason, and Bjorn. Jax tuned them out until, amidst his pretentious drivel, Ilyan said something that piqued his attention:

"...clearly King Brigan is too young and inexperienced to unite the rest of the Canyonlands to his ill-conceived notions—"

"Sorry—" Jax interrupted. "Did you say *King* Brigan?"

"That's right, Gray Knight," said Snake Eyes. "Much transpired while you were in Etheria."

Mason Drakeslayer cleared his throat.

Heir Duke of Solhelm once was he,
From fourth house straight to majesty
Chaos now spans the Canyonlands' sprawl
Since that fateful day of the Rise's Fall

Jax had always hated Mason's poems, but there was a smattering of applause from Ilyan, Jaira and a few other listeners. Gone was Jax's fleeting feeling of camaraderie with the arrogant High Prince.

Meanwhile, Jax's mind was reeling as they continued their conversation. According to Ilyan and Mason, High King Magnus was unfazed by Brigan's—that is, *King* Brigan's—soot, that just sounded wrong—declaration that henceforth Rengard would ally itself with the Knights of the Torch. Between the dual scourges of endless skyfalls and the relentless shadow wasting, Magnus felt certain that Evgard's southernmost keepdom would soon tear itself apart, then come crawling back to the Great Uniter on its hands and knees.

"My twin sister, Queen Ilona, performed her part well to the last," Ilyan said with pride. "The Canyonlands will likely never recover. Even now, rogue groups of dragonslayers band together, plotting to overthrow the foolish young king. I hope they succeed."

"Go to the void," Jax spat, automatically coming to his old squadmate's defense, in spite of their prior rivalry. But the brief moment of self was quickly overcome by Calyx forcing Jax back into silent complacency.

Ilyan turned up his nose at Jax, and when he next spoke, his voice was doubled with his wraith's. "The Builder's chosen host seems less... sophisticated than in ages past. I certainly hope he'll be compliant when we go to the Dragon Isles."

"He will be," Calyx overtook Jax's voice to assure his fellow wraith. Ilyan smiled back through wine-stained teeth.

Just then, a flash of blue-tinged dreamweave energy lit up the foothills and stony plain below. That was the Surgeon's signal—It was time for perhaps the most ambitious feat of psionics in the history of Evgard.

In perfect synchronization, every Psion runetraced. Jax's finger trailed the same blue light as the others, before they stretched out their hands toward the ancient, green-tailed comet streaking across the night sky.

Then, all together, the Psions *pulled.*

Jax instantly felt the bone-shaking jolt. His every muscle strained, and from his place nearby, Ilyan even began to tremble badly.

Many of the other Psions were shaking as well, and for a moment, Jax felt certain that even their combined might wasn't going to be enough to yank the comet from its course. But then, there came a shift in the air.

Standing atop the peak, the Soul Reaper at last lit up his psionic rune and held the legendary Veilblade high. The length of the Veilblade glowed with power, bright gold runes shining like starlight.

The hum from Streya's ancient weapon was palpable, and the tension in Jax's muscles eased slightly. At the same moment, the great green meteor tilted sharply.

Jax's heart began to pound at the sight of the millenia-old star at last falling. The promise of essentially infinite skystone was at their fingertips. Down in the stony valley, the soldiers readied themselves to fight the wild dragonkind that would surely hatch from the ensuing crater.

Drak... Jax could hardly believe it was working! He and the other Psions almost had it perfectly aligned to land safely in the valley before them—just far enough to withstand the impact, but still close enough to reach the skystone before too many dreklings could hatch and—

Woosh! A shockwave of pure violet dream energy erupted from the peak on which the Soul Reaper stood. The Veilblade twisted out of his grasp, as if suddenly imbued with psionic might of its own. It was resisting its wielder, with noble golden etherarchy refusing to mingle with the corrupted blue voidarchy.

As the Soul Reaper lost control of the Veilblade, the strain on the other Psions became overwhelming and Streya's Comet twisted off its forced course. No longer bound for the stony plain, it was heading straight toward the foothills.

Right where Jax and the rest of the Soul Reaper's elite forces were standing.

Green flashed, and panicked screams rose from the supposedly 'safe' place where Jax and the other elites stood. Dragons roared, some trying to dive away while others were forced by their selfish bonds to attempt to shield their riders from the oncoming comet.

As the heat from the rogue skyfall warmed his cheeks, Jax felt a surge of panic—Not for himself, but for Jade. While part of Jax felt he was deserving of the comet's fiery wrath, his dragon was innocent. His thoughts raced, searching for any possible way to save her...

A roar of thunder more powerful even than the noise of the comet flowed through Jax and Jade's bond. She stood her ground. Even if Jade somehow *could* have escaped with her life, she wouldn't abandon Jax the same way so many others had before her. Tremendous gratitude for his last real friend filled Jax as her power surged through his veins.

Jax may have had an affinity for working out, but he knew there was no way he could shift the immeasurable momentum of a centuries-old falling star alone. Still, rune blazing above his forehead, Jax thrust his hands outward toward the massive celestial rock.

Jax cried out from the strain, but didn't dare back down. He could feel Jade continuing to lend him her strength as he pushed with all his might. His ether well was draining fast.

It wasn't enough to push Streya's Comet a safe distance away. But rather than impact those gathered on the foothills directly, Jax was miraculously able to spin it so that it landed at the base of the foothills. A shockwave, accompanied by a ripple of emerald smoke, swept outward from the spot, violently knocking Jax and the others down.

Debris flew, and only Jax's quick telekinesis kept him from getting hit by a cascade of fiery rock. Nearby, he saw that High Prince Mason had activated some simple portal to keep him and his drake safe as well.

The rest of the elites were not so lucky.

Groans and cries sounded all around Jax, and he saw that many of his companions and their dragons were lying still. Bjorn's umbral dragon lay dead, having been forced to block Bjorn from the worst of the explosion. Bjorn himself lay unconscious but breathing, though his side looked badly burned. Sentinel markings lit his skin as his new regenerative abilities kicked in. Ilyan wasn't in great shape either, his leg having been smashed by a large boulder. In fact, Jax and Mason were the only ones still standing.

Jax's temples were throbbing from the use of so much etherarchy. Still, he found himself drawn to the newly formed, enormous skid mark that was the path the comet had carved in the earth on its way down. Likewise, Mason and Cosmos bravely took off toward the skyfall site to get the first look at the ancient comet.

Jax's evren, Jade, spread her four wings, and together they glided after them along the fissure. When the comet itself came into view, Jax gasped.

The sheer amount of skystone dotting the huge comet was dazzling. He'd seen skyfalls before, even ones that were abundant with skystone, but this... this put them all to shame. Through his bond with Jade, Jax sensed her hunger as the blinding white ether in the stones shone in her emerald eyes. For whatever reason, there wasn't a drekling egg in sight.

The pair alighted, and Jax slipped from Jade's back just as Mason and Cosmos disappeared around the skyfall's opposite side. Jax could sense Jade's hunger for the skystone, but she stopped herself just before lunging to take a bite; after all, to take in the skystone would mean her immediate advancement from second to third ascension.

If that happened, Jade thought, *I would only become a more powerful tool in the hands of the Gray.*

Jax knew it was true, and the guilt hit him hard. Calyx, on the opposite scale, had his own take on the matter:

All of the skystone must be for the Wraith King, he whispered in Jax's mind. *And us. You and I, Jax. It is as I promised—Together, we will build the greatest monument this realm has ever seen.*

Calyx's laughter was so deep Jax had to fight to keep it from manifesting through him. It thundered in Jax's mind, and he threw off his helmet, then pressed his hands against his temples in a futile attempt to silence it.

"Jax... *Jax!*"

The sound of his name jarred Jax. When he looked up, he was surprised to find the earnest face of High Prince Mason.

"Drakeslayer?" Jax said. "What're you—"

"You're not like the others, are you?" Mason rushed to insert.

"Huh?"

"You're not, I can tell. Quick—Think of something happy."

"What?" Jax's brow knit. Maybe he *had* hit his head on some debris. Either him or the High Prince.

"Think of something happy," Mason repeated, this time more urgently. "It banishes your wraith, if only temporarily, and seems to blur their memory as well. Trust me and do it now—There's no time."

Jax was still confused, but he immediately recalled one day when he was young, probably about fourteen or so. He was still living with Torsten in the tavern, the Naga's Head, but that day was one of those precious few when Solrac had come to take him away from that awful place.

Together, they'd traveled by winged kirin all the way across the Scarlet Strait to a beach near one of the Knight's safehouses on the northwestern shore of Rengard. Once there, Solrac and Jax had spent hours on the beach practicing psionics, lighting up runes, then hurling stones as far along the shore as they could, His Majesty the bloodhusky darting after them.

Solrac's praise of Jax's skill and His Majesty's eager tackles filled Jax's mind. Their presence was so expansive that, sure enough, Jax soon felt Calyx being forced to retreat, momentarily banished to the nether regions of the spirit plane.

Jax inhaled. His mind was quiet.

"Soot," Jax said as the lightness and clarity set in. "You were right."

Mason Drakeslayer nodded, and in his eyes Jax could see the same clarity, not usually present in the High Prince.

Just as misery draws dark in
So too, joy repels its sin.

"It's the only thing that's kept me sane," Mason went on. "But we have to hurry—We only have moments before others get here and see for themselves."

"See what?" Jax asked.

"Look."

Mason beckoned for Jax and Jade to follow as he and his drake led them to the other side of the meteor. While the first side had been peppered with skystone, this one was chock-full of...

"Dragon eggs?" Jax said. That much was certain—These weren't the craggy, lumpy shells of dreklings Jax had encountered numerous times before.

"Not just any dragon eggs," Mason said. "Do you recognize the shells?"

Jax racked his brain, trying to recall the distinctions between the various types of dragon eggs. Drake eggs were supposed to be scaled, wyvern eggs were leathery, and evren eggs looked almost like crystal. But these were different from any of those, their tiny scales crystalline in nature, each egg giving off a pearly, effervescent glow.

Jax's eyes widened. "Are these *all* true dragon eggs?"

Mason's urgency increased. "We can't let the Gray get their hands on these. They would do to them what they've done to Bjorn's umbral bond and so many others." At that, both Jade and Mason's drake, Cosmos, growled low in their throats. Jax knew Mason was right.

"But what can we do?" Mason despaired. "Even if we could get them out, there's no time to hide them—"

Jax set his jaw. "You're a Rifter, right?"

Mason frowned. "I suppose, but my power is severely limited. The ether well was a transplant, and while it revived me from the brink of death, it is incredibly weak, and despite all my training I still—"

"Trace this rune," Jax cut him off, kneeling down to draw a symbol in the dirt. It was a Rifter's rune he knew well—He'd seen Meleya draw it a hundred times, each time she'd accessed her rift hold.

Mason's brow furrowed with concentration as he reproduced the rune. The High Prince's expression twisted with the effort of opening and expanding the hold, but his determination outmatched his weakness.

Meanwhile, Jax raced to psionically pry each egg from the stone. While he couldn't move the eggs directly—psionics didn't work on living things—he could manipulate the rock holding the vast clutch in place on the ancient meteor. Jade and Cosmos helped too, lending their riders strength while carefully prying the eggs from the skyfall with their claws. Before long, Mason was closing his rift hold, now filled with a prize equal in worth to the vast horde of skystone on the other side.

Both Mason and Jax were exhausted. Already Jax could hear the Soul Reaper's force approaching the skyfall. Tonight, they would claim the greatest trove of skystone the realm had ever seen. Jax's wraith would be back at any moment, blissfully unaware of his and Mason's defiance. As drained as he was, Jax doubted he'd be able to resist Calyx taking over when he arrived.

To keep up appearances, both Jax and Mason began gathering skystone. But Jax took comfort in knowing that somewhere deep, deep within him, he was still capable of the smallest flicker of light.

CHAPTER 12: OROTHION

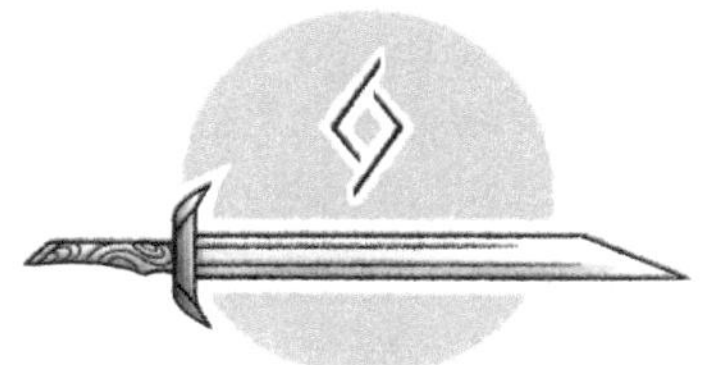

MELEYA

With so much to fill my time, the following weeks sped quickly by. As strange as it seemed, I loved falling back into the familiar routine of a soldier, waking up early to run drills alongside others preparing to fight for the same cause as me.

For the time being, I'd moved into my parents' extra room. At first I'd struggled to decide whether to live with them or at the barracks. The thing that ultimately convinced me that I'd made the right call was seeing Mom wave to Dad, Boone, and me as we came home at the end of my first day. Her face was bright as she eagerly served us the dinner she'd prepared. Afterward, I even helped her bake up some dessert.

When I wasn't at the training grounds outside the stronghold, I was with Sniff. He and I spent long hours on the outskirts of the redwood forest within Orothion's borders, me scrounging for mushrooms and berries while he hunted drakalope or gopherdrakes.

I needed those extra moments with my energetic evren. Not only had I missed him during my time in Etheria, but he was the only one under the stars who felt Blink's loss as keenly as I did.

Is she really gone forever, buddy? I asked him one day through our bond.

Sniff had replied by flying a loop, landing at my feet with his tail wagging and dragonfire green eyes shining. *Trrring! Not forever.*

You think?

Not think. Know.

That had gotten me smiling, feeling the first ray of hope I'd felt for Blink since her sacrifice at the netherstone. I gave Sniff a scratch behind his foxlike ears, then used rifting to throw a tree branch as far as I could see within the city's outer wall. Panting all the while, Sniff took off after it like a shooting star.

Meanwhile, Orothion bustled with activity. Diplomats came and went, passing through the town on their way to the castle. Elle's parents, who'd stayed on after the fateful banquet to help things settle, returned to Drakfell with the promise that they'd visit again soon. The royal family of Skygard, including Lady Vesta, eventually left Orothion to go back home to Keep Skygard, too. I was part of the group of soldiers that saw them off, and both Lady Vesta and Lady Annika saluted me on their way out.

Work continued on repairing the Skyforge dome on the terrace atop Orothion's tallest spire. They had a whole group of Astromancers forging skystone-infused starglass to try and patch it up, but there was nothing they could do to fix the etherlock since the Guardian-era technology had been lost. Kai's sister, Kari, spent a lot of time studying it, but even she hadn't been able to replicate its power quite yet.

Luckily, the other smaller etherlocks set all along the citadel wall were enough to keep the area safe from wraiths and wild dragons. Despite that, I did my best to keep a vigilant lookout for Xan and other Gray One activity, not wanting to take any risks as I safeguarded the Soul Reaper's voidshard.

Occasionally I'd see Vidya, though she kept mostly to herself, staying in her chambers and studying from books she'd borrowed from the castle's old library. I knew without asking that she was searching for information on how to sever her bond with her wraith. She secluded herself in Solrac's chambers for hours, sometimes days at a time, and I often found myself bringing her dinner just so that she'd remember to eat.

"Thank you, Meleya," Vidya said one day when I showed up bearing a steaming plate of fall-apart cattledrake roast with savory carrots and potatoes. She invited me in, already scarfing down her first bites as she shut the door behind me.

"Find anything today?" I asked as I took a seat in an excessively lush armchair. Solrac's taste in decor was evident throughout the fancy-yet-comfortable castle rooms.

Vidya found a place for her plate atop a desk that was strewn with books, scrolls, and even a few ancient clay tablets. "Most writing on how to attain voidarchy was destroyed by the Guardians before they died out—Trust me, I know. I spent too long searching for scraps of information like a drakking dragonmut hunting bones. Bones laced with poison," Vidya spat, taking a few more bites before going on. "Unfortunately, this also means most of the knowledge our people might've once had regarding voidarchy's *destruction* is gone along with it. There are myths regarding the scorching Everflame, of course, but nothing solid. Nothing real."

"I'm so sorry," I said.

Vidya sighed as she stuck out her chin. "Here, within the confines of the etherlocks, is the only place I'm safe. Or rather, the only place everyone else is safe from *me*."

I almost reminded her that I was in the same position myself, but instead I merely watched as she reached for the small wooden hand mirror she always kept atop the desk, her fingers tracing along tiny words carved into its back. In a rare moment of vulnerability, she sighed. "Drak, I wish Solrac were here."

"He'll be back before you know it," I said.

"Not necessarily." Vidya grimaced.

"What do you mean?"

Vidya eyed me. "I can count on your discretion, right, Meleya?" I nodded and Vidya sighed again. "Solrac believes he's not long for this world. He believes he's receiving omens regarding his imminent death—Apparently, it's something many Farseers before him have experienced."

"Stars," I said.

"It's always the same omen," Vidya went on. "A great gray dragon appears to snap off his head. He believes the dragon represents the Soul Reaper and his followers. When Solrac left for the Dragon Isles, he... Drak, let's just say his goodbye felt dangerously final."

"Oh, Vidya," I said, daring to get up from my chair so I could put a hand on her arm. I knew there was a strong possibility she'd push me away, but instead she clung to my hand, her eyes practically twitching as they struggled to hold back tears. I had no doubts she'd shed many while alone here day after day.

"I don't want to lose him again," Vidya said through gritted teeth, more to herself than to me. "*I'm* the one beyond redemption, the one whose foolishness led to all of this in the first place. It should be me who's doomed, not him!"

The way she said it made me think she wasn't just talking about Solrac, but someone else too, someone whom we both cared for dearly. My gut twisted as I replayed what had happened in Etheria with the Gray Knight—with *Jax*—over and over again, wondering what I could've done differently that might've helped him. I knew it wasn't up to me to save him, and I didn't feel guilt, only sorrow.

For the hundredth time, I recalled what Jax had said to me during his brief moment of clarity back in Etheria. Something about Streya's Comet. I'd relayed the information to my fellow Knights, but none had been able to make hide nor scale of it. Solrac seemed especially troubled by the information, but he'd been needed in the Dragon Isles and had to leave before the date of the comet's passing.

Only a short time later, Streya's Comet did appear in the skies. I, alongside several others, had watched the rare celestial event from atop Orothion's Skyforge terrace. Green light had streaked through the darkened sky far to the east, and then...

At once, the comet had made a harsh curve downward. Surprised reactions had arisen from those around me as the mighty meteor suddenly looked like nothing more than another skyfall, albeit a *massive* one. I'd frowned as I watched, and then Jax's words had finally made sense:

Streya's Comet... skystone... They're going to—

Soot. Could it be that the Soul Reaper and his followers were behind it? Did he really have the power to yank a legendary comet off its course?

It was all about the skystone, I'd realized. But drak, just what did the Soul Reaper plan to *do* with all of it?

I'd shared my realizations with Solvai and the other leaders of the Knights. While they shared my concerns, none of us had a clue what to do about it. For now, our only real option was to keep training, preparing for the worst come the convergence in the spring. We still had several months before that, at least.

I'd told Vidya about Jax's warning too, and it had both unnerved and comforted her. Like me, she believed it meant that Jax was still fighting, still clinging to his inner hero, the one who'd saved me more times than I could count.

Here in the lavish chambers, Vidya clung to my hand for another moment before returning to her dinner. After a minute, I spoke.

"Why don't you come down to my parents' cottage in town tonight? We and Boone were planning to play a few rounds of Fallen Stars, and I'm making honey fry bread. You should join us."

"I'm not sure. There were some more books I was planning to—"

"Please?"

Vidya's lower eyelids scrunched upward as she contemplated. Then, at last, she agreed to join us.

That night was the first of many Vidya spent with us. Pretty soon, Dad even invited her to join us at the training grounds. She was hesitant at first, but once we finally got her down there, she worked wonders. Vidya taught classes in which she helped the magi among our ranks learn to more effectively use their powers in combat, giving them both the gift of skill and confidence.

Of course, there were those who refused to train while in Vidya's presence—the Black Valkyrie had certainly left many Knights of the Torch scarred seemingly beyond repair. But the vast majority were willing to give her a second chance, especially the younger generation of soldiers.

Her skill as an instructor ultimately led to the betterment of the army as a whole. Besides that, I was grateful to see the purposeful light return to Vidya's midnight-colored eyes.

New recruits showed up at our gates every single day. Each new group gave me hope, since I knew that these were only a fraction of those willing to take up arms against the Gray. Scouts returned with reports of many towns—mostly in Skygard, Drakfell, and Evyndara—pledging their support for the Knights of the Torch.

It certainly appeared that, in many cases, High King Magnus's wanted posters featuring Elle and Aurora were doing the exact opposite of what he'd intended. People saw them not as a chance to gain riches, but as a rallying flag, invitations to join the cause and fight for a future led by a true dragon rider with the souls of the people in mind. Someone who saw magi not as a threat to be eliminated, but as a gift to our realm. As friends and equals.

Of course, there were those who felt the opposite as well. We heard tell of anti-magi uprisings, the likes of which rivaled those of the centuries-old Silver Crusades. I felt sick when I heard about the executions held by Evgardians unwilling to wait for Mage Hunters to come round the magi up.

That was the most disturbing piece of news—A messenger and his dragon had arrived to bring the Triarchy, the Knights' leadership circle, a particular scroll. By order of the High Crown, all magi would be required to report to Evyndara to receive the magi cure. Mage Hunters would be working overtime to fulfill the order, and any citizens caught harboring unregistered magi would be executed themselves. Those who complied, on the other scale, would be rewarded with both gold marks and the knowledge that they had done their part to 'make the realm a safer place.' The magi would be 'cleansed' of their etherarchy, then returned safely to their homes.

"I don't believe that for a second," I said when Solvai showed me the High King's proclamation. As the Sentinel representative of the Knights' Triarchy, she'd gotten an advanced look at the order from the High Crown. With permission from the other members of the Council, she'd taken it for further study. Solvai and I, along with our old squadmate, Edrea, stood beneath a firemaple tree in the courtyard outside the guards' barracks. The leaves had just begun changing colors, their normally fiery-red tinged brilliant gold on the tips.

"I don't believe it either," agreed Edrea, giving one of her signature scowls. "We saw firsthand what they did to those in the Asylum after they lost their ether wells. Captain Cenrik, for one."

"My mother and Meleya's for another," Solvai said.

"Besides, according to Vidya, the so-called magi cure process is volatile at best. Too many magi don't survive it," I added, thinking of Zerana. We now knew exactly what the cure really was: An excuse for the Soul Reaper to harvest ether wells and transplant them onto the souls of his own followers. I shuddered to think that someone out there had my Mom's ether well. Part of me wondered who, but the bigger part of me preferred not to know. Knowing would only make me angry.

"And all of this soot about purging the realm of etherarchy?" Solvai's hazel eyes burned as she smacked the proclamation with the back of her hand. "We know the Gray is just using this as a chance to build an army even more powerful than the one we fought in Rengard."

"The one your mother led, you mean?" Edrea said.

"Yes, Edrea," Solvai replied dryly. "That one."

"There you three are," came a masculine voice from around the corner, and the three of us turned to find two more members of our old squad heading our way: Cam, Edrea's burly stepbrother, and Erik, our sharpshooter with his trademark sketchbook tucked under his arm. The topmost page of his drawing pad showed his most recent piece of art: A picture of our squad as we currently stood, wearing the bright red cloaks of the Knights of the Torch.

The two young men took their places in our circle and Solvai let them get a look at the High King's proclamation. As the five of us stood there, I couldn't help but feel the absence of both Jax and Brigan.

Edrea must've been feeling the same, because pretty soon she asked Solvai, "Any news from the Canyonlands?"

When I'd learned what had happened to Brigan while I'd been in astral sleep, it had taken me a week to believe it. My heart ached for my friend; I could scarcely imagine how painful and daunting it must've been to lose one's family *and* inherit a kingdom all within the same hour. I wished I could be there for him now. We all did.

Solvai pressed her lips together. "Rengard's still in a very bad spot. There are more uprisings there than anywhere else, plus we just received word that there's a band of dragonslayers there bent on taking power and eliminating magi from the keepdom once and for all. They're using the attack from the Coven last Winter Solstice as well as the Rise's Fall to rile up the neighboring keeps. They don't care that both attacks came from those wielding *voidarchy*, all they can see is that magi were responsible. They're calling themselves 'mageslayers'."

"I don't like that," I said. The others voiced their agreement.

Edrea cleared her throat. "Any news about Brigan?"

Solvai's brows knit. "Another assassination attempt. It failed, luckily, since they didn't expect him to be as good as he is with a seaxe."

"Drak," I cursed. "Where was his high guard?"

"One of the assassins turned out to be a traitor *from* his high guard," Solvai replied.

"What Brigan needs is a proper high guard," Edrea said. "One with experience."

"You mean like Squad Reckless?" Cam asked.

"Exactly," Edrea said.

"We didn't exactly succeed when it came to King Axel," Erik winced.

"As long as Brigan doesn't try to make peace with a psychotic wild-shaping true dragon Liberator with an army of magi at her back, I think we'll be good—No offense, Solvai."

"None taken." Solvai shrugged.

"That's not a bad idea, actually," I put in. "The Canyonlands would be a fantastic ally for the Knights if only Brigan was given the opportunity to lead the way I know he can. If we can properly protect him, we could aid in that mission. Solvai, is there any chance you can speak with the Triarchy about transferring former Squad Reckless to the Canyonlands?"

Solvai tapped her chin thoughtfully as the whole squad hopefully looked her way. "I'll ask Cenrik. In fact, I've got to get going—The Triarchy is meeting soon."

She rolled up the proclamation and bade us farewell. The rest of us had the afternoon off from drills, and my squad dispersed.

As I watched them go, I couldn't help but worry. My family was in so many different places. Here in Orothion, across the Scarlet Strait in the Canyonlands... Only the stars knew where Jax was, and as for Asher and Elle...

Just thinking about Asher sent a pang of concern ringing in my chest. The thought of him facing General Kheradok in a duel to the death wasn't an easy one to swallow. But I'd seen him in action. Wherever Asher was now, I trusted that he'd overcome any lingering doubts and fight for the light like I knew he could.

Chapter 13: The Isles

Asher

The longship was fun at first. But after over a month at sea, the novelty had slightly worn off, and now I was about to fling myself overboard just to see if the sea was more interesting beneath the waves than it was staring at it from the deck. I wished we could've just flown the whole way, but there were just too many in our party for that to make sense.

At least with Elle's parents, the King and Queen of Drakfell, sponsoring our trip, we were traveling in style. The elegant longboat was sleek and white, with an ornate draconic figurehead at its prow. The sails were tan, and bore the Drakfellian fang crest. Atop the mast was a red flag flying the torch-like symbol of the Knights of the Torch.

The best part about the ship was its spacious deck, which left plenty of room for the handful of bonded dragons to stretch out and the crew to go about their business while I commandeered the middle for practice. Throughout the journey, I'd lost myself in training, spending every waking minute I could in the ring. I sometimes convinced members of the ship's crew to practice with me, but they'd grown tired of my astromancy ending the fight too quickly. Oddly enough, that didn't boost my confidence much. I needed to push myself harder and get even better. But I didn't feel like I had much to push myself *against*.

Especially since, before our departure, Kari had given me a gift: New and improved ascension armor, made from the scales Thorn shed after Zel and his lackeys had forced his third ascension.

And *soot* if it wasn't glorious.

As ever, Kari had outdone herself. The chest piece came with a set of pauldrons, one of which was larger, outfitted with an intimidating row of spikes that mimicked Thorn's spines. She'd designed an armored belt as well, complete with a place to clip on my father's skyseeker dagger. Finally, there were greaves to match the ascension bracers Kari had already made after Thorn's previous ascension. She'd arranged the coppery scales to fit in with the black, duplicating the patterns that grew on Thorn's hide.

The best part about it was the traces of Thorn's power that came with wearing the ascension armor. When I activated the armor's woodweaving power, it became hard like diamondoak, and grew to cover more of me too. The bracers became full gauntlets with overlapping plates that reached my shoulders, the greaves became boots, and the pauldrons extended into an impressive helmet with slanted eye slits and a crown of golden antlers like a more subdued version of Thorn's. Thorn loved that part.

I made sure to practice with the armor enough that I got used to its feel, but still spent a lot of time without it on so that I could keep practicing at a disadvantage.

Meanwhile, Elle had been training up her fighting skills as well. Determined to turn her sparring training into something useful in battle, she spent hours working with various members of the crew, as well as Aurora. Aurora used the opportunity to practice her illusion powers to project battle scenarios for Elle to take on. Elle was getting really good, and even better at funneling limited portions of Aurora's power into herself. Aurora's geomancy made Elle extra strong, and her hover-dashing was coming along nicely as well. Still, Aurora struggled with most of the Mystic powers, especially rifting.

Besides that, Elle spent a lot of time with her nose buried in a fancy copy of *Drekai Linguistics for Beginners.* Most Drekai spoke Evgardian, but she felt it was only right that she learn their language as best she could before we made port at Zolehiinu. According to the captain, that would be in only a few short weeks.

Elle and I hadn't exactly spent all that much time together during our travels thus far. For a while, I told myself it was because we were both so busy, but if I was being honest, there was more to it. I had to admit it: What Meleya had said right before I'd left Orothion had left me feeling confused. I felt a deep connection with Meleya, that much was certain, but was I right for her in *that* way? And was she right for me? Her parting words kept ringing in my mind:

Take fate by the reins and fly. She was right—there wasn't really a right or wrong in this. Only our own decisions, which would determine who we would become.

So I guess that was the real question: Who *did* I want to be?

When I was with Meleya, I felt confident. She saw me as a leader, despite having seen me during some of my most vulnerable moments. Plus, she was stupendously fun to mess with. That said, she definitely still had feelings for that son of a dragonmutt, Jax, whether or not she wanted to admit it. Try as I might, I couldn't get the conversation we'd had on the Skyforge terrace out of my head.

As for Elle, being with her pushed me to constantly improve. With her, I felt energized and hopeful, and our connection ran deep. But despite what Meleya had somewhat reluctantly confided about Elle still having feelings for me, Elle herself had yet to make that clear. She *had* kissed Kheradok, after all, and who knew if those feelings would resurface when she saw him again on the Dragon Isles. Maybe she'd play it safe, waiting to see which one of us would emerge from this duel alive.

That thought made my gut twist, so rather than continue to dwell on all these overly complicated thoughts and feelings that seemed to come with being a confused eighteen-year-old, I threw myself back into my training. From the sidelines Thorn gave a totally unrelated wyvern chuckle.

As I stood there on the deck running through my arsenal of moves, I found my gaze repeatedly drifting to where Elle was lounging atop Aurora's back. Elle's hair spilled across Aurora's scales as the free-spirited princess held her book above her in the air, mouthing the words.

I hadn't realized I'd been staring until Elle turned my way, her head upside down as she sprawled over her dragon's back, one eyebrow raised. Whoops—so much for focusing on my training. I instantly pretended I'd just been practicing a starglass spear spin move, but Elle clearly didn't buy it. She snorted and broke into an infectious grin.

"You know," she started, calling to me, "you could always try adding starglass weights to your wrists and ankles. If you train while impeded like that, once they're off you'll be even faster and stronger."

Intrigued, I gave it a try. I ran through my moves again, this time weighted down by thick, chunky starglass that clung to my bracers and boots. Sure enough, I started sweating in a good way.

"Hey, thanks for the tip," I said to Elle.

"No problem. It's something my father does when he trains."

From there, we carried on with our separate tasks once more. But even while wearing the starglass weights, I couldn't help but feel a little lighter now that the silence between us had been broken.

From that point forward, Elle and I fell right back into our old, comfortable friendship. I helped her practice speaking Drekai, and she helped me spar. Limited access to Aurora's etherarchy flowed through Elle, making her strong enough to match me. Most evenings, we flew Thorn and Aurora high above the longship so we could get the best view of the sunset over the sea.

Just a few days before our arrival in Zolehiinu, I woke up early to get in a little extra practice without my ascension armor. I'd just executed a move I was calling the 'skyfall strike' when suddenly my blade struck someone else's and came to a stop.

"Looking for a sparring partner?" Solrac winked. He stood before me with thick blond hair and a full beard, his face a mere echo of the one I'd always known. He'd been wearing the illusory disguise throughout the voyage to keep from drawing attention to the fact that he was the most wanted man in the realm.

"Always," I answered, assuming a battle stance.

Then, to my surprise, Solrac sheathed his long seaxe.

I cocked my head. "Pretty sure you're gonna need, you know, a weapon."

Solrac gave a rich, deep laugh. "I've already seen what you can do with that spear, Asher. You outclassed me long ago. You truly have an uncanny gift for outmaneuvering Seers."

"Hard to read a mind that doesn't plan." I shrugged. "So you *don't* want to spar?"

"On the contrary," Solrac said. "I just think it might be more useful for you to enjoy one last training session with your old mentor and fellow Astromancer, Boone."

At that, Solrac held up a wooden hoop with gold threads tied in a starry, crisscrossing pattern. I recognized the dreamweb instantly—The Farseer, er, Solrac, had given both Boone and me ones just like it when I'd first left Orothion for Rengard so long ago. Our dreamwebs had allowed us to access a sort of dream-realm training arena, which Boone and I had used to train together despite the hundreds of miles between us. Mine had broken en route to Rhana's safehouse, but it seemed the Farseer had procured a backup.

Grinning from ear to ear, I reached for the dreamweb, then funneled a little bit of ether into the small quartz tied in the center of the threads. At once, purple mist began to emit from the web, and soon my eyes glazed over.

Physically, Solrac and I were still standing on the deck of the longship, clutching the dreamweb hoop. But mentally, our consciousnesses had risen to the Astral Realm. Time would pass much slower here than back on the ship, so I could train for hours and still not miss breakfast.

While I'd technically trained with Boone here in this Astral Realm dream-pocket before, this was my first time since returning from Etheria. While the Ethereal plane was rife with color and texture, everything constantly churning with misty movement, Astra was far more subdued. The sky here somehow looked more like an ocean above our heads, a rich shade of purple filled with infinite stars bobbing in the waves of the dream energy. According to Kai, some experts speculated that each star was the light of some living being's consciousness, waiting to descend to this realm while in sleep or using relics like this dreamweb.

We appeared in a flash of light to stand on a wide training arena made from what I could only describe as dark glass. Every time we took a step, the dark, semi-clear surface rippled with purple light. Far below us stood a grove of tall, thickly clustered violet trees, and what looked like reflective pools of water everywhere, with trickles of liquid dream energy floating back up to that strange ocean dome of the sky. In some ways, it kind of reminded me of the Mirror Forest, only more purplish and dreamy.

But I wasn't worried about the astral forest—I was more focused on what was going on up here in the arena, one I'd been told Solrac had *made* with highly concentrated imagination. At least, that's how it had been explained to me. Stars, Mysticism could get weird. Luckily, I didn't much care about the intricacies of etherarchy the way Kai did.

We hadn't been standing there for longer than a few seconds before we saw a bright white spot streak across the endless, watery sky, then plunge downward like a skyfall to land atop the glass arena with a flash of light, which dissipated to reveal a wiry figure with stark white hair, leathery tan skin, and a scruffy beard. When he spoke, his northern drawl was as strong as it was the day we left Orothion.

"Well, ain't y'all a sight more welcome than a wyvernhog come home to roost in time for the yuletide holiday!" Boone said, tossing his tan dragonscale cloak over his shoulder.

Beside me, Solrac burst into laughter and embraced Boone. Now that we were in Astra, Solrac looked like himself again.

"Glad you could make it," Solrac said.

"You know I'd move the sun, moon, and stars for my oldest friend, Solrac," Boone said. "'Specially if it means helpin' out my favorite young Astromancin' protege!"

Meanwhile, Solrac was already backing up to the edge of the glass arena, calling back over his shoulder, "No going easy on him this time, Boone. How's... oh, I don't know, first to kill the other three times takes the victory?"

"Sounds as excitin' as a brawl betwixt scale-squirrels, and if you disagree, you ain't spent drak near enough time with scale-squirrels!"

That got a snort out of me even as my fingers twitched with anticipation. That was the other thing about Astra—Sustaining wounds or even dying here didn't mean a thing, since this was all essentially just a dream. It was exactly what I needed right now, since a duel to the *actual* death was what awaited me in the Dragon Isles.

We faced off, Boone's hands hovering over the starglass daggers holstered at his hips. Meanwhile, I summoned my starglass spear, followed by starglass weights to add to my bracers and boots.

Boone laughed. "You sure about that?"

"Gotta push myself, old man." I raised a confident eyebrow.

Boone raised one right back. "Your call, youngun." Then Solrac counted down from three, and the showdown began.

The last number had no sooner left Solrac's lips than Boone drew both of his curved starglass daggers and rapidly fired two ether bolts directly toward my chest.

Just as quickly, I whirled my starglass spear to deflect both shots. From there, Boone and I felt each other out with a few more lunges and jabs. During most of our prior training, we'd worked on specific skills, so this was the first time we'd sparred this freely. Having Solrac watching from the sidelines only egged us on. While Boone was a skilled ex-dragonslayer and Dragon Wars veteran, I was fairly certain he'd already taught me everything he knew.

Boone was keeping his distance so that he'd have the advantage of range from his ether blasts. But two could play that game. I charged my spear with ether and sent a comet-like blast of my own right toward Boone's chest.

Quicker than an ashviper, Boone twisted so his tan dragonslayer's cloak absorbed my shot, leaving a spiraling white mark on the scales.

Boone broke into a grin. "Woowee! Weren't all that long ago you could barely get a pitiful li'l drip-drop of ether outta that there spear! But now I reckon you're *almost* as good as me."

"Almost?"

"You had a good teacher." Boone winked, his eyes blazing gold as he infused his daggers with more ether. A mist of liquid ether now formed a cloud around his blades, amplifying his next flurry of ether blasts. Though I was able to block most of them, one slipped through my guard and hit me in the shoulder. With its power amplified, it literally blew me off my feet.

I skidded backward, and were it not for my levitation, I'd have slid right off the edge of the glass arena and fallen toward the purple trees below. As it was, I just barely managed to catch the edge.

Before I could so much as hover-swing myself back up onto the arena's surface, Boone started peppering me with another series of well-placed ether blasts. Within moments, I was falling through space, Boone's flurry so relentless that it rendered my levitation pointless.

As I crashed into the treetops, my dream self winked out in a flash of light. A second later, I reappeared in the center of the glass arena once again to find Boone laughing his head off.

"That's first kill to me, I'd wager," Boone said, blowing ether-smoke from the points of his daggers.

"Veteran's luck," I said, shrugging it off. "Figured you needed a win."

This time, I summoned two starglass scimitars crafted in Drekai style—With Mom in mind, I'd been training with them a little to add some variety—as well as a little extra starglass armor for absorbing those scorching ether blasts.

Boone grinned. "No extra starglass weights this time 'round? Whatever happened to pushin' yourself?"

Just for that, I hover-launched myself toward Boone, dodging his ether blasts left and right. But he was no slouch with levitation either, despite not using it as frequently as me. He sidestepped my scimitar slashes, and I switched to his tactic, shooting off more ether blasts of my own from the tips of my blades, which Boone continued to block with his dragonscale cloak. Our dance of astromantic fury had commenced.

Meanwhile, on the sidelines, Solrac had used imagination or whatever to conjure himself a fancy floating armchair made from the same darkened glass as the arena.

"Your mother, Asher—She grew up in the Dragon Isles, did she not?" he tried to strike up a conversation. Soot, was he sipping dream-cider from a goblet over there?

"That's right," I replied, ducking an ether blast and diving toward Boone's chest, nearly striking him before he parried with his daggers.

"I'm assuming she did not tell you much about her time there," Solrac went on.

"No." I grunted as Boone caught my next strike, shoving hard against my scimitar with one dagger. With the other, he barely caught me in the back. Were it not for my starglass armor, he'd have already secured his second win. Drak, this wiry old man was quick.

"Woowee!" Boone hollered. "You better watch yourself more closely than a narcissistic draccoon starin' at a pool!"

After briefly pausing to give my best goofy, bucktoothed draccoon face, I shoved Boone back with both blades, but he recovered quickly, forcing me to dodge another ether blast volley.

I was fairly certain that without Solrac's distracting chitchat—Soot, he was snacking from a floating platter of imaginary grapes now—I'd have been doing a lot better here. Then again, maybe that was part of Solrac's plan. Like starglass weights for my brain.

Determined to meet the challenge, I called to Solrac as I fought, "You wanted my mother to join the Knights, didn't you?"

Solrac shrugged, speaking with his mouth full. "I have a knack for spotting talent and putting it to its ideal use. Zerana had it in scales, and so does her son. Oh—watch your right side."

Sure enough, Boone was firing off another series of ether darts, these ones with sharp starglass cores in the center. My scimitars were blurs as they shattered each dart on impact.

Solrac continued between bites. "That is why I would like to invite you, Asher of Steel Rim, to have a seat on the council of the Knights of the Torch, where you and others will assist the Triarchy in making important decisions."

I stopped in my tracks. "What?"

Boone didn't miss a beat. Within a second, he'd pummeled me with a starglass core-ether blast to the face, and I winked out in a flash of light once more.

As I reappeared back at the center of the glass arena, I grit my teeth with frustration. That was two kills for Boone to my zero.

Boone grinned at Solrac. "I've always wanted to do that."

Frustration and adrenaline kindled a fire within me. In a burst of power, a mist of liquid ether surrounded me, amplifying my speed as I dove toward Boone. A streak of white and gold trailed behind me as we collided, and I sent him flying right over the edge of the glass arena. At last, it was *his* turn to disappear in a starry flash of light, only to come streaking through the air to materialize back in the center of the platform.

As Boone reappeared, I whirled on Solrac, who had added a variety of cheeses to his imagination-powered floating snack platter.

"Please tell me you're joking," I said. "Or that you have me confused with someone else—Someone actually cut out to sit on councils and tell people what to do."

"No, Asher, I'm quite certain." Solrac's tone was infuriatingly relaxed. "It's you we need."

Boone was already springing back into action, spurring me right back into the thick of things. Both of us were essentially glowing as ether-mist amplified our every movement.

"Everyone sees me as a joke!" I called to Solrac, trying to split my focus. "You've seen that for yourself."

"What both I and many others have seen is a young man who was instrumental in reclaiming Orothion. One who led the expedition into the Haze to uncover the secrets of the Netherstone. Asher of Steel Rim, whether you believe it or not, you just might be the greatest thing to ever happen to the Knights of the Torch."

"You literally hired me to be the team's *distraction*!" I protested. "I'm not like Elle, or Brigan, or you. I don't dream of inspiring the masses and leading them to victory. Scorch, I can barely even lead myself."

Yet even as I said it, the words didn't quite ring true. I did love seeing the reactions of others, especially good ones. What was more, it *had* felt good working with my friends to take back the Knights' headquarters so that it could once more be a beacon for true light. But none of that made me a leader, did it?

Meanwhile, Boone hit me with a hover-charged boot to the chest, then nearly downed me with a follow-up blast to seal his victory. But I rolled away just in time, hover-jumping high and landing at his back. From there, I stabbed him right in the back with my spear and he disappeared in another burst of light.

While Boone respawned, Solrac continued. "Then tell me, what *do* you dream of, Asher?"

Breathing hard, I first narrowed my eyes at Solrac's new dream-footstool and dream-palm fronds fanning him on either side. Then, I replied, "I… I don't know. Nothing, I suppose. Carefree days at the lakeshore and riding my dragon into the sunset."

Solrac sighed. "Yes, that does sound nice. But fate has greater plans for you. And I… well, I need to know that the Knights are in good hands. Perhaps those hands are unpracticed for now, but come what may, I'd like to know that honorable people like you are prepared to carry the torch. My own fate may be murky, but the omens regarding you are clear. You are destined to be a bridge—a beacon to which others can look for light."

By the end of Solrac's little speech, Boone and I were both back at it, bent on winning that final victory. Starglass and ether swirled across the glass arena.

"I don't care what the omens say, Solrac," I called, sweating. "You've got the wrong half-born."

In my frustration, I overcommitted to my next lunge at Boone, and I missed. Boone was easily able to redirect my starglass spear, knocking it from my hand. From there, he took advantage of my distraction and put me on my back with a swift elbow jab—Soot, this old man was tough.

Boot on my chest, Boone had thoroughly claimed the upper hand. He looked down at me, his dagger trained on my chest and his eyes fiery with golden Archonic light.

"You're right about one thing," said Boone. "I don't give a hoot about what them omens say neither. Doomsday Solrac's over there thinkin' the end is nigh and all that, but I say scorch it. I ain't gonna let fate control me.

"But melodramatic, future-spittin', gold campfires aside," Boone continued, "I know you, Asher. I seen you go from a plucky, talented boy to a warrior more skilled'na king spydra weavin' a drakefly trap. You done growed into an intelligent young Knight of the Torch, doin' his drakkinest to live the Code and share light with others despite what hardships come his way. You're one courageous son of a dragonmutt."

As I lay there pinned, Boone's words brought to mind my mother's Life Path. Courage. She wanted me to fulfill it for her; that much had been clear.

But stars if I wasn't frustrated by all of it. I was just some random outlander thief, but now I was about to face Kheradok, the esteemed General of the Dragon Isles. If I lost, Aurora and Elle, the true dragon and her rider with the potential to save Evgard, would belong to the Dragon Isles, not to mention I'd be dead.

The pressure, the weeks at sea, Solrac's insane proposal, and even Boone's unwarranted belief in me... it all came to a head I felt most potently in my heart.

My eyes burning with etherlight, I cried out as something seemed to explode from inside me. It wasn't like the full-body ether blast power I'd dubbed the astro-nova—This was almost the reverse.

Ether coalesced all around me as I sucked it all in. Boone's eyes reverted to their normal color, and both of his starglass daggers dissipated as their ether pulled toward me.

I shot into the air a few feet above the arena and Boone dropped to the ground. All the white, misty ether orbited around me in a series of concentric rings that crisscrossed my body.

From there, instinct took over. I thrust both hands out toward Boone, channeling all that ether into a massive, highly condensed ray of pure, blinding ether. He didn't stand a chance as he winked out for the third time.

When Boone reappeared, he was whistling and whooping. Even Solrac's fanciful spread and glass chair vanished as his focus was all on me.

"Yeehaw!" Boone hollered. "If that there ain't a breakthrough in astromancy, I don't rightly know what is!"

Solrac burst into applause. "Bravo, Asher of Steel Rim! Bravo!"

As their praise rang in my ears, my mind was still racing. Part of me still wished I'd taken Thorn and run months ago, leaving all these expectations behind. But I hadn't. Something in me had made me stay. Perhaps part of it was the people I cared about—Dad, Kai and Kari, Elle, Meleya, Solrac and Boone, and all my new friends too.

But deep down, I knew there was more to it. I *liked* being a Knight. I liked the purpose the Code gave me, even if I was still working to fully understand it. I wanted to keep choosing light, and that kept me choosing to stay. Staying so that I could...

Share light forevermore. The words of Mom's song came to mind, and my hand subconsciously went to my scarf. She'd said it had been given to her by her father, who had received it from his father before that. I had a duty to fulfill as part of that legacy.

I deactivated my etherarchy and landed back on the ground of the glass arena. My eyes returned to their regular dragonfire green as the misty rings of ether around me faded away.

Looking between Solrac and Boone, I wasn't totally sure what to say. Both of these men had invested so much in me, and somehow saw greatness in me, even if I had trouble seeing it myself.

"Thank you." I knew I could never articulate the depths of my gratitude, so I opted to keep things simple. "I'll consider it. But you have to promise me something, Solrac—"

"Yes?" The Farseer cocked his head.

"Don't you go dying on me just 'cause you think 'fate' wills it, okay? Boone's right about the omens; you can't let them dictate how you live your life."

For a moment, Solrac only offered a halfhearted smile. Then something in him seemed to click, and he looked me dead in the eyes and nodded.

"I'll consider it," he echoed my earlier sentiment with a mock tip of his nonexistent hat. Then he snapped his fingers, and at once the three of us winked out of—rather, *back into* existence.

My Astral spar with Boone and Solrac kept my thoughts occupied for the next couple weeks aboard the longship until at last, shouting from the ship's prow pulled all of my attention straight to something else.

I raced to the side of the boat, hover-dashing right on top of it to get a better look. The view took my breath away.

Tall mounds of earth dominated the western horizon. Everything was green and bursting with life, and a light patter of rain began to fall as we approached.

The closer we got, the more striking the thick green boughs of the scale cedars and the curtains of moss that hung from them appeared. The entire land was blanketed in a thin layer of smooth, white fog. It was beautiful, if not a little ominous.

For the briefest moment, I experienced another one of those residual Sight flashes from being woken too early from astral sleep. The ethereal aura of the land came alive before me in dragonfire green, the motion of it reminded me of dragons diving in and out of the rolling hills and mountains.

This was it—The place where Mom grew up.

We'd arrived in the Dragon Isles.

I'd already been to more royal galas than I cared to admit: Exactly one.

Sure, back then we'd been trying to steal a dragon egg rather than truly enjoying the event itself. But still, Keep Drakfell's extravagant feast featuring fancy food, stiff clothes, and dozens of uppity nobles desperately trying to impress each other hadn't exactly been my style.

But the welcome feast here at the Drekai palace was, in many ways, the opposite. Laughter and chatter abounded throughout the great hall as we served ourselves buffet style from platters heaped with steamed crawdrakes, spicy wild rice, flavorful cindershroom-and-potato sauce, and fire-hazelnuts sticky with sugar. I made sure to take notes on all of it for Meleya.

Our Evgardian-style clothing, though fine, made us stick out like sore scales. Elle wore her white ascension armor dress, Solrac a fancy, muted red cloak, and I my dark dragon-buffalo hide jacket. The other Knight representatives seated at various tables throughout the hall wore neutral colors as well. Only my turquoise scarf, which was tucked mostly inside my jacket's collar, matched the far brighter colors that dominated the clothing here.

Everything in the royal hall was exquisite, from the bronze, dragon-themed wall decor to the crisscross-patterned wooden doors. The doors didn't reach high enough to touch the ceiling or low enough to touch the floor, which added to the fresh, open feeling. About a dozen balconies surrounded the hall, and a forest filled with rich-smelling scale cedars surrounded the palace.

But perhaps the most fascinating part about the Dragon Isles' general atmosphere was its abundant use of psionics. Almost everything here had been enchanted to float. The dining tables and chairs we sat at didn't have legs, just runemarks. There were small, psionically charged dragon figurines slowly floating along near the ceiling. Decorative stones arranged from largest to smallest floated above one another, rigged with tiny streams of water falling down on them to form beautiful waterfall features.

There was so much to see, smell, and eat that I had a difficult time focusing on the dinner conversation. But sitting at a table with the Drekai Empress made behaving myself a must.

The Empress was a tall, fiercely distinguished woman in a long, green wrap dress. A pair of elegant horns adorned with emeralds swept off the back of her head, matching the shiny scales growing along her hairline, cheekbones, and shoulders. She wore a glorious, heavy-looking crown adorned with green dragon scales that matched the true dragon's heartscale she wore around her neck.

The conversation so far had been much more casual than I'd expected. Instead of tense or droning discussions about political affairs, upcoming duels, or potential alliances, the Empress and her two generals were chatting with us about music.

"There's nothing quite like the low, resonating sound of a didgeridoo," Empress Khaisa said fondly, her accented Evgardian perfect.

"I agree!" Elle replied with enthusiasm. "I heard one once during a festival near Drakfell's western border and I dreamed about it for the next three nights straight."

The Empress gave an infectious, bell-like laugh. "Not nightmares, I hope."

"Took the words straight from my mouth," Solrac chuckled, taking a swig from his drinking horn. The drinks were fantastic, something sweet and deep purple that they called honeyed huckleberry nectar. Solrac looked like his regular self once more, the illusory blondness having melted away the moment we set foot on Drekai soil—or rather, springy paaka moss, which covered most of the ground in the Isles. Here, Solrac was a free man, even respected by the Drekai for his work as the Farseer. Besides, the last thing we wanted to do was start off our potential alliance with any level of falseness.

"I've always found the ethereal notes of the ocarina quite soothing," General Kheradok added to the conversation. "My father taught me to play as a child, and I'd say the skill has served me well."

He and Elle exchanged glances and I fought a grimace, trying not to picture the kiss they'd exchanged back in the Mirror Forest. When Elle had told me about it, she'd sworn Kheradok had been the one to make the move, *and* that he'd initially come to kill her. But whatever his intentions, the sight of him now made me crack my knuckles under the table, one by one. Maybe I could bottle this feeling and save it for when I faced him in the arena.

"I'm rather a lute man if I do say so myself," Solrac put in, effectively halting my thoughts before they became too bitter. He made a strumming motion with his hands.

"Who knew the fabled Farseer had such hidden talents," Empress Khaisa teased.

"Legend by night, bard by day," Solrac said, leaving most of the table in stitches.

Only General Zora, Kheradok's co-leader over the Drekai armies, seemed grumpy and stiff, even down to her choice of clothing. While the other Drekai at the party wore comfortable, brightly colored sashes and pants, she donned fine bronze plate armor as if she were ready to march to war.

When asked about her instrument of preference, General Zora replied, "Do *raskalaata* count?"

She held up her heavy, oversized war boomerang. Solrac, Elle, and I scooted back, but Empress Khaisa just chuckled.

"Relax, Zora," she said. "*Kaiiki ja zii kazi*—All things in their season. Tonight is a night of celebration." Khaisa turned to us. "You'll have to forgive her. She just returned from the Canyonlands front."

"All is forgiven," Solrac replied. "On that score, I hope all is being made right after the end of the Dragon Isles' dispute with Rengard."

"Things are much better, yes," the Empress replied. "Young King Brigan has been most generous in providing reconciliation."

"Once Rengard settles, the Knights will be thrilled to have them as allies," Solrac put in.

"I'm sure," said Empress Khaisa, gaze shifting off to the side. Clearly, the conversation had strayed too near to politics.

I turned to Solrac, "*Kaiiki ja zii kazi*," I said, borrowing the phrase the Empress had used a moment earlier.

Empress Khaisa looked my way, smiling. "Your Drekai accent is impressive for someone raised in Evgard."

I shrugged. "My mom taught me well. She was raised here on the Isles."

"How remarkable. One of the southern isles, I presume? Most half-borns are from Jelziiki or Vaaza."

"I'm not sure, actually," I admitted. "My mom never said which one she was from."

Khaisa frowned, leaning slightly as she got a better look at the scales on the tips of my pointed ears. She opened her mouth to say something more, but at that moment, applause broke out throughout the hall and we turned to see that a group of Drekai entertainers had come in, taking over the central part of the room for their performance.

Some beat drums while others danced, spun, and jumped in time with the music, all while expertly wielding torches lined with green dragonfire. I ahhed along with the crowd. Some performers had psionic runes glowing over their foreheads as they telekinetically threw torches or even balls of fire. The fire seemed to paint the air itself with lingering streaks of light.

We enjoyed the show as we finished our meal. When the fire dancers finished, we burst into applause, with Solrac clapping and whistling the loudest of all. A few Drekai at other tables rolled their eyes and muttered '*Evgardiaanti*'.

We were just bringing our used dishes to a large washbasin when a man approached the Empress. He must've been some kind of advisor or something, with violet and black scales along his cheekbones, hairline, and shoulders. A fascinating white ether scar curled along his jaw, leaving a white streak in his hair above his ear.

"Empress Khaisa," he said. "You asked for me?"

"*Jhi*," the Empress replied. "I know you're no fan of large gatherings, but I wanted to introduce you to the visiting Evgardians since you spent so much time in their land." Empress Khaisa turned to our group. "Knights of the Torch, this is Zoren, one of my most trusted advisors."

We greeted the man. Solrac seemed to recognize him and called him 'The Ursadon', while Elle executed a curtsy. I was just in the middle of saluting the stoic, rather intimidating-looking soldier when he did a double take.

"*Zaavu,*" he swore, dragonfire eyes going wide as he looked at me.

"What? Did I spill on my shirt or something?" I looked down at my clothes, but found nothing particularly incriminating there.

"*Zu juuvi,*" Zoren said, pointing to my neck.

"What about Asher's scarf?" Elle asked when she recognized the word.

My hand flew to my neck where my mother's old gift was in its usual place, if not a little more neatly folded partially beneath my jacket's collar. General Kheradok and General Zora looked at the scarf with blank confusion, but Empress Khaisa gasped.

"*Zaavu ja ziivan!*" the Empress cursed. "How did I not realize?" She looked at me as if she were seeing a ghost. Then she muttered to Zoren, "Are you certain it's...?"

"*Jhi,*" Zoren replied in a hushed tone. He then spoke in Drekai, clearly expecting us Evgardians not to understand.

But I did.

"*I'd recognize that scarf anywhere. It's hers.*"

Hers. Soot, had they known Mom? But why would Mom have known someone as highly ranked as the Empress?

"What's going on?" General Zora asked. The rest of us were wondering the same thing.

"Nothing at all." Empress Khaisa struggled to regain her composure. Her eyes seemed to be welling with tears, her hands trembling as her stress mounted. Then she muttered something to Zoren before hurrying from the great hall.

"The Empress requests a moment alone," Zoren said, taking charge. "You will be escorted to your rooms now."

Zoren snapped his fingers and a servant appeared to usher us away. At least, he ushered Solrac and Elle away, ignoring their confused protests. As for me, Zoren asked me to stay behind.

"Empress Khaisa wishes to speak with you in a more private setting," he said once the others were gone. Then he led me out of the hall too. The generals tried to follow at first, but Zoren stopped them, saying it was the business of the Empress.

Finally alone, Zoren and I hurried down a long, open air hallway toward another building in the palace. From the moment he'd first looked at me, my stomach had been twisting into knots. What was happening?

"Zoren?" I asked.

When he didn't answer, I tried again, more forcefully this time.

"*Zoren?*"

He whirled on me, stopping in his tracks. The intensity of his glare literally made me stumble backward.

"Uh..." I started, my mind going blank. Zoren waited for me to continue, his gaze combing my face, hair, scarf, and everything else, taking in every detail.

"You," I started, heart pounding, "you knew my mother." It wasn't a question.

I thought I was prepared for the man's response.

I was so wrong.

"Yes," Zoren replied. "I knew Princess Zerana well."

Chapter 14: The Shield

Meleya

I was just about to head back to my parents' cottage outside Orothion after a long day of training. One of the last ones Squad Reckless was going to take part in for a while, since in a few days we'd be shipping out to Keep Solhelm. Solvai had arranged things to perfection—We were going to be King Brigan's high guard, at least for a month or so while the dust settled.

Kai's sister, Kari, would be joining us too, as King Brigan had specifically requested her assistance in building up some experimental wild dragon wards he wanted to test in the Canyonlands. Apparently she had big plans, as evidenced by the numerous crates and trunks of supplies she'd already packed for the journey.

As for me, there had been some deliberation as to whether or not it was safe for me to leave the safety of Orothion while bearing the Soul Reaper's voidshard. Ultimately, the Triarchy had decided that since Solhelm was only across the Scarlet Strait from here, as long as I left a few backup rift anchors here and brought enough skystone to get back at the first sign of danger, it would be alright. Sure, protecting the voidshard was my top priority, but that didn't mean I could spend my entire life running from Xan and the Gray Knight and whoever else might try to take it from my rift hold pantry.

That reminded me, I needed to make sure *Mom's* pantry was well-stocked before I left. Besides that, I still hadn't made a meal plan for the journey yet, let alone prepared everything we'd need.

I was just making a mental shopping list when I spotted someone coming in through the wide front gates of the stronghold. It was Shaya, her usually chipper mood somewhat dampened, with her long red hair tied in a high draketail style. I couldn't help but notice her hands, which, despite the warm early autumn day, were covered in a pair of thick, lacy black gloves.

I'd never seen Shaya without her gloves, or rather *a* pair of gloves. She must've had a dozen, all with varying levels of thickness. These gloves were shiny and black as ink, just like the shawl Shaya had knitted for my mother.

I'd thought about the shawl often since seeing it in Etheria the day my parents had told me about the new baby. The way the ethereal light had shone from it, like a protective shield around Mom's shoulders... The more I thought about it, the more I thought it looked almost exactly like the glow that emitted from Asher's scarf as seen from Etheria.

Hopeful that Shaya had answers, I leaned into my curiosity and called out, waving my arm. "Shaya!"

Shaya looked up to see me jogging over. She broke into a bright smile. "Meleya of Misthaven! How are you? Solei's blade—What a day, right?"

"I'm fine, thanks. Rough day at the refugee camp?"

Shaya gave an over-the-top sigh. "A new group of refugees just arrived, and so many of them are stricken with the shadow wasting it breaks my heart."

"Stars," I said, thinking of the poor, afflicted auras that Asher, Zerana, and I had seen while in Etheria.

Shaya went on. "The volunteer medics have been treating the worst cases as best they can, but two people went hollow today. There's just not enough liquid light to go around."

"What about the Lightwielders here among the Knights?" I asked. "Can't they make more?"

"They're already working overtime as it is," Shaya said. "It's how we keep up on our day-to-day supply in the first place. But creating even a small vial of liquid light can be taxing on a Lightwielder, depending on their proficiency. Besides that, we have to ship out a portion of our stores to Knights realm-wide, and I suspect some of the Lightwielders are selling vials on the black market. I can hardly blame them—There's a massive shortage all across Evgard."

Shaya sighed. "Aurora was helping to lighten the load before she departed for the Dragon Isles. That pretty little dragon is quite proficient with making liquid light. In fact..." Shaya lowered her voice. "Elle told me not to spread this around, but while you and Asher were in astral sleep, I once saw her purge the shadow wasting from a man entirely."

My eyes widened, and I recalled a town called Scorpio's Shadow—renamed Topaz Sierra—wherein I'd witnessed something similar. It had been hard to see through the crowd, and until now I wasn't even sure of what I'd seen happen to the little girl. But now that Shaya brought it up, it jarred my memory.

"Aurora breathed a white flame, didn't she?" I whispered back. "One whose touch scattered the Gray."

"Solei's blade, yes!" Shaya replied, barely able to keep her voice down. "A father of five, the whole left side of his body gray with the shadow wasting—healed completely in no time flat. I could hardly believe my eyes!"

"Stars, this is wonderful news!"

"Well, yes," Shaya said. "For the man and his family, at least. See, Aurora couldn't seem to manage the white flame again, not that Elle was thrilled about letting her try. Doing so drained Aurora so much that she slept for days. We were all so worried."

I nodded, intrigued by Aurora's power. Meanwhile, Shaya stuck out her chin.

"This whole situation is entirely unfair," she said. "Made worse by the fact that the High Crown has people terrified—Anyone showing even a hint of shadow wasting is getting yanked off the streets by black-and-whites from the Capital, then being shipped off to scorching Kolbohr."

"Isn't that a good thing?" I asked. "I thought Kolbohr was helping by taking in the shadow wasting victims when no one else would."

Shaya gave a bitter laugh. "And just what do you think the good-for-nothing King and Queen of Kolbohr are *doing* with them? Putting them up in luxury inns and feeding them bonbons?"

My spirits sank. "What *are* they doing to them?"

Shaya lowered her voice. "Word at the camps is that they're turning them into free, disposable slave labor. The refugees are desperate to protect anyone who catches the shadow wasting. Drakking nobles. And don't even get me started on the way Mage Hunters are rounding up every magi they can get their silversoot hands on thanks to High King Monstrosity's latest proclamation!"

She was practically breathing fire to match her hair. The tiny gold flecks in her eyes flashed as she balled her hands. Stars, those gloves were even thicker with lace than I'd realized.

"I cannot stand it!" Shaya steamed. "I just wish I could *do* something."

"Trust me, you are," I said. "Those refugees light up when they see you. Every smile is a strike against the Gray."

That got Shaya nodding, the fire easing somewhat. "I like that."

"Besides, maybe there's something else you could do," I went on.

Shaya gave me a quizzical look. "What's that?"

"I'm not sure yet. Shaya, the shawl you knitted for my mother... it's more than just a shawl, isn't it?"

At this, Shaya's expression went from curious to downright confused, so I told her about what I'd seen in the spirit plane, and the similarities it bore to the auras Archonic strikes produced when they protected against the gray.

"Do you have any idea what it could mean?" I asked.

Shaya frowned, her mind clearly racing a million miles a minute. "You had better come with me."

The library at Orothion was chock-full of cozy nooks and crannies, perfect for reading, studying, or—apparently—knitting.

A thick rug was set before a low-burning hearth with identical stone wyvern statues on either side. Shaya introduced the pair of them as Butch and Astrid Star-Catcher Hildegarde the Third.

"Were there Astrid Star-Catcher Hildegardes the First and Second?" I couldn't help but ask.

"We don't talk about them." Shaya winked, then gave a self-satisfied snort and promptly ducked behind Butch, who'd been hiding her wicker basket of knitting materials, including several spools of thick black threads. She and I sat together before the fire, the basket between us.

"First off, I probably ought to tell you about these," Shaya said, pulling off each of her thick, lacy gloves in turn, then passing them to me so I could get a better look. They were incredibly detailed, bearing patterns like a series of snowflakes held together by silky threads.

But even as I held them, they began to disappear in an evaporating cascade of golden etherdust. Within moments, they were gone.

"Your beautiful gloves!" I started. "I'm so sorry, I don't know what—"

"All is well," Shaya rushed to reassure me. "*Look.*"

She held out a hand and I leaned closer. There, winding up her fingers and palms, countless new, spydraweb-like strands were already forming and intertwining. New, faint lace where the old had been.

"What in the stars?" I asked.

Shaya gave a half-smile. "I can't stop creating shadowsilk any more than I can stop breathing."

"Since when?" I asked, fascinated as I watched the wispy threads curling along her palm.

"I've been this way my whole life," Shaya replied. "It used to be worse—Once, as a baby, I made a shadowsilk swaddle so thick I nearly suffocated. After that, my family always made sure someone was watching me. They hoped I'd learn to control it, but... obviously that still hasn't happened."

"Incredible," I said. Most magi didn't manifest powers until they were a little older. As for me, I hadn't shown signs of being a Rifter until the age of seven.

"As the years went by, I learned to keep the power contained to just my hands, but barring the use of silver manacles, I can't stop using my etherarchy, no matter what I do. That's why my parents kept me tucked away in the attic all throughout my childhood. Some magi can hide in plain sight. Not me."

"Soot," I murmured, my heart going out to her.

Shaya shrugged. "It is what it is. Since I make so much shadowsilk, I started weaving it into these threads."

She picked up one of the spools from the basket. "Part aldraka wool and part shadowsilk. The shadowsilk dissolves after about three days—unless I use it in my knitting."

"Why is that?" I asked.

"Thanks to these." Shaya pulled out a pair of shimmering knitting needles made from extra-strong crystal. I'd noticed them before, but hadn't put it together until now.

"They're made of skystone," I said.

"Precisely," Shaya replied, clicking the two sticks together twice. "Just enough power transfers into the threads as I knit, preserving the etherarchy in the shadowsilk indefinitely. Took me a while to figure it out, but when you spend years cooped up inside, you're not short on time."

I looked from the needles to the spools of shadowsilk-wool, fascinated. Shaya continued.

"I don't have a clue what you saw in the spirit plane, but that's my big secret." Shaya leaned forward. "Don't tell Trickshot I told you. She worries what people would do if they found out, even here."

"Your secret's safe with me," I promised. "Do you mind if I take a look into Etheria while you work?"

"Be my guest!" Shaya said eagerly. "I've always wondered what my aura looks like!"

As Shaya eagerly grabbed a spool of thread and started looping it around her crystalline needles, I traced the rune for the Sight. Her aura bloomed all around her, a vibrant yellowish-peach color, like a sunset before the sky gave way to darkness. Shaya squealed with excitement as I described it.

As she knitted, the yarn forming neat rows that hung between the needles, I saw the shadowy aura of the silk, as well as the golden aura of the ether from the skystone infusing into it. The shadowy aura of the silk looked nothing like the auras that clung to wraithkind; rather, it was light and shiny, coiling around itself like fine strands of hair floating underwater.

While the black-and-gold aura was undeniably beautiful, it wasn't the same as the white-gold halo I'd seen emanating from Mom's shawl or Asher's scarf. I watched as Shaya's creation grew so long it touched her lap, but still, no sign of anything like it.

"Hm," I said. "Is anything different than usual?"

"I don't think so," Shaya answered.

"I'll keep watching."

As Shaya continued knitting, we began to chat, first about growing up as magi in hiding, then about Shaya's work with the refugees and mine with the soldiers. Soon, the topic of our time at the Mage Hunter Academy came up.

"I remember you were always late returning to the dorm each night," Shaya said. "Something about an extra class with Mason Drakeslayer, if I recall."

"Ah..." I bit the inside of my cheek. "You mean the so-called 'class' that was really just an alibi for the High Prince to drop me off in an isolated grotto somewhere in Kolbohr for hours at a time?"

"No way!" Shaya's eyes widened.

"Way, I'm afraid," I said, then proceeded to tell her about those awful weeks. Shaya was a very good listener, and I opened up about the way I'd come to dread seeing Mason's face and even hearing his voice, because I knew it meant I had to go back to Scryer's Grotto. There, I'd pretend to search for the aura of the person he'd convinced himself was in possession of the Soul Reaper's voidshard. Night after night, I returned to that void, with no light in sight.

"Soot be upon that good-for-nothing High Prince," Shaya said, miming spitting into the hearth. "Meleya, that's awful."

"It's not a time I like to remember," I agreed.

"Solei's blade—You must've gotten strong."

"Strong?" I repeated. "More like the opposite. I shut out everyone I cared for out of fear. Even my best friends, Solvai and Brigan, as well as... as..."

"Jax?" Shaya supplied.

"Yeah." I looked down at my feet, where my indigo aura spiraled around my toes.

"Tell me about you and Jax," Shaya said, a hint of conspiracy in her gold-flecked eyes. "I'm a bit of a hopeless romantic, you see."

I exhaled through my nose, and for a split second, I considered telling her about Asher instead. "What Jax and I once had is..."

"I know," Shaya said. "But I love a good story all the same."

She was so eager and genuine, I couldn't refuse. Before long, I was telling her about meeting Jax at Outcast Outpost and about surviving the Dragon Mists together. Shaya listened intently, hungrily lapping up every word as she knitted.

Finally, I told her about the day Jax and I had blown off our classes at the Academy so he could whisk me away to that sunny mountain glade. I told her how he'd built a makeshift kitchen just for me, and about the sweet way he used to ramble when he had something serious weighing on his mind. I found I was smiling despite myself.

That was when I saw it: White-gold light began latching onto Shaya's threads, infusing them with the same shield-like halo I'd seen on Mom's shawl.

Excitedly, I got to my knees so suddenly Shaya jumped.

"Solei's blade!" she yelped.

"There it is!" I pointed, though I knew without the Sight, all Shaya could see was the silky black fabric she was making. "The shield! But where's it coming from?"

I visually traced the white-gold strands to the source, startling when I realized it was coming from... *me*.

All at once, I remembered the very first time I'd seen Shaya knitting back at the Mage Hunter Academy dorm. I closed my eyes, recalling that day before the hearth:

What are you doing? I'd asked her.

You might laugh at me, Shaya had replied before relenting. *It's just... I like to imagine I'm weaving happy memories into every piece I make.*

"You were picturing the time you bonded your wyvern," I said aloud. Shaya looked confused, but I pressed on. "And just now, I was remembering the glade. Shaya—they're memories."

Stars, could it be true? Were happy memories the final piece that turned Shaya's innate Archonic powers into spiritual anti-wraith shields? It seemed crazy, but I'd been to Etheria, where etherotters splashed in rivers of pure magic, conversations had color and texture, literal sparks flew, and long-lost mothers could embrace their not-really-dead sons. Of course it was possible. Anything was.

"Meleya, what's going on?" Shaya cocked her head, looking concerned for my sanity.

"Keep knitting!" I said giddily. "We may have just found something—Something that could give the Knights a vital edge against the Gray."

Chapter 15: The Bungalow

Asher

I was frozen. As in, I literally didn't move a muscle for what felt like several minutes, though for all I know it could've only been a few seconds. Soot, maybe it had been hours—Who was counting?

See, maybe if I didn't move, I could go back in time to before the Empress's advisor had spoken those two, life-changing words:

Princess Zerana.

Princess Zerana.

That meant... That meant Mom was a... That *I* was a...

What *was* I?

"If you'll hurry, please, Prince Asher." Zoren gestured for me to continue following him up the path toward the palace.

Prince Asher? I wanted to throw up.

I was so distracted as Zoren half-dragged my stunned frame that I didn't notice the moment when the covered walkway gave way to the springy paaka moss that carpeted the swamp. This man very well could've been kidnapping me, and I wouldn't have given a flying scale. As the torchlight of the Zolehiinu palace vanished behind us, it was all I could do to keep placing one foot in front of the other.

"Where are we going?" I finally dared to ask.

"*Kun Zuo*," Zoren replied, which I automatically translated to 'The Bog.' I did not feel reassured.

We finally reached a secluded beach. The sea lapped at the shore, and the low sunset in the west made the tall, dark sea stacks cast long shadows across the water. Looking back the way we'd come, I could see the distant splendor of Zolehiinu climbing up the low mountain above the foliage. The city was gorgeous, with hundreds of buildings set harmoniously amidst the trees and rivers, the layered, peaked rooftops reminding me of dragon spines. At its center, the palace gleamed like a crown jewel—the heartscale on the living dragon that was the city.

If I hadn't been losing my mind here as my entire identity fell apart, I might've actually enjoyed the view.

Through my bond with Thorn, I felt calming embers. He was at the dragon stables over the river nearer the palace gates, and didn't yet fully comprehend what was happening on my end. I tried to let my dragon soothe me, but not even he could keep my head from spinning as I numbly followed Zoren straight into the sea.

"Whoa, whoa, whoa," I protested, stopping in my tracks at the shoreline. "I'm going to ask where we're going once more, and this time, I don't want to hear something as vague as '*Kun Zuo*'."

"Place your hand here on the runestone," Zoren instructed, pointing at literally nothing.

I gave him my best blank stare. "You know, I'm honestly glad this is happening: You're crazy. Yep, that's it. You're insane, and all of this is some elaborate joke that—"

Zoren grabbed me by the wrist and placed my hand on the bit of air he'd been pointing to. Only it wasn't air—It was solid.

Before my eyes, whatever illusion had been cloaking reality melted away. My hand was in the center of an elaborate design carved into a heavy, jutting stone just shorter than I was. And it wasn't the only thing I'd been missing.

An entire network of buildings materialized, most of them psionically floating over the ocean amidst the stony sea stacks. Slats of telekinetic bridges connected the buildings, all of which came to a head at the largest building in the center.

"Welcome to *Kun Zuo*—otherwise known as the Emerald Eye dojo," Zoren said. "Some might think showing you this place is a risk, but I knew your mother well. If you're anything like her—and my observations thus far suggest that you are—then I'd be a fool not to let you in. Besides, after what we've discovered tonight, I doubt the Empress plans to let you out of her sight."

"Stars," was all I could manage as I followed Zoren onto a flat, psionically-floating stone. We stepped onto the stone, and runes glowed along its surface. Then, at a middling pace, the enchanted stone began to lift us up toward the balcony of the largest building.

We found Empress Khaisa inside, sitting in one of several chairs that had been placed in the corner of what looked to be a large, indoor training arena. Two Drekai advisors flanked her, and all three turned their full attention onto me the moment I entered the room.

"Is it true then?" one advisor asked. She wore an elegant wrap tunic and had a pair of spiraling horns.

"This is the half-born?" chimed the other, a wizened older man in black with impressively perfect posture.

"The scarf..." The spiral-horned woman reached toward my neck, but I recoiled.

"It's hers, Keskit," Zoren said to the woman. "I am certain of it. Besides that, look at him. You can see her in his features. The arc of his brows... the shape of his nose..."

"Zerana was always going on about your eye for detail, Zoren," the old man said.

"But this is impossible!" the female advisor, Keskit, fretted, turning Empress Khaisa's way. "I saw your sister die in the *zhatehlu ji kuniia* myself. You were there as well, Blademaster Zedek!" she addressed the older advisor.

"So was I, right before I left for Evgard," Zoren cut in. "I was never convinced of her death. The way she hesitated right before our Empress shot her dragonfire... Zerana never hesitated in a fight. And there weren't nearly enough ashes afterward either. Zerana's a Shadowbinder—She could have activated her invisibility at just the right moment, and none of us would have been any the wiser."

"The circumstances of Princess Zerana's death were suspicious at best," Blademaster Zedek agreed. "Reports over the years were mixed, but there were at least two instances of raiders claiming to have seen Zerana alive on the mainland. One claimed she was in some outlander town in Drakfell." He looked at me.

"Steel Rim," I provided, my voice coming out weak. "She came to Steel Rim with a raiding party. That's where she met my father."

"There you have it," Zedek said.

"Are we completely certain he's Zerana's child?" Keskit asked.

"He's my half-sister's son," Empress Khaisa finally spoke, looking up from her hands. "It's as Zoren said—One look at the young man would tell you that."

She rose, silky green robes trailing as she approached me. The Drekai Empress got a faraway look in her dragonfire eyes as she looked me over, reaching out a hand to touch the tip of one of my turquoise-scaled ears. Now that I was looking for it, I could see the resemblance between her and my mom.

"What I don't understand," Khaisa spoke softly, "is why she never returned home. Especially after our father's passing. He loved her so much." Her gaze went from neutral to barely subdued anger as she glanced at my scarf. For a second, I thought she was going to forcibly take it from me.

Zedek hung his head. "Emperor Khaz cared deeply for all three of his daughters. I can only assume Zerana did not know, or that it was not safe for her to come home at the time of his passing. Or..." He looked at me. "...perhaps she simply found happiness elsewhere."

Outside, I could hear the flapping of wings. For a moment, I thought it was a wild dragon attack, but when the door opened, I saw that it was Kheradok, tucking his wide black wings behind him and inviting himself in.

"Aunt Khaisa, please. I need to know what's going on," Kheradok said.

I could hardly believe my ears. *Aunt* Khaisa?

"It's only right that General Kheradok be here while we sort this out," the advisor, Keskit, said. "The half-born's existence affects him the most, after all."

"His existence?" Kheradok repeated.

Kheradok's expression went from curious to shocked, then deeply disturbed as Zoren and the others explained who my mother was. Who *I* was. The general looked at me as if he were seeing me for the first time.

"*Zehku?*" Kheradok said in disbelief. I recognized the Drekai word for...

"Cousin?" I said, equally dumbfounded. Suddenly, I was unable to stand by any longer. "Can someone please explain to me exactly what's going on? That is, what all of this actually *means*?"

There was a long, heavy pause before Empress Khaisa stepped up. Slowly, methodically, she told me how her father, the late Emperor Khaz, had been married twice. His first wife was an Evgardian, which caused quite the stir when my mother was born. Traditionally, she would have been the heir to the throne. But as a half-born, some had questioned her right to rule.

When Emperor Khaz's wife passed away shortly after childbirth, he married again. This time, his wife was a Drekai, generally regarded as a more appropriate empress. Khaisa was born shortly thereafter, followed by a younger sister."

"My mother," Kheradok put in.

"But when Zerana and I came of age, the people were discontented," Empress Khaisa continued. "Many supported Zerana as the firstborn, but there were also those who felt only a full-blooded Drekai should wear the crown. They called for a *zhatehlu ji kuniia.*"

"An honor duel," I translated.

"*Jhi.*" Empress Khaisa nodded. "*Zhaku* for short. I won the duel, but only because Zerana made a choice to effectively abandon her responsibility and claim to the throne. But she never formally conceded. Now, it is clear that my rule was never rightful. I have no children, which has always meant the crown would fall to my eldest nephew, Kheradok. But now that we know about Asher..."

"It changes everything," Kheradok said.

"Whoa, whoa, whoa." I put up my hands. "Slow down, everybody. Let's make one thing clear right away: I'm not an option when it comes to thrones and crowns and soot like that. The very idea is completely ludicrous."

"That's the way it works for the Drekai. Family is everything," Zoren said.

"Then *change* the way it works!" I said, panic setting in. I wanted to run. I wanted to bolt straight out of this room and take a flying leap over the scorching ocean, and I didn't give a flying scale if I didn't hover-catch myself.

As if I wasn't already living my worst nightmare, the old man, Zedek, got to his feet and said something that made it all ten-thousand times worse:

"I think we can all agree on what this means," he said. "The unmet demands of fate have called for history to repeat itself. The honor duel three days from now between Kheradok of Zolehiinu and Asher of Steel Rim will now be about far more than a true dragon or an alliance. About far more, even, than honor."

I held my breath. Everyone around me was nodding as the older man finished.

"It will be a battle for the throne of the Dragon Isles."

Khaisa and the others in that top-secret dojo took an oath to not speak of our discovery to another living soul until things could be properly arranged. They made me swear to do the same, which included not telling Solrac or Elle either, at least for now. This was Drekai business.

They doubted I could keep my word, so under the excuse of me needing space to mentally prepare for my duel, Zoren brought me to a special, private bungalow in the forest near the dojo. That was where I was to live for the next three days.

The bungalow was actually the most peaceful, charming place I could've possibly imagined. Per the Empress's request, Thorn was there waiting for me, perched at the base of a set of psionic stones that formed a staircase leading up to a quaint lodge in the treetops. I'd informed him of all that we'd learned—technically, my oath to secrecy hadn't mentioned *dragons*—and he swore to keep the secret too.

It will be alright, Thorn thought through our bond, along with a feeling like comforting embers, which I clung to with my entire soul. *You're still the same Asher.*

From the wide porch, I got the perfect view of a sprawling, majestic valley, filled with wildflowers and a lake reflecting the stars. The sight of it instantly transported me to Steel Rim. The view was so similar to the one from Kiivi Zariika, Mom's favorite cliffside overlook. Thorn joined me on the porch, humming softly. He must've noticed it too.

"This is your mother's old bungalow," Zoren said. "Only those closest to her knew about it. The Empress and I thought you might enjoy staying here."

Zoren was right. Inside, there were some soft, blackscale deer fur cloaks, a few stacks of books and some decorative rocks, some extra scimitars, and a couple of *kalaata*. Out on the porch, there was a very overgrown flower garden in a long, thin box.

"It's been largely untouched since she left," Zoren went on. "Khaisa didn't want anyone disturbing it. Despite their harsh final moments,

Khaisa loved her half-sister. Your mother, too, often spoke of how much she valued family, although she once confided in me her discontent regarding the way our people too often put honor before family. Honor, and in her words, personal pride. She said that during our last conversation together, the evening before her duel with Khaisa."

I'd been angry and confused earlier, but when I spoke now, my voice was slow and gentle as I stroked Thorn's scales. "Were you and my mother close?"

"I'd say so," Zoren said. "Princess Zerana was one of the first to tell me I had skill as a tracker. She was part of why I ended up joining the Emerald Eye, the team of agents sworn to serve the royal family since the age of the first emperor, Ash Ironscale."

"Ash Ironscale," I repeated.

"Without Zerana, I'd never have gained the confidence I needed to enlist with the group of agents bound for Evgard all those years ago," Zoren went on.

"What made you stay in Evgard for so long?" I asked, leaning against Thorn as we overlooked the valley.

"The same reason your mother stayed," Zoren replied. I could tell he wasn't used to speaking so openly, but I think he could tell how lonely I was feeling, or perhaps he was feeling a bit extra protective over his old friend's very confused son. "I fell in love. Soon after my team and I arrived on the mainland, we traveled to the Mirror Forest, where we were beset by umbral cougardrakes. I'd have died with the rest of them if someone very special hadn't found me."

Zoren shared with me a tragic story about falling for a young magi who'd been forced to join the Mage Hunters. The orphanage she'd grown up in had been caught harboring dozens of young, unregistered magi, and in order to get the Hunters to turn a blind eye to the others, she'd volunteered to join the Mage Hunters. As a rare Rifter, her skills were in high demand.

When she'd found Zoren sick with the shadow wasting and a scale's breadth from death, she'd brought him to the Academy's healers. He'd joined the Hunters too, hoping to fulfill his spying mission for the Drekai, but also because he'd have given anything to be close to the beautiful young woman who'd saved his life.

After graduating from the Academy, the pair of them were given the assignment to track and trap a psionic highwayman in southern Behrfell.

Despite Zoren's expert tracking skills, the thief continued to mysteriously evade his pursuers. It wasn't until later that Zoren discovered that his Hunting partner had been meeting with the rogue in secret. She'd fallen in love with him, and the two eloped, leaving Zoren bent on capturing the thief, a job that he'd obsessed over for more than ten years.

"What made you finally come home?" I asked.

"I had information regarding the Gray that I needed to share with my people. And, well... I finally learned a lesson I wish I'd learned much sooner."

"What's that?"

Zoren sighed. "Some hills are worth dying on, but there is also wisdom in a humble retreat. I was no longer able to justify wasting my time, energy, and skill on a hill *not* worth dying on."

As he spoke, I couldn't help but think about how I'd spent most of my life hating the noble class. I still got a bad taste in my mouth whenever I thought of the way the baron in Steel Rim had treated me. How so many of them flaunted their wealth while refusing to let poor and desperate refugees into their keeps. Kai and I spent years stealing from them, trying to earn enough coin to get our families somewhere safe. Nobles had always been the enemy.

And now, just like that, I was one.

And not just some random duke or count either, but a bona fide prince—and possibly the heir to an entire drakking empire.

Soot. I suddenly wondered if I was really ready to retreat from that particular hill. Part of me still felt like I needed the hill... As if it were a core part of my identity. *Could* I let it go, even if I wanted to? And if I did, would that just come off as two-faced and egotistical? As if, now that the rules benefited me rather than dragging me down, I was no longer against them? Drak, my mind was a mess.

"Is there anything else I can get you, Prince Asher?" Zoren asked, breaking my reverie.

"Don't call me that, alright?" I scowled. "Just 'Asher' is fine."

"Is that a royal decree, or just a personal preference?"

At that, I looked at Zoren's face, searching for any signal that he'd been joking. Other than the *tiniest* glint in his eye, his expression was utterly deadpan.

My jaw fell open. "Did... did *you* just make a joke?"

“Did I?” Zoren smiled mischievously. “Hm. Well, if it pleases ‘just Asher’, I will take my leave. Your servants will be here shortly to bring you food and whatever else you desire. If you wish to speak with me again, just let one of them know and I—”

“Thank you, Zoren. That will be all.” I nodded, then watched as he descended the psionic stone steps, leaving me alone with my dragon bond and my scattered thoughts.

“That was a friendly dismissal, not an order, by the way!” I shouted after him, but he was already out of earshot.

Back at the dojo, they’d made me swear an oath not to tell a living soul about what I’d learned tonight. But nobody had said anything about a dead one.

“Hey, Mom,” I said out loud, looking over the valley lit by a half moon. Here in her old bungalow, I tried to search for the peace I’d felt in her presence while in Etheria, the comfort she’d always brought me.

Instead, I found resentment—Cold, bitter frustration, burning inside my chest. This was her fault. If she hadn’t abandoned her duel with Khaisa, I wouldn’t be facing *her* choice—the choice she had refused to make—twenty years later. This wasn’t fair. It wasn’t right. I felt angry... and felt angry that I felt angry.

Tears welled in my eyes as I called into the oblivion, hoping in my bitterness that she could hear me now.

“Why, Mom?” I asked. “Why would you do this to me?”

For two days, I hardly saw anyone but Thorn. I’d expected that. For one, they didn’t want me to go accidentally break my oath and tell everyone who I really was. In fact, if Kheradok beat me in the honor duel tomorrow morning, they might never have to tell anyone at all. Kheradok would remain the uncontested heir to the Dragon Isles throne, they would get to keep their true dragon, and I would die quietly.

Yes. Honestly, that might be the best outcome for everyone. Imagining what would happen if I actually managed to *win*... soot. Sure, I wanted to secure the alliance for the Knights, as well as win Elle and Aurora’s freedom. But besides that, nobody—and I mean *nobody*—wanted *me* as heir. I was no Drekai. I was no Evgardian, either. A half-born halfway between both worlds.

Who *was* I, anyway? In truth, I was nothing more than a nobody who everyone was trying to shoehorn into being a somebody. Stars.

For hours, I teetered between hoping I'd lose the duel to wishing I could simply run away. It felt ironic that I was stuck living out the exact scenario my mother had tried so very hard to escape, as if she'd fled all the way across the world and wound up returning to the very same spot. And now, I was facing a choice between death and death—One death was literal, while the other meant letting my old identity die in the wake of becoming the heir to the Drekai throne.

But I *couldn't* just run away like she had—That would mean abandoning Elle and Aurora to the Dragon Isles, to serve against their wills for the rest of their days. Elle... Soot, I missed Elle.

I passed the time brushing up on my Drekai by way of some old Drekai-Evgardian language texts, and even read some interesting histories I found on the shelves. Naturally, I was most interested in the stories involving honor duels and duels of wills. I especially remembered the conversation Mom and I had had in Etheria regarding the differences between the two.

A zhavoi, *or duel of wills, does not end in death, but at first blood,* she'd said. *These are meant to settle matters of lesser consequence....*

A duel of honor is to the death over a matter of utmost significance. The extreme consequence corresponds to the extremity of what's at stake.

The records gave plenty of examples of duels of wills that had escalated into duels of honor, fought to the death. But I couldn't find a single example of things going the other way, *de*-escalating the situation. I found their culture's reliance on violence to be, frankly, pointless. Why would a nation ever condone, much less encourage, such needless bloodshed among its most promising young warriors? Frustrated, I'd shut the books. This was why I didn't read.

Instead, I pulled one of my mother's old scimitars from its display hook on the wall. It was an elegant single-edged blade, with a subtle curve near the tip. Gold designs were engraved along the base of the blade, and the teal wrapping on the long handle matched my scarf. The weapon was perfectly balanced.

With her scimitar in one hand and my father's skyseeker dagger in the other, I trained on an old practice dummy she had in a back room.

Something about wielding the two weapons felt right, one being from my Drekai side, and the other from my Evgardian.

Besides that, Thorn tried to keep me sane by flying me through the forest surrounding Mom's old bungalow. The chirruping, fog-laden woods were incredible and teeming with life. But even that couldn't snap me out of my destructive mental cycle. Maybe nothing could.

The day before the duel, I was looking over the rest of my mother's old belongings when I realized the decorative rocks sitting on her bookshelf were more than they seemed. Both psionic and illusion runes decorated their surfaces; when I touched one, it made me jump as it began to float and project an illusion.

A depiction of my mother's family manifested in the air above the hovering stone. It was like an incredibly realistic painting, but the figures were moving. I realized that this must've been tied to a memory, showing the moment the royal family had sat together, posing for a painting or something. This was much better than a painting, anyway.

In the illusion, Mom, Khaisa, and a third sister who must've been Kheradok's mother stood gathered around their father, Emperor Khaz. Despite the crown, the sight of the tall, proud man made me smile—I had his nose.

The memory-illusion included sound, and I heard the four of them laughing together. Mom gave Khaisa a playful shove, and Khaisa folded her arms as she pretended to be annoyed. That didn't last long, though, and soon the sisters were grinning once again.

I watched the scene replay several times, my heart growing heavier at each repetition. It hurt knowing that this perfectly content family had ultimately fallen apart, thanks to their own nation turning these two sisters against each other. And all over something as trivial as a crown.

The evening before the duel, Thorn was out hunting, leaving me sitting on the rooftop of Mom's bungalow. It was raining, and a normal person would've probably headed inside.

But if this was my last day among the living, I wanted to feel every raindrop slide down my face.

I wasn't sure how long I'd been up there, soaked to the skin with my eyes closed, when I heard a thud on the rooftop beside me. I recognized the sound of Thorn landing, and didn't open my eyes.

After a moment, I heard his voice through our bond: *Asher?*

"What?" I asked out loud, still focusing on the raindrops.

I brought you something, Thorn said. *I had to sneak, but it was worth it.*

It took a lot more energy than it should have just to open my eyes. But Thorn was right—It was so worth it.

Sliding from Thorn's back was Elle. Definitely not 'Eliana' this time—Just Elle. She wore a simple brown dress rather than her white armored one, and her hair was long and wavy, with beads of rainwater sliding down the strands. Aurora's heartscale shone like a white beacon on her collarbone. The downpour was making her squint in a funny way as she made her way toward me along the rooftop, but stars, I still found her beautiful. Like seeing a warm campfire after wandering the cold desert alone all night.

"No wonder I haven't been able to find you," she said, standing above me. "Is this part of your final preparation? They hide you away and isolate you in the woods?"

I swallowed hard. She didn't know.

Could I tell her? Did I want to?

No. For one, I'd sworn not to and, despite the doubts the Drekai royal family had, I refused to break my word. But even beyond that, I hated the idea of Elle looking at me differently right before my possible demise.

"Part of my preparation for sure," I said. "They all thought I talked too much, so they put me out here alone to help preserve my vocal chords. Throat's never felt better, actually."

Thorn flew off to give us some space. Elle sat down beside me on the rooftop, her dress making a slapping sound as she tucked her knees up and wrapped her arms around them.

We sat in silence for a long moment before Elle said, "How dare you."

I furrowed my brows. "Sorry?"

"You've got a lot of nerve, Asher of Steel Rim," Elle said. "Did you really think you could waltz into your scorched duel tomorrow without so much as saying goodbye to me? You lose so many points for that."

She was glaring at me viciously. I gave a nervous swallow as Elle continued to let me have it.

"I thought I was ready to watch this sky-forsaken duel, but I'm really, really not. I'm sick of playing it cool and acting like I'm above it all as this unflappable true dragon rider. The idea of losing you... I can't stand it."

She tried to wipe some of the falling rain from under her eyes, and it was hard to tell if there were tears there too. But Elle had finally stopped talking long enough for me to get a word in.

"What about Kheradok?" I asked quietly, bitterness creeping into my tone.

Elle raised an eyebrow, then shot back, "What about Meleya?"

My heart all but stopped. I was not expecting that.

"I'm not stupid," Elle said, then waited, looking at me expectantly.

In her bright amber eyes, I could tell all she wanted was the truth. To get on the same page again, whatever that meant. No more avoiding each other or sitting on vague frustrations and assumptions. With the duel tomorrow morning, there wasn't time to waste on any more games.

I told Elle about my spirit journey with Meleya. And I told her *everything*. How we'd braved the Haze together, then shared a kiss in that dark alcove. How I'd gotten to introduce her to my beloved mother.

Elle didn't get angry the same way I had when I'd heard about her and Kheradok's kiss in the Mirror Forest. Instead, she listened carefully, staying still and silent for a long moment after I'd finished.

Then, she just said, "Okay then. Now we're even."

"Excuse me?"

"I kissed someone else and so did you. So what? A kiss isn't a proposal."

"But it's not nothing," I said.

"So are you saying you love her?" Elle asked, raising her voice to be heard through the heavy rainfall.

Did I? I wasn't sure. Even in Etheria, I hadn't been *sure.* I thought of my last conversation with Meleya, and how she had told me not to hold back when it came to my heart.

"I care about her," I finally answered.

"I care about puppydrakes," Elle noted.

"She's kind," I said. "And smart."

"Agreed," Elle said. "Beautiful, too. What's more, your mother approves of her—I'll never be able to say that the way she can."

"I guess that's true," I said, faltering. "But..."

"But?"

"But..."

The tension between Elle and me was palpable, the torrential rain only adding to it. Her eyes were intense, bright with challenge to match mine as they waged a duel of their own in amber and dragonfire green.

"But," Elle said, this time with resolve, as if this were the answer to all of the confusion between us, "Asher, with us, there will always be 'but'. 'But what if?' or 'But why can't?' and on and on and on. Sure, we could move on from each other, but what if we gave up too soon? I'm the true dragon rider, destined to live a stuffy life at court, but what if that's not a good enough reason to give up on each other? Stars..."

Elle was on her feet now, practically calling into the storm for the goddesses themselves to hear.

"Maybe I shouldn't let thoughts of you run through my mind as I fall asleep each night, but what if I can't help it? Sure, the Seer dragon once told me to only let you into my heart if I wished for a fight, but what if that's a fight worth having? At first, I thought she meant a fight between me and someone else vying for your heart, and maybe she did. But what if the fight is between the different sides of ourselves? Which version of ourselves we want to be? And scorch, if I don't like who I am when I'm with you."

I was on my feet now too, arms ready to steady Elle if she started to slip down the sloped rooftop. My heart was still pounding as I took in the wild look in Elle's gaze, and the way the wind whipped her hair, free and unrestrained.

"You have to win tomorrow, Asher," she said.

"But—" I started.

"No." She shook her head, water sliding off the ends. "No more 'but this' or 'but that'. I know you're not ready to decide who you want to be just yet, so for now, the only 'but' we're allowed is this: Fate may not like it, *but* I refuse to let you go without giving 'us' a fair and honest try. Because stars, Asher of Steel Rim, I think *we* could be worth it."

She leaned in, and as her lips came closer, I could practically see two paths diverge before my eyes. In truth, my choices weren't about girls at all, but rather the two versions of me I might become:

On the one scale, there was Meleya. She was my escape, my ticket to a quiet, beautifully normal life.

On the opposite scale was Elle. I'd long been aware that being with her meant taking on far more responsibility than I felt ready for, and now... Well, with the threat of the Drekai crown all but literally looming over my head, that responsibility had just become a thousand times heavier.

But in that moment, I knew I just wanted to kiss Elle. I was cautious, not wanting to fall into the trap of loving the one I was with, but tensions were high, the storm was raging, and the idea of kissing this woman until I forgot about tomorrow's duel was incredibly tempting. Besides that, Elle's speech had gotten my heart thudding as I remembered each time she'd gotten me falling for her, again and again. What if she was right and *we* were worth it? If I lost tomorrow, we'd never get the chance to find out.

While I hesitated, Elle didn't. But the kiss she planted on my lips wasn't like anything I'd expected. Her face was all screwed up, her lips puckered into a tight 'O'. Frankly, it was without a doubt the most ridiculous, dissatisfying kiss anyone had ever experienced.

She quickly pulled away, and I gave her my most confused stare.

"What in the stars was that?" I asked.

"The worst kiss of all time," Elle replied. "One so bad, I absolutely *refuse* to let it be our last."

She took a few steps backward, enjoying the way she'd left my mouth hanging open. Her mischievous grin was like a bolt of lightning in the downpour.

"See you tomorrow," she said. Then she held up a hand, high in the air as if holding up a torch.

"Light the way, Asher!" Elle said, giving the rallying cry she'd been using to unite Evgardians to the Knights of the Torch's cause.

With that, Thorn flew back to retrieve her and took to the skies, leaving me standing there with nothing but hope, a racing pulse, and some very waterlogged boots.

When I finally climbed down from the roof, I didn't want to leave a massive puddle of water in my mom's bungalow, so I left my shoes and jacket hanging on the covered balcony to dry, then headed inside to build a fire and wait for someone to bring me dinner, hopefully with a warm drink of some kind.

When I stepped inside, I was surprised to find that my still-steaming dinner was already here, along with an unexpected visitor.

"Oh stars—Empress Khaisa," I said, inclining my head. The Empress had exchanged her emerald dress with a far more casual wrap tunic over pants. Her head was bare, her curling Drekai horns unadorned. She still looked regal, but far more approachable than she'd been that first day.

"Sorry if I kept you waiting," I said.

"*Nii kaata,* no trouble," Khaisa replied. "Tell me—*Ehta zezia zi Drekai?*"

She was asking about my Drekai language skills. Brushing up on it over the past few days had certainly helped, and being with Mom in Etheria had practically brought the language right back. Still, if I was being completely honest, my Drekai was only adequate at best, Although, I understood far more than I could say.

I replied in Drekai: "*I get by.*"

"*Good,*" Empress Khaisa answered in like. "*I need to know if the potential heir can hold his own in this country.*"

My mind seemed to sharpen as I focused on communicating in my mother's native tongue. She'd worked hard to teach me as best she could on her own, even while immersed in the Evgardian language in Steel Rim.

"*Please, eat.*" Khaisa gestured to the dinner table. She didn't have to ask twice. Like the rest of the Drekai food I'd tried while living here, today's prawn chowder tasted heavenly.

As I ate, Khaisa strode leisurely about the room, touching some of the old cloaks hanging on a rack and staring at the *kalaata* mounted on the wall.

"*Was she any good?*" I asked in my imperfect Drekai. "*My mother... Saw her fight much times with the scimitar. But the boomerang? Not much times. We just throw them together for fun.*"

"*She was incredible,*" Khaisa replied, unfazed by my linguistic shortcomings. "*But Zerana was good at everything she tried. She could pick up skills just like that.*" Khaisa snapped her fingers. "*She made our father so proud.*"

I sensed a hint of something like resentment in Khaisa's tone, and I wondered if there had been any sort of rivalry between the sisters. After all, they were so close in age. Looking at the Empress, I could even pinpoint specific features that she and my mother shared: the shape of their eyes, the way their hair fell, long and straight, down their backs. This really was my aunt, I realized. Had things been different, I might've grown up knowing this woman well.

"*What was she like? When she was young,*" I couldn't help but ask.

"*Zerana was a free spirit,*" Khaisa sighed. "*Some called her rebellious, but I knew that whenever she snuck out of the Zolehiinu palace to explore down by the river or hike Mount Khaalo, she did it not to disobey, but because of the valuziimi Zolehi inside her.*"

"*What's 'valuziimi'?*" I asked, unfamiliar with the Drekai word.

"*It describes the inner desire to wander and explore. A need so powerful we say it comes from the spirit goddess, Zolehi—*Solei, *herself,*" Khaisa explained.

I repeated the new word a few more times, committing it to memory. *"I think I have a bit of that valuziimi Zolehi myself,"* I admitted.

Khaisa laughed. *"I would be surprised if you didn't! You remind me so much of her."*

The way she said it, I couldn't quite tell if that was a good or bad thing. More likely, it was a painful, complicated thing. Here I was, some Evgardian-raised half-born, about to face the nephew she knew and loved in a battle for a crown I felt certain I didn't deserve.

As if reading my thoughts, Khaisa said, *"It's not fair, I know. This entire situation is frankly unprecedented. But... well."*

Khaisa took a seat at the table across from me. Carefully, she laid her hand on the table, palm up. The inside of her wrist and partway up her forearm was covered in marks—diamond-shaped tattoos, just like the ones Mom wore. Honor marks, each signifying a victory in a duel. Khaisa had even more than Mom had, which made sense, given how young Mom had been when she'd left the Isles.

"See here?" Khaisa asked, pointing to a spot in the middle of her forearm where there was a break in the interlocking diamonds, as if one tattoo had been skipped.

"This place belongs to the duel I had with Zerana the day she died. Or rather, the day she fled her homeland, rejecting the throne and her birthright. Many have asked me to take the honor mark for the duel, but I never could. It never felt right."

"Stars," I muttered.

"Stars," Khaisa agreed. *"Zerana had me beat in that duel. She was the superior warrior, and I am certain she would have made a superior empress, despite the foolish claims made by those who disliked her for being half-born. She was the eldest, the line hers by right. Your line, Asher."*

She held out a hand. *"May I?"* she asked, eyes flicking to my neck. With a degree of hesitation, I untied my scarf and passed it to Khaisa.

She clutched the fabric tightly in her hands, fingering the folds and the tiny markings I knew were ancient Drekai script. The lyrics to the song Mom had taught me.

"This scarf..." Khaisa said. *"It has been with our family for generations, since before we came to this land. When our father gave it to Zerana, I remember feeling both envy and relief. Envy for his confidence in her. Relief because it meant the burden of the crown would one day fall to her. But obviously she felt that burden was too much to shoulder."*

Continuing to stare at the heirloom, Khaisa went on. "*For years, I've feared that because of me, the succession would fall—for the first time—to a family outside of our own. One which does not recognize the urgency with which we must resist the Gray, the true threat to our nation—to our world. Kheradok's position as heir has long been a source of contention among our people, and soothing that has been difficult. But my nephew knows who the real enemy is, so I've always supported him.*"

Khaisa sighed, then passed me back the scarf. As I tied it back in place, the familiar fabric felt oddly foreign.

"*Do you know of Life Paths, Asher?*" Khaisa asked.

"*Mom told me about them, yes,*" I replied. "*Ideals that Drekai pledge themselves to at six... sixteen. Mom's was Courage.*"

"*And mine was Steadfastness. I believe I have fulfilled it well, despite my inadequacy.*"

The way she spoke reminded me so much of Mom. Mom had been my hero—brave, fiercely loyal, and family-minded. I saw so much of that in her sister.

"*I don't know you well, Empress,*" I started, "*but I'd say you've served your Life Path pretty scorching well.*"

That coaxed a soft smile out of Empress Khaisa. In her gaze, I saw something solidify, almost as if she'd gotten some kind of confirmation about me from our visit. I wished I could control when I had residual flashes of the Sight, because I was willing to bet her aura would've held clues to what she was thinking right now.

"*Well...*" She broke her gaze and rose. "*I suppose I should let you rest.*" As she headed towards the door, I found myself feeling surprised by how unsurprising I'd found her words. Shouldn't she be trying to rattle me? Put me off-guard ahead of my duel? Yet all she did was pause in the doorway to bid me one last farewell.

"*Good luck, Prince Asher, son of Zerana. Take courage.*"

Before I could so much as nod, she was gone, and I was left with the comforting sound of the rain pitter-pattering against the rooftop.

Fragment: The Hatchery

Kheradok

In Kheradok's estimation, the underground dragon hatchery at Zolehiinu was the most peaceful place in the entire realm. Drekai dragon keepers worked tirelessly to ensure the eggs were comfortable, and that each dragon hatchling's first moments with their chosen bond would be as ideal as possible.

Kheradok now surveyed the special area dedicated to true dragon eggs. Though the dearth of true dragons in Evgard was far more extreme, thanks to the slaughter of so many by ignorant Evgardians, not even the Drekai had many anymore. Even now, only two eggs lay in wait amidst the soft paaka moss nests in the warm, torchlit caverns. With a sigh, Kheradok recalled standing in this very spot not so long ago, playing the ocarina for a very special white dragon egg.

I remember too, Aurora spoke to Kheradok's mind as she stood beside him, her proud, pearlescent wings tucked behind her. *You played sweet songs for me almost every day.*

"That I did," Kheradok said, the regret evident in his tone. He'd lost his chance to bond Aurora, and she'd chosen Princess Eliana instead. Standing here, Kheradok couldn't help but reflect on the irony of it all: the Drakfellian King, Rodan, had robbed this very hatchery for the purposes of stealing Aurora's egg. Yet when she'd hatched, Aurora had somehow chosen the thief's daughter for her bond! It would have been humorous if it wasn't all so heartbreaking.

Once, Kheradok had felt certain that Aurora's bond with Eliana was not by choice. He'd even planned to release Aurora by killing Eliana, giving

Aurora the chance to become his dragon once more. But he'd quickly realized just why Aurora had chosen Eliana of her own free will. The princess was brave, just, and clever—a surprisingly worthy choice for a true dragon's trust, her despotic father notwithstanding.

Astonishingly lovely, too, Kheradok couldn't help but note as he stroked Aurora's flank. Thinking of the impulsive kiss he'd given her on the night he'd meant to end her life made Kheradok bite his tongue. He could still remember her sweet emberfern scent. Hear the sound of her voice.

"So is this where the Seer prophesied Aurora's death?"

Oh stars—As it turned out, he wasn't just hearing her voice in his mind. Kheradok spun around and there she was, Eliana of Drakfell, dripping wet from head to toe, signaling that she'd just spent a good while standing outside in the storm.

"My lady," Kheradok said, at once standing formally, "should you not get to your rooms to warm up?"

"I'm warm enough, thanks," Eliana said, striding his way to stand beside Aurora. There was a protective air to the way she placed a hand on Aurora's scales. The sharp look in her amber eyes was enough to get Kheradok to pull his hand away from the true dragon.

Kheradok cleared his throat. "And to answer your question, yes, this is where one of the royal Seers gave the omen regarding the white true dragon while Aurora was yet unhatched."

"What exactly was the wording of the prophecy?" Eliana asked.

"'Destined to restore the Guardian's fire, she will be trapped, sent to the great beyond of Etheria before her time.'"

The princess shook her head. "Not the Evgardian translation. Tell it to me the way it was originally given in Drekai."

Kheradok blinked, then did as she asked. "*Olaa zu khotaalo ka kalaat kun khaalo Eterilaaki, olaan jankiita, kun lokiika jakehti—*"

"Hang on," Eliana interrupted, brow knit in concentration. "*Olaan jankiita*—What's the translation there?"

"*Jankiita* means 'trapped' or 'bound'," Kheradok explained. "And *olaan* means 'she will be'."

"Or '*it* will be', right?" Eliana asked.

"I suppose so. *Olaan* could refer to 'he', 'she', or 'it'. But since the prophecy refers to Aurora, I think 'she' would be the most appropriate translation."

"Unless that bit is still referring to *kun khaalo Eterilaaki*—the Guardian's fire. 'It' being the fire, meaning it's *the fire* that's trapped, not Aurora."

"Your Drekai language skills are far more impressive than I'd realized," Kheradok noted. "Yes, I suppose that could be the case. But the second part of the prophecy is clear: *Kun lokiika,* 'the dragon', will be sent to the afterlife before her time."

Eliana pressed her lips together as if trying desperately to think of a way out of that part too. Alas, she couldn't find one. Aurora gave a soft growl and nuzzled closer to her grieving rider. If anyone could sympathize with Eliana's pain on that score, it was Kheradok.

Desiring to comfort her—and perhaps something more—Kheradok took a step closer to the princess. Her dress was wet with rain, accentuating the elegant curve of her back, and he gently placed his hand on her waist, pulling her closer...

The moment she realized what was going on, Eliana stepped away from his touch. "I'm sorry," she said. "Not again."

Not one to give up easily, Kheradok took the princess by the hand. "Why not?" he replied boldly. "Would you not agree that the pair of us together could do a lot of good? You are the Princess of Evgard's Western Badlands, beacon of the Knights of the Torch, and rider of the white true dragon. Even here in the Isles we know that High King Magnus himself sees you as a worthy rival. And as for me... you already know that I am the heir to the Drekai crown."

At that, Kheradok held his breath. He remembered perfectly the surprise—and intrigue—in Eliana's countenance when he'd told her of his rank back in the Mirror Forest. Kheradok felt the heat from her hand in each of his fingers.

Now, she held her head high and spoke with confidence. "You should know, I've just barely returned from speaking with Asher."

Kheradok froze. She must've been calling his bluff. If she'd just spoken to Asher, Kheradok had no doubt the half-born had told Eliana about his true heritage, and that *he* was also a contender for the Drekai throne and, by blood, one with an even stronger claim to it than Kheradok.

"*Zaavu,*" Kheradok cursed. "I—"

Eliana cut him off. "I care about him very much." With that, she pulled her hand away from Kheradok's, and even went so far as to walk around to Aurora's other side so that the kneeling true dragon was between them.

Stars, she *definitely* knew the truth about Asher, Kheradok was certain of it. She was playing the game well, no doubt waiting to see which of the men would win tomorrow's duel before—

Eliana pressed on. "Kheradok, you may be a powerful general and heir to a prestigious crown. Meanwhile, in the realm's estimation, Asher of Steel Rim is nothing more than a half-born outlander..."

Wait... Kheradok thought, taking in the sincerity in Eliana's expression. *She* doesn't *know!*

"...but to me, he's so much more." Eliana continued. "I'm sorry, Kheradok."

Kheradok's mind was reeling. Asher had been given the perfect opportunity to tell this woman of his lineage and all but secure her loyalty to him. Instead, he'd not only kept his promise to the Empress not to tell anyone the secret yet, but he'd also won the princess's affection on his own merit, perhaps even *despite* his humble upbringing. Kheradok's respect for both the princess *and* his cousin's sense of honor soared.

While Kheradok's emotions were on the slightly more chaotic side, externally he was all poise. "I understand," he said. "I expect that you're hoping for his victory come morning, then."

"Ugh!" Princess Eliana threw up her hands. "Is there any way tomorrow doesn't end in someone's death?" At her rider's distress, Aurora extended a comforting wing.

"I'm afraid not," Kheradok said. "The custom of honor duels is as old as the first emperor. And with so much at stake, I don't believe our people would accept anything less. This fight to the death, which began when I issued the challenge to your father, is already long overdue. Win or lose, it is the only path to a lasting peace and what will hopefully develop into a more amiable relationship between our cultures."

"But you're the Drekai General! Part of the royal family! Surely you can stop it."

Kheradok shook his head stiffly. "I cannot. If I win, I achieve peace by bringing honor to my people and restoring the white true dragon to the Isles where she belongs. And if I fail... Well, at least I will have brought my people another form of peace by way of an alliance with the Knights of the Torch in the battle against the Gray."

"This is exactly what I'm frustrated about!" Eliana fumed, the wet waves of her dark hair flying all around her and catching the warm torchlight of the hatchery. "This realm needs as much light as it can get, so why in the stars are two of our brightest fighting to snuff the other out? Doesn't that serve the Gray?"

Kheradok opened his mouth for his reply, but found he had none.

Eliana wasn't finished. "You know, for a military man about to engage in a duel to the death, you sure talk a lot of peace."

"Peace is my life path," Kheradok replied automatically. "The ideal to which I pledge my every action."

"So what's more important then—Achieving a form of temporary 'peace' through death? Or staying true to the core of who you are?"

Kheradok set his jaw, trying not to let on how deeply her words had pierced him. He felt like he was back in the Mirror Forest once more, blade in hand, fully prepared to take the princess's life in order to achieve the greater prize of reclaiming Aurora. Then, she'd made similar accusations that had garnered her not only her freedom, but Kheradok's respect. But now, Kheradok couldn't afford a lapse in judgement. Not with so much at stake.

"That choice is not mine to make," Kheradok replied.

"Then whose is it?" Eliana spat. "Empress Khaisa's? Your *aunt,* who's just supposed to stand by and watch her nephew either kill or be killed? What kind of supposed 'victory' leaves both sides so deeply scarred?"

"You... you don't know what you're talking about."

Zaavu. Kheradok turned away. Eliana's words were filled with aggression, but they reminded him of his mother, the very reason Kheradok had chosen the Path of Peace. She hadn't believed in the violence of the Drekai way either, which was why she'd left Zolehiinu and settled on a more peaceful Isle in the south where she'd met and married Kheradok's father. Both of Kheradok's parents had pledged themselves to the pursuit of peace, which drove their passion for helping those isolated into shadow wasting colonies. Both had contracted the disease, going hollow before passing away. Still, Kheradok hoped to live up to their legacy of peace in his own way.

Subconsciously, Kheradok felt the dull tightness of the scar on his back and recalled a hard-learned lesson—that even in the pursuit of peace, mercy could not rob honor. If it did, that peace would be false, worth less than that which had been sacrificed to achieve it.

His parents, virtuous as they may otherwise have been, had let their desire to show others mercy rob them of their very lives. Meanwhile,

Kheradok had achieved much by staying true to the traditions of the land he loved.

Expression hard, Kheradok spoke with conviction. "I will fight tomorrow. I must fulfill my duty, no matter the cost."

He gazed once more into Eliana's beautiful face. "And let the best man win."

Chapter 16: Solhelm

Meleya

The assassin was good, but he clearly hadn't expected a full squad of seven highly-motivated soldiers to meet him inside the royal study.

"Cam, block his exit!" Solvai barked the order.

Cam obeyed without hesitation, using his large, round shield and his wide frame to slip between the cloaked assassin and the window he'd come through. Cam slashed with his blade, but the assassin was agile, ducking and rolling out of the way in the nick of time.

Technically, he was more than agile—He moved with the speed of an Archon, the telltale golden warp trailing behind him.

Seeing the male figure with dark hair pulled into a tidy ridgeknot sitting at the desk, the assassin hover-bolted toward him, blade in hand. But Edrea was ready and waiting behind the desk. Her dragonhook spear would've skewered the assassin if he hadn't managed to arrest his momentum using a quick spurt of levitation.

The assassin doubled back, but Erik's crossbow bolt caught his dragonscale cloak, pinning him to the study's scalecedar armoire. With more of us closing in fast and nowhere to run, he chose to risk it all, expertly chucking his dagger toward the desk, infusing it with an extra hover-boost.

It was a killer shot, literally, but...

My portal ripped open to catch the dagger before it could strike. I placed the exit end of the portal facing the assassin—not in a way that would kill him, though I easily could have. With a satisfying *thwack,* the dagger lodged itself into the armoire so close to the assassin's head that it grazed his ear.

Striding up to the glaring assassin, I melodramatically yanked out the dagger and held it in front of his face. "I'll take that," I said with a self-satisfied smile. Stars, Asher must've been rubbing off on me.

Before the assassin could reply, a *thump* to his gut made him groan. The source of the thump was a burly young man with corkscrew curls and a penchant for sucker punches: Brigan's beefy cousin, Finn, who'd become one of Squad Reckless's temporary new members. Within a second, Finn had ripped Erik's crossbow bolt from the assassin's scaled cloak and had the man's arms pinned behind him in a painful-looking hold.

The man may have displayed the levitation skills of an Archon, but this wasn't the first dragonslayer we'd encountered since coming here. Finn scanned the man's clothing, eyes coming to rest on the slightly-larger scale fixed to his dragonbone bracers. It was the heartscale of a slain mythic dragon, which granted him limited access to its powers. Sure enough, when Finn snapped the scale off, the golden light in the man's eyes faded along with his ability to access etherarchy.

To add soot to scorchmarks for the unfortunate assassin, the dark-haired young man sitting at the desk finally showed his face—He wasn't King Brigan at all, but *another* favorite cousin, Finn's brother, Floki. Upon our arrival, he'd temporarily joined Squad Reckless too, and Brigan assured us both could be trusted. The assassin's head drooped in defeat.

"Well played, Squad Reckless," Solvai said.

The real Brigan took that as his cue, emerging from a storage closet. The orange crystal in his crown caught in the sunlight streaming into the study.

"Take him to the dungeon with the others," Brigan said with all the authority of a king. Finn and Floki gripped the assassin tightly on either side as they led him from the room.

Hardly missing a beat, Brigan returned to his desk. He cursed as he began to reorganize his papers. "Scorch. It's hard to get any work done when half the populace actively wants your head on a platter."

"This is what," Edrea started, "the third assassination attempt this week?"

"And the second dragonslayer," Cam added.

"Drak, Brigan," I put in, examining the assassin's dagger. It was actually quite nice, though the dragon skull ornamentation on its hilt was a bit much. "How did you survive before we got here?"

"Honestly, it's a miracle," Brigan replied, his gaze already fixed on a sheet filled with tiny script. "My cousins were working overtime—They're some of the few I can trust. I'm glad the Knights of the Torch let you come, even if it's only temporary."

"Well, it helps when a member of the sitting Triarchy is your squad captain," Solvai said with a smile.

Just then, the study door swung open and in swept a well-dressed young woman of about sixteen years with the same russet complexion as Brigan. She had his tight corkscrew curls, too, only hers cascaded all the way down her back.

"Was that *another* assassin I saw being dragged down the hall?" she asked, exasperated. "Are you okay, Brig?"

"Fine, Britta," Brigan replied, already moving on to the next pressing page in his stack. "What brings you back to the study?"

Britta looked down at the stack of sheets in her own arms and tapped the top one with a pen. She was Brigan's little sister, though she wasn't nearly so little as I'd remembered her being at the Winter Solstice Ball. After losing both her parents in one day and finding out her older brother was the new King of the Canyonlands, she'd had to grow up fast, and had already taken on the daunting task of managing Brigan's schedule.

"Just reminding you about your meeting with the nobles from Houses Scarlet Shore, Mesa, and Archdawn this afternoon. I know the new Duke of Archdawn was hoping to discuss plans for dealing with the shadow wasting outbreaks happening in Rengard's southwest."

"I'll be ready—"

Brigan had barely gotten the words out before Britta plowed on, scanning her notes. "Also, the Captain of the Guard from Dragonfire Bay arrived early. He comes bearing an update on the ceasefire on the Dragon Isles warfront. Besides that, some of the servants were wondering if you're planning to go ahead with the autumnal gala."

"Don't they know the keepdom is in crisis?" Edrea wrinkled her nose. "Who gives a flying scale about galas at a time like this?"

"Gauntlet down: Galas can be every bit as impactful as wars," Brigan said, and Edrea wilted. "Tell them we will be proceeding with the gala, but that the guest list will be limited so that we can ensure everyone's safety."

Britta carried on with her update on the keepdom's stare of affairs, and Brigan listened with measured poise. There'd been a lot of fallout after Brigan's initial proclamations upon becoming the Canyonlands' king.

First off, Brigan's decision to ally Rengard with the Knights of the Torch had caused more than a small stir. On top of that, his proclamation that henceforth all magi in the Canyonlands would be treated as free citizens had left many keeps panicking. In my estimation, their concern was unwarranted, since it wasn't like freeing Rengardian magi would somehow instantly increase their numbers and draw any more wild dragons than they would while living in secret.

To me, the bigger problem was the people taking Brigan's order *too* seriously. Some were disingenuously interpreting Brigan's order to indicate his endorsement of the imprisonment and execution of Mage Hunters. Already, Brigan had needed to send guards to protect the Hunters still living within the Canyonlands, helping them either get out unscathed, or else shed the blue cloak and relocate to keeps where they were unknown. It was all exhausting for my friend, and I'd had to remind him to eat meals and drink enough water on more than one occasion since our arrival.

"Oh," Britta said, swallowing as she flipped through pages. "Another one of these arrived as well." She passed her older brother a yellowed letter with an onyx black seal pressed into it. The seal bore the image of a dragon skull, and the sight of it got my entire squad gripping their weapons and casually scanning the room for more secret assassins.

"Soot." Erik narrowed his eyes. "What does the Duke of Skullheim want this time?"

Edrea scowled. "No doubt the same thing he always wants: the Canyonlands' crown."

"I'd bet good marks that he sent today's assassin too," Solvai grumbled.

Brigan opened the letter. There was nothing written inside it, just a map of the Canyonlands, labeled with the names of every sufficiently prominent keep from Solhelm in the north, where we were now, all the way down to Keep Rengard on the Rise in the south, just outside the Dragon Mists.

Carefully drawn lines cut across the map, representing the many canyons and gorges that peppered the redrock desert. The largest one of all, Rengard Canyon and the Ridgeback River that ran alongside it, divided the keepdom in half.

My gut twisted as I took in the messy, hand-drawn, inky lines splattered over top of the map. Dozens of keeps all over the eastern side of Rengard Canyon had been circled in black. One keep had been circled thrice, and someone had penned a quick icon of that same dragon skull beside its name: Keep Skullheim.

The message was clear. Brigan's self-declared rival for the crown, the Duke of Skullheim, was rapidly gaining support. Suddenly, the great canyon was beginning to feel like a battle line.

"His following is growing," Brigan murmured.

"How can that be?" Edrea said. "That old Duke of Skullheim is nothing but a foul, sinister murderer."

"In a way, that makes sense," Erik mused. "At least, the only other person I've ever met from Skullheim wasn't exactly friendly."

"You mean Bjorn?" Solvai said darkly. The mere mention of our former squadmate's name set my teeth on edge.

"Maybe all Skullheimers take a vow of meanness," Cam suggested. He looked around as if searching for someone to give him a shove of appreciation for his joke, but everyone was too focused. I wondered if I wasn't the only one who felt Jax's absence.

Edrea continued, "Anyway, I thought the forces we sent would've been enough to stop the Duke."

"I'd hoped so too," Brigan said, frowning. I frowned too, wondering how one grizzled, upstart dragonslayer had managed to not only evade capture, but to increase his army. He must've been more powerful than any of us had realized.

The Duke of Skullheim was yet to come as far north as Solhelm; I doubted he was strong enough for that yet. But reports said that he and his gang of former dragonslayers were calling themselves 'mageslayers,' doing their best to undermine Brigan's proclamation to free magi in the Canyonlands. They'd taken matters into their own hands, hunting down everyone who they even suspected of possessing etherarchy, then tying them to silver-painted posts and watching them suffer death by dragon and calling it justice. They wouldn't turn their back on the High Crown—If King Brigan wouldn't uphold tradition, they'd put magi in their place themselves. The reports had made me sick.

"It's like the Silver Crusades all over again," Brigan said grimly.

"I can't help but wonder if the Gray Ones are behind it," I added. "If chaos is their goal, they're certainly succeeding."

"Not for long," Brigan said, determined. He pointedly folded up the map and shoved it under the rest of his papers on his desk before turning back to Britta. "Now, unless there's something else, I really should get back to—"

"There is something else," Britta assured him, cringing.

I could tell Brigan was trying to keep from appearing overwhelmed as he waited for Britta to go on.

Britta paused. "Well... see for yourself."

She led the way to the window—Solvai made us do a scan for any hidden enemies first—and we peered down to where our third-story vantage point gave us a perfect view of the citadel's front gates. A small crowd had gathered, some supporting their friends and family who sported inky gray patches from the shadow wasting. Others carried blank-faced people who were completely gray. The hollow.

Even from way up here, I could hear their chants, asking for King Brigan the Lightbringer to heal them. My heart ached, and I noticed Brigan's expression soften too.

"I can send them away," Britta offered. "Or ask our medics to do their best without you."

Brigan cast one last look at the endless stack of papers on his desk before squaring his shoulders. "No. No, I'll go too. My liquid light vials have mostly refilled anyway. I won't be able to do anything for the hollow, but I'll do my best for the ones whose shadow wasting hasn't reached their hearts yet. Come on, Squad Reckless."

The rest of the squad was just as worried about our overworked friend as I was, but we knew he'd decided. Following Brigan, I started the guard's salute and the rest of the squad joined in:

"For Evgard, we serve. For her flag, we fight. For her people, we protect. For Evgard, unite."

I stood at the far end of the pier. Ocean waves crashed all around me as the twilit sky washed the sea in dim periwinkle light. A layer of fog hung over the ocean, and while it was beautiful, I found the muggy air wasn't much to my liking. For weeks, I'd felt as if I were perpetually covered in a thin layer of sweat.

Sniff skimmed the surface of the water, his four wings whipping up the cresting waves as he dipped them in again and again. He was supposed to be fishing for his supper, but the roiling ocean never ceased to distract my puppy-like dragon, even if he was now on his second ascension.

I felt his excitement through our bond, and nearly lit up the rune for the Sight so that I could see Blink too. But then I felt the vacancy in my chest and remembered. How long would it take for her essence to... recombine or whatever it was supposed to do? The thought of her never coming back made my heart ache.

My mind wandered to this week's meal plans, and I opened up my rift hold to check on my ingredients. While not on duty, I'd enjoyed visiting the kitchens here in Solhelm, where Brigan's chefs had shared some of their go-to recipes. I couldn't wait to try making their famous chili-lime oysters.

I scanned the shelves of ingredients, making a mental list. I was getting low on eggs, but we'd make it through the breakfast I was planning to make for the squad tomorrow. I'd need to stop by a market soon.

Unsurprisingly, my gaze inevitably found its way to the sack of rice in the far corner. Inside was the Soul Reaper's voidshard, and while I could still sense its dark presence constantly weighing on my soul, its impact had eased considerably. In large part, I attributed that to the brilliant etherberry glowing from its shelf inside my hold.

When Asher and I had awakened from astral sleep, I'd expected the etherberry bush to... I don't know, disappear? I certainly hadn't dared to hope it would remain accessible to me while in the physical plane. Yet there it was, thriving in the starglass pot Asher had made for it. I'd even plucked a few etherberries and shared them with my squadmates. They tasted just as sweet to my physical taste buds as they had to my spiritual ones, and it had topped my and Solvai's ether wells right off.

I had the strongest urge to plant the etherberry here in the physical plane, just to see how it would take to physical soil. That, and I could tell the little thing missed the sunlight. But I still wasn't sure where to plant it—Wherever it was, it needed to be someplace special. Somewhere its bounty could be shared, but not abused.

Satisfied, I closed the rift hold and continued watching the waves. Sniff had finally caught a fish, a big spiky dragonbass which he snapped up before alighting beside me on the pier.

Before I knew it, I found myself absently clutching the quartz crystal clipped to my belt. It glowed with the extra ether I'd filled it with this morning.

You miss him? Sniff spoke to me through our bond as he finished his fish. *Jax?*

I sighed. "Yeah."

It was true. Though I'd worked hard to ensure I'd been able to emotionally move on from Jax, I often wondered if I'd ever see him again. Did he still think about me sometimes? Was it wrong to hope he did?

And Asher? Sniff asked.

I thought about that. I'd've been lying if I said that I never thought about Asher, especially with him gone doing something so risky. I recalled our unforgettable flight through the ethereal skies, tethered by starglass to Blink as we soared like kites. I'd never felt more free. Part of me felt like I needed Asher to remind me how to have fun. But life consisted of more than games and adventure, and I found myself wondering—What did Asher and I each want long-term? I still didn't know.

Before long, I spotted Solvai and Brigan walking down the pier. The moonlight highlighted their faces as the three of us leaned against the pier's wooden railing.

"This used to be one of my favorite places to go as a kid," Brigan said fondly.

"I can see why," I responded, taking in the sight of the silvery starlight reflecting onto the endless water. A light breeze ruffled my hair.

It also caused my calf-length cloak to billow. The others wore the traditional black cloaks with orange trim typical of a king's high guard, but as for me, the cloak I wore was uniformly black. Solvai saw it catch the wind and nodded toward it.

"How has the shadowcloak Shaya made for you been working?"

"Really well," I replied as I held the finely woven fabric in my hands. Where it bunched, I could see the faint shimmer from the skystone-infused shadowsilk. Shaya had worked tirelessly to finish weaving and sewing it before I'd left for Solhelm, and made me promise to report on how well it protected me from ethereal attacks while away.

"If it works," Shaya had said, "we can start making more."

"My wraith hasn't bothered me since coming here," I told my friends on the pier. "Well... except for once."

"Really?" said Brigan. "When was it? Are you alright?"

"I'm fine," I tried to reassure him. "It was just after I'd arrived. I got careless and put the cloak away one night while I slept. Hours later, I woke up feeling a chill, and when I'd activated the Sight, Xan was there."

"What did she tell you?" Solvai asked kindly. My friends knew all about my wraith.

"Mostly lies," I replied. "The usual stuff. But some partial truths too. Those are much worse." I swallowed and fidgeted with the hem of the cloak. "She said that the Knights are using me for my powers by having me stow the voidshard in my rift hold. That the Knights are no better than the Gray."

Brigan, ever the analyzer, jumped in. "Let's break that claim down. Part of it is just another lie, plain and simple—the Knights are *far* better than the Gray, if simply by virtue of their aims. The Gray pursues chaos and destruction while the Knights pursue light, even if their individual actions aren't always perfect."

"That's true," I said.

"And as for the part about you having to keep the Soul Reaper's voidshard," Solvai put in, "do you need some relief from that, Meleya? If it's becoming at all overwhelming, I'm sure Solrac and the others wouldn't want you to bear it alone. Just say the word and we can try other solutions."

"No, it's not that it's too overwhelming exactly," I said. "Not anymore. I chose to keep the shard safe to protect those I care about. I don't regret that choice, and I want to be someone the Knights can rely on. I guess... I don't know. I just wonder if I'll ever really be... you know, *free.*"

"What does freedom look like to you, Meleya?" Solvai asked.

For whatever reason, Solvai's question utterly stumped me. As I stood there on the pier, surrounded by my two best friends and the smell of the salty ocean, my thoughts raced. I thought of my secret dream to care for my own vegetable garden, and wondered if such a little thing would ever be possible. If the Gray won, I doubted anyone throughout the realm would get to have those simple blessings.

When I didn't answer, Brigan chimed in.

"What if freedom isn't about circumstance?" he mused. "If it were, only those with the most ideal living situations would be considered 'free.' Some might consider a king or queen the most free of all. But as for me..."

Brigan sighed, then looked off towards the horizon. "Ever since becoming the King of Rengard, I've barely had a moment to myself. My time is no longer mine; rather, it belongs to the people I serve. But even though I've been more mentally drained than I've ever been before, I still find I'm satisfied with my life. Happy, even. Gauntlet down: Freedom isn't about circumstance. It's about choosing to be happy. Choosing light."

Solvai and I let Brigan's words sink in as we continued watching the darkening sky. Sniff was back flying over the water again. He wasn't hungry anymore, but he still wasn't quite ready to end his ocean playtime just yet.

My friends and I stood in comfortable silence for a few moments more before Brigan gave the biggest yawn I think I'd ever witnessed. Both Solvai and I chuckled.

"Sounds like it's bedtime for a certain King of Rengard," I said. "Something tells me you've got another big day ahead of you."

"Alright, alright," Brigan relented. "I've got to go meet with Kari about some of her anti-wild-dragon inventions, but then I'll go straight to bed. You two going to turn in too?"

A flute-like melody trilled in my heart through my bond with Sniff as my great yellow evren dove straight into another wave. I smiled. "I think I'll give Sniff another minute."

"I'll make sure Brigan gets back safely," Solvai said.

"Goodnight, Meleya," Brigan said, then called out over the water, "Goodnight, Sniff!"

Sniff responded with a gleeful evren chortle. As I watched my friends' retreating silhouettes, I couldn't help but feel grateful. I admired the way Brigan had stepped up and made the most of an impossibly difficult circumstance. I hoped I could learn to do the same.

As I stared out across the sea to the west, I thought about Asher. He too, had been put into a tough situation, called to sail across the sea to a land he'd never been to to fight a skilled, powerful warrior. The duel had to be soon now, and I could only hope that he rose to the occasion.

Chapter 17: Honor

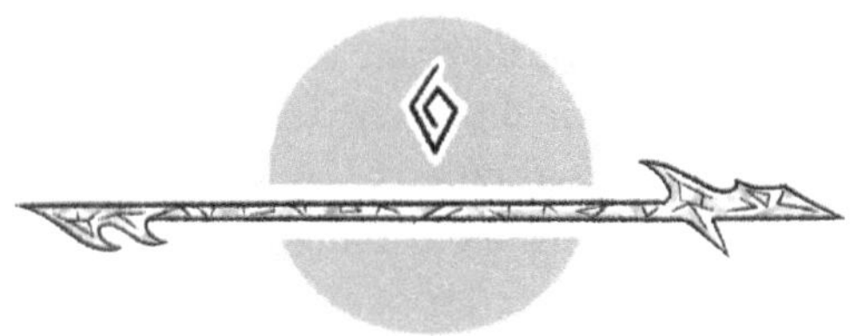

Asher

Just through that door lay the dueling arena where in just a few moments I'd be facing my death.

For whatever reason, standing there in the underground holding room beneath the arena, surrounded by racks of Drekai weapons and armor, I felt a sense of calm.

Well, mostly calm. I still paced back and forth, looking over the rows of scimitars, battleworn bronze chestplates and helmets, and an entire wall of *kalaata,* Drekai war boomerangs. The armor was exquisite, but so was the one-of-a-kind ascension armor Kari had made for me from Thorn's shed scales. I wore it now, though I hadn't yet activated its full, helmeted form.

I felt for my father's skyseeker dagger, clipped to its usual place on my belt. Meleya must've been rubbing off on me, because opposite the dagger, I'd added another backup weapon: one of my Mom's old scimitars from the bungalow. It felt good carrying both weapons, as if a piece of both my mom and dad were with me.

Staring at my reflection in a shiny bronze shield that hung on the wall, I saw what looked like a real warrior. My mom's turquoise heirloom scarf was secured in plain sight around my neck; between that and my ascension armor, I had something from Evgard and something from the Dragon Isles.

Thinking about my ascension armor got me—for the umpteenth time that morning—wondering where Thorn was. When I hadn't seen him again last night after Elle left, I'd assumed he'd gone out for a hunt.

But there was still no sign of him. When I felt at his heartscale, I could only feel soft, distant embers from him through our bond, as if he were sleeping. Was my dragon really out in the woods somewhere, snoozing through my duel? Honestly, that might be for the best. I didn't want Thorn to have to watch if things went poorly for me today.

Just then, there came a soft knock at the holding room door. When I opened it, I was surprised to find General Kheradok, looking duel-ready as well in his battleworn bronze chestplate and leg guards. He wore the same heavy gauntlet I'd seen him wear back in Keep Drakfell, the one that shot explosive balls of dragonfire. Hooray for that.

"May I enter?" Kheradok asked formally.

"Sure," I replied, gesturing to the room. "My armory-slash-pre-duel-holding-room is your armory-slash-pre-duel-holding-room."

"Thank you," Kheradok said, securely closing the door behind him. "Prince Asher."

"Oy. That still sounds so foreign."

"If you wish," Kheradok said, "I can simply call you 'cousin.'"

"Cousins who are about to do their best to kill each other. Nice."

"Historically, duels have often been fought between family members. Duels of wills to first blood, as well as duels of honor to the death," Kheradok said. "Father against son, brother against brother. In the case of your mother, sister against half-sister."

"It may be tradition," I said, "but that doesn't make it any less wrong."

"I actually believe you are right about that."

"Really?"

"I used to think peace was worth sacrificing everything for," Kheradok admitted as he absently touched a scar on his bicep. "But the more important lesson is balance. Balance between what is necessary for the good of the world and what is necessary for the good of the self." Kheradok grimaced. "It's a tricky balance to strike. As much as I am loathe to take a life, I feel I must honor my duty and the will of my people and do my best to be worthy of the heirship—as I hope you will."

"Are you asking me to go easy? Let you kill me so that the Dragon Isles isn't stuck with an heir as unfit as me?"

"On the contrary," Kheradok said. "From what I have learned of you since you so unceremoniously interrupted my honor duel with King Rodan, you are brave, caring, and wise, not to mention annoyingly fast. I want you to fight for the heirship with all you've got, as does our aunt, who spoke to me at great length regarding you last night."

I was so taken aback, I didn't know how to respond.

Kheradok continued. "From the moment you saved Rodan's life on the geyser fields of Keep Drakfell, I knew you were not a man who can be controlled. As an Archon, your heart guides you. These are qualities of a true leader."

"But until a few days ago, I'd never even *been* to the Dragon Isles. How could I possibly hope to rule it justly?"

"That is of little consequence if your heart is pure," Kheradok said. "Customs can be taught, but the spark within you cannot be."

"See?" I said, pointing to Kheradok. "Everything you say sounds like it's straight out of a book called 'How to Sound Epic and Be Legendary.' You were born to lead."

"So were you," Kheradok said. "That said, I certainly don't plan to go easy on you in the arena, either. At the end of the day, one of us will be named the heir and the other will ascend to Etheria. But whatever the outcome, Khaisa is glad to know that the future of the Isles will remain within our family."

Kheradok left soon after that, and time seemed to fly. It was as if only a few minutes had passed before Drekai soldiers were knocking down my door. They wore full battleworn bronze plate armor and layered helmets that masked their faces. One of them peered at me through his dragon wing-ornamented visor and said, "It's time."

"Sure is," I replied, my eyes flashing from dragonfire green to gold as I checked in with my ether well. "Time for a show."

The arena was a vast amphitheater built with the natural contours of the land. In Evgard, such stages were constructed with even stone seating, layered in neat rows. Here, some of the crowd sat atop wide rocks, others on thick tree roots, and others still on nothing but the layered paaka moss that climbed up on all sides of the sunken arena.

Last night's rainstorm hadn't let up this morning. If anything, it had gotten more tumultuous, the wind whipping the pelting rain into the layered rooftops of the Zolehiinu palace, which served as our backdrop. The occasional lightning strike lit the darkened sky.

The arena itself, as well as its seating, was largely protected from the storm anyway, thanks to a ring of totems all around us that put up a powerful psionic shield overhead. The rain skittered away, streaming down the face of the invisible dome.

The crowd hummed, the din increasing when Kheradok and I emerged on opposite sides of the arena. My heart thudded in my chest. The bad weather hadn't kept hundreds of Drekai from coming to watch, filling the seats and then some. More seating in the form of telekinetically-floating stones hovered throughout the amphitheater.

Stars. So much for my theory about Empress Khaisa and the others keeping the duel a quiet affair! It seemed half the city had shown up to see which side would fly away with the true dragon.

Speaking of which, there they were: Elle and Aurora, standing proudly beside Empress Khaisa in a special section for the royal family. Elle and Aurora had strategically been placed right on the arena sidelines so that the burgeoning crowd could see them and get a good view of what was at stake. Elle had dressed the part, looking elegant in her white armored dress with her pearlescent true dragon at her side.

Empress Khaisa's true dragon was there too, a mighty emerald green creature curled protectively around his bond. His third-ascension status made him significantly larger than Aurora, who was only on her second. Khaisa once again wore her regal wrap dress and heavily jeweled crown. I tried to picture Mom wearing something like that, but I couldn't.

Just outside the royal family's section was another special area for honored guests. Solrac was there with Trickshot and the other Knights of the Torch representatives who had accompanied us on our journey. I hadn't seen Solrac since the first day we'd arrived, and I wondered if he was worried about me. Khaisa had sworn her inner circle to silence regarding the secret of my heritage, which meant Solrac and the rest didn't yet know.

My spirits fell slightly when I didn't spot Thorn with them. Where was my dragon? If he was watching, I couldn't see him, and all I could feel through our bond were more of those relaxed embers.

There wasn't time to dwell on it though, because at that moment, Empress Khaisa raised her hands for quiet. When she addressed the people, her voice was amplified, likely with some kind of auditory illusion provided by her true dragon's power. She spoke in Drekai, and I noticed Solrac had a rune glowing over his forehead that translated what she was saying for him and the other Evgardians in real time. Elle, on the other scale, had her eyes closed, brow knit in concentration as she did her best to follow along.

"*People of the Dragon Isles,*" Khaisa boomed, "*I have called you together to witness a historic honor duel between two worthy opponents.*"

The crowd roared, their stomping feet even louder than the thunder. Those with wings flapped them while those with draconic tails thumped them against the earth. The whole mountainside seemed to come alive.

"*A duel of this caliber has not taken place in our land in many years,*" Empress Khaisa went on. "*For this fight is about more than mere honor.*"

The Empress paused for effect. The crowd leaned closer in anticipation. I knew what she was going to say next and held my breath, watching Elle and Solrac in particular for their reactions.

"*This is a battle for the Dragon Isles' throne.*"

As if to punctuate her words, lightning struck as the crowd erupted with yelling and more tail thudding. Khaisa had to amplify her voice further just to be heard as she explained the situation to her subjects, whose discord only grew once they realized exactly whose son I was. Across the arena, Kheradok stood stock-still as if it were the easiest thing in the world, but meanwhile, I was fighting just to keep my foot from tapping madly. My fingers twitched, itching to do something.

Solrac caught my eye. He gave me a knowing wink, then straightened his posture, and I naturally did the same. He seemed to be taking this new information in stride—That was, unless it wasn't really new information to him. I recalled our final sparring session in the glass arena in the dream plane.

You are destined to be a bridge, he'd said. *A beacon to which others can look for light.*

Soot, had he known even then? What exactly had his Farseer powers showed him about me?

Then I saw Elle. Zoren stood beside her, interpreting any Drekai words she might've missed. I watched comprehension dawn in her amber eyes as her jaw fell to the floor.

The shock in her expression quickly gave way to offense. She locked eyes with me, and though I most definitely couldn't hear her, I got the distinct feeling she was mouthing something like, 'Why didn't you tell me?'

I shrugged as if to say, 'It didn't come up.' She pressed her lips together, clearly reeling, but not wanting her pain to distract me from what I had to do.

The crowd was in a frenzy, and I could hear shouts, both in Drekai and accented Evgardian, assailing me from all sides:

"*Unworthy half-born!*"

"*No right to our throne—not even one of us!*"

"*Juuvi!*"

"*Juuvi!*"

"*Juuvi!*"

I recognized the Drekai word they kept repeating over and over as they pointed to my neck. *Juuvi*—scarf. They recognized it as belonging to my mother, or perhaps even her father, Emperor Khaz, before that.

Despite the cool autumn weather, I was sweating. Still, the showman in me kicked in, and I untied the turquoise square of fabric and held it high in the air. The crowd roared, many of the angry cries giving way to cheers. Empress Khaisa seemed to smile as I confidently re-tied the scarf around my neck. I may have been unsure about my identity at this point, but if there was one thing I was proud of, it was the fact that I was my mother's son.

Then, it was time.

Empress Khaisa began to count down, though I could barely hear it above the sound of pouring rain and the deafening crowd. Kheradok drew his scimitar. Something in me told me to summon my starglass spear, but I was momentarily frozen.

At that moment, however, all the noise seemed to disappear. Time slowed as I heard my mother's voice. Her clear, lovely voice, singing to me:

You are a link in a legacy of light
A chain that spans the ages

The words written on my scarf in ancient script took on a whole new meaning. I wasn't entirely certain whether I was having a residual Sight flash or whether I was just imagining the vibrant, dark turquoise mists of Mom's aura beside me. Either way, I had no doubt that Mom was here with me now on the Ethereal side.

I squared my shoulders, her continued support giving me the strength to stand tall. Death was no match for my mother, and I couldn't let facing mine get the best of me, either. Even if death seemed to be the easier of the two choices right about now.

Sent to tend with wisdom and might
Through bright or darkened stages

For this moment, all the resentment I'd felt over Mom hiding the truth fled my heart. Mom had wanted to tell me who I was, but she hadn't gotten the chance. Still, in all the ways that mattered, she'd told me *exactly* who I was.

My anxious twitching stopped. In my mind, my heart, or whatever it was, I heard several other voices, male and female, some with Drekai accents and some without. Was this side effect the result of being awoken early from astral sleep? The voices joined my mother's in ethereal chorus:

We will guide you
Ever beside you
Us who've come before

My eyes burned with golden etherlight as I summoned my starglass dragonhook spear and activated my ascension armor. My bracers became full gauntlets, and the fierce, black-and-gold-accented helmet grew to cover my head, the small, staglike-antlers that sprouted from either side of it reminiscent of a crown. Gripping my weapon, I assumed a battle stance, months of training just itching to take effect.

Do not fear
Your time draws near
Share light forevermore.

The competing sounds of rolling thunder and the raucous crowd came back into focus as Kheradok and I raced to meet each other in the middle of the arena.

The fight was fierce from the start, though neither of us came out right away with the full force of our etherarchy. First, we tested each other, my powerful starglass dragonhook spear clashing with his quick, precise scimitar.

The crowd roiled around us, but we were too focused on one another's movements to pay them any heed. This was between Kheradok and me—our long overdue fight to the death.

Though I normally would have had the reach advantage with my spear, things were never that simple when fighting a Rifter. Kheradok opened up a handful of portals which he kept close, slashing through them with his scimitar and targeting weak points in my armor.

I really had to focus as I blocked his blows with my spear and the diamondoak plates of my new ascension armor. Finally, I saw my opening, using a super-charged hover leap to gain some altitude before executing my 'skyfall strike' move.

White and gold trailing behind me, I blasted past Kheradok's guard, my empowered dragonhook spear slashing so quickly Kheradok couldn't fully dodge in time. He flung himself out of the way, tucking his wings around him as protection when he rolled.

When he returned to his feet a short distance away, his expression was set in furious resolve. My spear had pierced his leg armor, and blood now stained his pant leg on the outside of his thigh. It couldn't have been more than a flesh wound, but it got the crowd calling out and pointing.

Roaring, Kheradok spread his wings and took to the air, where he continued his portal-assisted assault from a more defensible position. I hover-dodged like crazy, and that was before Kheradok activated his etherarchy-enhanced gauntlet, launching a highly compact ball of emerald dragonfire.

"Uh oh," I muttered. I'd seen Kheradok's gauntlet in action before, and hover-dashed away from the smoking sphere...

...Only to find myself facing another one. Soot, Kheradok had anticipated where I'd run, and sent another through a portal—

Boom!

Both fireballs exploded in a shower of green flame coming at me from both sides. My armor took the brunt of it, but I felt the inherent ether within the plates being sapped up to keep the armor intact. Once my ascension armor used up all its latent ether, it would revert to its more humble form—still useful, but no longer able to regenerate me. The crowd ahhed at Kheradok's showy display.

I grumbled under my breath as my eyes burned with golden etherlight. Recalling my breakthrough in the magma-filled, turtle-laden caverns of Etheria's underground, I launched into the air.

My levitation swelled and, much to Kheradok's surprise, I clashed with him in mid-air. He may have been the one with wings, but that didn't mean he was the only one who could fly. Although, my form of hover-flying was much more difficult to maintain as a corporeal being than it had been as just a spirit. I felt my ether well draining, and knew I couldn't keep this up for long.

Blow for blow, Kheradok and I were equally matched. I was more grateful than ever for every ounce of training I'd done to this point. I'd never been more focused.

Our blades locked, our muscles tense as we faced off in strength. But I used the opportunity to send a blast of ether from the point of my spear straight into Kheradok's chest. The force threw him backward as a spiraling white ethermark bloomed across his battleworn bronze chestplate.

I whooped with excitement right along with the shouting crowd. Kheradok narrowed his eyes.

Then he ripped open a portal before me, his scimitar slashing through it with the speed of an ashviper. I threw myself into a mid-air backbend to avoid getting my throat slit, only to find myself dropping into range for Kheradok's *next* scimitar strike through *another* portal.

I rolled for my life, none too gracefully either. My levitation faltered, and I dropped back onto the paaka moss, gasping as I got the wind knocked out of me. I scrambled to right myself.

From there, I *kept* scrambling as another series of rifts began to pursue me, knowing full well that, if I stopped, Kheradok's blade would whip through whichever portal caught me first.

"Soot," I cursed under my breath. Kheradok was skilled. What was more, his portalling style was so different from Meleya's! Nicknamed the Snowstorm, Mel was constantly dodging in and out of portals or sending her opponent through them to keep them disoriented. Kheradok's style was more like a meteor shower, each hyper-focused rift packed with a precise, deadly strike. Everywhere I went, portals followed.

"You can't run forever!" Kheradok taunted.

"You'd be surprised!" I called back. But thinking of the Snowstorm had given me an idea.

I continued my hover-path around the arena both on the ground and in the air as several of Kheradok's rifts pursued me. Several, but not all. There were a handful of rifts holding still directly beside Kheradok that he'd been slashing through at range.

I swerved straight toward one that had the telltale white interior of an entrance portal. Thinking I was coming at him again, Kheradok assumed an airborne battle stance.

I kept on course right up until the last second, then executed a harsh, mid-air pivot.

Confused, Kheradok watched my preemptive dodge. Meanwhile, the momentum of his pursuing portals continued. As I'd planned, the first of the black-tinted exit portals that had been on my tail vanished right through the center of one of Kheradok's white-tinged entrances. I added a mist of liquid ether to enhance the incoming effect.

A surge of satisfaction filled me as the 'eclips-plosion' lit the arena. White ether dusted the paaka moss like snow, and Kheradok went flying so high he momentarily broke through the arena's psionic barrier that blocked the rain. When he dropped back down to land on the deep green moss, he was soaked to the skin and his beloved scimitar was nowhere in sight. The helmet he'd been wearing was gone as well, and white ethermarks spiraled along his wings. Kheradok groaned.

"*What in the stars was that?*" he mumbled in Drekai.

"That was the 'eclips-plosion'," I replied in Evgardian. "And this one's called the 'just encase'."

Taking advantage of his disoriented state, I blasted Kheradok's hands and feet with ether, forming starglass trappings that bound him to the earth. I came to a stop over him, spear poised to strike.

Adrenaline was rushing through me, but despite it, I hesitated. Kheradok... As much as I wanted to hate him for kissing Elle, deep down I knew he was a good man. And more than that, he was family. How could I—

"*You must finish this, Asher!*" Khaisa shouted from the sidelines, though I sensed her agony. The crowd roared.

My moment of indecision cost me my opening. While starglass bound Kheradok's hands, he'd still been able to activate his gauntlet. Dragonfire glowed through the crystalline restraint for just a moment before the starglass shattered.

I shielded my eyes from the hailstorm of green flame and starglass shards. Meanwhile, Kheradok tore open another portal, this one leading to a rift hold. From within, Kheradok grabbed a second scimitar, this one longer than the last, with a blade whose edge shone with... Soot, was that silver?

Sure enough, when Kheradok touched the blade to the other starglass bonds, they dissolved into etherdust. Within a second, he was back on his feet, slashing toward my starglass spear. The silver in the blade's edge completely disintegrated my weapon on contact in a flurry of etherdust.

Meanwhile, Kheradok kept coming at me, and the spectators shouted as I was forced to block with my gauntlets. The silver in the blade made my arm guards revert back to ordinary bracers, and they lost their extra diamondoak aspect entirely. With each new chink, a few more black scales broke off.

I gasped as Kheradok's forthcoming blow bruised my arm and maybe even fractured something. Biting back the pain, I drew both of my backup weapons.

Crossing my father's dagger and my mother's scimitar before my chest, I blocked Kheradok's next blow.

Meeting him blade to blade sure beat trying to last with just my broken bracers, but it quickly became clear that Kheradok's lifetime of training with a scimitar *far* outweighed my three days in the bungalow. Only my hover-speed kept me from going down, but I was using up ether faster than a drakalope running from a frenzied craghopper. Stars, I'd certainly trained a lot with Boone.

I held my own in our vicious back and forth for as long as I could, barely able to keep Kheradok from annihilating me. Drak, that sooty silver-edged blade of his had really changed the game.

After locking both my weapons in place with his, Kheradok shoved his gauntleted hand into my chest. At once, green flames began to spark.

"Not again," I groaned, half for the drama and half genuinely sick of getting blown up.

Kheradok's dragonfire bomb blew me backward. I went skidding across the arena, losing my helmet somewhere along the way. My ascension armor was working overtime trying to heal me, but based on how much pain I was in, it was just about out of ether. It would recharge with time, but that was one thing I didn't have. The crowd's shouting was deafening, and I could tell many of them thought Kheradok was moments away from ending it for good. Ending *me* for good.

Dazed as I was, when I looked up, I realized I'd come to a stop very near the royal family's private section, with the rest of the Evgardians nearby on the sidelines. Solrac, Elle... they were calling for me to get up. I wanted to, but soot, I was exhausted.

Then I saw Khaisa. Though her expression was rigid, I saw the pain in her red-tinted eyes. Maybe it was Mom still influencing me from beyond, but I realized that the Empress was reliving the day she'd lost her sister. The day her family fell apart. Now, it was happening all over again. Kheradok was her beloved nephew while, in me, she saw Zerana. No matter who won today, her family—*our* family—would lose.

My hair had come loose, dark strands whipping into my face. Though the psionic barriers kept the torrential rain out of the arena, they could do nothing against the wind.

I forced myself to my feet just in time to dodge Kheradok's scimitar as it materialized through a portal. Rolling to the side, I avoided his follow-up strike through a separate portal, though I couldn't help but notice that Kheradok was slowing down too. He hadn't used his wings since they'd gotten hit with my eclips-plosion, so that was a good sign for me.

Despite his growing fatigue, Kheradok roared as he summoned another onslaught of portals to surround me. I had no idea which one he'd strike through, but I was just as determined to finish this as he was.

When his next slash came, I was ready, having re-sheathed Dad's dagger. My irises burned with golden etherlight as I hover-ducked to avoid Kheradok's deadly blow.

But before Kheradok could pull his arm back through the rift, I grabbed hold of it and yanked hard.

Kheradok cried out as I wrenched him through his own portal. He tumbled into me, disoriented. I nearly had him there, but Kheradok was quick, throwing up a large, catch-all portal between us so that I couldn't get to him with Mom's old blade.

I hurried to hover-dash around it, but by then Kheradok was back in a fighting stance. We crossed blades again, battered and drained. Kheradok's wings were tense with pain, and my wrist was screaming. One way or another, this was it.

When Kheradok's next series of portals split the air around us, I knew what I had to do. I felt a swell of power within my chest, my frustration with this whole situation mounting the same way it had during my final sparring session with Boone in the dream realm.

Astromancers specialized in the manipulation of pure ether. I'd never felt that more keenly than I did now, drawing in every drop of ether I could reach.

Astoundingly, Kheradok's portals turned to dust and streamed toward me like ethereal rivers. I saw more ether bleeding from his forehead as I drew from the dregs of his ether well. A deafening crack from an ether-filled crystal embedded in his gauntlet competed with the thunder as it, too, fed my theft.

Even those spectators lining the arena's edge weren't immune. Ether streamed from every magi within range, all of it coalescing into white-gold rings of ether, orbiting around me at high speed.

Eyes blazing like golden infernos, I hovered above the arena. My whole body hummed with power, begging to be directed into something.

My gaze locked onto Kheradok. He was staggering, weakened. Taken off-guard and completely vulnerable.

I thrust my hands toward him, and all of that ether surged his way. A wave of ether washed over him, solidifying into starglass and locking his entire body into place.

Gripping my mother's scimitar, I approached. My own fatigue was barely more than a memory now as I trained my blade on Kheradok's chest. The throng of onlookers was in a frenzy.

When Kheradok looked at me, it was with the fire of a warrior's acceptance. Blood trickled from his nose and he held his head high. He knew what came next.

The only problem was, I didn't. Lightning flashed, as if scolding me for my hesitation.

"End it!" Kheradok snarled. All around me, Drekai voices called for the same.

But louder than all of them was the voice only I could hear: *Don't make the same mistake I did,* my mother spoke to my heart. *Have courage, Asher. Have courage.*

At once, I made a decision. Whether it was right, wrong, or somewhere in between, I had no idea. But for now, all I could do was *act.*

"End it!" Kheradok shouted once more.

"I plan to," I replied.

My eyes still ablaze, I pulled all of the ether I'd just used to surround Kheradok. The starglass reverted to swirling, misty ether once more, spinning all around me. Kheradok dropped to his knees, weaponless, drained, and accepting of his fate.

As for me, I redirected all of that ether toward the center of the arena. I bit my lower lip in concentration as I recalled the memory stone I'd found in Mom's bungalow.

The shouting crowd went almost silent as my starglass took shape; after all, I'd been practicing my precision with starglass for years.

Then, it was finished: a larger-than-life starglass statue of the late Emperor Khaz and his three daughters, piercing the darkness of the storm as it glowed from within with the light of so much ether. The family was smiling, their laughter captured in this moment of love and connection.

The crowd murmured. Some recognized their faces, I was sure of it. But I hadn't expected to hear so many muttering words like *'jumalaai'* and *'Izikaii'*—Goddesses and Allfather.

Oh stars. It absolutely looked like a statue of the three goddesses, Streya, Selene, and Solei, surrounding their loving father.

Moving quickly so that I didn't lose my nerve, I turned to the watching crowd and hovered next to the statue to catch their attention. In the relative quiet, my voice carried across the arena.

"You've all seen duels of will escalate into duels of honor! Today, you're seeing the opposite!"

I landed beside Kheradok's kneeling form, then guilelessly offered him my hand. Some onlookers began to protest. Kheradok looked up at me, horror in his gaze.

"You can't do this," he said. "You do not understand what it means!"

"I understand exactly what it means," I told him, then called back to the crowd once more. "I drew first blood! I'm turning this honor duel into a duel of wills!"

Then, I repeated the most important parts in Drekai, so that my intentions would be clear to all: "*Zhaku ka zhavoi! Kuniia ka voiima!*"

Honor duel to will duel. Honor to will.

My voice only reached the first few rows, but those spread the word like wildfire. '*Kuniia ka voiima*' soon rang throughout the amphitheater.

"You cannot do this," Kheradok insisted, even more emphatically than before. He was practically pleading with me, there on his knees. "To do so demonstrates that you do not see that which is at stake as a matter of consequence! You belittle the potential treaty between the Knights and the Drekai, as well as the value of the white true dragon! You show the Drekai nation that you see our throne as naught!"

"Those things *are* as naught!" I said, aware that the nearest spectators were hanging onto our every word. "Everything we're fighting over is of *no* consequence compared to what enemy we truly face: The Gray."

From her place at the edge of the arena, Empress Khaisa's eyes were glistening with... stars, was that pride? Emboldened, I continued, speaking even louder. Significantly louder, I realized, as someone—probably Solrac, though I couldn't be sure—used their illusion etherarchy to amplify my voice.

"Squabbles over treaties and who controls what dragon—even the thrones of great nations—*None* of it matters. Not really. So take my scorching hand already, *zehku.*"

My eyes burned with fire as I extended my hand to Kheradok once again. Understandably, Kheradok seemed increasingly less bent on convincing me to drive my spear through his heart. At last, he took my hand and let me pull him to his feet. The crowd roared.

With the brilliant white light of the starglass statue shining behind us, Kheradok and I faced the crowd. Both of us were bruised and exhausted, but at last, united.

In Drekai, I called out across the arena. "*If we are to survive the Gray, we are better off with a capable warrior like General Kheradok alive and well!*"

Cheers rose. It could've been my imagination, but I thought I spotted a flash of deep turquoise mist flowing throughout the throng—Mom doing what she could to rouse her people's auras from the spirit plane. Near where the Empress stood, I saw that Elle was cheering as loudly as the rest, and my heart swelled.

I tried to find Solrac, too, but he was no longer in his seat. In the back of my mind I wondered where he'd gone, but there was so much else to focus on.

"*Zaavu,*" Kheradok swore as he beheld the cheering throng. "So much for tradition."

I leaned closer to Kheradok. "Not all traditions are worth keeping alive. Honor is a worthy tradition—when it doesn't turn into personal pride."

"That," Kheradok said, grimacing as he gave his ether-scarred wings a painful-looking test flap, "is a hard-learned lesson. One I won't soon forget."

It was hard to say where it began, but soon the crowd began to chant. One thing seemed to echo across the Dragon Isles:

"Jaaril Asher!"

In Evgardian, we had two words that fit, but in Drekai, we needed only one word for 'prince' or 'heir.' Prince Asher. Heir Asher.

Stars.

The crowd of Drekai was looking to Khaisa, waiting for her to make the official call. As she had before the match, she raised both hands to bring the arena to silence. Her voice amplified, Khaisa confidently declared:

"*Long live Prince Asher, grandson of Khaz and son of Zerana—Heir to the crown of the Dragon Isles!*"

The cheering, wing-flapping, and tail-thudding was deafening as dozens of spectators surged into the arena. The nearest Drekai soldiers from the arena's perimeter fought to surround Kheradok and me, practically doing battle just to keep the throng at bay.

Only then did it hit me just how drained I was. The rush of adrenaline I'd felt while dueling Kheradok was fading fast, and now my whole body hurt, especially my throbbing wrist. Besides that, after pouring everything I had into that statue, I was so low on ether that my chest felt tight, and my heart was working overtime just to keep me on my feet. Kheradok appeared to be in a similar bind as he pressed his fingers to his temples.

At least someone must've noticed how badly we needed healing. A trio of guards wearing layered helmets pushed ahead of the rest to get to me.

"Here, drink this," one guard said, passing me a vial. "It will help with the pain." Was it just me, or was there something strange about her Drekai accent? It was hard to tell with so much yelling and shoving going on.

Assuming it was some kind of remedy to help with my wound, I chugged the liquid. At first it was like sweetened water on my tongue, but the aftertaste was something like ashes. I supposed not everything in the Dragon Isles could taste good.

Wordlessly, the most muscular of the three guards took me by the arm and began guiding me away. His grip was surprisingly tight, his fingers practically digging into my skin.

"Ease up, big guy," I said in Evgardian, then switched to Drekai. "*Are we going to the healing rods?*" Mom had once told me about Drekai healing rods, which used stones charged with Sentinel regeneration etherarchy to heal anyone standing close enough. I'd always wondered what it felt like.

Although, the cuts Kheradok had given me using the silver blade wouldn't be affected.

Where was Kheradok, for that matter? I tried to look for him, but it seemed other guards had taken him elsewhere.

"*Hello?*" I prodded the guard's shoulder. "*I said, are you taking me to the healing rods? And where's Kheradok, is he coming too?*"

The guard grunted something that might've been a 'yes,' but I could barely make it out. My hearing felt suddenly muddled and my vision was becoming blurry. A wave of nausea crested within my stomach and it took all my focus not to vomit. Soot, I must've been more exhausted from the duel than I'd originally thought. The third helmeted Drekai soldier appeared on my other side to prop me up as we hurried from the arena.

Through bleary vision, I realized they'd taken me back to the underground holding area where I'd been before the duel began. *Of course,* I thought sluggishly. *There must be a medic here waiting to heal me... away from the crowd...*

While the female warrior with the strange-sounding accent shut the door to the holding area behind us, the two holding me up hurried to help me out of my ascension armor to get a better look at my wounds. Soot, everything hurt. They shoved the armor into a corner.

"*Hey! Be careful with that!*" I tried to protest, but then the tall guard put a hand to my chest and the worst of my wounds began to knit closed. I recognized the telltale feeling of Sentinel regeneration etherarchy, what my armor had been doing before it had run out of power.

But... wait. Even my silver wounds were healing. I wasn't mad exactly, but alarms began flickering within my mind. That shouldn't have been possible.

I narrowed my eyes, seeing double.

My confusion multiplied when I saw Solrac lying on the floor with silver chain whips binding his hands and feet. And soot, was that more silver crowning his head?

What was going—

Before I could even complete the thought, I cried out as a burst of icy pain shot up my wrists. Silver manacles now bound me, effectively cutting off my etherarchy.

"You're not Drekai soldiers," I mumbled. I tried to grab one of the scimitars resting on a nearby rack so that I could make a strike against my three kidnappers. But thanks to my blurry vision and increasingly lethargic movements, the muscular fake guard easily stopped me in my tracks, roughly shoving me to the floor.

Hands bound, I groaned as my head hit the ground harder than I would have liked. Not that I would have liked my head to hit the ground at all. Stars... I was seeing stars.

Banging sounded in my ears, along with faraway voices ordering for the door to be opened.

"Hurry!" said the tallest of my captors, the one who'd healed me, as he removed his helmet. Beneath it was a vaguely familiar, hard-faced young man with a wild mohawk and even wilder eyes. "They'll force their way in soon."

I tried to call out for help, but my voice failed me. I couldn't even get to an upright position.

"Grab them both," another captor ordered. It was the female one who'd given me whatever draft was making the room tilt. With grim horror, I realized that without her bad attempt at a Drekai accent, I recognized her voice.

"Helga, you stalker," I croaked, trying to point.

She ripped off her Drekai helmet to reveal a pair of thick eyebrows lowered over cruel eyes. She bent over me, and with a smirk, Jaira of Whitestone Hall said, "No escape this time, Prince of the Dragons."

"Oh Helga," I mumbled. "Your obsession with me... It's... highly undignified..."

Jaira looked so thoroughly annoyed with me I thought she might slap me across the face. Instead, she glanced toward my collar.

Then she called to their third disguised companion, the muscular one who'd thrown me to the ground. "You sent his dragon back to the goddesses, right?" Jaira asked.

The third fake guard threw off his helmet, and my heart clenched with anger when I saw Jax's face.

"Taken care of," he replied gruffly.

"Thorn?" I muttered, practically choking. Panic seized me as I grabbed for the heartscale around my neck, expecting to feel cold nothingness. Instead, a tiny spark of relief filled my chest as I felt more of those low, sleepy embers. Despite what Jax had said, Thorn wasn't dead.

"Well then," Jaira said. "He won't be needing his heartscale anymore. Take it, Gray Knight."

Jax pried the black-and-copper heartscale from my weakened grip, then yanked hard to snap the cord.

By now, the banging coming from the other side of the door made the hinges shake, and the yelling was deafening. Jaira snapped at her companions.

"Set the snakes, Diamondback!"

The mohawked guy sneered, then held out his long arms as two silvery snakes adorned with runemarks slithered from his sleeves and onto the floor. From there, they slunk away to only the stars knew where.

Jaira snapped again, "Let's go!"

They didn't waste another second. Jaira produced a small stone, which she threw to the ground. Blue light arced up from it, cleaving a man-sized portal in the air.

Solrac in tow, the mohawked kidnapper vanished through the portal. Jaira was next.

Jax moved toward me, and I knew it was our turn. With the world appearing as a mess of muddled shapes and my limbs barely functioning, I knew there was nothing I could do to stop him as he tossed me over his shoulder like a sack of scales.

"You're a sootfire, Swan-spawn," I managed.

Jax's reply was terse. "You won't be so cocky when you're strapped to the Surgeon's table, Dragon-boy."

Then, only seconds before I was certain those outside would have ripped the door from its hinges and barged in, scimitars at the ready, Jax dragged me through the portal and it winked shut behind us.

FRAGMENT: THE DREAM

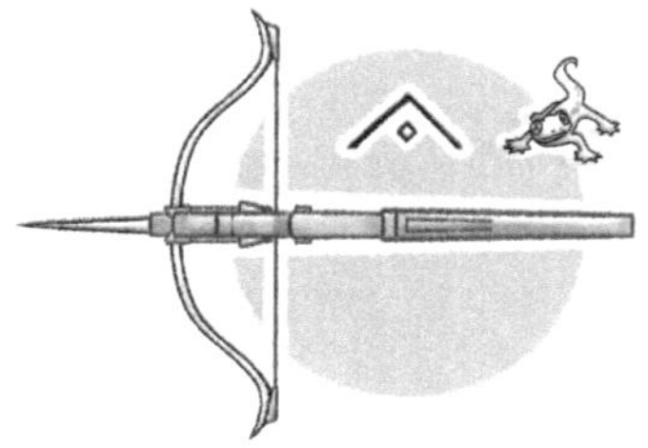

KAI

Not for the first time, Kai had fallen asleep in the library. He'd been studying late into the night, and it turned out that Orothion's copy of *Omen Reading For Scalebrains* made for a halfway decent pillow.

He'd been going over omen interpretation until his eyes hurt. Even since before the quest from the Mirror Forest, he'd been seeing the same things every time he lit an omenfire. Sometimes, he'd even see such visions *without* lighting a fire, their power so strong they'd assault Kai's mind without warning.

Tree, Tower, Moon—The words he'd scribed in his notebook were burned inside his mind. First, a great white tree he thought might represent the Knights of the Torch or even the mysterious Everflame.

Next, a foundationless blue tower forged from crystal. That one had kept Kai up late for many a night, especially since Asher and Meleya's return from their sojourn to the spirit plane. The netherstone they'd found at the Haze's center... It looked an awful lot like the tower Kai kept seeing in his visions. The only difference was, the one Kai's omenfires had shown him was far larger, with three floating tiers near the top. The same triangle-and-diamond symbol found upon Orothion's etherlocks overlaid the tower in a sinister sapphire blue. Besides that, a constellation shaped like a great sword shone behind the tower, the stars within it pulsing between void blue and brilliant gold.

What could it mean? Kai wondered. *Is something even worse than the Hazes coming for Evgard?*

And then there was that drakking blood moon, red drops watering the steps of Orothion. A name was written on the moon, but it was blurry, and no matter how many times he replayed the vision in his mind's eye, Kai couldn't make it out.

And, on top of it all, there was the recurring vision of Meleya leveling her seaxe at Asher's chest while he screamed. That one worried Kai most of all, because although it made no sense—Meleya would never hurt Asher—Kai was certain that this particular future was coming very soon. With each new manifestation, the omen somehow felt more concrete.

Ugh, Kai thought. *I'm just not cut out for this whole omen thing.*

No Seer is, came a reply through Kai's bond with his evren. Flint was in the dragon stables, having awoken when he felt his rider's inner turmoil.

Sure they are, Kai countered. *All magi are predisposed to various aspects of their etherarchy. Rarely is anyone truly expert in every facet of their inherent power set. I've spent years developing my skill with illusions, so what's the point of my training with omen reading when there's a ninety-nine percent chance I'll* never *master it?*

Because there's a one percent chance you do, Flint replied with the steadfastness of a mountain. Kai knew better than to argue with his dragon bond, who had only become more strongwilled since reaching his second ascension.

Trying to clear thoughts of visions and inadequacy from his mind, Kai sat up in his chair and stretched. Looking over his desk, he found the usual stack of books, his journal, open to his notes regarding the omens that so plagued him, and a little figurine of a stonescale evren carved from cindercone pine wood.

All of his stresses melted when he picked up the carving. It was an excellent likeness, from the spikes on Flint's jaw to the way his tail curled up when he was happy. Solvai had made it for him as a gift before she'd left for Solhelm.

Drak, Kai wished she were here. Prior to Solvai's departure, the two of them had fallen into a routine where she'd sit beside him at the desk carving while Kai studied. They'd share their favorite parts of the day for a while before falling into comfortable silence. That was the best thing about Solvai—Like Kai, she didn't need constant conversation to be perfectly content.

Unable to stop himself, Kai runetraced and a perfect rendition of a memory bloomed within his mind. Nothing special, just Solvai's face, smiling at him. Then again, what could've been more special than that?

For a long moment, Kai just watched the memory. How many freckles did it take to reach perfection? He started counting.

But Solvai's freckles were infinite. Innumerable, just like the number of things Kai liked about her.

At last, Kai decided that if he wasn't going to sleep, he might as well get started on the day's tasks, starting with the daily Glint check-in. He reached out to his ethereal familiar, only to find her mental presence ready and waiting for him.

We have news to report, creator! Glint imparted to Kai in her calculating gecko way as her silvery little form crawled from his boot and onto the desk. *A ten on the 'urgency' scale!*

What is it? Kai transmitted back, instantly alert.

There was a pause, and Kai could sense that his ethereal familiar was mulling something over. At last, she replied.

The news comes from Glint Eight, who is assigned to Princess Eliana of Drakfell and charged with observing the proceedings regarding the Knights' voyage to the Dragon Isles.

I know, Kai thought back, his heart beginning to pound. *What happened in the Dragon Isles?*

Glint paused before responding, *We must follow protocol and check in with Glints One through Seven first.*

We must... Are you kidding me?

Kai protested, but Glint insisted that Kai could handle learning the news just a minute later. Following the regular procedure regarding the daily check-in was perfectly acceptable—vital in maintaining order, even. After all, Glint was not a barbarian. Kai sighed, having only himself to blame as Glint reported on the findings of each Glint copy in succession.

Glint One had been assigned to Solrac, but as of yesterday, she'd somehow been dismissed. Kai had found that suspicious, but when he'd resummoned her into the physical plane here at Orothion, her report had been inconclusive. Glint One had felt the brush of silver, which had instantly prompted her dismissal, but between the jostling around in Solrac's boot and the stormy weather, the circumstances surrounding the event had been chaotic. Kai had planned to send another copy, spawned from Glint Eight, to Solrac soon.

Moving on, thought Glint in a hurry.

Glint Two was with Kari. Though sunrise was still hours away, Kari was currently hard at work. King Brigan had given her a spacious workshop in the castle at Keep Solhelm, and already she'd put together some noteworthy prototypes for inventions that she hoped would deter wild dragons.

All proceedings regarding Kari's activity are normal, Glint reported, blinking up at Kai from the desk.

Okay, Kai thought back, annoyed. *But what about Glint Eight? What's going on with Elle? Is it about Asher? Is he okay?*

Shh.

"Shh, yourself!" Kai growled aloud.

Really? Glint blinked at him.

Kai sighed. *Carry on.*

Glint Three, of course, was here in the library, curled up in the lovely little bookshelf nook Kai and Solvai had made for her. Her large, mirrored eyes were sad, the same way they'd been for weeks. After learning that Jax was the Gray Knight, Kai had unsummoned Glint Three as a precaution. She'd been completely surprised by the revelation, since Jax had left her behind in her terrarium at the Mage Hunter Academy. She'd been munching on the large supply of spiny crickets Jax had caught for her, patiently awaiting his return, only to find herself being forcibly re-summoned to Orothion.

Glint Prime offered her usual condolences to Glint Three concerning her attachment to Jax, then moved on.

As for Glint Four, she had never been more content. During the quest team's Orothion infiltration, Zel and his lackeys had discovered her in Asher's boot and dismissed her. Kai had offered to re-summon her into the physical plane since, but Glint Four insisted she was perfectly happy where she was, enjoying an extended vacation in the astral plane, far away from spastic half-borns with an affinity for jumping from great heights. Kai had agreed to this arrangement only because Glint Eight was already going to the Dragon Isles with Elle, and she assured Kai that she'd be able to split into Glint Eight B or even Glint Eight B Alpha should the need arise.

Glint Five was assigned to Ivar, and was currently overseeing his and Boone's work with the armies here at Orothion. All was going well regarding their preparations to face an army of the Soul Reaper's followers come the convergence of mythic stars. Well, as well as things could go—Despite Solrac-slash-the-Farseer's assurances that such a formidable fight would come, the omens hadn't been all that clear on the specifics. All they knew was that that was the day their enemy would make their move against this realm once and for all.

As for Glint Six, she had been reassigned to Solvai. Glint Prime had to keep Kai from getting too fixated on checking in on her well-being.

Level ten urgency, Glint reminded Kai before moving on.

Glint Seven, who had been assigned to Valla, was out of range. It was a strange phenomenon. While Glint Seven could not communicate using words or images, the rest of the Glint network could sense the faint emotions of their sister Glint. Wherever she was, she was very happy. Kai caught the slightest inkling that she was surrounded by paper. Books, maybe? Either way, the other Glints insisted she was quite alright, and that according to Glint Seven, Valla was too. Kai wasn't exactly satisfied with such a vague, emotion-based report, but he accepted it for now. If anyone was hopeful for Valla's success, it was Kai. After all, she was currently following the same path that had led to the disappearance of Kai's—

Glint Eight, status report! Glint Prime's little gecko voice instantly honed Kai's focus.

What is the news? Kai asked, leaning closer to the unblinking gecko perched on his desk.

From there, Kai watched a series of events unfold before his mind's eye, all from Elle's perspective: Asher wearing his sleek, powerful ascension armor, facing down General Kheradok of the Dragon Isles. Khaisa, Empress of the Dragon Isles, addressing her people. She spoke in Drekai, and Kai shared Elle's confusion as her limited language skills only clued her in on one or two words. Something about a historical duel... a fight about more than just honor...

At that point, a frenzy broke out. The crowd was shouting madly, all pointing to Asher, who stood there with his shoulders back and chin high. Kai's brow furrowed. What had the Empress said?

"What's happening?" Elle asked, and Kai felt her rising tension.

A Drekai man with purple scales—Stars, was that the Drekai Mage Hunter, the Ursadon?–leaned close to Elle, translating for her.

Elle's emotion surged. "Asher's the crown Prince of the Dragon Isles?" she gasped, her gaze honing in on Asher.

Kai literally felt the intensity of her glare through the memory. She called to Asher, though her words were swallowed up in the din of the crowd.

"Scorch, Asher, why didn't you tell me last night?"

Elle's mind continued to reel, and Kai caught the briefest glimpse of a rooftop and a rainstorm before the Glints filtered Elle's memory with an almost protective air. Apparently they'd had a conversation up there last night that had intrigued Glint, though the mirror gecko assured Kai that he did not need to know more. It was up to Asher to confide in Kai on this one. Kai accepted that.

From there, the Glints gave Kai a vicarious front-row seat to a duel of epic proportions. Asher and Kheradok clashed even more fiercely than the lightning overhead, the crowd's shouts and stomping feet causing the ground itself to vibrate.

Glint replayed it all quickly, highlighting the most important fragments. Kai watched with wide eyes, fists clenched as he waited to see what the outcome would be. He sensed Elle's fear on Asher's behalf throughout the memory, and was emotionally right there with her as he watched his best friend nearly die multiple times.

After an exceptionally noteworthy breakthrough in his powers—Kai would have to jot down some notes on that for future reference—Asher chose not to kill Kheradok, but instead channeled his rage into building a statue. Soot, Asher really was the most unpredictable guy in the realm. Still, the gesture had done wonders to win over the people of the Isles.

"Drak and soot and scales..." Kai murmured as the memory ended. He still couldn't believe it. Genuinely, this defied all logic.

Desperate to gather all the data he could to somehow try to comprehend this impossible development, Kai grabbed a Lightwielder's torch and began to scour the library. He was alone here, and it took him some time to find the section containing genealogies. Even then, there were only a few scrolls containing any information on the Drekai.

Kai brought the scrolls back to his desk and pored over them. These were out of date, only recording the royal line as recently as Emperor Jihn and his wife, Empress Riiza. But if Kai's understanding via context clues and Glint's research assistance were correct, those two were the parents of Emperor Khaz, who was—apparently—Zerana's father. *Jaarila* Zerana... the firstborn daughter of the Drekai Emperor. Indeed, by blood, that made Asher a viable contender for the throne. More than that even, since he was from the line that technically should have precedence over even Empress Khaisa herself.

Stars, it was a lot to take in. The other Knights needed to know, but he probably shouldn't wake them just yet. Then there was the matter of Akayto... Drak, Kai *had* to find Akayto. Did he know Asher was the lost Prince of the Dragon Isles? How could he *not* have known? Then again, if he had known, wouldn't Asher have known too? And if Asher had known, he'd have let Kai know, even if it was supposed to be secret. Soot, *especially* if it was supposed to be secret! And since Kai didn't know, it could only be assumed that Asher and Akayto hadn't known either... *ugh!*

Kai had no sooner lost control of his whirling thoughts than a ruffling noise behind him made him jump. It seemed Kai wasn't alone in the library after all.

He spun around only to find himself nose to beak with a large black bird. Violet eyes stared back at him and Kai yelped, flinging himself backward straight into the desk.

"Ow..." Kai muttered as he righted himself. At once, he realized it was the Farseer's—er, Solrac's—mythraven.

"Hello," Kai said when the bird just kept looking at him. "Can I help you?"

Kai must've been tired, because he could swear the bird just nodded. Then it opened its beak, and thick, purple smoke poured from its maw like a rushing river that swallowed Kai whole. Kai's eyes rolled back, and his head dropped onto the desk as he instantly fell asleep.

Kai opened his eyes moments later, but he was no longer in the library at Orothion. Instead, he stood on the deck of some kind of ship? That couldn't be right—there was no water. The ship was flying, or rather, floating in a river of pure ether. Drak, he'd seen an ethereal river like this before, while combing Asher's memories of the Spirit Plane. This was a ley line.

To make things even stranger, when Kai looked down, he saw that he was wearing rich, floor-length red robes. Drak, these were the robes of the *Farseer!* What was going on? What kind of dream was this?

"There you are."

Kai flinched at the sound of the familiar voice. He turned around, eyes wide as dragon eggs as he took in the sight of a scarred woman with dark, angular eyes and enough weapons on her person to outfit an entire squad. A strange, forest green mist surrounded her.

"Valla?" Kai asked, his deep, resonant tone making him jump. It seemed he had inherited the Farseer's mysterious voice too.

"You can cut the dramatics, Solrac," Valla went on, speaking quickly. "Before I give you the full report on my quest so you can relay it to the rest of the Knights, I've got something to say. Something personal."

"Oh," Kai replied, taking a step backward and putting up his hands. "Valla, I wouldn't if I were—"

But Kai's voice and appearance were still that of the Farseer, and Valla cut him off with a harsh 'sh.'

"Don't try to stop me," Valla pressed on faster than an approaching ocean wave. "I need to say this, Solrac. I should've said it months ago, but I've lacked the courage, and I'm not too proud to admit that. But you need to know I'm over you."

"Valla—"

"*Hush.* I doubt you've been all that worried about my heart all this time, but I just needed to put yours at ease. I'm alright. At least, in that way."

"*Valla,* there's been a mistake—"

"The only mistake was mine in holding on for so long. Don't try to comfort me, Solrac. Like I said, I don't need it. In fact—"

"*VALLA!*" Kai shouted, wildly waving his hands—which were covered by the red-scaled ascension gauntlets of the Farseer. "Please, I'm begging you—For your sake and mine, *stop!*"

Valla's eyes narrowed to slits. "How dare you try to rob me of the opportunity... to..."

She trailed off as Kai runetraced. The golden runes were charged with the power to break illusions, and they shone from over Kai's forehead as their power took effect. A moment later, the epic Farseer persona had melted away to reveal plain old Kai.

Feeling completely embarrassed, Kai cleared his throat. His voice was back to normal too. "Um... hello."

At the sight of him, Valla's cheeks were a deep shade of rose, her eyes wide with mortification. She tried to speak, but only a series of stutters came out.

Desperate to pretend none of that had ever happened, Kai asked, "Where am I, and how in the void did I get here?"

"That's what I want to know," Valla grumbled, looking down at her hands. They held a dreamweb tied with a black raven feather, a glowing white crystal at its center. "This was *supposed* to let me reach the Farseer, not you."

A shadow crossed Valla's face. "Wait... Solrac... He's alright, isn't he?"

"As far as I know. He's in the Dragon Isles." Kai shrugged, still trying to wrap his mind around what was going on. He recalled the various times Solrac had invited him to join him and Valla in calling upon the Farseer. Of course, Kai now knew that Solrac had been projecting a Farseer illusion all along, most likely using the mythraven. But despite the charade, the dreamweb's power was real. Kai hadn't used dreamwebs much himself, but he'd studied the concept at length. The purple smoke was evidence of Astral influence—Kai wasn't *really* on this ship; rather, his dream-self had been transported to it thanks to Valla activating the dreamweb. The only question was, why had a relic meant to summon the Farseer—

"We don't have much time," Valla said. "I can already sense that our connection isn't strong—You keep fading in and out."

"I do?" Kai looked down to find that Valla was right. His whole form was flickering like mad. When he squinted, he could make out the shapes of Orothion's library. It was kind of disorienting. Waking up would be all too easy.

Valla rushed on, the green mist surrounding her spiraling with urgency. "Pass this message along to the rest of the Knights—We're on the path to the Everflame."

"We?" Kai cocked his head. "Who's 'we'?"

Valla pressed on as if she hadn't heard, and based on Kai's flickering, maybe she hadn't. "We even know where it is, but we can't—scorch, I'm losing you, Kai. Kai, you should know... Hang on... get the captains!"

Valla called for the captains of the ship, and within moments Kai spotted two figures running up behind her. At the sight of them, Kai completely froze. Though they were engulfed by neat clouds of coral and copper mists, he'd have recognized their faces anywhere.

Soot and scales, Kai must've been dreaming. Well, technically he *was* dreaming, but not in *that* sense exactly—

"Kai!" Kalari's voice kept him from overthinking anything. Kai ran to meet her, throwing his arms around her shoulders, only to discover that his dream self was only illusory and couldn't actually feel her. Kai went right through her, his dream form barely disturbing the misty, coral-colored clouds of her aura. Beside Kalari, Kaidan stood dumbfounded, his copper aura practically still as he took in the sight of his son.

"Valla, I thought you said you were contacting Solrac!" Kai's mother exclaimed.

"I thought I was," Valla murmured, her face reddening all over again.

Kai was still in shock. Mom and Dad were dead, everyone said so. Well, at least they always said they were *probably* dead. Kai had come up with reasonable statistics regarding their survival a thousand times, always clinging to that tiny chance—approximately one-to-five-point-five percent—that they were still alive but, for whatever reason, unable to come home. At one point, he'd even thought one of them was secretly the Farseer.

Seeing them now put a fire of hope in Kai's heart so bright hot tears pricked his eyes.

"We're all really here, aren't we?" Kai asked.

"Well, I suppose that depends on one's definition of 'really' and 'here'," Kai's father said, his copper aura now concentrating near his head, almost like an orbiting crown. "If you mean 'really' as in not-hallucinating and 'here' as in our respective consciousness are currently capable of interaction, then yes, yes we are. But in reality, of course, your corporeal form remains in the physical plane while your mind has travelled 'here' via dreamweave etherarchy. Meanwhile, *our* physical forms truly are 'here', inhabiting what I could only categorize as an alternative interdimensional space adjacent to that of the physical plane in which you reside—"

"We're in Etheria, honey," Kalari cut in, always one to get right to the point. "Trapped here all these years."

"It's not like astral sleep, either," Valla hurriedly put in. "We're *physically* trapped here."

Etheria. Kai's mind was reeling. That explained why Mom and Dad hadn't come back for him and Kari. They must've wanted to, but couldn't, stuck in the spirit plane and surrounded by wild magic with no way home. Kai felt like crying for joy, but his form was still flickering and it didn't look like he had much time left before their connection was fully severed.

"But we believe we've found a way out," Kai's mom went on. "The Everflame."

"The Everflame? It's real?" Kai's eyes widened.

"Oh, it's real," Kaidan said. "We know exactly where it is, too."

"But we can't get to it," Valla jumped in. Her gaze kept jumping back to the dreamweb she held. The crystal in its center was dimming fast, and along with it, their connection. It must've been especially draining for it to connect them across planes like this. Kai could feel himself flickering even more, and Orothion's library was manifesting around him more plainly by the second.

"Mom? Dad?" Kai said. The sensation barely made sense, but as he squeezed his physical eyes shut, his dream eyes opened wide and Mom and Dad came back into focus. Drak, they had to hurry.

"Where's the Everflame? Why can't you get to it?" Kai asked in a rush.

"The way is blocked," Kalari said. "Only a Guardian can open the gate. But we have a plan..." Her words became muddled as the dreamweb's power further drained. "Get to Evgard's central nexus... waterfalls... only a Guardian..."

Kaidan picked up then, his words just as fragmented as his mom's. "...plenty of magi... one of each type except Rifter... hoping a relic will suffice..."

"What was that, Dad?" Kai asked, straining.

Valla answered instead. "The bottom line is..." Her voice faded. In the library, Kai could see the light of sunrise beginning to stream onto his desk. Staying asleep was becoming impossible.

"... just tell... we'll keep trying!" Valla finished.

"Keep trying what?" Kai asked, brow furrowed. He blinked, over and over again, but it was no use. The dreamweb was spent, and he was waking up.

"Mom, Dad!" Kai shouted, reaching out his rapidly fading hand. He could barely see the ship now, only the outlines of their faces.

Their lips were moving, but Kai heard no words. Still, his mother's eyes communicated her final message with perfect clarity as she mouthed what Kai thought was, "We love you."

The next thing Kai knew, he was awake.

Fragment: Origin

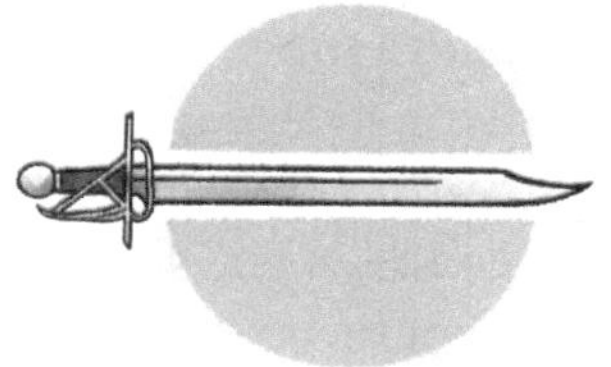

ELLE

Elle hadn't been allowed to see Asher *before* the duel, which had put her in a rather grumpy mood. Then, she hadn't been allowed to see him *after* the duel, which had amplified her grumpiness into righteous indignation. *Then*, when she wasn't allowed to see him over the *next few days* while he 'recovered' from the duel—apparently by Asher's own request!—she'd nearly gone crazy with worry.

Elle was certain the Drekai healers were doing their jobs well, of course, but she simply couldn't rest easy until she'd seen Asher in person. For one, she had to make sure he was well.

And for another, Asher had *a lot* of explaining to do.

"Prince Asher," Elle muttered as she paced back and forth on the balcony of her quarters. "Scorch."

He'd known the other night on the roof, Elle was sure of it. Yet somehow, he'd kept his big mouth shut. A medium-crazy laugh escaped Elle. Now, Asher outranked *her!* Drak, this changed everything. Yet, at the same time, it changed absolutely nothing. Stars, Elle was glad she'd made her intentions so clear the night before the duel. She couldn't stand the thought of Asher thinking she only wanted to be with him because of his newly recognized status. Now, whether he chose her or not, at least he'd never have to doubt.

"Then again," Elle mumbled aloud with equal parts anxiety and annoyance, "it's been three days since the duel without a sign of Asher, so maybe all of my hopes for our future are purely hypothetical anyway!"

Growling like a grumpy drachidna, Elle flopped back into her comfortable, pillow-laden wicker chair. From the balcony, she had the perfect view of the misty scalecedar forest that surrounded the Zolehiinu palace. Stars, this place was gorgeous. She had no doubt the spectacular view was a reflection of her chambers being among Zolehiinu's finest, thanks to Aurora's exalted status as a true dragon.

Here in the Dragon Isles, dragons were given special accommodations alongside their riders. While Aurora had a luxurious stall at the shared dragon stables that floated over the river, she preferred staying here on her balcony connected to Elle's room.

The balcony was as big as the room inside, and fit for a royal true dragon. One side was blanketed in soft green moss and wildflowers, while the other side featured a sandy area and stacked boulders that formed the perfect spot for sunbathing. A few more psionically charged stones floated there too, angled so that water flowed down them before pooling at the bottom, allowing Aurora to drink.

Now, Aurora was darting around the mossy area in pursuit of a sky-blue spitfire. Elle knew that the Drekai army used spitfires—serpentine lesser dragons with a pair of triangular wings that ran along the length of their bodies—as lookouts. They were small enough to perch on your shoulder, but had decorative frills they could flare out around their faces to make themselves look larger. For the past half hour, this one had been having the time of its life playing tag with Aurora.

In an attempt to be productive, Elle cracked open her Drekai language study book. She'd no sooner found her place than she heard a soft, Drekai-accented voice calling from below.

"Excuse me, but I think my spitfire is on your balcony."

Elle was at the balcony's edge in a flash. Peering down, she saw a young Drekai woman with light blue scales on her hairline, cheekbones, and shoulders looking up at her. She was probably a few years older than Elle, and had a trio of charcoal pencils sticking out of her blonde draketail hairstyle.

"Cute little blue one?" Elle asked. "He's here—Come on up!"

When the blonde Drekai woman spotted the spitfire frolicking with Aurora, she let out a sigh of relief. The spitfire flicked his tongue at her, then went right back to playing. Both Elle and the young woman laughed, and Elle invited her to sit down for a refreshing drink while they waited for the little creature to tire himself out.

"I'm Elle, by the way," Elle said as the pair sat down with glasses at a stout wooden table there on the sandy portion of the balcony.

"The Evgardian true dragon rider." The blonde Drekai nodded. "I saw you at the banquet the night your party arrived. My name's Zaria."

"Well, Zaria," Elle said. "*Juuka zavaaka.*"

"*Zakohi!*" Zaria replied. "Your Drekai isn't half bad!"

"At least until I have to talk about something beyond the weather or asking where to go to relieve myself," Elle laughed. Zaria laughed back.

Together, they sipped their drinks, a deep red concoction that Elle thought tasted like subtly sweet cherries. It, like everything else she'd tried here, was delicious.

"Mm," Zaria said. "So, what's it like being bonded to the white true dragon?"

"I didn't realize so many people here knew about Aurora." Elle blushed.

"Aurora, that's a perfect name," Zaria said, watching the dragons play. "It's a shame when people name their dragon bonds before they've met them. Good names are supposed to fit their owner, like a snug pair of gloves." Elle smiled. It would be good to have a friend here in the Dragon Isles. She answered Zaria's question candidly.

"Honestly, at first, being bonded to Aurora was a little nerve-wracking. I was so desperate to be perfect that I kind of became a shell of myself. But a friend helped me realize that she chose me for a reason. While I'm always striving to do my best and improve, I'd like to think that Aurora's bond amplifies the best of me... if that makes sense."

"Absolutely," Zaria said, beaming. "I understand a thing or two about feeling inadequate. But if the Allfather trusts me to perform my task, the least I can do is believe in myself."

Elle smiled. "Are all Drekai as religious as you?"

"Not all, but most, yes," replied Zaria. "We are an honor-bound people determined to serve our ideals. Each Drekai chooses a life path to follow, and together..."

Zaria slid from her chair and onto the sandy ground. With an artistic hand, she began drawing in the sand, several squiggly lines that briefly coalesced before swiftly branching out again. At first, Elle thought it might've been the symbol for the Knights of the Torch, but Elle quickly realized it was a tree.

"Our distinct paths all weave together into a great tree," Zaria explained. "Ultimately, each of us must branch out to bring prosperity to our homeland. Yet and at our roots, we remain as one—children of the Allfather."

Elle joined Zaria on the ground to get a better look at her drawing.

"That's beautiful," Elle started. "And in some ways, true for our whole realm. At the end of the day, our identities as Drekai, Evgardian, magi, Knight, Mage Hunter, dragon rider... they don't really matter much, do they?"

Zaria shook her head. "It's like the half-born *jaaril* said after the duel—All our petty squabbling serves only to distract from the real enemy. His choice to shift the honor duel to the death into a duel to first blood moved many of us, as did the beautiful monument he created. Family has long been one of our most sacred ideals, and yet, I believe we've allowed it to become poisoned in our pursuit of pride." Zaria shook her head. Her lips formed a soft smile as she went on.

"I see Prince Asher as a symbol of hope. Hope that together, our two nations may be stronger than either will have ever been alone. That one day, the whole *realm* might become family. With any luck, the signing of the treaty today will mark the beginning of a new age of unity. You've got a role to play in that as well."

Elle nodded solemnly. "Will you be at the treaty meeting then?"

Zaria nodded, and Elle thought she saw a flash of nerves cross her new friend's face. "In fact," Zaria said, "I'd better get going. Some last minute things to prepare—*Taiva!*"

She was calling to her spitfire, and Elle recognized the word for 'sky.' That must've been the spitfire's name.

Sure enough, the little guy came gliding toward Zaria then perched on her shoulder, his scaly body shuddering as he settled in. His presence seemed to put Zaria at ease.

"You had fun, eh, little one?" Zaria smiled, first at the spitfire then at Elle. "See you tonight then?"

"See you tonight."

Relief flooded Elle when she saw that Asher was, in fact, at the meeting, which was taking place in the same great hall wherein they'd had their first meal upon arrival. Now, however, every table had been arranged in a large square, all the chairs facing inward so that everyone could see each other. The Empress and her core advisors sat at the table at the back of the grand hall.

Elle didn't waste a second before racing around the tables toward Asher's seat. For a moment, Elle thought about behaving like a proper princess, but in the end, she couldn't help but embrace him. At least she refrained from squealing and squeezing him.

"Here I was thinking you wanted to score some more points," Elle rushed. "But leaving me in the dark for *three days*? Come on, Asher of Steel Rim. Or, should I say Asher, Prince Who Absolutely Outranks Me Now?"

Elle had expected a scorching good quip from Asher to counter that remark, but instead, all she got was a mildly amused chuckle. That, and a stiff pat on the back.

"Good evening," Asher said mechanically.

Elle arched an eyebrow, her lips quirking into the mischievous grin she knew Asher liked. "What kind of soap have they got you washing in? You smell different." Elle loved Asher's outdoorsy scent, but today he smelled strangely like lavender and grapes.

There was a slight pause, as if Asher were trying to decide how to respond to Elle's subtly flirtatious comment. At last, he replied, "I hope my odor is to your liking, Princess."

His awkward attempt at banter got Elle to snort. What sort of game was he playing today? Normally, she had no trouble reading Asher's energy and matching him quip for quip. But today? *The pressure must be getting to him,* she thought, not without sympathy. After all, hadn't she recently gone through a similar phase herself? This must've been so difficult for Asher—to go from hating nobles all his life to learning he was a *prince!* Elle couldn't even begin to imagine the jumble of thoughts and emotions that must've been going through his head.

"Forgive me, but we'd best take our seats. It is good to see you, Eliana."

Asher walked off, but Elle's heart sank. Okay, something was definitely off with Asher. Besides the uncharacteristic stiffness and utter lack of wit, he'd called her *Eliana*, not *Elle*. Drak, she needed to talk with him alone after this. She'd hate to see this whole Prince-thing kill Asher's spark the way her role as true dragon rider had once nearly killed hers.

And anyway, Asher was right about one thing: It was time to take things seriously. This meeting could potentially change the fate of the realm forever.

She took her seat while Asher took his own on Empress Khaisa's right-hand side. Meanwhile, most of the Knights of the Torch were clustered together along one row, with Solrac right in the middle. He looked deep in concentration as he pored over a stack of papers, and kept putting up a finger for silence each time another Knight tried to speak with him.

Sitting opposite Asher, on Empress Khaisa's left, was Kheradok. He briefly made eye contact with Elle, and her mind flashed back to the night before the duel, when they'd discussed sweet Aurora's fate while in the hatchery.

Destined to restore the Guardian's fire...

For the umpteenth time, Elle thought of the various times she'd seen Aurora breathe her glorious white flame that healed the shadow wasting: once for a little girl in Topaz Sierra, and again for a man at the refugee camp outside of Orothion. Aurora had tried to recreate the flame on multiple other occasions, but to no avail. It wasn't something she could do on command, only when something inside her felt compelled to do so.

While Aurora's power was great, Elle worried for her. Each time she'd performed such a healing, the endeavor had exhausted the white true dragon of her strength so much that Elle could sense it through their bond. That was why she'd sworn Shaya and the others who'd witnessed the miracle at the refugee camp to secrecy. Still, Elle couldn't help but feel that in hiding this gift she was no different than Kheradok, who'd tried to spare Aurora her dark fate by leaving her unhatched and suppressing her light.

Through her bond with Aurora, Elle felt a warmth like the sun's rays. Though the feeling was meant to bring comfort, Elle only felt dread at the thought of losing her beloved dragon.

Momentarily, Empress Khaisa stood, cutting through Elle's thoughts and bringing the chatter in the room to a halt.

She spoke Evgardian for the benefit of the Knights, then gave a brief speech about how she hoped this new alliance would prove vital in protecting our realm. She praised Asher for his courage during the duel, and declared that the Drekai would accept his drawing of first blood and seal the treaty.

"The true dragon Aurora, and her rider, Eliana of Drakfell, are hereby released from all claims—past, present, and future," Empress Khaisa declared. "Furthermore, the Drekai and Knights of the Torch will enter into an alliance in preparation to face our most ancient mutual enemy:

the Gray. As Khaisa, daughter of Khara and Khaz and reigning Empress of the Dragon Isles, I will sign first."

She did so as one advisor produced a document. Elle herself had read over its contents, and felt a thrill as the Empress finished signing with a flourish. This was the first formal alliance between Drekai and Evgardians since the dawn of the realm as they knew it. History was being made here.

Next, the Empress held out the pen to Solrac to sign on behalf of the Knights of the Torch. When Solrac stood, Elle couldn't help but notice the uncharacteristically vacant expression in his eyes as well as the peculiar stiffness with which he moved toward the head of the tables. He took the pen with a mechanical air, too; it was nearly enough to make Elle say something.

Apparently, she wasn't the only one who noticed something was off. After narrowing his eyes at Solrac, one of the Empress's advisors, Zoren, spoke up.

"I believe the true dragon rider should be the one to sign. After all, she stands among the leadership of the Knights of the Torch, does she not?"

There were some murmurs—followed by a brief clarification that Elle was, in fact, of age, if only recently—and then the next thing she knew Elle found herself with a pen in hand. The thrill she'd felt earlier only strengthened as *she* got to be the one setting the future in paper and ink.

From there, the exchange of information began. The Knights went first, sharing everything they knew about the Gray. Solrac remained oddly quiet as those surrounding him explained what they knew of wraith bonds from the Black Valkyrie, as well as the information Asher and Meleya had collected during their unique spirit journey into the Haze. Elle kept expecting Asher to chime in, but he too stayed weirdly quiet.

The Drekai seemed exceptionally interested in what Asher and Meleya had found at the center of the Haze. Many took notes as others asked questions regarding the netherstone, including Kheradok.

"The netherstone you discovered," Kheradok said, "was it of ancient make? Guardian Era in design?"

"Yes, according to reports," one Knight said, gesturing to Asher, who gave a vague nod. "We suspect that more of these netherstones are causing the Hazes throughout Evgard in the physical plane too. Some of ours speculate that while these strange, crystalline monuments might've originated in the physical plane, they've been dormant in Etheria for the past thousand or so years."

"What we don't understand," another Knight butted in, "is why they're affecting the physical plane only now. And only in certain areas."

"We can answer that," came a timid Drekai voice. All the attention turned to Zaria, the young blonde Drekai with the pencils in her hair whom Elle had met earlier that day. Her cheeks pinked and Elle noticed her sky blue spitfire curled around her shoulder giving her a little nudge.

Empress Khaisa stepped in. "Drekai and Knights, allow me to introduce Zaria, one of the Dragon Isles' leading historians. Zaria has spent the last several years investigating and documenting the *khaamu*—the wraiths. If there are no further questions for the Evgardians, I'd like to invite Zaria to share her findings."

Zaria hefted an enormous portfolio onto the table where she sat. As she organized her pages, Empress Khaisa continued.

"Zoren's journeyings throughout Kolbohr have yielded valuable information as well. As one of my most trusted advisors and longtime agent of the Emerald Eye, he will aid Zaria in presenting the information we Drekai possess regarding the Gray."

Zoren and Zaria exchanged looks. Then, Zoren cleared his throat.

"To fully grasp the scope of what we face, we must first go back to the beginning of Evgard," Zoren began. While Solrac's storytelling always came with a flair of melodrama, Zoren's tone was somber, though no less intriguing, given the nature of the information he was about to divulge.

Meanwhile, Zaria had begun to paint. As in, she was holding a paintbrush, enchanted with golden runemarks, which she swished expertly through the air. As she did, illusory images began to take shape, a sort of watercolor-esque quality to them. She kept glancing down at pages from her portfolio she'd spread out on the table before her, using them as references for the illusion-powered art her paintbrush relic allowed her to compose.

Vivid landscapes appeared in the air, shimmering and slightly translucent. Rengard's ruddy canyons, snowy Behrfell, the epic cascades of the Capital... Elle even spotted the craggy, geyser-ridden badlands of Drakfell, her home.

"Before either Evgardian or Drekai set foot on this land, there were dragons," Zoren said.

At that, Zaria's paintbrush produced a flurry of illusory, watercolored dragons that ran and soared across the varied landscapes. Elle's pulse flew at the sight of such mighty creatures and raw, malleable earth.

Suddenly, one painted dragon loomed large over the rest. The glorious, third ascension true dragon with blood-red scales appeared to roar, his wide wings outstretched.

Zoren continued. "For centuries, third ascension true dragons ruled territories of their own, with drakes, wyverns, and evren living among them in peace. But the dragons weren't fulfilled. Alone, they could never achieve the same degrees of sentience and control that comes with being bound to a rider."

With a flick of her enchanted paintbrush, Zaria shifted the colors of her art to reflect night, the lone true dragon now roaring into the emptiness of the starry sky.

"When the first Evgardians came by skyboat," Zoren went on, "the dragons rejoiced. The greatest true dragon of them all, a wise, ruby-scaled creature, soon bonded the Evgardian leader, a man named Theok."

At this, Zaria painted a silhouetted man reaching out toward the dragon, who promptly offered him his heartscale in return.

Elle recalled tales of Theok and how he'd led his people out of their dying lands and into this one by skyboat from her history lessons. Blessed with an extraordinarily long life, Theok was said to have been the last of the original Guardians. All of the stories surrounding Theok were shrouded in mystery, but Elle knew that all legends were born of at least some truth.

"Both Drekai and Evgardian myth alike speak of Theok's great power," continued Zoren. "Granted the ability to access all nine types of etherarchy, the great Guardian Theok and those who followed him tamed this wild land. According to legend, Theok was liberal with his power, bestowing the Guardianship upon those he believed would best serve the people. Some wielded all nine types like he did, while others wielded only a few and were called skymages."

Zaria's brush produced other silhouettes, male and female, many of whom stood alongside watercolored drakes, wyverns, and evren in a variety of colors. Between Zoren and Zaria, the entire room was transfixed, and Elle was no exception.

"Thus did Evgard enter its first era of peace and prosperity. With the Guardians at the helm, they built a remarkable nation, their innovation remaining unmatched even today, establishing Evgard's shining Capital city at a rare intersection where ether freely spans both the physical and ethereal planes."

Zaria's illusion wiped clean before showing the High Citadel, nestled amidst a glorious network of waterfalls. The waterfalls appeared to flow with pure white ether, which glinted off of the magnificent black and white castle.

"Thanks to the information shared by our new Evgardian allies," Zoren said thoughtfully, "I would surmise that Theok and his contemporaries chose that spot because it was an ether oasis, an intersection of numerous ethereal ley lines."

Several listeners nodded their heads, including Elle. That made perfect sense. Notably, Asher didn't give any reaction at all, despite having been the one to have collected said information about the ether oases and ley lines. Stars, what was wrong with him today? Even Zoren narrowed his eyes in Asher's direction before going on.

"Alas, one of Theok's chosen Guardians was not satisfied. Though most Evgardian histories regarding this man were destroyed, those that survived refer to him as "the Gray Revenant."

When he said the name, Elle felt a few of the hairs on the back of her neck stand on end. This dark feeling only worsened as Zaria painted a shadowy man wearing jagged armor and a helmet with eye slits that glowed sapphire blue.

"The Gray Revenant sought to enhance his own power to the level of the three goddesses and the Allfather," Zoren went on gravely. "To achieve this terrible ambition, he turned to voidarchy."

At once, the whole color palette Zaria had been using went from bright to dull and almost grayscale as blue streaks of watercolored lightning backlit the shadowy man. A frayed cloak trailed from his back, its hem having been shredded to threads.

"Since the dawn of time, the *khaamu,* or wraiths, have lain in wait, craving the one thing they can never truly have: a physical form."

Shadowy, watercolored wraiths surrounded the Gray Revenant, amorphous beings with wispy forms and vivid blue eyes. Some bore jagged writing in white across their faces, and Elle could see glowing blue cores pulsing from within their chests.

Elle shuddered. She'd heard tell of these beings, and even heard that Asher and Meleya had faced them in Etheria. Scorch, was this what they really looked like?

"Since time immemorial, one wraith had stood above the rest as the most ancient and powerful. We Drekai call him *Khaamu Khizaari*, the Wraith King. He whispered to the Gray Revenant, promising him power, wealth, and immortality. Soon, the two were blood-bound."

Zaria's art flowed from the brush, depicting the man pricking his finger on the sharp tip of a thin crystal—a voidshard. The act etched a name on the shard, and his eyes burned with more sinister sapphire light.

"Many followed the Gray Revenant. Using corrupted astromancy, they erected monuments to the Gray called 'netherstones.' Once infused with rifting etherarchy, these acted as lesser gateways between Etheria and the physical plane. Through these, the Gray could enter this realm and poison the souls of men and women, as well as the very land itself."

Elle's heart pounded as she watched the images dramatize Zoren's tale. Pieces were falling into place.

"Stars," Elle murmured. "The Hazes." A few of her fellow Knights muttered in agreement.

Zoren continued spinning his historical tale. "Then, one thousand years ago, only a few short years after Evgard's founding, the Gray Ones nearly pushed Evgard into what they call the Gray Age, or the Age of the Wraith—An era of darkness, wherein the Gray nearly swallowed the whole of this land. Desperate to save their new home, Theok and the other Guardians, as well as their bonded dragons, combined their etherarchy to banish these netherstones, one by one, into Etheria."

"Zoren," one of the Knights, a medic called Trickshot began. She spoke Zoren's name with a certain familiarity, and Elle could tell that Zoren knew her as well. In fact, he seemed rather glad that she was here.

"What sort of etherarchy is that, if I may ask?" Trickshot asked.

"A specialized kind of rifting," Zoren responded. "While Evgardians have lost the banishment rune to time, we Drekai remember."

With that, Zoren nodded to General Kheradok. Kheradok instantly stood, traced a complex rune in the air, then opened a small, gold-rimmed portal. He pushed on the rift, which in turn devoured a mug set before Trickshot's place at the table. The rift winked out, and the cup was gone.

"Without an exit portal, that which is banished becomes trapped in the spirit plane," Kheradok explained.

“Hmph,” Trickshot said. “Lucky I wasn’t thirsty, eh?”

There were a few scattered chuckles, which helped ease the heaviness that had settled over the assembly. Next, another Drekai advisor piped up, an elderly but strong blademaster that Elle thought she had heard referred to as Zedek.

“When a group of Rifters channels their power together, it multiplies. Our people have used this form of etherarchy only in times of great need, when great darkness plagues this plane.”

“My father, Emperor Khaz, ordered exactly such usage on the Evgardian city, Misthaven, years ago,” Empress Khaisa said. “When he learned that the magi sanctuary, set on the border of the Dragon Mists, was secretly being run by members of the Coven of the Gray Ones, he sent spies. They reported that the Liberator and her followers there were helping the Soul Reaper move his voidshard from its hiding place in the Mirror Forest to a new one in the Dragon Mists. The Mists’ mysterious and unpredictable powers have kept its location shrouded from the probing of Seers for many years. We lost many good agents trying to track it down.”

Zoren looked somber as he picked back up. “Just when the Gray Age appeared imminent, Theok and his Guardians were able to successfully banish each of these netherstones, but they could not destroy their dark power. Knowing this, the Gray has lain in wait, waiting for the Guardians to slowly die out, so that they could resume their prior efforts and have no one powerful enough to stand in their way. Even as recently as the last few months, the Coven of the Gray Ones has been hard at work, pulling these netherstones back into the physical plane, where their numbing power has begun to spread like a flood throughout our lands.”

“How is the Coven doing this?” Trickshot pressed.

“Once again, rifting,” Empress Khaisa said. “Still, we believe our agents have managed to stunt the Coven’s progress on that score.”

“How’s that?” Trickshot asked, and Elle found herself leaning forward in anticipation of the Empress’s answer.

“Thanks to the Rifter Purge enacted by the late Evgardian High Queen, Rifters in Evgard have become increasingly scarce. Our agents tracked down the one the Coven was using to pull the netherstones through, a man named Torsten, and took care of him.” At that, a couple of Drekai exchanged grimaces, as if doing so hadn’t been pleasant. Elle had never heard of this Torsten person, but the sound of his name made Trickshot blanche.

Zoren took over again. "The bottom scale is that while the Coven is no longer able to restore more netherstones into this plane, the ones they've already brought in are spreading their darkness rapidly."

"And, unfortunately," Zaria piped up, "as of yet, we've been unsuccessful in destroying any netherstone we've come across. It's little wonder the ancients resorted to banishing them."

Zoren nodded. "Meanwhile, cases of the shadow wasting continue to increase both on the Evgardian and Drekai sides. If the Gray is not stopped, it's only a matter of time before the Wraith King and his followers get what they couldn't last time."

"Last time..." one Knight muttered. "How *did* Theok and the others finish off the Wraith King—this Gray Revenant character—last time?"

Zoren looked down. "The legends are scant, since after destroying the Gray Revenant, those who followed the Guardians saw to it that nearly every document describing the use of voidarchy was burned. Suffice it to say, the Guardians and their dragons severed the Wraith King from his host, scattering the wraith's essence so completely they believed he would never be able to reform."

Zaria had started painting her illusions again, showing white blotches of paint essentially erasing the shadowy Gray Revenant.

"Unfortunately," Zoren said, "they were wrong."

Zoren had everyone's full attention once more. Elle settled in to listen.

"While I was unable to acquire the Soul Reaper's voidshard," Zoren went on, "I was able to ascertain the names written thereon. These names took me to Evgard's north, a small town in Kolbohr called Gloomhaven. A sorry seaside village where the sun never shines."

Zaria was prepared for this part of the story as well, and soon the room was gazing at her beautifully rendered scene of a dismal town shrouded in gray fog, its craggy cliffs rising up to meet a stillwater bay.

"During the Rifter Purge enacted by High King Magnus's mother, many children born with teleportation etherarchy were abandoned, left on the streets, in the wilds, or worse. One such child was found and taken to a small Sanctuary of Streya in Gloomhaven."

Zaria's brush was flying to keep up, painting a depiction of a sickly, emaciated boy of no more than eight or nine, standing before a chapel of the Mind Goddess, Streya. Elle marvelled how, for all their cultural differences, both the Drekai and Evgardians worshiped the three primal goddesses, along with their respective symbols: the sun for Solei, the moon for Selene, and the stars for Streya. Stars adorned the chapel Zaria painted before them.

"The Sisters and Sons of Streya that ran the Sanctuary had their hands full," Zoren said. "There were too many secret magi children to care for, and while I suspect they did their best, some things inevitably slipped through the cracks. Young Kjell, for that was the boy's name, felt isolated, and eventually robbed the Streyan's coffers and struck out on his own."

Zaria showed the boy, now slightly older, leaving the Sanctuary. In the image, one Sister in black robes called for him to return, but the boy didn't listen.

"While the Sanctuary now lies abandoned, some records survived," Zoren continued. "I was able to trace Kjell's next steps. First, he retreated to a cove near Gloomhaven's stormy northeastern sea. There lies a series of grottos, filled with potent, corrupted ether geysers that I believe are remnants of the Gray Revenant's ancient tyranny."

As Zaria painted the dreary scene, Elle could practically feel the cold emanating from the dripping stones. Tide pools dotted the ground, and bursts of misty blue light from small springs lit the caverns where the boy crouched alone.

"This place, called Scryer's Grotto, was once pure, a haven among the Guardians to watch over the various keepdoms. That is, until the Gray Revenant turned on them, corrupting the etherarchy there and using the great scrying crystals said to be hidden there to spy on his enemies. The cavern is well-guarded, and I was unable to get to the deep caverns where these crystals reside. But Seer relics were able to show me glimpses of what happened there not so many years ago."

At that, Zoren produced a dreamweb. The wooden hoop was tied with threads, with several tiny fragments of crystal suspended along them. Zoren explained that the crystals held bits of memory, and were taken from the grotto and other places in Kolbohr. Seer etherarchy infused into the relic had allowed Zoren to learn of Kjell's journey.

"Here in the grotto," Zoren said, "young Kjell began to truly embrace his 'friends'."

"Friends?" Elle whispered, not liking the sound of that. Across the way, a few of the Drekai who'd heard the tale before grimaced.

"The other children at the Sanctuary had accused Kjell of talking to shadows, but the reality was even more heinous. In the isolation of the grottos, he'd been using the Sight paired with the lunar cycles to speak freely with the wraiths."

The illusory painting showed the young man surrounded by wraiths, their eyes casting blue light onto his gaunt face. Stacks of books and scrolls lay before him too.

"Kjell began to read. He used his skill with rifting and the Sight, as well as the scrying crystals in the grotto, to seek out the oldest libraries the realm over. He devoured everything he could get his hands on regarding voidarchy, the Gray Revenant, and the almighty Wraith King who'd bound himself to him. He became obsessed with the god-like power the Guardians once had." Here, Zoren shivered, then exhaled and resumed his retelling.

"Using this knowledge in conjunction with his wraith companions, Kjell began to experiment. He was able to identify magi by their ether wells using the Sight, then kidnap them and drag them back to the Grotto."

The images Zaria now painted were even darker and more sinister. Kjell was older now, and Elle hated even the watercolored depiction of him bending over a magi lying still upon the ground.

"Many magi died as Kjell tried time and again to tear out their ether wells," Zoren continued, the faintest trace of anger creeping into his otherwise even tone. "He failed dozens of times, nearly dying himself as he tried to stitch the ether wells of these expired magi onto his own soul. But eventually, he saw his first success."

A crystalline object, glowing white with ether, hovered over the chest of a silhouetted man. Then the image shifted, and the glow emanated from Kjell's chest, now a vivid blue instead.

"A second success soon followed." Zoren spoke grimly. "Once Kjell had three ether wells, he at last felt like he was ready—Worthy of notice by the most powerful wraith in Evgard's history.

"Kjell had learned well the ways of the *khaamu,* of their constant struggle for power, and their willingness to consume one another in order to come out on top."

Zaria raced to paint the scene as Zoren went on. "Night after night," he said, "blue fires burned within the grotto as Kjell sacrificed the wraiths he'd once called friends, scattering their essences to the farthest reaches of Etheria. Each sacrifice brought him closer to summoning the Wraith King.

"Despite Theok and the Guardians' combined efforts to permanently rid this land of the Wraith King, such was ultimately sufficient to restore his life force. Agnai, for that is his name, had risen again. He appeared to Kjell, who begged him for the chance to become his human vessel."

Even in the inherently beautiful watercolor style, the monstrous wraith that Zaria painted into existence was enough to set Elle's nerves on edge. A shadowy crown of jagged spikes rose from his head, and though Zaria's depiction left the specifics indistinct, Elle could tell hundreds of words had been scratched onto his featureless face. Cold, glowing blue eyes glittered as they stared at Kjell's likeness.

"Agnai protested at first," Zoren said. "Kjell was no hero of men, not proud and strong like the countless other human vessels the Wraith King had inhabited before. But, using the stolen ether wells he'd stitched onto his own soul as evidence, Kjell convinced Agnai of his cunning. *He* would succeed where even the Gray Revenant had not—by striking at the very heart of Evgard from the inside."

From there, the illusory paintings showed the same voidshard from earlier, this time, Kjell's blood watering its planes. In its red wake, Kjell's name appeared opposite Agnai's.

"With Agnai as his bond, Kjell became the Surgeon or, as we know him, the Soul Reaper. He offered his services to High King Magnus, who struggles to keep the splintering keepdoms united. The Surgeon offered a solution to the magi plight: Remove their ether wells."

"Of course," Trickshot said. "Without their ether wells, the magi would no longer draw wild dragonkind! Magnus gets to be Evgard's salvation—"

"—And Kjell and the Wraith King get infinite ether wells to build their army of corrupted skymages," Elle finished, sufficiently horrified. "One even more powerful than that of the Gray Revenant."

"It was a risky plan," Zoren said, nodding. "At first, Magnus was hesitant—He wanted proof that the magi would survive the process. That this would truly be a mercy to them. He funded the Soul Reaper's experiments in secret and eventually began to see consistent success. Many magi lives were lost during this process."

"Including that of my sister, Zerana," Empress Khaisa said, her neck flexing with emotion.

The room fell silent in memory of Zerana. Elle looked to Asher to gauge his reaction, only to find that he had none at all. His expression was blank.

Elle was more certain than ever that something was very wrong with him, and she couldn't stand by any longer.

It wasn't very proper, but Elle stood, then began carefully skirting around the table. Kheradok and a handful of others gave her a quizzical look, but Elle whispered, "*Taiika jehn kiiljuni.*" She didn't actually need to relieve herself, but hadn't been able to resist using one of the few Drekai phrases she had in her arsenal.

Zoren carried on with his tale. "It wasn't until Magnus's son, Mason, fell ill with the shadow wasting that the Soul Reaper was able to win the High King over completely. The Soul Reaper promised to restore Mason, which he did, but at a terrible cost: Mason became wraith-bound, a foreign ether well stitched to his soul serving to sustain him."

Zaria was painting Mason Drakeslayer now, but Elle was too focused on getting to Asher to notice. Scorch, this was a large room.

"The only way to stop history from repeating itself is by severing Kjell's bond with Agnai, the Wraith King," Zoren said. "Agnai cannot operate here without a body, and without his Gray One, the Soul Reaper is no more than a man."

Now Khaisa spoke back up. "My father lacked the information we've since gathered, but he understood this well. He and my mother sent many sets of agents to Evgard in search of the token of the Surgeon's bond with the Wraith King: the Soul Reaper's voidshard."

"I was among these sets." Zoren nodded, a shadow crossing his face. "My unit and every other since has failed in our quest. I was able to discover the names upon the shard, which led me north, but the shard itself remains out of reach."

"Not anymore," Elle said, the carrying quality of her own voice all but startling her as she paused her trek across the room. Everyone turned to Elle, curiosity burning in the Drekai's expressions.

Elle straightened. "The Soul Reaper's voidshard is in the Knights of the Torch's possession. Thanks to the valiant efforts of our own Meleya of Misthaven, who keeps the shard safely stowed in Etheria by way of her rift hold."

Blinking stares met Elle, and only a horror-struck Zoren seemed to have the wherewithal to speak. "Meleya... *Meleya* has the Soul Reaper's voidshard? I knew she'd read the names on it, but are you telling me that dark relic is in her possession?"

"I am indeed," Elle confirmed. Unable to contain herself, Empress Khaisa stood and broke into a genuine smile.

"This alliance has thus far proved itself most beneficial," she said. Others from both sides chorused their agreement.

Meanwhile, Elle had resumed her journey toward Asher, having just now reached his side. She frowned deeply as she observed him sitting there, hands neatly folded in his lap, looking straight ahead as if fully engrossed in the topic at hand.

Yes, something was *definitely* off.

"Asher?" Elle whispered, kneeling down to match his level.

"What is it, Princess Eliana?" Asher replied. "Oughtn't you return to your seat?"

"*'Oughtn't'?*" Elle repeated in disbelief. Additionally, what was with the strange violet sheen to Asher's skin? She could only make it out when she was looking hard, but as Elle focused, it became more and more clear. Asher... he was shimmering, as if he weren't real at all.

Meanwhile, the council's conversation carried on. The Knights and Drekai were discussing the voidshard, and what lengths they expected the Soul Reaper might go to in order to get it back. The Knights shared what they knew of the Veilblade, and how the Black Valkyrie suspected the Soul Reaper hoped to use his voidshard in order to attune it.

"Asher?" Elle whispered again. "Who do I meet on this eve of darkness?"

Elle knew Asher was as aware as any true Knight of the Torch that the proper response to the passphrase was, 'One who carries the light.' She waited with bated breath.

Asher seemed completely focused on the conversation, but cocked his head before whispering back. "Darkness? The sun hasn't yet set, so I can't imagine what you mean."

Elle's heart sank as her resolve rose.

The group discussion had turned to the convergence of mythic stars. It seemed that Seers among both the Drekai and the Knights had been seeing it in their omenfires, leaving both groups certain that, come spring, the Soul Reaper intended to make his move.

"This makes sense," one Drekai said. "Our most sacred texts all attest that the night of the convergence is when the barrier between the physical and spiritual planes is at its thinnest."

"So what does the Soul Reaper plan to do that night exactly?" another Drekai asked.

Trickshot responded with sobriety. "Scorch... he has the Veilblade... I think he means to tear the veil between worlds..."

With equal grimness, Zoren finished her sentence, "...and let loose an infinite horde of wraiths on Evgard and the Isles alike."

No sooner had the last word fallen from Zoren's lips than Elle brought the whole council to a sudden halt by drawing her saber. Erupting with shimmering green and violet flame, she plunged it into Asher's side.

Gasps filled the room, and for an awful second, Elle thought she'd made a terrible mistake.

But when Asher's illusory form began to dissolve into blue etherdust, those gasps of shock turned to ones of anger. Within a second, the illusion completely gave way, leaving behind a small, silvery snake coiled upon Asher's seat.

Drekai and Evgardian alike began to yell, looking around in confusion. Zoren sat very near Asher, and while some panicked, he narrowed his eyes, scanning the faces of the other members of the assembly.

Elle knew what he was doing, his years as the legendary Mage Hunter, the Ursadon, having trained him to recognize the telltale signs of etherarchy. In an instant, he'd locked his gaze on Solrac. Sure enough, now that she was looking for it, Elle could see that same violet sheen shimmering from Solrac's form.

'Solrac' was already trying to quietly slip away, but Zoren wasn't about to let that happen. He swept across the room, whipping out his blade with the speed of an ashviper. Within another second, Solrac's illusory form was dissolving too, leaving behind another copy of that same silvery snake.

Trickshot demolished the intruder snake with a bolt from a miniature crossbow she'd kept sheathed at her hip, while Zedek used some kind of dreamweave etherarchy to freeze and capture the one that had been projecting the illusion of Asher.

"*Zaavu!*" Zoren swore. "These familiars are the work of the Mage Hunter, Ilyan. He works closely with the Soul Reaper."

"Soot!" Trickshot echoed the curse, locking eyes with Zoren. "Does this mean the Gray knows we're aware of their plot?"

"Would it matter to them if they did?" Zedek mused darkly.

"And more importantly," Elle spoke over the mad racing of her heart, "where in the stars are Asher and Solrac?"

Fragment: Diamondback

Jax

Jax brought up the rear as their party trekked across Drakfell's lonely geyser fields. They kept to the northeast, avoiding the cities clustered towards the Badlands' southern end, whose inhabitants had allied with the Knights of the Torch at the behest of King Rodan. They stuck to out-of-the-way scaledeer trails, having set aside their highly recognizable Mage Hunter's cloaks for less conspicuous garb. Jax still wore his heavy plate armor as he traveled, though. Hiding within this shell felt natural now.

Bjorn walked at their party's rear, his umbral dragon bond having been killed back at the crater where Streya's Comet had fallen, while from the head of the group, Jaira rode a gray, third ascension void-wyvern with awful, lightning-like blue cracks riddling his hide. His eyes were wild and sapphire blue, and with Jaira possessing its heartscale, the unfortunate creature had no choice but to obey her.

The void-wyvern had some limited rifting powers, which was why she'd been given to Jaira for this quest. His power had allowed them to skyskip, a trick Jaira had apparently learned from observing some group of Knights of the Torch over the summer. She'd been assigned to follow them, though she'd been tight-lipped regarding details, specifically *who* she'd been tailing. That was probably for the best. Either way, skyskipping allowed Jax's party to travel across vast stretches of sky very quickly, and was how they'd reached the Dragon Isles in time for the duel. It was also how they were going to get back to Kolbohr in time for the full moon and the Soul Reaper's next round of surgeries.

After a long morning of skyskipping, the void-wyvern's power was drained, so the group had to walk through the damp-smelling geyser fields. Despite the dragon's fatigue, Jaira made him carry her while Bjorn stalked behind, occasionally jabbing the creature with the end of his jagged silver dagger to encourage it to keep moving. Each time, Jax's instinct was to make him stop, but Calyx's presence in his mind was strong and Jax continued choosing to do nothing.

Meanwhile, Jax's evren, Jade, used the claws on the hinges of each of her four wings to walk alongside her bond. Draped across her back like freshly hunted scaledeer were none other than the Farseer and the newly-discovered Prince of the Dragon Isles. Or rather, Solrac and Asher, chained in silver so that they couldn't access their etherarchy. In addition to that, Jaira kept the two of them drugged on low doses of astralock. They had brief spells of muddled consciousness, but had slept almost the whole journey from Zolehiinu so far.

Jax still couldn't believe it. What he'd learned while watching the duel in the Dragon Isles still rang in his ears. Asher, of all people, was a *noble*. And not just any noble—The heir of a mighty nation!

Once again, Asher of Steel Rim shines so brightly that you fade to nothing. Calyx's deep, guttural voice filled Jax's mind. *But do not worry, Jax. I will help you build something that ensures you are remembered throughout the ages.*

As usual, Calyx's demeaning remarks and vague promises grated on Jax's heart and mind. He thought about using Mason's trick to keep his wraith at bay, but somehow even something as simple as thinking a happy thought seemed exhausting to Jax right now. In fact, Jax had hardly used the trick since Mason had taught it to him. Calyx had been extra present ever since the day Streya's Comet fell, and Jax was just so tired.

Jax had mixed feelings regarding what he and Mason Drakeslayer had done back at Streya's Comet's skyfall site. So far, neither he nor Mason had said or done anything about the vast clutch of true dragon eggs hidden inside Mason's rift hold. How could they? They were both servants of the Gray, bound as strongly as Jaira's umbral dragon. Still, when he thought of the dragons he and Mason had saved from this same, miserable fate, he felt that tiny flicker of hope flare within him.

The Badlands were hot, and Jax's plate armor weighed heavily on his shoulders. He removed his helmet to wipe the sweat off his brow.

He'd just re-tied his maroon bandana around his forehead and was about to return the helmet to his head when a gentle breeze rustled his wild, steely hair. It felt so refreshing on his scalp that Jax changed his mind about redonning his helmet, instead tossing it into Jade's saddlebag as they walked.

As he did, Jax got an extended look at Solrac and Asher lying there. Solrac was out cold, eyes shut and limbs limp. But Asher was starting to wake up. For whatever reason, the astralock didn't last as long with Asher.

Probably his crazy Archonic system working overtime to burn it off or something. Jax sneered.

Groggily, Asher turned his head and caught sight of Jaira sitting astride the chronically growling void-wyvern.

"For shame, Helga," Asher muttered, clearly less than fully coherent. "Give Skippy a break already."

"Skippy?" Jaira twisted in her saddle to shoot Asher an annoyed look.

"What's his name then?" Asher mumbled, his arm flopping as he tried to point to the miserable wyvern.

Jaira lowered her thick eyebrows as she swung off the dragon's back. For a second, Jax thought she'd taken Asher's advice to heart, but rather than walk like the others, she sauntered back to where Jade carried Asher and gave him a sharp elbow to the face, followed by another dose of astralock. She then went straight back to riding Skippy—er, the wyvern.

"Soot." Asher rubbed his face. "Not my nose! That's one of my top five handsomest features!"

Asher glared at Jaira, then craned his neck the other way only to find himself looking right at Jax. The pair locked eyes.

Jax waited for Asher to make some dumb, mumbled joke. Would he mock Jax about failing to kill him in Etheria? Call him Swan-spawn? Or would he just get angry at Jax for what he was doing to him now? That's what Jax would've done.

Instead, Asher asked one groggy, albeit genuine question:

"Why?"

Almost immediately, Asher's eyes grew heavy and he started muttering something nonsensical about some massive craghopper named Karl, but that one simple word shot through Jax like a bolt from a crossbow.

Why?

Why *was* Jax so resentful of Asher? And why was he doing this to him?

Asher deserves this. Calyx's voice was oppressive. *Life comes easy for him. Everyone loves him—Your own father prefers him. Your mother esteems him. Even Meleya, the only woman you ever really loved—*

Shut up! Jax ground his teeth together. *None of that is Asher's fault—It's just who he is. He's not trying to cut me down.*

Of course he is.

No, he's not. Jax was angry. But it wasn't Asher he was angry with. It wasn't even Calyx.

It was himself.

Without the helmet on, Jax had a full, panoramic view of the surrounding landscape. They were crossing the Badlands' vast geyser fields, vents of water shooting from the earth at intervals all around him. While they were too far north to attract attention, now that they'd gotten past some of the tallest foothills, Jax caught sight of a sprawling city on the shores of the Dragonstorm Sea.

It was Keep Drakfell, the city where they'd run their heist to steal the true dragon egg. Jax even thought he could make out the tiny streams of steam rising from the Dreamy Drakalope tavern, in whose basement was housed a secret Knights of the Torch hideout.

At once, a memory filled Jax's mind:

Jax sat alone at the crowded bar of the Dreamy Drakalope, his head in his hands. Behind him, patrons laughed and drank as they relaxed in their seats within the tavern's unique hot springs. But Jax wasn't in the mood for revelry. Not when Kari had just broken things off with him.

"Anything I can do for you, handsome?"

Jax looked up as the barmaid tapped his shoulder. She was pretty, and Jax was certain her question applied to more than just Jax's drink preference.

"Not unless you can somehow change the past and, oh, I don't know, keep me from messing up everything like I always do?"

Jax's reply was clearly more than the barmaid had bargained for. She shrugged her shoulders and hurried away, leaving Jax in peace.

Peace that lasted about two seconds before a certain pointy-eared someone invited himself to take a seat beside Jax at the bar and promptly ordered drinks.

"Get lost, Dragon-boy," Jax said. He was in no mood for Asher's show-offy antics.

"I just thought you could use a drink," Asher said.

"You look like you could use another punch to the jaw."

Asher held up his hands. "Spare us the bar fight. Look, I'll go if you really want me to. I just figured it might help if you talked about your breakup with Kari."

Jax turned to Asher and was surprised to find not a trace of either mockery or gloating in his dragonfire green eyes. Asher hadn't exactly been subtle about his disapproval of Jax's relationship with the girl who was practically his older sister... but there was no mistaking the sincerity in his present gaze.

"How'd you know?" Jax furrowed his brow.

"I've known Kari for a while. Plus, you storming out of the hideout helped."

Groaning, Jax pushed his fingers through his hair. The condensation from the many hot springs inside the tavern made it stick up even more wildly than usual. "What's wrong with me? I really thought she was into me."

"I know she was into you," Asher replied as the bartender returned with two bubbling glasses. "So what happened?"

For a moment, Jax thought about telling Asher to scorch off again. Jax didn't need this. He needed...

Drak, *Jax realized. What he needed* was *someone to talk to.*

Jax began slowly, opening up about how painful it had been when Kari ended things. Kari was the first girl Jax had let himself be vulnerable with. Jax had just begun to let her see his insecurities, but in the end, it was just as Jax had always feared: He was unloveable.

Then Asher gave Jax some insight into Kari's all-or-nothing personality. He swore Jax shouldn't take it personally, since all of Kari's life, she'd been perpetually moving on to the next big project. It had nothing to do with Jax somehow failing.

Asher didn't know it, but that had been exactly what Jax had needed to hear.

Jax took his first big swig of the drink in front of him, and the taste of alcohol burned in his throat. He coughed, then swore.

"Drak. I don't do alcohol."

"Oh. Sorry," Asher said. "I forgot. Mystic."

It was true, alcohol clouded most magi's senses, and for Mystics, it was nearly impossible to runetrace while intoxicated. But Jax's sobriety had everything to do with seeing what it had done to Torsten. Memories of his adoptive father momentarily assaulted Jax. He recalled the large man standing above him, bottle in hand and darkness in his eyes. Absently, Jax bit his lower lip, where the scar he'd received during a particularly nasty alcohol-fueled tirade had never fully faded.

"Keep your voice down about that," Jax told Asher. "But even besides that, I don't do alcohol."

"Why not?"

"Just... reasons." Jax wasn't ready to open up about that part of his life, even if Asher had proved surprisingly sincere. Maybe someday they could be close enough for that. The thought gave Jax hope.

Jax propped his elbows on the bar. "Thanks for the insight, Dragon-boy. Maybe you're not as big a drakpat as I thought."

"Gee, thanks," Asher replied. A sort of understanding passed between them, and Jax knew Asher wouldn't go around blabbing about their conversation. He was grateful for that.

As Asher returned to the hideout, Jax couldn't help but think he may have been wrong about Asher all along. After all, nobody else had bothered to check on him.

For one moment, Jax's petty jealousy seemed stupid. Asher wasn't his enemy, not really.

Maybe, just maybe, Asher could be a friend.

"You're not Jax."

Back in the geyser fields, Asher was pointing at Jax, his eyes half-closed as the newest dose of astralock began to take effect.

"What?" Jax asked.

"You're not Jax," Asher repeated, mumbling. "Your disguise is close, but you gotta take those dumb sleeves off. Real Jax would... never miss a chance to... to show off his shoulders..."

Asher trailed off, catching sight of Solrac still passed-out beside him. Asher snorted at the sight of him, then stammered, "Who hunted this giant drakalope?"

Jax froze. Asher may've only been half-conscious, but his semi-coherent musings had cut to Jax's very soul. Not the part about Solrac being a drakalope, but what he'd said before.

I'm not Jax, Jax thought. Then he repeated it aloud under his breath. "I'm not Jax. What... What am I doing?"

Nothing, Calyx's voice came through loud and strong. *You chose nothing, remember? You left the old Jax behind—You are the Gray Knight now, stronger than ever. Impossible to hurt.*

But even Calyx's tauntings seemed hollow now. For whatever reason, Asher's silly, simple statement had given Jax a burst of clarity. He didn't know how long it would last, but Jax clung to it with his entire soul. Just to the south, a geyser thundered as it shot a fountain of water into the sky.

“This isn’t me,” he said again, silently shedding the plated gauntlets that covered his hands. Perhaps he wasn’t Jax now... But maybe he could be again.

Calyx hissed as Jax removed his tassets, greaves, and finally his oversized pauldrons and chestplate. Soot, he felt like he could breathe again.

Jax’s mind was racing. He needed to take action as quickly as possible. If Jaira and Bjorn got Asher and Solrac back to the Soul Reaper’s lair, they didn’t stand a chance of coming out alive. There was no time to waste.

What are you doing, Gray Knight? Calyx said, his voice so loud it rang in Jax’s ears. *Remember, Asher took everything from you. Solrac abandoned you.*

But Jax was no longer listening, too busy adjusting the harness that held his twin axes on his back as he made his plans. Could he take out both Jaira and Bjorn alone?

Through his heartscale, Jax felt a swell like thunder from Jade. He wouldn’t be alone. Carefully, Jax started toward Jaira and Bjorn as the geysers awaiting eruption bubbled and hissed.

Think of the release, Calyx pleaded, a note of panic creeping into his deep, netherworldly tone. *Choose nothing once more.*

“No,” Jax replied out loud. Maybe his clarity wouldn’t last, but for now, it was all he had.

Feeling more like himself than he had in months, Jax muttered, “I choose light.” Instantly, positive memories filled Jax’s head, from running wild heists with Boone to the little yellow mirror gecko, Three, munching on a spiny cricket. The memories were simple, but powerful enough to chase Calyx from his mind.

Jax felt bad about taking down a girl, but Jaira absolutely deserved to have a heavy metal chestplate chucked at her head. Her eyes rolled back as she slipped smoothly from her saddle and flopped into the dirt. Jax darted toward her unconscious form; if he could just get that astralock, maybe he could—

Wham!

Bjorn reacted more quickly than Jax had anticipated. His fist took Jax in the chin, pain erupting as blood began to drip onto the long sleeve of Jax’s tunic. Jax instantly knew that it’d been no ordinary punch.

Sure enough, a row of sharp, rock-solid diamonds sprouted from each of Bjorn’s knuckles. More diamond spikes ran in a ridge up Bjorn’s arm, mingling with... Drak. Bright blue Sentinel patterns. Bjorn had been wearing his new Geomancer's silvermark for a while now, but this was the first time Jax had seen Bjorn's newly stolen powers in action.

Two geysers roared nearby, sending plumes of steam into the sky. The surge of water caught on the wind, blowing a warm mist across Bjorn and Jax's bodies.

Bjorn laughed as he cracked his bloodied knuckles. "I've wanted to do that for a *long* time. Consider it payback for that time we brawled in the courtyard on our first day at the Academy." Bjorn whipped out his sinister silver dagger, jagged and irregular after a bout with silverbane, while Jax reached for one of his axes.

"Think about this carefully, Gray Knight," Bjorn taunted as the two young men faced off in the increasingly active geyser fields. A sharp, mineral tang rode the breeze, and Jax suddenly realized the eruptions were probably Bjorn's doing too—as if the geysers were responding to the Geomancer's agitation. "You really wanna switch sides *again*?"

"Yeah, I do," Jax replied, still feeling like he'd just glimpsed the sun after months of darkness. He wasn't about to let the light out of his sight for even a second.

With a burst of confidence and maybe a little melodrama—Hey, he was Solrac and Vidya's son, after all—Jax crossed his arms and took hold of the long sleeves of his tunic. Then, Jax ripped both sleeves off at once.

Meanwhile, Jade gave a mighty roar from her place beside Jax, the sound accentuated by the trio of geysers bursting nearby. She'd already set Solrac and Asher down carefully against the adjacent ridge, and Jax heard a half-conscious Asher cheer.

Not averse to some theatricality of his own, Bjorn gave a blood-curdling, maniacal yell as blue Sentinel markings pulsed along his skin. More chunks of diamond sprouted from his back and up his neck. In a puff of blue mist, a whole ridge of them momentarily replaced the mohawk on his head as well. Jax felt his guts twist.

Drak, this guy was insane.

Insane, but not stupid. Knowing he couldn't take on both Jax *and* Jax's second ascension evren simultaneously, Bjorn darted for where Jaira lay unconscious in the dirt. In one swift motion, he snapped the cord from around her neck. Then, the poor creature's heartscale in hand, Bjorn forced the feral, exhausted, third ascension void-wyvern to bare its teeth at Jax and Jade.

"Get him," Bjorn ordered.

The dark dragon had no choice but to oblige with vigor. He dove toward Jax, but Jade leapt in the way and the two dragons went rolling, just missing an erupting geyser. The other dragon was larger, on his third ascension, but Jade was fighting for something she cared about. Some*one* she cared about, despite all of his recent mistakes.

Invigorated, Jax and Bjorn rushed to meet each other. In one hand Bjorn wielded his silver Mage Hunter's seaxe; in the other, his jagged dagger. When both weapons came at him, Jax blocked with his twin fanged axes, locking Bjorn into a battle of strength.

Muscles straining, Jax shoved Bjorn back, causing him to stumble and drop his sword. In the background, Asher gave a drowsy 'whoop.'

"You show that sparkle-gem monster!" he called.

Bjorn snarled Asher's way as he righted himself. Jax used the leeway to runetrace, blue light trailing from his finger. Soot, he wished it was gold. Nevertheless, both of his axes floated into the air, then simultaneously shot toward Bjorn.

Bjorn was a whirlwind, blocking Jax's axes in turn with his dagger and geomantic diamond armor alike. Meanwhile, Jax barrelled in to give Bjorn a punch to the gut.

Not a moment later, Jax heard the telltale rumbling of another geyser about to erupt nearby. With a mighty telekinetic heave, Jax grabbed hold of Bjorn's tunic and hurled him toward the bubbling pool.

Whoosh! Just as Bjorn was about to land, the jet of scalding water blasted into the air. Bjorn shot upward right along with it, roaring as the water scalded his torso, then rolled off the spray and landed on the ground with a pronounced thud.

The geyser might've killed a lesser foe, but Bjorn was a Sentinel now. As such, his regeneration powers kicked in immediately. Angular, sapphire blue patterns spread across his arms, neck, chest, and shoulders, which Jax could see through Bjorn's hole-riddled, sorry excuse for a shirt.

Enraged, Bjorn howled like he'd come straight from the jaws of the void itself. He charged toward Jax, who telekinetically pushed against his axe in order to leap over his foe, then landed and whirled around to face Bjorn once more.

The battle continued. Bjorn landed a few diamond-spiked punches along with a graze from that pesky dagger of his, but Jax pushed through the pain, determined to take him down. To Jax, the fight was about more than petty jealousy or a thirst to prove himself—He was finally fighting *for* something, and drak did it feel good.

Off to the side, Jade roared as she used the spike on her nose to leave a nasty gash across the umbral wyvern's flank. The beast shrieked in rage.

From the sidelines, Asher chimed in with a seemingly inexhaustible supply of groggy whoops, whistles, and the occasional, "Are you seeing this, drakalope?" directed toward the still-sleeping Solrac.

As stupid as it was, the encouragement fed Jax's inner fire. At last, with a psionic pull that ripped Bjorn's boots out from under him, Jax pinned Bjorn beneath his knee, then wrenched the Geomancer's dagger from his grasp and held it firmly against his throat. Calyx's voidshard burned in Jax's pocket like a plague, but still, like it or not, the bond with the wraith *did* make Jax immune to silver.

A cloud of warm vapor from the geysers speckled both their faces as Jax wound back his fist, ready to deliver the punch that would undoubtedly knock Bjorn out. From there, he'd grab 'Skippy' the wyvern's heartscale to end his brawl with Jade, then use the remaining store of astralock to drug Bjorn and Jaira before getting Solrac and Asher back onto Jade's back and flying them down to Keep Drakfell—

Before he could implement his plan, however, something silvery shot out from the shroud of geyser mist, and Jax gasped for breath as Jaira's chain whip wrapped around his neck. He dropped the dagger, allowing Bjorn to free himself. That sooty split second had flipped the scales, and now it was Bjorn pinning Jax beneath his crystal-armored knee. Jax cried out in pain as Bjorn drove his diamond knuckles into his shoulder, blood watering the earth.

"Should've kept your armor on, eh, Gray Knight?" Bjorn spat in Jax's pain-contorted face.

Sensing her rider's distress, Jade tried to disengage from her fight. But the larger wyvern caught her tail and forced her off course, and her flank grazed the scalding water of an active geyser. Jade roared in agony.

"Jade!" Jax shouted, but Bjorn only pressed his razor-sharp knuckles deeper into his skin.

"Say goodnight, Gray Knight," Bjorn taunted, raising his wicked dagger over Jax's throat.

"Not today," Jax growled, pushing back against it with telekinesis.

“Diamondback, wait!” Jaira snapped, appearing over Bjorn’s shoulder. Her voice was grating, but at least she had a satisfying dragon egg-sized bump on her head from where Jax’s heavy piece of armor had hit her.

“You can’t kill him,” said Jaira forcefully. Jax frowned. The geysers boiled and spat, and a damp, coppery scent swept across the fields.

“Why not?” Bjorn said, still locked in a veritable arm wrestle with Jax’s telekinesis as it pressed against his dagger. “We’ll just replace him with another Psion. New cure patients come in every other week; we’ll have plenty of ether wells to choose from.”

“He and his wraith still have a job to do,” Jaria overruled him. “That’s all I know. Traitor or not, the Surgeon needs the Gray Knight alive—for now. Besides, once his wraith takes over again, this little moment of weakness won’t matter.”

Bjorn looked incredibly annoyed to have been robbed of his potential kill. Still, he did as Jaira said, dropping his dagger in favor of shoving his other diamond-studded fist into Jax’s opposite shoulder to keep him incapacitated. Jax roared.

Meanwhile, Jaira seized the opportunity to pour several drops of astralock down his throat. Jax sputtered, trying to eject the sickly sweet concoction, but the damage had already been done. Jax knew he didn’t have long before he’d be out cold. He needed to act now—Needed to get a warning to his friends, or *something*.

“Jade!” he shouted as he struggled against Bjorn’s iron hold. “Jade!”

At last, he spotted her struggling toward him. Her side was badly scalded, but at least her wings appeared to be alright. Through their bond, he felt her loyal, stormy energy reaching out to him.

“Take his heartscale!” Bjorn called to Jaira, who started forward. Jax only had seconds remaining.

After desperately tracing a telekinetic rune with his finger, Jax ripped Jade’s heartscale from his own neck and tossed it into the air, dodging Jaira’s greedy fingers and sending the scale flying towards Jade. His dragon had already been through a forced bond once before. Jax wasn’t about to let that happen again.

His vision already growing blurry from the astralock, Jax barely saw the rich green heartscale slip into Jade’s own saddlebag. No longer able to communicate through their bond, Jax shouted aloud:

“Go, Jade! Go!”

Jade spread her wings, but the umbral wyvern moved to stop her again and gave her a gash across her underbelly. Even with their bond dulled, Jax could sense her agony over leaving him behind. She glanced toward Solrac and Asher's unconscious bodies, staggering as she tried to move toward them. If she tried to help them, Jax would only lose her for good.

"Go!" Jax shouted again, his voice breaking on the plea.

Using her second ascension power to call out to his mind even without their bond, Jade replied, *I'll go to Orothion—Get help.*

With those parting words, Jade barely dodged a blast of sapphire dragonfire from the umbral wyvern as she took to the skies, heading south towards her goal.

"Never mind the drakking evren!" Jaira said. "Get the Gray Knight tied to the wyvern with the others. Scorch, this'll slow us down."

Jax tried to fight back, but the astralock had left his limbs limp and his mind muddled. He'd lost, and now he'd suffer a fate as bad as Asher's and Solrac's. With that depressing thought, he felt Calyx's presence reassert itself in his mind.

Once again, you have failed, Calyx's whisper dominated Jax's mind. Jax felt him trying to slip back into control.

I may be a failure, Jax thought back to his detestable wraith, *but drak if one thing is certain: I'm* never *letting you control me again, Calyx.*

We shall see... Calyx gloated as more bursting geysers seemed to punctuate their internal sparring.

Then, Jax's consciousness slipped away as the astralock took full effect.

CHAPTER 18: DESIGNS

MELEYA

The smells of savory crab and tangy grilled pineapple reigned alongside me in the Keep Solhelm kitchen. I wasn't in too much of a hurry yet, but I did need to get these scaleberry hand pies into the oven double quick so that they'd have plenty of time to cool. I wanted to pack them up with plenty of time remaining before our ship left port.

That's right—Today, after about a month in Keep Solhelm, Squad Reckless was finally returning to Orothion. Now that the situation here in Solhelm was more secure and Captain Gunnar had managed to vet essentially the entire guard to ensure their loyalty to the rightful king, we were free to go. Brigan's cousins were now leading Brigan's permanent high guard.

I was going to miss it here—Brigan most of all—but I was also excited to get back to Skygard to see my parents again. I especially wanted to check in on Mom and the baby, as well as Vidya. Soot, I even missed Dusty. Besides that, I was eager to hear how things had gone in the Dragon Isles. Would there be any news upon our return? We hadn't heard anything so far, though not for lack of trying. King Brigan wrung his intelligence network as best he could, but news from the Dragon Isles had always been scant and difficult to verify. The best I could do was look up at the stars each night and hope that Asher was seeing them too.

Anyhow, the regular cooks weren't going to be back for another hour, so I had the place to myself. The kitchens here at Keep Solhelm's castle were extravagant, and while I enjoyed them, I actually much preferred the more humble kitchens I'd worked from before. I'd especially loved the one in the Broughkin Arms tavern, and I couldn't help but think of the little bunker kitchen back on the Rise. And, of course, the beautifully imperfect kitchen in the glade above the Mage Hunter Academy.

After feeding my squadmates lunch, I'd sent them off to pack. I stayed behind to wrap up the leftovers and, since I was already packed, I figured I may as well throw together a quick dessert to bring along as well.

I'd just begun cutting butter into my flour mixture when a young woman with dark curls and a smith's apron strode in, her face buried behind a tall stack of notes. Not looking up, she half-nodded to acknowledge my presence before grabbing a scorchapple from a basket on a shelf.

While Kari had accompanied us to Solhelm, she wouldn't be returning to Orothion with us today, having requested to remain behind to continue working on her experimental anti-wild dragon inventions.

"Okay if I take this?" Kari asked, holding up the apple.

"It's not my kitchen, but I bet the cooks would be fine with that," I replied. "Or, if you want, we have some extra crab wraps with pineapple salsa leftover from lunch. I'll make you a plate."

At last, Kari glanced up from her notes, her eyes widening when she saw me. "Meleya! Sorry, I was just working."

She set her notes down and pulled up a chair. Meanwhile, I pulled out a plate and began to fill it for her.

Kari sighed. "There just never seems to be enough time for food. Why do we humans have to eat so often? Three whole meals a day? Ridiculous!"

"I like it," I said. "Three chances to slow down and take care of yourself. With any luck, while connecting with those you love."

"Huh. I never thought about it like that. Maybe I should stop working through lunch every day." Kari laughed

I placed a plate of food in front of her, and she inhaled with satisfaction. "This sure beats a lonely little apple," she said, digging in. I smiled before returning to my pie crust.

Kari didn't get three bites in before glancing longingly at her stack of notes. She put a finger on the top one, tilting it toward her to read through something... then saw me watching her and immediately pushed the stack of notes away. We chuckled.

"What are you working on exactly?" I asked, sprinkling flour onto the countertop.

Kari's eyes lit up. Her mouth was full of food, but I was fairly certain she said, "Would you like to see the designs?"

Within a second, she'd spread a whole selection of note-covered sketches across the countertop, right up to my floury section. Hopefully she didn't mind a little pie crust on her blueprints.

But while Kai was overly neat about things like that, Kari didn't seem to mind. Her drawings were well done but rough, her handwriting so hurried I could hardly read it. But she knew exactly what each note said as she outlined some of the basic principles of a few of her and Brigan's ideas.

One featured a tall rallying post with a small trove of skystone kept in an impenetrable cage of reinforced dragonforged steel at the top. These were meant to act as beacons, set up strategically far enough from civilization that they would draw wild dragons elsewhere, leaving the keeps alone.

Another design she and Brigan had been collaborating on involved incorporating a silver-based component into a stucco for the outer walls of keeps. He hoped that the silver would deter wild dragons *without* making the magi living in the cities uncomfortable. That one needed some more experimentation before it was ready. Long term, Brigan even hoped to use some of the excess silver we'd seen at the Mage Hunter Academy. Of course, a lot would have to change before that would be feasible.

She went through more sketches, each more intriguing than the last. I was impressed, both with Brigan for contributing so heavily to such ingenious designs, and Kari for making each vision logical. As I worked with my dough, it took a surprising amount of mental energy just to keep up with it all, especially since Kari talked really fast.

"Besides all that," Kari said, "Brigan—er, King Brigan—wants to involve bonded dragons more in the guard, and also to stop the nobility from hoarding all the skystone so that there's more to go around when it comes to ascending our dragons. Think about it: A soldier with a third ascension dragon bond is far more effective as a defender. He's already working to implement that strategy. Stars, he's clever."

She looked up fondly as she said it, and I raised an eyebrow. Then I used my non-floury elbow to gesture to one page half-covered by another.

"What's that one?" I asked.

"Oh, that," Kari started, pulling out the page. It bore a quick sketch of a triangle with a diamond sprouting from each of its three points. The shape of an etherlock, the devices the Guardians of old built to protect Orothion, both from wild dragons and wraiths.

"That," Kari went on, "is a fairly new idea I've been toying with—rather, a new iteration of a very *old* idea. I haven't had much time to experiment with different alloys yet, but I've been wondering if we can recreate an etherlock's anti-voidarchy capacity."

"Really?" Now it was *my* eyes lighting up.

Kari fed off of my interest. "See, right before we left Orothion, I took a hard look at the Skyforge dome. You know, the one you asked me to help you blow up?"

"Ah, yes. *That* one." I smiled.

"Well, it turned out to be one of the stronghold's primary etherlocks," Kari said. "Remember how Zel and his followers had to literally change the composition of the metal in order to get that voidshard to corrupt it and allow wraiths in?"

"Yeah," I replied, recalling the way the metal all around the voidshard had turned a cool shade of gray rather than the warm, brassy tone of the other etherlocks I'd seen.

Kari rushed on. "Well, I got some samples, both from the corrupted portion of the framework and the original stuff nearer the base, and it turns out there's a reason the whole thing blew up so easily when we hit it with the amplified eclips-plosion. I isolated the elements within each sample, and there's one very specific one missing from the gray, corrupted portion."

"Which element?" I bit.

"Gold." Kari beamed. "I immediately went to Zel's cronies we've still got chained up in the dungeons there. Turns out, one of them was a Geomancer. He said that Zel had asked him to isolate the gold within the etherlock's frame and extract it. But get this: He couldn't do it!"

My brow furrowed. "Why not?"

"That's what I wondered, too. *Then* the guy went on to say that when Zel forced *Lady Vesta* to use her geomancy to do it, it worked. Can you guess what made the difference?"

I chewed my lip as I lightly kneaded my dough. I remembered my few interactions with Lady Vesta, including the moment she turned on Zel once she knew her niece was safe.

"Lady Vesta wasn't wraith-bound," I said as it dawned on me. "Zel's other Geomancer was, wasn't he?"

"Yes!" Kari exclaimed. "It got me thinking, what if—"

"Gold stops voidarchy the same way silver stops etherarchy," I finished, my eyes growing wide.

"Exactly! That's my theory, at least."

My mind instantly began spinning. If Kari's hypothesis was true, it would change everything. Replicating Guardian-era technology was just a start.

Of course, even if it turned out to be true, it wasn't a solution. For one thing, gold was incredibly rare. There was no way we could equip an entire army with gold weapons the way the Mage Hunters did with silver. They'd had centuries to mine and stockpile it, whereas the convergence of mythic stars was in a matter of months.

Besides that, as Kari said, this was still only a theory. They'd need a lot more proof before they could call for any sort of large-scale mining operation, and that was only *if* the Knights could gain access to any gold mines.

Kari continued musing on the matter. "Based on our admittedly sparse observations, plus some logical speculation, it just makes sense, you know? Now, I obviously haven't been able to test the theory, since I don't exactly have any willing participants who happen to match the very specific criteria of being a magi whose ether well has been darkened by voidarchy but they're also on the Knights' side."

"Vidya," I said right away.

"The Black Valkyrie?" Kari sounded wary.

"If you're trying to counter voidarchy, I guarantee she'll want to help," I said firmly. "I'll ask her when I get back to Orothion."

Kari still didn't quite seem convinced, but she half-agreed before returning to her meal. In an effort to keep herself from defaulting back to her work, she stacked her papers and pushed them off to the side.

"So, Meleya," Kari began between bites, "I can't help but notice your dragon is on his second ascension."

"Sniff? Yeah, Solrac ascended him before we left on the quest to Orothion." I began rolling out my crust into one large piece.

"But you don't wear his scales," Kari observed.

"You mean ascension armor?" I asked, and Kari nodded.

It was true. After Sniff's ascension, I'd meticulously gathered up his golden-yellow scales and saved them. Even now, they were stowed inside my rift hold. At first, I'd left them there because there hadn't been time to forge me any ascension armor before we'd left for the quest, but even once things had settled down a bit in Skygard following my and Asher's escapades in Etheria, I hadn't brought them out again. If I was being honest, there was still a small part of me that felt I didn't deserve to wear the scales after all the mistakes I'd made.

Thinking of Etheria reminded me of Blink's ascension, and the promise Zerana had made when she'd gathered her spirit scales. Zerana said she'd have my *spirit* ascension armor forged and brought to me. This wasn't the first time I wondered what that might be like, and what discrepancies there were between spiritual and physical ascension armor.

Kari went on. "Anyway, If you haven't made plans yet, I'd love to use Sniff's scales to make your ascension armor."

I stopped mid-roll of my rolling pin. "But aren't you *way* too busy for something like that?"

"Oh, but designing armor is my favorite thing to do! It's the perfect mental break between other projects. Please?"

The light in her eyes was so sincere that all of my excuses fell flat. "Alright," I agreed. "I'll leave Sniff's scales in your workshop before we ship out."

Kari got so excited she literally giggled. I smiled as I grabbed a knife to cut out the hand pies.

"I'm excited to see what you come up with," I said. "Your inventiveness is incredible. I'll never forget the first time I saw silverbane in action—It helped save my parents in Keep Rengard, you know."

Kari waved a hand modestly. "Silverbane was a group effort. I couldn't have done it without Asher helping me discover liquid ether. And of course, Jax put in hours of work extracting spydra venom."

I perked up at the mention of Jax. "You worked closely with Jax then?"

"Did I ever! In more than one capacity, if you know what I mean."

Kari winked, and I froze. Suddenly, I knew exactly what she meant. My heart dropped into my stomach.

"You..." I started lamely. "You and Jax... the two of you... oy."

Kari was completely oblivious to my discomfort. "What can I say?" she laughed. "I can't resist a dummy with big muscles."

I didn't *mean* to slam the knife down so hard into my dough that it left a dent in the countertop. Drak, I felt bad about that.

"Jax isn't dumb," I replied, much too defensively.

Kari narrowed her eyes. "Wait... Jax served on your squad in Rengard, didn't he? Were you and he...?"

I ground my back teeth together. There was no way to hide the truth now, and I nodded slowly.

Kari burst into laughter. "Stars! Does that make you kiss number seventy-one?"

My face grew hot all the way from my nose to the tips of my ears. Yes, technically I supposed I *was* 'kiss number seventy-one', but I certainly didn't feel like just another number in his lineup. Jax hadn't seen me that way either, I was sure of it.

From there, Kari began to chatter animatedly about Jax, going on about everything from how silly he was for tearing the sleeves off his tunics to how wild it was that he'd become the Gray Knight.

"It must've been so mind-blowing to see him in Etheria like that," Kari said. Most of the Knights had heard the story by now.

"Yeah, it was," I replied, trying to respond like a normal person as I busily filled each hand pie with a scaleberry compote. It wasn't easy to keep my voice even though, since I was growing more and more frustrated by the second.

Oddly enough, it wasn't learning that Jax had been with Kari that bothered me. Rather, it was the casual way that Kari spoke of him. As if Jax of Blackfjord were just some fun little fling when, to me, he'd been so much more.

I channeled my anger into pinching pie crusts. The way Kari talked about Jax's current struggles didn't sit right with me either—As if they, and he, were fascinating data points we were observing from a vast distance rather than a good man we'd both known well, falling prey to the darkness. I'd once fallen prey to that same darkness myself. But while I'd had friends to catch me when I'd fallen, Jax was all alone out there.

But I'd seen the way Jax's vibrant tangerine aura had broken through the gray shell in Etheria. Jax was still fighting, I was sure of it. Instinctively, I reached for my quartz.

"So, what then?" Kari asked.

I blinked a few times to refocus on Kari's face. Stars, I'd completely missed what she'd just said.

"Sorry, what was that?" I asked.

"I said, what would you say to Jax if you saw him again?"

"Oh," I said, somehow dumbfounded by the question. Carefully, I arranged the hand pies on a baking sheet as I pondered.

What *would* I say to him? A hundred different responses crossed my mind, but the one I kept coming back to was: 'I'm sorry.'

I knew none of Jax's mistakes were my fault. Still, I couldn't help but wonder how much simpler everything would've been for both of us if I'd only trusted him back at the Academy. If I'd confided in him rather than pushing him away, where would we be today?

Drak. A film of tears covered my eyes and I had to look away. Luckily, I was able to cover my emotion by putting the pies into the oven.

Hoping to distract Kari from her question, I cleared my throat. "You gonna stick around until these come out of the oven? I made extra."

"Mmm, I wish," Kari said. "Unfortunately, I have to go. Brigan wanted to meet this morning to go over some additions to the skystone beacons. He's been calling for a lot of extra meetings with me lately actually—Not that I'm complaining. I honestly love how hands-on he's been with all of this—"

"Kari?" I cut her off.

"Yes?" She cocked her head.

There was a long, tense pause as she met my serious gaze. Then, I said, "Brigan isn't a dummy either."

The silence between us was thicker than dragonhide, and I watched as understanding dawned in Kari's gaze.

"I know," she responded, her tone genuine. I nodded.

From there, Kari gathered up her papers and headed for the door. Just before disappearing into the corridor, she turned back.

"Thanks for the meal, Meleya. Don't forget to leave Sniff's scales in my workshop before you leave so I can get to work on your ascension armor."

I exhaled. "Thank you."

"You're welcome."

Throughout our journey across the Scarlet Strait, I'd wondered if there would be any news upon our arrival.

And holy scorching stars, was there.

"Asher's a *what?*" I asked, utterly blown away by what Kai was saying. Kai and his stony gray evren, Flint, had met us at the docks below Orothion's cliffside castle. After giving Solvai an incredibly darling hug, Kai had broken the news—or more likely, told us a very strange joke, because I couldn't bring myself to believe a word that came out of his mouth.

"Asher's the Crown Prince of the Dragon Isles. Heir to the Drekai throne, in fact."

"*Asher?*" Solvai's eyes were as wide as mine. "As in *Asher of Steel Rim?*"

"I know," Kai said. "*I know.* But I've quadruple-verified my sources, not to mention interviewed every Knight we've got who has even an inkling regarding Drekai succession. It's true. Asher had no idea until he arrived, of course. You know that turquoise scarf he always wears? Word is that it's a royal family heirloom they recognized upon his arrival."

"Drak," I swore under my breath. A pit was forming in my stomach as I wondered how Asher had taken the news. No doubt it had cut him to the core.

"Is he alright?" I asked.

"That's the other thing." Kai grimaced. "Asher... he's missing."

"Missing?!" I repeated, my heartbeat spiking.

"Solrac too," Kai went on. "They were taken just after Asher won his duel against General Kheradok and replaced with illusions, courtesy of the Mage Hunter, Ilyan. We think they're bringing them to the Soul Reaper—He's been after the Farseer all this time. Asher... Drak if I know what they want with him. Anyway, the Drekai Empress has sent out search parties, and so have the Knights. Between our combined forces, I'd say we have a roughly fourteen-point-eight-percent chance of rescuing them, but that's not taking into account any sort of time restrictions. Soot, I should make a table..."

"What else can we do?" I asked, my heart beginning to pound.

Kai shrugged. In his eyes, I saw the same desperation as I was just now beginning to feel. Solvai took Kai's hand.

As for me, I gripped the hilt of my sword, wishing I knew where to stick it. Worry bloomed within me so strongly I felt dizzy. Asher and Solrac had been taken by the Soul Reaper, and only the stars knew what they had in store for them.

Chapter 19: The Cage

Asher

If I had to describe my surroundings in three words, those words would be:

Cold.

Eerie.

And 'someone-please-get-me-out-of-here-right-now.'

I'd seen my fair share of inescapable prison cells, yet this one was somehow the most hopeless. Rather than bars of iron or even silver, the ones that trapped me now were forged from pure, vivid blue lightning, presumably the result of some kind of intense lightwielding voidarchy. Every time I got within an inch of the bolts, they sent a shock through me that put me on my back.

Something told me my starglass key trick wasn't going to work this time.

I'd been drugged on astralock when Jaira and her manic, mohawked sidekick threw me in here, but now that it had worn off, I could see my surroundings perfectly through the narrow spaces between the lightning bars. I was in a massive room with curved windows that let in the light of billions of stars. Down below the loft where my cage was situated lay the biggest telescope I'd ever seen, tilted skyward. Piles of raw skystone were everywhere, absolutely radiating power. Unfortunately, try as I might, something about the lighting cage kept me from being able to draw any of it in. I could use my power inside the cage, but couldn't seem to affect anything outside it.

I'd been pretty mentally out of it for most of the journey here, but I'd overheard enough to be certain of it: I was in the Soul Reaper's lair.

Bordering my cage was a terrifying laboratory, complete with operating tables equipped with silver chain straps. No doubt this was where all those magi had gone to receive the so-called cure. As if that weren't enough, rows of shelves filled the lab, lined with glassy jars that contained odd-looking, glowing crystals. Almost all of them were broken in some way: shattered into pieces, covered in fissures, or cracked right down the center. They reminded me of skystone, but there was something different about them, something even more ethereal than the valuable, ether-filled gems that fell from the heavens. I got the feeling I'd seen things like them before.

"Ether wells," came a husky voice from within my cage.

He must've noticed me staring at the jars. Cautiously glancing over my shoulder, I regarded my unlikely cellmate.

Jax sat in the corner of the lightning-forged cage, just out of range of the electrocuting bars. His gaze was shadowed. As ever, I tensed up just looking at him, ready to summon my starglass spear in a second.

I couldn't remember many details about the journey here. I had vague memories of Solrac being with us, but upon arrival, Jaira and Bjorn had taken him to a separate holding cell made entirely from ether-blocking silver. Apparently, they weren't willing to take any chances with the legendary Farseer.

That left me with Jax, the guy who'd abandoned the Knights in favor of the Gray. The Gray Knight who'd hunted Meleya and me down in the spirit plane, nearly killing us both. Jax of Blackfjord, the very reason I was trapped here now, facing my doom.

My memory was too hazy to remember exactly why Jaira and her companion had turned on Jax, or why he was a prisoner, too. Something about a fight with the mohawked guy, Bjorn? Had Jax really turned on the Mage Hunters? I couldn't be sure.

Most likely, his presence here was all a part of some convoluted trick. The one thing I knew for certain was that this guy despised me as much as I had once despised his mother.

"Most ether wells break during soul surgery," Jax explained darkly, nodding to the rows of crystal-filled jars. "The ones that don't, the Surgeon stitches to the soul of a new host."

When I didn't respond, Jax swallowed. "You can bet your dragon's heartscale we'll be next."

"Why hasn't the Soul Reaper harvested our ether wells already?" I asked.

Jax squinted toward the stars through the windows above. "The surgeries work best at midnight under a full moon, or some soot like that. Without my dragon's help, we arrived later than planned and missed the full moon. So we have a few more weeks."

"A few more weeks," I repeated, mumbling as I absently began pacing the length of our enclosure. The square, voidarchy-powered cage was so small I could pace its length in three long strides.

I hated this feeling. Trapped in such a small space with someone who utterly despised me. Unable to do anything but await my turn on the operating table.

"The Surgeon's been waiting for you," Jax said, his eyes still in shadow as he looked down. "My wraith... he's stronger here. He says you're to be a crucial element in the convergence. That your power will bring about the downfall of Evgard."

"I'm not the one whose runes burn blue," I retorted, instantly knowing I should've held my tongue.

Jax's jaw tightened and his muscles twitched. I braced myself, ether flowing into my fingertips as I prepared to summon my spear. Even before he'd given himself over to the Gray, I knew Jax's temper was as strong as his punches. Although, I doubted Jax would settle for a simple fistfight when he still had those twin fanged axes strapped to his back. When they'd left us here in our lightning prison, Jaira and Bjorn had allowed Jax's axes to remain with him, almost as if they were hoping the two of us would tear each other apart.

Judging by the look on Jax's face, they very well might get their wish.

"Why did you turn on the other Mage Hunters?" I dared to ask.

Jax snorted, then trained his gaze upon the floor. "So you *were* conscious for that."

"Not entirely," I said. "Just enough to be confused. From what I saw, one minute you were binding me in silver, drugging me and saying you'd killed my wyvern. The next, you're fighting your new friends."

"I didn't touch your drakking wyvern," Jax said. "I just gave him enough dreamberry juice to keep him from following us. Thorn doesn't deserve to get caught up in this."

Relief filled my heart. That explained Thorn's drowsiness the day of the duel.

"So Thorn doesn't deserve it, but I do?" I asked. "And Solrac?"

"Solrac," Jax muttered under his breath as a flash of something dark crossed his face. He winced, mouthing something as if talking to someone I couldn't see or hear. His mutterings got louder, until finally Jax said, "Of course Solrac wishes *you* were his son instead."

He started getting to his feet, and I automatically assumed a defensive stance. It took me a moment to comprehend what Jax had said.

"That I was his... What's that supposed to mean?" I asked.

"Solrac," Jax said through gritted teeth. "He's my real father. Not that drunken idiot, Torsten."

That took me aback. "But everyone said—"

"I know what they said! They lied—they *all* did. My entire drakking life has been nothing but lies! And you... you're at the heart of it all."

I was still processing what he'd just said about Solrac, but Jax's eyes were burning with an inner fire. White energy began to coalesce between my fingers as I prepared to defend myself.

"Me?" I asked. "What in the stars do *I* have to do with your messed-up life?"

"Everything!"

"Well that's super clear! Thanks for explaining!"

"Everything and everyone I ever cared about, you took from me!" Jax raged. "You have *everything!*"

"Wrong!" I shouted. "I don't have a *mother!* Thanks to *your* mother and the sky-forsaken Gray *you* follow!"

Jax gave a yell as he wrenched one of the axes from his back. I gripped my now fully-formed starglass spear.

"Scorch you, Asher of Steel Rim!" Jax shouted. "You're a smug, moronic pile of soot!"

"And you're an arrogant, wraith-bound traitor!"

"I should've ended you in Etheria! Then again in the Dragon Isles!"

"Well, now's your chance!" I cried, holding my spear out to the side and leaving my chest exposed. "Do it, if you hate me so much!"

Jax gave a yell, a pained cry from the very jaws of the void. Then, as if the words surprised even himself, Jax shouted again.

"It's not you that I hate!" Jax hurled one of his fanged axes—not at me, but at the lightning bars of our prison. There was a sizzling sound as the crackling blue barrier dropped the axe to the ground, leaving a fiery black burn mark across the blade. The axe lay there, smoldering against the floor.

"It's not you that I hate..." Jax repeated, more to himself than to me. He breathed heavily, his eyes wild as a dark glint settled over them. His muscles twitched as he stared at the axe, then the lightning.

My heart stopped as Jax took his first step toward those crackling bars. Then another. Then...

"Jax..." I said, but he didn't break his stride.

"Jax," I called more forcefully now. "*Jax!*"

He was reaching for the bars when, in what might've been the stupidest move of my life, I grappled the broad, insanely muscular Jax from behind.

"Let me go, Dragon-boy!"

"No!"

Jax struggled, but I held fast. I'd held onto both a bucking craghopper and a thrashing ursadon before—I could handle a nineteen-year-old young man. Even one as strong as Jax.

Using all my might and maybe just a little bit of levitation etherarchy, I finally wrenched Jax away from the bars. He was delirious, and I was able to maneuver myself between him and the wall of the cage, pushing back against his shoulders.

Eyes burning gold, I flared my ether. Starglass appeared along my hands, binding me to Jax. He wasn't going anywhere without taking me with him. He pushed against me and my boots scraped along the floor until my heels were only an inch away from the lightning.

That was when Jax locked eyes with me. Time came to a standstill as I watched every drop of tension drain from his body.

Little by little, I watched as the fire in his deep midnight irises faded away. Then, his gaze became frantic as he took the time to really consider exactly what he'd been about to do.

Jax choked on a sob as the first wave of tears began to stream down his face. I let my starglass disappear as, trembling, Jax collapsed to the ground.

I went down with him, holding him as he buried his face against my shoulder. I clung to him just as fiercely now as I had only moments before.

"It's too late for me," Jax began to ramble as sobs wracked his body. "I'm broken beyond repair. I thought by choosing nothing—by... by handing over my choices to someone else—that I'd absolve myself of the consequences. The pain, and the drakking guilt, too. But each day, I just fall deeper and deeper into this sickening pit. And now, I'm in so deep I'll never be able to climb back out. I don't deserve freedom. I don't even deserve the void."

As he wept, I felt my own chest constrict. Tears pricked the backs of my eyes.

My first instinct was to think of a lighthearted distraction. A clever quip or random question to avoid confronting the heaviness or pain.

Instead, my voice cracked as I replied, "You're as free as you choose to be."

Jax swallowed. "What?"

The lump in my throat grew. "My dad said it to me before I first left Steel Rim with the Knights of the Torch. I thought I knew what he meant by it then, but now I'm not so sure. Freedom... I used to think it was a luxury that only those born noble or privileged got to enjoy. Something *they* purposely withheld from the rest of us. But after what happened—what I learned in the Dragon Isles..."

"You mean after you found out you were a Drekai prince," Jax said, a slight edge to his voice.

"...I've never felt more trapped," I finished. "Even before you and the others showed up. It's like you said: My entire life was built on nothing but lies."

For a while, my words hung in the air, almost seeming to placate the very air we breathed. Finally, Jax sighed.

"Remind me again why we hate each other so much?"

"Girls, mostly," I laughed. "Honestly, though, I think we both just really like attention; it's only natural we'd each see the other as a threat. I mean, stars, do you have any idea how cool I thought you were the first time we met?"

"Oh, please," Jax scoffed.

"No, I'm serious." I stood firm. "Technically, it was even before we met, when Kai and I tried impersonating you and Boone to get into that Knights of the Torch meeting. I remember how well everyone treated Kai while he was in your body, like you were someone they really respected and looked up to. And then later, when we *did* actually meet while fighting off those dreklings, I could tell right away how strong you were. Honestly, I think part of why I viewed you as a rival was because it felt good to think of myself as someone worthy of being compared with you. Well, that and the way you kept calling me Dragon-boy..."

Jax smiled, then let out a deep breath.

"You really thought I was cool?"

"Well, the sleeveless tunics were a bit much... but other than that, I'd swear it on my mother's memory."

After another moment, Jax pulled away. As we sat facing each other in our tiny prison, he pressed his palms against his eyes to try to dry the tears. When he looked at me again, I didn't see loathing in his red-rimmed eyes. I saw loneliness.

"You were never my real problem, Asher," Jax said. "It was my own stupid jealousy. I thought your light shining brighter meant mine had to dim."

"That was surprisingly poetic," I noted. "Then again, maybe not so surprising, considering your father."

Jax scoffed, but there wasn't anger in it, not anymore. "It's funny. Before I knew the truth, I thought Solrac was perfect. But now, I'm angry with him, too."

"I know how you feel," I said. "My mom... she never told me who she really was. Who *I* was. She never flat out told a lie, but stars if her omission of the truth doesn't feel like one."

The thought of my mom threatened to put a lump in my throat once again. Glancing through the lightning bars of our cell, I saw the operating tables of the Soul Reaper's laboratory. The ones that would eventually claim us, too—either for death, or the 'cure.'

Jax must've known what I was thinking. "I'm sorry about your mother," he said.

"This is where she died," I said softly. "I wonder if she was as afraid as I am."

"More afraid, I think."

Jax's comment surprised me and got me a little defensive. "My mom was one of the bravest people the realm's ever seen," I retorted.

"Knowing you, I don't doubt that." Jax shook his head. "What I meant is, I'll bet she was terrified—not for herself, but because she had someone back home. A son whose mom would never come back."

That did it. My tears started right back up again. I put a fist to my lips and squeezed my eyes shut, and realized Jax wasn't just talking about my situation. It had been under different circumstances, but Jax's mom had left him too soon as well.

"Mom was my favorite person in the world," I said. "But I haven't lost her, not really. Being with her again in Etheria taught me that. Even the deepest wounds can find a way to heal." I looked at Jax. "The worst mistakes, too."

Jax pressed his lips together. "You really believe that?"

I nodded. "Your mom is living proof of it. Even from beyond, my mom kept urging me to give her a second chance, and I'd bet my scarf she'd say the same thing about you. It's never too late to start choosing light again."

Jax grimaced, but this time, I thought I could see the newfound resolve behind it. Then, sighing, he turned away from me and looked towards the lightning bars of our prison.

"So, Dragon-boy," he said. "Any ideas on how to get out of this void?"

The next morning, Jaira and Bjorn had come for Jax, looking a little disappointed to find that we hadn't murdered each other. Five or six masked, gray-hooded soldiers accompanied them to ensure we didn't try anything as they used a relic to part the lightning.

"Watch out or you'll be next, scale-skin," Bjorn taunted as he and Jaira dragged Jax to one of the operating tables and strapped him in. I wondered if the Soul Reaper had decided to perform soul surgery on him early, despite the moon not being full.

Muscles bulging, Jax strained against the silver mesh straps. With his ether well having been corrupted by his wraith, the silver no longer affected him, but still, Jaira tied him down so tightly I could see the straps digging into his wrists and ankles.

"Where's the Soul Reaper then?" Jax asked through clenched teeth. "Coming to take my power? That's fine—I don't want it."

Jaira laughed. "So eager to lose your ether well, are you? But it's not that simple. No, we're here to ensure you still serve the Gray. You have a job to do, Gray Knight, and the Surgeon's asked to make sure you're still up to the task."

"What do you mean—"

Jax's question gave way to an agonized yelp as Jaira lashed him with her silver chain whip, cutting a long red gash across Jax's upper arm. Jaira gave a wicked grin.

"That," she began, "was just a taste of what's to come if you don't properly do your job. But don't worry, proving your loyalty is simple: Let your wraith back in control. Show us you won't let the Surgeon down."

"I won't," Jax said. "My mind is mine and mine alone. I'm never letting Calyx take over again."

"I was hoping you'd say that."

Jaira's whip flashed again, this time leaving its mark along Jax's exposed shoulder. Jax rapidly sucked in air.

"Bjorn?" Jaira said, offering her counterpart a turn.

Manic light in his eyes, Bjorn was all too eager. Blue Sentinel markings appeared on his skin as he used voidish geomancy to sprout a row of razor-sharp diamonds along his knuckles. Without so much as a pause, Bjorn threw a punch at Jax's face. A row of fresh scratches soon stood out beside the one that had only just begun to scab over, evidence of Jax's fight with Bjorn on the journey here.

Jax cried out, and so did I.

"Hey!" I called. "Back off, Spike!"

Bjorn turned my way, glaring daggers at me from across the lab. "It's Diamondback, actually," he growled.

"I don't care what cute little nickname you go by," I said. "Keep your gem-encrusted hands off of my friend!"

Bjorn just rolled his eyes, then returned his attention to the operating table.

"The Surgeon just wants to know that you and your Gray One are still capable of finishing your job," Jaira cooed. "After all, you are 'the Builder'. Just show us those sapphire eyes, Gray Knight. Then we'll stop, I promise. Diamondback will even heal you."

"No." Jax set his jaw.

Jaira tsked, then lashed him again with that awful whip, this time along Jax's cheek. At the same moment, Bjorn used his dagger to cut a torturous line across Jax's left forearm. Jax arched his back, trying in vain to break free.

My gut twisted. I hated being forced to watch, unable to do anything to stop Jaira and Bjorn's sick torture. As they continued trying to break Jax's spirit, I attempted to launch ether blasts and starglass shards at them from between lightning bars. But the cage had been designed with impenetrable blue energy suffusing the space between the bars, thick enough that each blade of starglass hit the wall with a feeble sizzle, vanishing into etherdust on contact.

"Don't do it, Jax!" I shouted. "You're as free as you choose to be!"

Jax understood, and I sensed resolve in his expression. He may have been physically bound, but his mind—his thoughts and choices—were still his own.

"Let the wraith in!" Jaira shouted, ignoring me as she hoisted the whip over his body.

"Choose light!" I called.

Jax didn't move. When the next lash came, it cut his ear, and blood dripped onto the table.

Eventually, Jaira and Bjorn realized their efforts weren't going to yield any results. They untied Jax, then roughly shoved him back into the lightning cage. He was bleeding from multiple wounds and one eye was nearly swollen shut, but nevertheless I could detect some of his old swagger in the way he moved.

"Don't think this is over, Gray Knight," Jaira snarled. "We'll be back—for as long as it takes to break you."

Then she turned on her heel, and after one last lunging hiss toward the cage, Bjorn followed.

I scrambled over to Jax. "Are you okay?" I asked, knowing he wasn't. Each cut dripped blood and his jaw was already looking bruised from Bjorn's punch.

Jax spat a mouthful of blood, then gave me a half-smile. "I'm better than I've been in months. I don't give a flying scale what they do—I'm never choosing nothing again."

Jaira and Bjorn kept true to their promise, returning for Jax every day. Each day they tortured him, Bjorn made sure to carve another tally mark on Jax's arm with his silver dagger. Besides the tally marks, they healed him enough so that there wouldn't be any permanent damage—they didn't want to ruin the vessel of one of their most powerful wraiths—but otherwise left him bruised and battered. But to Jax, nothing was worth allowing his wraith, Calyx, to reclaim control.

Each time, I shouted encouragement from the cage. Eventually, Jaira got so fed up with me that they started gagging me before each session. Jaira and Bjorn were relentless, as if they were punishing Jax for betraying them. While Bjorn had dark etherarchy of his own, I sensed deep jealousy from Jaira, who had none. I knew for a fact she'd had lightwielding powers at one point, but she'd somehow lost them. She now channeled that resentment into beating Jax, who had powers beyond anything she'd ever dreamed of, but refused to use them.

Every time they threw Jax back into our cage, he freed me from my gag and I did my best to help him with his wounds. I was no healer and our materials were limited, but I drew from our meager water supply to at least clean his injuries and used delicate starglass to sort-of-bandage the worst ones.

With the impending full moon looming over us, we did our best to keep each other from giving in to the fear. We reminded each other that we were Knights, and that Knights chose light.

After about a week with no results, Bjorn tried a different approach. When table-bound Jax saw the mohawked maniac pull out the bottle, he tensed all over.

"Get that away from me," Jax said.

Bjorn grinned wickedly, as if he'd known the alcohol would strike a nerve. "Why, Gray Knight? Afraid of a little drink?"

Relishing in Jax's vain protests, Bjorn poured three glasses of the dark liquid—draquila, if I had to guess. Jaira and Bjorn raised theirs in a toast.

"To the Soul Reaper," Bjorn said, then took a massive swig.

Next, both Jaira and Bjorn set their drinks down and swarmed Jax. Jax thrashed, pressing his lips together as Jaira pinched his nose and Bjorn held the glass to his lips. When Jax at last had to take a breath, Bjorn poured the draquila down his throat.

Jax sputtered and coughed, but it was clear most of it had gone down. Jaira taunted him.

"Just let your wraith in already, Gray Knight. Show us your eyes."

"I... I won't." Jax's eyes were tinted red, and my heart wrenched. If I hadn't been gagged, I'd have been screaming at Bjorn and Jaira. It was clear he hated this form of torture even more than the gouges and bruises.

Jaira and Bjorn made him down the entire tall glass, but I watched with pride as Jax didn't break. When they finally threw him back into the lightning cell and left, Jax looked like he was going to be sick. I made him a bucket from starglass.

"I'm so sorry," I said once he was finally able to help me untie my gag.

"Me too," Jax replied, sweat beading all over his face.

"You don't have to tell me," I said hesitantly, "but, if I can ask, what's your problem with drinking? I know you're a Mystic, and alcohol makes it harder to runetrace, but is that all?"

Jax looked up at me, his eyes still rimmed with red.

"That's part of it." He sighed. "But mostly it's because of how I saw it affect my father—Well, not my real father, I guess, but the man who raised me from the age of six until I was old enough to join the Knights. Well, 'raised' might be giving him too much credit, but he kept a roof over my head, anyway."

"He made you tough," I offered, trying to give a positive spin.

"Yeah, well maybe I didn't want to be tough," Jax spat, then stopped himself and took a deep breath. "I just wanted to be a kid. Was that too much to ask?"

"No," I said under my breath. "It's not." We sat in silence for a few minutes before I went on.

"Think Bjorn and Jaira will try it again tomorrow?"

"What does it matter?" Jax shrugged. "It won't make a difference—I'm not letting Calyx into my head. Nothing could make me, not now that I've made my decision. I've tasted the Gray, and it only offers lies. I'm never going back."

"Choose light," I said, and Jax nodded.

"Choose light."

Chapter 20: The Trap

Meleya

The smell of creamy drakalope and cindershroom sauce over rice filled the room. Meanwhile, hungry refugees eagerly clutched their dishes as they waited for their meals. The line seemed endless, but Shaya and I were serving them as quickly as we could.

"Thank you," a little boy said as Shaya passed him a steaming bowl.

"You are most welcome," she replied, her smile bright. "Though the one who deserves thanks is Meleya here—she's the cook."

I blushed as the child thanked me, too. Shaya winked at me, knowing full well how much I didn't like getting called out. I loved watching people enjoy my food, but I didn't need the world to know I'd made it.

Orothion's east tower bustled with activity as over a hundred skyfall refugees ate and socialized. Turning the largely unused tower into a refugee center had been Shaya's idea, and with a lot of convincing, she'd gotten Vesta and the other leaders on board. Before long, many of us had gotten involved, all collaborating to ensure our guests had proper bedding, water, and—in my particular case—delicious food. Even my father's ethereal familiar, Dusty the draccoon, liked to hang around, crawling up the walls and making the children laugh. I threw him scraps of leftovers whenever we had them to spare.

As for Shaya, she practically lived in the east tower. She loved chatting with the refugees and helping the medics tend to those who'd been afflicted with the shadow wasting. She'd knitted more shadowsilk blankets, shawls, and socks than I could count, which I now understood might've made the biggest difference in keeping any Gray shadows at bay. She'd been thrilled to hear that I'd hardly suffered any attacks from my wraith since I started wearing her shadowsilk cloak, and was determined to start making as many of them as she could.

Of course, there hadn't been much time to sit down and weave, what with all the work to be done for the onslaught of refugees. Nevertheless, I couldn't help but admire Shaya's diligence. Whenever anyone commented on her work, she said something along the lines of, "Nothing says 'enjoy the void' to High King Magnus better than full bellies and smiling faces. Solei's blade—He won't be shipping *these* people off to Kolbohr!"

When I wasn't cooking for the refugees, I was either discussing baby names with Mom, whose belly was growing rounder by the day, or training with the other soldiers under Captain Cenrik, Commander Boone, my dad, and all the other newly appointed commanders. Despite the Triarchy's pleading, Rhana had opted to stay behind at her cabin in the Mirror Forest. It was too bad, since her experience would've undoubtedly made a difference, but someone had to look after the safehouse and its dragons, and there wasn't anyone else she trusted enough to delegate such important responsibilities to.

Since by now it was common knowledge that Archonic power was the most effective type of etherarchy against the Gray, the commanders had sought out the help of any Archons among our ranks. The Shadowbinders would line our blades with shadowfire while the Astromancers would either infuse an edge of pure ether or starglass. The effects wore off after a while, so they had to re-infuse the blades at the onset of every training session. Whenever it was my turn with a starglass edge, it reminded me of fighting in Etheria. That blade Asher had made me, with the snowflake design, had been one of the handiest I'd ever fought with. In a perfect world, Asher would've been right here with us, teaching his fellow Archons some of his niftiest moves, but for the moment it was all we could do to hope that he was still alive. On that front, I had all the faith in the world; This was Asher, after all. Trouble was his middle name, but he always managed to squirm his way out of it in the end. Right?

As for the Lightwielders, the third type of Archon, they usually didn't have enough ether to spare for training purposes. They were needed basically 'round the clock, using their powers to fill vial after vial of liquid light for shadow wasting victims all over the realm, not to mention keeping the shelves sufficiently stocked here at Orothion's medical wing. Inspired by Brigan and Bolt, the dragon keeper had requested some ascension scales from all the lightwielding dragons to make vials of liquid light that would refill on their own. Even so the medics had been growing worried about how little there was to go around.

After finishing up the mountain of dishes that'd been left after serving the refugees dinner, I'd returned to the cottage only to find out that Dad and Dusty were off meeting with Cenrik to go over battle formations, and Mom was already asleep for the night. Rather than stay inside alone, I reached out to Sniff through our bond.

He'd been about to start his nightly hunt, but changed his plans immediately at my request to go flying. I met him at the dragon stables, where he tackled me to the ground with excitement.

Laughing, I scrambled back to my feet, then held out a little jar of ground peanut paste I'd prepared for him earlier. He eagerly licked the jar filled with his favorite treat clean.

When he was done, I climbed into the saddle and we took off. The sky was nearly as picturesque as the one in Etheria as the sun set and the full moon rose over the redwood forest just northwest of the stronghold.

Sniff and I flew together a lot lately. When it was just the two of us together, high in the sky, it gave us time to remember Blink. Often, I'd search my heart, willing the sound of drumbeats to play within it. Once or twice, I'd thought I felt something, a soft, faint pounding. But it must've all been in my imagination.

My pitch-colored shadowcloak fluttered behind me as we flew. It wasn't strictly necessary out here, since I knew that even the forest within the stronghold's walls held enough etherlocks to keep wraiths at bay. Still, I liked to wear the cloak as often as I could. It had worked so well in Solhelm, and besides, I'd always been one to keep a backup of everything.

Sniff and I flew for long enough that I lost track of time. I wasn't sure how late it was when I spotted firelight rising from the ground amidst the enormous redwood trees. Curious, Sniff and I flew downward.

We found a ring of torches lighting the vast surface of a giant redwood stump. The stump was perfectly smooth on top, forming what I quickly realized was a stage. Boone was sitting on the lip of the stump stage, playing a slow, lilting melody on his harmonica. To my surprise, the only person there with him was Vidya. She was standing center stage, singing along with Boone's playing. Her voice was beautiful and rich as it sailed towards my ears:

Oh Leo, Leo, stay with me, long past the winter's chill
Far longer than the summertime, my heart shall love you still
Don't go, my Leo, into night, don't leave me here alone
For thoughts of eternity without you are as bleak as ashen stone

I recognized the old love ballad from my many years traveling with the nomads. It was an ethereal, haunting melody, but also a happy one that was popular at weddings and festivals. Now, listening to Vidya sing, I realized just how badly she must be missing Solrac. She'd been putting on a brave face ever since learning about his capture, but I knew not a moment went by that she wasn't thinking about him. If it weren't for her wraith keeping her grounded here, I wondered if she'd have gone off in search of her husband herself. Stars, I wished that Shaya had already started making more shadowcloaks.

As I alighted from the saddle in front of the stage, Vidya waved for me to join her up there. Without a crowd watching, I happily obliged. My voice harmonized with Vidya's as we reached the chorus:

Drink the water, dearest love
Of everlasting life with me
Drink the water, blessed above
That I may be the wife of thee
For years. At least, this, as a start
Nothing short of forever will satisfy my heart

Boone's harmonica swelled as he fell into the music. Vidya gestured to me, an invitation to take the second verse. I was no great soloist like her, but my soft soprano echoed through the forest. Glancing toward the woods, I noticed the black-feathered mythraven perched in a nearby tree, cheerily listening to the old ballad. It must be missing Solrac too.

Oh Leo, Leo, trust in us, e'en when the world seems gray
Though voids and darkness round us close, my love for you shall stay
I'll find you, Leo, beyond the stars, and with your hand in mine
We'll turn each nightmare into light, two souls now one entwined

We sang the chorus once again, our harmony ringing like soft chimes thanks to the acoustics of the forest amphitheater. When Boone's harmonica finished with a sweet flourish, we just stood there in the stillness for a moment. The sounds of night seemed to be listening too.

Finally, Sniff couldn't help himself. He let out a sort-of-musical roar-slash-howl, which caused a few nearby birds to flee their nests in search of safer ground. Boone, Vidya, and I laughed.

Among the birds, Sniff spotted a few plump dragonbats taking to the skies. I sensed excitement and hunger through our bond, and since he'd called off his hunt for me earlier, I sent feelings of encouragement to him. He took off after the bats, disappearing into the redwoods.

"Woowee!" Boone whooped. "That there song, Leo's Ballad, were the one my Auriana done sung me when we gave each other these." He held up his wrist, showing off the beautifully woven marriage bracelet there. I'd noticed it long ago, but had never dared to ask about it.

"Drak if her voice weren't prettier than the sunrise over the Evyndalian sea," Boone continued fondly. Then he chuckled. "Scorched memories're seared into my mind. Flowers in her hair. Rainstorm in the distance makin' us hurry through the vows. Old Kodi standin' by lookin' more pleased'na baby ursadon just found a honey-laden hive o' scalebees."

Vidya and I exchanged smiles. "Who's Kodi?" I ventured.

Boone grinned. "That old rascal, Kodi. He were the best dragon bond that ever drew breath. Lost him durin' them sooty Dragon Wars, but some nights, like this one, I don't feel like he's all that far away."

He tilted his face upward toward the full moon, and I wondered if he might be right. The tan, dragon-scaled cloak Boone always wore caught the moonlight, and for a long moment, the three of us shared peaceful silence... a silence that Boone soon broke with another melodic interval from his harmonica, this one far more lively.

"Woowee!" he shouted. "It's been far too long since I done played an ol' Bramblewilds jig!" Boone gave another whoop before launching into another song.

Vidya and I laughed, then began clapping along. I was no dancer, but she leaped and twirled across with a former acrobat's grace. The firelight seemed to step up as her dance partner, flickering orange and bright.

Boone was in the middle of his next song, a jolly tune that reminded me of singing birds, when the sound of beating wings pulled my gaze skyward. My heart jumped when, at the same moment, another musical melody began to sound from my bond with Sniff.

Yet while Boone's song had been cheerful, Sniff's was filled with ascending panic.

I froze. *Sniff?* I asked. *What's wrong?*

Sniff responded, *Look up!*

I did, and found four dragons silhouetted against the moon. Sniff led the way back toward our stage, while behind him I counted one evren, one wyvern, and one... Stars. One true dragon, shining in the moonlight.

My breath caught. "Is that Aurora?" I asked aloud, and Boone's song came to an abrupt stop.

Sure enough, the true dragon's scales shone pearlescent white, and a female rider with long, dark waves sat astride her. Elle was back! I recognized the wyvern as Asher's mount, Thorn, and my gut twisted when I saw that he was riderless. As for the other evren, she was badly wounded, a scabbed-over injury along her flank that looked infected. It seemed to be taking all of her energy just to stay aloft.

I squinted at the evren, then did a double take. *Sniff,* I asked through our bond. *Is that... Jade?*

In affirmative response, Sniff gave a mighty roar. Faster than the others, Sniff landed first. Elle dove downward too, the dragons flanking her close behind. Hurriedly, I traced a rune and opened up a portal for poor, exhausted Jade to get herself to the ground without having to expend even another ounce of strength on flying. Sniff and I rushed to her side.

"Drakkin' drakefish!" Boone exclaimed. "What in Solei's blue sky's happened to y'all? Princess Eliana, ain't you s'posed to be retunin' from them yonder Dragon Isles with the rest of the Knights and the like? Why are y'all out here on your lonesome?"

Elle's hair was tangled and her travel dress was torn. When she spoke, her voice came out hoarse and rushed. "The rest of the party is on their way, but I couldn't wait. Not after hearing about what happened to Asher and Solrac. Aurora and I were faster, and..."

The rest was clear. Elle had done what I'd considered doing myself a hundred times—taking my dragon and going out to find Asher and Solrac myself. But while logic had kept me grounded, Elle *did* have a tendency to let her heart take her off script.

"Whoa there, missy!" Boone put up his hands. "First things first—You need to slow down and catch your breath."

Hurriedly, I retrieved my canteen of water from Sniff's pack and handed it to Elle. She drank deeply, some color returning to her cheeks. Meanwhile, Thorn eagerly lapped water from one of the many nearby puddles, while I made another portal to help Jade drink from the rainwater too without having to get up.

"You and Aurora came alone?" I asked Elle once she'd finished hydrating.

"Thorn came with us... not that he'd have listened if I told him not to. After leaving Zolehiinu, I wasn't sure where to go, but I naturally gravitated toward home in Keep Drakfell—That's the fastest route to Kolbohr, anyway."

"Kolbohr?" I repeated.

Elle nodded. "That's where the Soul Reaper's lair is."

"She's right," Vidya confirmed, both of us listening to Elle with growing dread.

"We ran into Jade along the way," Elle went on.

"Jade..." Vidya truly looked at the injured green evren for the first time. Her face went white. "Jax's dragon."

Jade gave an exhausted roar before speaking to our minds. *Jax and two other Mage Hunters kidnapped Solrac and Asher from the Dragon Isles. But Jax... he turned on the Hunters.*

"He did?" I asked, a flicker of hope flaring within my heart. Jade nodded and went on.

Jax tried to save Solrac and Asher, but they overpowered him. They've taken him to the lair as well.

"Scorchin' scatbeetles!" Boone swore. "What's all this soot and nonsense about some old lair? What're them ghost-followers gonna do to 'em there?"

"The Soul Reaper's lair is where he performs the soul surgeries," Vidya said grimly. "The Surgeon has long sought the ether well of the Farseer. It's the only one he lacks to become his voidish version of a Guardian. As for Jax and Asher..." Vidya looked away.

Or rather, she looked *up*.

"The moon." She pointed. "The Soul Reaper always performs his surgeries at midnight beneath a full moon, when the physical and spiritual planes are most aligned."

"That's tonight, ain't it?" Boone said somberly.

"Drak you and fate, Solrac," Vidya cursed and pressed her lips together. "The surgeries will begin within the hour."

Elle squealed, and my stomach dropped. Sniff let out a soft whine.

"Well, drak and a half," Boone said. "Ain't no way we can get to Kolbohr that quick. Drakkin' keepdom's halfway 'cross the realm!"

"It might as well be on the sun," Vidya said miserably. "Even with skyskipping, it would take us weeks to get there. By then, they'll have lost their ether wells, or worse."

Vidya's face screwed up. It was what she'd feared for weeks: Solrac's prediction regarding his imminent death. Only to make it all ten times worse, their son was in that same peril, too.

Not so, Jade's voice sounded in our minds once more. We all turned to the green evren, and I put a hand on the scales along her neck.

"What do you mean?" Vidya asked, and I sensed both skepticism and hope mingling in her expression.

Check my saddlebag, Jade instructed, and when Vidya did, she first found Jade's heartscale safely stowed inside. Jax had put it there to ensure the Hunters couldn't forcibly bond his dragon. But at the very bottom of the bag, Vidya found a small, round stone marked with runes. Rifting runes.

"That's a rift anchor!" I exclaimed. "Will it take us to Asher, Solrac, and Jax?"

Yes, Jade responded grimly. *The Mage Hunter, Ilyan, slipped it into my pack before we departed. He said his visions required it, but not for Jax and the Hunters' use. Having no desire to go to the Soul Reaper's lair, I didn't tell Jax about the anchor. The Hunters didn't have enough skystone to use it at such a great distance, anyway. But I believe here at Orothion, you do.*

Vidya carefully turned the stone over to reveal a carved symbol of an unadorned mask with vacant eye holes. A pointed crown sat upon its head, encircled by a series of nine diamonds. The mere sight of it made Vidya grimace.

"It's an invitation," she said, "for anyone who dares come for the Soul Reaper on his home territory. Whoever uses this portal is walking straight into a trap."

"A trap we have to spring," I said, "if we want a chance at rescuing our friends."

"Then spring it we will," Boone said, hands already going to the hilts of his starglass daggers.

"Hang on," Vidya said. "We can't just go rushing into the Soul Reaper's lair. Even if we brought an army, we'd never make it out alive. Solrac, Jax, and Asher... we'd doom them, as well as ourselves and any unfortunates foolish enough to join us."

"Then we don't bring an army," I said, determined. "All we have to do is get them through a rift to bring them straight back here to Orothion. One rift. I've got an anchor in the stronghold already. And if we die..." I thought of Zerana. "Well, that wouldn't be the worst thing that could possibly happen."

My choice of words got to Vidya. Hesitantly, she began, "With my shadowbinding keeping us invisible, perhaps there's a chance we could evade capture. But my wraith..."

Vidya swallowed, and I could tell she was verging on panic at the thought of her wraith taking control. I recognized the expression well.

Without hesitation, I shed the shadowcloak Shaya had made for me. I'd told Vidya about the cloak before, and the idea intrigued her, though I wasn't sure if she fully believed in its power. At least, she doubted it would work on someone who was wraith-bound, especially when that wraith was as strong as hers.

Still, wordlessly, I clasped the cloak around Vidya's shoulders. It was black, like the swan-feathered one she used to wear, but this one felt entirely different.

"It's not perfect," I said as Vidya felt the fine threads, "but it helps. You *will* be strong enough. Trust me."

Vidya set her jaw. Whether she believed that or not, she knew she couldn't stand by while her family needed help. "I have to go alone," she said. "I won't risk any of you on this mission."

"I'm the one who can rift us back," I said definitively. "I'm coming."

"Me too!" Boone said, giving one of his curved starglass daggers a twirl.

"And me," Elle said, getting back to her feet.

"Sorry, Princess," Boone said. "But you ain't goin' nowhere."

"Boone's right," Vidya said. "You need to regain your strength after your journey here. Besides, the Knights—scorch, the whole realm—needs *you*. We can't risk the face of the uprising."

"Asher's life is on the line. I'm coming."

"*All* of our lives are goin' to be on the line," Boone insisted. "Don't be foolish now, Princess Eliana."

"But—"

"But nothin'."

Frustration and determination mingled in Elle's amber eyes. Boone and Vidya were right, Elle *should* stay behind. But I recalled the bond we'd formed under the scorpio mountain, and knew I had to do for her what I hoped she'd do for me if the scales were swapped.

"Let her come," I said. "Like we said before, we're going straight in and straight out. And even if things go awry, Elle's a strong fighter. We could use her."

Elle's eyes shone, and I could tell Boone and Vidya wanted to argue further. But there really wasn't time to argue.

"We'd better not live to regret this," Boone relented.

"Streya help us all," Vidya agreed.

Right on Elle's heels were some equally determined dragons.

What about us? Thorn asked, and Sniff sniffled in agreement.

"Sorry, buddy." I caressed Sniff's neck. "But a big yellow evren wouldn't exactly be conducive to a stealth mission. Nor an even bigger black wyvern either, Thorn." Thorn deflated, and Boone went over to reassure him that we'd do everything we could to save his rider. Elle hugged Aurora's neck in farewell too, and Vidya spoke with Jade, checking if there was anything else we should know before departing.

Meanwhile, I pulled Sniff aside. Not only did I need to give him one last good scratch behind the ears, but I needed to give him a special assignment of his own. We ducked around the edge of the stump stage, and I kept my voice down as I told him so that the others wouldn't see or hear.

Sniff nodded along as I spoke, a serious light entering his normally playful eyes. When I asked if he could handle the job, he nodded with as much sobriety as I'd ever seen him exhibit.

Now my turn for request, Sniff spoke to me through our bond.

"What's that?" I asked.

Sniff surprised me when, all at once, he was tackling me to the ground again. My elbow splashed into a shallow puddle, but I didn't care as Sniff licked my face. A loving string of musical notes played inside my heart.

Promise to come back? Sniff requested.

"I will," I promised, praying to whatever goddesses might be listening that I'd be able to keep my word. "Now hurry and get Jade to the dragon stables so that the keepers can tend to her wounds."

On it, Sniff imparted back, then flapped his wings and led the other three dragons back above the canopy.

When I returned to the group, Vidya, Boone, and Elle had finished preparing for our mission. But while Vidya knew all about the layout of the Soul Reaper's lair, it was hard to put together a solid strategy when we didn't know exactly where the Soul Reaper and his followers had put the rift anchor's exit stone. Initially, I was worried that we'd rift straight into some kind of silvered cage, but Vidya assured me that they wouldn't risk the silver stopping us from coming through.

"There's still plenty of skystone in the stronghold's basement armory from Zel's hoard," Vidya said. "That'll be more than enough to get us to the lair."

"And what about the return journey?" I asked. "Will we need to bring skystone with us so I can rift us all the way back?"

"No," Vidya answered.

"Why not?" Boone asked.

"Trust me," said Vidya. "Finding skystone in the lair will be the least of our problems."

A beat of silence came next. I wished there was more time to put together a stronger plan, but midnight crept closer with every passing second.

I looked between Boone and Vidya, who in many ways had become like a grandfather and a second mother to me. Then I met Elle's gaze, her amber eyes full of determination, anxiety, and love. Thinking of what was at stake, I could relate. I knew we should've been afraid, too, and I was certain that fear would come. But for now, we stood strong. This was it—Solrac, Jax, and Asher needed us.

Without another word, the four of us headed back toward Orothion and the skystone that would power the rift anchor. From there, it was on to Kolbohr and our likely doom.

Chapter 21: The Soul Reaper

Asher

By the night things finally changed, Jax had accumulated twenty-six dagger slashes along his forearm. The moon was finally full, hanging above those curved, glassy windows like a great eye staring into the lightning cage where Jax and I were trapped.

First into the lab that evening was a thin man with a thick, silvery snake draped over his shoulders. I recognized him immediately as the Mage Hunter, Ilyan.

Behind Ilyan trailed twenty or more masked, gray-robed guards, all armed with seaxes, halberds, and a few runemarked staffs. They stood in a tight formation behind Ilyan and his snake as they settled in the middle of the laboratory.

"Why so many?" I muttered to Jax.

Jax was troubled. "I don't know. It looks like they're forming up for a fight."

Next came Jaira and Bjorn, who carried between them a semi-conscious man with tangled dark hair and what was once a very well-trimmed beard.

"Solrac," I said, my eyes widening. He was visibly thinner than he had been when we'd arrived, and he was practically drowning in silver chains, twisting every which way over his limbs and torso. A thin, silver circlet crown adorned his head, effectively blocking any chance a Mystic like him would ever have of channeling etherarchy.

Solrac was mumbling to himself, a string of disconnected thoughts. I caught only bits and pieces:

"Don't come... Too dangerous... Swan, snow, scales, and starglass... Four come in, four go out. Or is it five? Fate is but a pen in our hands."

Ignoring his ramblings, Jaira and Bjorn tied his arms and legs to the operating table, yet Solrac was already wrapped in so much icy, painful silver that he barely noticed the new, silvered bonds.

As they strapped him down, Solrac caught sight of Jax and me standing at the edge of our prison.

"Jax!" he called weakly. "Oh, my boy. Don't worry—The tower will not be your legacy!"

"The what?" Jax was perplexed. Solrac was clearly delirious.

"Asher!" he continued. "Your bane... will be your salvation."

Jax and I exchanged deeply concerned looks. What was he talking about?

Ilyan let out a self-satisfied chuckle. "I wouldn't count on legacies or salvation if I were you two. The silver has badly affected the Farseer's abilities, for I too, have foreseen the omens surrounding this night and, trust me, it does not end well for your side."

Before either Jax or I could respond to that smug, snake-loving Mage Hunter, a new voice echoed throughout the laboratory:

"Now now... This night does not have to end badly, either for our own beloved Gray Knight or for our esteemed guest, the long-lost Prince of the Dragon Isles. That decision lies with them."

The sonorous, doubled voice chilled me to the bone. The hairs on the back of my neck stood on end, and I wanted nothing more than to run far, far away. But intuitively, I already knew there would be no running away from this nightmarish creature—not without a fight.

"Soot," Jax swore under his breath, backing away from the edge of the cage.

I narrowed my eyes to get a look at the newcomer. He wasn't a large man, but his very presence was imposing and inescapable, like the sun behind closed eyelids. Tattered gray robes that paid homage to the look of the wraiths I'd seen in Etheria trailed to the floor. His face was thin, his hair ashen, and his irises... soot, they looked like glowing fragments of shattered cobalt.

The weapon hanging at his side was equally formidable. The longsword gleamed, its hilt reminding me of a shining star.

The Mage Hunters and gray-hooded lackeys watched with reverence as the man strode toward the lightning cage. Many inclined their heads, calling him 'Surgeon.' Jax backed further away when he came close, but as this ghastly man made unbroken eye contact with me, I stood my ground.

Surgeon... Of course. So this was the legendary Soul Reaper, the man the Drekai feared above all others, whom the Knights of the Torch claimed would be the downfall of Evgard. I pondered what to say to him for a grand total of half a second.

"It's about time you showed up!" I started, instilling as much melodrama into my tone as I could. "I've got a laundry list of complaints about my stay here—For one, this suite is incredibly chilly. The food is awful, and would it kill your staff to give us bedrolls? Honestly, the service here is disgraceful!"

Jaira, Bjorn, and every masked guard in the room froze. I guessed no one had ever sassed the Soul Reaper before. They looked to their master for a response.

"You are as bold as the stars predicted you would be, Asher of Steel Rim," he said, voice as even and creepy as before. "I certainly hope you will choose to join us before the night is through."

I forced a laugh. "Nah, your lackey, Zel, already offered. If you think there's a chance of me joining you, you're as delusional as you are badly dressed. I mean, come on—You'd think with all this skystone, the man could afford a robe that isn't falling to shreds."

Jaira looked both horrified and ready to skewer me, as did most of the Soul Reaper's followers. Bjorn alone seemed enlivened by the possibility of the Soul Reaper violently retaliating.

But as for the man himself, he simply stared, those unblinking eyes still locked onto mine. I fought to keep the casual expression on my face while inwardly my heart was thudding with terror.

Agonizingly slowly, the Soul Reaper cocked his head. At last, he spoke again.

"Within the hour, it will be midnight. Tonight, beneath the full moon, the veil between worlds will be at its thinnest, and I will begin my soul surgeries. The Farseer will be first..."

The Soul Reaper turned to groggy Solrac with fire in his eyes. "I will finally have the powerful Seer's well I have long sought in order to become the first Guardian in a thousand years. But, dear Prince Asher, if you wish, I will end tonight's surgeries there."

He turned back to me, something dark and ancient in his gaze. "I will offer you the same opportunity I offered your mother when she lay on those very tables: *Join us*. The omens have long predicted your crucial role on the day of the convergence of mythic stars. I offer you the opportunity to select the side that will emerge victorious."

"How many times do I have to tell you no, you blue-eyed creep?"

I wasn't sure if it was a blessing or a curse that the Soul Reaper was suddenly too distracted to respond to my—probably ill-conceived—comment. Either way, the man was fixating on my neck or, more specifically, the turquoise dust scarf I wore there.

"*Shava tu kalavira...*" he muttered in a language I'd never heard before, then took a cautious step backward, as if momentarily afraid. Finally, his expression returned to ice.

He reached for me, and I flinched as his hand went right through the lightning bars as if they were nothing. I knew this guy was hyper-powerful, with almost every type of etherarchy at his disposal. Was he somehow countering the lightning's effects with shadowbinding by phase-shifting through it? Prisoner or not, Kai would've been taking notes for sure.

Whatever the case, those thin, icy fingers were suddenly clutching my scarf, yanking it straight off of my neck.

He held it for a moment, his expression triumphant, but also twisted, as if merely holding the scarf brought him intense physical pain. As for me, I felt exposed without it, and nearly grabbed for it then and there.

A second later, I desperately wished I had.

Without a moment's warning, the Soul Reaper pulled the scarf back toward himself and held it against one of the cage's crackling lightning bars. The lightning flared, and seemed to fight against something within the scarf. For a brief moment, I thought I saw a halo-like burst repelling the cage's voidarchy, causing the lightning to momentarily dissolve. But in the end, it was no use.

I gave a strangled cry as I watched the scarf blacken and burn, leaving behind nothing but a pile of thin, golden threads upon the floor. My mother's scarf. An heirloom that had been passed down in my family line for generations.

But I knew it was even more than that. Tears blurred my eyes as I helplessly watched blue flames eating away at the final relic that had tied me to my mother. That simple square of fabric was what had allowed her to protect me even from beyond the grave. One moment it was here, and the next... it was completely gone.

Not a moment later, I heard the voices. Without the connection to my spirit-protector mother, an onslaught of cold, sinister voices thundered like a wild storm inside my head:

Join us, Asher.
Let me in—I can grant you power unlike anything you've ever felt before.
Think of it, Asher. You can make them all pay for what they've done to you.
Join us! Join us! Join us!

They were so loud, I was barely conscious of Jax kneeling beside me, cursing as he looked at the ashes of what had long been my most precious possession. The Soul Reaper watched me, as if fully aware of exactly what his dark followers could do now that Mom's scarf no longer protected me.

"Perhaps you'll change your mind soon enough, Asher of Steel Rim," the Soul Reaper mused, an empty almost-smile on his gaunt face.

I wanted to scream as the voices in my head threatened to overwhelm me. But what I heard next forced me to focus.

"Is everything in place for tonight, Overseer?" The Soul Reaper turned to Ilyan.

Ilyan nodded eagerly. "Yes, my liege. They'll take the bait, I'm certain of it. Each time I consult the omens, they show me the self-same thing: A blizzard beneath a full moon on the night we sacrifice the Farseer. With this fine group of Coven acolytes under my command, and the monsters from the fathoms below at the ready, we will be more than prepared when she arrives. By morning, your voidshard shall be restored to you once and for all."

My mind was racing, my thoughts battling with the onslaught of voices. She... blizzard... voidshard... He couldn't be talking about Meleya, could he? No. She was safe at Orothion. Her coming here... that wasn't possible, right?

Ilyan went on as if quoting some prophecy: "'*Where the half-born goes, his bane will follow.*' Tonight, I foresee that the Snowstorm will fall."

Chapter 22: The Break-In

Meleya

Lift your eyes up to the sky
We condemned here to die
See all those beautiful stars
And know they're not really that far
They say we're not alone
And we're going back home
Lift your eyes up to the sky!

Through the rift, Solrac's voice rang out loud and clear as he sang an old, rhythmic song written hundreds of years ago during Evgard's bloody Silver Crusades. It sent chills up and down my arms as I remembered the last time I'd heard it sung around a nomad's campfire, accompanied by tales of magi bound for the executioner's block, raising their last words in chorus.

"Son of a dragonmutt—Will someone shut him up already?" Jaira's voice sounded through the gold-rimmed portal as well, though she didn't know it.

Vidya, Boone, Elle, and I stood silently together in the basement of the Orothion stronghold. An untold quantity of skystone surrounded us, lighting the musty room adjacent to the underground armory. The Knights had tapped into some of Zel's skystone hoard, selling it to provide supplies for the Knights, but most of it remained exactly where the elderly half-born traitor had left it, saved for a time of need.

Like now.

It turned out the Gray followers had placed the exit end to the rift anchor smack in the middle of the Soul Reaper's laboratory. A cold energy emanated from within the rift, and the Mage Hunter with the silver snake, Ilyan, stood directly in front of it, with nearly a quadruple squad's worth of masked, hooded, gray-robed acolytes behind him, armed and ready.

But though the portal was wide open, providing us with a perfect—albeit white-tinted—window into the lair, Ilyan and the others didn't even flinch. He may have been a Seer, but he couldn't see what was happening literally right in front of his nose.

Part one of our half-baked, all-crazy plan was working. Before opening the portal, Vidya had enchanted the anchor with powerful shadowbinding etherarchy, allowing her to make the rift—and us, standing just outside it—completely invisible.

Skystones drained one by one as we held open the rift that spanned keepdoms. Through it, Vidya, Boone, Elle, and I got the lay of the lair.

I realized right away why Vidya hadn't been worried about bringing skystone along to power our return journey—the entire lair was practically bursting with the ether-filled crystals. They stood out on shelves, tables, chairs, and even sat on the floor in piles. Some stacks rose even higher than I was tall. I shuddered to think of what evil purposes the Soul Reaper planned to use it for.

The lair consisted of both a laboratory and an observatory. From here, I could see an enormous telescope pointed toward vast, curved windows that let in the light of hundreds of stars, as well as the round, full moon.

Meanwhile, in the loft portion, we saw Solrac lying on some sort of horrible-looking operating table. Silver bound him from his head to his feet, and I winced as I took in the sight of his gaunt face and unkempt beard.

Standing above him were Jaira and Bjorn, dressed in their Mage Hunter uniforms. But it was hard to focus on them when the Soul Reaper himself was in the room. A chill ran through me as I finally beheld the man I'd only ever seen before in shrouded nightmares.

Despite not being very tall or having a particularly strong physique, his very being radiated power. Just his tattered gray robes and the gleaming, starry longsword he kept sheathed at his side made me want to shut off this portal and march right back to my parents' cottage without looking back.

But Solrac's wasn't the only face we saw. There in the corner of the laboratory loft, trapped in some kind of voidarchy-powered lightning cage, I saw Asher.

Elle grabbed my hand, amber eyes wide as she spied him through the portal. As for me, the revelation about Asher's true heritage filled my mind. Looking at him now, I didn't see some long lost prince of the Dragon Isles. All I saw was my friend, his eyes shut tight, hands pressed against the sides of his head. He looked terrified, and I prayed he was okay.

And there, inside the cage with Asher, a hand on his shoulder as he spoke to Asher in low, reassuring tones was...

Jax.

I witnessed their interaction with confusion. When the three of us met in Etheria, Jax—as the Gray Knight—had tried to kill Asher in cold blood. And even before he'd changed sides, Jax had never bothered to hide his loathing of the goofy, pointy-eared Archon. So what in the stars had changed?

Watching Jax now made my heart melt. Drak, I felt like I hadn't seen him in so long. I'd seen his spirit in Etheria, true, but he hadn't been himself. That much had been evident in his aura, shrouded by the stifling gray mists from his wraith. But now, I could plainly see that he'd regained much of his former self. I squeezed Elle's hand back.

But his face... Oh, stars, Jax's face. Bruises and cuts, some old and others fresh, covered Jax's jaw, nose, and forehead. Everywhere I saw skin, from his neck to his arms to the shoulders exposed by his sleeveless tunic, looked like it had been hurt in some way. My heart ached as I wondered what they'd put him through.

Through gritted teeth, Boone muttered so quietly I doubted the illusion of silence Vidya had cast over us would've even been necessary. "Soot be upon them fools who done this to that boy."

"You know Jax well?" I asked, keeping my voice imperceptibly low as well.

"Jax'n I've been workin' together under Solrac for many a year," Boone replied. "I love that headstrong youngun more'na javelina loves a good prickly pear. That rascally li'l astromancin' trainee of mine, Asher, too. And as for Solrac... he an' I have been through more soot together than the sun and the wind." Boone's eyes narrowed, his expression filled with loathing. "Them scorched Gray-lovin' lunatics done picked the wrong old craghopper to antagonize, I'll tell you that."

"It's time," Vidya cut in, straining from having to split her focus between so many types of etherarchy.

Looking around the armory, I realized she was right. The skystone here was draining fast, and while we likely had several more minutes before we were in any real danger of running out, it was time to act.

"Ready, Meleya." Vidya nodded my way. I nodded back.

Vidya's eyes flashed lightning blue as she dug deep to access more of Zerana's shadowbinding power. At the same moment, I traced a rifting rune.

With Vidya's impressive shadowbinding cloaking my rifts, I placed an invisible entrance portal of my own directly in front of the one made by the rift anchor. Then I spotted a relatively safe place within the laboratory, far off to the side behind a particularly large pile of skystone—That's where I put the exit.

Then, together, the four of us stepped through my hidden rift, leaving the safety of Orothion for the uncertainty of the Soul Reaper's lair—-Well out of sight of Ilyan and his minions.

The second we stepped into the lair, I felt it, an oppressive darkness that seemed to claw at my heart and stifle all hope. In what Trickshot had described as a side effect of being woken early from astral sleep, I caught a flash of ethereal gray mingled with sapphire blue. In the background of my thoughts, I could almost sense faint, garbled whispers. Not true wraith voices, not quite, but like the shades and echoes we'd encountered so often in the Haze while in Etheria.

So as to not rely on my inconsistent flashes, I traced the rune for the Sight, and at once the dark, spiritual reality bloomed before me with awful clarity. This place was *crawling* with wraithlings, their shadowy gray forms so thick it felt like looking through a dust storm. While these minor wraiths weren't capable of proper communication, the nearest ones nipped at the fringes of our spirits as if trying to stifle the light. I could tell from my friends' downcast expressions that the shades and echoes were taking a toll on them too.

It seemed only one spot remained free of wraithlings, repelled by a halo-like aura visible only in the spirit plane. That aura was emitting from Vidya's shadowcloak, forging a white-gold barrier between her and the darkness. The cloak was doing its job—Vidya's powerful wraith remained distant.

Now that we were out of sight and the invisible portals had dissolved, Vidya let out a breath of relief. Even with three ether wells, such a complicated use of her powers had taken a lot out of her. Still, her reprieve was short lived, since the next part of our plan relied on her skills as well.

We could hear voices echoing within the lair from where the operating tables were. As Vidya invisibly slipped away to set the next part of our plan in motion, Boone, Elle, and I listened in.

"Midnight draws near," the Soul Reaper said, his deliberate, doubled tone chilling me to my core as he approached Solrac's table. "We can feel the ethereal plane aligning."

Ilyan piped up next. "The Snowstorm will be here any moment, my liege."

My heart stopped at the sound of my moniker. Soot, had the rift anchor been meant for *me* all along?

Suddenly, a long-suppressed memory clawed its way to the forefront of my mind. When I'd first arrived at the Knights' safehouse in the Mirror Forest, each new arrival had been subjected to questioning by Kai. My interview with Kai had been long and arduous, and ultimately I'd learned that his hesitancy regarding me had had everything to do with one of his recurring visions. The scene he'd shown me had left me feeling sick.

My Sight rune dissipated as I recalled sapphire stars hanging in the air around me as I stalked toward a table, void-blue fire dancing in my eyes and a murderous expression on my face. My heart lurched as I realized it was an operating table—like the very ones here in the lab—and that Asher was strapped upon it. I'll never forget the sound of Asher's scream as I leveled my seaxe at his chest before the vision went black.

Dragonbumps appeared on my arms. I wasn't capable of hurting Asher, right? A jumble of nerves wrestled in my stomach as I thought of the shadowcloak—the one on Vidya's shoulders.

I'd no sooner formed the thought than a harsh, raspy voice from within my head nearly made me jump out of my skin.

Snowstorm! What a welcome surprise!

Drak. I fortified my mind against the onslaught I knew was coming.

You must let me in, *Snowstorm! Together, we could challenge the Wraith King! Bring this lair—and all of the Gray—to its knees.*

Leave me alone, Xan, I warned.

Think of it! Xan pressed. *We can save Asher, Jax, and Solrac. Just put me in control, and we* can *do this!*

For one awful second, the thought tempted me. But Asher's scream from the vision resounded in my head, and I knew I couldn't let Xan in tonight. I *wouldn't.*

We can't challenge the Soul Reaper, I mentally replied.

Ah, but with the power of the Soul Reaper's own voidshard, we could! Together, you and I would—

I said, leave me alone! I cut her off. At my words, Xan had no choice but to shrink away, hissing as she momentarily retreated from my mind.

"We cannot wait any longer, Overseer," the Soul Reaper was saying. "The time has come for me to take my final ether well."

"Of course." Ilyan bowed. "I and mine will await the arrival of the Snowstorm. You must focus on your task."

Suddenly, I heard a clinking sound from beside the operating tables in the middle of the loft. Soon after, protests arose from Asher and Jax's cage.

"Get away from him!" Jax shouted.

"Stop that!!" called Asher. But the pair's continued protests fell on deaf ears.

We couldn't directly see what was happening while hidden behind the skystone, but I carefully traced a pair of small portals into being. One I set before Boone, Elle, and me, and the other I placed just off to the side, facing the main room. It was still well-hidden behind another stack of skystone so that those within the lab wouldn't see it, but using the rifts as a sort of angled periscope, Boone and I could just make out what was going on on the other side through the white-tinge of Etheria.

Ilyan and his small army of masked acolytes were still staring at the rift anchor in the middle of the loft—waiting for me, apparently. Meanwhile, I froze at the sight of the small, sharp blade the Soul Reaper held in his practiced fingers. The blade looked to be made of blue starglass—voidglass—and had a shimmering edge that might've been dream energy of some kind. Over the Surgeon's forehead, I saw the rune for the Sight.

He was using it to see Solrac's aura, I realized. Or, more specifically, his ether well.

I tensed, feeling tempted to burst into the lab to put a stop to this, whatever the cost. Soot, was Vidya ready yet? Before my misguided instincts could take over, Boone put a hand on my arm.

"Careful now," Boone breathed. "I know we've all been eagerly awaitin' your baby sister's corporeal debut, but for now, you're the only unofficial grandkid I've got."

Hating this helplessness, I crouched back down behind the skystone stack, shivering as I felt the wraithlings close in around us. Huddling closer to Boone, I continued watching through my periscope portal.

"Normally, I grant subjects the gift of being unconscious during soul surgery," the Soul Reaper said. "But not you, mighty Farseer. I want to see the etherlight leave your eyes."

Even Jax and Asher's protests gave way to silence as the Soul Reaper bent over Solrac's forehead, voidglass knife in place. I held my breath. Was this it? The moment Solrac had predicted, wherein he would die at the Soul Reaper's hand? The moment Vidya had feared for so long? Drak, where *was* Vidya?

Just before the Soul Reaper could make the incision, more singing pierced the lair. Only this time, it wasn't Solrac.

Jax's foot stomped in time as he sang, his tone low and rich as he continued the same song Solrac had started earlier:

When your head's hanging down
And your doomed for the ground
Lift your eyes up to the sky!

The singing startled the Soul Reaper. Jax kept going.

May swift fall the blade
Ours the truer crusade
Lift your eyes up to the sky!

Though he lay at blade-point, mere moments away from losing everything, Solrac joined in the following chorus, as did Asher as he caught on.

Lift your eyes up to the sky
We, condemned here to die
See all those beautiful stars
And know they're not really that far
They say we're not alone and we're going back home
Lift your eyes up to the sky!

As the three voices blended in harmony, the very energy of the lair seemed to shift. I felt a spark of hope rising within my chest as I looked up to the brightly shining stars through the windows of the observatory.

But despite his initial surprise, the Soul Reaper ultimately didn't care if Solrac went out singing or silent. Through my periscoping rifts, I helplessly watched with grim fascination as he placed his knife over the center of Solrac's forehead, then made the first incision. Solrac's voice shuddered, but he kept singing right along with Jax and Asher. I didn't dare try anything too soon since, according to Vidya, soul surgery was a volatile process, and the simplest slip could have devastating results.

I cringed, though the small blade didn't draw blood. It didn't even cut Solrac's skin at all, instead going straight through to his spirit. My heart thudded so loudly I worried some masked lackey would hear it.

But a much louder thud from the other side of the lair rendered that even less likely. At once, the Soul Reaper's blade halted in place. He withdrew it, and Jax, Asher, and Solrac stopped singing as everyone looked toward the sound.

My heart continued to pound as the Soul Reaper hurriedly scrawled a few runes in the air before he, Jaira, Bjorn, and several others stepped away to peer over the edge of the loft and into the observatory portion of the lair. Ilyan and many of his acolytes remained, their gazes still locked onto that exit rift anchor, pointlessly waiting with bated breath for it to activate.

Over the balcony's edge, a single swan stood at the foot of the telescope, its wings a light, pearlescent gray. It was Vidya's ethereal familiar, one of six identical starswans. No doubt the Soul Reaper's followers would recognize the Black Valkyrie's iconic creation, but if anything, that would only add to the effectiveness of her distraction.

Next, the sound of beating wings came from high above our heads. Two more pale gray swans were flying up near the curved windows, backlit by the stars and the full moon. Murmurs broke out among the followers of the Gray, and I heard Jaira and a few others muttering: 'the Black Valkyrie'.

Their gazes followed the swans as yet another appeared, perched on the loft's balcony railing. But as for me, I turned all of my focus onto *my* task. Vidya was giving us a window, but it wouldn't be a very big one. Ilyan and his acolytes would make this difficult, but they were watching the rift anchor, not the operating tables or the lightning cage. There wasn't time to come up with a better plan, or even to come up with a mightier and less petrified person to carry it out. There was only me, and I had to try.

My mind raced as I raised my finger to runetrace. My studies at the Mage Hunter Academy had taught me that I could rift silver directly through my portals, but that if any silver touched the gold rims, the portals would dissolve instantly. The operating table upon which Solrac lay was pretty well laced with silver, and a portal large enough to encompass the whole table would have to be pretty wide. The bigger the portal, the higher the risk that someone would see and stop us. And as for Asher and Jax, I could only hope they would think quickly enough to run through my portal once it appeared inside—

A strangled gasp yanked my attention from the rune I'd started. At first, I saw nothing through my periscope rift, but within a moment, two once-invisible figures melted into plain sight.

The first was Vidya, who'd been fiddling with the silver straps pinning Solrac to his table, and the second was the Soul Reaper himself. For a moment, I was confused—Wasn't that the Soul Reaper staring out over the balcony with the others? But already that illusion of the Soul Reaper was dissolving, making it clear that the true Surgeon was the one putting Vidya in a telekinetic chokehold. Soot! How had he known where she was?

Then I remembered which rune hung over his forehead. Invisibility worked on physical eyes, but with the Sight activated he'd have seen Vidya's spirit. Soot.

The Soul Reaper held Vidya by the collar, telekinetically pulling the fabric tighter as he yanked her into the air, her feet kicking at nothing as she struggled to free herself.

Then, with a twisting motion of his hand, the Soul Reaper channeled astromancy, forming a tall, blue-tinted starglass post that shot upward against Vidya's back. Next, a thorny ironclaw vine appeared as the Soul Reaper used woodweaving to wind the plant up the post and around Vidya to hold her in place. The vine bound her so tightly she could barely move.

Everything happened so quickly that Vidya was already completely trapped before any of the others, Knight or Gray, registered what was going on. Surprise colored every expression as they all turned to see the action unfolding.

"The Black Valkyrie!" Jaira pointed. "I knew it was her!"

"Mom!" Jax looked confused and more than a little worried.

As for Solrac, he regarded his wife with solemnity. "Streya help her," he muttered in prayer.

"Dearest Black Valkyrie," the Soul Reaper said, not missing a beat. "How long it has been. We are glad to see you back—We had begun to miss you."

"I can assure you, the feeling is not mutual," Vidya bit back. Eyes blazing sapphire, she accessed her shadowbinding powers to phase shift directly through the ironclaw vines, then dropped to the ground, landing in a battle stance as she whipped out her dragonhook spear. Shadowfire sprang to life lining the blade.

Normally, the mere sight of Vidya would've sent anyone with an ounce of sense running for the hills. But the Soul Reaper simply laughed.

"You could've been great—had a place at my table in the Age of the Wraiths. Yet here you are, unworthy of either the Gray *or* the so-called light..."

He glanced through the windows toward the full moon, clearly eager to get back to work while the veil between worlds was at its thinnest. "Dear, foolish Black Valkyrie, did you really think you could defy fate, retrieving your precious Farseer on your own?" He laughed again.

Then his fractured eyes narrowed. He cocked his head as if he were listening to something—or, more likely, some*one*.

The rune for the Sight still burning blue over his forehead, the Soul Reaper made the most painstakingly slow head-turn of all time. Mason Drakeslayer had once told me that the Soul Reaper's skill with the Sight was severely limited when it came to discerning colors, but apparently he had no trouble seeing our auras through large piles of skystone.

"Although, traitorous Valkyrie," the Soul Reaper spoke coldly, "we see that you have not come alone. Come out, dear Knights. Let us not cower in the shadows like ignorant, filthy animals. Are we not among fellow intelligent, civilized creatures?"

"Welp," Boone murmured to Elle and me. "So much for stealth."

The three of us gave each other one last nod, then rolled in opposite directions, each of us leaping out from behind the skystone with weapons blazing.

For Boone, literally.

Fiery white ether burned from each of his twin curved daggers, ready to shoot. I was vaguely aware of the rest of the laboratory reacting to our entrance. Jax and Asher's calls were something between pure shock and 'get the void out of here', while Ilyan sputtered something along the lines of, "But how? The Snowstorm is a true master of deception!"

Before I could marvel at the idea of someone thinking *I* was even mildly deceptive, Boone called out:

"Dragonfire in the hole!"

Without further ado, he ran toward the Soul Reaper with ether blasting from his forward-curved daggers. Elle came hot on his heels, a ripple of green-and-violet dragonfire blooming to life along the edge of her saber as she made for Jax and Asher's cage.

But with a demonically casual wave of his hand, the Soul Reaper used telekinesis to raise two large chunks of skystone into the air. The stones absorbed both Boone's ether and Elle's dragonfire instantly.

At the same moment, Vidya's black spear thrust toward the Soul Reaper's back. When her blade sprouted through his chest, my breath caught. Had she struck him down, just like that?

But when Vidya retracted her spear, the Soul Reaper was still whole and standing. Drak—more shadowbinding ether had allowed him to phase shift, essentially transforming parts of his body temporarily to shadow and making him virtually untouchable. Orbs of inky black shadowfire flew from both sides as the Soul Reaper forced Vidya back from where Solrac lay.

While my companions distracted the enemy, I was runetracing, concentrating on the anchor I'd left back at Orothion. I drew from the skystones surrounding me, my ether well brimming with power even as I drained it, forming a portal large enough to swallow Solrac and his silver-laden table. All I needed was enough time to get him and the others through before—

Suddenly, my rift evaporated as another rift—this one lined with blue—overcame it. The Soul Reaper was forming a portal too, this one a curved, translucent dome—much like the one I'd made to protect Asher, Zerana, Blink, and me in Etheria. His reflective rift shield encompassed himself, Jaira, and Solrac's entire operating table, effectively shutting mine out. Right away, I tried to form a portal *below* the dome, only to learn that his encompassed the floor beneath the table as well. He did *not* want to risk losing the Farseer's well, not even for a chance at reclaiming his voidshard.

The strikes Vidya, Boone, and Elle had tried to level at the Soul Reaper reflected right back onto them. Vidya only narrowly missed getting stabbed through the shoulder by her own spear. Boone hollered as he leaped to dodge one of his redirected ether blasts.

"These old bones ain't meant for leapin' 'round no more!" he noted.

The Soul Reaper didn't pay any of it heed as he set right back to removing Solrac's ether well. Jaira grinned wickedly from within the reflective dome as she handed the Soul Reaper his tools.

There wasn't time to waste. I'd have to figure out how to get to Solrac later, but for now, I focused on opening up a portal within the lightning cage so that I could at least get Jax and Asher out—

I screamed as, out of nowhere, someone grappled me from behind. Someone far taller and stronger than I was, his arms lined with razor sharp spikes of... soot, were these diamonds sprouting from Bjorn's flesh?

"Welcome to the void, ethercursed." Bjorn's savage whisper filled me with terror.

I could hear Jax and Asher calling my name and shouting strings of curses at Bjorn, but my primary attention was on the icy burn of the jagged silver dagger Bjorn was pressing against my neck. I could tell he was just itching to slit my throat.

"Stay your blade, Diamondback!" Ilyan hissed. From its place draped over his shoulders, his actual snake hissed too. "We need the Snowstorm alive if we are to guarantee the retrieval of our master's voidshard!"

Ilyan was right—While there was a good chance the contents of my rift hold would reappear alongside my body after my death, there was also a chance the items would show up in places that meant something to me. My parents' cottage in Skygard. The bunker back on the Rise. The secret glade that Jax had taken me to after weeks of being trapped in Scryer's Grotto, equipped with its very own kitchen just for me—or any number of other possible locations. Ilyan was careful and logical, unwilling to risk losing the shard by ending me. Not if there was a surer way.

While masked acolytes swarmed Vidya and Boone, Bjorn's grip on me tightened. I could tell he really wanted to disobey Ilyan's order.

Bjorn may have had me restrained, but still, my finger traced through the air. Before he could make another move, I ripped open a portal directly beneath his right foot. The sudden drop through the floor threw him off balance, and he had to put out his hands to catch himself.

The trick gave me the window I needed to spin out of Bjorn's grip and right into another waiting portal. I vanished into Etheria, then right back out again, directly beside the blue lightning cage. Elle was there too, having broken free from the fight. Asher stood opposite her with veins of blue lighting crackling between them.

"Mel!" Asher exclaimed as soon as I appeared. "*Stars*, you two shouldn't have come, but I'd be lying if I said I wasn't glad to see you! Both of you."

Elle tore her gaze away from Asher to look at me, likely planning to exchange a knowing glance. I just found myself staring at the two of them, momentarily frozen as a hundred thoughts crossed my mind in the blink of an eye.

Seeing the way Elle looked at Asher, her feelings were clear. But as for me... Drak, I wasn't nearly as sure of mine. I'd have expected to feel a twinge, some kind of resentment at the thought of them together. But to my surprise, all I found myself thinking about was how grateful I was that someone else cared enough about Asher to want to see him safely home.

Then I saw Jax, the sapphire of the lightning contrasting harshly with the much deeper, richer midnight blue of his eyes. Rather than rush forward as Asher had, Jax hung back, looking at me like I was a ghost as his hand gripped something tied to his belt. At once, I realized it was his quartz, and almost subconsciously, I touched my fingers to mine as well.

Pulling me from my momentary trance was the sight of a tiny mirror gecko crawling onto the toe of Elle's boot. Was it just me, or were little Glint's eyes darting rapidly back and forth between the four of us?

I shook my head to clear it as I spoke to Jax and Asher. "Get ready to run. I'm sending you two back to Orothion."

I'd no sooner lifted my finger than both Jax and Asher were all but yelling at me.

"Like the void," Jax protested.

"We're not going anywhere without the rest of you!" Asher insisted. Jax gave a fierce nod of agreement.

My finger flew, my entrance rift appearing inside the cage. Within a second, both Asher and Jax were emerging from the exit rift at my side.

I could tell Elle wanted to wrap her arms around Asher, but with an onslaught of gray-hooded acolytes headed our way, there just wasn't time. Glint hurriedly darted to the relative safety of Elle's boot.

Both Elle and I drew our swords. Elle lit up more light-like dragonfire along hers, while I activated a portal shield infused with reflective power over my left arm—just like the Soul Reaper's dome, but on a smaller scale.

Meanwhile, to my left, Asher summoned his starglass dragonhook spear. On my right, Jax drew both of his fanged axes and set them telekinetically hovering above his ready hands as he assumed a battle stance.

"Time for a show!" Asher cried, as together, the four of us engaged the enemy.

Chapter 23: Acolytes

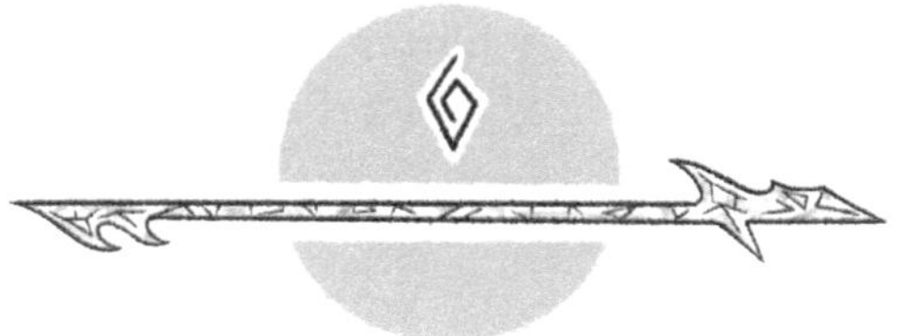

Asher

I fought with the spastic, borderline-manic energy that can only come from someone who's been cooped up in a cage for far too long.

My starglass spear was a blur as I charged it with hover-levitation power to speed up my swings. I was everywhere at once, surrounded by a mist of swirling liquid ether that amplified my every move as I knocked down each new Coven acolyte that rose against us.

Elle defended my back, her fiery saber trailing light as she crossed blades with an acolyte using woodweaving etherarchy to shoot grasping tendrils from the butt of his wooden staff. Despite her cutting them off and burning them to ashes, the tendrils stubbornly kept regrowing.

As much as I hated the idea of Elle and Meleya being here in the voidish armpit of Evgard that was the Soul Reaper's lair, I was glad to have them fighting alongside Jax and me. Jax's axes were positively flying, keeping Coven acolytes scrambling.

Just then, Bjorn's bone-chilling battle cry reverberated throughout the lair as he—quite literally—leaped into the fray. While the general chill here felt as if it was dragging my spirit down, this guy thrived on the darkness. Diamond spikes caught the light of a thousand skystone shards as Bjorn sailed toward Meleya with a vengeance, his jagged silver blade held at the ready above his head.

Meleya was ready for his attack, raising her portal shield so that Bjorn's dagger went right through it, then emerged harmlessly from the exit portal near her feet. When Bjorn's dagger-wielding hand shot out from it, she stomped on it. Bjorn howled.

Across the way, Boone was shooting like mad, his daggers all but glowing as ether blast after ether blast left curling white marks on our enemies' bodies. He whooped.

"Woowee! I tell you what—All of y'all ghost-followin' drakpats needa get yourselves to a sanctuary an' purge yourselves of this drakkin' Gray soot like your ever-livin' souls depended on it!"

Rather than seek religion, the nearest gray hood lashed a silver chain whip Boone's way. The whip took out Boone's left dagger and earned the acolyte a deeply offended, wrinkly look from Boone.

"Scorch you silversoots and your flashy, flailin' flogs," Boone scolded.

Just then, a crackling sound whipped my attention to the side. A Coven acolyte gripping a jagged halberd had just activated his lightwielding power. From within his mask's eye holes, blue light flashed as lightning lit up along his weapon's blade.

He seemed to think that blade had my name on it. I hover-dodged to avoid getting zapped, all the while complaining.

"Oh, buddy—You have no idea how sick I am of blue lightning right now!"

Using my spear, I channeled so much starglass onto his halberd's head that it tipped right onto the floor with a massive *clink!* The Lightwielder continued grasping the shaft, which dragged him downward too.

I took advantage of his awkward position, infusing him with hover-energy and flinging him into the loft's balcony railing. Once there, I encased him in starglass that trapped him in place.

"One down," I started. "Only about a zillion more to go."

There weren't actually infinite Coven acolytes coming for us, but with how badly we were outnumbered, the thirty or so masked men and women—not to mention Bjorn and Ilyan—seemed endless. Still, we didn't have to take them all down. All we had to do was figure out how to free Solrac before it was too late, then Meleya could portal us all out of here.

Speaking of Meleya, she was still engaging Bjorn. Her portals were doing wonders to keep him at bay, but the man they called 'Diamondback' was far bigger than she was, and relentless. I wasn't entirely sure what he had against Meleya specifically, but he was clearly taking great satisfaction in assaulting her with his jagged silver knife. Nearby, I could tell Jax was just itching to get at him, but he was rather preoccupied defending against three acolytes at once, and even with his telekinesis, he wasn't about to be free anytime soon.

As for me, I was about to step in when a certain Drakfellian princess beat me to it. Elle was probably the only person I knew who preferred dresses even during combat, and soot if she didn't make even her humble, worn-out travel dress look good as she spun into the fray, sword ablaze with light. She blocked Bjorn's diamond knuckles, her added strength from her true dragon bond surprising him. The auroral flames wreathing her saber burned him and, with a yelp, he leaped backward, manic eyes going even wider. Then he snarled, diving toward Elle to exact revenge.

But Elle's move had given Meleya all the window she needed. As Bjorn dove, Meleya's portal ripped to life before him to swallow him up. He vanished, only to reappear through the exit portal, which Mel had placed horizontally...

...Right in front of me.

She'd given me the perfect opportunity. Before disoriented Bjorn had even landed, I'd pulled the same thing on him as I'd done to the Lightwielder: infused him with levitation. He slammed into the balcony railing, where I encased him in starglass beside the other guy—though, for good measure, I trapped Bjorn there upside-down.

"That, my mohawked friend, is what I like to call the 'just encase'!" I called. "Enjoy being a jewelry display stand, Diamondback!"

"You're an idiot." Meleya rolled her eyes, then wiped the sweat from her brow. Elle gave a deep, genuine belly laugh.

"You know, I think he adds just the right sparkle to the room there." I busted up too, though Meleya raised an unamused eyebrow at the pair of us.

Deeply dissatisfied with his new position, Bjorn let out a hair-raising yell before raising an upside-down, diamond-spiked fist and chipping at the thick starglass encasing him. At this rate, that would keep him occupied until we were gone.

Already, more acolytes had forced Meleya and Elle back into action. A pair of seaxe-wielders were making their way toward me when a cry pulled my attention to the center of the laboratory.

It was Vidya, desperately trying to break into the reflective rift dome that sealed Solrac in with Jaira and the Soul Reaper. Coven acolytes were swarming her too and, despite her prowess as a warrior, one Shadowbinder had apparently gotten through her guard as black, disintegrating shadowfire licked along one of the pale gray swan wings sprouting from her back. She had no choice but to retract the wildshaping-empowered wings, though based on her expression, the pain remained on her back. That would no doubt leave a scar.

From where he'd just downed another acolyte, Jax shouted, "Mom!"

Recklessly abandoning his fight with yet another gray hood, Jax raced to his mother's side. Based on the number of foes Vidya faced, he'd need backup, so I followed close behind, drawing from a skystone or two along the way to top off my ether well.

Jax and I reached Vidya at the same time. While Jax's telekinetically-charged axe turned one enemy's dragonhook spear into kindling, I formed a starglass shield to block a blade bound for Jax's back. Jax spun around just in time to watch my starglass blade take the acolyte down.

"Thanks," Jax said, then looked up. "Astromancer!"

Sure enough, a gray hood using levitation like mine had hover-jumped high and was coming at us from above, a flock of razor-sharp starglass shards surrounding him. He clearly hoped to skewer all three of us.

"Boost me!" I shouted, and Jax instantly sprang into action.

The telekinetic shove upward on my boots perfectly complemented my jump. I met the other Astromancer in mid air, hovering as I whipped up a highly concentrated astro-nova and focused it directly onto him.

He wore a mask, but I was willing to bet that, beneath it, his jaw dropped as a wave of misty, pure ether blew him and his entire starglass arsenal back, his gray robes aflutter as he dropped straight off the edge of the balcony.

As I landed, I saw that Jax had returned my prior favor, having taken down another acolyte whose silver crossbow bolt would've undoubtedly pierced straight through me had Jax's telekinesis not redirected it. Jax and I exchanged glances, giving each other a single nod of respect.

We continued to fend off Coven acolytes while Vidya did everything she could to break through that reflective rift dome. She slammed against it with psionically charged weapons, tried to torch it with shadowfire... but each new impact was only redirected right back into the rest of the laboratory.

With each passing second, Vidya's attempts grew more and more reckless. When she desperately stabbed straight toward the Soul Reaper behind the barrier, her spear came right back out, grazing her arm and leaving behind a black shadowfire burn. Vidya cried out, dropping her weapon to the floor with a clatter.

Jax rushed to her side to ensure she was alright, but it was painfully clear that she wasn't. Eyes red with rage, Vidya reached toward the impenetrable dome.

"No!" she cried.

I turned to get a better view at what was happening with Solrac beyond the shimmering, translucent surface.

One look told me that it was already too late.

My heart sank. Through the rift, I saw Solrac lying there, unconscious... or worse. The Soul Reaper stood over him, triumphantly holding up Solrac's crystalline ether well. The fist-sized, ether-filled crystal was shrouded in scarlet mists, fresh from Solrac's aura.

Meanwhile, I could feel the darkness creeping ever closer to my core. I had no idea what was going on in the spirit plane, but I suddenly recalled the way it felt being in the Haze—as if hope was nothing but a memory, or a dream.

Vidya dropped to her knees in anguish, relentlessly calling her husband's name. Beside her, Jax cursed the Soul Reaper as he defended her in her grief.

The wraith-bound Surgeon paid them no heed as, within the rift dome, Jaira held up some sort of runemarked silver mirror. Now the Soul Reaper could see himself as he used his voidglass tools to stitch Solrac's ether well to his own soul at the level of his head, like the final jewel in a crown.

I felt sick as I took in the scene. Solrac... he was alive in there, right? But he was so still, his expression dangerously peaceful. I couldn't be sure.

Even as the fighting raged on throughout the lair—blood speckling her tunic, tears staining her face—Vidya began to rhythmically pound on the floor. Then, she began to sing.

Chapter 24: Snakes

Meleya

When you've done all you can
And you've run out of plans
Lift your eyes up to the sky!
You'll live on in the minds
Of those you've left behind
Lift your eyes up to the sky!

The sound of Vidya's heartbroken ballad penetrated my very bones. Even from here on the opposite end of the balcony where Elle and I battled gray hoods, it gave me the conviction to keep fighting.

At the very least, Vidya's song seemed to unnerve our enemies; I couldn't help but feel that the song was somehow shifting the aura of the room.

There was one way to test my theory.

"Watch my back!" I shouted to Elle, then hurriedly traced the rune for the Sight. As Etheria bloomed to life before me, I gasped.

Like before, I saw that the lair was utterly filled with wraithlings. Churning gray mists, piled atop one another like a wall of stormclouds, their blue eyes lighting the darkness.

But many of the shades and echoes… they were fleeing. Scattering in the wake of a ribbon of golden light, which emitted from where Vidya knelt singing. The look of it reminded me of the gold rim of a Rifter's tear. With a start, I realized the rich, powerful stream of light *was* the song, weaving through the Gray and banishing it like a wildfire amidst dry prairie grass.

Vidya's voice broke as an enemy got past Jax, forcing her to bear arms once more. As she stopped singing to return to the fight, the golden light faded and the mass of wraithkind retook control of the room.

"No," I muttered. The song's ethereal power had been giving us an advantage. I couldn't just let that go.

Brandishing my seaxe as a gray hood appeared to battle me, I threw caution to the skies. I was far too fascinated to feel embarrassed, and picked up the song at its chorus:

Lift your eyes up to the sky
We condemned here to die

"What are you doing?" Elle asked as she fought.

"The spirit plane..." I said, the light from the Sight rune aglow upon my forehead. Sure enough, as I sang the hopeful shanty, the ethereal, golden ribbon began to cut its way through the lair once more, diminishing the wraithlings' power.

"Sing with me!" I called to Elle.

She still looked confused, but she trusted me. I brandished my long seaxe and Elle swung her fiery saber while her beautiful voice joined mine in harmony:

See all those beautiful stars
And know they're not really that far
They say we're not alone
And we're going back home
Lift your eyes up to the sky!

Through my ethereal eyes, I saw the gold ribbon growing wider and stronger. Dozens of wraithlings burned in its wake while more still fled its light.

Though he clearly didn't understand it, I sensed the Mage Hunter, Ilyan's, mounting frustration. While he hung back from the fight himself, blue runes shone from over his forehead as his hands moved through the air. A moment later, the thick, silvery starspitter snake over his shoulders burst into a whole slew of smaller snakes. They tangled around his boots in a roiling pile.

"Get the Snowstorm," Ilyan ordered, thrusting a hand toward me.

The snakes obeyed, slithering toward Elle and me like a monstrous ocean wave. The sight of them sent shivers along my skin, but I leaped into action nonetheless.

A portal ripped along the floor before Elle and me like a gaping, gold-rimmed chasm. The wave of snakes poured into it like a living waterfall.

That was the entrance rift. As for the exit, I formed several smaller portals, which distributed the aggressive dream-snakes pretty evenly amongst the nearest Coven acolytes.

Our foes' yelps were like music to our ears as Ilyan's snakes snapped and spat their dreamweave energy at them. The bites and blasts drained their stamina, and I even saw one fall asleep on the spot.

"Brilliant!" Elle commented.

From there, my friend seized the opportunity. With a flying leap—no doubt charged with some kind of minor levitation afforded her by Aurora—Elle crossed the rift chasm and darted toward the snakes' source.

At the sight of the princess's fiery saber, Ilyan's face went pale. He'd always been one to hang back from such in-person fighting, preferring to let others get their hands dirty instead. But Elle wasn't about to let him skulk back to the shadows, not this time.

She got the Mage Hunter on the run, pursuing him down the staircase that led into the observatory below. Glancing over his shoulder, Ilyan shot the odd dreamblast her way but, with graceful agility, Elle dodged each one. She must've been practicing with Aurora's hover skills in hopes of keeping up with Asher.

With Elle chasing down Ilyan, that left me to face his remaining snakes and his army of acolytes. After all, I was Ilyan's primary target.

My trick of turning the snakes against their allies didn't last long before the gray hoods caught on. A couple had pulled out silver weapons, which they used to dissolve my portals by hacking at their rims.

I expanded my portal chasm to fully encircle me, leaving me on a patch of floor that reminded me of the lone redrock mesas back home in the Canyonlands. But despite that, the snakes were starting to leap across the gap to get at me, and I cried out as one latched onto my ankle. At the same time, another sank its teeth into my elbow, while a third spat a blue-violet dream dart from its fangs right into my neck. A wave of exhaustion swept over me as my runes dissolved, and it was all I could do to stay on my feet.

Soot, this was not good. More snakes were coming, and I couldn't fend them off alone. But Elle was still down in the observatory, and Jax, Vidya, and Asher were occupied battling Coven acolytes of their own—

With a loud, long 'whoop', Boone came for me. Starglass daggers blazing, he shot the dreamsnakes one by one, starting with those closest to me. His precision was astounding, and soon enough, he'd cleared a path to reach me.

"How's about a little ether dart for a midnight snack, you slitherin' sons of dragonmutts?" he called. "You like ghosts? I'll give y'all ghosts!"

The sound that came out of Boone's mouth next was one I could only describe as something between the neigh of a dragon-horse and the garbled wail of a banshee-owl. Whatever you called it, it was enough to give the nearest snakes pause, and I could've sworn they looked deeply disturbed.

Meanwhile, Boone charged up both of his next shots, then combined their power into one highly concentrated blast. The white explosion that followed was enough to send nearly every remaining ethereal familiar dreamsnake straight out of the physical plane.

Boone was mid celebratory whoop when the nearest Coven acolyte, who must've been a Psion, yanked him upward by his tan dragonscale cloak, then dragged him violently through the air, catapulting him right over the edge of the balcony.

She released her hold over him then, and Boone began to fall.

I had a new portal up and going in a flash. I caught Boone inside it and dropped him out the exit back in front of me.

But I wasn't finished yet—I reversed the scales, and soon the Coven woman who'd launched Boone was falling through a portal of her own, emerging exactly where she'd tried to drop Boone.

Before me, Boone tipped a nonexistent hat. "Well, thank you kindly, missy!" He plucked a skystone from the nearest pile and used it to refill his ether well.

"It's like you told me." I smiled. "Us snowheads gotta stick together." Then, side by side, Boone and I went to face the next round of enemies.

Chapter 25: Captain Cal

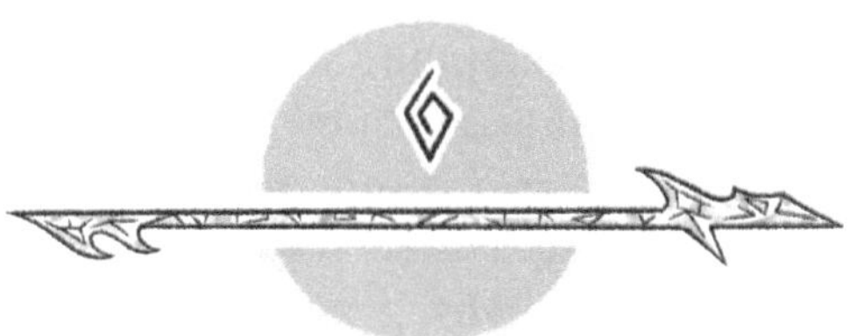

Asher

From the corner of my eye, I saw Elle dart down the staircase and into the observatory in pursuit of that snake-making Seer, Ilyan. Naturally, I wanted to go after her, both to protect her and ensure she'd be back in the loft in time for our escape. Although, it looked like that escape was gonna take some time, since none of us were about to leave without Solrac, dead or alive. Anyway, I trusted that Elle could handle herself against Ilyan. He was crafty, to be sure, but his etherarchy was more tactical than purely offensive, almost like the Gray's version of Kai.

Right on cue, I heard a gut-twisting sound like the squish of a thousand fish slapping down onto the deck of a ship, followed by a heinous, wet-sounding draconic roar, and I hover-dashed to the balcony railing faster than a skyfall.

Sure enough, Elle had Ilyan cornered, but the snobby Seer clearly had another trick up his sleeve. From whatever insidious fathoms lay below the lair, he'd somehow summoned a half-dozen amphibious monstrosities.

The draconic squids—roughly the size of Thorn on his third ascension—squeezed into the observatory through whatever shadowed doors lay hidden below. They were horrible, beaked creatures—water drakes, but with six curling, thrashing tentacles sprouting from their backs like wings, built for fighting on both land and sea. All six beasts were gray, with curling smoke trailing from their flesh, and their eyes were blue. Umbral.

I knew exactly what they were from the stories my dad used to tell me, though I'd never seen one before now. These were krakendrakes, deadly predators of the sea and the bane of nautical skyseekers.

They moved toward Elle with such synchronicity that I was almost positive they were being mind controlled. Sure enough, more runes glowed from over Ilyan's sweaty forehead, and his expression was etched with concentration as he cowered in his corner.

But there wasn't time to sit around marvelling over Ilyan's technique—though I was certain Kai would've wanted to take a few notes. As I stood there, several sets of squishy, gray tentacles were already lashing Elle's way.

Elle slashed at the nearest one with her saber, but one lightning-fast tentacle slapped her into position so that another could coil around her. The slippery tentacle squeezed, pinning her sword-arm to her side as it hoisted her into the air. She screamed.

Without a moment's hesitation, I flung myself off the balcony. Infusing my jump with hover-energy, I launched toward Elle and the army of krakendrakes.

I became a veritable cyclone, white ether mist trailing behind me as I levitated in a tight circle surrounding Elle. My spear cut through several krakendrake tentacles with a satisfying yet totally disgusting *swish*. The krakendrakes roared.

I sliced the tentacle holding Elle clean off, and it released its hold over her. From there, I swiftly came to a stop directly below her, catching her way more smoothly than I deserved.

As Elle clung to my neck, her amber eyes were bright. I gave her a wide, crooked smile.

"So, I guess that's five points for me then?" I asked.

Elle's gaze shifted abruptly to something just over my shoulder. While still in my arms, she reached up behind me with her saber, and I heard another wet *swish* as she relieved yet another roaring krakendrake of its tentacle.

"And three for me," Elle said, arching a brow.

Both of us grinning as if we weren't in an actual fight for our lives, Elle and I sprang back into action. Her skirt sailed as I set her down, and the two of us engaged the very angry krakendrakes.

I quickly realized why skyseekers at sea feared these things. Besides having sharp fangs, webbed claws, and six lashing tentacles on their backs, a pair of thinner tentacles with diamond-shaped clubs on the ends curled out from just behind the spiked draconic ruffs on their jaws. Each club was filled to bursting with tiny, wicked-looking barbs.

While I was busy going spear to claw, one of these clubs gave me a hard slap right on the back. Pain bloomed from a hundred different pinpricks as I felt little beads of blood soak into my shirt. No doubt that had ruined my nice dragon buffalo leather jacket.

"Oh no, you don't, Captain Cal!" I called. "And I'll leave it up to you to decide whether that's short for 'Calamity' or 'Calamari'!"

The next time the barbed tentacle came for me, I grabbed hold of it. "Whoa!" I shouted as the surprisingly strong tentacle whipped me to the side. Captain Cal the Krakendrake was trying to shake me off, but my grip was fierce. When the not-so-good Captain tried to toss me upward, I used the momentum and just a hint of hover-dashing to fling myself onto her back.

I was still holding one of Captain Cal's foremost tentacles as I sat astride her, and when she tried to smack me with the other one, I grabbed hold of that one too. Those nasty barbs were just itching to draw more blood, so I hurriedly covered each club with a hearty layer of starglass. Before Captain Cal knew it, I was gripping those tentacles like reins on a dragon-horse.

"Let's ride, Captain Cal!" I hollered as the krakendrake began to buck and thrash. It spotted Elle battling one of its siblings and moved to take a bite out of her, but I yanked on my makeshift reins, and she jerked her head sharply to the side.

By this point, Captain Cal had definitely had enough. Using four of its back tentacles, it seized each of my limbs and raised me up above her back.

"Whoa there!" I protested as Captain Cal began to pull each one in a different direction. "I don't like where this is going!"

Clearly, neither did Elle. Having finished setting her current krakendrake project on fire with her sword—stars, that was why this place suddenly smelled like a seafood cookout—she whipped around to hurl her saber straight into rearing Captain Cal's exposed chest.

Captain Cal gave a mighty final roar before its umbral form began to wisp away into nothingness. The pressure eased on my limbs as I fell through the smoke, using levitation to hover-catch myself.

"Whew!" I said, scrambling to retrieve Elle's sword. "Consider yourself caught up on points, Princess."

"Why thank you, *Prince.*" Elle winked as she caught it by the hilt.

Before I could decide whether to appreciate her quick response or resent it—Soot, in the heat of battle, I'd nearly been able to forget about the whole Prince of the Dragon Isles thing for a moment—a thunderous, doubled voice pierced the laboratory. It wasn't a booming voice; rather, it was the kind that got the hairs on my arms standing on end. Elle and I automatically covered our ears.

"Behold, the mighty Wraith King!" The voice echoed. "The first Guardian to grace this land in over one thousand years!"

There was a *whoosh* of icy wind that brought the temperature of the lair down several degrees. Soot, could I see my breath now? Besides that, the already empty sapphire light dimmed.

Elle and I exchanged glances. The others!

Together, Elle and I raced upstairs to the laboratory loft. My hover-dashing got me there first, but she was close behind.

After his self-aggrandizing proclamation, the Soul Reaper had now gone perfectly still within his protective rift dome. His fractured blue eyes were wide and distant, as if he were seeing something other than what was in front of him. All the fighting seemed to have come to a momentary stop as the Coven acolytes watched their master, unsure of what came next.

Just then, the Soul Reaper's concentration on whatever etherarchy he was performing peaked. His reflective rift shield exploded in a flurry of blue-tinged dust. That instantly spurred Meleya to action, tearing open a portal of her own. She grew it wider and wider, doing her best to finagle it so that it could scoop Solrac straight inside without bringing the Soul Reaper along for the ride. The rest of us prepared to move.

But that was when the Soul Reaper seemed to return to the present. He psionically flung a single silver coin—probably a Mage Hunter's coin—toward Meleya's rift. That small piece of silver was enough to destroy even her mighty rift, and Meleya cursed with frustration.

But the Soul Reaper wasn't finished. Before our eyes, he took on what I can only describe as his full wraith form. All sense of his underlying humanity fled as gray mists encompassed him from his head to his toes, each feature being swallowed up as he appeared to emit a darkened reverse-glow.

Next, he swept over the edge of the loft as dark geomancy enhanced his size to practically fill the observatory portion of the lair. He loomed over the loft—Soot, his head alone was at least as tall as my arm now!

Gray shadowfire and a sapphire glow burned all across his misty, inhuman limbs. Soulless blue eyes glittered beneath his jagged, smoky crown, and spine-chilling white calligraphy adorned his otherwise featureless face. Besides that, I thought I could almost see the residual glows from his nine stolen ether wells—three on his brow, three across his chest, and three along his core like a belt.

Suddenly, his arm morphed at the wrist to form an enormous, jagged wraithblade. The mere sight of him put me in a cold sweat. Even the Mage Hunters and Coven acolytes shrank back in fear.

Only Meleya moved, her finger flying to try and reform her portal yet again. I raced toward her with Elle hot on my heels.

But the Wraith King stopped Mel's portal before it could even get started. I'd just reached her when a bitterly cold blast of shadowfire traced a precise line along the floor to cut the area directly behind Meleya off from the others. Jax, Vidya, Boone, Solrac... Just like that, they were behind a thick, impenetrable wall of flame.

As for Elle, more icy shadowfire cut between us like a knife. Elle's protests were swallowed up as she too vanished behind the fiery barrier.

Within a second, it was just Meleya and me on the balcony, surrounded by a ring of fire, looking up at the great Wraith King like a couple of scaleshrews facing down a wild third ascension wyvern.

"We see now," the Wraith King reveled in his icy, doubled tone. "We can foresee all!"

I highly doubted that. Sure, the Wraith King had just stitched the most powerful Seer ether well in the realm onto his soul and was now apparently enjoying some insane visions. But I'd spent enough time around both Kai and Solrac to know that omens were always uncertain, shrouded in mystery and symbolism.

"You two," the Wraith King said, looking down on us. "Asher of Steel Rim and Meleya of Misthaven... We can see it now. Your powers will be key in the coming convergence of mythic stars. And we are at last greater than the Farseer and his Guardians! With you two at our side, we will rise—"

"Whoa, whoa, whoa," I started, my casual tone deliberately undermining the Wraith King's grandeur. "I'm going to stop you right there, Mister

Wraith King. Sorry to break it to you like this, but neither of us is going to choose your side."

The Wraith King either didn't hear me or else willfully ignored my moronic retort. He continued musing as his powerful, fiery form roiled and cast a sinister pall over the lair.

"This is why this foolish Farseer wanted the pair of you for the Knights of the Torch! You, the Prince of the Dragon Isles, whose astromancy surpasses even that of the Guardians of old. And you, the Snowstorm, who holds the key to unlocking the Gray Age. Give us our voidshard, and we will make you rise."

While Meleya didn't shout out with the same cocky sarcasm as I had, her defiant words cut just as deep.

"Our fates are not yet written in the stars!" Meleya called. "And I will *never* give you that voidshard!"

The shadowy, oversized Wraith King narrowed his glowing sapphire eyes. In this form, they were the only real feature on his face, aside from the seemingly infinite scrawls of white markings that adorned its surface. Writing, all of it in some kind of sweeping wraith script I didn't understand.

The Wraith King then extended his hands toward us. I summoned thick starglass armor and even a starglass shield, ready to brace against a physical attack.

But I hadn't been prepared for the voices.

A surge of netherworldly voices assaulted my mind, ten times worse than it had been while I was still trapped in the lightning cage. Unintelligible hissing from what felt like hundreds of shades and echoes mingled with the thunderous shouts of more powerful, full wraiths:

You will never be free, Asher of Steel Rim!

The Knights, the Drekai, they have the wrong man! What will they say when they discover what a disappointment you are?

You are good for nothing! A worthless distraction! A fraud!

Each new claim played right into my innermost fears and insecurities. I dropped my starglass weapons, allowing them to dissolve as I shoved my hands uselessly over my ears. I wanted to scream, run, disappear—*anything* to tune them out. Soot, without my mother's scarf, I was more alone than I'd ever before been. The voices... I'd always thought they were supposed to be blatantly evil, the lies they told easy to dispel. But the things they said... weren't they essentially accurate?

Even your mother did not believe in you enough to tell you the truth! This is her *fault, not yours!*

"Augh!" I cried. I was feeling stifled, as cramped and confined as I'd been inside that underground alcove in Etheria.

But just like in that ethereal alcove, Meleya's voice pierced through the din:

"Asher! *Asher!*"

I looked over to see her face. She must've been hearing the voices too, their hisses tailored to her. But despite that, she was there to anchor me.

"Asher, rise above the noise!" she said.

"I can't," I replied through gritted teeth.

"You've got this, Asher. I know you do."

Though Meleya said it, it was my mother's voice I heard speaking her words. Though the Gray fought to claim me, so did the light. Mom, Dad, Meleya, Solrac, my other friends... they believed in me. And for now, their confidence would have to be enough.

Somehow, my choice to do as Meleya had said and rise above the noise was enough to, if not stop, at least dampen the storm that raged within my mind. Setting my jaw, I looked up at the Wraith King.

"Sorry, Wraith King, but I guess the third time's not the charm. I've already chosen light."

Chapter 26: The Name

Meleya

The mighty Wraith King's eyes glittered with hate as they looked down on Asher. Then, as if blinking away a pesky fly, he turned his attention on me.

"Asher of Steel Rim is a fool," his double timbre thundered. "But you, Snowstorm, are not. You have tasted of our great power; for you, there can be no going back. Join us as we unite the realm."

But before I could echo Asher's rejection, Xan's cold, raspy laughter echoed inside my mind.

I know you better than he—I know you would never *serve the Wraith King. Am I wrong, Meleya?*

No, I replied. *But—*

We must *take him down before he destroys everything you love! Only we have the power to end this and save thousands.*

You know I'll never let you control me again, I mentally shot back.

A small vow to break to save your realm.

"Well then?" the Wraith King pierced the internal argument. "What is your answer?"

I squeezed my eyes shut. There had to be another way out. There was always another way.

Boom.

The sound of a drumbeat in my chest jarred me. It couldn't be Blink—she was gone. While Sniff assured me that she'd eventually reform, there was no way she'd already done so.

Boom-boom.

Eyes still shut, I once again traced the rune for the Sight. When I opened them, I saw not Blink, but Zerana's spirit standing before me in Etheria.

I inhaled as I took in the sight of her dressing me—at least, dressing my spirit—in armor. Gleaming, silvery armor forged from the scales Blink had shed during her ethereal ascension.

Zerana had worked wonders, and now the scales formed a beautiful piece that covered my spirit torso. She was also busily tying on my new spirit bracers too, which were lined with more of Blink's glorious scales, with spirit crystals like the ones in Zerana's ethereal scimitar interspersed among them.

"Zerana," I breathed. Thanks to the full moon bringing the spirit and physical worlds near, I could just make out her voice, though whether I heard it aloud or with some kind of spirit-hearing I couldn't be sure.

She, too, was singing.

My work will go on
In that great world beyond
Lift your eyes up to the sky!
Where waters are sweet
Broken souls are complete
Lift your eyes up to the sky!

Through my ethereal vision, I saw that the golden ribbon formed by the music had expanded. Sure enough, it seemed to have torn open a crack like a rift, and through it, more auras were beginning to appear. Spirits like Zerana. Stars, were they coming from deep Etheria?

Ethereal eyes shining, I basked in their mounting radiance as the incoming spirits joined Zerana in singing the ballad's chorus. I got the feeling—something about the faintness of their glows—that while our song had summoned them, their time here was only temporary.

"She's here, isn't she?" Asher suddenly said. "I can feel her."

Though Asher wasn't a Rifter and couldn't access the Sight, I'd always felt he had a strong connection with the spiritual, and not only because of the scarf that tethered his mother to him as a *khaviila*. After all, the scarf wasn't there now. It certainly helped that tonight was a full moon, when the veil between the spirit and physical worlds was at its thinnest.

Looking up at the Wraith King with eyes that spanned both planes at once, I noticed the strain in his dense, shadowy, gray aura. Maintaining this form wasn't easy for him, which helped explain why he was granting us time to think. Stars, he truly hoped Asher and I would join him. What kind of potential must we have? What sort of limitations must he?

Asher hummed along with the spirits as ether coalesced in his hand—the one that wasn't holding his spear. Before long, he'd formed a glorious starglass long seaxe with a snowflake-like pattern on the hilt. It was the same one he'd first made me in Etheria. He held it out to me.

"We've faced monsters like this before," Asher said. "This one's just got a really big head."

I locked eyes with Asher. "So, are we gonna do this?"

Asher's turquoise aura swelled with determination. "Absolutely."

I took the starglass blade.

Whether our next move was born of inspiration from what we felt from the other side, desperation to save our friends, or sheer insanity, Asher and I ran toward the edge of the balcony, straight toward the monstrous Wraith King.

Improvising, I opened an entrance portal flush with the balcony's edge. Our war cries echoed as Asher and I dashed through, emerging in mid air only a short distance from the Wraith King. Our legs pedaled through empty space.

Asher activated his levitation to propel himself forward, wildly hurling ether blasts. He was essentially flying as he assaulted the Wraith King like a hornet taking on an ursadon. An increasingly *angry* ursadon, I might add, trailing gray smoke throughout the observatory as he swatted futilely at his seemingly insignificant foe. After this, I highly doubted the Soul Reaper would still want Asher on his team.

"Eat starglass, Ghost Breath!" my friend cried.

As for me, I set up a series of reflective portals face-up in the air, then used them like stepping stones leading straight to the Wraith King's chest. I clutched my starglass seaxe, ready to drive it straight into his core.

But as I approached, time seemed to expand. With the Sight still going, I could see through the Wraith King's shadowy exterior—directly into the soul of the man underneath it.

There, beneath the thick haze of gray, was the faintest spark of pale, flaxen yellow. The aura, while distinct, reminded me a little of the one belonging to my squadmate, Erik. Sweet, shy Erik, who I'd come to think of as a younger brother.

The sight of it made my breath catch. I thought of Jax's spirit in Etheria—the proud tangerine trapped by that dark, gray shell. This was different, of course, but in some ways, it really wasn't.

I dove through my final portal, adjusting it so that it was no longer reflective. Instead, I placed the exit end high, near the Wraith King's jagged, shadowy crown.

As I fell through the air right past his face, I pulled back my seaxe, instead using a different kind of backup weapon.

"Kjell?" I asked, speaking the name I knew was written on one side of the Soul Reaper's voidshard.

The sound of it completely stunned the monster. Gray mists burst as he involuntarily shifted, reverting from his geomantically enhanced form. I caught myself in another portal, which deposited me on the ground near the foot of the massive telescope. There, as I had before only in dreams, I found myself standing eye to eye with the Soul Reaper.

No, not with the Soul Reaper. With Kjell.

His irises faded from that fractured sapphire to light brown. Through the Sight, I saw more hints of flaxen yellow emerge from deep within the gray.

He just stared at me, his expression neutral so that I couldn't tell if he was seconds away from stabbing me with that demonic wraithblade on his arm he'd conjured earlier or offering me a mug of scaleberry cider. Clearly, he hadn't heard his true name uttered in so long it had shaken him to his very soul—his *true* soul.

But our brief moment of human connection was short-lived. The brown of his eyes zapped back to lightning blue, and before I knew it the Soul Reaper had reached out with his non-bladed off hand and put me in a chokehold. Sentinel markings shone through his tattered sleeves, and I figured he must've been boosting his strength through a Wildshaper's totem of some kind.

"Give us the voidshard, you insolent child," he seethed.

Straining, I choked out a defiant, "Never."

"We will kill you where you stand!"

I just glared back, daring him to follow through, though I knew he wouldn't dare. Not when there was a chance of the contents of my rift hold reappearing somewhere he couldn't reach.

Frustration burning in his gaze, the Soul Reaper loosened his hold around my neck ever so slightly, then used his other hand to trace a rune, opening a portal beside us.

He yanked me through with him, and the pair of us appeared in the laboratory loft once more. The shadowfire was gone, and I saw that the battle between Knight and Gray had resumed in full force. Dead krakendrakes lay sprawled upon the floor, their tentacles still spasming like fish out of water. I saw more than one gray hood there as well, though, to my relief, my friends were all still alive.

They weren't in great shape, though. Blood speckled their clothing and Vidya looked to be cradling a broken arm, but I thanked the stars they were alive. No—I thanked the spirits, whose auras I could still just see at my friends' backs thanks to the Sight.

The Soul Reaper roughly shoved me to the ground. I yelped as my knee twisted awkwardly. Of all of the injuries I'd sustained thus far, this one hurt the most.

Looking up, I saw the Soul Reaper's hands flying as he performed many forms of etherarchy at once. Without a hint of regard for their safety, he telekinetically shoved his own masked guard away from their respective duels with my fellow Knights. Then, as if out of nowhere, an army of ironclaw vines sprang to tie up my friends. The plants, infused with the Soul Reaper's powerful woodweaving voidarchy, seized each of their limbs, keeping them from using their powers.

Boone thrashed against the vines as he dropped his starglass daggers. Elle's scream cut short as one vine gagged her. As for Jax and Vidya, the plants wound around their hands to keep them from being able to runetrace. Vidya had escaped the ironclaw's hold earlier by way of phase-shifting, but one look at her now told me she was in too much pain, too spent to pull that off again.

Besides the vines, the Soul Reaper conjured dozens of voidglass shards, all facing toward my friends like a flock of hungry, razor-beaked dragon birds. One false move and my friends would bleed out, and that was only if the Soul Reaper didn't choose to psionically stab them at will.

"Stop!" I cried weakly, my heart thudding at the sight of each of their auras—Vidya's lavender, Boone's rich sepia, Elle's amethyst, and Jax's orange—all swirling and twisting with panic.

That was when Asher came hover-dashing into the fray, running along the ceiling's curved windows like a star shooting across the firmament.

"Let them go, you great big—"

We never got to hear whatever insult Asher had cooked up. Quick as a flash, he vanished into the rift the Soul Reaper had suddenly thrown up right in front of him.

To my horror, the exit portal deposited Asher directly onto the operating table beside Solrac's still form. Asher groaned, landing hard on his back as the Soul Reaper used quick telekinesis to tie the silver bonds around his arms and legs.

"Dearest apprentice!" the Soul Reaper said. From the fringes, Jaira instantly stood at attention. "Begin the petulant dragon prince's soul surgery and place his ether well in a jar alongside our other prizes, then we shall decide which of our servants shall be the fortunate recipient. If Asher will not unite with us willingly, we will take his power for our own."

Chapter 27: The Operation

Asher

I was trapped.

Tight silver bonds sent an icy burn along my wrists and ankles, nullifying my etherarchy. Before I could even think about trying to somehow channel without my hands, Jaira wrapped her silver whip around my chest once, twice... I wanted to scream as it completely cut me off from my power source, but even that capacity was currently out of reach.

"This will be so satisfying," Jaira said, reveling in my pain.

"Oh Helga, what would your father say?" I asked through gritted teeth. I could tell something in my words unnerved her, and just for that, Jaira tightened the silver chain, eliciting a cry from me.

I was vaguely aware of Meleya and the others shouting in the background. Elle was gagged, but her muffled shrieks tugged on my heartstrings. I wished I could get out of this if only to spare her the pain of watching it.

From there, Jaira pulled out a strange, glass bubble etched with runes. Runes I recognized as those meant for accessing the Sight.

Jaira smashed the glass against the side of my operating table, and a soft, wispy smoke filled the air around us. As it dissipated, I realized that she'd used the relic to cast an enchantment that made Etheria visible within our immediate vicinity. That way, she'd be able to see my ether well while she worked.

As for me, muted versions of Etheria's splendor flashed before me, fragmented and confusing. It reminded me of the way I'd felt when I'd first fallen prey to astral sleep, blinded by the colors and the lights, overwhelmed and sick. Jaira's harsh magenta aura looked like a hailstorm all around her.

Seeming to indulge in every facet of my torture, Jaira selected a delicate voidglass blade from the lineup she'd laid out. My heart thudded in my chest, and my voice came out just a bit higher than I'd have liked.

"Before we get started, let's discuss the pros and cons of you savagely ripping my ether well from my soul, why don't we? I'll go first. One con is that my new friends in the Dragon Isles will *not* be happy about this. Another is that I really, *really* don't want you to—"

"Shut up, half-born," Jaira snapped. "You won't be able to talk your way out of this one."

With that, she made the first incision.

I inhaled sharply as a harsh, numbing sensation sprouted from my chest, its chilling tendrils reaching out from there. It felt nothing like getting cut with a physical blade. Bleeding would have been far preferable to this cold, sinking feeling as the unnatural blade severed a core part of what made me *me.*

I could feel my ether well resisting each cut, fighting to remain with me. This soul surgery process... It was unnatural. Disgraceful, twisted, and wrong. But bound as I was, I couldn't do a thing to stop it. Was this how my mother had felt?

Jaira's focus was intense. I could see that plainly through the mediocre Sight relic's enchantment as her magenta aura storm turned even more turbulent. Panic, anger, and terror all built up within me until I cried out, channeling as much power as I could straight from my own ether well.

As I did, there was a massive flash of ether, and I heard a sickening crack that seemed to reverberate throughout the lair. My chest ached, as if icy water had spilled across it.

Jaira let out a string of curses, and I quickly realized why. In a pair of tongs she held a crystal—my ether well. At least, part of it. For rather than a natural, crystalline shape, the fragment she held was jagged along one side. Cracked. Split right down the middle.

"Drak, you scorching sootfire!" Jaira swore, her eyes blazing with fury. As for me, I couldn't speak for the horror and spiritual anguish. My chest felt at once frozen and like it was on fire.

I was vaguely aware of Meleya shouting my name. For a second, I thought I saw the beginnings of a gold-rimmed rift split the air above me, one that might've been large enough to swallow me, the operating table, and even Jaira in one swift motion.

But then I heard the Soul Reaper's magnified double tone overwhelm every other sound in the room.

"We would not do that if we were you, Snowstorm!"

Meleya screamed, and even Jaira and the other acolytes turned to watch the scene unfold across the balcony. Despite my agony, I craned my neck to see. They were too far away to be affected by the Sight enchantment, and I was grateful not to have to wade through the fragmented mists and colors.

With a flick of his wrist, the Soul Reaper slowly pressed the tips of his floating voidglass spikes against Vidya, Boone, Elle, and Jax's hearts. The four of them cried out in pain.

"Stop it!" Meleya pleaded, and at her word, the Soul Reaper psionically wrenched back the spikes.

The villain laughed coldly. "That is your greatest flaw, Snowstorm. Arrogance. You think you can save everyone by your wits and wills alone. This will be a hard-learned lesson, then. Give me the voidshard, or watch me kill your friends one by one."

Meleya blinked several times in rapid succession, and I wondered if she was hearing more voices.

Meanwhile, Vidya called out, her voice ragged and broken. "Don't do it, Meleya! None of our lives will mean a thing if he gets his hands on that voidshard!"

The Soul Reaper pressed. "Who will it be first, Snowstorm? The traitorous Black Valkyrie who has taken you under her wing? Or perhaps her equally traitorous, weakling son? Ahh... Perhaps you wish me to dispose of the beloved true dragon rider the Knights falsely believe will be their salvation?"

"I... I..." The impossible choice loomed over Meleya like a wave about to pull her under. I fought against my bonds with all I had, but to no avail.

"That there's a mighty weighty decision to place on a young lady's shoulders," Boone suddenly called out. "How's about I make the choice instead?"

Then Boone was suddenly on fire—not with orange or green flames, but a white blaze of pure ether. With awe, I saw him pulling extra power from the nearest skystones, sucking the crystals dry. He was drawing power from the magi among the Coven acolytes, too, draining them so quickly that a few collapsed to the ground.

The pure power began to orbit him in a series of concentric circles, just as it had during my breakthrough in the dream realm's glass arena, and again in my duel with Kheradok. Boone was pulling the same move—It seemed even an old drake could learn a new trick. But it didn't look like Boone was about to make a statue.

Boone burned so brightly I had to shut my eyes. Jaira gasped, and I heard screams from a few of the Soul Reaper's lackeys, including Ilyan, who had been nearest to Boone. Once the initial burst of etherlight faded, I saw him clutching at his eyes. Stars, had Boone blinded him?

The next thing I knew, Boone was channeling all that etherfire in a combined shot from his curved daggers, straight at the Soul Reaper. The Soul Reaper lost focus on all of his voidarchy, staggering back as he tried to shield himself from the glaring light.

He must've activated some sort of defensive voidarchy, maybe phase shifting or something, since the blow didn't paralyze him as I'd hoped. But when the light dissipated, the Soul Reaper was staggering backward, and I saw a large, stark white etherscar rising along his neck, chin, and one of his cheeks. The scar wound along his skin with a hundred tendrils of shining white, and I doubted it was going to fade anytime soon.

Despite everything, I found myself whooping in Boone's honor. Meanwhile, Boone wasn't about to let the Soul Reaper's momentary distraction go to waste, and neither was Meleya. The pair shot toward him, weapons at the ready.

But despite his disfigurement, the Soul Reaper was quick to collect his wits. Enhanced by his wraith, he had a set of portals up and running quicker than I'd have thought possible. He drew that long, starry blade from his side and shoved it through the entrance.

At first, I wasn't sure where the exit portal was. Then, a stifled grunt all but stopped my heart.

Across the room, Meleya screamed at the sight of the otherworldly, bone-white blade protruding from Boone's chest. The Soul Reaper's portal was at his back, and I watched in horror as he yanked the blade back, leaving Boone with blood soaking into his shirtfront.

Shock froze me, as it did the rest of our allies. Boone looked down at his chest, then up, his gaze meeting each of his fellow Knights in turn. When he looked at me, I could practically sense his acceptance.

Then Boone turned to Meleya, his breathing coming in erratic gasps. All other sounds seemed to come to a halt as he forced his final words to come:

"Take care of yourself, snowhead."

Chapter 28: Ghost

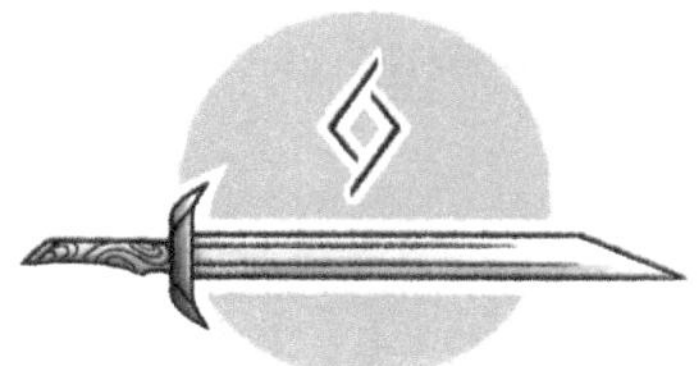

Meleya

I wasn't sure if I screamed again or not as Boone's body fell. After all, my gaze remained fixed on the place where he'd been standing, for I still had the Sight rune glowing and, in the ethereal plane, I saw his spirit, now translucent, still proud and upright. For a moment, time seemed to stretch as I watched him.

The body now lying on the floor was lifeless, but Boone's rich, dusty tan aura still clung to his spirit, as vibrant as it had been only a moment ago.

Tears filmed over my eyes as I watched what happened next. First, a large, translucent spirit-dragon, an evren, appeared, four wings extended. The creature had wide antlers, and its coloring reminded me of a brown-and-tan rattledrake. With a start, I realized he matched the mottled scales of the scaled cloak Boone always wore.

I could just make out the sound of a mighty roar as the evren landed beside Boone's spirit. At the sight of him, Boone's whole face lit up. He threw himself at the creature, taking hold of his antlers, and began to playfully wrestle with him.

Their moment was cut short as another spirit appeared. Her aura was a light periwinkle, and her translucent hair flowed all around her in wild coils. She wore a warm, beatific smile as I watched her tap Boone's spirit-shoulder.

When Boone saw her, he seemed to forget everything. He swept her into his arms, lifting her high as she laughed. I could've sworn I heard him call her by her beautiful name: Auriana.

When he spun her around, I suddenly became aware that Boone was singing.

To those who remain
On this side filled with pain
Lift your eyes up to the sky!

Boone's wife, for I was certain that was who she was, joined in the song.

Though long is the night
Morning breaks with the light
Lift your eyes up to the sky!

I could hardly breathe for the sobs that wracked my chest. A whole chorus of spirits were singing, all around the laboratory, their song battling against the pervasive Gray. Their souls stood by crying Elle, and they burned at the mighty wraiths looming behind Vidya and Jax. Even Asher, lying trapped on that table, was surrounded by a grouping of vibrant souls, led by his mother, Zerana. She seemed to hold his hand as he cried out in horror, unable to see all that I was seeing.

Then the Soul Reaper's voice brought me back to the present. Despite the distraction, he'd already recaptured Jax, Elle, and Vidya in the vines.

"Who will be next, Snowstorm?" he boomed. Though he used an auditory illusion to enhance the grandeur of his voice, I couldn't help but feel that it paled in comparison to the powerful song from the spirits. His petty games and trickery didn't matter in the long run, I could see that now. Still, the spirits of Boone, his wife, and his dragon bolstered me, and I knew I had to do all I could to get those of us who remained home.

I swallowed, trying to collect myself. "Kjell, please—"

"Do not think that little trick will work again, foolish girl!" He stalked closer to me with every word. "Open the rift hold!"

Though her presence was weakened by so much ethereal light, Xan rasped within my mind. *Open the rift hold! We can use it to destroy him!*

"Don't open the rift hold!" Vidya shouted desperately. The Soul Reaper jabbed her with another starglass shard and she bit back a howl. Jax yelled in protest, and from the operating table, Asher screamed while Jaira snapped at him to hold still. She was bending over him again, heinous voidglass tools glinting with sapphire light.

The Soul Reaper was now close enough that I could feel his chilly presence like a wall of ice.

"Last chance," he said, his breath like a creeping winter wind on my forehead. "Open the rift hold."

Yes! echoed Xan.

"No!" wailed Vidya.

The song of the spirits swelled, emphasized by the thrumming of drum beats I felt through my ascension armor. I inhaled deeply, then raised my finger to runtrace. Light trailed behind it as the rune for accessing my rift hold appeared in gold over my forehead.

Xan hissed in anticipation. The Soul Reaper leaned closer.

The rift tore open and I thrust my hand inside, my fingers closing around something small and thin:

My little canister of ghost pepper spice.

I pulled it from my rift and shook it hard toward the Soul Reaper's face, the ruddy, ultra-spicy powder landing directly in the Soul Reaper's wide-open eyes. He screamed like something from the void as he lost all concentration and dropped my friends from their ironclaw bonds.

Friend and foe alike appeared dazed.

Nobody had seen *that* coming!

I beckoned to Vidya, Jax, and Elle, who quickly shook themselves from their stupor, then all four of us bolted toward the operating tables.

My rift hold had only been open for a moment, but it had been enough time for Xan. She filtered in and out of my ethereal pantry in the blink of an eye, then appeared beside me, her smoky form roiling with rage. *It's gone! What have you done with the voidshard?*

You think I'd have brought it with me here *of all places?* I mentally shot back. Standing proud, I recalled the favor I'd asked of Sniff before coming to the lair. I knew my loyal dragon bond would keep the voidshard safely at Orothion, out of enemy hands, be they the Soul Reaper's, Xan's, or anyone else's.

Xan's shrill hiss was both livid and final. *Then you are useless to me! Farewell, Snowstorm.*

Then, I saw her shadowy form sweep across the laboratory, toward the operating tables and directly into...

...Jaira.

Chapter 29: Voices

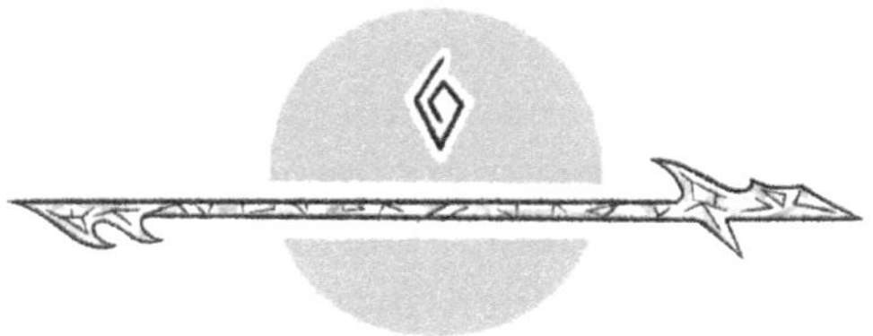

Asher

Jaira was already a psychotic maniac, but all of a sudden, she somehow took things to the next level.

First she dropped the voidglass scalpel she'd been about to use to cut out the rest of my broken ether well. Then her body began to tremble with power, her eyes shining with vivid blue light. With the lingering effects of the Sight enchantment still functioning, I saw ethereal gray smoke rising from her silhouette.

"Yes," she said, nostrils flaring. "Finally!"

She stood, and in her iron grip I saw a long, thin crystal appear, pulsing with sapphire light. A voidshard. On one side, I read the name 'Xan.'

Without a moment's hesitation, Jaira jabbed the sharp point of the shard into her hand. A single bead of red blood slid down the crystal, another name etching onto the plane in its wake: Jaira.

Oh soot—She'd just bonded a new wraith, hadn't she?

Jaira cackled as lightning crackled all around her and a mist of blue-tinged, corrupted ether pulsed. Soot, her powers were back too!

When Jaira spoke, another, raspier voice now overlaid her own. "We will make them all bow before us now!" She cast her fully sapphire eyes down toward me, still strapped to the table.

"Starting with you," she finished.

She seized the fallen scalpel, murder in her eyes. She'd already placed one half of my broken ether well into a jar, and now she was coming for the rest. Heart pounding, I cringed backward, feeling exposed and utterly helpless. Already, I felt the void within my chest where I'd once felt only power.

Hope was nothing but a memory. Here in the lair, there was only fear. Besides Jaira, the voices were back and stronger than ever, their shouts and hisses blocking out the light. I tried to be strong, but how could I? My astromancy... it was—

I can erase the pain, Asher... One netherworldly voice suddenly rose above the rest. Through my fractured glimpses of Etheria via the Sight, I thought I saw a lean, gray figure, his featureless face looking over me.

"You... you can?" I murmured, latching onto the thought.

That was when I heard it—Mom's voice, calling my name. Though it was softer, fainter than that of the Gray One, it cut through the darkness like a single ray of light. Like the brightest star in the velvety night sky, the one Dad had called 'the Anchor.'

If you can find the Anchor, Dad had said, *you'll always know where you are and where you're headed.*

With Jaira's threatening, wraith-bound form above me, blade raised, I knew where I was headed. I shut my eyes, prepared for the bittersweet escape.

But Jaira's soul-stab never came.

I cracked one eye open as Jaira made a sudden choking sound as someone yanked her back by her Mage Hunter's cloak and tossed her backward through a gold-rimmed portal, which dropped her as far away as I could see—right off the edge of the balcony.

Standing in Jaira's place was none other than Meleya, having reached me first thanks to her rifting. The intense blue light of the lair glowed behind her like a halo, mingling with the tendrils of vibrant indigo from her aura. The Sight rune glowed from over her forehead, but in her eyes, I saw blue light reflected, light I now realized was coming from the spirit plane. A whole mass of Gray Ones was here, their sapphire eyes narrowed as they surrounded me, hungering for my soul. The tall one I'd seen earlier was leaning over my chest, as if feeding off of my hopelessness.

I caught a flash of deep turquoise too, flanking Meleya. Mom. Besides that, warm, silvery light momentarily seemed to glow from Meleya herself, and I remembered the scales of her spirit dragon, Blink.

Meleya's expression was set in rage and she raised high the starglass seaxe I'd made for her and leveled it at my chest. Silver light from Blink's power and teal from Mom seemed to race along the edge of Meleya's sword, infusing it with higher power.

Meleya arrested her blade's momentum an inch above me, but she'd struck her true target. The blade cleaved through the swarm of wraiths and they dissolved in a swell of golden light, and I felt an instant lightening as Solrac's strange words from earlier replayed in my head:

Your bane will be your salvation.

Once the Gray had fled, I saw Meleya's face, once more devoid of ferocity, with loving concern having taken its place. At once, gratitude for her filled my heart. Following her eye line to my chest, I realized that my shirt was open, revealing a white ether burn spiraling out from the area over my heart. It looked like the mark left by a dying star, the white tendrils contrasting harshly with my copper skin. The sight of it made me dizzy as panic began to rise within me once more.

Meleya quickly shook herself out of her stupor. The Soul Reaper was still screaming in agony—despite my horror, I *had* to give Mel props for throwing hot pepper spice into the eyes of the realm's most dangerous super-villain—but I knew we were already on borrowed time. She began to runetrace.

Within another second, Elle was there, untying my silver bonds. The sight of my chest made her gasp.

"Oh, Asher," she said.

"Nothing but a scratch," I halfheartedly joked as she worked. For whatever reason, my mind suddenly recalled the moment during the battle at the geyser fields so long ago in Keep Drakfell, the day Elle's father had nearly executed me. While I'd thought she'd betrayed me, Elle had appeared during a time of need, bringing both Thorn's heartscale and my ascension bracers. I'd been wounded, and her fingers had trembled as she tied them on me.

Now, her fingers worked with confidence and haste. There'd be time for nerves later, once we'd put this scorched lair far, far behind us.

Meanwhile, Meleya's rescue portal to Orothion had at last split open. Though Boone's power surge had emptied a large amount of the skystone here, Meleya drew from the rest, and it was more than enough to form the gateway from this void to that sanctuary.

Vidya was ready and waiting, having already untied Solrac. I still couldn't tell if he was dead or alive as Vidya used telekinesis to hold him up. Telekinesis didn't work on living things, but I wasn't sure if her power was affecting his body or just his clothes.

"Go!" Meleya told her, and she and Solrac vanished through the white-tinged rift instantly. Jax was right there too, and I nearly choked again when I saw that he was carrying Boone's body.

A second before he could step through the rift, however, a sharp hiss pulled his attention back into the laboratory. Though Ilyan was still cowering in a corner, clutching at his eyes, he was using his freshly reconstituted megasnake to see for him. The creature struck quicker than lightning, its fangs sinking into Meleya's leg.

She gasped as the dreamweave venom drained her stamina. She tried to shake it off, but she was too focused on keeping the rescue rift going. I struggled to rise, but Elle wasn't finished untying me quite yet.

Jax moved like the wind, hurriedly propelling Boone's body through the rift before darting toward Meleya. Charging his clothing with telekinesis to pull himself forward even faster, he was at her side in a flash, decapitating the snake with his axe and dissolving the ethereal beast into a flurry of blue dust.

Meleya gave an audible sigh of relief as she stabilized. She was still exhausted, but the rift was going strong.

Meanwhile, rather than get back to the rift as any normal person might've done, Jax stayed put to protect Meleya—and, I realized, to protect *me*. By now, the bravest of the Coven acolytes had sufficiently come to their senses. A handful approached Meleya, that diamond-spike-mohawked maniac, Bjorn, at their head.

"No sanctuary for you, ethercursed," Bjorn said.

"Jax..." Meleya started, but Jax was already fulfilling her unspoken request.

"Just like at the Winter Solstice," Jax said as his axes began to spin before them like a shield, deflecting Bjorn's geomancy-powered spikes in mid-air."Hurry!" Meleya called out to Elle and me as she labored to keep the rift going.

"Almost finished..." Elle replied. "Got it!"

The silver chain fell away from around my torso, and I hurried to sit up. I must've done so too fast, because the burning from my chest intensified, causing me to groan and nearly fall onto the floor. Elle caught me under the shoulder, her added strength from her bond with her true dragon allowing her to prop me up easily. I leaned against her as my legs wobbled.

“Go!” Meleya cried, nodding toward the portal. Behind her, Jax was keeping the increasingly large group of Hunters and acolytes at bay with his axes and telekinesis, but only the goddesses knew for how long.

As Elle dragged me toward the portal, I felt the tiniest resistance spark to life inside me. To my right was Elle, pulling me one way. To my left, I saw Meleya watching me with her large, brown eyes. With the residual effects of the Sight relic still hanging in the air, I could see fragments of their auras as well. Mel’s wild, brilliant indigo was familiar to me. And Elle’s... hers was a glorious, royal purple, burning like a beautiful beacon. Though I’d technically never seen it before, it somehow felt familiar too.

The logic of it all was simple—Meleya had to come through the rift last, otherwise the portal would deactivate. But for whatever reason, I felt like I was making a choice.

My mind raced as I staggered toward the portal, my thoughts crossing faster than the blink of an eye. Meleya and I had been to the void and back, quite literally. Memories of our adventures in Etheria flashed through my head—Travelling to the netherstone, fighting off shades, jumping on the backs of lava turtles. The way she’d stilled my heart in that underground alcove, and flying with her on Blink while tethered by those fine starglass links.

In a lot of ways, *Meleya* had been my Anchor.

Elle was pulling me toward safety. Soot, Mel was begging me to let her. Still, I locked eyes with Meleya, a weighty question I couldn’t quite put into words on my exhausted, no-doubt delusional lips.

“Mel?”

Chapter 30: Destiny

Meleya

I was a split second away from shouting at Asher, who'd paused just before stepping through my rift. But as I was about to let him have it, I saw something in his dragonfire green eyes that gave me pause. Maybe it was the way he looked from Elle to me, or perhaps it was the churning of his aura that clued me in—Asher was asking for my permission.

Asher of Steel Rim had been there for me when I'd been at my lowest. Though he'd driven me crazy at first—he still did more than half the time—he'd also pulled me out of the darkness I'd buried myself in while at the Mage Hunter Academy. I may have been his salvation here, but he'd been mine long before tonight.

Yes, our destinies had long been entwined. But fate was a pen we wielded ourselves.

"Go," I assured him, the word tasting final in my mouth.

Asher blinked, then gave me a sober nod. "Thank you." Then, quick as a flash, he stopped resisting, allowing Elle to pull him through the portal.

There wasn't a moment to waste. With only the two of us left, I turned over my shoulder, hoping to find Jax ready to go.

Instead, I found him locked in combat with Bjorn, who'd somehow managed to drive him even further away from my rescue portal. More Coven acolytes were there too, as well as one final krakendrake, being compelled to action by a gray-robed Wildshaper who sat astride it.

The krakendrake grappled with Jax, holding him in place. Bjorn laughed and gave Jax a diamond-spiked punch across the face. Jax's head jerked to the side, where he saw me holding my rift.

"Go!" he shouted at me, his eyes pleading.

The krakendrake gave a watery roar as it slammed Jax hard onto the ground, keeping him pinned beneath its tentacles. Jax groaned, trying to wrench free, but he couldn't use telekinesis on anything living, and the chronically squirming tentacles were too much even for his significant physical might. His axes were nowhere to be seen.

"M, go!" Jax called again, his voice strained and desperate.

"But..." I started. All around me, the skystones were draining fast. Our window was closing—not to mention the Coven acolytes now coming for me.

"We aren't finished with you, Builder! Not until you perform your task!" Bjorn snarled at Jax.

Whatever the specifics of that meant, the message was clear: The Gray wasn't about to let Jax go, and my own window to get out was closing.... Closing...

I looked toward my rift where Asher had just disappeared, then back at Jax. At the sight of him, a wave of emotion rushed through my body. Tearing up, I recalled that long ago day in a sunny mountain glade, when Jax had shared his greatest fears with me.

Voice breaking, I said, "I swore never to leave you behind," then wrenched the twin heartscales from their cords around my neck and tossed them through my rift. Then I shut the portal, allowing the Coven acolytes to restrain me from either side.

Jax shouted so hard it thrashed his voice while they shackled me in icy, painful silver. But when I looked back at him, the starlight wreathing him as it shone through the vast windows, I had no regrets.

Echo 3

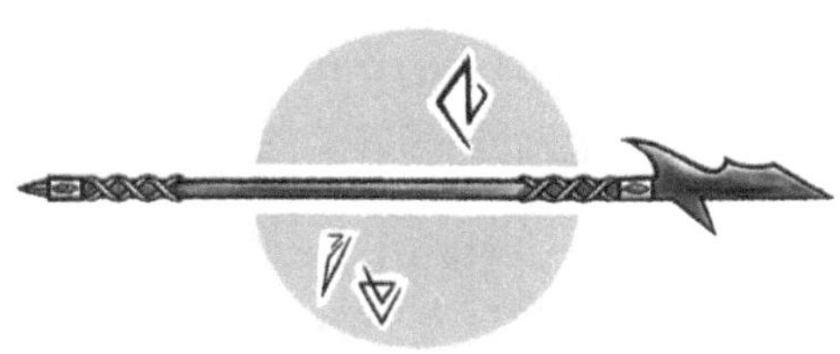

Vidya

When the portal stopped, so did Vidya's heart.

"No," she said with a frantic edge. "*No!*"

She clawed at the empty space where the rift had been with such madness that she ended up on the floor. Once there, she began beating the floor so hard her fists became bruised and the pain in her broken arm flared so badly she nearly retched.

Despite that, when a pair of arms grabbed her from behind, she did her best to thrash out of their grip.

"Vidya," a gentle voice started.

"Let me go!" she shrilled. "Meleya's still back there! And Jax... Jax... JJ..."

Words gave way to sobs as Vidya allowed the Knight to pull her off the floor. Shaya held Vidya tightly.

"There there," Shaya spoke soothingly, her light eastern accent a comfort. "Take slow, deep breaths—That's it."

The irony that it had once been Vidya holding and soothing infant Shaya wasn't lost on Vidya as she let the young woman lead her to a bed in the medical wing at Orothion. Once it had begun sputtering the first time, nearly opening again and again, Ivar had been wise in following his instinct to bring his daughter's rift anchor here. Besides that, he'd summoned a veritable army as backup, three whole squads of soldiers ready to meet whatever Gray might've come through that rift.

While Vidya was all but hysterical, Ivar stood as still as a statue. He clutched two heartscales to his chest, the last things that had soared through the rift before it'd closed, a mumbled prayer repeated over and over on his lips as he willed the rift to open again. Just once more. Guilt racked Vidya—She was certain it wouldn't.

Already Asher lay on one bed while Boone's body lay on another, covered in a sheet. Another bed held Solrac, though Vidya couldn't see him due to the number of medics surrounding him.

Vidya's mind was so addled she barely registered what the chattering medics were saying. The head medic was shouting orders from the center of the huddle, that much was certain. Surely he wouldn't be doing that unless Solrac was still alive, right? Vidya recalled the way his limp form had slumped against her as she dragged him through the rift, and her already breaking heart shattered further. Shaya sat beside her as a healer tended to her wounds.

The medical wing wasn't just filled to bursting with medics and soldiers; there were also members of the Knights' Triarchy and other leaders. Most were still just trying to piece together what had happened. Several questioned Vidya, though at first she harshly told them all to scorch off. It wasn't until several long minutes later that Vidya finally told her tale to Solvai, the Triarchy's demure Sentinel who Vidya knew was the Liberator's daughter.

Solvai listened with measured attention, though Vidya could tell that, inwardly, the young woman was terrified over the fate of her dearest friend, Meleya. Indeed, the very thought of what the Soul Reaper and his followers were doing to both her and Jax made Vidya's gut twist.

Vidya dug her fingernails so hard into her palms they left crescent-shaped marks. She *had* to believe that Meleya and Jax stood a chance, however slim, of escape, or at least of survival.

Finally, after what felt like hours, the medical wing began to calm. Men came for Boone's body, and Vidya overheard discussion regarding preparations for a burial ship. Boone. Boone, whose harmonica sat forgotten on a bedside table near the window until Dusty, Ivar's ethereal draccoon, soberly came to collect it to bring to his creator.

Vidya clenched her teeth as the memory of the Veilblade piercing Boone's chest struck her like a bolt of lightning. Almost worse was imagining how a mere year ago, Vidya would've been complicit—even an active participant—in heinous deeds just like it.

Before long, the wing was practically empty. There were just a handful of healers sitting at a corner table and making plans, and the three patients, Solrac, Vidya, and Asher.

Solrac still hadn't moved, his eyes all but sealed shut. Still, when Vidya slid off of her own bed—*scorch,* her back and arm hurt—and sat beside his bed and placed a careful hand on her husband's chest, she felt its rise and fall. He was alive, at least for now.

"So there is a limit to my punishment," she whispered as her tears splattered against his inert body. "Please come back to me, Solrac, I need you now more than ever. Please." Though not in the same way as Solrac, Asher was strangely still as well. His typical excess energy appeared to have been spent as he sat up in his bed, staring down at his bandaged chest. Around the edges, Vidya could see the tips of the star-shaped burn mark from his botched soul surgery.

Despite their protests, Asher had sent his friends away as soon as he'd been able to think clearly. Vidya couldn't blame him for wanting some time alone after what he'd gone through. Elle had been especially reluctant to leave Asher's side. But while her injuries had been minimal, the medics had insisted she go to her rooms to get some real rest. After all, prior to the events in the Soul Reaper's lair, Elle had already been travelling for days on end from the Dragon Isles. Her exhaustion overcame her, and at the medics' insistence, she'd finally left.

With the medics still deliberating amongst themselves in the corner, Vidya spoke to Asher. "They say the initial pain from soul surgery only lasts a few hours."

The words felt hollow even as they fell from Vidya's lips. Still, she wanted to comfort him. Something in her compelled her to it; a warming in her chest. This wouldn't have been the first time she'd felt the soft push from Zerana's influence, bits of her spirit lingering in her ether well. For a moment, she wondered if Solrac's well might influence the Soul Reaper in a similar way, perhaps inspiring him, however subtly, to save their son.

When Vidya had learned that Zerana had, in fact, been a lost heir to the Drekai throne, she hadn't been surprised. Her skill and grace had always felt out of place in Drakfell's outlands. Even Ilyan had suspected that she was lying regarding her birthplace when they'd brought her into the lair, making note of his suspicion in their records. Oh, to go back in time to that fateful day! Guilt for what she'd done to Zerana crippled Vidya far more than any of the wounds she'd sustained in the lair that night.

Though she was once again safe behind Orothion's anti-voidarchy wards, Vidya pulled the shadowcloak Meleya had given her more tightly around her shoulders.

Asher didn't respond for so long, Vidya had begun to think he hadn't heard her.

"Jax will be okay," he suddenly spoke, though his eyes remained glued to the floor.

Vidya straightened. "What makes you say that?"

"First off, Jax is far stronger than anyone realizes. Nothing will break him." A fierce loyalty colored his tone.

"And besides that," Asher went on, "they need him for something. Something his wraith is meant to do before the convergence, that they can't accomplish without him. Jaira called him 'the Builder'—Does that mean anything to you?"

Vidya winced. "Not specifically, no."

"Well," Asher said, "As long as Jax holds out, they'll keep him alive. Trust me."

"Scorching stars," Vidya said, something between a curse and a prayer of gratitude. The Soul Reaper had kept Vidya in the dark on many of his plans and the intricacies of wraithkind, but she'd gleaned at least one valuable lesson: The Wraith King's ancients each possessed certain unique skills—specific positions, so to speak, on their council. It was part of why she'd assumed the moniker of Black Valkyrie—her wraith bond, Exusha, was the Warrior. She shuddered to think that her son's wraith, this 'Builder', held a position so vital to the Gray.

Both bolstered and alarmed, Vidya sat back in her chair. She and Asher sat in silence for several more minutes. Meanwhile, Vidya stared into Solrac's face, lined with exhaustion from what he'd been through in the lair. His hair was a tangled mess, his beard far longer than either of them would have liked. His left cheek was marred, too, something she hadn't noticed during the fight earlier. They'd cut a new silvermark over the Psion's symbol on his left cheek, this one that of a Seer to reflect the power he truly possessed. At least, the power he'd possessed before this night.

The sun was just rising when Asher broke their silence once more. "When Jaira was carving my ether well out, it... it cracked," he said. "What exactly does that mean for me?"

Asher was looking up now, pained wonder in his dragonfire eyes. Vidya swallowed.

"It's difficult to say, since each case is unique. Most magi whose ether wells break die. In some cases, the magi's power is altered in some way, divided into fragments. In al—" Her voice cracked, and she took a moment to recompose herself. "In almost all cases, the ether well's power is lost. Deadened completely, and made useless."

"Useless." Asher winced as he repeated the word. Vidya grimaced, but she'd never been one to sugarcoat things.

More time passed, and exhaustion, both mental and physical, soon overcame Vidya. She climbed into the hospital bed nearest to Solrac, then shut her eyes.

She'd just started drifting off when she heard soft, frustrated grunts. She cracked one eye open and caught sight of Asher, hands outstretched, as if preparing to brandish his starglass spear.

The medics had momentarily left, and Asher clearly thought he was finally alone. He thrust out his hands again, willing his etherarchy to come.

"Come on," Asher muttered under his breath. "Come *on.*"

But try as he might, his irises refused to flash gold.

Vidya closed her eyes, careful not to let Asher see that she'd noticed. Then she held Solrac's cool hand as exhaustion finally overtook her.

Fragment: Mantle

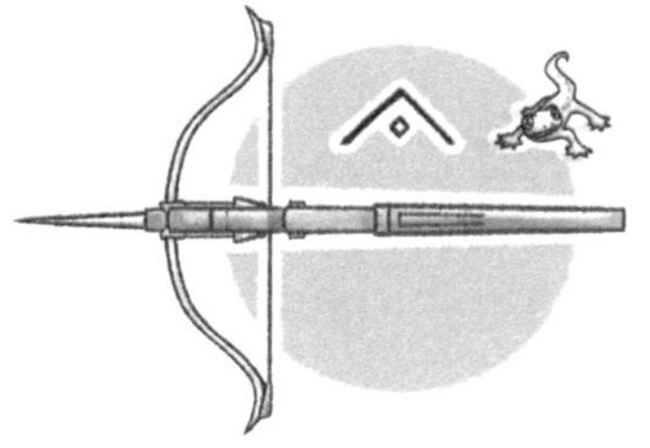

Kai

Kai hadn't been able to sleep all night. Every time he closed his eyes, fragmented dreams assaulted him in flashes of gold and sapphire light.

In the dream, Solrac stood tall and resolute while a great, shadowy gray dragon swept toward him, jaws wide. Kai tried to call out to him, but Solrac only closed his eyes in stoic acceptance of his doom.

But just before the gray dragon could snap Solrac's head off, a brilliant blast of white light impacted the dragon's maw. Curling, etherscar-like patterns bloomed across the beast's neck and jaw, and Solrac turned to his rescuer in surprise.

Boone ran toward Solrac, starglass daggers blazing. Kai's dream had no sound, but Kai got the sense Boone was shouting in defiance as he shoved Solrac aside, taking his place before the gray dragon.

Now the monster turned his ire onto Boone. Yet just as the dragon's razorsharp teeth closed around him, the pair of them vanished into curling smoke.

Kai cried Boone's name, only to startle at the sound of his own voice. His voice wasn't his own... It was Solrac's.

Suddenly, the whole vision shifted, and Kai found himself strapped to a table, watching a scene unfold to his side. A scene he found chillingly familiar.

Radiant stars hung overhead, and Asher was strapped to a table just like the one where Kai lay. He thrashed as he tried to free himself as gray mist surrounded him. Wait... not mists. Wraiths. A whole slew of them, feeding off of Asher's light.

The next thing Kai knew, it was Meleya now looming over Asher, expression set in rage as blue light danced in her eyes. But the light... it wasn't coming *from* her eyes. It was only a reflection of the source of her anger—the wraiths feeding off of Asher.

Kai already knew what came next. Meleya raised her seaxe high, then fiercely leveled it at Asher's chest. Only she wasn't slashing into Asher—She was destroying the wraiths. In the wake of her weapon, the Gray Ones burned and fled.

Kai woke with a start. It took him several moments to recognize his bedchamber near Orothion's library. He blinked several times, trying to shake his disorientation and get his breathing back under control. Drak, he was covered in sweat.

This wasn't the first time he'd woken from nightmarish visions, and he found himself wishing he were a child again. Back then, whenever a dream left Kai nervous, his parents would come into his room and sit with him, chatting or reading until both his pulse and his mind had calmed back down. But now... well, now he could only hope that his parents were making progress on their strange, ethereal mission. It helped knowing Valla was at their sides.

Almost subconsciously, he reached for his black notebook and opened to a marked page. On it, he'd scrawled every fragmented piece of information that his parents and Valla had been able to communicate to him regarding their mission to find the legendary Everflame.

The way is blocked, Kalari had said. *Only a Guardian can open the gate.* Kai wasn't sure what sort of gate she'd been talking about. His parents had gone on to explain that they had a plan... something about getting to Evgard's central 'nexus', waterfalls, and finding a rifting relic, whatever all that meant.

"Streya help them," Kai found himself muttering. He'd never been much for praying—he preferred more logic-based responses to trials—but it couldn't hurt to cover one's scales.

Momentarily, Kai heard voices in the hallway outside, though there was no way it was morning yet. He couldn't make out every word, but they spoke quickly, their footsteps hurried. Something about the medical wing... a rift anchor...

When Kai heard Asher's name, he flung off his blankets, then dressed as quickly as he could before darting into the hallway and racing to the medical wing.

The entire wing was a panoply of chaos. Despite the unholy hour, the place was bursting with people, some shouting, others crying, nearly everyone in some sort of hysterics. Medics rushed from place to place, carrying bandages, salves, and vials of liquid light.

Through the wall of people, Kai glimpsed Asher. He was battered, and his eyes were wide with shock, as if he'd just seen horrors far worse than Kai's nightmare. When Kai spotted the sharp, white burn mark on his chest, Kai had no doubts. Princess Eliana was all but glued to Asher's side.

Vidya wasn't in good shape either as Shaya practically forced her into a hospital bed. And stars, was that Solrac lying there too? For a second, Kai panicked, but then he saw that Solrac's chest was still moving, up and down, however shallowly. Besides them there was Boone... oh drak, Boone! Kai's gut twisted as he recalled his dream. With a sinking feeling, he realized he wasn't surprised to find him in such a state.

Everyone was shouting, and Kai soon found himself pushed to the fringes of the action as he slowly began to piece it all together. They'd gone to Kolbohr with a rift anchor... rescued Asher and Solrac, but both had undergone soul surgery and lost their ether wells. At least, *Solrac* had lost his ether well. Kai wasn't exactly sure what had happened with Asher...

Kai was reeling, still trying to make sense of it all when the sound of his name made him jump.

Kai.

Kai turned, expecting to see someone standing right behind him. But there was no one.

Thinking he must've imagined it, Kai refocused on the action. Not five seconds later, though, he heard it again.

Kai...

Kai narrowed his eyes. He recognized the deep, resonant voice as that of the Farseer. But that made no sense, since Solrac was *very* unconscious, lying on a hospital bed, surrounded by chattering medics. There was no way—

Kai!

Kai whirled around, this time his gaze coming to rest on the window. There, perched on the stone sill, was a large, black bird with runemarked feathers. It was the Farseer's mythraven, its shiny black eyes fixed on Kai.

Then suddenly, wings.

With a *whoosh* that made Kai jump, the mythraven swooped overhead, the tips of its wings brushing against his head. It flew above the mayhem, straight out the door and into the hallway. Everyone was so focused, they didn't notice.

The deep voice appeared in Kai's head once again. *Follow.*

Curiosity got the better of Kai, and he did just that.

None of Kai's maps of the Orothion stronghold had shown him the hidden tunnels leading to the secret cove. In fact, Kai was fairly certain the mythraven had led him through several illusion-cloaked doorways he doubted even the Triarchy knew about. Glint popped her head out of his boot, intrigued.

In the end, the tunnels had let out into a surprisingly homey and tastefully decorated cove. A soft sort of tingle fell over Kai's skin, and he could tell the place was positively humming with power.

At the far end of the cove, a high-backed chair sat before a roaring, golden fire. Kai recognized it as a Seer's omenfire, and got the feeling that this one had been burning for a very, very long time. The room somehow smelled like spiced scorchapple cider, which Kai found quite pleasant, despite his confusion. What was this place?

The mythraven alighted atop the back of the chair, and Kai did a double take. For a moment, it looked like someone was sitting in the chair, but upon closer inspection, Kai realized that it was just the Farseer's rich red robe. The Farseer's gauntlets were laid on the arm rests, and his gnarled, antlered staff was leaning against the chair as well.

"What's going on?" Kai wondered aloud. Glint looked up at him, sharing his confusion.

All at once, several of the runes along the mythraven's feathers began to glow gold. The robes shimmered. Things went hazy, then suddenly, Kai wasn't looking at empty robes any longer.

The Farseer was sitting regally in the chair, staff in hand and the mythraven perched on his shoulder. Glowing eyes stared from within the hood, a brilliant skystone suspended between them.

"Hello, Kai of Steel Rim," the Farseer's deep voice resonated throughout the cove.

Kai tensed. This wasn't adding up. Yes, he knew the Farseer persona was often projected via illusion, but Solrac was passed out in the medical wing several stories above the cove. And besides that, even if Solrac *did* survive this, he was no longer a magi, his ether well having been stolen by the Soul Reaper.

Feeling ridiculous, Kai spoke to the illusion. "Solrac?"

At the sound of the name, the illusion pulled back the hood of his robes. Sure enough, Solrac—or rather, an illusion of him—smiled at Kai, even throwing in a little wave. Glint's already wide eyes grew even larger.

"Hello, Kai of Steel Rim," Solrac repeated the phrase, his accented voice as chipper as ever. "If you are receiving this message, it means I am dead."

Kai's jaw dropped. He'd *just* seen Solrac upstairs, in bad shape, but definitely breathing. Though, as Kai pondered it, he recalled reading about relics Seers could infuse with pre-loaded messages. If Solrac had used something like that, with the mythraven as a vessel—all of those runes on its feathers had to be for something—he might not've accounted for his survival in the Soul Reaper's lair. When he'd infused the relic with this message, he'd planned on being dead.

"Yes, yes," the Solrac-Farseer illusion continued. "I have no doubt that this is a time of great mourning amongst the Knights. But I have taken every precaution to ensure my passing will not leave you all in dire straits. Many Farseers have come before me, and on my honor, I swore to continue this long and noble legacy."

Kai's stomach was in knots. Trembling, he put a hand on the stony cove wall to steady himself as the illusion grandly went on.

"The convergence of mythic stars draws near, and with it, the night the Knights will finally face the Gray. Now more than ever, the role of Farseer will be absolutely pivotal. For centuries, the Farseer has served as a light for the Knights, a resource to which they can turn for truth, and a patron to protect them against the forces of darkness."

"Oh stars..." Kai was going to be sick. But the illusion didn't notice as it carried on.

"My turn to take on the mantle came at an inconvenient time as well," Solrac continued, a wave of regret crossing his illusory face. "But such things rarely come when we feel ready. And, Kai of Steel Rim, whether you believe it or not, you *are* ready."

Kai vigorously shook his head, shutting his eyes tight as if he could will the illusion away. He'd sunken all the way to the floor now, cowering on his knees, hands in fists as they grasped the hem of his tunic to keep from trembling.

After that, the illusion went silent for a long time. So long, in fact, that Kai finally cracked open his eyelids to see if the Solrac-Farseer illusion was still there.

It very much was. Solrac was beaming down at him.

"Dearest Kai," the illusion finally continued as Kai shakily got to his feet. Whatever relic was powering the pre-meditated message must've been enchanted to wait for Kai's eye contact before delivering the message Kai had been dreading from the start:

"You are now the Farseer, and though it may not feel like it yet—" The illusory Solrac raised his finger in triumph, "this is the greatest thing that could've possibly happened!"

Epilogue

Mason

When Mason Drakeslayer arrived at the Soul Reaper's lair via rift anchor, he hadn't expected to find the place looking like the aftermath of a cyclonic storm of squid and skyseekers. Scorch, that sounded like the makings of a poem—Mason mentally logged the phrase.

Both the observatory and the laboratory loft above were in a state of utter disarray. Half-empty skystone crystals mingled with scorchmarks on the floor. Tables had been overturned, glass shattered, and gray cloth shredded to bits. Coven acolytes littered the ground, some moaning and nursing wounds while others lay still. One poor chump had been pinned to the loft's balcony and encased in starglass, his posture indicating he'd been there for a while. Taking pity on the bound man, Mason drew a silver Mage Hunter's dagger and relieved him of his starglass bonds.

Ilyan, who'd been the one to alert Mason that something was afoot, was standing atop the upper balcony, protectively clutching the silvery snake he always kept draped over his shoulders. He was scowling, and something was off about the detached way he was looking over the observatory. Mason quickly realized that was just it: Ilyan *wasn't* looking—he'd been blinded. Whatever had done it must've involved a lot of ether, since Ilyan's irises and pupils had gone a shimmering shade of white. At the moment, he was actively cursing out Bjorn for not being able to heal him using his Sentinel regeneration powers. Still, it appeared that Ilyan was already adjusting to his new affliction by using his ethereal familiar as his vicarious eyes. At once, the nickname 'Snake Eyes' took on a whole new meaning. Mason would have to write that one down later too.

From where Mason stood down in the observatory area, he could see Jaira busily working up in the laboratory loft. But before he could join his companions, Mason spotted the Soul Reaper. He wasn't far, standing near a wall as if inspecting it.

Suddenly clearing his throat, Mason asked:

From krakendrakes to sightless Seers,

What in the stars just happened here?

The Soul Reaper startled at the sound of Mason's voice. The Soul Reaper's startle startled Mason, since his master had *never* jumped like that. He was always calm, collected, and in control. Eerily so, in fact. Scorch, what had happened here to make him so on edge?

At once, Mason realized what he'd been doing there by the wall, which shone with thinly-plated silver, giving it an almost mirror-like quality. He'd been looking at his own reflection, as if disturbed.

When the Soul Reaper turned Mason's way, the High Prince understood the reason. The Surgeon's fractured, glowing blue eyes had gone bloodshot, despite the pulsing wildmarks surrounding them. His regenerative Sentinel power was clearly hard at work, trying to heal whatever damage had been done, but from the looks of things there'd remain some lasting scarring; Mason tried his best not to let the shock register on his face.

But that clearly wasn't what so unnerved the mighty Soul Reaper. Even now, the wraith-bound man held a hand to an intense, pure white mark that crawled up his neck and onto one side of his jaw and face. The brilliant mark contrasted harshly with the Surgeon's otherwise dark and ghostly appearance, and something about it shook the powerful Soul Reaper to his core.

The remnant of light mars the gray, said the voice that lived within Mason's mind. *It erases the marks of the Wraith King's accomplishments.*

Mason wasn't sure what his wraith, Dasai, meant by that, nor did he want to find out. Best to leave the wraiths to their doings, that was Mason's philosophy—just do what was needed to pacify them and then stand out of their way. Once Dasai got what he wanted, he'd help Mason get what *he* wanted. Dasai had been promising that for months, and despite his doubts, Mason believed it was true. He *had* to believe it.

Upon seeing Mason, the Soul Reaper quickly recovered his composure, or at least the illusion of it.

"Walk with us, Drakeslayer," the Soul Reaper said, his doubled tone sounding as confident as ever. He beckoned, and Mason grimaced as he sidestepped a severed krakendrake tentacle on his way to join him. Together, they headed to the stairs toward the lair's laboratory loft.

"At last, we have taken the Farseer's ether well for our own," said the Soul Reaper.

"Finally!" blurted Mason as relief washed over him. Hopefully, this would keep the Soul Reaper satisfied for a long while.

"Indeed," the Surgeon continued in his doubled monotone. "The Black Valkyrie and some Knights of the Torch tried to rescue him, but they were too late to stop the surgery. Ultimately, their attack was but a minor inconvenience."

"Right." Mason gulped as he stepped over another dead krakendrake. "Super minor."

Mind your sarcasm, lest you make the great one angry, Dasai scolded him. *Insolent human...*

Mason had never *wanted* to be wraith-bound. But when he'd woken up from his coma with a stolen ether well and a powerful Elder Gray One whispering into his mind, Mason knew he only had one choice: Embrace the darkness, for if he lost his wraith, he may well lose his life. The Gray was all that sustained him now. Still, every once in a while, defiance would creep its way into Mason's consciousness, and he'd let happy memories purify his mind once more. He'd gotten both the defiance and most of his happiest memories from his late mother.

You need me, Mason's wraith reminded him. *I own you now, Drakeslayer.*

Of course, Mason thought in response. Still, buried more deeply within Mason's consciousness than the Gray One could penetrate, Mason knew that wasn't entirely true. None of his companions, including the wraith, knew that Mason still held an entire trove of invaluable true dragon eggs within the confines of his rift hold. The hold was his and his alone, as was the secret. Only Jax of Blackfjord knew about the eggs, and scorch if Mason wasn't clinging to this shred of goodness like his life and sanity depended on it. Once the Gray fulfilled their promise and Mason was reunited with his deceased mother, Mason hoped to be able to look her in the eye without complete shame.

Still, the weight of carrying the true dragon eggs was close to breaking Mason. With such a weak ether well, maintaining the rift hold was a constant strain. Mason found he was always tired, and longed for an opportunity to relieve himself of the burden.

As Mason and the Soul Reaper ascended the stairs that led to the laboratory loft, Jaira called out.

"She's ready for soul surgery, great Soul Reaper! If we're quick, the full moon's potency should still be sufficient. And one more thing—Now that I'm wraith-bound once again, I want her ether well!"

Jaira's borderline-crazed tone made Mason frown. The Soul Reaper had asked that no additional magi be brought in for soul surgery this lunar cycle. Mason should know since, as the standing head of the Mage Hunter Academy, he was overseeing the awaiting magi being held by Hunters in various holding cells in Evyndara. Mason knew the Surgeon had asked for no new victims—er, patients—because he wanted to dedicate his whole focus to finally obtaining the Farseer's well. So who was this 'she' Jaira was—?

Mason's heart froze as they reached the top of the stairs and found Meleya of Misthaven strapped to the operating table. Her limbs were bound in silver, and her face was set in proud indignation as she fearlessly stared Jaira down.

Then, Meleya spotted Mason.

Her expression crumbled instantly. Mason felt his gut twist as he took in her fear at the mere sight of him. And how could he blame her? For months during her time at the Mage Hunter Academy, Mason had isolated her, forcing her to complete tasks for the Surgeon with Mason as his liaison. Of course she shrank at the sight of him. Mason couldn't help but think that no subject should ever have to look at their leader that way.

"Of course you won't be the recipient of the Snowstorm's ether well, Jaira... or should I say Lightbane," Ilyan chimed in, his snake guiding his footsteps toward them as his milky white eyes stared blankly ahead. "Why would the great Surgeon reward you when you botched the half-born's soul surgery?" Ilyan gestured to a jar containing a fragmented piece of crystal surrounded by wisps of turquoise mist. Mason thought it better not to ask.

"Besides that, your new wraith is yet untested," Ilyan continued. "You must work to prove she can be controlled, her power harnessed to serve the Wraith King. And for another, the Surgeon is more intentional with his ether well bestowals than that. You currently possess lightwielding, as well as astromancy from before you... *lost*... your other Gray One. Now you lack only shadowbinding to become the ultimate Archonic skymage. The Surgeon plans to make Diamondback here his ultimate Sentinel skymage.

Meanwhile, in order to become the ultimate Mystic, all I lack is the ether well of a Rifter. Surely the Snowstorm's well will become mine. Isn't that right, great Surgeon?"

The Soul Reaper appeared to hardly be listening as he took slow, deliberate steps toward where Meleya lay bound. His eyes appeared glazed over, and brilliant, sapphire runes had begun to glow over his forehead. Seer runes, Mason realized. His new ether well, the mighty one he'd taken from the Farseer himself, was now fully functioning.

Just as he reached Meleya's side, the Soul Reaper paused. His eyes returned to their regular state, and he slowly cocked his head, something several shades eerier than a smile in place on his face.

"No one will be taking the Snowstorm's ether well." The Surgeon fixed his gaze on Meleya. "No. You see, for our aims to succeed, we need her... intact. Take her below."

Scattered protests broke out at that. Jaira's voice rose above the others.

"But great Surgeon, we can't put her down there. That's where we've only just locked up the Gray Knight!"

"That's right," Bjorn snarled. "We thought some solitary confinement would be just the thing to get the Builder to finally comply."

Jaira continued, "If you want us to put Snowstorm below, we should move the Gray Knight elsewhere—"

"*Silence!*" The Soul Reaper roared with such power that Mason wondered whether he was burning ether to amplify his voice. "Leave the Gray Knight right where he is. The omens are clear. Send the Snowstorm to Scryer's Grotto with him."

At that, Meleya's eyes went wide.

"S-Scryer's Grotto?" she stammered. "No... no, please, don't put me back there. Please, *please*!"

Once again, Meleya locked eyes with Mason. And once again, Mason felt the guilt rise in his chest. Still, wraith-bound as he was, Mason felt Dasai twisting his expression into a cruel smirk as he watched Bjorn drag Meleya down the stairs toward the door that led to Scryer's Grotto below.

The echo of the heavy door slamming made Mason wince, and he automatically took a step toward the staircase as if to follow. But then the Soul Reaper returned his attention to Mason.

"As for you, Drakeslayer, we are glad you have come," the Surgeon said. "We have a special task for you."

Mason stood tall. "And what might that be?"

"You see, we still require our voidshard. Without it, the Veilblade will not serve us, and we will not be prepared come the night of the convergence of mythic stars. But now that I see the future with such clarity, I realize that we will not obtain our shard by way of force, but with finesse."

A hungry light entered the Soul Reaper's eyes. "That is where you come in, Drakeslayer. As the son of High King Magnus, the Great Uniter, who better to lead a mission to Orothion than yourself?"

"Orothion?" Mason's brow knit.

Jaira protested. "But all of Skygard is enemy territory. Orothion is where the Knights of the Torch's headquarters is!"

Sapphire ire sparked within the Soul Reaper's eyes as he whirled on Jaira. Apparently, she'd contradicted him one time too many.

Runes flashed over his forehead as he thrust his hand outward. Telekinetically propelled by her clothing, Jaira flew backward and crashed into a pile of skystone. The crystals clinked and clattered while Jaira seethed. Her irises flashed bright blue, and Mason thought he saw hints of lightning sparking along her fingers. She muttered under her breath, but as Ilyan eyed her, she bit her lip and calmed herself.

"As I was saying," the Soul Reaper carried on, ignoring Jaira. "Our dear diplomatic Drakeslayer has been second to none when it comes to winning over the nations of our great realm. We believe it is time we made peace with the Knights of the Torch, do you not agree?"

The question took Mason off-guard. Of course he wanted peace with the Knights and Evgard. That would change everything! On the other hand, he knew the Gray was cunning, always playing from multiple angles. How could he trust the Soul Reaper?

You have no other choice. Mason knew his wraith spoke the truth. *Not if you want to succeed in your goal.*

The Soul Reaper gave another ghostly smile, though the bright, tree-like ether scar on his neck and jaw undercut the effect. Still, his cold, doubled voice set the hairs on Mason's neck standing on end.

"Do as we say," he said, slowly cocking his head as the Seer runes across his brow continued pulsing with their spectral, sapphire glow, "and you have our word: You will be reunited with your mother soon enough."

End of Book 4

The story continues in The Skystone Chronicles, Book 5

A Brief Guide to
EVGARD

By Blake & Raven Penn

Scan here to see the guide online

THE SKYSTONE CHRONICLES

Mystic

Mind

Seer

Seers are Mystics that can access telepathic runes. Some of the more basic runes enable them, to read minds or see omens of the future, while more advanced runes can enable mind control, precognition, and memory wiping.

Method of Accessing Ether

Mystic ether wells are located in their minds. They trace runes of golden etherlight in the air to achieve mythic effects. Mystics must Know the correct runes and have the right intention behind them, and each rune requires a certain amount of ether. Once the rune is completed, it appears over the Mystic's forehead.
Runes can also be carved onto objects to save time. This is most commonly seen with runemarked wands or staffs. We once met a certain Mystic who'd even carved psionic runes onto a whisk. The meringue was delicious.

Shared Power: Dreamweave

All Mystics can access the Dreamweave. In the most basic terms, the Dreamweave deals with illusions.
This can manifest through simple runes to trick the eyes, or more advanced runes to trick the other senses. Some runes enable the use of dreamblades—weapons made of focused, purple dream energy that passes through physical objects, but drains the souls vitality and the victim's stamina. Quite inconvenient when someone blasts you midway through a meeting about the end of the world.
Additionally, the Dreamweave can be used to make illusory bodies for ethereal familiars, which, for lack of a better term, are almost like a solidified imaginary pet.

Psion

Psions are Mysitcs that can access teleKinetic runes. More basic runes enable pushing, pulling, or holding objects in place. Psionics only work on non living things (like rocks or metal), and they require more ether to move things that were once living (like wood or leather.)

Rifter

Rifters are Mysitcs that can access teleportation runes. The most basic runes involve making portals through Etheria (the spirit plane), while more advanced runes allow them to make anchors, rift holds, and access the Sight to see into Etheria itself. Rifters can ony open portals to places they can see or to an anchor.

Sentinel

Body

Method of Accessing Ether

Sentinel ether wells are located in their core, near the belly button. Their mythic powers are more instinctually driven, and generally require a physical totem of some kind for use. A Geomancer's totem might be a volcanic stone or granite, while a Wildshaper's might be a wolf's fang or a dragonhawk's feather. A Woodweaver's totem could be a leaf or a piece of amber.

When Sentinels access their ether, golden patterns appear on their bodies around whatever area is being affected.

Wildshaper

Wildshapers are fauna-based Sentinels. They can take on aspects of and transform into animals for which they have a totem. This is commonly used to enhance senses or gain a creature's strength or agility. Full transformations are typically accompanied by a cloud of golden ethermist. Careful—that desert finch perched on your sill might not be what she seems.

Geomancer

Geomancers are earth-based Sentinels. Using a totem take from a certain environment can grant them aspects of power related to that environment. A totem of sandstone might be used to make sandstorms, while a stalactites totem could grow into a large club. A common use we've seen is to make one's skin hard as stone, so try not to make any Geomancer enemies. Trust us, they know how to take a hit.

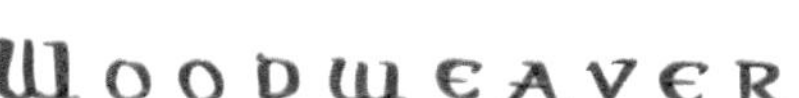

Woodweaver

Woodweavers are flora-based Sentinels. They can use their ether to manipulate and even generate plants based on what totems they have. Some use this power to keep an endless supply of freshly-grown arrows in their quiver or grow diamondoak armor. Others maintain their crops even throughout the winter months. Some have even discovered the secret to making plant servants, called Folians.

Shared Power: Regeneration

All Sentinels share the power of regeneration. This enables them to use their ether to heal wounds. They can train to heal themselves more quickly or learn to heal others. Sentinel regeneration does not work on wounds caused by the anti-ether metal, silver.

Archon

Spirit

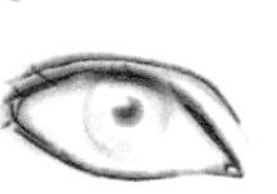

Lightwielder

Lightwielders are Archons that manipulate light. Different forms of light carry different properties. Commonly, lightwielders use lightning for raw power or liquid light to heal. Lightwielding can reveal things hidden using etherarchy. Less commonly, these Archons can concentrate light into blades or barriers of a weightless, solid material called Luxite.

Method of Accessing Ether

Archon ether wells are located in their hearts. They achieve mythic effects through the will of their spirits. When they command ether, their eyes glow gold. When an Archon learns a new way to use their ether, it is typically through a "breakthrough" during a moment of intense emotion.

Shadowbinder

Shadowbinders are Archons that manipulate darkness. Solid darkness forms shadowsilk, while darkness in its plasmic form makes shadowfire that slowly disintegrates anything it touches. It's actually quite useful in sewer systems. Shadowbinders can even use their affinity for darkness to turn invisible and pass through objects.

Shared Power: Levitation

All Archons share the power of levitation. This entails Archons using their ether to manipulate how they move. It's most commonly used to make themselves lighter and faster, through hover-jumps and hover-dashes. Levitation has its limits, and in the past thousand years, we've only met one who learned how to use this ability to fly. An Archon manipulating their movement in this way leaves a faint trail of warped golden light behind them as they go.

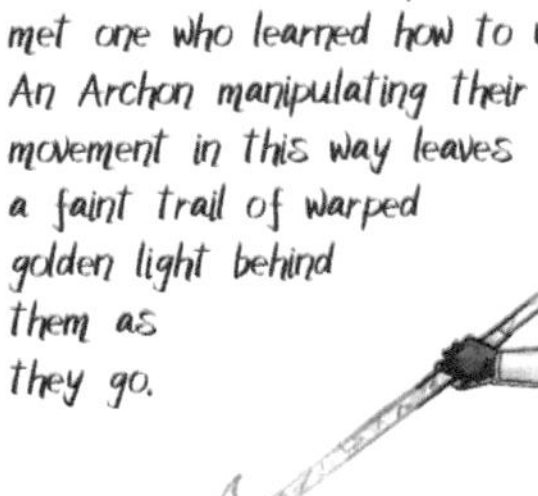

Astromancer

Astromancers use ether to manipulate ether itself. They can condense ether into starglass objects that will last a day, or blast ether directly. Ether leaves a white mark, and hurts both physical and ethereal creatures. It can stop dream energy as well. Some Astromancers can even sense where ether is, and what type is being used. Very few can give their ether away, and even fewer can take it from others. We think it's a latent astromantic sense in dragons that enables them to hunt magi by sensing their ether wells.

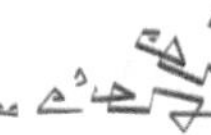

DRAGONS

Dragon Bonds

All dragons have a heartscale. It's found on their chest, near the heart. Dragons and humans can forge a bond if the dragon gives the human their heartscale. This grants the human power over the dragon, while enhancing the dragon's own cognitive abilities.

Drakes

Drakes are dragons with four legs and no wings. They're commonly built like this world's panthers or tigers, but more serpentine. They vary greatly in appearance, though most are large enough to carry two human riders on their first ascension.

Evren

Evren are dragons with four wings and no legs. They have small claws on the joint of each wing which they can use to crawl, but evren are much more suited to the air. They tend to have more canine features, almost like this world's flying foxes. Evren prefer to sleep hanging upside down from trees or cliffsides, and are usually only large enough to carry one human rider at a time until their second or even third ascension.

Wyverns

Wyverns are dragons with two wings and two legs. Their wings have well-developed claws at the wing joint, allowing them to navigate the ground far better than evren, though not as well as drakes. They are the most snakelike of the dragons, and tend to have longer necks and tails. When it comes to size, they're generally larger than evren, but smaller than drakes.

Ascension

Evgardian nobility jealously guard the secret to dragon ascension. Still, we suspect the trigger to a dragon's ascension has something to do with their hunger for ether. When a dragon ascends, their ability to communicate grows, and they advance in mythic power, if they have any. Third ascension is the highest level of dragon ascension that we currently know of.

Ether Hungry

Dragons love ether. They will take it from any source they can find, even human magi. It is for this reason that magi are outlawed in Evgard—their ether is what draws wild dragons to the Keeps.

True Dragons

True dragons are what your world generally thinks of as simply... dragons. They are great, intelligent, flying beasts with armored scales, four legs, two wings, and a tail. They vary in color, length, size, and style of horns. Every true dragons can command all nine types of etherarchy as well as breathe dragonfire, which produces an ultra-hot, emerald-green flame.

Since the Dragon Wars, true dragons are incredibly rare in Evgard.

Dragon Eyes

The eyes of dragons are a burning emerald green, just like their dragonfire. All dragons (as far as we know), even lesser dragons, share this trait.

A note on true dragon eggs

Usually no larger than a fist, True Dragon eggs harbor immense power. Their shell tends to be scaly, with a color matching the scales that the hatchling will have. Hatchlings are always bigger than the space the egg could have contained, which implies they must have some form of rift hold within them. The shell ought to be saved for its mythic properties.

Dragon Blood

While true dragons have gold blood, the blood of drakes, wyverns, and evren is more bronze or copper in color. Some like a few drops in their draquila, but it was a little acrid for our taste.

Evgardian Creatures

Draconic Animals

There are countless draconic animals in Evgard. From draccoons to wyvernhogs to aldraKa, the draconic lifeforms have supplanted most non-mythic animals. Some of our favorites are Kirin, which are draconic horses, and lutradons, which are large, scaly otters. There's nothing more fun than splashing around and riding a lutradon in the riverbank.

Ethereal Familiars

Ethereal familiars are not well understood. Born of etherarchy, these creatures act as an extension of the magi who created them. They develop their own distinct—and often strong—personalities as well (we once had rather an interesting encounter with a passive aggressive shrew). While all magi types technically have the capacity to create one, Mystics tend to do it most, using a complicated set of runes that manifest on the sKin of their familiar.

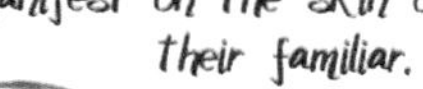

Umbrals

Umbrals are creatures corrupted by the shadow wasting. They fade until they become a smoKy gray version of what they once were. They have lightning blue eyes. The bite of an umbral spreads the shadow wasting, though it will not turn humans or dragons fully umbral.

Etheria
the Spirit Plane

The world of spirits, though invisible to most, overlays the physical plane or the one wherein we reside. While many features, geographical and otherwise, align in both planes, there are many discrepancies. Accounts from the handful of people who have returned from Etheria report mystical journeying, otherworldly creatures (both light and dark), and visits from loved ones from beyond the grave.

All of Etheria is divided into either a Haze or a Haven. While within a Haze, the world around you appears dark and dismal, shrouded in gray and frothed with danger. The sun itself looks dim on its ethereal ring spanning the gray sky. It is not clear to most Evgardians what causes the Hazes.

Meanwhile, while in a Haven, all appears light and good. At the center or each Haven lies an 'ether oasis', a fountain or pure ether where spirit creatures gather.

Spirit Creatures

There are too many spirit creatures to number, but we will feature some we encountered while in Evgard here.

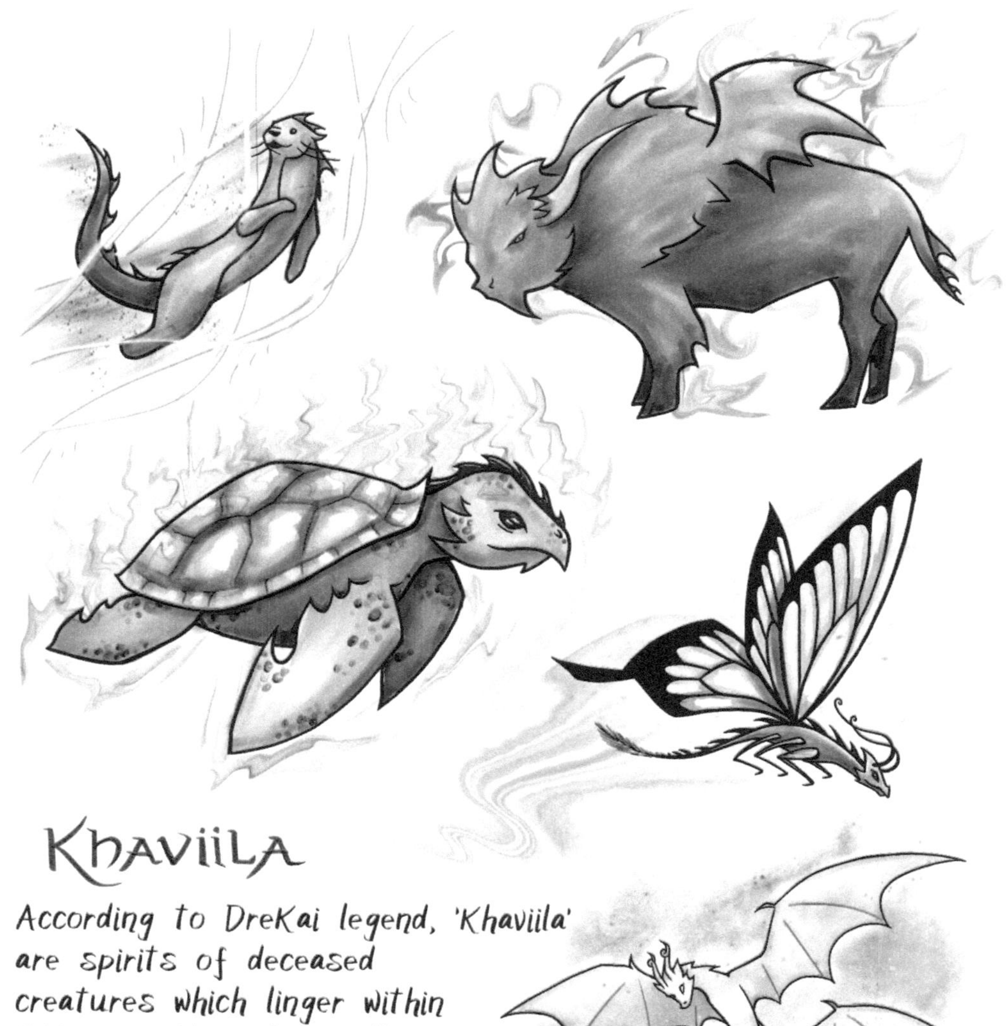

Khaviila

According to DreKai legend, 'Khaviila' are spirits of deceased creatures which linger within Etheria rather than fully move on. They dedicate themselves to protecting a specific, still living person, connected to them by an object of some kind.

Ethereal Auras

Scan to see in color

Everything in the physical world has a spiritual form, which emits an ethereal aura. Many Rifters have speculated regarding the meanings of aura colors and textures, but the science of auras is uncertain at best.

We've included a sample of known auras amongst various Knights of the Torch, along with some possible interpretations.

The Skystone Chronicles

the DRAGON Isles

West of Evgard, across the Izmara, lies the proud nation of part-dragon people Known as the DreKai.
Their land is beautiful,
albeit quite damp in our experience.

The Capital city, Zolehiinu, roughly translates to "house of Solei"

A perpetual mist blanKets the scalecedar forest floor. Their architecture seamlessly blends etherarchy and nature, and a preponderance of Psions leads to many teleKinetically floating elements, from buildings to staircases to their iconic carved totems which they infuse with various powers.

For centuries, a secret agency called the Emerald Eye has served DreKai royal family.

the skystone chronicles

DreKai Customs

Honor Duels and Duels of Wills

A people driven by sKill and honor, the DreKai often settle disputes by way of single combat. There are two distinct types of duels. The superior is a ZhaKu, or duel of Honor. These are fought to the death, over matters of great importance, such as the fates of lives, tribes, or nations. The inferior of the two duels is called a Zhavoi, or duel of wills. These are fought over matter of lesser consequence, such as disputes over land, dragons, or personal disagreements.

For each duel won, a DreKai receives a diamond-shaped tattoo called an 'honor marK.'

Life Paths (ElaaKa Kuu)

At the are of sixteen, each DreKai, half-born or otherwise, most choose an ideal to which they dedicate their every action. Warriors often pledge themselves to the path of Strength, SKill, or Bravery Craftsmen might choose Creativity or Generosity. Others still select paths liKe Family, Love, or Peace. Often DreKai carry a toKen of some Kind that reminds them of their chosen Life Path.

the Soul Reaper's Lair

According to our sources, the Soul Reaper's lair is located somewhere on the eastern shore of the Keepdom of Kolbohr. The lair is comprised of and observatory and a laboratory.

Acknowledgements

Howdy, dragon riders! It's time to give some thanks. As Boone might say, we're more grateful'na wyvernhog sittin' pretty in his pen durin' a fine turkeydrake dinner!

As always, we couldn't have gotten this book done without the help of our amazing family. Between your encouraging words in the face of our angsty-artist moments to the infinite hours of babysitting, you were literally vital to this fantastical endeavor. Our parents are absolute champions. Alex and Kimball, you were vital. And to our kids, thanks for your patience, perseverance, and prayers that 'Mommy and Daddy can sell a lot of books.'

Our beta readers deserve a major shoutout as well. Your genuine reactions—for good or for 'wait what did I just read?'—really got this book to where it needed to be. We relish every laugh, gasp, tear, and excited squeak. So a big thank you goes to Michaela, Auriana, Kimball, Eli, Amy, Cathy, Eden, and Ella. Additionally, thank you to every one of our amazing ARC readers, especially those who helped us catch those last-minute typos!

Another major hero of Team Skystone is our editor, Nadav Laemmle. We are honestly blown away by the way he takes these stories to the next level. As always, thank you, Nadav!

And finally, a massive thanks to YOU for reading (or listening to) this book! As indie authors, every reader makes a huge difference. If you liked Dragon Knight, please let us know by leaving a review. That's the best way to get other readers to give these books a chance.

May you always choose light, burn bright, drive out darkness, and light the way.

(Link to leave a review)

About the Authors

Blake and Raven Penn fought through epic battles and twisted love triangles to finally find each other. They both studied script writing in college, and now deign to turn their film and comedy experience into novel writing. Through sunshine or the dreaded Utah Valley inversion, they spend their days tending their wild offspring and dreaming of dragons. Aiming to write fantasy adventures that would keep their former teenage selves up reading long past midnight, Blake and Raven hope to brighten a world in desperate need of light.

To contact us, you can reach out via skystonechronicles.com or follow us on social media @blakeravenpenn. Also, be sure to sign up for our newsletter for updates and to get a free short story set in the land of Evgard!

www.ingramcontent.com/pod-product-compliance
Lightning Source LLC
Chambersburg PA
CBHW020917310726
48980CB00011B/929/J

* 9 7 9 8 9 9 3 7 7 3 2 1 6 *